# PRAISE FOR HEATHER GRAHAM'S
## BESTSELLING CIVIL WAR SAGA . . .

## *Glory*

"A breathtaking story that encompasses every emotion, every human trial and triumph during a time of turbulence and change. Hurrah for Ms. Graham for bringing many little-known and fascinating historical events to life."              —*Romantic Times*

"Everyone who has read a Heather Graham Civil War novel knows they are in for a delightful reading experience. . . . *Glory* is another triumph for Ms. Graham."          —*Under the Covers Book Reviews*

"Compelling. . . . Graham sure does have a way with heroes."              —*The Romance Reader*

## *Surrender*

"Refreshing, unique, classic. . . . Assured narratives, deft characterizations, and fast-moving plots are givens. Graham does it better than anyone!"
                              —*Publishers Weekly*

"Wonderful characters . . . brilliant!"
          —Harriet Klausner for *Painted Rock Reviews*

*continued on next page . . .*

# Rebel

"Magnificent . . . enthralls you with scorching sensuality. . . . Skillfully combines a captive/captor romance with a powerful historical novel . . . sizzles with action that never stops."      —*Romantic Times*

"Successful, sensuous romance."      —*Publishers Weekly*

# Captive

"Passion explodes . . . packed with a high degree of sensuality and enlivened with rich historical details."
      —*Romantic Times*

"One of the most versatile, prolific and popular writers in the romance world. . . . *Captive* is a thrilling love story . . . of an impossible, unthinkable love."
      —*Newman Times-Herald*, GA

# Runaway

"Graham lights up the sweet savage swamps. . . . [Gives] readers exactly what they want. . . . We pant for more."      —*Kirkus Reviews*

"If *Runaway* is any indication . . . Graham will own the bestselling list for some time to come."
      —*Affaire de Coeur*

# Triumph

Heather Graham

A SIGNET BOOK

*To Donna Rausch*
*with lots of love, thanks, and*
*prayers for a beautiful lady.*

SIGNET
Published by the Penguin Group
Penguin Putnam Inc., 375 Hudson Street, New York, New York 10014, U.S.A.
Penguin Books Ltd, 27 Wrights Lane, London W8 5TZ, England
Penguin Books Australia Ltd, Ringwood, Victoria, Australia
Penguin Books Canada Ltd, 10 Alcorn Avenue, Toronto, Ontario, Canada
M4V 3B2
Penguin Books (N.Z.) Ltd, 182–190 Wairau Road, Auckland 10, New Zealand

Penguin Books Ltd, Registered Offices: Harmondsworth, Middlesex, England

First published by Signet, an imprint of Dutton NAL,
a member of Penguin Putnam Inc.

First Printing, January 2000
10  9  8  7  6  5  4  3  2  1

# Prologue

# Home Fires

*Fall, 1864*
*The West Florida Coast, Near Tampa Bay*

The sky was strange that night. Though dark, the lingering effects of a storm at dusk had left crimson streaks across the shadowy gray of the sky. A cloud passed over the moon, which seemed to glow with that strange red light. Tia McKenzie shivered, feeling an uneasy sense of fear and foreboding. Indeed, the color of the blood that stained a country torn apart seemed to touch the night, and the house that stood before her.

Ellington Manor had once been one of the finest examples of a large working plantation in the South. Once. Once the white-columned porches had borne fresh, snow-colored paint, and elegant ladies in their silk, satin, and velvet had swept up the stairs of the Greco-Federal home, had laughed, teased, danced, flirted, and prayed for the right Southern boy to come along.

Then had come the time when Southern troops had trained on the lawn, and Southern boys had given out their boastful battle cries, and in time, all those good Southern boys who had graced the steps along with the beautiful girls had been called forth to war. There they had fought, and there, by the tens of thousands, they had died.

Looking up at the now decaying, weed-covered facade of Ellington Manor, Tia felt a familiar pain sweep through her. She had come here often as a girl. She had danced here, laughed here, and imagined the world to come. Now the lawn was overgrown, the paint was gray and cracked and faded, the dense Florida foliage was encroaching, steps were broken, windows smashed, and spiders spun their webs where once youthful trysts had taken place. Old Captain Ellington had died early on at Manassas, and young Captain Ellington, who should have inherited the house, had died at Shiloh. Not even his bones had come back. Miss Liza Ellington had loved her family home and would have never let it come to this ruin, but she had gone forth to war as well, contracted measles while nursing boys at a camp outside Richmond, and died there. Her remains, at least, had come home, and lay beneath the marble angel in the family graveyard behind the main house.

Yet tonight, there was a small beacon of light within. Colonel Raymond Weir, Florida regulars, had come. Her friend, her countryman. Once upon a time, he had been a boy upon those steps, flirting with the girl that Tia had been. She had seen him since then, and she knew that he had lost none of his youthful ardor for her. Indeed, with time, his feelings had become something deeper, while she, herself, should have been in sympathy with his cause if not his intent—he meant to burn out a known Union sympathizer.

Yes, she should have understood. She should have shared his fury. Except that . . . .

The Union sympathizer was her father.

Tia could hear the sounds of men and horses from the dilapidated outbuildings to the south of the main house. Weir's men were here, preparing to attack. Just as she had been warned. Five companies of them, ten to twenty men remaining alive within each of those companies. They were to ride out at Weir's command, eating the miles between here and Cimarron—her father's property, her home. The house was to be burned to the ground. Her father, should he survive the shelling, was to be given a mock trial and executed. While her mother . . . well, word was that Weir would turn a blind eye to whatever might become of the devoted wife of such a traitor. Raymond Weir was a Confederate officer taking military law into his own hands. This was what the war had become.

The soldiers had yet to see Tia; she had come alone. She had watched the house, biding her time. She was afraid tonight, afraid as she had never been before. In the last few years of the war, she had grown hardened and wary, but she had also learned courage—sometimes by accident. Tonight would be no accident. She had to stop Raymond, or at the least, delay him. Help would come, but only in time, because between her family and her state, life was divided. Her father was a Unionist, her brother Ian a Yankee hero. She and her other brother, Julian, a year younger than Ian, were ardent Rebs. Once she had believed in her cause with all the passion in her heart, but that was when the war had been fought on more decent ground, when honor had still meant something to men in both blue and gray.

She had left an urgent message for her Rebel brother to get hold of her Yankee brother, and she knew that help would arrive at her father's home. For a moment she breathed deeply, bitterly regretting that she could not call upon another Yank, but there was no help for it—he was fighting in the North—and if she'd possibly had the time to reach him, she wouldn't have known where to do so. It was only because Ian's wife had just had another baby that she dared to hope he had reached Florida, and would receive her message. So she'd come here herself. She had no choice. She had to buy time.

How? she asked herself for the thousandth time. How? All things *could* be done, she reminded herself. She had ridden from the camp alone, traveled nearly a hundred miles in just a few days—alone. How ironic, for her father would be furious; the men in her life would all be furious. But still—how could she waylay Raymond Weir?

Then the answer came back the same as it had each time she had asked herself.

*Any way that she could.* Tonight, she wasn't a Rebel. She'd done enough in the name of the great "Cause." Played dangerous games, begun by sheer chance perhaps, but perpetuated in the name of all that she had held dear—honor and freedom, and what few pathetic, battered lives she might save. And she had paid a strange, anguishing price for those efforts, swore she'd not ride out again . . . but tonight . . .

She couldn't back down. *Her father . . .*

Yet playing her very strange role in the war had been one thing. She had hurt no one except herself. While now . . .

What she planned was wrong. *She didn't want to do it . . .*

Stop. No time for morality, no time for thoughts of honor—or even promises given at another time when the world had seemed to spin too quickly. She couldn't stop the war. Nor could she help the fact that love must come before battle—she would die for her parents, for her brothers, for any member of her family. But she didn't intend to die here tonight.

*No! Merely trade her heart and immortal soul for the lives of those she loved.*

She was grimly aware of how it might all go. Weir would see her, of course. He had said that he would always do so. Perhaps he would allow her to plead and beg and flirt . . .

Then he would apologize, tell her that he was sorry, but her father was a traitor born and bred, to be hanged that very night if not shot down dead . . .

He would think himself the victor—he wouldn't know that she had bought the time she needed, all that she had come for that night. Her father employed a lot of men—black, white, Seminoles, Creeks, Germans, Irish, and more—in his defense. But Weir had made arrangements to meet up with another cavalry unit from the north of the state. Her father would fight, but his forces would be overwhelmed unless his Yankee son or some other soldiers—friend or supposed foe—brought reinforcements before the battle commenced.

Now. Time to move. To act.

Tia nudged her horse, moving quickly and quietly forward into the front yard. She rode straight to the steps that had once graced so many a lighthearted soiree. There, in a pool of light cast out from within, she slipped from her horse's back and started to the porch.

"Halt!" commanded a thick voice, and a slim picket stepped from the shadows to accost her. "Madame, what—"

"I need to see Colonel Weir, sir. You may tell him that Tia—"

"Why, Miss McKenzie!" the man gasped, recognizing her, his gaunt cheeks turning red. "Why, yes, Miss Tia, I'll tell him right away. It's Thackery, ma'am. I met you at General Roper's ball, soon after the battle of Olustee."

"Oh yes, good evening, sir." Thankfully, she did have a reputation as a devoted Rebel herself, despite her father's being a Unionist. But the way the man looked at her, with a gaze between guilt and pity, she knew he had to be wondering if she was aware of their purpose that night. She shouldn't have been, except that a soldier who had seen her own sacrifices had told her about the treacherous plan. The official government had long ago determined to leave her father be. His empathy for the Union was known, but he had chosen to practice a staunch neutrality throughout the war. Soldiers from both sides had, upon occasion, found a haven for a dying man there. Cimarron cattle had fed a number of Yanks, yes, but their cows had often fed the Confederacy as well. Tia dug her fingers into her palms. This was an act of judgment by a few men with power and troops, a depredation, one that must be stopped.

Thackery opened the front door to the house and started in. Tia followed him, despite the fact that he had surely wanted her to wait.

Raymond Weir was standing before the fireplace, hands clasped at his back. His uniform was threadbare, but very properly worn. He was tall, a formidable man with long blond locks, bright blue, seemingly all-seeing eyes, and a handsome face now richly darkened by the sun, despite his cavalry hat. He turned quickly at the sound of their entry, frowning as he saw her.

"Colonel, sir, Miss—"

"Tia!" Raymond exclaimed. Then he gazed sternly at .Thackery. "Private, I haven't time tonight for visitors. Especially Miss McKenzie."

"Don't blame your soldier," Tia said quickly. "I followed him without permission."

"I can't see you now, Tia," he said gravely, and had the grace to flush. "I have business this evening. What are you doing here? I'd heard you were with Julian."

"I was heading home," she lied, meeting his eyes, "and I heard you were in the area." She hesitated. What was she going to do? "I felt I had to see you!" she declared passionately.

Raymond looked at her, then past her to his soldier. "You may leave us, Private Thackery."

"Are there orders, sir? For the men?"

"When the time is right, I'll give the orders, Private."

"Aye, sir!"

The private saluted sharply, then turned to exit the house. The heavy wooden front door closed behind him. Raymond stared at Tia. She held her ground, returning his stare. A log snapped on the fire. He lifted a hand toward a sideboard that held a crystal decanter.

"Tia . . ." he murmured softly, emotion naked in his voice. Then he cleared his throat. "We've nothing so fine as sherry to offer, Tia, but I imagine you've become accustomed to the coarser taste of a good Kentucky bourbon over the years?"

"Before the war, sir, I became familiar with Kentucky bourbon," she said and walked to the decanter, pouring out shots for both of them, the larger for him. She walked to him boldly then, offering the larger whiskey. He took it from her, studying her with longing—and suspicion. Once, he had courted her properly, flattered her to no end. She had flirted with him, entranced by his attention. He was a striking man, as impassioned about the South and their state as she had once been herself. She still loved her state, but she loved her father more. She had come to despise Weir.

"So," he said, not touching his whiskey, "why have you come?"

"Because . . . I heard you were here," she said, staying close. She had to hope that he hadn't heard rumors regarding her relationship with a certain Yankee. She had to keep Raymond here. Stall him. Play out this charade!

Oh, God. She was going to go to hell. And maybe quite soon—if Taylor were ever to discover what she was doing this night.

She didn't dare think about that now. Steady blue eyes were upon her. "As I said," Raymond reminded her, "I have business tonight, I'm afraid. Tell me—why have you come?"

This was it! The time to act, and act well, she warned herself. And so she lowered her head, fingering her glass of bourbon. "I have come because . . ." *Why?* "Because I have seen too much death. I thought my work with Julian was so important . . . but I . . ." She looked up, amazed that she had managed to bring a glistening of tears to her eyes. "I have realized that life, so precious, slips away too quickly. We can't be obliged to hold to the same restraints that might govern us were the world more fair. Time has new meaning, sir, as does life itself. I have come to regret my . . ."

Her voice trailed off. The whiskey was suddenly taken from her fingers, set upon the mantelpiece with his own empty glass. He held her hands tightly, staring into her eyes. "You regret your refusal to marry me? Can it be?"

She lowered her head again, nodding. *Yes, of course, that was it. They could have a marriage ceremony. That would take time!*

He lifted her chin. "I will still marry you, Tia. In a heartbeat. I have always thought you were the most beautiful, compelling creature in the world. Before the war, I was taken with your dreams, with your fierce desire to see the world, to know people and places. And since the war, I have seen your dedication, your devotion, your courage. I have always been in love with you, will always be in love with you. And yet . . ."

His voice trailed of. *And yet,* she thought, *you would*

*hang my father, you bastard!* Maybe he didn't realize that although she disagreed with her father, she had never been his enemy. Too many fathers, sons, brothers, and cousins had faced one another down with rifles and bayonets in this war. She loved her father. More than any cause, dream, or ideal.

"Tia . . . tonight, tonight I'm afraid I can't. Duty demands my time."

She touched his cheek gently with her fingertips, meeting his eyes. "Duty can wait. I've learned that war will go on—and so it can wait. You're right. I'm so sorry I refused you. It was a mistake. Marry me now, right now!" she urged him.

He shook his head sadly. "My troops ride without a priest or any manner of minister," he told her. "There is no one to marry us. I cannot tell you how very sorry I am, since you will come to your senses after this night and want no more to do with me again."

"Why would that be?" she asked softly, trying not to let him see how desperately she searched for another way to stall him.

He stared down at her, hesitating. He apparently believed that she didn't know the truth regarding his plans for the evening. It would never occur to him that what he planned was so wrong that he had been betrayed by a Southern soldier. "The things we must do in this war . . . we never know what the future will bring, do we?"

"It has been the war, the things I have done, the way I feel that I must serve until the end that have caused me to give up all hope of personal commitment," she told him. No, he didn't know the truth of her life either. Few men did. Those who knew had sworn themselves to secrecy. Anonymous in her deeds, she was a heroine. If the truth were known . . .

*Taylor knew!* she reminded herself. *And she had sworn to cease her part in the war. She had tried to do so. But now, now, here she was . . .*

"So you have loved me, too?" he queried with a hopeful doubt.

She forced a tender smile. "You are handsome, sir, a gallant cavalier of my own beliefs. What is there not to love? I thought that I had nothing to give until the war ended, but I've come to realize that so much is stolen from us, so many sweethearts will never know their lover's embrace . . ."

"My God, what a pity I have to leave!"

"No!"

She stopped, breathless, gritting her teeth very hard and looking at Raymond again. "Ray, I came tonight because I'm afraid of the future, afraid that I'll never experience life fully. I earnestly desire to take what . . . happiness I may before it is snatched from me."

He smiled, yet the sadness remained in his smile.

"I told you; I have to leave," he said with weary resolution. "The war—and death—beckon to me, even now."

"You mustn't leave me . . . not yet!" she insisted desperately.

"Yes, I must—"

"Not now, when we've both been so honest. When . . . death is always so near. You mustn't go, not when . . . not when I simply crave . . ."

"Yes?"

She opened her eyes wide upon his. She was losing him. She must do something. She couldn't . . . she had to. She spoke softly. "I want to know . . . love." The world seemed to spin.

"My God . . ." he breathed. Then he frowned. "Tia, do you know what you're saying?"

"Yes, as I know that you will ride out tonight, die for the Cause if you must, and I will then grow into a bitter old maid, without ever having tasted . . . life."

"My God . . ." he breathed again.

Then his lips were on hers and he crushed her to him. The strength of his hold, the ardor of his kiss were overwhelming. For a minute, she felt a rise of panic. Of revulsion. She could not do this. She wanted to scream. Then she reminded herself that any price, any despicable act must become her willing sin, for her father's life was at stake.

She drew herself from his arms, though, again alarmed at the strength within them. She looked toward the door, hesitating. There had to be a way to buy more time. "Isn't there a place more private?" she whispered.

"Yes. Upstairs, one bedroom has been swept, the bed remade with fresh linens found in a chest. I rested there earlier."

She nodded, slipped from his hold, and started for the stairs.

Just then, the front door burst open, and Private Thackery entered the parlor. Raymond stiffened, reminded of his quest that night. "Colonel, sir, the men grow restless. They—"

"I will be right with them," Raymond said with a sigh.

Silently, Tia swore to herself. She was losing him. She must not. Where she stood now, high against the wall of the stairway, only Raymond could see her. She loosened her long dark hair from the twist at her nape, her eyes meeting his. One by one, she began to unbutton the ceaseless closures on her bodice. She had done this too often, she thought a bit hysterically. She was becoming far too adept with buttons. She needed to slow down.

Ray was staring at her, then he looked from her back to his soldier. He was wavering. She almost had him.

"Sir!" Thackery said.

Thankfully, she had greatly reduced the amount of clothing she wore in the last years of privation. Ray started to turn away again. No. She slipped the bodice from her shoulders, her eyes riveted on his, and waited, bare-breasted, determined that he would not leave her.

Raymond looked back to Private Thackery.

"The time is not quite right. Thirty minutes; I will be with the men in thirty minutes. Tell them to be ready to ride at that time." *Thirty minutes! Would it be enough? If Ian had gotten her message, he would ride straight to Cimarron. He would have ridden across the state faster than she. Tia would delay the attack as long as she could.*

Private Thackery exited.

"Yes, by God, privacy. You, alone . . ." he said.

Tia continued up the steps, her heart slamming against her chest. A knife. She should have brought a knife. She could have executed him as he had intended to execute her father. But she didn't think that she could kill a man in cold blood. Not this way. If she were facing a man with a gun while she stood on her father's property, surely, she could shoot to kill. But murder, in this manner . . . It didn't matter anyway; she didn't have a knife.

"To the right," Raymond said. He was behind her, just inches away. She continued down the hallway, veering to the right as he had instructed.

She thought she heard a sound. Something. Movement in the house. Perhaps it was the whisper of the wind against the rattling, decaying old manse. Or perhaps she was at last losing her mind, fearing that God would strike her down for this act.

"The door there," Raymond said. Apparently, he had heard nothing. Her imagination.

She entered a room. Moonlight, still that strange, unearthly shade of red, filtered through the open drapes. Once, this room had belonged to the master here. A handsome mantel stood against the left wall. A large bed faced the windows with their fluttering, now tattered draperies.

"The bed is clean, the sheets are fresh, tended by my men," Raymond said softly.

"So you said," Tia whispered. And suddenly, she could do nothing but stand there, watching the eerie color of the night spill upon the room. She felt very cold. She started to shake, Oh God, of all the things that she had done, this was the worst.

"My love . . ." A whisper, and Raymond was behind her, swiftly. His hands moved upon her bare arms. He drew her against him. His lips touched her neck. She clenched down on her teeth, hating him. He shifted the fall of her hair, pressed his mouth to her shoulder. Then she felt his fingers on the tiny buttons that closed her skirt, felt it fall away, felt his fingers then entwine on the cord that held her pantalettes, and then they, too, had fallen, and the strange, bloodred dusting of moonbeams fell upon the length of her bare flesh. It had been all too easy for him. She needed more time!

"Come, my love . . ."

*Come.* Good God, how could she endure his touch when she had known another . . .

"Look at the moon!" she entreated, walking toward the window.

"Tia, the moon, like the war, will come again."

"It's a beautiful moon, yet shaded in red—"

"There's no time for talk."

His scabbard and sword were cast aside. His cavalry jacket and shirt were shed.

"I need another drink, Raymond. This is new to me."

"Madam," he said curtly, running his fingers through his hair. She had denied him too long in life, she realized. And now that she had offered him what he had so long wanted, he had no more patience. "I remind you— you invited me to this room. Shall I leave?"

"No! You mustn't leave!"

He lifted her, bore her down on the bed. He rose above her; his eyes met hers. Her heart hammered; she couldn't breathe, couldn't follow through with this. She was going to scream, to laugh, scream, beat against him . . .

"My love!" he said again, and kissed her fingertips.

"My—love," she whispered in return, but she choked on the words, fighting the tears that suddenly stung her eyes with a vengeance. She had to stop this; she could go no further. *My love! She had heard those words before. Spoken in another man's voice . . .*

"Oh, good God!"

The furious, mocking exclamation suddenly exploded from the shadows.

*In another man's voice!*

A deep-timbred voice, husky and mocking, suddenly thundered out of the red-coated darkness in the room. Not just another man's voice—*his* voice.

Yes, his. It couldn't be! She was losing her mind; she had recalled that voice from memory, and brought with her memory the flesh-and-blood appearance of the man. Oh, God, her guilt had played havoc with her mind—he couldn't possibly be here. But he was. And he had been here, following them through the shadowed house!

Yes, he was here. She saw only a shadow then, hovering above her, but she knew it was him. She knew his voice so well—knew it in laughter, taunting, as he taunted now. She'd known it gentle upon rare occasions, and sometimes, oh God, yes, sometimes she'd known it in fury, as furious as it was now, as dangerous as the portents of the bloodred color that danced upon the moon.

She froze. Her blood seemed to congeal, colder than ice. She felt Raymond atop her. Felt her own nakedness. Taylor's deep voice struck her again like a whip.

"That's it—I've had it with this charade!" Taylor announced. And then she saw his towering form more clearly, and she felt the fiery tension of his very presence. *Felt! Oh, God, she couldn't look his way!*

"What in the name of the Almighty?" Raymond demanded. "Taylor! You!" he spat out.

But the sound of steel could suddenly be heard in the room, and in the eerie touch of moonlight, Tia saw a flash of silver—and the touch of a sword at Raymond's throat.

"Stop. Stop right now!" Tia cried. The sword rested just at Raymond's jugular. Taylor's eyes remained riveted upon Tia as he gritted his teeth.

"Ah, good, I have your attention," Taylor said.

She should die right now, Tia thought.

Because certainly, *he* would kill her later.

She closed her eyes, praying that the night itself would disappear. *He* was not supposed to be here; he was supposed to be in the North! Good God, if she'd imagined he was near, she would have swallowed all pride and thrown herself on his mercy, begging his assistance rather than chancing this desperate game she now played. She knew that he would have helped her father.

"I'm sorry," Taylor said, "but this charming little domestic adventure has gone quite far enough. Colonel Weir, if you will please rise carefully."

"Damn you, Taylor Douglas! You'll die for this. I swear it! How did you get in?" Weir demanded, rising, swallowing down his fury at the interruption—by a hated enemy.

"I entered by the door, Captain."

Thankfully, Tia thought, the scene was not as wretched as it might have been. Raymond Weir's trousers were still in place. But then again . . .

The point of Taylor's sword suddenly lay between Tia's breasts.

"Tia, get up. And for the love of God, get some clothing on. I grow weary of finding you naked everywhere I go—other than in our marital bed, of course."

"Marital bed!" Raymond repeated, stunned.

"Ah, poor fellow, you are indeed surprised. A fact that might spare your life, though I had thought of you before as something of an honorable man, just a fanatic. But yes, I did say marital bed. You hadn't heard? Though it grieves me deeply to admit, the lady is a liar and a fraud. She can marry no one for she is already married. She is wily, indeed, a vixen from the day we met. All for the Southern Cause, of course. She will play her games! But what of that great cause now, Tia?"

Humiliated, Tia braced herself against the fury behind the sarcasm in his words. *What would he do?* She'd sworn not to play the role she'd managed to make quite famous when they'd first met. Well, tonight, she had not ridden as the Lady Godiva. She'd tested his temper before. Never like this. But he *had* sent her home, sent her *away*. And he hadn't written, or even sent word.

And she'd had no choice in this!

So thinking, and finding refuge in anger herself, she caught the tip of his blade and cast the sword aside as she leapt from the bed. She wanted so desperately to find some dignity in this situation—difficult when she stumbled desperately in her search for all her clothing.

She could feel her husband watching her. She was amazed he hadn't simply killed her.

"Tia?" Raymond said, and the sudden streak of naked pain in his voice gave her so much pause that she had to remind herself that he had meant to kill her father. "You are *married* to him."

"Yes."

"But you came to me . . . tonight!" he rasped out, wanting to believe that she had desired him.

"You were going to attack Cimarron," she said, adding bitterly, "and kill my father."

Raymond shook his head. "Your father . . . no, Tia. I meant to seize the property, nothing more."

"That's not true! My father was to be killed—executed."

Yes, it was true. The truth of it was in Weir's eyes. He was, in his strange way, an honorable man, and found lying difficult. "I would have spared his life—for you!"

"How touching," Taylor interrupted, his voice a drawl that didn't hide his fury. "Tell me, Tia, was that explanation for him—or me?"

She moistened her lips to speak, but she was too hurt, angry, and ashamed to address Taylor. *I would have come to you!* she wanted to cry. *But I didn't know where you were, and there was no time! You must understand, my father's life is at risk . . .*

She couldn't explain. She lashed out instead. "Taylor, you're being a truly wretched bastard. You don't understand anything!" she screamed, her fingers trembling so hard she couldn't get her buttons fastened. Both men were staring at her.

She'd made a mistake with her bitter words, she quickly realized, for Raymond suddenly made a split second decision to defend her honor.

Her honor. It was laughable, for she had none left.

But Raymond made a dive for the sword he had so hastily discarded in his eagerness to be with her. He barely drew it from the sheath before the sound of crashing steel erupted in the night. Raymond's sword went flying across the room, and the tip of Taylor's blade was once again pressed to the Rebel's throat.

"Taylor!" Tia cried out, and at last dared look at her husband. "Don't . . . murder him. Please!"

No, she had never seen such anger, so barely controlled. They had met and clashed before, they had argued, indeed, the war had never burned more brightly than between them. But this . . . fury that now compelled him was such that she longed to shrink away, to run, to flee. Indeed, death itself would be far easier than facing what she must. He was tall, standing an even inch above Raymond, so filled with tension that the constriction of his muscles seemed evident even beneath the cut of his blue cavalry frockcoat. His eyes, a striking, curious hazel seemed to burn tonight with a red-gold fire as deadly as the haze about the moon. His features, very strongly and handsomely formed, were taut with his efforts to control the sheer fire of his anger.

She wanted so badly to cry out to him again. She had no words, but she wanted the anguish in her voice to convey what had been in her heart.

"Please, don't . . ." she said simply.

Those eyes rested upon her. Fire in the night.

Then Taylor gazed back at Raymond. "I've no intention of doing murder, sir. We are all forced to kill in battle, but I'll not be a cold-blooded murderer. I've yet to kill any man over a harlot, even if that harlot be my own wife."

Tia felt as if she'd been slapped, struck with an icy hand. And yet it was at that precise moment that she realized their situation. Good God! The yard was filled with soldiers! Rebel soldiers, enemies who could take Taylor down, *murder him,* without a thought!

"Call me what you will," she cried, "but your life is in danger here, and you fool, there is much more at stake! There are nearly a hundred men outside preparing to march on my father's house— "

"No, Tia, no longer," Taylor said, and his gaze focused upon her again. "The men below have been seized. Taken entirely by surprise. Quite a feat, if I do

say so myself. Not a life lost, Colonel," he informed
Raymond.

"So you'll not murder me. What then?" Raymond
asked.

"I believe my men are coming for you now, if you
would like to don your shirt and coat."

Raymond nodded, reaching for his shirt and frockcoat.
The latter was barely slipped over his shoulders before
two men appeared in the doorway. Yankee soldiers.

"To the ship, Colonel?" asked one of the men, a
bearded, blond-headed fellow of perhaps twenty-five.

"Aye, Lieutenant Riley. Have Captain Maxwell take
the lot of them north. Meet me with the horses below
when the prisoners have been secured."

"Sir?" the lieutenant said politely to Raymond.

Raymond looked at Tia. He bowed deeply to her. She
dared do nothing but look back. The perfect soldier,
Raymond accepted the situation—and the metal restraints slipped on his wrists by his Yankee captors. They
departed the room.

She remained dead still, waiting. She couldn't face
Taylor. She wanted to cry out again, burst into tears,
throw herself into his arms . . .

If he were to kill her, would anyone blame him? She
had put his life in danger often enough, willingly at
first—he was, after all, the enemy.

Or had been.

And he would never believe that she hadn't wanted
to do what she'd done tonight, that the ties he had
bound around her had been there, invisible but strong,
a web he had woven that held her with far greater
strength than the piece of paper that proclaimed them
man and wife. She had fought him so often. Now, when
she wanted peace, to pray for his forgiveness, he stared
at her with no mercy.

*But could that matter now?* she asked herself. *She had
prayed that Ian would come, her brother the enemy, with
his Yankee troops, and he might have been the one to
fight and save his inheritance. Ian hadn't come; Taylor*

*had, and he would make her father safe. Cimarron would
be saved. She had been willing to pay any price . . .*

*And this, it seemed, was the price.*

So she braced herself. Waiting, at least, for a blow to
fall. For him to touch her with some violence. She could
feel it in him, feel it in the air, the way he must long to
hurt her!

He came to her. Powerful hands gripped her shoulders, his fingers biting into her flesh. She met his eyes.
His arm moved, as if he would strike her with all the
force of his fury.

No blow fell. He pushed her from him. She closed her
eyes, shaking, looking for the right words to tell him that
she hadn't wanted to come here, that she would have
come to him . . .

She heard him turn from her, walk away, head for
the stairs.

She didn't know what foolhardy demon stirred her
then, but she found herself flying after him.

She caught him upon the stairs, stumbling to get ahead
of him, to force him to face her. And then she couldn't
speak, she stuttered, faltered, and tried again. "Taylor,
I—I—they said he meant to kill my father."

"Step aside, Tia," he said simply.

"Taylor, damn you! I had to come here, I had to do
what I could to stop him. Can't you see that, don't
you understand?"

He stood dead still then, staring at her with eyes still
seeming to burn with the red-gold blaze of the ghostly,
blood-haunted night. She had lost him, she thought. Lost
him. Just when she had begun to realize . . .

"I understand, *my love,* that you were ready, willing,
and able to sleep with another man. But then, Weir is a
good Southern soldier, is he not? A proper planter, a
fitting beau for the belle of Cimarron, indeed, someone
you have loved just a little for a very long time. How
convenient."

"No, I—"

"No?" His voice alone seemed to make her the most
despicable liar.

"Yes, you know that—*once* we were friends. But I . . ." She broke off, fighting the wave of tears that rushed to her eyes now. What was it? He was the enemy! And yet, staring into the gold steel of his eyes, feeling him there above her, knowing his anger, knowing how he leashed it now, knowing the scent of him . . . and remembering . . . the touch of his fingertips on her skin . . .

And she knew then, quite startlingly, clearly, despite the circumstance, just how very much she loved him. Had, for quite some time. Neither duty, debt, nor honor had given her pause tonight. It had been the way she felt about him, loved him, him, only him.

"Please!" she whispered.

He slowly arched a dark brow. And then he reached out, touching her cheek. "Please? Please what? Are you sorry, afraid? Or would you seduce me, too? Perhaps I'm not such easy prey, for I am, at least, familiar with the treasure offered, and I have played the game to a great price already. When I saw you tonight . . . do you know what I first intended to do? Throttle you, you may be thinking! Beat you black and blue. Well that, yes. Where pride and emotions are involved, men do think of violence. But I thought to do more. Clip your feathers, my love. Cut off those ebony locks and leave you shorn and costumeless, as it were—*naked* would not be the right word. But what if I were to sheer away these lustrous tresses? Would you still be about seducing men—friend and foe—to save your precious family and state? Not again, for until this war of ours is finished, I will have you hobbled—until your fate can be decided."

Hobbled . . . *imprisoned*. Did he really intend to make her a prisoner of war? He had threatened it before. It didn't seem to matter now. Too much had gone too far out of control.

"I—have seduced no one else. I . . ." She was again amazed that tears threatened to choke off her speech. "I'm not a harlot, Taylor!" she managed to whisper. Her eyes met his.

Then she gasped, startled and afraid, for he suddenly

reached out for her, drawing her into his arms. His lips
were punishing as they crashed down upon hers, forcing
her mouth apart, kissing her deeply, with passion, with
anger . . . regret, perhaps, a tumultuous series of emotions that left her shaking, bruised . . . and longing for
more. His fingers threaded into her hair, arching her
neck. His palm cradled her cheek, fingertips stroked her
throat and beyond, his touch then seeking more of her,
tracing the form of her body beneath the thin cotton
fabric of her bodice. She felt his fingers over her breast,
his palm encompassing, thumb rubbing over her nipple,
stroking, eliciting. A sweet weakness pervaded her. She
wanted to fall against him, feel again a time she had
known once at war . . . and let it become peace. She
would have gladly given herself into his arms. She
wished, prayed, that his anger would cause him to sweep
her up, carry her back up the stairs to the scene of her
almost-sin, and there, assert his right to be with her,
punish her with a wild ravishment, remind her that she
had sworn to be his, enemy or no . . .

Yet he pushed away from her. "Ah, Tia, what a pity!
I'm not at all sure of your motives at the moment, but
for once, when you are apparently ready to become a
willing wife with no argument to give me, there remains
too much at stake for me to take advantage of your
remorse. There's a battle still to be waged."

She drew back, frowning. "A battle? But you've
stopped Captain Weir from the war he would wage
against my father."

"Tia, you little fool! Weir was only a half of it! There's
a Major Hawkins with militia from the panhandle who
will bear down upon Cimarron at any moment now. I
don't know if Ian ever received word of this, or if Julian
knows somehow. You apparently learned about it. But
I may be the only help your father will have."

She stared at him, stunned. "Dear God! I'd forgotten
there would be more troops. I've got to get home!" she
cried, and she turned, running frantically down the remaining steps.

"No! Tia!"

She didn't make it to burst out into the night. She was caught.

By the long ebony flow of her hair. How ironic.

She cried out, but found herself whirled back inexorably into his arms. Meeting his eyes. Again, they were fire. Fire, and fury. His fingers bit into her as he held her. "You're going nowhere."

"My father—my home—"

"Your enemy will save them for you," he informed her bitterly.

"No, please, you have to let me ride with you. I beg of you, Taylor, in this, I swear, I—"

"Make me no more promises, Tia, for I am weary of you breaking them."

"But I swear—"

"This fight will be deadly, and I'll not have you seized by either side as a pawn in the battles to be waged."

"Please!" she begged, but even as she desperately entreated him, the front door burst open. She didn't turn. Her eyes locked with his. She heard soldiers, and knew his men had come—for her.

"Gentlemen, take my wife to the ship, please. They'll not be surprised to find another McKenzie prisoner at Old Capitol."

One of the soldiers cleared his throat politely. "Mrs. Douglas, if you will . . ."

She lowered her head, stepping away from Taylor's hold. He released her all too quickly.

She looked up at him again. "No!" she said softly. Then she cried out, "No!" and she turned, and did so with such speed and with so great an element of surprise that she was able to tear past the two Yankee soldiers who had come for her.

She raced down the steps. Those faded steps where ghostly couples had danced and laughed in days gone by.

She called out for her horse, and, thank God, Blaze, her blessed, wondrous mare, trotted in from the trees, just as Taylor burst out behind her.

She leapt upon her horse. Taylor wouldn't shoot her

down. And no one else could catch her. No one had such a mount. Except, of course . . .

Taylor himself.

"Home, girl, home!" she told Blaze, nudging the animal.

She lowered herself to her horse's haunches and sped into the night. She knew the trails. They were the paths of her youth.

Soon, the light of the house faded behind her. Only the bloodstained moon remained high above to illuminate the night.

The earth seemed to tremble; mud flew. She felt the great workings of the animal beneath her as they raced. And then she realized that she wasn't alone in the night, that *he* had come in pursuit, that he was almost upon her, with his men following behind.

"Please, God!" she prayed to the night. She had to get home. She had to see her mother, her father, Cimarron. "Please, God . . . !"

But God was not with her. Taylor was an expert horseman; he leapt from his own mount to hers, drawing in on the reins. She twisted on the mount, trying to fight him. Her efforts brought them both crashing down from the horse to the ground. She tried to rise, tried to fight again. He caught her flailing fists, pinned them to the ground, straddled her. Again she felt his eyes, and his fury, and still she gazed up at him desperately. "Please, Taylor, please, for the love of God . . ."

He stared down at her, gold fire in his eyes, and she was suddenly reminded that this was the way that they had met, on a night when a legend was born.

"Please, please!" she whispered. "Bring me home! Let me be there. Bring me home tonight. I'll stay by your side, obey your every command! I'll surrender, I'll cease to ride, I'll turn myself in to Old Capitol, I'll put a noose around my own neck, I swear it, Taylor, please, I'll—"

"Love, honor, and obey?" he demanded harshly, a tremor of some dark emotion in his voice.

And she realized that he, too, was thinking that this night was ironically similar to the one in which they had met. Was he wishing that he had never come across her in the woods?

He was suddenly on his feet, drawing her up. "You'll ride with me!" he told her harshly. "And go where I command, stay away from all fire! Blaze can follow on her own—she knows the way."

"Yes!" she promised, and she was amazed at first that he would show her this much mercy after what she had done, but realized then that if they didn't ride now, ride straight, ride hard, they would not reach her father's property in time.

As it was, they raced the horses almost to death. She rode before him, and yet twisted enough to estimate the strength of the troops following behind them. Sixty to eighty men. How many had come against Cimarron? Would Ian make it home? Would there be other help?

The night sky remained bathed in blood. Indeed, when they neared Cimarron, coming from the south below the river that would be one line of defense, the white plantation house itself was steeped in the blood.

And ahead! Far ahead, defenses had been erected against the river and men were already busy at the work of battle, shouting, taking places behind newly erected earthworks. She could hear her father shouting orders; she could see men running to obey. His workmen, and men in blue and . . .

Men in gray. *Both* of her brothers had made it here, she saw. Her heart was suddenly warmed. *Even in this horror, blood was thicker than water, friendship mattered, and a good man was a good man!*

Then she froze.

Tia saw her mother, her beautiful mother, still lithe and slim and golden blond, racing hard across the lawn with some all-important missive for her father. A foreboding filled her.

Someone, a defender at the rear of her father's house, called out, accosting Taylor's party as they approached the yard. "Halt, or be shot!"

"It's Colonel Douglas, here to defend with the Mc-Kenzies!" Taylor shouted, sliding down from his mount.

Beneath the bloodred sky, Tia could see soldiers loading a half-score of Enfield rifles onto a gunboat positioned on the river. Most of the men at Cimarron were behind the earthworks. Her mother was not. Tia jumped from Friar before Taylor realized her intent.

"Mother!" she shrieked, racing across the lawn.

"Tia!" she heard Taylor shout, his voice harsh with a desperate warning. "Tia!" she heard him shout again, and she knew he ran after her in pursuit. But she couldn't stop. Her mother was in danger. She had nearly reached Tara, who was still unaware of the soldiers taking aim at the earthworks.

Again, she saw the soldiers, heard the chain of command to fire . . .

She reached Tara, threw herself before her, trying to bring them both down.

"Tia!" her mother exclaimed, just before she heard the roar of the guns.

Fire tore into her.

In a field of crimson, she clung to her mother.

Then they were falling, falling . . . crashing to the earth together.

Dimly, she heard the cry that tore from Taylor's lips. She heard his shouts, the fire that emitted from his Colts in rapid succession. Then, he was beside her, on his knees, and she was staring into his eyes. Fire eyes, as gold as a blaze, eyes that had condemned her, held her, imprisoned her, and now . . .

She reached up to touch his cheek. His striking, powerful, ruggedly beautiful face was blurring before her. It seemed that her whole life began to flash before her eyes . . . no, not *her* life but the life that he had given her, filled with tempest, trouble, passion, fury . . . oh, yes, fury, but still life with a soul, with spirit, with love—

*Their* life . . .

Before the war had come here tonight, to Cimarron.

# Chapter 1

# A House Divided

**Winter, 1863**
**Eleven Months Earlier**

"Tia! Tia! Miss Tia! There's someone coming!"

Tia McKenzie froze at the sound of alarm in Private Jemmy Johnson's voice as it filtered to her through the trees.

"Ma'am!" he whispered desperately. She heard him clear his throat. "I don't mean to interrupt your privacy, but . . ."

Here she was, totally vulnerable in a manner in which she had seldom been since the war had begun, and someone was coming.

"Miss Tia, I know you're . . . in an awkward state, but . . ."

*Awkward?* To say the least.

Ah, yes, "buck" naked, as the boys called such a state of complete undress. She had thought that they were deep enough inland to avoid the contact of any troops, indeed, any human inhabitants of the state, much less the movement of enemy troops.

These days, it was apparently no longer possible. New strategies were afoot. Right when they were most beleaguered by illness, malnutrition, and a lack of medical supplies, the enemy had chosen to make a new assault, hoping to cripple the most important war effort of the state—feeding an army.

She traveled with a pathetic, ragtag group herself. Three privates so green they were barely old enough to shave, and two sadly injured men, the latter being the

cause of her sudden determination that she had to strip
down to the buff to bathe away the encrusted dirt and
blood that had seemed to cling to her body with greater
vigor since they'd begun this hasty journey. The last action by the old camp along the river had left two youngsters—and they were no more than that, truly—with
minie ball injuries that were far too often fatal. Her
brother, Colonel Julian McKenzie, had performed the
surgery which had thus far saved their lives, but soon
after, they had broken camp. The fellows who could do
so pulled somewhat to the north while she and Julian
had determined to take these fellows on a southwest-
wardly trail which would bring them to an old Creek
camp, where they could seek shelter until the fellows
healed enough to return to the front. She'd been down
to one change of clothing—a sad state of affairs if she
were to look back—but now seemed the time for that
change. Indeed, she would be close to home once they
reached the Creek camp, and there might even be time
for the indulgence of returning to Cimarron, and throwing herself into the gentle care of her mother, father,
and other loved ones there—until she returned to the
field to resume assisting her brother.

"Miss Tia!"

Jemmy's voice came to her again. Ever more
desperate.

She had to think, to *unfreeze!*

Her horse stood by her side, but her clothing lay on
the opposite bank. She was soaking from head to toe,
though she hadn't yet had a chance to wash her hair,
which waved down her back and shoulders like a sweeping black cape.

The soldier would be in front of her any second.

"Stop where you are. Get the men, and—go!" she
ordered, her voice full of sudden authority.

"Go?"

"Yes, go! Get away quick. I'll follow."

"We can't leave you!" Jemmy said frantically.

She heard him moving along the pine-carpeted path
toward her. "Don't you dare come closer, young man!

Take our injured and move along. I know these trails better than any one of you, so get moving. I'll see who comes, and circle around to join you on the trail."

"But Miss Tia—"

"Damn you, listen to me. I gave you an order. Go!"

She had no rank, of course. She wasn't even in the militia. But if truth be told, she possessed the simple authority of all she had learned in years of helping to patch wounded men back together again, of learning when to strike and when to run. She'd been a very properly brought-up young woman when it all began, but though privileged, she'd been the child of what she considered to be enlightened parents. Her education had been thorough. She'd longed for more, for travel to far distant lands, a chance to view the great pyramids of Egypt, the castles in England, the palaces in France. Instead of those dreams, she'd spent years with men. Young men, old men, handsome, gallant, rude, charming, educated. And when the war came, she'd met them from every backwoods hole in the state. Rebs and Yankees. She'd seen them survive, and she'd seen them die. She'd sewn them up, and she'd bathed them down. She was far more familiar with male body parts than she'd ever imagined . . .

So in truth, she reasoned suddenly, slightly amused with the realization, she had some authority, much experience, but little modesty left.

"Miss Tia, someone is coming quickly now." Jemmy was standing there. So much for the question of modesty.

"Yes, I know, Jemmy. If you please . . . oh, never mind."

She rose, still indecisive. It wasn't Jemmy's fault. He was a boy, one who had lied regarding a few months to a year to get himself into the service—he wasn't yet eighteen, she was certain. Not that she was so ancient herself, but as far as the war went, she was old, very old.

Now, of course, he was staring at her, stunned. Of course. She was "buck" naked. But not really. She had very long hair, ebony in color, thick and lustrous. It fell over her shoulders, down her back—and her front—and blanketed the most strategic points of her form, she assured herself.

And so she stood on the trail, thus enwrapped, and stared at the now frozen, gaping Jemmy. "First, snap your jaw shut, soldier, this is war. As you said, someone is coming fast. It is likely to be the enemy. And we have injured. So go now—and I mean it! You get our men to safety, and Blaze and I will be right behind you, once we see the enemy, and what he is after—and draw him away from you, if need be."

Jemmy suddenly seemed to find his mind and senses. "No! You're a woman. We can't leave you. We can take on the enemy—"

"The hell you can!" she swore flatly. "My sex doesn't matter—can't matter!—now. I've been in this too long for such consideration. Longer than you, far longer than you. Listen to me! Would you kill our injured? Go."

"But—"

"Go! And don't you mention a word of this to anyone, Jemmy Johnson, or I'll shoot you down myself, do you hear? Take our injured down the Seminole trail. Move fast. I'll take Blaze along the eastern route, hopefully drawing any rider who would follow, and after I assess the enemy strength, I'll change course and meet up with you by nightfall."

"Yes, ma'am!"

To her relief and amusement, he saluted. She saluted back, then regretted the action—wondering just how much of her long, concealing hair she had readjusted so that it didn't quite conceal anymore. He tried to look into her eyes, but his gaze kept slipping. Then, as she had ordered, he turned and fled. She saw him and their little party of injured hurry along the trail, disappearing around the bend and slinking into the old Indian trail, just as she had ordered.

As soon as they were swallowed by the foliage, she started across the little tributary, thinking that she would regain her clothing, but she had barely taken a step when she realized that she could just hear the sound of hoofbeats against the soft earth and that someone was coming closer and closer. Blaze was on this side of the trickling little tributary of the river.

She would never manage to have both her horse and her clothing. The situation was desperate. Seconds were ticking away. She had to do something, make a decision.

Clothing . . . horse?

*Clothing!*

No! She had to make the right decision to protect the injured men who were in her care. What was a little *bareness* when death might be the alternative?

What in God's name had made her decide that today, of all days, she just really had to give herself a complete and thorough scrubbing?

Maybe the enemy would pause for water, and just go away.

*Maybe he wouldn't be the enemy.*

Just as that thought filled her mind, a rider came into view, a tall man on a tall horse. His face was hidden beneath the slant of his plumed, wide-brimmed hat, and his shoulders were encased in a *Union*-issue, cavalry frockcoat.

He was definitely the enemy, she thought, her heart sinking.

And he certainly wasn't hiding his identity as a Yank.

He was but one man. A lone rider. Tia felt a sense of relief, and even superiority—she knew this terrain as few men did. Her home was across the state, but she had learned her geography from her father and her uncle, whose Indian blood had led him in dozens of merry chases across the terrain throughout the long, treacherous, and deadly Seminole wars.

And yet . . .

*Who was he? What was he doing? Not exactly a spy, for he was in full uniform. A scout? Yes, searching for troop movements, perhaps even looking for her own little pathetic band of injured and raw men who were, in truth, little more than children playing at being soldiers.*

Just what would she do if he were to note that they had followed the old Indian trail.

*He was a lone man . . .*

But well armed. He had come with a sharpshooter's rifle tied across his saddle, a Spencer repeating rifle in a case below it, and a pair of six-shooting Colts holstered in the gun belt that rode his hips. Mean weapons. And something about the easy, agile, and assured way that he moved seemed to testify to his ability to use them.

The boys had already ridden on. If he followed them, there was no question in her mind—at least half of them would be dead.

Coming into the copse, the Federal cavalry scout paused. Felt the air, listened, surveyed the landscape. Hoof prints, near the water. Broken and bent branches.

*Yes . . . someone was near.*

By dusk, the slender offshoot of the St. Johns was an exquisite place to be. Pines rose in green splendor, shading the little tributary, while shimmering rays of the dying sun broke through here and there to cast diamond sparkles upon the darkening water. A lone wading bird stalked the far side of the water, long-legged and graceful.

A crane. Tall, snow white except for its legs, it was the focal point of the glorious picture there. The bird was so still that if it weren't for the creature's coloring, it would have blended with the scene. Like any predator, however, this creature of ethereal beauty was sleek, cunning, and careful. It waited; it watched. Its stillness was so complete that it might indeed have been a painted picture that Taylor Douglas stared upon, a picture of serenity and peace.

*The woman was much the same.*

*Yes! The woman.*

*Was she alone? Perhaps now . . .*

*But she hadn't been before! And so . . .*

Though she was dead still, low and flattened against a pine, he saw her. *Or part of her. She was well concealed by the foliage. Still, strangely, he sized her up within his mind.*

Slim, graceful, striking, like the bird. Like the crane, she watched, and she waited.

And, he thought as well, like the crane, *she was a predator. No one watched and waited and calculated in such a manner without intending to strike.*

He dismounted from Friar, his bay horse, named for his deep brown color and long shaggy mane. He stretched in a leisurely manner, then hunkered down by the water, dousing his face, yet surreptitiously studying her there, across the water.

*Yes, she watched.*

*She thought herself hidden, and indeed, he could see little of her, a long slender arm, a wealth of dark hair, a face as stunningly sculpted and delicate as that of the most elegant of belles. Her eyes were dark, large, hypnotic . . .*

*Pinned on him.*

*Ready for battle. To spring to pounce. She waited merely for the right moment . . .*

Was she unaware that he had seen her? Most probably. His eyesight was exceptional. It was one of the gifts that made him an incredible marksman, as well as a good scout. And he knew this area as few other men did, just as he knew, indeed, that the Southern forces of Captain Dickinson—little Dixie—were in the near vicinity. He knew he was close to an encampment, and that he would find his prey.

And yet . . .

He had expected nothing like this. He couldn't help feeling a certain sorrow. *Had the Southern forces become so low, so pathetic, and so depleted that women were doing the work of the army? And so thinking, he couldn't help remembering back to the beginning of the war, when the reckless bravado and confidence of the men who would be soldiers had brought about the pointless tragedy that would scar his own life.*

No. This was different. This girl was here by no accident.

He threw more water on his face, adjusted his hat, and whistled for Friar to come to the water. Keeping low, his hat brim over his eyes, he surveyed the area around the little tributary. A number of roads here, different ways to go—different ways out. He rose slowly, seeing that beyond the obvious, there was a trail heading into what appeared to be thick foliage. It was as he stared at the trail that she suddenly made her presence known.

He'd thought himself a hardened soldier. But she stunned him, froze him in place.

She swept his breath away.

She was sheer audacity.

For suddenly, she stepped from her hideout among the pines in all her glory. Sheer, *naked* glory. A magnitude of splendor that wiped the mind clean, stealing into the senses, the fantasy of dreams. She was slim, compact, her form clad in nothing other than the superb blanket of her hair, falling down in rippling waves of pure ebony to cover her breasts, belly, and thighs in a manner that teased in the wickedest way . . .

"Good day, Yankee."

For a moment, he couldn't answer. He saw her smile.

"Madam," he said, his jaw tense but working.

"You're in a Rebel state."

"I am."

"So . . . I assume you're looking for rebellion, soldier?" she called in a taunting voice. "If so, then come this way."

To his amazement, she dashed off in a web of ebony grace, the stole of her hair flying about her in a cloud like a raven's wing, only to resettle as she sped along the pines to a trail just southward of their position. Still paralyzed with simple shock, he watched her.

Then he swore, bursting back to life.

Hurtling himself into his saddle, he urged Friar to take a wild plunge into the river. At its greatest depth, the water was only four feet, but there it rose in mighty showers and rushed back upon him in shimmering cascades.

By the time he had crossed the river, she'd mounted a large handsome horse—a far finer animal than he had seen in most of the South. And there, on the trail, she sat, a naked beauty cloaked in nothing but the black sable of her hair, staring his way. Her limbs were long, ivory, striking against the darkness of the horse's coat. Her face, though shadowed by that magnificent head of hair, again appeared young, striking . . .

And cunning.

She might have been startled, just at first, that he had so quickly crossed the water and found her upon the trail. But she gave that little thought, kneed her horse, and tore down the pine-carpeted trail.

Deeper and deeper she rode into the green darkness of the trails. Pines, oaks, webbed with ferns and mosses, created a rich canopy above them. She knew the trail, he thought. No one who didn't know the trail would ever dare ride its length so recklessly. Nor could they follow such a twisted course with such great speed for so long a time.

Only a fool would follow so recklessly! he thought.

And yet . . .

He followed. She was leading him astray, he knew. Tempting him from all his intent. Only a fool would follow, yet he was certain that, just as she would lead him away—she would lead him back again.

After twenty minutes of a heavy gallop in her pursuit, he came to a small bubbling brook. He was amazed that she had a horse with the speed and stamina to elude him so long. The Southern states had begun the war with the best horses—life in the South had been far more based upon the farm and the hunt than that in the North, and the majority of the best breeding stables had been in the South. But war had taken its toll on horses just as it had on humans—far too many of the Southern horses were little but flesh and bones.

Not to mention the horses that had been casualties of war, rotten carcasses next to their masters upon the killing fields of the fight.

He was lucky to have an exceptional mount himself. Friar was from Kentucky, a horse bred from specially chosen stock for both strength and speed. He still thought that he might have overtaken the woman if the trail hadn't been so narrow and treacherous. Perhaps it was best to wait. Give her time to knot her own noose . . .

She had just crossed the brook when he reached it. Still, he reined in. It seemed a good time to hold off, back away. To wait. And to watch. She wasn't without sense, or was she? She would surely know that she had to slow down her horse. To own such a creature, and to ride it so well, she must be aware that she would kill the animal if she raced it into the ground. But what did he know of her? Maybe she would consider the act of eluding him to be worth the life of the horse. Then what? They were deep in the midst of nowhere, far between the habited lands of either coast. She would have to care about the life of her horse.

Very soon, she would have to slow down, walk her mount, allow it water.

He dismounted from his horse, and hunkered down by the water. He drank, looked around. She had definitely crossed the brook. He would wait, let her move on without being chased. She would see that he had stopped, and perhaps believe that she had lost him, that his pursuit was finished.

Never.

He was determined.

*Why? She was a wanton little fool. Good God, didn't she see the risks?*

He gave himself a shake, gritting his teeth, stiffening. He hadn't felt this encompassing web of pain and bitterness enwrap him in a long time now. There had been a goal in his life, a quest, and he had pursued it. The past was over; he didn't know why this incident was forcing him to recall events he had long since pressed to the back of his mind—and soul.

It was the war.

*Damn her . . .*

He would pursue her because of the war.

Whatever she had led him away from, she would lead him back to.

# Chapter 2

~~

Tia raced on after she was certain that her pursuer had given up the chase. But then she reined in, aware that she was riding Blaze into the ground. A cruel thing to do to such a fine, blessed animal! She patted the horse's neck. "Good girl! You are worth your weight in gold, you know? You can outrun almost anything on four legs, eh?"

She fell silent. Dusk was coming, and here she was, alone on an old Indian trail—stark naked. She felt chilled and very uncomfortable.

And unnerved.

She had never felt so alone. And yet, of course, she wanted to be alone. She needed to be alone. Totally alone.

Far, far away from . . . *him.*

Had she definitely lost her pursuer? She whirled around on her mount. He hadn't followed. She had probably lost him at the brook. So . . .

If she rode back on an even narrower, highly over-grown path, she could reach the brook by just moving a little to the south and west. If she had lost him at the water, she would emerge downstream of him, return to where she had been—and regain her clothing. Alone, she was moving so much more quickly than her party could possibly be going, she would have no problem catching up with them on the very path they had taken—once she was decent again.

"I know, you need water. So do I. Naturally, you need it more," she acknowledged, patting Blaze's neck again and urging her down the narrow path. She was careful all the while, feeling chilled and ridiculous. She was not accustomed to riding naked. The woods suddenly seemed to be filled with all manner of eyes.

She swore at herself, and gave her full attention to the trail. She looked up at the sky, hoping she had a few hours of light left. She couldn't begin to imagine being stuck out here, riding alone, naked on her horse—in the dark. "This has to be one of the insanest things I've done as yet, Blaze, though I admit, I had wanted adventures out of life. However, I had wanted to tour the pyramids of Egypt and the like, not the backwoods of my own home!"

As she had planned, she returned to the brook by way of the downstream trail. She dismounted quickly, drinking deeply from the fresh water, then leading the thirsting horse to drink as well. She looked around herself. Nothing . . . or no one. Just a brisk forty-five-minute trot and she could be back to her clothing, pretending that this wretched episode had never occurred.

Yet just as she was congratulating herself on being safe, she saw the huge brown horse with the long, thick mane—and the Yankee riding the animal. The rider had eschewed the trail all together—he came racing straight through the water, his speed uncanny, his body leaning low so that he was all but one with the animal.

She shrieked with surprise, tearing for Blaze, leaping up on her horse with a speed and agility born of sheer panic. She managed to seat herself on Blaze . . .

But that was all.

The huge brown horse was upon her.

As was its rider.

The man made the leap from horse to horse with the sure certainty of a circus performer. She screamed wildly, twisting in a vehement denial of what had happened, only to find his arms around her, the horse rearing, and the two of them plummeting to the ground.

She struck hard, but he struck harder, having somehow come around her as they had sailed to the earth to take the brunt of the fall. For seconds, she couldn't breathe, think, or shake herself from her state of pure surprise that she lived, yet lay on the ground. Then she realized the very serious—no, desperate!—nature of her predicament, and she tried to rise. His arm came around her. She jabbed an elbow into his rib, heard him grunt and groan. She tried again to jackknife to her feet, only to find him catching her, spinning her down again, and this time, straddling her, capturing her viciously flailing fists, and pinning them to her sides.

"All right, madam, who are you, and what is your game?" he demanded.

She drew in a ragged breath, staring up at the man, seeing him in truth for the first time. He was perhaps twenty-five to thirty years old, with striking hazel eyes that seemed to hold her with a greater force than the powerful hands that had pinned her wrists to the ground. His hair was dark, rich, and certainly askew at the moment, nearly as tangled as her own. His features were haunting . . . handsome features, a face well defined with clean lines, broad cheekbones, squared jaw, ample brow, and a dead straight nose. Yet the years had woven a tension into those features, and he might have been younger than he appeared. Fine lines teased around his eyes, and his mouth; she had never felt such a sheer force of will in a man. He seemed furious, and exceptionally contemptuous, as if her behavior were a personal assault and not the result of her stupidity. His hardened, rough-edged anger—along with the fact that she was in an entirely untenable position— brought back her own bravado. When all was lost and panic threatened, there was nothing left to do but keep fighting.

"Who the hell are you and what is your game, sir? Though you are no 'sir,' no gentleman, ah! But then again, you're a Yankee in a Southern state, are you not?"

"Who are *you*?" he repeated, snapping out the words.

Her name? Good God, she should die rather than give her name! What if he knew Ian? There were tens of thousands of troops, of course, but this fellow was cavalry, like her oldest brother. And he was in Florida, where Ian was sent often enough. And even if he didn't know Ian, Lord! He could give out her name and . . .

"Who do you think?" she spat out, bitter, furiously aware now that she *had* been caught—and far more than a little afraid, no matter how hard she fought to remain calm and seek any advantage for escape. "I'm Lady Godiva, of course."

That, at least, seemed to amuse him a bit. The smallest hint of a smile teased his lips.

"Then what, my dear lady, is your game?"

Her game . . .

She was pinned to the ground, stark naked, by a stranger. A young, powerful stranger with arms of steel and eyes that belonged to a cheetah. She was humiliatingly aware of the rough feel of his clothing against her bare flesh. Her hair . . . yes, her hair was still her cloak, yet it left so very much to be desired. Indeed, what was her game?

"No game, sir. You scared me, I ran . . . leaving my clothing, I'm afraid."

"What a liar you are!" he said smoothly, the gold cheetah eyes seeming to burn into her.

"I beg your pardon, but I am telling you the truth! Your arrival on the south side of the river kept me from my clothing—"

"And you just happened to be way out here, a good Southern lass, stripped bare and bathing in a little tributary far, far from the nearest civilization?"

"I was simply out riding, sir."

"From where?"

"From where? Well, from . . . um, my home, of course."

"And where is that?"

"Oh, well, I come from . . ."

"Yes?"

"I won't give away the location of my home to the enemy, sir. Suffice it to say that I live near, that I was out riding."

"No, you weren't."

She was alarmed to see that no argument on her part

would change him. Again, the seriousness and foolishness of her situation struck her, and she started to shake. He was all too aware of her distress as well, which naturally brought her temper rising again, even while her better senses warned her that she might well be in danger of both rape and murder, and there would be those wretches who might think she had brought about such a horror by her own wanton behavior.

"Sir, you are apparently an officer—"

"A Yankee, as you noted."

"As an officer of the Federal army, I charge you, sir, to rise, and to cease bringing such discomfort to a lady."

"A lady?"

"Yes! You must release me. Now!"

"Perhaps I'm not a Yankee officer."

"What?"

"I could be a deserter, with a stolen frockcoat. A man on the run from both Federal and Confederate law, a desperado, glad of any treasure to be found in the way of money, cash, goods, clothing—or human flesh."

She froze, staring at him, every inch of her flesh burning, terror seeming to wrap around her like the tentacles of an octopus. Somehow, she kept staring at him without blinking. And she told him, "Kill me then, and quickly, and steal what you will. My horse is all I have of value."

"Now, Madam Godiva, what man would want to kill you quickly, without enjoying the good sport to be had first?"

The deep crawl of his voice had a very serious edge, and yet staring at him, reading the harsh lines and character in his still striking face, she didn't believe that he was a deserter.

"Do what you will quickly, slowly, but threaten me no more!" she charged him, yet then she couldn't help but cry out, "Just exactly what is it you want?"

"I want to know your plan, Miss . . . er . . . Godiva. I mean, most obviously, you were trying to lure me away from something. What?"

"I don't know what you're talking about! And if you're an officer—"

"A might-be deserter," he reminded her.

"You are no deserter, you are a Yankee officer, and you must follow some rudimentary code of conduct. Yankees *are* accredited with atrocious manners, but this . . ."

"Bad manners? If I were to rape and murder you, madam, you would consider it nothing more than *bad manners*?"

"You are no cold-blooded murderer!" she cried. And perhaps, at last, something in her voice reached him. She heard the grating of his jaw, but something changed just slightly in his eyes, in the way he watched her. "If you would be a gentleman . . ."

"Oh, dear, Miss Godiva, I'm so very sorry," he said. He eased his hold on her wrists, then released them. Sitting back on his haunches without casting any great weight upon her, he crossed his arms over his chest. "If you think to shame me, you've come across the wrong man—at the wrong time. And in the wrong state of dress, I'm afraid. I do remember learning manners concerning the fairer sex, but in those classes, the ladies tended to have clothing on the bodies to whom one was to be so polite and correct."

"Would you please stop speaking to me in such a sarcastic manner? This is wretched and cruel, and obviously a terrible discomfort to me."

"Young woman!" he snapped, suddenly furious and leaning over her. "Have you lost your mind? Every day that the war lingers longer, there are more deserters roaming the woods and forests, more desperate men about, more men who wouldn't give a damn for the value of your life much less your virtue! Now who the hell are you and what the hell are you doing out here?"

She gritted her teeth, aware that he was right in many ways. She was frightened, as she had seldom been frightened in all her life.

"Yes!" she admitted. "Yes! I was trying to distract you! But you needn't fear—I kept you from no great troop movements, no desperately desired spy . . . just a few wounded men, seeking solace and healing!"

He stared at her for a very long time, then at last, he rose, and for a moment, her distress was greater, for without his frame to conceal her, she was all the more unclad. Yet as she awkwardly tried to rise and sweep her hair around her nakedness, he slipped his frockcoat from his shoulders, reached impatiently down to help her rise, and encompassed her in his coat. Her teeth were suddenly chattering.

"It's a Yankee garment!" she murmured, painfully aware that it was a laundered garment, with a hint of masculine aftershave about it, along with a faint scent of leather and tobacco, scents she associated with a time long ago, her father's drawing room, her brother after a day's hunt, so long ago.

"Do you want to give it back?" he asked, hands on hips.

Without his coat, he still cut a strong and imposing figure. His cotton shirt had somehow remained white, and the breadth of his shoulders seemed even more visible. His flesh was bronzed by the sun to a deep copper, and that, with the striking rise of his cheekbones, reminded her of someone she knew, but could not place.

She hugged the frockcoat to her. "No, I don't want to give the garment back. I thank you for the courtesy. But . . . now that you know I'm actually an innocent caught by circumstance, sir, you'll forgive me if I wish to part ways—"

"An innocent?" he inquired with dark skepticism.

"Yes, really! And I'm about to be on my way—"

"What?" he lashed out succinctly.

"I'm going," she said, then sighed with impatience. "I go my way, you go yours. You're a Yankee, I'm a Rebel, but since there's no one else here, just us, no real war about, it seems we should just go our separate ways."

"Lady Godiva! Not on your life!" he informed her.

She stared back at him, growing uneasy again. She lifted her chin. "I'm leaving," she informed him, turning about. But she didn't manage to leave.

"Take one step toward your horse, madam, and I'll

drag you down to the dirt again, and this time, I promise, I will not let you up."

He spoke quietly, with an almost pleasant warning, and yet, she was very afraid he meant exactly what he was saying.

She hesitated, spinning back to him.

"Then what is your intent?" she demanded.

"Well, first, we'll go back for your clothes. After all, I wouldn't want you thinking that Yankees *can't* be gentlemen."

"My clothing, good. That will be another honorable courtesy. And what then?"

"Then . . ." he said, his voice trailing.

"Yes!" she hissed. "Then—what then?"

"Then . . . we shall see," he said simply.

She turned to head for Blaze again, but then started as she felt his hand fall on her shoulder. "Oh no, my dear Lady Godiva," he told her.

She twisted around to meet his eyes, her own wide with innocence.

"You said that we were riding back. I was merely attempting to reach my horse—"

"You'll ride with me," he said, and turned her toward him, adjusting his way-too-big frockcoat over her shoulders. "I wouldn't want you tempted to run naked into the woods again. Alone."

"But—"

She never went further with her protest. His hands locked upon her waist and he set her upon his own mammoth gelding, slipped up behind her with the same uncanny agility she had seen before, and lifted the reins. She felt his chest at her back, his arms around her. Renewed anger and a wretched shaking seized hold of her at the same time. She didn't want to fight at the moment—or move. Movement only made things worse. She'd shared a greater intimacy with a stranger in a matter of minutes than she had known with any man in her life—father, brothers, and patients included.

"My horse—"

"She follows behind us," he assured her.

"There is no need to do this," she said, trying not to sound as if she pleaded too desperately. "I am no threat to you—"

"You are mistaken. You are a threat, to me—and to yourself. In fact, your intent is to be an incredible threat."

"But—"

"You were moving with soldiers, madam, weren't you? By your own admission," he reminded her.

"Yes, but—"

"You are bold enough to entice a soldier into the woods with a display of the . . . the barest beauty. Clever enough to try to lie your way out of any predicament. So I wonder, who are you? What other sacrifices do you make for your war department? Give me your name."

"I think not."

"I think so."

"Do you plan a Yankee torture?"

"I plan to have the truth."

"Then you explain yourself, and quit playing games. What do you intend to do once we have retrieved my clothing?"

"Why, remove you from the war. Take you into custody. Find out more about you. Perhaps in St. Augustine we'll discover that dozens of men have been lured to their doom by the wiles of the Lady Godiva."

"No!" she protested in horror. St. Augustine! She had kin throughout the city, some there permanently, some coming and going, her oldest brother being the worst of them. She would not, could not, be dragged to St. Augustine. Oh, God, Ian would . . .

She didn't even want to imagine what Ian would say and do. And her father would find out, and her mother . . .

"You have to let me go."

"No."

"But—"

"You will remain in my custody until I can give you over to the proper authorities, and that is that. You should thank me, you little fool! Keep up a lifestyle like this and you are sure to be ravaged if not slain. It's my fondest hope that your father is a good, stern Southern fellow who will quite simply find a good hickory stick and a wood shed and leave such an impression on your—dare we say bare?—flesh that you never think of such foolhardy behavior again."

She lowered her head slightly. Her father had one hell of a temper, for sure, but he had never raised a hand against any of them in anger. What would he do now? It wasn't his violence she feared. It was his disappointment. She adored him, had always adored him, as she did her mother. She'd been a normal child, she thought, angry and rebellious at times, but the last years had shown her time and time again that she'd been blessed, and she never, ever wanted to cause her parents harm. Or shame. They had all chosen their ways; they had even been encouraged to know their own hearts. Her father had never called anyone a traitor, though the name was thrown at him often enough because he refused to say that he had come to terms with secession.

"Don't you think you've chastised me quite enough for any father?"

"Not in the least."

"I did what I had to do."

"And I'm doing what I have to do."

"So I should be repentant—and grateful? Well, you bastard, I'm not sorry!" she proclaimed suddenly, tossing her hair back. "There were injured men who would not survive your dragging them to St. Augustine!"

"Oh, we'll find them," he assured her in such a way that she was chilled.

She shook her head again. This time, with her hair playing havoc beneath his nose, he sneezed.

"If you don't mind . . ." he began.

"I do mind! You must leave those men alone. They are just children, just boys, too young to be in the service, don't you see? But the state is so desperate, so many men are dead, rotting in Southern states that are actually far north of us! There is no militia left—" She broke off, realizing that she was telling a Yankee in just

what horrible a condition the state's defenses were in.
"Well, of course, troops will be sent back. There is an
action that will surely go on to the north, there are so
many troops, North and South accumulating . . . in that
arena, of course, we have thousands of men—"

"Madam, neither of us is a fool."

"You must make no attempt on those boys! And you
must leave me alone. I'll escape, you know, and if I have
to, I'll kill you—"

"Thank you. I'll be forewarned. I believe we have now
come back to where we began. In fact, I think that pile
there might be your clothing."

Yes, they had come back to where they had begun.
Where she had been such a fool, delighting in the feel
of being really clean after so much blood and dirt . . .

There lay her clothing. Dried out over the log where
she had laid it.

He leapt down from the horse, reaching up to her.
With little choice, she accepted his arms. Yet, before he
would lift her down, he asked her, "What is your real
name, Godiva?" he asked her.

"Godiva—that is all!" she told him.

"I will find out."

"Will you? What is your name, sir? Tell me, so I can
always remember the incredible rudeness of the invading
Yanks," she demanded.

He grinned, but it seemed his teeth grit audibly for a
number of seconds. "Ah, if you are Godiva, then call
me Captor of Godiva, so it seems, madam. And I am
no invader." He lifted her to the ground. "Madam, if
you'll allow me . . ." he said, bowing with a polite flourish. Then he walked to the pile of clothing, bent over,
and one by one began to retrieve her garments. His
broad-shouldered back was to her. Pity she had nothing
to throw against it! She thought again about running,
but she had learned how quickly he could move. And
she did want her clothing.

He turned at last, taking a few leisurely steps toward
her. Impatiently, she strode forward, snatching her cloth-

ing from him. With it clutched in her hands, she demanded, "Do you mind?"

He grinned. "Yes, actually, I do. It's just a shade nerve-wracking to turn one's back on you. Just now, you considered an escape—but luckily for you, dear Godiva, you chose reason over stupidity."

"The gentlemanly thing to do—"

"That does not seem relevant here, does it, since you enticed me into the woods in something—shall we say—slightly less than a lady's apparel?"

She swung her back on him, dropped his frockcoat, and quickly dressed. Despite her bid for dignity, she tripped over her pantalettes. When she turned back to him, cheeks reddening, he was somewhat attempting to conceal an amused smile.

"What now, sir?" she demanded.

"I'll take my coat back." He came forward to retrieve it. He stared into her eyes, then reached to the ground for the coat she had dropped. Standing before her, he slipped the garment back over his shoulders. His eyes never left hers.

"And now?" she queried.

"We follow the path we should have taken."

She shook her head suddenly, with honest passion. "You don't want to find my injured lads. I swear to you that they are harmless—"

"We shall see."

"If you chase them, they will think they have to fight."

"Madam, I assure you—"

"Don't you see, they're young! They'll think they're honor-bound to die. All men seem to come into this wretched war thinking that they're obliged to die! Please . . . !"

She was startled to realize that she had reached out, touching his arm. She felt the hardness of his muscle beneath the fabric of his clothing. He was fit, rugged, in good shape. Not an officer whose men did his bidding while he sat back himself. His men . . .

He was here on his own. Did he command others? Or

had he gained his rank through his prowess with the weapons he carried?

She gazed at her hand where it rested on his arm. Met his eyes again. Snatched her hand away. She didn't want to touch him. She didn't want to think of him as being human, much less male, and a male in a healthy and rugged good condition which would make him all the more a very dangerous adversary.

She knew she was flushing as she stared at him.

"They don't need to die," she whispered. "Honestly. It would be like the murder of children."

"You can't begin to imagine how many children have died," he told her curtly.

"But . . ."

"I've no interest in causing further harm to your injured. Still, Godiva, you will come with me. And we will see this through. Together."

He turned around, heading toward the horses. Watching him, frustrated, furious, and more afraid than ever of his strength and determination, Tia remembered the small ladies' Smith and Wesson she carried in her skirt pocket.

With his back to her, she quickly dug in her pocket, reached for the weapon, curled her fingers around it, and pulled it out. She aimed it dead center on his spine.

"Sir!"

He swung around and paused when he saw the gun.

"Now—you will come with me. My prisoner." Feeling elated, she kept the gun level on his heart, but approached him, her eyes narrowed, her gait suddenly light. "Ever hear of Andersonville?" she asked quietly.

"Indeed, I have," he said coolly.

"Say your prayers, soldier," she told him, "for you will be going there."

"I think not," he told her.

"Why? I will shoot you, you know."

"Will you?"

"Do you doubt it?"

His narrowed gold eyes assessed her. "I don't know you well enough to know just what you will do. You do ride around the woods naked. Maybe you would shoot a man in cold blood."

"Don't tempt me!" she warned.

He stared at her for a long moment, then said, "It's growing late." He turned, starting for the horses.

"Stop, you fool! You are my prisoner. I am very capable with a gun. My marksmanship is excellent."

He ignored her. She gritted her teeth hard. She didn't want to shoot him. He was the enemy, of course, but he was a flesh-and-blood man. She couldn't just shoot him down, but he was simply walking away. "Stop, I mean it!"

Again, he ignored her.

She fired—intending to shoot into the dirt.

Except that . . . she didn't shoot at all.

He swung back around, slowly arching a brow. She stared from the gun to him, and back to the gun again.

"You didn't think I'd leave you with a loaded gun, did you?" he queried.

"But . . . how . . ." she began, and then she realized that he had quickly, subtly found the gun when he had gone to collect her clothing—when he had turned his back on her.

And now . . .

Now he thought that she had been ready to shoot him down in cold blood.

The color drained from her face as he stared at her.

She turned to run.

She went no more than ten feet before she found herself spinning, then crashing back down to the earth again. And he was straddling her, pinning her down. She couldn't breathe. She could only feel the heat from the fire in his eyes.

"Lady, trust me!" he said softly. "From here on out, *you* are *mine*."

# Chapter 3

〰

"Yours! Oh, no, you are mistaken," she promised him icily. "I'm not yours—or the Union's. I don't belong to any man or state or government. I'm not property—"

"As no woman—or man—should be," he interrupted quietly.

She caught her breath, well aware that he was suggesting she fought for what was called the "peculiar institution" of slavery.

She didn't owe him any explanations, nor could she possibly care what this stranger thought about her, her ideals, ethics, principles, or the reasons for any of her behaviors. And still, she found that she was defensively lashing out at him. "Kindly release me, sir. I don't belong to any man, and I don't own any men—or women or children. Neither do any members of my family."

"Who are you then? Where is your family? Tell me that, and I will gallantly help you to your feet."

She pursed her lips, staring at him stubbornly.

"I can wait."

She smiled icily. "Good. I can wait, too. I have no desire at all for you to try to behave 'gallantly' in any way, shape, or form."

"Fine. We'll both just wait."

To her horror, he stretched out beside her, an arm and a leg continuing to pin her to the ground. Infuriated, she started to struggle, only to find that she did nothing but edge more closely against his blue-clad frame.

And he watched her. Watched her with those large hazel eyes of his. Again, she felt a strange shivering sensation while meeting his gaze, as if she knew him, or should know something about him. And she grew desperate to free herself from the intimacy he forced.

"Catherine," she lied. "My name is Catherine—Moore."

That was all it took. He rose, offering a hand down to assist her with all the gallantry he had promised. She would have none of it, of course. Petty, childish, perhaps, but he could hang before she would accept the slightest assistance from him. She scrambled to her feet on her own, eyeing him warily all the while.

"And now?"

"Now we ride."

"My horse—"

"Will follow again."

She shook her head. "You're being unnecessarily cruel to a good horse, Yank. The added weight—"

"Your weight is nothing," he assured her dismissively, which made her want to draw up to her full height. Except that she was petite, which didn't seem at all fair. Her brothers were giants; even her mother was tall.

She wanted to be formidable.

"You're mistaken—" she began, but he interrupted her curtly.

"I will have your silence, madam!"

"I don't have to—"

"I can gag you."

She gritted her teeth again, standing with her arms folded firmly across her chest. "Be glad you did find the bullets in that gun, Yank. It doesn't take a wrestler to fire a lethal shot!"

"I stand forewarned. Now you shall stand silent," he said. He just looked at her and spoke with a low, almost pleasant tone. She had been threatened, really threatened, and she knew it. She lifted her hands, arching a brow, not willing to give him the last word, nor really willing to be silent.

And so she watched him.

Minutes later, she thought that the most distressing thing about being with the stranger—other than fearing for her life and future—was the uncanny way he seemed to have of *knowing* exactly where people had been, and where they had gone. He picked up on the trail taken by her party of green soldiers and injured men, though he barely glanced at the tracks in the pine-strewn trails, nor took time to study broken and bent foliage and trees. He quickly assessed the area, set her upon his horse again, and mounted behind her. Then they started riding. And despite the time he had taken pursuing her, capturing her, and returning to this spot along the river, she knew that they would overtake the others. Whether they did so before or after they reached the old abandoned Indian camp, she couldn't quite determine.

But they would find her little party of injured. That was a simple fact.

"You should just take me in," she told him suddenly. "I am the famed Godiva. I have led thousands of men to their deaths, I have caused ships to crash, I—along with General Lee perhaps, and blessed Stonewall, while he lived, and a few others—have almost single-handedly kept the Confederacy in the war. I have—"

"Graced many a stage, I imagine?" he queried dryly.

She bit her lip, lowering her eyes. Once upon a time, her mother had thought to find her livelihood on the stage. Long ago, before she had met and married her father. She certainly hadn't inherited her mother's golden coloring, but perhaps she did carry within her a certain talent for the dramatic—and as he had suggested, bald-faced lying.

"Take me in, I warn you. I am dangerous. If you wait for darkness, terrible things may happen. I'm not even human, really. I'm a shape-changer. I—"

"The cabin lies just ahead, and I imagine your men are within it," he said flatly.

"And what could you possibly want with my injured?" she queried.

"To see who they are," he told her.

"Green boys."

"Maybe, maybe not."

"But—"

"You've lied about everything."

"I'm not lying now!"

"But there's no way for me to tell that, is there—Catherine?"

The way he said the name was chilling. As if he knew she had lied even there.

"I warn you—given the opportunity, I will shoot you down before I'll let you injure a single one of those boys."

"If those boys are who and what you say, they are in no danger from me."

"And if they're not, you may be dead yourself in a matter of minutes!"

"I don't think so."

She didn't need to see his face to feel the strange hazel piercing of his eyes. She wondered again what it was that seemed so familiar about him, when she was sure she didn't know him. He reminded her of someone, and she couldn't quite place who, or why.

"Think about it—I could be leading you into a real trap," she warned quietly.

"I'm thinking, and I don't believe that you're leading me anywhere at the moment," he replied, his voice a very soft drawl. Then it struck her—he might be wearing a Yankee uniform, but he hailed from somewhere in the South.

She twisted around to accost him. "What kind of a traitor are you?"

"I'm true to my convictions, and that makes me an honest man. I wonder if there is any honesty in you whatsoever."

She turned again. The light had begun to fall. She might have lost her own way here, as familiar as she considered herself with the area. But he was right; they were almost upon the old Indian cabin in the woods.

"What do you think you're going to do? Barge in and shoot down a half-dozen men?" she inquired desperately. "Because, of course, they'll be forced to shoot at you if you come after them."

"Not if you keep them from doing so," he said.

"What? Why should I stop them?"

"Because you want them to live."

"The odds are—"

"That not one of your 'green' boys will get off a single shot before I mow them all down." It didn't sound as if he was bragging—merely stating a fact.

He reined to a halt along the trail right before the cove with the small cabin. It had been built and abandoned many years before, during the Seminole War, when the Florida Indians had built their homes with native pine before learning that they had to run so often and so fast that it made far more sense to build platform houses with nothing but thatch roofs—houses above the ground and the vermin in the swamps where they were finally forced.

Since those days, the cabin had been used often enough. Lovers had known it as a place to tryst; hunters and fishermen had found it a haven in the woods. It was known, however, only to the locals.

Or so she had thought.

"Well, Godiva?" he inquired.

"Let me down. I'll tell them not to fire. Except, if you think you can drag my wounded boys back to be seized for a wretched Yank camp—"

"All I want to do is see your wounded boys, Godiva."

That was difficult to believe. And the Yankee's Spencer repeating rifle didn't just look dangerous, it killed, "mowed" men down, just as he'd suggested.

"Let me down then."

This time, he dismounted from behind her. She braced herself to refuse any assistance to dismount from him.

She needn't have bothered. He didn't offer any assistance, and when she met his strange gold eyes as she dismounted on her own, she saw that he was fully aware she would have prided herself on her refusal of anything he offered. She felt let down—and furious.

"A hand might have been polite and proper."

"And you probably would have spit at it. Go, see to your men. Call one of them out and tell them to hold their fire."

She walked toward the cabin, tempted to run inside, take cover, and see that he was blasted. But she just didn't dare. Instinct warned her that this man meant business, and no cover would make her, or the boys, truly safe from his intent.

"Jemmy! Jemmy Johnson!" she called. "It's—" She nearly stated her name, then quickly caught herself. "It's me! Please, come out!"

The old, weather-beaten door to the cabin opened. Jemmy Johnson, Enfield in hand, stepped out warily. She was glad to see his caution, although it wasn't quite enough.

"Miss T—" he began carefully.

"Private!" she interrupted quickly. "The enemy is among us, but he has sworn to let us be if we are all that we say we are. Hold your fire. Command the others to hold their fire."

"But Miss T—"

"Jemmy, for your lives, and for the blessed love of God! Do as I say!" she pleaded. "Weapons down."

"Hell, Jemmy!" someone bellowed from within the cabin. "I ain't holding no weapon! I'm trying to keep Stuart here from bleeding to death!"

It might have been a lie; it might not. But the strange Yankee seemed to go by gut instinct as well. He went striding by Tia and straight into the cabin, his Colts secured to the gun belt at his waist, his Spencer held easily in his left hand.

Easily . . .

She was certain he could spin it around and fire in seconds flat.

She followed behind him quickly.

No lie had been spoken by Trev McCormack, the eighteen-year-old standing by Stuart Adair, one of the two patients. He had been laid atop a rough wooden workbench where Trev kept shifting to put more pressure on his friend's bleeding calf wound. Hadley Blake, the second wounded man, had passed out, and lay with his head supported by a saddle blanket in a corner of the dusky cabin. Gilly Shenley, one of the unwounded

recruits, searched the cabin for a proper stick with which
to form a tourniquet for Stuart's dangerously bleeding
wound.

"Move, boys, let me see the source for that," the Yankee commanded. They stood dead still, staring at him.

"Move!" he snapped.

And they did.

Tia almost cried out as she watched him grip Stuart's
calf and survey the damage. He stared at her. "Come
on, Miss Godiva, you've surely had some medical training! Get some bandages ripped, a tourniquet going—"

"Can't find a sound stick—" Gilly complained.

"Break up that old broom over there. Come on, lad,
a young thing like you can surely snap that pine bough!"

Gilly did as told. Tia quickly ripped up her hemline,
glad that he meant to do his best to save Stuart's life,
humiliated that he was telling them what to do. Hell yes,
she knew her business, and if he hadn't steered her away
from her boys, they wouldn't be in this predicament!
She could have stopped the bleeding; she'd worked with
her brother through the majority of the war, and she'd
dare say she was as competent and efficient as most surgeons in the field.

Still, he was more efficient, she had to admit. Within
seconds, a tourniquet had been fashioned, and the bleeding was slowing. A few seconds more, and it was coming
to a halt. And he was telling them how to release it. She
was glad she hadn't stopped him, or made any comments. What mattered here was not who did what, but
that a man's life had been saved.

"Private Gilly, there, is that your name?" the Yankee asked.

"Private Gilly Shenley, sir!" said the boy, a straw
blond with a sad little scraggle of chin whiskers. To Tia's
sheer annoyance, he then saluted.

"I need you to go to the brook and bring me back a
large quantity of the moss that forms on the stones
there. We'll put some new stitching in here and get a
poultice on the wound, and he should heal just fine."

"Yes, sir."

"Also, I need some wild mushrooms, the black-tipped ones. Do you know which ones I mean?"

"I can go," Tia said. "I know exactly what—"

"No, he'll go," the Yankee said, his eyes hard on her. "I'm assuming you can do excellent stitches?"

Her needles and a length of surgical thread—supplied to her by her cousin Jerome McKenzie, one of the few men still successfully running the blockade—were in her pocket. She withdrew them, then stared at her needle for a moment, well aware she had no matches left with which to burn the tip. Then she was startled as the Yank withdrew a box of matches from his pocket and lit one.

She held the tip of the needle in the flame to sterilize it, then threaded the needle, and proceeded very carefully to mend the tear ripped around the young man's wound during their forced flight.

She felt the Yankee watching her for a while, and when she was done, she looked up and saw the first light of approval in his hazel eyes.

"Perfect," he said.

"I've had experience," she told him dryly.

"You've been in Florida the whole war?"

"I have, and I assure you, we've had a constant flow of injuries and disease."

"I wasn't suggesting that your talents were wasted here. I was just thinking how appreciated they might have been during the really tragic battles when tens of thousands of men fell in a single day."

She shrugged. "I don't know what good I would have been elsewhere. I learned everything I know from . . ." She hesitated, not wanting to give herself away in any manner.

"She learned from her brother, the best surgeon in the field!" Trey McCormack provided.

Still watching her, the Yank slowly smiled. "The best surgeon in the field! And who might that be, Private?"

"Don't you tell him, Trey! I don't want this man knowing my name, and certainly not that of my brother. I don't want my brother—"

"Or yourself?" the Yank suggested, interrupting her.

"I don't want my brother jeopardized in any way!" she finished.

"But Miss Ti—"

"Trey!"

"Yes, ma'am."

The Yankee didn't force the point, but still she felt uneasy, aware that he was studying her, perhaps seeing more than she wanted him to see.

"What now?" she asked him.

"We wait for Gilly to get back with the poultice."

"I can make the poultice. I'm as familiar with the healing qualities of mosses and molds as most physicians."

"More so than most, I imagine," he said.

"Are you a physician yourself?"

He shook his head, hesitating slightly. She realized he had decided not to reveal too much about his own identity. "I have a witch doctor or two in my background."

"What?"

"Never mind. Like you, I've learned from experience."

Gilly came back in then, breathing hard, but carrying the moss and the mushrooms in his mess plate.

"They need to be mashed together . . ." the Yankee began.

"Truly, I do this well. Let me make the poultice," Tia said. "Gilly, you can help me. Bring them just outside. Bring your mess plate."

Gilly did as she had ordered. He knelt down by her side when she found a fallen log to use as a worktable.

"Gilly, don't turn around and look back as I talk to you, do you understand?"

"Don't turn around?"

"Gilly, we've got to take him by surprise somehow."

"Take him by surprise? But he hasn't come to hurt us."

"Gilly! He's a Yankee officer—he isn't coming through to applaud us on medical technique!"

"But Tia, he just saved Stuart's life."

"Yes, and I'm grateful for that, though if we hadn't been running, Stuart might not have ripped his previous stitches so badly! The point is, Gilly, we can't chance letting him leave, going for help, and bringing a score of men to take us in."

"A score of Yankees—"

"The state is riddled with them now, Gilly! They've decided that we are to be taken, that we are a danger. Troops are amassing to the north of the state, west of Jacksonville and St. Augustine. We know that they've decided on making a real movement against us here. Trust me, please, Gilly, if he leaves here, he might come back with plenty of reinforcements!"

"And how do we stop him?"

"By surprise, somehow by surprise!"

"Have you taken note of his weapons?"

"Yes, of course, and I'm sure he's adept at using them. We need to divert his attention, and you'll have to take him from the back. It will be our only chance."

"You want me to shoot a man in the back? I don't care if this is war, Miss Tia. That's cold-blooded murder. There are still such things as honor in this world, and if we survive the war, no matter who wins it, I'm still going to have to live with myself."

She stared at the very young man who seemed to know his own purpose so well. "I understand. I'm really not suggesting cold-blooded murder, though how our actions out in the field aren't murder, I don't know. You don't have to kill him. Taken by surprise, he can be knocked out. We can leave him hog-tied and immobile and we can move west again, hook up with Dixie's troops, and then, our wounded will have a far better chance of survival!"

"Leave him tied? There's varmints aplenty out here, Miss Tia."

"I'm sure he'll untie himself. I can only pray that it will take him time."

"But how will we divert him?"

"I don't know yet!" she admitted, exasperated. "Be ready for my signal. When you get the chance, warn Jemmy and Trey."

"Miss Tia, we can move Hadley now; but if we were

to try to move Stuart, I'm afraid the bleeding would start up again."

"Have we got any food on us?"

"What?"

"Food, Private, food. To eat!"

Gilly shook his head. "First you want me to shoot him down. Now you want to invite him to dinner, Miss Tia?"

She sighed, losing her patience. She was dealing with children here! Children already shot up in the defense of their native state, she reminded herself.

"I'm simply trying to buy time."

"We've spent a lot of time out here already," Gilly commented. "Is the poultice done?"

She looked down where she had been busy mashing mushrooms and moss together. It was amazing to see how mechanical her actions had become. The war had so inured her that she could function without thinking. She didn't know if that was good or bad.

Moss and mushrooms were now one pulpy mass, ready to be applied, and bandaged onto the wounded limb.

"Let's go in. And yes, we're inviting him to dinner. We're buying time."

Tia brought the poultice in; Gilly followed behind her. In the cabin, the Yankee was busy with Trey and Jemmy, seeing to the comfort and well-being of their other wounded man, Hadley Blake. The Yank had carried a small bottle of some kind of liquor in his frockcoat pocket. He was in the process of bathing Hadley's wound, this one in the lower arm.

Though he didn't turn around, Tia knew that he was instantly aware that they had returned. His eyes were fixed on the wound. "Your brother is one hell of a surgeon, all right—if he's the one who worked on this boy."

"He is."

"This arm should have been lost."

"He's excellent at saving limbs," she murmured, and she couldn't quite keep the pride from her voice.

The Yank stood. "The poultice?"

"Here."

"Go ahead. Tend to the other boy. I'm sure you know your business."

She stared at him, then walked on over to the worktable where Stuart lay, twitching restlessly now and then.

The boy was very young. Perhaps only fifteen or sixteen. The youngest of this sad little band, she thought, though he had certainly lied his way into the militia. She smoothed the hair back from his forehead. "Help me, Trey."

Trey came to her side.

"Think a splash of that whiskey would do well here?" she asked the Yank.

"Indeed." He stepped forward, bathing her fresh stitchery. Stuart Adair groaned and twitched again. Already, though, his face had more color.

Whiskey often seemed to be the best cleanser they had. Julian had commented that the wounds cleaned with whiskey often seemed to heal the best as well. She dabbed the wound dry, quickly and expertly applied the poultice, then bandaged the leg neatly.

"There's the remains of an old straw bed over there; let's get him on it," the Yank said.

With tremendous care, they moved the wounded boy. When both the injured lay in deep sleep, Trey asked, "Think they'll make it?"

"Half of it is in the spirit, boy," the Yank said. "Yes, I think they'll make it."

"How about joining us for some hardtack stew?" Gilly suggested. "Yank, you are most welcome to anything we've got."

"Well, you can melt down some hardtack with that clean brook water—I'll pick out the maggots. And maybe I can come up with something a bit better. Give me what's left of that broomstick, son."

Gilly found the broken broomstick and handed it to the Yank. He exited the cabin, not seeming to care that his back was to them. And yet it wasn't the right time to strike—Tia knew it. She shrugged to Trey, and followed him out.

The Yankee walked down to the brook. He stood curiously poised over the water.

"What the hel—sorry, Miss Tia. What on earth is he doing?" Jemmy demanded.

"I don't know . . ." Tia murmured, and she felt uncomfortable again, watching the Yank. As if she knew him. Or should understand something about him that she hadn't quite placed in her mind.

Suddenly, like lightning, he moved. When he straightened, he had a huge catfish dangling from the broomstick.

"Hell, yes!" Jemmy cried, delighted. "Oh, sorry, Miss Tia—"

"Quit apologizing for swearing!" she said with a sigh. "This is a war."

"Yes, ma'am, sorry, ma'am. I'll get the cooking fires a-burning!"

"Now, wait . . ." Tia began uneasily. She didn't want any gifts from the strange enemy.

But they weren't waiting. They hadn't really eaten in almost forty-eight hours, and they hadn't had a decent meal in months. A fire was quickly lit. Gilly was an expert at what was called hardtack stew, a meal made by boiling hardtack and adding in bacon grease—or real, smoked bacon, which the Yank had in his saddlebags, and in this case, the hardtack stew made a filling side dish for the main course of the very delicious, fresh fish. The Yankee stranger supplied coffee as well, and laced each cup with a sip of the whiskey. To Tia's alarm, by the time the moon had risen high in the night sky, the boys were looking up to the Yank as some kind of god.

Washing their utensils with Jemmy by the brook, she told him sternly, "He's still a Yank. He's dangerous, and you boys can't forget that."

"Yes, Miss Tia, but you said we needed to buy time. We've bought some time. Trey and Gilly are in the cabin now, getting some of the soft stew into Blake and Stuart. We're giving them the strength to run when the time comes, right?"

She nodded. That much was true.

"We'll also try to get them a night's sleep. It doesn't look as if the Yank's going anywhere yet. But don't go forgetting that he's the enemy."

"No, ma'am."

"In the morning . . ."

"Yes?"

"I'll get him to accompany me down to the brook somehow. You boys follow. I'll keep him occupied. Then you can come in and take him by surprise. You're going to have to move with speed and certainty. Can you do it?"

"I may be young, ma'am, but I know my duty."

"Good."

They returned to the camp.

The tall Yank alone remained by the fireside, standing with a tin camp cup in his hand while he watched the fire die down. He cut a very dashing figure in his handsomely fitted frockcoat, one booted foot set against a log, his head slightly bowed.

Again, she had the eerie feeling he knew the minute they drew near; his hearing was uncanny, as was his eyesight.

He turned to them as they reappeared. His eyes were the pure color of the blaze in the fire, and something about the way he looked at her was just as dangerous.

Jemmy paused with her by the Yank. "I'll go on in and see how our injured boys are doing, getting their nourishment down," Jemmy said.

"You do that, soldier," the Yank advised.

Jemmy left, a bit awkwardly.

And Tia found herself alone with the Yank once again. She felt his gaze as he assessed her with his fire-glowing eyes, a slight smile on his face. "Perhaps you should run in with your valiant, protecting army," he told her.

"Perhaps I should."

"Ah, but you think you should keep an eye on me."

"Perhaps."

"So why do you look like a bird about to take flight? Are you afraid of me, Godiva?"

"No."

"But your heart is beating a thousand times a second, so it seems. I know that look on your face, so wary . . ."

"You don't know me at all!"

"Every inch of you."

Her heart was indeed beating a thousand times a second. And still, she lifted her hair from her neck with a bored nonchalance. "I would appreciate it if you'd quit being so rude as to remind me of my most uncomfortable folly."

"I wouldn't remind you, if I were able to forget!" he said, still smiling, and she didn't know if he was in the least serious, or if he simply enjoyed his game of taunting her.

He indicated the log. "Sit, Godiva."

She stared at him uneasily. She should say good night—then run to the shelter of the cabin and the security of her boys.

He knew her hesitation, and smiled.

"Be reckless! Brave, bold, confident! Take the risk. Courage, Godiva! Indeed, I think you're going to need it."

"There is no risk in sitting with you!" she countered, but it was a lie, for suddenly . . .

She felt as if she were indeed in the greatest danger she had yet encountered.

# Chapter 4

⁓

"Coffee with a shot of whiskey?" the Yank suggested. "I did make the offer earlier, though you refused me."

"Why, naturally, sir," she said, "I am quite careful with a stranger, when that stranger is an enemy."

"Ah, so speaks the Southern Belle!" he taunted.

"So speaks a war-weary, wary young woman, sir. Do you think you can make me drunk?"

"Drunk? You? From a single shot of whiskey?" She wasn't sure whether or not to be offended by the amusement in his eyes. "Not at all. I have a feeling that proper lady though you may be, you're quite familiar with whiskey and other spirits."

She ignored his tone then. "Fine. I'll have coffee with a good strong shot of whiskey. You're right—I am familiar with spirits."

He poured her coffee and added a generous dose of the whiskey. She accepted it, watching him.

"So . . . you're staying through the night?" she asked him.

"I am."

"What if you fall asleep, and we cut your throat?"

"You won't."

"Why not?"

"Because if I hear one of you near me—which I will—I'll put a bullet through flesh so fast there won't be time to scream."

She shivered at his tone, then huddled into herself, sipping her coffee, hoping that he hadn't seen her reaction.

But he was suddenly closer to her, hunkered down in front of her, his eyes searchingly on her own. "Did you intend to slit my throat, Godiva?" he inquired.

"No," she murmured uncomfortably.

She swallowed a huge sip of coffee, burned her mouth, and almost choked. She stared at him again, then shook her head. It was odd to have him so close again, and alarming to feel that she was coming to know him in some small way. Odd, the things she noticed, like the size of his hand, the rough texture of his palms, the length of his fingers, the neat, clean cut of his nails. She swallowed hard, wishing she did not feel so unnerved, and that she could find him to be a far more repulsive person. "Why are you staying here? Why haven't you moved on?"

He shrugged, still too close. "I have my reasons."

"We're just what I said we were, a small party of children. Injured children at that, as you can see. And very, very tired," she added, sighing.

"Then relax," he suggested. "Put your head back. Sit upon the ground there. Let the fire warm you. It is, in truth, a spectacular night. The air is cool, but the fire is warm. The stars remain beautiful in a clear, ebony sky. Rest."

"Rest?" she inquired. "With you? Lie down beside a rattler?"

He laughed easily. "Oh, Godiva! I think your fangs are probably far more dangerous than my own."

"But—"

"Had I meant to hurt you or molest you in any way, lady, I have certainly had my opportunities, don't you think?"

She lowered her lashes, flushing.

"Lie back on the saddle and blanket there." He rose, indicating the spot with a sweep of his arm. "The pines are soft beneath the blanket; the canopy of the sky is certainly a lovely one tonight."

Near the log, before the fire, he had laid out his saddle, saddle blanket, and army-issue bedroll. She was

amazed to realize just how welcoming and comfortable
it all looked.

But then, it had been a long day.

"You had intended that as your own bed," she said
politely.

"Lady Godiva, it is yours."

"But—"

"Allow your enemy to be valiant."

She rose as well, meeting his eyes again as they stood
before the fire.

"Fine, I will steal your bed. If—"

"If?" he interrupted her. "If I make no assumptions
that your being in my bed means that, er, you wish to
be in my bed. Trust me—I had no intention of doing so."

"Fine!" she said. She turned away from him, taking
the few steps to the spot. Then, after she had stretched
out, pulled his camp blanket around herself, and closed
her eyes, she added a soft "Thank you."

"My pleasure, Godiva."

He didn't touch her, but he was near. She heard him
sit down upon the log again, and though she didn't open
her eyes, she knew that he kept his gaze upon the fire,
and that he was thoughtful.

Would he tire? she wondered. Sleep soundly?

Soundly enough that they might surprise him in his
sleep?

No. She was certain that assaulting him in the night
would mean certain death. And not for him.

Yet would the morning be any better?

Perhaps, if she was any kind of seductress at all. If he
had come to trust her at all . . .

She was so tired, yet surely, far too nervous to sleep.
He was there, sitting beside her on the log. So close. His
presence unlike any she had known before.

Strange, but that enemy presence lent a certain security to the night. She stretched like a cat, then eased
more deeply into her makeshift bed, feeling a luxurious
sense of comfort. The weather was so cool—a Florida
winter, coming in earnest. The air seemed refreshingly
sweet around. The bedroll was warm where she was

cold, and the saddle and blanket did make a fine pillow. Half-awake and half-asleep, she slit her eyes, and she could see the fire as it flickered and danced in the night. She was exhausted. Indeed, she'd been so tired, and then so full of catfish, and then the coffee spiked with the whiskey . . .

The world fogged. She was still so keenly aware of him. And she strangely thought that he smelled good; he was bathed, shaven, smelling of soap and leather, clean and rugged. *Yet why did something about him seem familiar? Why did it seem she should know something, understand who he was, what he was . . .*

The answer eluded her. Her eyes closed further. She could dare to trust him tonight. So that she could betray him come morning.

It was easy to sleep, and yet later, she awoke, shivering.

The fire must have died.

She rose slightly and saw that he was up, stoking new life into the fire.

He heard her, sensed her, knew that she was awake.

"Cold?"

"No, not really."

"Yes, you are."

He came to her. With his unnerving agility, he was down and beside her before she even realized his intent. She started to move, to protest, but he set an arm around her firmly. "I mean you no harm, Godiva! Trust me, you hardheaded little wild thing. I'm only trying to warm you."

"I don't want the warmth of such an enemy."

"Didn't anyone ever tell you, Godiva, that we don't always get what we want?"

"No!"

"Then it's time someone did. Lie down, sleep."

She gritted her teeth. She hadn't quite realized the scope of his strength; the arm around her was like an iron clasp. She closed her eyes, protesting no more. She could hardly entice him to join her down by the stream in the morning and flirt with him so engagingly that he'd forget his back if she fought being near him while they slept.

It would just have to be a wretched night. One in which she would never find any rest again.

But she did sleep. Comfortably, and very deeply. She was amazed to feel the coming of the sun against her cheeks, hear the chirping of birds.

The world, she thought, could be so strange. War everywhere. Men killing men. But the birds let out their calls as usual, the sun rose each morning, winter came, and the breeze was fresh. And it was possible to waken in the morning and believe that there was no war . . .

Except that, when she awoke, he was there. Beside her as he had been. She had twisted and turned and— mortifying as it might be—she had used him. Used his form for added warmth, curled into the curve of his body, turned into it again. And now she looked his way.

She had slept beside the man, through the night, and she didn't even know his name.

His eyes opened, hard on hers, and she realized that he hadn't lied, that the softest whisper of sound, a bare hint of movement, awoke him. She'd done nothing but open her eyes, and she had awakened him.

Or had he already been awake?

She thought that was the case. He had awakened and lain there without moving. Not to disturb her? Or to study her. But there they lay, his eyes now on hers with just inches between them, their bodies all but entwined.

She instantly pushed away, forgetting all thought of seducing him into an entrapment. She awkwardly struggled to her feet, backed away from him, and turned, fleeing toward the brook.

Her heart was hammering, lungs heaving. She felt hot and cold, and hot again.

The water beckoned. Bubbling over the little rocks midstream, powder blue, except for diamond-like crystals that rode the surface, gifts of the sun.

At the brook, she fell to her knees. She splashed her face, half-soaking her gown, and so she opened her bodice at the throat. The water was wonderful, so cleansing.

More and more. She scooped up big handfuls of the fresh, cold water, and dashed it against her face, her neck, her collarbone. She delved into her voluminous skirt pocket again and found what had become her most cherished possession—her horsehair toothbrush. It was wearing thin, but then again, this was war.

Fortunately, Christmas was near. And one of the blessings of being a civilian was that she could go home, and at Cimarron, her mother would give her a new toothbrush, maybe even understanding just how much such a small item meant.

"I've got baking powder," she heard.

She stiffened. He'd followed her. Already.

Were any of her men even awake yet? Would they arrive in time if she were to distract him here—now?

And then, that thought didn't really matter—she realized just what he had said.

Baking powder! A great luxury for cleaning teeth, now that she was so constantly on the road and on the run.

She jumped to her feet, spinning around to face him. He walked toward her, taking a leather satchel from his frockcoat and handing it to her. He remained amused, and yet he seemed to understand. She accepted the gift, knelt to the water again, and felt the delirious, sensual pleasure of really cleaning her teeth. She ran her tongue over and over them, delighting in the smooth feel.

When she rose and turned toward him, ready to thank him, she realized that Trey and Gilly were hovering near the rear of the pines. She lowered her eyes quickly, moistened her lips. Then she looked up at the Yank with a bright smile. She moved an inch closer to him. He still smelled like soap and leather, not at all repugnant. This was doable. She lay a hand against his frockcoat, aware that her bodice was opened to what she hoped was a temptingly low position. She looked up into his eyes. "Thank you. I'd thought you'd be the most horrible person in the world. A monster. But you've cared for men. You've looked after their health, their welfare. I don't know what you really want, why you're waiting, but . . ."

"Yes, but—go on."

He was challenging her. He didn't seem easily seduced in the least.

She bit her lip.

"But you're really not a monster."

"Can you be so certain? We are all different things to different people, aren't we? Maybe I am a monster."

"Well . . . I've talked to you now."

"Yes."

She offered what she hoped was a winning smile.

"Slept through the night with you."

He was watching her, but smiles and flirtatious talk didn't seem to create the smitten effect she had hoped for.

His hand curled over hers where it lay upon his chest. He was a towering man, gazing down at her. She drew his hand to her lips, pressed a soft kiss against it, led it to her breast. A fine hand, large, long-fingered, the palm calloused. He was a man who worked with those hands, and yet, they were still somehow quite fine. And when his hand lay against her flesh . . .

She was startled to find herself the one shaken by the contact. A lightning sizzle of heat seemed to flash through her. She was hot, cold, weak.

"I don't see you as a monster," she whispered.

"No?"

She shook her head slowly, then she rose on her toes, coming closer, closer, closer. She saw the fire in his eyes. His head lowered toward her own. She felt the pressure of his lips, and again the flash of fire, the touch of his tongue, and a feeling so hotly, damnably erotic . . .

Then suddenly she was spinning, forced around before him, and locked with her back against the wall of his chest as he pulled a Colt—and aimed it at Trey and Gilly, who had been rushing for him.

"Don't make me shoot," he warned with deadly quiet.

They both stood still, ashamed, looking at their feet, at one another, at him, at Tia.

"Don't shoot them!" she cried out. "They meant you no harm."

"No harm—other than a bullet in the back?" he suggested.

"No, that would be—"

"Foolish, since it might have killed you as well!" he said angrily. She felt his arm tighten around her waist.

"No, sir. We never intended to shoot you. That would be murder. We never intended that, sir," Gilly said.

Perhaps the Yankee believed him. "And Private, it wasn't exactly *your* plan, was it?" the Yank inquired.

Trey shifted uneasily. "No, sir."

"Go back to the cabin," the Yank advised.

They were green boys. They had been raised as gentlemen. They stared at Tia, afraid, awaiting her word.

"Go back to the cabin. I imagine I'll be joining you shortly," Tia said.

"We can't leave if you intend her harm," Gilly said. His Adam's apple was wiggling, but his words were admirably brave.

"On my word, gentlemen, the lady will remain unharmed."

"Go on back to the cabin," she murmured. It might be the only way the man would ever release her.

And at last, the two turned, as told. If they lived, she thought, they would be good men. She stood dead still, barely daring to breathe as they left.

Then suddenly, abruptly, and with a frightening force, the Yank spun her again in his arms. "Let's finish what we started."

"What?" she cried with alarm.

"We'll finish what we started. You were saying . . . I'm not a monster, my lips were on yours, my hand . . . fingers, they were in a delightful realm of exploration."

"No . . ."

She was certain that she'd said the word, that she'd voiced the protest. And yet . . .

Was she afraid? The word was so weak, a whisper on the air, nothing real, just a breath.

No, it was him, the relentless force with which he touched her . . .

She felt his lips again, his kiss, deep, hot, wet, seeming

to delve into her being and her soul. She set a hand against him, to push him away. She didn't know if he so much as felt her fight, if it meant anything to him, or if her intent was lost against the very power of his embrace. And she wasn't sure at all how it happened, but her bodice was opened completely, her breasts were bared, and his hands were upon them. She was backed against a tree, aware that as he kissed her—a searing, ravishing kiss, almost indecent in itself, seeming to consume both thought and honor—she was sliding to the cool ground. But he was with her. He was there to break her fall, to catch her, hold her, embrace her. The air was cool, but her flesh seemed ablaze. She must protest with a greater urgency, stop this madness raking her system, parting her lips, giving way to the force of his kiss, the heat of his passion. Dear God, where was this leading? Couldn't she put up a better fight. Oh God, not a better fight, just a fight at all . . .

Then suddenly, his lips broke from hers.

He stood. Towering there, he straddled her prone body from above, looking down at her. She met his eyes, confused, then aware of her half-naked state, flushed cheeks, damp, swollen lips. She jerked her bodice together, shimmied on her buttocks to a sitting position against the tree, staring at him. "What—" she gasped, moistening her lips, searching for words, "What—"

"What, indeed? I mean, you had been seducing me, right? Pretense, we both know that. So . . . were you supposed to be able to claim that you were callously ravished by a vicious Yank? Take my hand, get up. I have no intention of destroying the fragile flower of any *sweet, innocent* Southern woman."

She could hear just how sweet and innocent he considered her to be.

Her honor seemed as broken as the South.

"Oh, get away from me!" she cried, rising, the tree a fine bulwark behind her. "The men might have managed to take you this time."

He laughed. Very rudely. "Oh, Godiva, I don't think so! The men were gone, weren't they? They had refused to leave you without my word that I'd cause you no harm—"

"And you lied!"

"Never. You are not in the least harmed."

Oh, he was mistaken! Her pride and self-respect were damaged beyond redemption!

"Your conceit is unbearable! Get away from me. If you truly mean no harm—"

"I never meant harm, but you are dangerously over-zealous in your determination that you can outwit an enemy, and you certainly have and do intend great harm," he warned her. His voice was suddenly so angry that she bit into her lip, backing away. "You will find yourself caught in an awful backlash, you little fool. Setting out to hurt others may well be dangerous. You came upon me. You don't know who is out there, you truly don't know the full scope of what the war has created, and in your quest to destroy your enemy—"

"I'm not trying to destroy you—"

"Ah, there you have it! Fundamentally, we disagree. But damn you, you will listen to me. I'm trying to make you give a care for your own life and safety—"

"Hey, Yank!"

Tia was startled. If the Yank was, he gave no sign.

Still, she sprang hopefully to her feet. Reprieve.

It was Trey calling. Enfield in his hand, he was running through the pines, anxious to reach the brook. Breathlessly he called out, "Dixie's coming. Dickinson and his troops, sir. Fifty, sixty men, coming this way."

Dixie. Captain Jonathan Dickinson. He and his cavalry were often all that had defended the state of Florida. She'd been hoping to meet up with him.

And now . . .

The Yank had been looking for Dixie, as well, she thought, her heart thundering.

"Trey! You've given him Dixie's position, damn it!" she swore suddenly. "That's exactly why he has stayed with us, what he's been waiting for! He's been searching out Dixie's position, and we have led him to the very place!"

"No!" Trey protested. "No, that's not possible. He's been a decent human being to us. I've just given him a chance to leave!"

"Knowing Dixie's position!" Tia spat out. And it was true. He'd been out scouting for Dixie and his troops to begin with—he had just stumbled upon them. And they had given him the information he'd wanted.

"You needn't give your young soldier there any kind of a reprimand. I've known Captain Dixie to be in the area."

"You were looking for him."

"Maybe."

"And now you know exactly where he is."

He shrugged, and she wondered if he was even out to destroy Dixie—or if he had just come to make certain of the man's movements. Dixie was a small man—almost as small as she was herself. But he was a formidable soldier, and he'd kept the Yankees jumping many a time.

"Well, Godiva," the Yank said, "you've suggested that you want me gone. That I should leave, that you wanted to be quit of my presence. I think that time has come. And indeed, I feel assured for your personal safety— you're with your boys here, and soon enough you'll have the escort of larger forces."

"Are you insinuating that *you've* kept me safe in any way?" she inquired incredulously.

"Godiva, I'm sure you really don't understand all that's out there!"

"Enemies of my state, my *country,* are out there, that's all I know!" she informed him heatedly.

"I think I will be on my way," the Yankee said. He saluted Trey, who saluted in return. Then he startled Tia by drawing her to him with a frightening strength.

"A warning here," he said, and his voice grated. "A warning with true wishes that you survive the war with mind, body, and soul intact. Behave, Godiva, for yourself—and lest your good Southern parents discover their daughter's wanton ways!"

She lifted her chin. "Well, I just have to thank God you don't know them and that you will never darken their door!" she informed him. Oddly, her voice betrayed her—wavering just a hair.

"Ah! I've touched a nerve, have I? I'd quite begun to think that impossible. My, my, ravished in the woods— and she would have endured! A fine sacrifice for the great Southern Cause! Yet mention Mother and Father and . . . perhaps I do know them, my dear. Oh, Godiva! Do take care! You are far too reckless, and trust me, you never know just what wolves do lurk in the forest on the prowl for naked beauties!"

With a deep, mocking bow, he turned from her.

And disappeared into the pines.

# Chapter 5

"Why, I'm telling you, sir, it's the truth, this is God's own free man, I swear it! And I promise you that I am a free woman myself, and have been since the day I was born!"

"Listen, darkee, ain't no person of color leaving here without a look over by the bounty hunters."

"I can't be detained! And neither can my brother, nor his wife here! He's one chance of a good job, and if I don't have him spruced up by tomorrow morning—"

"Get out of the line!" the white soldier shouted, his face turning red, the veins in his neck all bulging.

Curiously, Sydney found herself walking forward. She knew the voice of the woman talking. It was Sissy.

Sissy, with whom she had lived in Washington. A beautiful, extremely intelligent young black woman who had performed espionage for the Union. Who had worked with Jesse Halston, the man who was Sydney's—

Husband. Yes, and actually, Sydney was married to Jesse partially because of Sissy. Sissy had been privy to her moments on the night she'd been arrested, and so, in a roundabout way, she was partially responsible for the fact that Jesse had felt honor-bound to marry her— and get her out of Old Capitol.

Sydney, not sure at first what she was doing, excused herself, cutting through the line. She addressed the balding, sallow-faced officer in charge.

"What is the problem here, sir?"

She saw Sissy's eyes widen even as the officer stared at her, looking her up and down. Sissy knew that Sydney had gone to visit Brent, but perhaps she hadn't been expecting her back on the same day she was evidently returning home from some trip south herself.

A dangerous trip for a free black woman—especially one who had already been seized by slave hunters, and given over to a man with designs of becoming her master. A man responsible for the whip scars that littered Sissy's back.

"Ain't no darkees goin' by me, ma'am, and I don't care how prissy their language might be. Book learning!" He spat into the dirt.

"This darkee, sir, works for me," Sydney said imperiously.

"Does she, now?" the man demanded. "Thought you were a Southern woman, Miss McKenzie. You are Miss McKenzie, right? I seen you about a year ago, working down at the Chimborizo hospital then."

"Why, yes, I was there!" She smiled, grateful they'd hit common ground.

"Ain't no darkees getting by me, miss!" he insisted again.

She met Sissy's eyes and frowned, wondering what on earth had tempted Sissy to do something so stupid as to leave the safety of Washington.

"You don't understand. I give you my word that she is a free woman."

The soldier hesitated. "Maybe I ought to call my colonel in."

"Maybe you had best!" Sydney said. "My God! My eldest brother risks his life daily against the Union blockade to keep the South alive, and I have just come from seeing another brother who risks his life daily to save our soldiers! I have put my own life in peril again and again, sir, and you are trying to make my life difficult, denying me the right to leave my own country with my own servant?"

He cleared his throat.

"That, ma'am, is the point. You are attempting to return to Washington—a hotbed of illegal activity!"

"Call your superior, sir. Now! Or, I promise you, they will hear about this in the highest of government—and military—circles!"

That made the man pause. "Fine. You can take the darkee with the big mouth. Too bad she ain't somebody's slave—a good whomping might shut her up and show her her place! But the man and his wife stay."

Frowning, Sydney looked around Sissy at the tall, emaciated-looking black man and the thinner woman at his side. They looked forty, but probably weren't much more than twenty, she thought.

"Sissy—"

"Why ma'am, I told you my mommy died just outside Manassas, and that I was coming for Del here and his wife, Geraldine!" Sissy told her enthusiastically.

Sissy had told her no such thing. And she doubted that this man was Sissy's brother. But who was he. And what in God's name was Sissy doing?

Sissy suddenly let out an awful wail. "I can't leave my brother, Miss Sydney, ma'am. What with my momma newly dead and all—"

"Sir!" Sydney interrupted, "I'm telling you this woman is in my employ. I'll vouch for her and the others," she said firmly.

The soldier seemed indecisive. "There's word you married a Yank, ma'am."

"Word is true. But it hasn't changed who I am, or where I was born, sir. You said that you knew me. I helped hundreds of men in that hospital, sir."

"But you're going through the lines to return to your new husband in the Northern capital. Why should I take your word?"

Sydney knew she was capable of being extremely assertive when she chose. Partially because she had inherited her facial structure from her grandmother's family—she had strong, wide cheekbones, a dead straight nose, and wide eyes beneath a clear, defined brow. Yet her eyes, green as a forest, were from her mother, and it was from her mother as well that she had learned to be assertive and determined—and courteous, of course—all in one.

"You should take my word, sir, because I have offered it, and I promise you that I do not do so lightly."

"You have your papers?"

"Yes, of course, I have travel papers. I am on personal business, family business, and nothing more. My papers to leave the North were approved by General Magee, and my permission to return to the North was signed by General Longstreet just yesterday!"

"All right, then, ma'am, take your people and pass on through. I can't, however, promise you any safety from here on out. You're still some distance from the Yankee lines. But there ain't been much action of late."

"I know that, sir. Thank you for the warning. Sissy, come along now—with Del and Geraldine."

She squared her shoulders, lifted her chin, and walked on by. Slowly. An orderly from her brother's surgery remained with the crude wagon he had managed to allow her for transportation back to the North. Corporal Randall's skinny roan mare was tied to the rear of the wagon. When they reached Northern lines, he would leave her with the conveyance, and return to her brother's surgery outside Richmond.

She prayed that Sissy was walking along behind her—slowly. But she didn't turn back. She reached the wagon, and the young dark-haired man with the scraggly beard and blade of grass in his teeth. "Corporal Randall, we've company for the trip back."

Randall arched a brow.

"One of my servants, and her kin."

Randall looked over her shoulder, inspecting the three people following behind her. He spat out the blade of grass.

"You ain't bringing contraband slaves North, are you, Miss Sydney?"

"Heavens, no! May I remind you, I went to prison for my *Rebel* espionage."

"Just checking, ma'am. You do have a Yank husband now."

"Indeed, sir, I try not to condemn him for his loyalty, and I pray he will not condemn me for mine." She turned to Sissy and the thin pair who hovered just slightly behind her. "Up in the wagon, and let's go."

Sissy, her "brother," and his wife crawled up into the rear of the wagon. Sydney took a seat next to Corporal Randall, and he flicked the whip over the backs of the mules made available for her transport. Randall rode with his eyes straight ahead as they started out, then he turned to look at Sydney. "You do know these folks?"

She sighed. "Sissy has worked with my husband, Corporal. I met her through him. She became my servant because of her work with my husband. She was born a free woman, but Corporal, at one point she was seized as property and richly abused by her master." She stared at Randall. "It is possible, Corporal, to be a loyal Rebel, and deplore what monsters do to other human beings!"

Randall looked ahead again, a small smile playing on his features. "Miss Sydney, you don't need to go getting your dander up around me! I never did cotton to the idea of one man owning another. But then again, I never did cotton to the idea of the Federal government telling a *Virginian* what to do and what not to do. Still, I think we'd best get these mules moving, since folks are mighty touchy these days about all aspects of the war!"

Close to the enemy lines, Randall climbed down from the wagon and looked up at her. He shook his head with a sigh.

"I don't much like leaving you."

"I'm almost within Yankee lines."

"Well, that's just fine. As long as you meet up with Yankee troops. There's too many misfits in this war now, and you may meet up with men who have no loyalty in any direction."

"Deserters?"

"Deserters, drifters . . . trash. White and black. You take care now, you hear? Move fast. And get within those Yankee lines."

"Thank you, Corporal Randall. I promise you, I'll move with all speed."

"You do that for me," Randall said, untying his horse's lead from the rear of the wagon. He mounted his mare and came back around by the wagon, where Sydney had now taken up the reins. "God guard you," he said, saluting Sydney.

"And you." She smiled, saluting him in return. "Stay well!"

"I will! Wish you would have stayed with us, Miss Sydney!"

*Maybe I should have done exactly that!* she thought. She should have just stayed with Brent, assisting him in his surgery.

What had brought her back? The husband who'd had no desire to see her since the machinations of their marriage?

Christmas. It was nearly Christmas. She needed to be there, in case he came back. Only because he had done what seemed to be the honorable thing in marrying her, she felt she owed him at least the appearance of a home and a wife loyal to him, if not to his country.

Corporal Randall saluted again, called out to the mules, and when they had started up their journey again, he turned his mare, and left. When Sydney was certain they had ridden far apart down the long path, she turned around and called out sharply to Sissy where she sat in the rear of the wagon. "Come up here!"

Sissy, she had come to realize, could play any role. She had seemed as meek and mild as the most timid servant girl when they had met—but then, she'd been following Sydney around and spying on her spying activities! This small, beautiful, remarkable young black woman had a tempest and passion in her soul too often hidden by the thick, dark lashes that could conveniently sweep over her eyes when she didn't want her thoughts known. Now, she came forward as Sydney bid—carefully, lest the jerking gait of the mules send her crashing over the side of the wagon.

Taking a seat next to Sydney, Sissy informed her,

"You might have said 'please,' " and her tone was no less imperious than any Sydney had ever used herself.

"I might have, but I'm hardly in the mood!" Indeed, she cracked the whip over the backs of the poor mules with such a sharpness that the sound sent them bolting down the path. The wagon creaked and jolted; in the rear, the thin woman moaned, and Sydney gritted her teeth, irritated that Sissy could make her so foolishly angry.

"You've told me often enough that you know masters who are not only kind, but *polite* to their slaves."

"You're not my slave, you never have been, and you know darned well I never owned any slaves whatsoever. So don't play word games with me right now, Sissy, not when you might have risked my life back there."

"Your life was never in any danger," Sissy said.

"Oh yes, it was! Unless this really is your long lost brother—which I do not believe! So let's be honest and open here—are these escaped slaves? Have you forced me into a position of betraying my own country?"

Sissy turned on her. "Have you betrayed your own conscience?"

"My conscience, ethics, morals, heart, et cetera, are none of your business. You've used me, and we remain in danger."

"I didn't use you—you came forward to help me of your own free will."

"Yes! But I didn't know that you were trying to smuggle slaves out of the South! It's illegal."

"Only when you're in the South."

"We're still in the South!"

"Barely," Sissy assured her. Then she added quietly and desperately, "And I would have used you, yes! I am ready to use anyone, do anything, to help free people who are kept in bondage."

"Oh, my God."

"You've seen my back!" Sissy told her heatedly.

"Not every slave is viciously beaten."

"Look at those two!" Sissy implored her. "Do they

look as if they've been cherished and tenderly cared for?"

Sydney had to turn around—and admit that Sissy was right. The pair with her, overworked into an early old age, were stick-thin, sadly emaciated.

"You could see some real scars on his back!" Sissy said.

"Maybe he deserved them. Maybe he lied or cheated or—"

"Or tried to escape," Sissy said flatly.

"You're missing the point here. You have no right to make me a part of this!" Sydney insisted. "I am a Southerner—"

"You're Jesse's wife now."

"It doesn't change the fact that I think the North should let the South go!"

"Well, the North isn't going to let the South go."

Sydney shook her head. She was angry, unnerved, uncertain, and angrier still because she didn't want to be at all uncertain. *Yes, good God, these poor people most obviously and desperately need their freedom.* But she had gone to a Rebel camp, she'd been born a Floridian, and she had gone with her state, and there she was— *helping escaped slaves!* She shouldn't be doing it, it went against the laws of *her* country, the Confederate States of America, and yet . . .

She didn't believe in slavery, she had never believed in slavers, and she knew that her grandmother's people had often helped escaped slaves. There had even been large communities of escaped slaves who had taken on the Indian ways and become known as the Black Seminoles. The Indians, so constantly persecuted, had stubbornly resisted white efforts to find escaped slaves, often at the peril of their own lives.

And yet . . .

The persecution by the army had also been so rigorous that most Seminoles had readily embraced the Confederacy—the Union uniform was so very much hated by those who had managed to flee the mass migrations to the West.

It hadn't seemed to matter that many of the vicious men who had hounded the Indians had simply changed uniforms. To most Seminoles and other Indians in Florida, the Union uniform was a hated symbol, and so it would remain. Her father, her brothers were all Rebels. The irony of the contrasts in what they believed in and what they were fighting for suddenly seemed incredibly great.

"What you have done to me is a presumption on our friendship," Sydney began again angrily.

"Friendship? Was I your friend—or your servant?" Sissy demanded.

"Oh, my God! Here I am, risking my life, getting you through the Rebel lines, and you have the nerve to goad me. Let's see—were you my friend? Lord, no! You had me arrested!"

"I didn't have you arrested. I merely knew you were out to do some harm to Union troops, and I followed you, and listened—"

"And spied on me, and had me arrested."

"Jesse arrested you."

"Thanks to you."

"Well, then, he married you—and got you out of prison, right? So it all ended well for you, didn't it?"

"Oh, wonderfully! It was a forced marriage, and we hate one another—"

"He never hated you," Sissy interrupted. She looked at Sydney, her dark eyes serious and questing. "You hated him—because you thought he was betraying you by forcing you to remain here. Well, you were a fool. He let your brother go when it was against everything he believed. By forcing you to stay behind, he gave Jerome a better chance to escape. He kept you from danger. He arrested you because he had to. And I don't think you hate him at all. I think you're fighting a stupid war that you don't believe in yourself."

"And I don't care what you think!" Sydney flared.

"Sydney!" Sissy said suddenly, her face gray. "There's someone . . ."

Sydney fell silent, listening. There was a commotion

in the brush ahead. She felt the color drain from her own cheeks. She'd been arguing with Sissy out of anger— she hadn't thought that they might really be caught by Rebel troops.

Who was ahead?

A voice suddenly seemed to crack out of the air, as if God were speaking.

"Halt! In the name of God and the Union, halt!"

She reined in quickly, realizing that Corporal Randall had risked his own well-being, taking her as close to Yankee lines as he had. A soldier stepped onto the trail, rifle in his hand.

"Who are you and where are you going?"

"I have my papers right here, sir," Sydney said.

He came to the wagon, glanced over her travel pass, her and her company, and told her to move. "Farther up, you'll be asked out of the carriage, ma'am."

She thanked him and started down the road again.

Ahead was another stop. The road here was filled with soldiers. Tents and cooking fires were to one side of the road; a number of soldiers stood against trees nearby, drinking coffee, cleaning weapons, taking their leisure. Sydney crawled down from the wagon with her papers, nodding in return to the soldiers who acknowledged her presence. She felt their eyes watching her every step. She was unaccountably nervous leaving Sissy and her friends in the wagon. She'd left the South with these people. That should have been the hard part. She was tired now, with a blazing headache.

She handed the Union sergeant her papers. He stared at the papers, then he stared at her. He stared at her papers again, then peered into her face for the third time. She shifted from foot to foot and sighed with deep and obvious aggravation. "My papers, sir, are in perfect order."

"There's a McKenzie here in your name," the sergeant pointed out. "You kin to Colonel McKenzie?"

This was Union territory.

*Which Colonel McKenzie?* she was tempted to ask.

She knew that he was referring to her cousin, Ian, the

*Union* colonel. She was tempted to tell him that she was also related to Julian, her cousin and Ian's brother, but a Confederate colonel, and then there was another Colonel McKenzie, Colonel Brent McKenzie—her brother, the surgeon she had just gone to see. Then, of course, there was her other brother, naval Captain Jerome McKenzie, the one she had used when trying to leave the South—but mentioning his name to Federal forces often caused a severe reaction since he continued to run circles around the Union blockade.

Was she trying to make good use of renowned names here?

If so, naturally, there was still that other colonel she could mention . . . Colonel Jesse Halston, United States Cavalry, just like the one McKenzie relative she was ready to claim at the moment.

"I am a first cousin to Colonel Ian McKenzie, United States Cavalry," she said, but she knew by the man's sudden, snickering smile that he knew exactly who that made *her.* The McKenzie who had been instrumental in more than one prison escape from Old Capitol, the McKenzie who had helped break out her brother and a number of her countrymen dressed as a ladies singing group. She'd also helped her cousin escape by suggesting he slip into a coffin.

Yes, she was one of the McKenzies who had actually resided at Old Capitol for a while. Perhaps she could get into a friendly conversation here with this man and explain it all. Tell him how she had tended Jesse first in Virginia when he had been a wounded prisoner in the Confederate States of America. How much she had started to like him there, and how liking him had made her see more than ever that the war was a tragedy in which friends and brothers, fathers and sons, could walk out on a field any day, be ordered to fire—and shoot one another down.

But then Jesse had betrayed her, threatening to call out the guard should she attempt to leave the city with her brother Jerome.

Then came the part the guard would really like—there

she was, a good Rebel stuck in the heart of Washington. Before she knew it, she was passing information, and before she knew it, she was a Rebel spy. She hadn't come here with designs on espionage—she had really, truly just fallen right into it. Then, in a nutshell, Jesse—assisted by *Sissy,* who had ostensibly been living with her as a servant!—had learned what information she was to deliver, disguised himself to receive the information and prove her a spy, had her arrested, and seen her sent to Old Capitol. The man who had then been her downfall and total nemesis had come around at the urging of her cousin-in-law, Rhiannon McKenzie, Julian's wife. Because she'd asked Rhiannon for help—afraid that all her male kin would feel honor-bound to storm the Yankee citadel for her release. Rhiannon had gone to see Jesse. And Jesse had come to the prison—where she was incarcerated because he had tricked and betrayed her. There was only one way to get her out, and that was because of his own reputation as a heroic cavalry commander. He could marry her, and take responsibility for her future actions.

Would telling the man any of this help? No.

"Sergeant, you have no right to detain me in this manner," she told him firmly. "My papers are in perfect order."

"You went back behind Rebel lines, Miss McKenzie."

"*Mrs.* Halston," she hissed impatiently. It seemed ridiculous that he was giving her trouble—for once in her life, her motives had been strictly within the law. "And my husband has been out of the city—fighting. He was wounded, imprisoned, and wounded again—fighting for the Union, sir. But without him being here, I took the time I was left alone and went to see my brother. He is not a spy, nor engaged in any manner of undercover activity whatsoever—he is a surgeon. I hadn't seen him in a very, very long time. I left the city with permission from General McGee. But now I am back, because my husband is a Union soldier. This is his home, and this is where I will wait for him. Now I am weary, and I want to go home. Please let me pass!"

To her surprise, the man seemed to take a slight step back. "Mrs. Halston, you've got to realize that Washington, D.C., is a hotbed of snakes and spies. And with your known Rebel activities, I'm not sure it's such a good thing for you to be coming and going. Whether you are or aren't guilty of carrying information—"

"I am not carrying information!"

"Who are these people with you?" he demanded suddenly.

"What?"

"The Negroes?"

She straightened to her full height. Although the man naturally remained taller, she was aggravated enough to feel as tough as a little terrier. "This is a free woman who resides in Washington, and for your information, soldier, she has done the Union great favors upon many an occasion!"

He looked over at Sissy. "The Union—or other darkees?"

She stared at him, horrified and infuriated. "President Lincoln has taught us that the major issue we're fighting over is slavery! I can imagine being challenged in the South, but how dare you detain me here any longer regarding the Negroes in my company!"

"Look, Mrs. Halston, the city is teeming with refugees and darkees with no jobs and no place to go."

"This is Mr. Lincoln's city, and they will reside here. Let me pass now with these people, or so help me, sir, I will somehow see to it that you are very, very sorry for the difficulties you have caused me!"

The soldier suddenly looked as irritated and angry as she herself felt. "You should have never been let out of prison, Miz McKenzie, and that's a sad fact."

"But I have been let out!" she replied with soft vehemence, but as she turned away from him, he had a rejoinder for her.

"Leave it to a half-breed!"

She didn't know if he had meant for her to hear him or not. But it was the wrong night for him to come out with such fighting words.

She swung back around on him, catching his jaw with a sturdy slap that must have stung like the venom of a hundred bees.

"Quarter-breed soldier, and you can count on it. We just keep fighting and fighting, one way or the other. We are survivors!"

"Why . . ." the soldier began, incensed, his cheek reddening, his hand rising reflexively to touch the spot where she had struck him. "Why you—"

"Breed? Rebel? Just what would you like to call me?" she inquired. "Take care, sir, with what you do, since you must recall, you are dealing with someone carrying the blood of pure savages in her veins!"

She was startled by a sudden sound of applause. Swinging around, she saw that the group of Yankee soldiers standing by the trees had been watching her. They had kept their eyes on the entire altercation.

"Teach him his manners, ma'am!" a young soldier called out.

"And if he takes another step toward you, don't you worry none, we'll do some of the teaching for you!" another man said. He wore a sergeant's stripes on his arms as well, an older man, with rich gray whiskers, heavy jowls, and a round, muscled body. "Are you forgetting you're speaking to a lady, Sergeant?" he demanded sharply.

"The lady has been a Confederate spy!" the checkpoint sergeant argued.

"If we had to hang every lady in Washington who had lent a sympathetic ear to the South, we might be plumb out of ladies in the capital. As to Mrs. Halston, well, doesn't seem to me she's doing anything much against the Union now. Looks to me like she might be doing something for those poor people there in that wagon. There's been refugees by the hundreds piling into the city—I can't see what harm Mrs. Halston's bringing in two more can do to anyone."

"Why, she's Jesse's wife, is she?" a cavalryman asked. "Why, then, here's to you, ma'am. Jesse saw fit to marry the lady, and she seems like a fine, fierce beauty to me. To Jesse's wife!" he declared.

The rest of the soldiers let out encouraging calls, clapped, and saluted her, appearing to be well entertained—and pleased with her show of courage. Flushing, she was tempted to bow, while at the same time, she wanted to run away. She'd been attacked for being a Southerner, then for trying to help blacks into the city—and then for her own Indian blood!

"Sergeant Walker!" one of the men, an artillery colonel who had been leaning against an old oak, called out sharply, approaching the guard on duty. "Let the lady pass!"

"Lady! But, sir—"

"Sergeant, let the lady pass!"

"But—"

"Now!"

Sydney met the colonel's eyes. He looked fifty—like the darkees, he was probably twenty years younger. His hair was stone gray. His eyes were as old as the hills. She managed a small smile to him in acknowledgment.

"Thank you, sir."

He bowed low to her. "Mrs. Halston, my pleasure."

She hurried swiftly back to her wagon, crawling up to take the reins.

She felt incredibly weary—and confused. It didn't help that Sissy was staring at her with pride. "My, my!" Sissy said softly. "It's a Rebel Yank!"

"I'm not a Rebel Yank!" Sydney lashed out. "Honestly, I wish you were my darkee! I'd skin your hide!" she threatened.

Sissy broke into peals of laughter.

"You made me a conspirator in stealing contraband!" Sydney charged her.

Sissy shook her head. "No, Mrs. Halston, you just helped two human beings gain their freedom and their lives. I thank you with all my heart, and I know that God himself thanks you as well. Sydney, you were magnificent!"

Sydney shook her head. "Sissy, I didn't want to be

magnificent! What I did was wrong, your tricking me was wrong—"

"The end defends the means, Sydney—Machiavelli."

"What is a slave doing reading Machiavelli?" Sydney asked.

"I was educated, Miss Sydney. Don't you see—it's all in the education."

Sydney shook her head, staring at Sissy. "Hundreds of people, thousands of people, have no education. Plantation slaves surely aren't all like you, Sissy! What will they do, how will they manage? This war will leave a world destroyed. Farms will be ruined, people will be homeless, and when this fighting is over, new fighting will begin. Life will be horrible."

"But freedom is the first step!"

"What is freedom if people starve?"

"Freedom is not feeling the crack of a whip on your back, Miss Sydney. It's knowing that your sons and daughters aren't going to be sold off to a master in another state who may or may not be a good man. Freedom, Sydney, think about it. You knew prison. Isn't freedom worth any cost?"

Sissy pleaded so eloquently.

Sydney shook her head slowly. "My God, Sissy, I don't know. I just don't know."

Sissy smiled. "I still say thank you! And when Jesse hears about this—"

"Oh, my God, don't you dare tell Jesse!"

"But—"

"No! I mean it. I swore I wouldn't be involved in any kind of espionage."

"But you just helped—"

"Sissy, you must understand! We were behind Rebel lines. We could have been arrested, killed!"

"You were determined and brave."

"Don't you dare tell Jesse! You promise me!"

Sissy reached out suddenly, touching a strand of Sydney's deep auburn hair. "Soldiers watch you and waylay you, Miss Sydney, because you are beautiful."

"For a quarter-breed," Sydney breathed through half-clenched teeth, and she was startled to realize the bitterness she had felt at the soldier's remark. She had seldom felt the stigma of prejudice; her grandmother might have been a Seminole, but her grandfather had been a McKenzie, and though her parents had chosen to live deep in the unsettled south of the state, she had attended dinners and balls at her uncle's house in Tampa, as well as those she'd been invited to throughout the state, and in her mother's native South Carolina as well. She was a child of privilege—very rich, no matter what her bloodlines. No man had ever dared taunt her, not with her brothers and cousins. And yet, sometimes, she had heard whispers when she entered a room. Heads turned toward her . . . men and women watched her, and sometimes they thought that it was such a pity that she should be "tainted" with Indian blood. She had never felt tainted—she had known nothing but love and pride from her grandmother's people. Before this war between the states, she had determined that she would never play a marriage game—she would far rather become a reclusive, but educated and intriguing, old maid. If and when she married, she would marry for love, and love alone, and if society happened to be against that love—and she had foolishly fallen for a man too weak to defy society—then she would surely fall out of love as quickly as she had fallen into it.

But then she had met Jesse, and he had found her background interesting, not tainted. He had fascinated, he had charmed . . . but he had been the enemy, and he had betrayed.

And still . . .

He had married her, and asked nothing of her. What came between them had nothing to do with color, race, or creed. It had simply been North and South.

"Miss Sydney, you silly *mostly* white child. It's because of all that you are that you're as stunning as you are!" Sissy said, shaking her head. "And yet . . ."

"And yet what?"

Sissy shrugged, but kept her eyes level on Sydney's. "Well, there are whites, you know, who consider a man or woman black, no matter how pale that black may be. Great-grandmother, great-great-grandfather . . . and you know, in your heart, *you know,* that there are lots and lots of slaves with the white blood of their masters running in their veins. But did you know, Miss Sydney, just how many whites consider an *Indjun* just as color tainted as a black man, and any amount of color tainting makes you just as colored."

"Sissy, you're not going to get beneath my skin and change me into a rabble-rousing fool like Harriet Beecher Stowe because I have Indian blood!"

Sissy shook her head again. "Sydney, I don't want to change you into anything. I just want you to realize that the world can be a hard, wicked place."

"I know that."

Sissy turned toward the road and the night. "Jesse is a real cavalier. He sees people." She turned to Sydney. "And he loves you."

"That's why he prefers the battlefield to coming home," Sydney murmured.

"I fell in love with a white man once," Sissy said quietly.

She was being baited, Sydney knew. But she couldn't help herself. "All right, Sissy. What happened."

"He lied and insisted he owned me, then he raped me, and we had a child."

"Sissy! I didn't know you had a baby—"

"I don't have a baby anymore. It was a healthy boy, but before he was born, my white 'owner' fell out of lust with me. He sold the baby."

"Sissy, I'm so sorry—"

"Don't be. You see, that's the world. He could lust for a Negroid woman, but certainly never, *never* marry her. Can you imagine, he *sold his own child*!"

"No, I cannot imagine," she said. "And yet, such things are true."

"Jesse *married* you. Just to help you, to keep your family safe, for God's sake!"

"I know that Sissy—"

"He'd be very, very proud of you tonight."

"Sissy, don't you even *think* about saying anything to Jesse. You don't understand the promise I made. You must swear not to say anything to him."

"But—"

"Swear!"

Sissy sighed. "I promise, *Mrs.* Halston. I promise."

"Good!" Sydney said firmly. She cracked the whip over the backs of the mules once again. They were close to home.

No, home was far, far away. Where it was warm. Where winter's frost never seeped into the bones . . .

And yet, she was suddenly anxious for her home away from home.

She wanted to crawl into darkness, away from everyone, and try to understand just what she was fighting for herself.

# Chapter 6

H ome.
   Tia opened her eyes, not quite sure what had awakened her.

Sleeping was pure luxury. Her bed in her father's house was imported, her pillows were of goose down, her sheets were soft cotton, and in the coolness of the night, the quilt that covered her was warm and encompassing. Far different from the thin camp bed she had made her own at her brother's now constantly moving field hospital.

She knew that what they saw of the war was nowhere like what occurred in other places; the skirmishes they saw couldn't begin to be as severe as the fighting in the other areas. Casualty figures from battles fought across the South—and into Maryland and Pennsylvania—were staggering. Fifty thousand killed, wounded, missing, in a single day. Even seeing a battlefield so strewn could probably not even sink into the soul. Yet, no matter what the numbers, death was an individual thing, and she had watched men die, and each individual death had been a terrible thing. But others had lived, and that made the camp beds, the horrible food, the mosquitoes in summer and the damp cold in winter all bearable. She loved her brother; Julian was one of the best surgeons in the world, she was convinced. And from the beginning, she had wanted to come with him to his surgery. Her parents had never suggested that nursing in the wilds was not a suitable occupation for a lady—as had been the case with innumerable young women when the war had begun—but everyone in the household had teased her about the luxuries she would be leaving behind. She smiled, holding her pillow close to her chest. She had, indeed, shown them all. She might be an ivory-skinned "delicate little thing" to all appearances, but she had found her own inner strength serving in the field. She had gone from her down pillows to straw without a blink; she had bathed in cold springs—to tremendous ill effect, she might add!—she had stood by while wounded men had screamed in anguish, and she had never faltered or turned away when Julian had given his orders for help. She had stitched wounds, soaked up blood, cleaned out infected injuries—the stench of which had scarcely been bearable. She had done it all—forgoing all luxury, and maybe even proven something to herself. She had to admit, though, that at the beginning, it had been terrible. Far more terrible than she had ever imagined—and she had been sorely tempted to run home. She had never let it show.

It was so good to be home—there was nowhere in the world like Cimarron. The plantation sat upon the river coming in from Tampa Bay. Winter could become chilly, but never deadly cold, and on mornings such as this, the breeze just touched the chintz curtains by the latticed door to the balcony that surrounded the house. The rear of the house faced the river; to the front was the grand entrance; to the east lay the sloping lawn and, down from it, a thick pine forest filled with lush hammocks and fresh water springs. It was as if life went on forever here as it had before. And yet . . .

There were changes, of course. Most of her father's best horses were gone. Last night, though there was coffee in the house, they'd saved it and had a chicory brew after dinner. Candles were more carefully doled out; slivers of soap were collected to be molded again. Lying in bed, feeling the cool breeze slip through the latticed door, Tia felt her heart beat a little faster. Cimarron was strong. A little citadel unto itself. The house stood, the servants and workers remained, all was as it had been, except . . . the war was slowly coming here, too. There was no deprivation yet as there had been elsewhere. All across the South, people had lost their homes to the invading armies, they'd been robbed, their possessions "confiscated." Refugees roamed the larger cities; invading armies sometimes stripped properties of all available food and supplies, then burned homes and barns to the ground. Some officers, North and South, tried to stop the pillaging of their troops. Sometimes they were desperate to feed their men. No matter what the intent, with hungry armies to be fed, the land was stripped. And it was the women left behind, with the old and feeble, with little children, who often paid the price of war. Tia had heard it said that the war might have been over now if it weren't for the patriotism of the women of the South, of their determination to accept any hardship. She wasn't so certain. It was one thing to be full and warm and in good health and be patriotic; quite another to be starving and homeless, with a dream left in the ashes.

It was especially good to come home now. Assisting Julian, when their hospital had remained in one place, had been one thing. She had felt strong, secure, and confident in what she was doing. She had even felt very mature—*old!*—as of late, with so many so very young new recruits joining the militia. But with the renewed interest recently shown the state by Yankee forces, situations were becoming very perilous. Julian had moved the surgery. And she had taken the injured and eventually—after being so rudely delayed—met up with Dixie's troops. That wretched no-name man!

Dixie's men had delivered her safely home the previous afternoon. They'd been polite, courteous, and a pleasure to ride with. They were, she thought, the true backbone of the state, especially when so many regular troops were so constantly stripped from the state to go north. After Christmas, she was determined, she would join up with Julian again, wherever he was. His newly acquired wife, Rhiannon, was an excellent assistant, but she was expecting their first child any day now, and besides, any field hospital always needed whatever competent help could be had. But for now, home was good.

A place to repair the wounds done to her confidence, convictions, and sense of security by that awful man.

Tia clenched her teeth at the thought of him. While he hadn't brought the full force of the Yankees down on Dixie, he had seen to it that the Yankee troops and supply wagon Dixie had intended to take had been reinforced. The Rebels were forced not only to forgo their plans to confiscate desperately needed supplies, but to run as well, since the Yankee forces guarding the supplies were so many, and so well armed.

A twinge of uneasiness and guilt assailed her.

It might have been worse. Much worse. Except that . . .

According to rumor, some of the Yankee troops had been led astray. Led down the wrong path by a vision suddenly appearing in the woods. All of Dixie's troops had escaped and survived.

The vision in the woods had disappeared, so it seemed. They had told her all about it late in the night when they had rejoined her and the injured men at their rendezvous point fifteen miles westward, on the old Indian trail leading to Tampa.

There was a brief tapping at her door, then it swung open. "Good morning, dear!"

Her mother, Tara, came sweeping into the room. She was tall and elegant and very blond; in her mid-forties now, her hair was still her crowning glory, without a strand of gray among the gold. Her smile could still light up a room, Tia thought, grinning herself while burrowing more deeply into the covers. Her mother *looked* fragile, but she was all steel inside. No matter what her thoughts on a subject, she could temper her words. Jarrett McKenzie's determination to remain as neutral as he could in the war had been a difficult stand among his neighbors, but his wife supported him with total passion—and diplomacy. Each time one of her sons came home, she managed to keep the politics out of the matter of family love—quite a feat, since, throughout the country, some fathers and sons had sworn never to speak again for the stand taken by the other. Her nephews and nieces, ardent Rebels all, remained welcome in her home at any time. Injured soldiers, from either side, received the greatest care possible. Representatives from both armies came to Cimarron at times to negotiate various matters—prisoner exchanges, evacuations of newly occupied areas, surrenders, temporary truces.

Tara pulled open the draperies, allowing the sun to flood into the room.

"Mother, that's cruel," Tia groaned, sinking more deeply beneath the covers and casting an arm over her eyes to shade them from the sudden light.

"You've been sleeping nearly ten hours."

"But I'm home for Christmas!"

"And you chose to go to war with your brother," Tara reminded her. "You have no rank, no commission. No one pays you, and no one forces you to stay."

Tia sat up in the bed, staring at her mother, who had gone to throw open the latticed doors. The air that rushed in was cool. Tara seemed reflective, as if, looking out the widow, she saw the past, and not the coolness of the winter's day.

"You didn't stop me from going!" Tia reminded her, curious that her mother seemed so strange about the situation.

But Tara turned to her then and smiled. "You made a choice, and I admire the choice you made. You've helped your brother tremendously; God knows how many lives you may have helped to save. But I'm still glad you're home. Every time one of you leaves this house . . . well, I am afraid I'll never see you again. I hear the lists of the wounded and the dead, and . . ."

Tia jumped out of bed, running over to her mother, throwing her arms around her. "I'm certainly safe, Mother. And Julian is a surgeon—"

"A reckless one! Your father and I are neither deaf—nor stupid. We hear what goes on. And even when Julian does remain in his field hospitals, Ian is out there . . ."

Out there on the wrong side, Tia thought. But she didn't say anything. This was her father's house. And she adored her brother, no matter what his personal ethics decreed he must do.

"Oh, Mother, you mustn't worry."

"And the sun shouldn't rise," Tara murmured, pulling away slightly, studying her daughter's face. "You're too thin."

"Which is good, since I'm short."

"Not short, darling, petite."

"Short. What happened to me? This is a family of giants—even you're tall."

Tara sighed. "Petite, Tia, is just fine. But you're not short, really, your height is average at the least, and among other women, you might even be considered tall. You're only a bit smaller than I am—it's just that your brothers and your father are so very tall—"

"And bossy."

"—and therefore, you feel *short* in comparison."

"Is that all it is?"

"You really are just about my same size."

"Am I?"

"Just like me," Tara said.

Tia laughed. "I'm dark as night while you're pure sunshine."

"All right, so you have that fabulous head full of ebony hair, and indeed, your father's deep, dark, fathomless eyes! You are your father's daughter!" Tara said, smiling and hugging her tightly once again. "In most things!" she murmured, then pulled away. "Anyway, I'm glad you're home. And tonight, you will be your father's daughter in pure diplomacy, if you don't mind. I can't tell you how happy I am that you did come home for Christmas, what with the boys away and even Alaina and the babies staying in St. Augustine. It really isn't fair, you know, this war—it's not only destroying our country, our land, and—my God—an entire generation of young men, but I'm a grandmother, and I don't get to dote on my grandchildren, spoil them terribly, and hand them back. For that reason alone, I'm so happy I have my precious little daughter home—"

"Little! There you have it!" Tia said with a sigh.

"Sorry, dear, it's just a manner of speech. You are the baby, and always will be."

"Ah . . . be careful there, Mother! Aunt Teela thought Sydney was her baby, and then Mary made an appearance when everyone least expected it!"

"Well, that's true, but most likely your father and I are quite done, and that leaves you in the position of 'baby' and 'little.' "

"A baby old maid!" Tia sighed.

"Through your own choice," her mother said, somewhat sharply. Then she smiled. "But you're here and I'm so glad—"

"And you mentioned diplomacy. Why do I have to be diplomatic? Oh, Mother, don't tell me that Father has invited forlorn Yankee friends in the peninsula to come to Christmas dinner—"

"Your father would never do anything so foolhardy. This remains a state in rebellion, and the Yankees do not hold Tampa as they hold St. Augustine. Your father is a man of tremendous courage who does not lie about his views—but then, again, neither is he an idiot. He does not taunt the Rebel forces who control the state, and he respects the fact that the state did vote for secession."

"So what is going on?"

"Exchange negotiations."

"Exchange?"

"Some Florida militia boys have been taken by Northern troops, and some fresh young Yanks out of St. Augustine were seized trying to pillage a farmhouse west of the city. We're having some officers to dinner to make arrangements to exchange the boys for Christmas."

"What kind of officers?"

"*Kind* of officers?" Tara repeated. "Gentlemen, I imagine."

"Mother! *Which* officers? Union men? Confederates?"

"One of each, of course."

"Wonderful. The war will wind up being fought over the dinner table!" Tia said.

"There will be no fighting at the table."

"Is Ian coming?" Tia asked hopefully. "Is he going to be one of the Yankee officers?"

Tara shook her head. For a moment, Tia could see the strain in her mother's features, and yes, the war had aged even her. She never held her children back, and yet Tia saw briefly then the agony that she suffered, never knowing where they were.

"The last I heard, Ian was in Virginia again," she said. "When he is in the state, he is seldom able to come here. Alaina is praying to see him in St. Augustine sometime soon. He sent her a long letter, but God knows when he'll be in the state. Sometimes I pray he stays far away. It seems to me that people grow more bitter all the time, and there are plenty of fools and fanatics here who would gladly shoot a man in the back or hang him from the highest tree for his determination to fight for his own conscience."

"Ian is a remarkable survivor, Mother," she assured Tara. "He will come home when it's all over."

"Yes, of course. Well, I've a thousand things to do. And you needn't worry unduly. I'm acquainted with both officers coming here tonight. So are you."

"Oh? Who is coming?"

"Colonel Raymond Weir."

"Hm," Tia murmured. "Well, he is a pleasant gentleman."

"You should think so, dear. You used to flirt outrageously with him."

"He is attractive," Tia agreed. Tall, blond, handsome—a planter who loved his horses, his land, a good bourbon, and the smell of leather. Sometimes, he enjoyed one too many a good bourbon, but her friend Sally Anderson had told her once that all good Southern men were supposed to have a fondness for bourbon, and if it led them to start a few fights here and there, such was the substance of life. Men, in general, she thought, did tend to overindulge occasionally, but he was never rude or abusive to her when he drank; indeed, he tended to become more wistful. Then again, few men dared bother

her much—she had her father's watchful eye and that of two powerful older brothers. If that wasn't enough, she had her two male cousins to the south, reputed to be somewhat "savage" because of their Indian blood. Sometimes, she had felt a little too protected. Sometimes, as her mother had said, it had made her an outrageous flirt—she had dared anything.

But she had liked Raymond Weir, very much. And she had loved the attention he paid her. Naturally, too—before the war—it had been wonderfully flattering to have the attention of a man so admired by many other young women. She knew he had wanted to marry her. She had always hesitated, flirting but keeping just a bit of a distance between them. She'd had her dreams of seeing the world, and though he was wonderfully handsome, smelled just fine, and seemed to have no disgusting habits—such as chewing tobacco and having the juice running through his beard, drinking beer and whiskey and passing gas all night, and the like—she was looking for something just a bit more before settling down to plantation life. She wanted, at the least, a grand tour of Europe. What she really wanted was to see the pyramids in Egypt, the lands of the Crusades, the Parthenon! So she had held him at bay . . .

And the war had come.

"It will be nice to see Raymond again."

"And you will behave, of course?" Tara said sternly.

"Behave?"

"The poor man was madly in love with you at one time, you know. So now you must behave. Don't tease him mercilessly."

"Mother!"

"Tia, my darling, I pity the man who loves you. You flirt, you tease, you become interested in a man, and if it seems that he is becoming too interested in you, you throw the poor fellow right over!"

"Mother!"

"It's true. But since Raymond is a Confederate with the loudest Rebel yell in the war, and your father has

Unionist sympathies, I suggest you take great care not to create any arguments."

"I would never cause Father trouble!" she protested.

Tara smiled. "You've changed, my darling, with the war. Matured. With little choice, I'm afraid. Now you sometimes behave as if you're determined to become an eccentric spinster."

"Easy, when so many men are dead!"

"So many are dead," Tara agreed. "But you are young, Tia, and there will be men in your life. When you first began noticing the attention of our local swains, you changed your crushes even more quickly than President Lincoln changes generals! As soon as you had charmed them into being smitten, you brushed them off like so much dust on your boots."

"I did no such thing. I tried to be friendly and kind to everyone, but sometimes certain people would just take kindness too seriously."

"You are kind—and compassionate," Tara said softly, then grinned. "Just pure hell on those who would love you!"

"Pure hell? Mother, you told me a lady isn't to use such a word, much less in regard to her daughter—"

"I'm sorry, dear. You're so right. Speaking the truth can be such a burden!" Tara teased. "Anyway, be kind to Colonel Weir. But be careful."

"I did think about marrying him, you know," Tia admitted.

"He's a fine man," Tara said. There was something reserved in her tone.

"*Hm* . . . it sounds like there's a 'but' in there."

"I'm not sure if he's the right man for you."

"I'm not sure, either," Tia admitted. "But should I marry him just because you want me to be kind to him?"

"You should never marry for any reason but love," Tara said gravely.

Tia smiled, swirling around her bedroom and landing back on the bed, her fingers laced behind her head. "Mother, you are completely unorthodox! Most parents tell a daughter she must marry whom they say, and you encourage romantic notions!" She rolled across the bed again, looking curiously at her mother. "Strange, since I've heard you married my father on the spur of the moment, all to escape a rather dastardly villain, and that it had nothing at all to do with love."

Tara set her hands on her hips and inched up her chin. "You're an impudent girl, Miss Tia McKenzie. I adore your father and you know it."

"Ah, but love came!" Tia teased this time. "Naturally, since there is no finer man than my father."

Her mother stared at her for a long moment before saying softly, "A fine man, but you and Julian have disagreed with his teachings."

Tia sobered, sitting up Indian style, pulling her toes beneath her. "I don't disagree with him, Mother, but the state of Florida—"

"The state of Florida is full of fanatics who cry glory again and again. Like Colonel Weir. His passion for this 'cause' is so dedicated he sees nothing else—that is why I'm not at all sure he's the right man for you, whether he is still madly in love with you or not!"

"Really?" She and her mother were startled by a deep-voiced comment coming from the doorway. "I'm not sure if there is a right man out there for you, little sister. Mother, you're absolutely right! Pity the poor fellow who loves her! She is hell on men."

They both spun around. A man stood in the doorway. A Union soldier, yet very welcome in this Southern home. Tall, dark-haired, blue-eyed, filling the doorway with his presence.

"Ian!" Tara cried.

Tia followed suit, echoing her older brother's name. "Ian!"

As one, they rushed to the doorway. Tia stood back, letting her mother embrace her oldest son. Tara was shaking; there were tears in her eyes. She blinked them away quickly, looking him over carefully for any sign of injury as Tia took her turn, hurtling into his arms, hugging him tightly.

"Ian, how on earth . . ." Tara murmured.

"I came in by ship, Mother, south of here. We're holding some ground by the gulf. I was hoping to reach St. Augustine and Alaina and the children but—"

"Oh, my God, Ian, I want you to be with your wife and children, but please tell me you didn't come here just to leave immediately?"

He shook his head, blue eyes sparkling as they met his mother's. "If Alaina received my latest despatch, she should arrive before supper time tonight."

"What a Christmas gift! Two of my children home . . . and my grandchildren on the way!"

Ian looked over his mother's head to his sister. "Julian?" he queried. There was just the slightest trace of anxiety in his voice.

"Julian is well, but in the north of the state," Tia said quickly. Her brothers had met at times during the war. Never enough.

"I saw him after Gettysburg, but not since."

"He's very well; I left him just about a week ago. Rhiannon's baby is due soon." She hesitated a minute, remembering that as far as the war went, her brother was her enemy. "He had to break camp, change the position of his hospital, and he didn't want to travel with her any more than he had to right now, so . . ."

"So he won't be home for Christmas," Ian murmured.

"I'll have a grandchild, and I haven't even met his wife," Tara said.

"Don't worry, she's absolutely gorgeous," Tia said, and couldn't help adding, "for a Yankee, that is."

"A Florida Yankee," Ian reminded her.

She made a face at her brother, then remembered she hadn't really hugged him. "Oh, Ian!" she said, and threw herself at him. He caught her, embracing her, holding her very tightly for a minute, just as she held him. The family had always been close—they'd squabbled as children, but had immediately risen to one another's defense at the least provocation. The war made time shared between them all the more precious. Would they have been this very close if they hadn't seen that lives could be shattered in a split second with the explosive sound of gunfire or a cannon's charge? Yes, Tia thought. They had been taught the importance of their family; they had been lucky to grow in an environment ruled by parental love. They would have always cared, but they had seen so many people die that they had learned that each time they came together might be their last.

Grinning at Tia as he set her down, Ian said, "You will love Rhiannon, Mother, quite honestly. Naturally, she shares an intelligence as yet not realized by my young sibling here, but one with which you and Father are well versed."

Tia countered, "Ian, your own wife sees the intelligence of our belief in a loose confederation of states, in which decisions are made at far more local levels regarding the lives of those—"

"Children!" Tara chastised. "It's Christmas, and there will be no talk of war for Christmas."

"It's Christmas Eve," Tia corrected. "And there will be talk of war." She made a face at her brother. "We're hosting an exchange."

Ian nodded. "I know. There's to be a prisoner exchange."

"If you're aware of what's going on," Tia asked, "why are they risking another man in enemy territory when the negotiation is taking place in your father's own house?"

"These arrangements had been requested before I knew I was coming south—by a Southern colonel, I understand," Ian said. "Naturally, the situation proved provident for me—an added reason to be sent south."

"And what was the other reason?" Tia asked.

He stared at his sister for a long moment. She curled her fingers into her hands. Her brother was an exceptionally impressive man with his cool blue eyes, dark hair, and towering height. Every inch a colonel. And a Unionist. "The Northern armies are keeping General Lee moving, though he had hoped to go home for Christmas as well, I was told. I've had few nights in a bed since the Gettysburg campaign myself, but since other men are busy in the field, I've at last gained a reprieve. I'm grateful for the time given me. I can see my wife, my children, my mother . . . my sister."

She was sorry to feel suspicious—but she knew there was more reason to Ian's being there than time off for hours spent in the saddle. Many men had yet to make it home at all since the beginning of the war. Ian had probably been sent here because of the renewed conviction of the Northern powers that Florida needed to be stopped.

"Ian—" she murmured.

"I'm home for Christmas, and that is why I'm here," he said firmly. He looked at his mother. "Who is coming for these negotiations. Anyone I know?"

"Ray Weir and Taylor Douglas."

Ian shrugged. "Weir is all right. He'll bait me, but I'll be a perfect gentleman and ignore him, of course. And it will be a pleasure to see Taylor again."

"Who's Taylor?" Tia asked. The name seemed familiar.

"You don't remember him?" Ian asked curiously.

"No."

"He's our cousins' cousin," Ian said.

"We're our cousins' cousins," Tia protested.

"Other side. Uncle James's mother's sister's grandson. See the connection?" Ian asked. "We played as kids, but maybe you were too young to remember. Taylor was a class ahead of me at West Point."

"Another Yank?" she inquired tartly. She remembered now, not the man, but the fact that her cousins had talked about him often enough.

Ian arched a brow with a half-smile. "Since we know that good old Ray Weir is a righteous Rebel, then Taylor Douglas must be the Yank. We're having *negotiations,* dear sister. You need one party from each side of the question to negotiate."

"I'm merely mentioning that status quo," Tia said sweetly.

"My darlings, I'm so delighted to have you—and yet you're both giving me this ferocious headache," Tara said.

"No more talk of war, Mother, I promise,"

"Not until tonight, at any rate," Ian murmured. His eyes met his sister's, and he smiled, and she was suddenly just glad to see him, glad about Christmas, glad to be home—and blithely unaware of what the night would bring.


Cimarron.

Taylor Douglas came upon the house in the late afternoon. A slight fog lay upon the ground, just touched by the dying rays of the sun which had managed to stretch across the seasonally metallic sky. The house seemed to rise like a Greek-columned castle on a fairy-tale hill, though the best that could be said for any of the land was that it had a small roll—by Tampa Bay, there was nothing that could remotely be considered a hill. Still, the fog gave the house a strange magical cast, he thought, amazed at his own touch of whimsy. Magical indeed—it stood against the flood of passions that had ruled the foolish and the sane for so long now.

He had ridden by himself here, in full uniform. There had never been such a time when so many different companies of soldiers were roaming the state—Confederate and Federal—but it was equally true that a man could traverse miles without coming upon anyone who would care about the color of his uniform.

War was often for the rich—or those who had something to lose. Many small farmers in the state were totally uninterested. Life was always simply hand-to-mouth, and food would be sold to any man with money, especially if it was silver or gold.

Even in the South, people were becoming wary of Confederate currency.

If he had, however, run into Rebel troops, it wouldn't have mattered. His papers certified his right to be here. He'd been assigned to the state by his own government. He'd been requested for the negotiations by none other than his old West Point professor Robert E. Lee. There had been few men he had admired like Lee, and owing to his exceptional marksmanship, Taylor had piqued

Lee's interest. He had been a guest at Lee's beautiful home, while he had hosted the Lee family himself once at his father's Washington town house. He knew what it had cost Lee to leave the Union; the greatest Southern general of them all had been loath to break up the country. But he fought for the South, and though Taylor disagreed with his decision, he had to respect it, just as he prayed that Lee respected his decision to stay with the Union.

Taylor was glad to be leaving the main body of the war behind—at least for a time. He had a pleasant assignment for a change. Visiting a fine house, enjoying Christmas Eve dinner in the company of good people, and making arrangements for exchanges—a matter of life, rather than of battle, blood, and death.

He had been to Cimarron once, years and years ago, having come with James McKenzie, his mother's first cousin.

"Taylor!"

He was startled to hear himself suddenly and cheerfully hailed. Seeing the rider who raced across the long sloping lawn toward him, he grinned and waved in return with pleasure and surprise.

A moment later a handsome black stallion came to a perfect halt before him, and he found himself greeting Ian McKenzie, heir to this vast empire—should it, and he, survive the war.

"Ian!" he greeted his old friend. "By God, what are you doing here? Indeed, what am *I* doing here if you're here—now that's the real question!"

Ian dismounted from his horse, blue eyes alight as he approached Taylor, extending a hand in welcome. Taylor accepted it and leapt down from Friar, embracing the other man briefly, then drawing back with a grin. "Well, you look hale and hardy."

"Much to the chagrin of my brother, I believe," Ian said, smiling as well. "Before becoming his wife, my sister-in-law apparently mentioned that I was the 'stronger' looking of us two, which Julian took rather offensively. I'm afraid that our side is known to eat better, although I'm quite sure, were he able to make it home more often, my mother would see to it that none dared call him slim."

"Cimarron remains as impressive as always," Taylor said. "I'm sure he could become fat as a house himself were he able to remain. How are the rest of the McKenzies—have you any news? I'd heard that Sydney married Jesse Halston and was living in Washington, but I wasn't able to see her before I was sent here."

"Sydney is well; I saw Jesse after Gettysburg," Ian said gravely. "She'd been getting into a few fixes, helping the family out of Old Capitol, until she managed to find a place in prison herself. He's responsible for her now, and I'm assuming he'll be a good influence."

"Good—to our way of seeing the world," Taylor commented.

"Good as in safe," Ian said flatly.

"Safe is certainly good," Taylor said. "But what are you doing here? I wouldn't have needed to come if—"

"Well, then, I'm glad that no one, including me, knew that I might be able to make it here for the holiday," Ian said. "I promise you, there will be no hardship in spending Christmas with my family."

"I'd certainly not meant to imply such a thing. It's just that—"

"You'd asked not to be sent to the state, right?" Ian said.

"A request long granted, now denied," Taylor agreed. "I find it very difficult to be here."

Ian studied him. "For many reasons, I imagine," he said quietly. "Well, still, for the holiday, we're glad to have you here. My parents are delighted."

"They remember me?"

"My father forgets almost nothing, which can be quite a thorn in the side, since he can remind us all of transgressions many years gone by!"

"How does he manage with your brother a Rebel, and our mutual cousins casting their lots with the South?"

Ian hesitated just briefly, studying Taylor's face. "He watched his own brother battle an unrelenting army during the Indian wars—he has no quarrel with his brother, or his brother's children. As to Julian, he is glad that his younger son is a healer rather than a killer. And my sister—"

"She remains at home, with your parents? I must admit, I don't remember her. She was but a babe in arms, I think, when I came here with James. And I don't think she ventured to my mother's place with you when we were all children."

"Tia. She was just a toddler when you visited here with Uncle James all those years ago. She is home; you will meet her now. And thankfully, you will do so in my father's presence, for she seldom argues with him. In her heart she believes herself a Floridian first, rather than a Confederate, but certainly not a Unionist! She helps Julian with his injured, and so my parents believe her safe in his keeping, although I don't think they realize how often they might be parted. I worry about her frequently, but I do trust my brother to keep her well behind the lines."

"I haven't asked about your wife and children," Taylor said.

Ian's smile was very quick then. "They are here. They arrived just a few hours ago. In fact, I had just left Alaina sleeping and come out for a ride when I saw you emerge from the trail. My God, but it was good to see my wife—" He broke off abruptly, looking downward as if he inwardly cursed himself for his thoughtlessness.

"I'm sorry—"

"Don't be," Taylor interrupted quickly. "I would be a sorry fellow to despise others for their happiness. I shall be delighted to see Alaina. And your little ones. The boy is Sean, right?"

"Sean is now nearly three, and Ariana is almost two. They are pure mischief."

"Good for them."

"Come along to the house."

Taylor led Friar alongside Ian as they approached the rear of the house. At this time, it appeared that the docks by the river were quiet; all in fact, seemed quiet.

"How does your father manage here?" Taylor asked.

"Without the Florida Rebs burning him to the ground?" Ian asked.

"Frankly, yes."

"Well, he's acted as a go-between upon many an occasion. He hasn't involved himself in any espionage activity—in short, he's done nothing illegal."

"That hasn't always stopped either side from burning out those they consider to be traitors."

"Well, there's also the matter of his employees," Ian said.

Taylor grinned. "I knew I was being watched—before you appeared."

"By at least a good twelve men." Ian pointed to the loft of the barn far beyond the rear of the house, and to a guard tower along the river. "My father is like a nation unto himself. Throughout the years, he has gained the unquestioning loyalty of dozens of men. He has given work to outcasts, foreigners, blacks, Indians, Asians, and good white men of vision. The South would have to be able to spare a small army to take my father down; that time has not as yet come. I pray it never will. Then, again, to the Rebel forces, my father has bred one traitor—me. But my brother is known to save more lives than they can acquire in recruits these days, and my sister is wildfire and passion and adored by anyone who comes in contact with her—who would burn down the home that belongs to such ardent Rebels as well?"

"I imagine the danger remains."

"Always," Ian agreed. "Mark! Mark Espy, where are you, lad? My God, it's getting foggy tonight. Mark, come take our horses to the stables, will you, please? And show Colonel Douglas how well we care for our animals here!"

"Yes, sir!" A young, mixed-blood stableboy came running from the mist that had settled around the wide verandah that encircled the great plantation house. He grinned, taking Friar's reins from Taylor.

" 'Andsome fellow, sir!" the lad complimented.

"Thank you. Friar is his name; he'll be glad of a warm stall."

The boy grinned, leading the horses away. Even as he did so, the rear door of the house opened and banged. Two little urchins came running out into the mist, heedless of it, fast as cannon balls. They were followed by the whir of a woman, racing after them.

"Sean! Ariana! Don't you follow your brother when he's being bad, young lady! Your grandmother told you to stay in the house. Hey, you hellions! Ian, you wretch, you got the child you deserved—he doesn't listen to a thing. Ariana, you are a sweetheart, good girl. Stay here, on the porch—naturally you're an angel! Now you, come here, Sean, don't you disappear on me in this wretched fog!"

The voice was familiar.

She didn't seem aware of Taylor or Ian because she was so intent on tearing after the little boy who was squealing with wild pleasure as he raced outside, eluding her pursuit.

"Tia, it's all right. I'm here, I've got him," Ian said, scooping up the boy.

"What?" she cried, still running, apparently afraid she would lose the child.

Suddenly, the fog whirled and lifted.

She came flying through it, crying out as she saw a full-grown man in her path. She couldn't stop her impetus.

She plowed head-on into Taylor. He tried to catch her, lost his own balance, and fell backward to the ground.

He stared at her.

She stared at him.

Huge, thick-lashed dark eyes widened against the sculpted ivory pallor of her face.

He stared back, stunned.

She screamed, trying to rise.

He didn't let her. For a brief moment, his fingers vised around her arms. And he smiled grimly.

"Godiva!" he said softly.

# Chapter 7

❧

"Tia, it isn't the whole Federal army, coming to take your precious South," Tia heard her brother say.

No, this was worse.

He was really there. The dreaded no-name Yank. He was on her lawn. Touching her again. He knew her. He knew Ian. He was here, at her father's house.

Oh, God . . .

She was staring down into his tawny eyes, eyes that seemed to glitter and narrow now like the devil's own. She could feel the force in his fingers, feel the length of him beneath her. She wanted to yell at God. What was this wretched irony?

Ian was reaching down to help them both. His son clung to his neck. Even as he leaned over, Taylor came quickly to his feet, drawing her up along with him. She was so shaken she couldn't stand. He steadied her; she shook him off.

"Tia!" Ian said sharply.

She closed her eyes, looking down, fighting to breathe. It was her father's house. There were to be negotiations here, discussions that would free Rebel prisoners.

*Oh, good God, he could give her away! And he might share the "rumor" that "Godiva" had appeared again, disconcerting and confusing the Yankee troops when they should have been in hot pursuit of Dixie and his men.*

"I—I—" she stuttered, teeth chattering, face surely as ashen as death.

"Tia, I don't believe you've ever met Colonel Taylor Douglas," Ian was saying sternly. "He is more than a guest; his grandmother is Uncle James's aunt. As I mentioned before, he is a cousin to our own cousins."

"No—no. We haven't met!" she said quickly. She stared at the wretched enemy who was now a guest in her own home. *He would give her away, certainly, and he would take pleasure in the disaster he would cause!*

"Miss McKenzie," he said, politely doffing his plumed cavalry hat and bowing. He rose, staring at her again. "Of course, we *have* met."

"I . . . I . . . I . . . no, we couldn't have. I would have remembered. I don't know many Yankees, I . . . I . . . I . . ."

He smiled politely, arching a brow as her voice trailed off. She had run out of words.

He shook his head. "How sad you don't remember!"

"You have met?" Ian inquired. Her brother sounded very suspicious, Tia thought.

"No . . ." Tia protested.

"You were a babe-in-arms," Taylor said pleasantly, "so I can understand why you've no memory of my coming here."

She felt dizzy. Weak-kneed with relief. And yet by the way he was smiling at her . . .

He could still give her away.

Her jaw seemed locked. It was an effort to speak. "Welcome to Cimarron, Mr. Douglas. If you'll excuse me, I left Ariana on the porch. Sean McKenzie, come with me, and leave your father be with his guest. We'll go on in and find Gram, shall we?" She took Sean from his father. Her three-year-old nephew offered her a beautiful smile, curling his fingers into the length of her hair. "Auntie Tia, cookie, please!"

He was an angel now. Why not—he'd brought her running out straight into the arms of the very devil himself.

She spun around, hurrying toward the house with Sean in her arms. She could hear her brother and Taylor coming behind her. She found Ariana, big blue eyes wide as saucers, on the porch, waiting for her just as she'd been told. "Come, baby," she said, hiking up her niece as well. "Let's go upstairs to the nursery. Where I used to play. Have you been on the rocking horse yet? A friend of your great-uncle carved it for me when I was just as big as you are now, Ariana!"

Tia heard the men enter the house behind her; she heard her mother calling her name from her father's den. She pretended that she did not. She hurried up the stairs with her two charges in tow. On the second floor, she noted that her brother's door remained closed—Alaina, his wife, remained within. Alaina had arrived soon after Ian, and since the hours the two spent together tended to be scarce, Tia had at that moment decided that she was going to give her older brother the best Christmas present she could—time alone. She'd effused about how exhausted Alaina must be after having to cross the peninsula so carefully in the company of other civilians on their way to Tampa Bay. She'd swooped down on the children and told Alaina and her brother to get some rest. Of course, the last thing they wanted in one another's company was rest, and that was surely obvious to them all. Alaina and Ian had both been very grateful—her sister-in-law's smile had been well worth her effort. She even knew her little nephew and niece, since Julian's Rebel camp hospital in the pines hadn't been that far down the St. Johns River from the Yankee stronghold at St. Augustine, where Alaina lived as the war raged on. Most of the time, the children were good with her. Today, as she'd read to Ariana, Sean had grown bored—and escaped. And although there were others on the plantation who might have taken on the task of watching her brother's precocious toddlers, she had wanted to be with them. She adored them.

The nursery was at the far end of the hall. It was filled with cradles and cribs, books and toys, the blocks with which they had all played, the rag dolls which she herself had dragged around for years. The nursery hadn't changed. Her parents had always assumed that their children would grow, marry, and bring home their own children. The rocking horse sat in the center of the room.

"Sean, you haven't ridden this mighty steed as yet! Take a seat, my good man!"

Sean sat on the rocking horse. Ariana, apparently growing sleepy, curled into Tia's arms as she took a seat in one of the large rockers. She felt her own heart thundering against her chest as she tried to remain calm. *He was in her house. A guest. The no-name monster had a name and title now, and he was in her house, talking to her brother, and probably her father as well.*

"Charge!" Sean called from his rocking horse. "Charge!"

Ariana smiled angelically at Tia and closed her blue eyes. Tia kept rocking. The door to the nursery suddenly opened. She tensed.

"Tia?"

She exhaled with relief. It was Alaina, a golden blond with eyes to match, a Rebel in her heart as well, but a woman who had fought her own wars, had found her own peace, and lived—with a faith that would not fail her—for the day when the war would end.

"Tia, thank you so very much!" Alaina said, walking into the room. Tia drew a finger to her lips, indicating that Ariana slept in her arms.

Alaina nodded, coming to the baby and taking her from Tia. She hugged her daughter close to her, smiling at Tia above the baby's head. "I know I'm lucky. Some wives haven't seen their husbands since this madness began. My God, I live and breathe for the days when he can come back, but I live in terror as well, always afraid that . . ."

"That the next thing you'll hear is that there was a battle, and you cringe every time they read the list of the dead," Tia finished softly for her.

"I'm going to put her to bed in our room,." Alaina said. "I'll be right back for Sean!"

"Alaina, please, take your time."

"I can't take too much time. Raymond Weir and his attendant have arrived. Your father and mother are serving drinks in the den, and your mother wants us down as quickly as possible. Taylor is here, too."

Tia arched a brow. "You know Taylor as well?"

Alaina smiled. "Of course. He's a second cousin to Sydney, Jerome, and Brent. I grew up near them, you know that. He was with your Uncle James frequently enough. I can't believe the two of you never met!"

"We did."

"What?"

"When I was an infant," Tia said quickly. "So I've been told."

"He's been trying to stay out of the state; it's very difficult for him to be here."

"It should be," Tia muttered.

"It's difficult for Ian to be here as well," Alaina said.

"I know, and you know I love my brother—"

"Of course. Just—well, don't hate Taylor for being a Yankee. He really is an exceptional man. I had an awful crush on him when I was a child."

"Lovely," Tia said. Alaina didn't hear the sarcasm in her voice.

"I'm surprised you didn't meet him again. He was just ahead of Ian at West Point. They were both with General Magee when the war broke out, though assigned to different duty."

"How nice," Tia murmured. "He's kin to my own cousins, and friends with my brother."

"Yes, so this should all go very well. I mean, Ray Weir is representing the South, and Taylor is here for the North. Conversation should be smooth, the exchange pleasant—and Christmas peaceful for us all!" Alaina's smile was infectious; Tia smiled in return. After Alaina had left the room, Tia rose and walked over to the rocking horse, where Sean still played.

"Charge!" Sean called again, swinging an imaginary sword in the air. He smiled at Tia. "My father is a great cavalry officer!"

"Yes, he is," Tia agreed.

She turned around, aware that someone stood at the door to the nursery. She thought Alaina had come back, and then she was simply *afraid* that Taylor Douglas might be there. But it was Raymond Weir, tall, handsome, his blond hair long, curling around the collar of his gray uniform dress coat, his carriage very dashing.

"Raymond!" she said, relieved.

"Tia!" He swept off his hat and bowed, every inch a gentleman.

"Sir!" Sean said, and saluted sharply.

Raymond Weir looked at the child gravely before saluting in return. "Ian's boy?" he asked. She nodded, then smiled and whispered, "But far too young to be the enemy!"

Ray Weir smiled, but it was a slightly stiff smile, as though he didn't seem to have much sense of humor about the war itself. He stared at Tia then, his hat in his hand.

"No enemies here," he said softly. "My God, Tia, it's good to see you. You've been near me, and yet so far from me, for so long. I've been so anxious to see you. I know you've been with Julian through most of this; I almost craved an injury to come to see you."

"Desire no wounds on my behalf, I beg of you!" she said. "Survive this wretched war, Ray, if you would do me any favors."

"I would do anything for you," he replied.

She lowered her lashes, aware of the passion in his voice. If the war had come later . . . might she have been married to him? Or was her mother right—had she just been a horrible flirt totally unaware of what she wanted, or afraid to cast her fate beneath the power of any man? He was very good looking, charming.

*And what would he think if he knew of her latest war efforts?*

"It's so very good that you are here," she said. "Almost like old times. Before . . ."

"The war," he said.

She nodded.

"I admire your father's efforts here. It's a pity he doesn't see the true future of his state. He will, I believe, in time."

Her father's position had been exactly the same since

the very beginning. He was not going to change his mind.

"Perhaps we can forget out positions for a Christmas celebration tonight," she said.

Ray didn't answer; Alaina came sweeping back into the room at that moment for her son. "The baby is down. Sean, time for bed, my darling. Oh! Ray! How good it is to see you here alive and looking so very well!"

"Alaina! What a pleasure to see you as well."

"You were looking for a moment's rest and stumbled upon the nursery instead?" Alaina asked.

Half-laughing, Ray shook his head. "No." He inclined his head toward Tia. "Your mother most kindly showed me to a guest room. I'd heard a rumor bandied about downstairs that Tia was with the children, so I ventured here on my own."

"As long as you didn't come to the nursery looking for peace and quiet!" Alaina said.

"On the contrary. I was looking for something wild!" he said.

Alaina arched a brow, glancing at Tia. "Well, then. Sean, my love, let's go. Tia, your mother is anxious for you to come down."

"Then I will do so right away," Tia assured her.

Alaina departed with Sean. Tia walked to the door. Ray remained there, his eyes upon her gravely. "You've grown more beautiful with the years. I'd thought that impossible. You've matured. You've held my heart and haunted my dreams for years, you know."

"It's very sweet for you to say so, Ray."

He caught her hands, turned them over, kissed the palms. She met his eyes and was flattered, and also bemused by the strange stirrings she felt inside. She cared for him; she had always cared for him. He was handsome, dashing, reckless, and wild—the very pinnacle of Southern manhood. He would be right for her, and she felt . . .

Good. She needed a friend in the house tonight.

She smiled suddenly. "You're beautiful, too."

He laughed. "Thank you, ma'am. And I thank God for this chance to be at Cimarron—with you here as well!

"My mother . . ."

"Is anxious for you, yes." He stepped back, the perfect gentleman. He would want the perfect Southern bride, bred to proper behavior, courtesy, tact, discretion—and chastity—at all times. She felt a flush warming her face.

"Excuse me."

She fled from him, hurrying down the hallway, then down the length of the stairs. She walked quickly to her father's study. The door was open. She entered.

Her father was seated behind his desk, as dark, handsome, and impressive as ever. Her brother, her father's very image, stood by the side of the desk while pointing out some of her father's books to their guest—Taylor Douglas.

Her heart slammed against her chest as the men turned at her arrival. Douglas stood as tall as her brother, clad in a fresh white shirt and dress cavalry frockcoat. In the lamplight, she noted the thick, straight, raven darkness of his hair, the clear hazel of his eyes, and the cast of his cheekbones. She'd been blind, she thought. She had seen something familiar in him when they had met; she should have seen certain resemblances to her cousin Jerome, as in the very dark, straight hair that was a sure sign of his Indian blood.

She stared at him.

He stared at her.

Someone cleared his throat. She blinked.

Reeves, her father's very dignified valet, who had been at Cimarron as long as her family, was serving whiskey and sherry. He frowned at her, noting the way she stared at their guest, then arched a brow as she frowned back— but she reached properly for a sherry instead of the whiskey she suddenly craved.

"Tia, finally!" her father said, rising.

She swallowed the sherry quickly. "I'm sorry, Father. I'd not be late to this roomful of Yanks, except for the fact that I've dearly missed those little hellions my brother has bred. My time with them is precious as well!"

She noted her father's frown and instantly rued her flippancy. She swept on over to his side, kissing his cheek. "Ian, I do envy you your children."

"Naturally, they're my pride and joy," Ian said, "but you needn't envy them. You'll surely have your own."

"I may delight in being an old maid aunt!" she assured him, finishing her sherry.

"Do you remember Taylor Douglas, Tia?" Jarrett asked.

"No—I had not remembered him," she said, staring across the room at Taylor and wishing that he wouldn't look at her the way that he did, as if he knew her far too well. "But we have met now."

"Yes, we have met. And been formally introduced," Taylor said politely, his eyes remaining upon hers, his slight smile seeming always to be a threat. "Indeed, may I say, sir, that your daughter's warmth and charm have made me feel as if I've known her for quite some time."

"We welcome everyone at Cimarron, don't we, Father?" she said. Jarrett arched a brow at his daughter, and she knew that he was doubting her ability to be polite and charming to a Unionist guest. Turning to Reeves, she added, "I would love another sherry, Reeves. I taste nothing so sweet when I'm away."

"Yes," Taylor said agreeably. "The road is hard— *bare,* so frequently, of necessities."

She felt color flood her cheeks again, and she was delighted when Ray Weir made his appearance at her father's side.

"Ah, Ray, join us!" Jarrett said. "Please, come on in. Reeves, if you would, a whiskey for the colonel."

"Thank you, Jarrett," Ray said, accepting the drink offered to him. He lifted the glass. "To life!"

"To life!" all those in the room agreed, raising their glasses.

"Colonel Raymond Weir, Confederate States of

America . . . Colonel Taylor Douglas, United States of America," Jarrett said, formally introducing the two.

They assessed one another, both behaving with professional etiquette intact.

"Colonel," Ray said, nodding.

"Colonel," Taylor acknowledged.

"You are from here, sir?"

From hereabouts mainly, though I have spent some time away."

"It is my home, sir, with no time away," Ray said.

"So I understand," Taylor said.

"At this point, we should, perhaps, leave you gentlemen to your arrangements," Jarrett said. "Dinner will be at your leisure."

Several hours would pass before dinner. Apparently, there were a number of prisoners to be exchanged, but privates could only be exchanged for privates, corporals for corporals, lieutenants for lieutenants. Unless, of course, two privates should be bartered for a sergeant, or three sergeants for a major, or two privates and one sergeant for a lieutenant.

Reeves, coming and going from the den to refill whiskey glasses and offer cigars, assured the household that both men were adhering to a gentlemanly manner—when the discussions grew heated, they did so quietly. At seven-thirty, word came from the study that they had nearly solved their differences, and would be delighted to join the family for dinner at eight, should that be convenient.

Awaiting dinner on the verandah in the company of her family, Tia felt a sense of warmth and contentment unlike anything she had known for a very long time. Though their discussions could not help but include allusions to the war, it was not the war they discussed. Alaina talked of life in St. Augustine, and of Risa, Jerome's wife, with whom she lived. Risa had departed a few weeks earlier for the North—it had been some time since she had seen her father, the Union general Magee, and not having the least idea where her husband was at the moment, she had chosen the time to bring her son to see her father. Tia told her parents about Julian's wife, Rhiannon, and how she had really been the one to step in when Jerome had been seriously injured on one of his last forays. There were no arguments, only sincere conversation, and Tia, seated by her father on the steps on the porch, was glad simply to lean against the bulwark of his frame. If only . . .

Ray and Taylor appeared on the porch.

"Gentlemen, the matter is resolved?" Jarrett asked.

"Sir, it is," Ray assured him.

"And we offer our most sincere thanks for your hospitality," Taylor said. "As do the men who will be exchanged. It has been agreed as well that those men will no longer fight, but accept honorable discharge and return to private life."

Tia looked at Raymond Weir, certain that Taylor must have been mistaken in their agreement; the South could not afford to exchange men—and then not use them to fight.

But Raymond Weir stood listening, and making no correction to Taylor's words. Her father rose, announcing that they should adjourn into the dining room and enjoy the evening meal with thanks for the holiday— and the occasion.

With the children in bed, Alaina and Ian sat down next to one another at the large dining room table. Her father and mother were at opposite heads of the table while Tia found herself between Raymond and Taylor.

Passing biscuits.

Her father said grace, and then conversation at first revolved around the food, the house, the weather, and Christmas Eve.

Then, after the food had been served and Tara complimented, Raymond said, "Since we're looking to the Christmas season, I find it my duty as an officer and a gentlemen to make fair warning to you, Colonel Douglas, and to you as well, of course, Colonel McKenzie, to remove yourselves from this section of the state as soon as you are able, following the holiday. Sentiment is high against the enemy, and men captured after the transaction we've completed this evening are to be dealt with harshly."

Tia was aware of a piece of bread crumbling in the hands of Taylor Douglas, to her left. He did, however, maintain his poise. "I thank you for your warning."

"They are confiscating property as well, Colonel Douglas, so I've heard. Perhaps you should consider some quick sales. Such things have been done in the North, as you are aware. Robert E. Lee's wife's Arlington House was seized—the Union refused to accept payment of the taxes from anyone other than the owner, and that poor crippled lady, forced to flee, could not return."

"I'm afraid it was a very horrible act," Taylor agreed, looking across the table at Ian, who had given him some signal that they would maintain peace, no matter what. "Master Robert is a great man, and a great leader of men, and perhaps it is this very recognition by his friends in the North which makes it so difficult for them to accept the fact that he's their enemy."

"Ah, they will hate him more when he defeats the Union," Raymond said, shaking his head. "It's true, however, no offense meant, sirs, that traitors should be dealt with harshly. I might be interested in purchasing some of your property, Colonel Douglas."

"None is for sale."

"You risk a fortune."

"Not so great a fortune. I would make a gift of my property in the south of the peninsula to my second cousins, the James McKenzies, before selling it. And as to my home in Key West . . . the Union navy is firmly ensconced there. The property south of St. Augustine . . . well, at the moment, it is a no-man's-land. But I thank you for the offer."

"I have every reason to believe, Colonel Douglas, that European powers are ready to recognize the Confederacy as a sovereign state, and so will turn the tide of war."

"Again, sir, I say—I will wait."

"We run circles around you. Why, even our women drive your so-called soldiers to distraction, sir!"

"What women would that be?" Tara interrupted, her voice sweet but firm and she tried to dispel the growing argument.

"Why, madam, I've heard through good sources that we've a wild Rebel maid riding through the pines and leading the enemy astray. I heard this from Captain Dickinson's own men. They had been sent to seize a reinforced Yankee supply wagon, and were nearly run down by the number of soldiers suddenly put on duty, when a beautiful vixen, all in the bu—"

He broke off, staring from Tara to Alaina to Tia. He flushed.

"Yes?" Tara insisted.

"Well, she's a flame for justice, of course," Raymond said.

"But what were you about to say?" Tara insisted.

Tia concentrated on spearing a piece of fresh tomato. She felt her own face growing red. Felt tawny eyes upon her as Raymond continued to look for the right words.

"Well, they, er, they have a name for her."

"And that is?" Alaina insisted. "Please, Colonel Weir! You have two women with Rebel sympathies at the table, though we respect the beliefs of others around us—my husband and in-laws included, of course! Tell us about this vixen of virtue, or whatever she may be!"

Tia stared across the table at her sister-in-law. She wondered if there was a certain wistfulness to Alaina's question. She'd practiced serious espionage at the beginning of the war, and had she not been caught by her own husband, she might well have been executed. To the best of her knowledge, though male spies had suffered the ultimate penalty for their service to their countries, North and South, though it had been threatened, no woman had as yet been legally killed.

But Alaina was fascinated.

Raymond Weir looked across the table at Alaina. "Well, they call her 'Lady Godiva,' if that makes a proper explanation. Apparently, she shouted the name out at some point herself, and as it's so fitting, it seems to have stuck."

"Godiva—she rides around the countryside *naked*?" her father said, sounding angry and shocked.

Tia wanted to sink beneath the table.

"One would think that someone would stop a woman from such reckless and dangerous behavior," Ian said. "Maybe she doesn't realize how many men could be killed, thinking they owed it to her and all Southern honor to ride in her defense."

Alaina coughed suddenly, and the sound ended in a little squeak. Tia realized that her brother had squeezed his wife's hand beneath the table and that he was staring at her suspiciously.

She stared back, and though they were both trying to behave entirely circumspectly at the table, Tia could see that Alaina was furious that Ian would be suspicious.

From past history, maybe Ian had a right to his suspicions. But it was all so long ago. And of course, Alaina was entirely innocent.

"In all honesty, in many situations, the South has been quite desperate," Tara said. "Perhaps this woman was doing all she could to divert the soldiers, in order to save lives."

"But it's an interesting situation, isn't it?" Taylor Douglas said suddenly. His fingers rode over the rim of his wineglass and he stared down at it as he spoke. Then his eyes suddenly met Tia's. "To take soldiers by surprise at first might gain a few a reprieve. But few men, North or South, are entirely fools. I imagine the next time this Godiva appears, she could be in grave danger indeed, since men will know that she is out to do nothing but mislead them."

"It's amazing how stupid men can be at times!" Alaina announced.

"I'd not cast aspersions upon your gentle sex, Mrs. McKenzie, but one might say the same of women as well—since we do have this Rebel spy running around as naked as the day she was born."

"You seem to speak from experience!" Raymond said.

"Sir, were you diverted from some quest by this fair Rebel? Do you have knowledge of this vixen that I do not?"

Tia stared at Taylor, praying her face wasn't a dead giveaway. He hesitated.

She thought her heart would stop.

"I believe I saw her," he said gravely after a moment. "Yes, I admit to being a victim of the lady."

"Victim!" Tia muttered, then hastily bit her lip.

"Did you know her?" Alaina asked. "Did you know her—personally?"

He looked at Alaina. "Why would I know her?"

"Sir, you're from this state. Surely you attended some balls and barbecues, and would know if she was the daughter of a planter, a politician, or, say, a Florida botanist?" She stared hard at Ian, referring to her own father with the last.

Taylor Douglas smiled. "The child of no botanist I knew as a child. The lady I came across was definitely not at all blond."

"But she could have disguised herself, and acquired a wig," Ian suggested.

"No," Taylor said flatly. "I assure you, she was not blond. She did not wear a wig."

"How could you be so certain?" Alaina demanded, then her face flooded with crimson as she realized what his answer would have to be. "Oh!" she gasped in embarrassment.

"*Did* you know her, sir?" Raymond demanded harshly.

And again, Tia waited, her heart stopped, her lungs on fire. She couldn't bear it any longer. If he didn't answer, she'd scream and leap to her feet, and they'd all think she was crazy, and her father would know . . .

"I have been gone from the social arena of the state for quite some time. It is unlikely that I would have recognized the lady as the daughter of any one man," he said at last.

Tia felt as if she could pass out right into her plate. He wasn't going to betray her.

Not now anyway.

"Cigars and brandy, gentlemen?" Jarrett said. "It's such a balmy night, I thought we might enjoy our after-dinner drinks outside on the porch."

"As you wish, sir. Ladies . . ." Taylor rose, bowing to the women at the table, and followed his host out of the house.

"Ladies . . ." Ian echoed, rising, bowing politely, and following suit. Raymond Weir did the same.

"That went fairly well," Tara murmured. "No swords were drawn."

Tia didn't stay long in the salon with her mother and Alaina. Restless and needing to calm her nerves, she exited the house by the way of the back door and walked slowly around the verandah until she neared the front. She could hear the men speaking.

Eavesdropping, her mother had always warned her, was rude—and it often exposed one to things one would rather not hear about. The men were discussing Godiva—a topic she definitely did not want to hear about—but from the subdued tone of their conversation, it was clear that Taylor had not betrayed her secret.

Fortunately, their conversation did not last long. Tia heard Taylor thank her father for his hospitality, then she listened to footsteps entering the house, and muffled voices from within as the men met with her mother and thanked her as well for the evening.

Then after a few moments, she heard nothing more. She walked around the verandah, and was startled to find that Raymond Weir was still there, standing on the porch and looking out into the night.

"Tia," he said softly. She smiled, approaching him, yet wishing she did not feel so uneasy.

He inclined his head, his eyes pleasantly raking the length of her, his smile flatteringly appreciative.

"It's really good to have you here, Ray."

"If only this were a loyal household. How wonderful it would be, Tia, if your father would only realize that he must cast his fate with his state!"

"He loves the state, Ray, adores it."

"You, Tia, are all that is good in our life, in our state, in our being!"

She smiled. "Very poetic, for a solider, sir."

He reached out, taking her hands, drawing her to him. His hands covered hers. "Tia, marry me."

She didn't answer. How strange. She had joked about there being no men left to marry. He was the perfect mate. A rebel soldier, a brave man who led well and fought hard. Smart, handsome, passionate . . .

*A man who might want a woman such as Godiva, but never marry her!*

She was startled, but did not pull away, when he leaned down and pressed his mouth softly to hers. A kiss . . . she waited. For passion, for feeling . . .

What was she expecting? It wasn't as if she was experienced. And yet . . .

*Yet she was. She'd felt a kiss before, filled with passion, boldness, a spark, a flame, a fire, a threat, a warning, and a promise . . .*

Taylor. Taylor Douglas.

She pulled away from Raymond.

"I love you, Tia."

She shook her head. "Not . . . not now, Ray. The . . . the . . . war. My father, my own—well, I have my own duty within it."

"I love you," he repeated.

"And I . . ."

*She what?* She didn't know what she felt. Attraction? Disappointment? "Ray, when the war is over . . ."

"I can't wait for the war to be over."

"Maybe there will be another time."

"There will always be another time. I will take any time, Tia, that you give me. You, in any manner, in any way you wish."

He stepped back, bowed with a flourish, and headed back into the house. Tia walked out on the lawn. The fog had lifted. The night was beautiful. The curve of the moon was naked in the sky.

"Good night . . ." she murmured aloud.

"Good night, Godiva!" a voice replied.

She turned quickly, looking up—the voice had come from the upstairs balcony. There he was, Taylor Douglas. He had shed his frockcoat, and in the cool evening, he stood in only a white cotton shirt. It, and the dark tendrils of his hair, were being lifted slightly by the breeze.

"Don't say that!" she whispered furiously.

"Good night!" he repeated, and smiling, he turned and disappeared.

Cold.

Christmas Eve, and it was so damned cold.

Well, at the least, Brent McKenzie thought, hunkering down by the fire at the small house near the hospital he had taken for his quarters, his situation had changed somewhat.

He'd been called back to work on soldiers coming in from the battlefront.

There were so many of them.

Tonight, he wondered why he had wanted to be a doctor. From surely the strangest duty in the war—trying to help soldiers with syphilis and educate what seemed like an entire army of camp followers on how not to spread venereal disease—he was back helping men whose bodies had been shot, stabbed, sliced, and bombed to bits. Either way, it seemed a bitter detail. Even on Christmas eve, men were coming in, wounded in encounters beyond the city. Grant had been put in charge of the entire Union effort. He had made his own headquarters with the Army of the Potomac, and he'd ordered Meade to take Richmond. Lee's weary soldiers did their best to clock the army movements made by a man whose motto was that war should be as terrible as possible—that way it would end.

Brent was tired, he was worn out, and he was cold. He hadn't even gotten used to Christmas away from home. Christmas usually meant a crisp, cool day—but with the sun shining, his home surrounded by the blue of the sky and the sea and the green of the grass and the foliage. And flowers. His mother loved plants, herbs, and flow-

ers. Teela always had flowers for Christmas. A wealth
of them.

It was late. He'd been invited to dinner by a number
of officers, but he'd had a boy come in with possible
gangrene—and he'd refused to wait even a day to see
the wounded young soldier, knowing how quickly infection could flourish. He'd taken the leg, something he had
been very sorry to do. But while he was a good surgeon—a damned good surgeon who usually attempted
every possible miracle to save a limb—he knew when to
take a limb as well. The gangrene had been serious. He
could only hope it hadn't spread through the boy's
system.

Last Christmas, he reflected, he'd been far from home.
Sydney had been with him. And actually, Sydney had
been to see him not so long ago, but he had known,
what seemed like a very long time ago now, when he'd
treated Jesse Halston after the Union cavalry man had
taken five bullets, that his sister had been falling in love
with him. Sydney had gone to Washington to arrange
for prisoner exchanges, wound up helping their brother
escape instead—and marrying Jesse Halston. He was
glad. He liked Halston, and he'd been glad to save his
life. Now Sydney was back in Washington, waiting.
Hopefully, Jesse Halston had enough rank and power to
make it home for Christmas.

Hopefully, he wasn't lying dead on some forlorn
battlefield.

Brent picked up the poker, stoked the fire, and reflected on the war. Strange. He'd hated being sent to
deal with the prostitutes and the men with their sexual
diseases. Giving lectures on the use of condoms. But
after a while, he hadn't hated the duty so much. The
prostitutes had been people, many of them warm, sad,
caring, funny, wild individuals.

Face it, he told himself. He'd been forever changed by
the experience. In many ways. He'd be forever haunted.
Because of Mary.

He'd treated her father until he died. And, Brent reflected dryly, he had thought that the colonel's beautiful

young daughter had been his mistress, and he'd made quite a fool out of himself, and an enemy out of her.

He jabbed the fire with a vengeance, wondering where she was tonight.

The flames flickered high and bright, blue and red. He set the poker down and warmed his hands before them. After a moment, he pulled off his military jacket, loosened his shirt, and walked over to the Queen Anne chair that sat on the hooked rug before the fire. An elegant cherry-wood occasional table by the chair carried a decanter of brandy. He poured himself a glass and spoke to the fire.

"Cheers, Doctor McKenzie. Merry Christmas."

He nearly threw his glass up when he received an answer.

"Yes, cheers. Merry Christmas, Doctor McKenzie."

The brandy sloshed as he leapt to his feet, spinning around to stare at the doorway to his bedroom. *She* was there. Mary. Either that, or the war had cost him his senses. His imagination had run riot. He was now stark, raving mad.

Her huge silver eyes were steady on his, her hair loosened around the snow-white robe that was all she wore.

"Mary!"

"Yes."

"What in God's name are you doing here?" he demanded, frowning fiercely.

She walked into the parlor before the fire. He thought that her hands were shaking but she reached down for the brandy decanter. "Do you mind? I thought I should help myself before you spilled it all."

He lifted a hand. "Go ahead," he murmured, still staring at her with astonishment. Yes, it was her; she was real. As stunning as a little snow queen in the white robe. She smelled of fresh soap and rose water; her hair, in the firelight, seemed as soft and sleek as sable. She seemed a pure assault on his senses. He had been exhausted; suddenly he was wide awake. He had been cold. Now his flesh seemed on fire, touched by lightning. *She isn't wearing a thing beneath the robe,* he thought.

"I'll ask you again," he said, and his voice barked out far more harshly than he had intended. "What are you doing here? How did you get here . . . in this house? How did you find me?"

"You were easy to find. I simply asked where you had been transferred. One of your orderlies pointed out your quarters in this house. It wasn't locked, or guarded in any manner. I let myself in. You should be more careful. The city of Richmond is teeming with refugees, some of them desperate men. Some people are fleeing the city again, afraid of Grant, and stealing everything in sight on their way out. Amazing, isn't it? Our countrymen aren't all noble soldiers and physicians. Some are simply cowardly thieves."

"Mary, *why* are you here?"

She tossed the brandy down and set the glass back in a deliberate gesture, her eyes downcast. Then they met his again.

"You said that I owed you; I always pay my debts," she told him.

"What?"

"I'd heard that you were here. My father . . . I owe you for all that you did for my father. I—I always pay my debts. It's Christmas. It seemed like a good time."

"So . . . you're here to . . . pay a debt?"

"Yes," she said quickly, her eyes falling from his once again.

He couldn't help it. He reached out, caught her hand, and pulled her to him. She wasn't wearing a thing beneath the robe. He lowered his head, kissed her. Her lips trembled. God, they were sweet. His kiss deepened. Her lips parted. Her body, pressed to his, was warm and supple and perfect. He cupped her breast, marveling at the feel, shuddering as the sensation in his fingertips seemed to work into his groin.

He caught himself, pulled away from her. "Damn you, Mary!" he swore angrily. "You don't owe me! I was angry when I told you that; you owe me nothing at all for your father. What the bloody hell do you think of me, that I wouldn't help any man when he was dying?"

She stood just feet away from him, shaking, her eyes shimmering like sterling with a hint of tears.

"I do owe you for what you did for him."

He took the single step back to her, taking her into his arms, lifting her chin, meeting her eyes. Her lips trembled. He felt himself shaking. "Mary, Mary! You little fool. I will not make love to you because you feel that you owe me any debt! I was angry, jealous, hurt— an idiot."

She lowered her eyes, leaning her head against his chest.

"Would you . . . would you make love to me . . . if I told you that I simply wanted to be with you? That I've spent every day since you left trying to figure out how to come to you, how to tell you . . ." Her voice trailed away in a whisper. He wasn't even sure he had heard her correctly. His fingers shaking, his blood burning, he caught her chin, lifted her eyes to his once again.

"What?"

"I want to be with you. I need to be with you. I have nowhere else to go now."

"Mary, you shouldn't be here just because there is nowhere else—"

"It's not that, you fool man! I want to be with you. I admire you, I am intrigued . . . I am curious—for the love of God, I am willing! Don't tell me you can't use me—"

"Use you?" he interrupted, frowning.

But her thoughts were elsewhere. "Here, at the hospital. You know that I'm more than competent, that I can anticipate your needs."

"Can you anticipate them all?" he murmured softly.

"Brent, please. I know I've arrived quite strangely, out of the blue. But I had to come here, and I had hoped that at Christmas . . . well, you would feel at least something for me."

"Mary, it wouldn't be right. You are not that kind of woman."

"What kind? Sensual—seductive?"

"Oh, my God! Mary, trust me . . ." He paused, looking at her. Silver eyes glittering, hair streaming down her back, robe parting to provide just a peak at the roundness of her breast, the rouge of her nipple, the narrowness of her waist, curve of her hip . . . "Trust me, you do know how to seduce!"

"Brent . . . please . . ."

"Mary, please . . . what?"

"Hold me tonight. Let me be with you. Make . . ."

"Make love to you?"

"God, yes!"

"But Mary, come the morning . . ."

"Brent! I planned this for a very long time. Yet in my dreams, you made it much easier for me. Brent—I am all but throwing myself at you. You must not be so cruel as to refuse me!"

He was lost—or found. He was not sure which. "God forbid that I should be cruel," he said.

She smiled. He swept her up. Her arms curled around his neck.

"Merry Christmas," she said softly.

Merry Christmas indeed. It was cold outside, but it was as if he had died and gone to heaven.

# Chapter 8

~~~

He had ruined all hope of sleep.

As Tia paced across the floor in her bedroom, she kept hearing his voice over and over again, mocking, taunting. *Godiva.* Had he been threatening her?

Yes, of course, he was threatening her. Sometime, tomorrow, he would tell her father the truth. Tell him who she was, what she was doing.

Her father would kill her.

Worse. He would be disappointed. *Shamed.*

She had to see Taylor. Talk to him.

What was she, mad? She couldn't just go tapping on his door; she might wake up her parents, or her brother, or Alaina, Reeves, Lilly, someone else in the house.

She opened her doors to the balcony. The night had grown cool, but not cold. She stepped out in her bare feet. She'd seen him just outside on the rear balcony, near his room. Without really planning out her intention, she suddenly sped around the balcony, came to the guest doors, and hesitated. No, don't think, you won't *act!* she warned herself. She opened the door, slipped inside.

It was dark, but a whisper of moonlight filtered in. She could just make out the bed, and she tiptoed over to it.

She saw his form, shoulders bronze, the muscles starkly defined against the white sheets. In the shadows, he seemed to be soundly sleeping. She hesitated, then sat at his side. "We need to talk. Please, listen—"

She nearly cried out as he turned, arms sweeping

around her, bearing her down into the bed. He whispered something. She couldn't make it out. A name?

She strained against his chest with her palms, her anxiety growing. "We need to talk, I need you to listen to me."

Beside her, one leg draped over her, his arm around her waist, she suddenly realized that he hadn't been sleeping at all. He had probably seen her from the moment she'd reached his doors to the balcony.

"Miss McKenzie! Just what game is it you're playing now?"

"Colonel Douglas—"

"Yes, it is. Surprised?"

"No, of course not, I—"

"What the hell are you doing? Wrong room, Godiva? Were you looking for your gallant Southern lover? He who would accept anything from you, anything at all?"

"You wretched eavesdropper! You are the rudest individual—"

"Rude? For repeating the truth? I could be far worse."

"We need to talk."

"We? You and me? Oh, so you came in the dead of night—dressed, I'll admit, but my Lord, Godiva, this is seductive material!—to talk. To me."

"I was not looking for Raymond!" she insisted.

"As you say. How charming. You were looking for me in this lovely sheer gown. Coming purposely into my room. I'm deeply flattered, and not a little stirred, I must say."

"Stop it! I'll call my father, my brother, the whole Confederate army!"

"Stop it? May I remind you, you came after me."

"I didn't come *after* you."

"And make up your mind—are we calling your father, or the Rebel army? My defense will be based entirely on the identity of whom we summon."

"Listen to me, I wasn't coming after you—"

"You're in my bed."

"Please—!"

"So you *were* looking for good old gray-clad Colonel Weir," he said. "Mistake, I might add."

"How dare you insult Colonel Weir! He's loyal and fighting for his state, and he is determined, and a gentleman still, and—"

"A good man. That I don't doubt."

"Then—"

"He is a fanatic. He has read too much Machiavelli. The end defends whatever means is required to reach it. He will destroy this state before he allows it to return to the Union."

"We haven't lost the war!"

"You will."

She stared up at him, the tawny eyes now on hers in the night, the very handsome, currently grave structure of his face. She felt almost compelled to reach out and trace the line of his cheekbone. Nor did it seem quite so terrible to lie there, being touched by him, and she suddenly thought of her brother's closed door and all of the things she had missed by committing herself to the war. She gritted her teeth, furious with herself, wondering what was wrong with her that she could lie there with an avowed enemy who seemed to take the most perverse pleasure in taunting her and want to touch him. The warmth that spread through her seemed like a taste of evil, and yet—heaven help her—she desired it.

"I didn't come to talk about the war."

"Now I'm really flattered. You've come to seduce me?"

"No!" she protested, then realized the volume of her voice and swore softly at him. His smile further infuriated her. "Damn you, stop it!"

"I haven't done a thing."

"Stop doing what you're not doing!"

He smiled again, shook his head, then sobered. "All right, Godiva, talk."

"You haven't given me away as yet," she breathed, looking into his eyes.

"I have great respect for your father, brother, and

mother," he told her. "It would not benefit them to know of your evil deeds."

"What I did was not evil. It was accidental. You must understand. You were there."

"I was there once," he said softly. "Godiva also led a company of men down a merry path when they had nearly taken Captain Dickinson and his troops. How many other times has she ridden since then?"

"That's the only time, I swear it. I didn't mean to—"

"You are quite frequently naked by sheer accident for a well-bred Southern girl, are you not?" he demanded.

"I wouldn't say 'by accident'; it was spur of the moment, sheer desperation—"

"I really should tell your father. Because you have to stop what you're doing."

"You can't tell him, please—"

He leaned closer to her. "You will get yourself killed. And when your body is found, they will know, and their grief will be compounded again and again. And I will be guilty of a terrible crime against them, because I knew."

"Please . . ."

"Tell me that you'll never do it again. No matter what the circumstances."

She caught her breath, staring up at him.

"It's the only way, Godiva."

"I won't do it again. I didn't mean to do it, as I said—"

"No matter what the circumstances."

She gritted her teeth very hard. "No matter what the circumstances."

"Then your secret is safe with me."

Barely daring to breathe, she looked into his tawny eyes, praying he was telling the truth. Then she realized again her circumstances. She lay flat on his bed, his leg cast over her, his hand upon her waist.

This time, *he* was naked.

And she realized it in such a manner that her eyes widened in panic and her flesh burned with a flow of blood. "Well, then, I—I—"

"Ah, you suddenly see the real danger in the enemy!"

he taunted, leaning close again. "Good. But you needn't try to run so suddenly in sheer panic, dear Miss McKenzie. What did you think, that I would suddenly lose control in your father's house, rape his daughter in his own home?"

"No, I—I—my God, it's just that—"

"Shush!" He suddenly brought a finger to his lips. She had heard nothing. Yet he quickly moved over her, leaving the bed, striding to the doors to the balcony. He held still there, and she bit her lip, trying not to watch his lithe, bronze form in the shadows. His broad shoulders and well-muscled arms seemed to ripple with each play of moonlight, and she couldn't help but notice the way his torso narrowed to a lean waist, that his buttocks were as tightly muscled as the rest of him, that his legs were long and powerfully built.

He moved like one who had grown up with danger—like her Uncle James and her cousins, who had known the suffering of the Seminoles. In silence, he watched at the latticed doors, and heard what she did not. He turned back into the room, finding his trousers and slipping into them.

"What are you doing?" she whispered.

"Be quiet, and stay there," he commanded.

A second later, he was out on the balcony. And a moment after that, she heard him cheerfully hailing someone who was also out on the balcony.

"Ah, Colonel Weir! Did you find you couldn't sleep as well?"

"Colonel Douglas," Weir returned. He sounded awkward.

"It's a beautiful night." Taylor said. "From here, this gracious house, with the sky so dark, the stars so bright, it is almost possible to forget the war."

"I never forget the war, sir."

"No, I imagine that you do not," Taylor agreed, and Tia could hear a note of irony in his voice.

*What had Ray Weir been doing on the balcony. By her room?*

"I think, sir, that what we accomplished here tonight

has been good work," Taylor continued. "There is so much bloodshed; when lives are spared, it is a decent thing at last."

"But freedom, sir, has always come at a cost! Sometimes, lives must be the price paid for a nation to survive."

"True enough. That lessens the value of no one life." Taylor said. "Well, sir, I didn't mean to interrupt you if you desired a private vigil in the night. But then . . . is that the door to your guest room? Were we given such close quarters? How interesting an arrangement by our gracious host."

"That . . . no, that is not my room. I am around there to the river side of the house. I—I merely decided to walk around the house, admire the architecture."

"Ah, I see. Oh, of course, I believe that is one of the family rooms. Ian's room—no, it is his sister's room, I think."

"Perhaps," Weir said stiffly.

"Good God, I didn't interrupt a secret tryst—" Taylor began with horror.

"No, indeed, sir, that you should suggest such a thing against the daughter of the house!" Ray said angrily.

"No offense intended, sir. It is simply that your admiration for her, and hers for you, is quite obvious."

"She is the most beautiful creature I have ever seen," Raymond said. "I have loved her forever."

"Curious that you never married. She was of age before the war, I believe?"

"I should have pursued my suit, sir. The lady longed for travel and adventure. I thought that she should see the world she craved to see, before becoming a proper wife. Yet, I always believed that she loved me."

"Well, the war will end," Taylor said.

"One day, indeed, I believe she will be mine."

"Good luck to you, sir."

"Yes, good night," Raymond told Taylor. "Were you returning to bed?"

"I thought that I'd enjoy the stars awhile longer.

Don't let me delay your stroll around the house any longer, sir."

"Yes, er, good night, then."

Tia waited, sitting up in Taylor's bed. A minute later, he reentered the room and came to the bedside. Now, somewhat decently clad in his trousers at least, he sat at the side of the bed. She noticed for the first time that he wore a gold chain around his neck with a medallion; it rested against the bronze of his chest.

She noticed, as well, that he wore a gold band around the ring finger of his left hand.

"I believe your lover was looking for you—heading for your room. I would not deprive you two of a romantic encounter, but I didn't think you'd want him discovering that you weren't in your room—indeed, that you were visiting me. You might want to slip back into your own room before someone else comes looking. There probably will be bloodshed here this evening, should someone find you here."

"No one would think that I had come for an illicit affair with a Yankee," she assured him.

He smiled. "Then just how would you explain your appearance?"

"You suggested that I come here, because . . . because I might know who Godiva is! Because I must warn her . . . that the Yanks may know who she is, that—"

She broke off. He was laughing softly. "And you think that your parents would believe that I enticed you into my bedroom *to talk about the welfare of a strange woman*?"

"Why not?"

"Oh, come, Tia, you're not a fool. You know that poor Colonel Weir lusts for you, in agony, so it seems. You teased an army with your perfection—and they followed you blindly. No, either your father or brother—or Weir—would want to kill me. There would be duels, and three people would die."

"And those people would be?"

"I would not be among them."

"My brother is one of the best swordsmen—"

"I am better."

"Your arrogance knows no bounds."

"Godiva, go back to your own bed, and leave me be."

"There would be no contest, sir!" she said, angrily rising. "I would simply tell my father that it was the truth, that you dislike me, have no desire for me—"

"Godiva, I never said that I had no desire for you!" His voice was deep, husky, and yet, for once, it seemed to hold no amusement. He stood before her, and though she was angry enough to strike him, she found herself not doing so, but standing very still as he reached out, his fingers touching her face. His head lowered to hers. She remembered the feel of his kiss. His lips were so close. They nearly touched hers. And still, she didn't move. His body was close as well. She could almost feel the hard-muscled structure of his torso against her breasts. "But," he murmured, "thank God, I would never be like that poor besotted Colonel Weir, never fool enough to love you, Godiva."

He was no longer touching her. Nowhere near so close. She felt a rush of cold air, as if wind swept in around her.

Fury filled her.

And she lashed out, her palm a blur, ready to hit him hard.

She never touched him. Her arm was captured, she was spun around, and she found herself enwrapped hard against him, her back to his chest, his arms around her tightly, fingers lacing just below her breasts. And his whispered warning touched her ear where he spoke softly against her. "You need to take care with that temper, Godiva. And with your welfare. Behave, I warn you. Keep your promise, keep yourself safe."

"What do you care?" she choked out furiously, her fingers working at his to earn her release.

"Your brother is my friend, your cousins are my kin, and your father is a truly great man."

"They are not your concern."

"Then perhaps I should simply tell them the truth."

"No!" she said, and went very still. "No."

"All right, then. I'll be careful not to mention you at all, should I be speaking with any of your kin. You take care not to talk about me as well."

"I wouldn't be talking about you."

"I could come up in conversation. And I wouldn't want you discussing various aspects of my person with which you shouldn't be familiar—after all, we have now both seen one another in the all-together."

He was taunting her now, he knew, and ready for the explosion of anger that ripped through her. Chuckling softly, he held her tightly until the fullness of her fury had abated. Then his amusement seemed to fade, and a somber quality fell over him. "Go to your own bed, Godiva. But heed my every warning, because I will tell the truth of the matter if I see no other way."

She stood some distance from him, still so livid she couldn't find the right words to say.

"I might be reprieved," she managed at last.

"I don't think so."

"It's a war, sir. You could be killed."

"And you could be killed, you little fool, and that's the point of this."

"Good night, Colonel. With luck, we'll never meet again."

She turned to flee with dignity.

He caught her arm. She wrenched at it. "Wait!" he grated. "Don't you want to see if the coast is clear?"

She bit her lower lip, drawing blood, lowering her head. He stepped past her.

A silent tread.

"Go," he said softly.

And she did.

Christmas Eve.

There was no reason why Sydney couldn't have gone home to Florida. Her husband lived in Washington, so it was where his wife should be, but since she hadn't seen her husband since their impromptu marriage in prison, she *should* have gone home. She didn't even live in his apartment. She still shared with Sissy and with

Marla, an Irish friend, widowed in the war, who had helped in her old spying days. Her borrowed space, her only privacy, here in Washington was a tiny ten-by-ten room in the apartment the three women shared near the White House.

Washington was cold. Wretched. Patches of ice, a vicious wind. Home meant the sun, and during those very few times when the temperature dipped into the thirties, there was still warmth from the sun. Home meant her mother, her father, her new baby sister. Perhaps Jerome would even be there; God knew, her oldest brother could move with unbelievable speed when he chose. And even if she hadn't made it home—Brent was less than a hundred miles south of here. She could have, perhaps, reached her sister-in-law in St. Augustine, or cut across the state and spent the holiday at Cimarron with her aunt and uncle.

She had to quit thinking that way. There were a dozen other things she might have been doing rather than what she was . . .

Risking her life again like an idiot!

Driving her wagon, Sissy at her side, she neared the Southern picket line.

"Ho, there!"

Today, the officer in charge appeared to be about twenty-five, lean, sad looking, and very cold. He wore a lieutenant's insignia. A worn scarf was wrapped around his neck. He shuffled back and forth on his feet, his rifle held easily in his hands. She drew in on the reins, ready for his questions. He smiled at her, bringing his hands to his face. Blowing on them. He wore gloves, but they were riddled with holes.

"Good evening, ma'am. May I have your papers? State your business."

She handed him her traveling papers. "I came south with letters from the fellows at Old Capitol, with proper permission from the Yankee authorities to do so. There, Colonel Meek, whose troops have headed on back toward Harper's Ferry, received the letters, and signed for my return to Washington."

The officer stared up at her. "Mrs. Sydney . . . *McKenzie* Halston?"

She nodded.

He smiled suddenly. "If you see your husband or your cousin Ian, tell them Rafe Johnston sends his best."

"You rode with my cousin Ian?"

"And your husband. With Magee. I heard your brother married Magee's daughter. Always thought it would be Ian."

"They're all doing very well," Sydney said. "I . . ." she began. But then she froze. The sound of a sneeze came from the back of the wagon.

Johnston stared at her. She stared back. She felt the blood drain from her face. Even as he looked at her, she saw the future flash before her eyes. He would arrest her. She was an avowed Southerner-heading north with runaway slaves. There could be a trial. There might not. They might hang her tonight, make an example out of her, prove that the South could not tolerate spies and traitors, even among their womenfolk.

She saw Johnston lower his eyes, and then he looked at her again. And he knew exactly what she was doing.

But he handed her back her papers. "Merry Christmas, Mrs. Halston. It's a good time to pray for peace."

She exhaled on a soft sob. "Merry Christmas, Lieutenant . . ." She lifted the reins. Her fingers were numb. She couldn't hold them. She inhaled again, remembered the embroidered bag she carried at her side—and the gift she had carried in case she had managed to see her brother.

Gloves. Good, calfskin gloves, both soft and resilient. "Lieutenant . . . these were for my brother Brent. I was never able to see him. Please . . ."

"No, ma'am, I can't take those." His eyes told her that they might be considered a bribe.

She shook her head. "Please, I wanted so badly to give them to someone to whom they might mean something. Please . . ."

He looked at the gloves in her hands, looked at her,

into her eyes. He took the gloves. "Thank you. Hurry on now."

She grasped the reins, cracked them, calling out to the mules. They rode on.

"God bless us!" Sissy breathed.

"We're still in Rebel territory. And we've the Yanks to get through. If we encounter a wretched son of a gun the way we did last time . . ."

"We won't," Sissy said with assurance.

Sissy was right. It was Christmas Eve. The Yankee pickets, like their Southern counterparts, were melancholy. They wanted the war to be over. They wanted to be home. All along the lines, they sang Christmas carols.

The officer who stopped her on the road barely looked at her papers.

No one sneezed.

They passed on through to the city, and arrived at last in a dark alley off South Capitol Street, near the African Methodist Episcopal ministry of Reverend Henry Turner. Washington might mean freedom for the slaves, but it did not assure them a good life, or even a decent meal. Reverend Turner had always been a passionate man about helping his fellows, so tonight, Sydney drove Sissy and the two men and three women they had met just below the lines to the alley where Turner would meet them, and find them a place to stay.

They blessed Sydney as they came from the wagon, one of the men carrying the beaten, pregnant young girl whose story had inspired Sydney to risk her own life again and come south for the contrabands.

One of the women came around the front of the wagon, looking at Sydney with her huge dark eyes. She grabbed Sydney's hand and tried to kiss it.

"Please!" Sydney whispered. "Go on now. Merry Christmas."

"God bless you, ma'am!" said one of the men, a huge black field hand.

"And you," she murmured. She was flushed; embarrassed. She shouldn't be doing this. But when the message had reached the house about the dying girl, she'd been busy feeling sorry for herself, and angry with herself for not leaving Washington.

"I'll go with them to the Reverend," Sissy told Sydney. "Are you going to be all right?"

"Yes, of course."

Sissy shook her head. "Marla isn't even at the apartment. She went off to spend Christmas with old Mrs. Lafferty and the orphans."

"I'll be fine. I'm very tired."

"I'll be back tomorrow morning sometime."

"We'll find a good Christmas dinner somewhere," Sydney agreed.

She left Sissy, and took the wagon back to the livery near the apartment. "It's late for you to be heading home alone, Mrs. Halston," the night man told her.

"I'll be fine."

It was past midnight, she realized, but not so strange, for in wartime, there always seemed to be someone out and about. She passed a group of officers sharing a flask over a street fire. They tipped their hats to her, watching her curiously. She nodded, and hurried into her apartment.

A fire burned in the cozy living room. There was a note left on the mantle from Marla:

> Syd,
> I'm off to play Santa the best I can to the little ones.
> Major Cantor brought a roast—it's on the dining room
> table—and a delicious claret. (I know it's delicious; I
> tried it.) Left you a steaming bath and my gift, lavender soap. It may not be steaming when you return.
> Left a kettle by the fire.
> Love to you, Marla.

Sydney smiled. She might be far from home, but at least she had a few friends. She shed her cloak and her boots in the living room. She walked into the darkened bedroom, where even there, a fire had been left burning. It was the only light in the room, illuminating the tub. She touched the water. Still warm. The kettle rested by the fire. Taking a thick pot holder, she poured the steaming water into the bath and began to shed her clothing. As she stepped from her skirt, her travel papers fell from the pocket. Weary and anxious for the warm water, she left them where they lay, and sank into the tub.

She closed her eyes and leaned back.

After a moment, she felt a very strange, uneasy sensation.

She opened her eyes.

She froze.

Jesse was there. Across the room, seated in the one armchair in the far dark corner. Stripped down himself to uniform trousers, boots, and white cotton shirt, eyes grave, handsome features somewhat leaner than they had been when last she'd seen him. He watched her in silence.

"Jesse . . ." she breathed, stunned.

He stood, walking toward the tub.

"Where have you been?"

"Been?" she echoed.

"It's after midnight. Where have you been?"

She thought desperately for an answer. Her mind was blank. She shrank into the water, hugging her knees to her chest, greatly unnerved. "I . . . I can't discuss the situation right now, Jesse. I wasn't expecting you."

"Obviously."

Her eyes narrowed. "I haven't heard from you in six months!" she snapped. "In fact, you told me to get an annulment."

"But you didn't. Where have you been?"

"Out!"

"Out where?"

"It's really none of your business, and you have your nerve, interrogating me here, now, in the bathtub. If you'll just get out of my room and let me finish and dress—"

"I married you, Sydney," he said softly, leaning down, bracing his hands on the side of the tub. "Then I did the very gentlemanly thing—and rode off to war. Tonight I'm back. Where have you been?"

She met his eyes, sharp, hazel, and unrelenting. Six months. A long six months. He had changed. She lowered her head, remembering when he had been a Confederate prisoner and she had been his nurse. She remembered the way he had looked at her then, the charm in his voice, the sound of his laughter, the gentleness of his touch, the way she had longed to see him each day.

She looked up again. He wasn't the same man.

"I was out—with friends."

He turned away, picking up the papers that had fallen from her skirt. He read through them. They fell from his hands, drifting back to the floor. "Letters from dead Rebs, eh, brought south?" he asked.

Then suddenly he turned. And his hands were on her shoulders, and he was dragging her dripping and protesting from the tub. "My God, you promised, you swore!" he raged at her. "You swore there would be no more espionage, and I gave my word for you, that there would be no actions against the Union in which you were involved. My word! I gave *my* word for you!"

She had never, ever seen him like this. He was the one always in control, a man who did the right thing, thoughtful, considerate, courteous—if determined. When he had prevented her from leaving the city with Jerome, when he had arrested her—when he had married her—he had been in control. Even after the wedding. *He had walked away.* Not now.

She couldn't even respond. She stood before him with soap and bath water sluicing from her form, and she couldn't find the right words to defend herself. No! She hadn't betrayed the Union, but she had ridden south . . .

His arm suddenly jerked back and she braced herself, gritting her teeth, certain that he meant to hit her. Six months, six months between them, and this was how they met.

No blow landed upon her. But his hands were suddenly upon her again, and he was shaking her, and then he thrust her from him, and in the small space of the tiny bedroom, she fell back, tripping so that she fell into the tub again. Water spewed up and around her. Her fingers closed around the soap.

She threw it. He saw the missile coming and ducked. Then he stared at her, and she knew she was in trouble.

He made a dive for her in the tub again. She struggled, trying to free her arms. She was dragged back out anyway and caught again before the fire, where she kicked and writhed to get free. "Let go of me, you oaf. You want an annulment, you'll have an annulment so fast your head will spin, Colonel Halston!" she swore. It did her no good.

"Liar! I trusted you!" he hissed. "Like a fool, I thought your word meant something." He didn't begin to release his hold, but used his weight to press her toward the foot of the bed. This time, she fell backward on the mattress. He followed her down.

"Get away from me, get out of *my* apartment. My word does mean something, you horrible *Unionist.*"

"Rebel spy."

"Yankee bastard."

"Indian!" he shouted at her.

"And God help me, but I'd love to scalp you!" she taunted him in return.

"Where have you been?" he repeated.

"None of your business. Leave me alone!"

"Not this time. You're going back to Old Capitol, my dear wife. This time, you will stay out of trouble."

She sucked in her breath. "Fine! Send me back. There will be an annulment."

"I will."

But he hadn't moved. He still lay atop her, his shirt as soaked as she was.

"Send me back!" she whispered. But she didn't mean it. God, she didn't mean it. She hated prison. And hated the fear that one of her brothers, her father, or her other kin would die to free her from such a place. And yet . . .

"Do it! Send me back!" she repeated.

"Not yet."

"Yes, now . . ." The feel of his body was a fire against her. She'd been so afraid so many times that he didn't come because he was dead. He wasn't dead; he was alive and well—he had just stayed away from her. "Do it!" she cried, and she started slamming her hands against him. "Do it, do it, do it . . ."

He caught her wrists, shook his head. "I came home to spend Christmas Eve with my wife. It is a long, hard, lonely war. I intend to spend it with her."

His mouth found hers. Seared into it. She tried to close her lips, twist her head. Tears stung her eyes; her lips parted in a sob, and suddenly she was kissing him back. She'd fallen in love with him easily. Trying to hate him had been hard. Fearing for him daily had been torture. Waiting, and waiting, and waiting . . .

And now this. His kiss, the touch of his hands. A feeling of hunger, of rage, of fear. His wet clothing was a tangle around him. She was chilled and hot at the same time. Aware of where they were going, and thinking that I should never have been miserable, praying that she would love him . . .

Just his kiss, his touch. Heated, evocative. Awakening a hunger that left her clinging to him, and still afraid of the unknown. He was passionate, but impatient with his anger. She tasted his lips; her fingers curled into his hair. The kiss did things, and still . . .

She screamed and choked, and wanted to die. Her nails dug into his shoulders. He went rigid, waited. His eyes met hers. Hers closed. And he began to move again, giving no quarter. She still thought that she would die. The pain remained . . . but something grew out of it as well. She gritted her teeth, trying to push him away. She burrowed against his shoulder his chest, suddenly wanting more, moving with him, wanting . . . wanting . . .

Sweet mercury filled her, as molten as a spill of steel, sweeping away strength and anger and every other thought except elation for the moments that lifted her to ecstasy. She clung to the magic, and to his arms, and then she was drifting down again, and she was cold and sore and caught in the tangle of the sheets and his clothing.

He lay beside her, no apology spoken. After a few

moments, he rose, shedding his disheveled clothing. She shivered, watching his body in the moonlight. He was perfect—except for the scars. The bronze of his shoulder was marred by the white line where he had been injured at Gettysburg. He'd probably receive another promotion because of that scar—bravery under fire on the battle-field. And of course, so many officers had died. It was a time when replacements might readily be given credit.

She looked lower, swallowing. There had been that time when they had both been intrigued, when they had flirted, when they had fallen in love. A time when they had been friends. Then there had been their marriage . . . and now, when nothing seemed right at all, there was this time of intimacy. God, how she had dreamed of being with him! Laughter, champagne perhaps, all the right tenderness, whispers in her ear. She hated him, hated him for con-demning her. An echo of pain seemed to linger within her, and still . . . she wanted him to lie down beside her.

He came back to the bed, wrenching the covers with her still upon them. "Get under the sheets and blanket," he said brusquely. "You're shaking."

Ah, what gentle, endearing words on this occasion!

"I'm not cold. I'm angry. I want you away."

"You're freezing. Do as I say—for once."

"Because this is Washington, and you think you have all the power?"

"Because it's logical."

She rolled away from him, trying to rise. She was drawn back; the covers brought over her. He lay down beside her. She stiffened. He didn't allow her to do so. He drew her against the warmth of his own body, held her there. She closed her eyes. There were so many things to say. She didn't say any of them.

Then she felt him.

His lips, a brand against her nape, her shoulder, her backbone. His hands, cupping her breasts, sliding down her ribs, her belly, to her groin. Fingers pressing, stroking . . .

This time, something suddenly caught within her. Wildfire. She turned to him, guided by instinct, touching, tasting, kissing, in a frenzy. Desire spit, rose, spiraled, teased, and taunted. His mouth was everywhere on her. Each touch elicited a burst of fire. She twisted, writhed, and trembled, and when he was within her again, she arched to his every thrust, feeling impassioned, fevered, hungry . . .

The world seemed to explode. The war was over; life had ended. Diamond glimmers of bursting light broke a black satin heaven, then there was nothing more. And it seemed to take forever and ever to drift down and realize that he was with her, shuddering as well in the aftermath of climax.

It was wonder, pure wonder. And she was in love again, ready to admit to him what had happened, how she had become involved, how it was actually the South, her own heritage, and everything she stood for that she had betrayed. She'd never do it again. If it hadn't been for the kindness and justice of Lieutenant Johnston, she might have been caught, but . . .

He stroked her hair. "There will be no question of an annulment now," he said.

"No," she whispered, turning into him, her face against his chest. He smelled delicious. Muscle rippled beneath her touch. His warmth was encompassing.

"My God, I shall be sorry to see you back in prison."

She stiffened. Drew away. "In prison?"

His eyes touched hers. Deep hazel, grave. "Did you think that I was so desperate for your love that I would be seduced and demented—and forget that you *lied— that you made a liar and a fool out of me*?"

She jerked away from him. He reached out, preventing her from fleeing when she would have left the bed.

"Get away from me! Get your hands off me! Call your guards and have me arrested tonight, though on what charges, I do not know! Call them now! Old Capitol seems a wonderful place to sleep, as long as you do not sleep there as well! You're right, I'll be among my own people, my own kind, sleeping with Rebels rather than *snakes*!"

"Get back in here."

"No!"

"Sydney—"

"You intend to arrest me again; do it."

"Not tonight."

"Why not tonight?"

"There's time."

"No, there's not! I could cause an entire uprising; force the South to win the war while you sleep!"

Aggravated, he caught her around the middle and pressed her back down. She couldn't believe the pain she was feeling.

"I hate you!"

"Sorry. It's a war."

"Yes, it is. So arrest me this minute—or let me go."

"No."

And he didn't let her go. He lay down beside her, keeping a firm hand upon her. She twisted, turning her back to him, but aware of his arm around her.

Christmas Eve . . .

A time of peace.

She had never felt more at war.

# Chapter 9

D awn.
    The sun was rising; the sky was clear; the day was beautiful. And far in the south of the Florida peninsula, it was warm.

James McKenzie stood by the little inlet of salt water that created a lagoon on his property and looked out far past it—far to the sea beyond. He stood shirtless, his bronze chest muscled and honed, and barefoot, the warmth of the salt water running over his feet. He loved the water; he loved the sea and the warmth. His attire might not be exactly proper, but then, they were far to the south of real civilization, and he'd been called a savage often enough in his life. Down here, on his own property, his attire was his own concern. He gave it little thought as he continued to stare at the sea.

His son was out there. Somewhere. His oldest son, Jerome, trying to find new ways to slip the Union blockade and bring supplies to the state and the Confederacy. He had watched the water through the night and into the morning, hoping against hope that Jerome might make it home for the holiday.

There was no sign of a ship. He didn't despair. He had to believe in the ability of both his sons—and his daughters!—to survive the war. At the moment, however, he wasn't particularly worried about the girls. Jennifer, his child by Naomi, his first wife, was home with him. She and her son, Anthony—now a handsome, precocious young boy of six—had been with him since Jarrett had brought her home after her husband's death. Disguised as a man, she had begun some very dangerous spying activities, been caught and nearly hanged. His nephew, Ian, had managed to save her, and since then, she had tried to exist without thinking about the war—despite the fact that the state remained Rebel, and Union navy ships out of Union-held Key West far too often came near their shore.

Then there was his daughter Mary—born just last year and quite a surprise to both him and his wife, Teela. She had given him tremendous fear at the time of her birth, fear that she would die in childbirth, but she and the baby were well now, saucy, sweet, toddling around, allowing them to smile in the midst of their worry for their other children. James had lost a wife and child to fever during the Seminole War; he knew the anguish of it, and often prayed that, were he to be given one gift from God, it would be to *not* outlive any more of his children. Brent, he thought, might be safer than Jerome; Jerome was brash and reckless, and renowned for his daring escapades against the Yanks. Brent was a doctor, a surgeon, dedicated to life. James liked to believe that he would have the sense to take care for his own.

But then there was Sydney . . .

Reckless, passionate, as any warrior of old. She had been with Brent in Charleston when South Carolina had seceded. She had become a nurse in Richmond. She had gone to try to exchange a Yank for her brother when Jerome had been captured.

Then, recently, she had married the Yank.

A damned fine fellow, he had been assured.

But Sydney had been living in Washington ever since, and he longed to have her home. Staring out at the water, he wondered about heading north to suggest to her new husband that Sydney might fare better back in her own home while the war raged.

No one thought, of course, that he should do it. Teela told him he had too hot a temper, that he'd be demanding his daughter—something he didn't have a right to do, since Sydney had married the man by choice, had written about him before, and apparently loved him. But it was too long for a father to wait to see his child. Especially when it was Christmas.

"Father?"

He turned, surprised to be discovered there, by the lagoon pool, at this early hour. It was Jennifer. She was maturing now, in her mid-thirties, into a very serene and dignified woman, more beautiful, he thought, with each passing year. She had her mother's hazel eyes, a nobility to her native features, a gentle smile, and at least, an inner peace. She came to him, and he slipped an arm around her shoulders. "Father, he is smart enough not to come. He knows the navy men will be keeping a close eye out for him now! They know Jerome loves his family." She was silent for a minute. "I imagine Risa is by the sea today, as well. Looking out."

"Risa is in St. Augustine. Teela urged her to come to us, but she was afraid that she would hear he had come to the north of the state somewhere, and she wouldn't be able to reach him."

"He's not a fool. He is safe. And we just received that letter from Brent; he is well, but very busy—"

"You'd think they'd stop killing for Christmas, wouldn't you?" James said softly.

"We have a long letter from Sydney, as well, you know, brought by one of Captain Dickinson's men."

"I know."

"Father, I wish I could ease this all for you somehow."

He drew her closer, setting his cheek against her dark head. "You do. You and Anthony and Mary. Have I told you how much I love you lately, daughter? How very precious you are?"

"Father, I—"

Abruptly she stopped speaking. "Look, Father, look!"

He'd been staring out to sea, and so he hadn't seen the man lying half in the water and half out at the far side of the lagoon beneath a giant palm.

"My, God, it is a man!" Jennifer breathed. She pulled from James, and started running around the pool.

"No! Wait!" James called firmly. He didn't know if she would heed him or not, and so he started to run himself. He caught her arm, pulling her back. "Wait! If he's alive, he may be dangerous!"

He passed his daughter, aware she still followed behind him, but at least she was at his back. As he neared the body, he drew the knife he always kept in a sheath at his ankle before falling down to his knees in the wet sand by the body. He rolled the soldier over, thinking that the man must be dead.

Not dead . . . a pulse ticked at his throat. Weak, but there. He looked at the uniform. Union cavalry. More cavalry—damn the cavalry! He was a lean man, young, with sand-encrusted blond hair and burned skin.

"Father . . ."

"He's alive."

James studied the man's face. A smear of blood grazed his temple, coagulated now with a matting of hair and sand.

"We have to bring him in! Help him," Jennifer said.

"He's Union, Jennifer."

"So . . . so is Ian! And Taylor stayed with the Union as well. They are both men you care about, nearly as close as your own sons."

"Jennifer, your husband was killed by Union fire."

"And I was saved by my cousin Ian from a hangman's noose. Father, you can't mean to let him die because he is a Federalist! What if a Union woman were to find Brent or Jerome or Julian injured? Oh, my God, does that matter—"

He looked at his daughter carefully. "No, I just want to remind you of the past, of the years gone by. There was a time when you wanted even Ian dead!"

"Perhaps. But both you and Ian taught me to live past bitterness. You wouldn't just let a man die. I know you!"

James sighed. This was trouble, pure trouble. But Jennifer was right; he wouldn't let any man die.

Yet he'd cut the bastard's throat himself without blinking if he awoke to threaten his wife or children or six-year-old Anthony.

"Father . . ."

"I have him, Jennifer. Run back and tell Teela quickly

that I'm bringing . . ." He paused, smiling ruefully. "Tell her I'm bringing her a wounded Yank for Christmas. It's just what she's always wanted!"

Christmas morning. Tia could not help flirting atrociously with Weir, aware that her easy laughter was heard by her enemy, that he listened to her teasing comments, saw the way she laughed with Weir—sharing conversations about the past. She intended to dazzle Weir, but she didn't know why, because it felt dangerous and wrong. She caught her sister-in-law's warning eye, and knew that Alaina was perplexed and worried. Still, she couldn't help herself.

The morning was, however, truly enjoyable after breakfast ended. The children awoke but weren't in the least hungry, since they were anxious only to open their gifts. They tore into the bright packages containing games and toys, laughing and running around. Their eyes were bright; too young to know that a dark cloud remained over the state and a country divided.

Then gifts were distributed to the adults as well, those that the family naturally exchanged, and those which Tara saw to it were available for her guests.

For Raymond Weir, a large smoked ham.

For Taylor Douglas, a miniature tintype of a woman, formed into a delicate silver frame that would easily fit into a soldier's knapsack or pouch.

Tia had never seen it before. She didn't even know what it was at first, but it traveled around the room and everyone complimented the workmanship. Taylor Douglas gazed upon the gift, then looked at Tara. "It's a kindness beyond all I might have imagined, Mrs. McKenzie. With all the responsibilities you have here, that you thought to do this . . . that you were able to obtain this likeness . . . well, madam, I am deeply grateful."

Tara smiled happily. "You sent this to James's wife, my sister-in-law, Teela, soon after you were married. Teela and James lost their home to fire a while back. During the rebuilding, she sent us many things which had been saved, to keep for her. This picture was among them. When I heard you were coming here, I knew that Teela would be glad for you to have it again."

The framed miniature had reached Tia. She looked down. The woman in the tintype was delicately blond and very beautiful. Her smile was sweet and winning. Her eyes had a faintly teasing nature to them.

She was his wife.

Her fingers felt cold and awkward. What did it matter? She had prayed she'd never see him again. He'd done nothing but humiliate her.

And now this.

They had shared a strange intimacy, and he was a married man.

He was looking at her. She handed the miniature to him. "She is very beautiful."

He nodded, and turned away.

"Tia, will you help me with the eggnog, dear?"

"Yes, of course, Mother."

"We'll move on into the music room, gentlemen."

"And ladies, Papa, and ladies!" Ariana, sitting in her grandfather's lap, reminded him.

"Oh, yes. And ladies, of course." He smiled across the room at his daughter-in-law. "Ladies, do forgive me."

The others laughed. Despite the very presence of the war in their house in the form of the opposing colonels, the house seemed filled with Christmas spirit.

Only Tia seemed to have lost her sense of joy. "Are you all right?" her mother asked her as they joined Lilly in the kitchen, preparing a tray of eggnog—with and without whiskey—for their company.

"Yes, of course, Mother, I'm fine."

"Has the colonel been pressuring you?"

"What?" she asked guiltily. Could her mother have possibly realized that there was *something* between her and Taylor Douglas?"

"Ray Weir. I do feel a bit sorry for him. He looks at you constantly."

"Oh . . . well. He did mention marriage again."

"And?"

Tia shrugged. "I reminded him there was a war on."

Tara nodded. "Then take care with him, my dear. Don't tease him too mercilessly. He's becoming very much a military man."

"And what does that mean?"

"That he might want to take the law into his own hands at some point."

"But—"

"Never mind, Tia. I didn't mean that many military men aren't fine human beings—such as your brother, Ian. But power is strange. Men take hold of it sometimes—and want more and more. You just don't always realize your own power."

"What is that power?"

"Youth and beauty," her mother said, smiling.

"Oh, Mother—"

"Come, dear, you're going to deny me, say that I think you're beautiful because you're my daughter, and that is all. You're simply very, very beautiful, and the rest of the world agrees. Most obviously, Colonel Weir thinks so."

"Colonel Weir . . . and who else?" Tia said, surprised by the words herself, and very surprised by their wistful quality. "Oh, Lord, how silly of me, how petty in the midst of all this—"

"Tia, I will not say more. I'll not have it all go to your head!" Tara gave her a tight hug. "Let's go do carols. This is a very precious occasion, with you, Ian, Alaina, and the babies, and I will not see the day slip by!"

Drinks were served. At her father's insistence, Tia joined her mother at the piano. They had often played together and even more often, sung together. Her mother's stage training coupled with a really beautiful soprano voice had made her an excellent teacher, and Tia knew that many of the harmonies she did with her mother were exceptionally pretty. She was tense at first, uncomfortably aware of both Weir and Douglas, but after a while, Ariana, joining in, had her laughing, and they did fun songs with the children, then medieval carols. Realizing that at one point Taylor Douglas was watching her with an intrigued speculation, she found herself suddenly striking the keys in a rousing rendition of "Dixie." Her playing was perfect, her voice even more so, full of the emotion that could make a song great.

Yet when she had ended, the room was in utter silence. She met her father's eyes, and saw his anger and his disappointment that she had forgotten that their guests were there for *peaceful* negotiations, not to fight the war in their living room.

Then Raymond Weir began to clap.

Politely, Taylor Douglas joined in. Then the others as well. She felt the blood draining from her face, knowing that her father did not applaud. She quickly began to play "Silent Night." Ariana crawled up on her lap. She sang with the baby's pretty little voice joining her own, a few sibilant *s*'s making it all the more charming. Still, she wanted to sink into the woodwork.

She had ruined the spirit of the day.

Finishing the song, she kissed the baby on her forehead, set her alone on the piano stool, and turned to her father. "Excuse, me, Father . . ."

And she fled.

She couldn't crawl into the woodwork, but she could go riding. Fly through the cool winter's day on Blaze, and feel cleansed by the air.

"Tia!"

Her father hadn't called her, her mother had. She pretended not to hear.

She didn't dare take time to change. Exiting the house by the rear, she ran down the sloping lawn to the stables. Billy Cloud, one of her father's Seminole men, was whittling by the door. "What are you up to, Miss Tia?"

"Just a ride, Billy."

"Take care that you follow the property line, Miss Tia."

She hesitated. "Why, is something wrong?"

He shrugged and looked up at her with sage dark eyes. "War is wrong, Miss Tia. The Vichy house due east of here was burned down last week. No troops will admit to it, but they say that Mr. Vichy was selling his cattle to the wrong group of people. You take care where you're riding."

"I will, Billy, I promise."

She went in for Blaze, bridled her horse, but didn't bother with a saddle. She left the stable, waved to Billy, then raced for the forest trail.

Sydney awoke slowly. She opened her eyes, wondering why she felt so groggy, sore . . .

And suddenly cold. She shouldn't be cold. It was Christmas, and she should be home, where it was warm . . . home with her mother, father, family.

She hadn't been home in a very long time . . .

But home was different now.

She sat up quickly, remembering that Jesse had come, remembering the night. Remembering the way that he had held her, infuriated her, and held her again. She was tired because she had barely slept; each time she had drifted to sleep, she had awakened to sweet sensation, seduced awake, and in dreams. The words that had come between them had made them more certain enemies than ever, but she had loved him before . . .

And she loved him still, despite the damage to her pride, the bitterness he felt for her, certain she had betrayed him.

She looked swiftly around herself in the small bedroom, and then saw that he was there, standing in front of the mantle. He was dressed, in full uniform, hair clean and smoothed back. He held his hat in his hands as he stared at the flames, his expression grave. Though he didn't turn, he knew that she had awakened, and he spoke to her softly.

"Sydney, I'm sorry. By God, so sorry. But I see no help for it!" he said.

"Help for . . ."

He turned to her. Ever the officer, gallant and straight, thoughtful now in his words. She thought of the way he had touched her in the night, and more; she thought of the way he looked at her, at the gentle, teasing things he had said in the past.

"I swore for you," he told her. "When we were married, I swore that you would cease all spying activities. On my own honor, I swore for you."

She looked down, not knowing what to say, whether defending herself with the simple truth would suffice or not.

"Jesse, I've done nothing. I swear to you now, I'm innocent of any wrongdoing against the Union."

"I wish I dared believe you."

"How can you care for me, as you claim, and not believe me?" she cried out.

He smiled with a bittersweet curve to his lips. "I've seen your work firsthand, Sydney. I know that you are passionate about your cause."

"Jesse, I haven't seen you in six months. I left here once to see my brother Brent—"

"Who happens to serve just outside Richmond."

"I wasn't carrying any government or military secrets, Jesse. I just went to see my brother. He's been assigned back to military hospital duty after having been on a special project . . . dealing with disease."

"Yes, I know where Brent is working, Sydney. I make a point of keeping track of your family, the best I can. Luckily—and with ill luck for the many who are killed— the Army of the Potomac and the Army of Northern Virginia are constantly circling one another. Brent was sent to try to educate some of the illustrious Southern camp followers, and stem the rising tide of venereal disease. Now he's back trying to patch up the wounded, who flow in as constantly as we circle one another. That explains the past. What now?"

"I went to see him again."

"You were not gone long enough to have traveled to Richmond."

"How on earth can you know that?" she began with annoyance.

Again, he offered her a very wry smile. "Spies," he said softly. "Sydney, why were you gone when I arrived? Where had you been?"

"I . . ." she began, then hesitated. Did she have the

right to tell him? Would he accept what she and Sissy had done as being a good thing?

She lowered her head. "I'm not at liberty to tell you," she said.

"Sydney, for the love of God—"

"Yes, for the love of God." She looked up at him, suddenly damning him. "There is no such thing as trust between us, is there?"

"Sydney, how can there be?"

"Then if you'll excuse me, I'll dress—and you can arrest me."

"Sydney, don't be ridiculous. I'm not leaving this room."

"Then stay if you choose."

She threw off her covers and rose, ignoring him as he stood by the fire. She gathered fresh clothing from the small wardrobe in the corner of the room, turning her back on him to dress. She had barely stepped into pantalettes when she felt his hands on her shoulders, his whisper at her nape.

"Sydney—"

"Jesse, leave it be!"

He spun her around to meet him; stroked out a long, tangled lock of her hair, ran his knuckles down her cheek. She wanted to fall against him, lay her head upon his shoulder, feel his comfort—and his passion. She pulled away from him, her green eyes hard as jade.

"Leave me be, Jesse. Leave me be."

To her surprise, he did. Uttering a harsh oath, he turned away from her, heading for the door.

He paused there.

"House arrest, Sydney. I won't have you thrown back into Old Capitol."

"Indeed—even Yankees might ask about my current crimes!"

"If you won't tell me—"

"I can't!"

"Then you leave me no choice," he said.

The door opened, and he exited. The door slammed in his wake.

It was Christmas. He would come back, she thought. But he did not.

Following Tia, Taylor reached the stables to find a tall, muscular fellow standing at the stable doorway—swearing. If Taylor remembered correctly, it was Billy Cloud, Jarrett McKenzie's head groom, whose features more than hinted of his Indian blood. He saw Taylor, flushed, and excused himself. "Colonel! I beg your pardon, I was in thought regarding a problem."

"No explanations are necessary, sir, but what's the problem? Perhaps I can help."

"Her father's the only man who can ever help with that hellion!" Billy said, shaking his head with exasperation.

"Are we referring to Tia McKenzie?" Taylor asked, grinning slightly.

"We are." He peered at Taylor suddenly. "You're kin to James McKenzie. And to Osceola."

"Distantly, yes."

"We'd heard you were coming. I remember you from many years ago. It's good to see you again, sir—though in a strange uniform."

"Billy, the men who brutally pursued our people in this uniform have split, just as the nation has split. I thought about it long and hard before I chose the path I did."

"Did your dream visions lead you to your quest?"

Taylor smiled. It had been a long time since he'd been with the Seminole people. "Under the influence of the black drink—and stone-cold sober—I made my choice. You have stayed with Jarrett McKenzie."

"Oh, I think some of those swaggering braggarts in Confederate uniform are complete asses," Billy said, and grinning, he added, "I will get your horse. You're leaving?"

"I'm going after Miss Tia."

"Good, you will save me the trouble. Her father's men guard the circumference of the house, but outside the grounds here . . . I tell her not to ride into danger. She promises she will not and does so anyway. She doesn't think she lies because she refuses to see danger when it stops her from doing what she will."

Billy brought Friar from his stall and went for the saddle while Taylor bridled his horse. He thought that Billy's assessment of young Miss McKenzie was right on the money—she didn't think, and she didn't see danger. She did what seemed right for her at the moment. She didn't even see the danger she was causing in her father's own house. She had no idea how her every word and movement were affecting Raymond Weir.

"Thank you, Billy," he said, and grinned, stepping back.

Taylor followed the path Tia had taken. It was a clear shot to the woods, and once there, he could easily follow her trail. The area was exceptionally beautiful, the floor blanketed in pine needles, the trees forming canopies of green darkness overhead. He cantered through the trails at first, then slowed, certain she had stopped somewhere ahead. He dismounted, walking the distance, until he came to a copse around a beautiful, freshwater spring. She was seated upon a log, legs curled beneath her, staring at the water.

"Too cold to dive in?" he inquired.

Startled, she swung around, eyes widening, then filling with anger as she looked back to the water. "How did you find me? Billy told you where to go?"

He walked over to her log and stood by it, then hunkered down, folding his hands before him, staring at the crystal clarity of the water as well. He didn't gaze at her. He didn't need to. It seemed that she was a memory in his mind's eye. Her eyes were very dark, mahogany dark like her father's—a strange twist of inherited traits, since James's family, with their Seminole blood, all had light eyes, blue or green. Tia's very coloring was part of her beauty. The depth of her eyes seemed endless. The color seemed to match the sable luster of her hair. Her cheeks were fair. Pure ivory and cream. And her features were delicate and beautifully formed. Soft rose naturally blushed her cheeks, her lips were the deep red of wine, generous, full, beautifully formed. He remembered too clearly the taste of them.

"No one needed to tell me where to go," he said. "You're easy to follow."

"Why did you follow me? I left the house to escape."

"To escape what?"

"Mainly you," she said, turning to stare at him.

"Or perhaps your father's disappointment?" he suggested. She turned away quickly, and he knew that he was right. She had wanted to get to him—and so her stirring rendition of "Dixie." She hadn't gotten beneath his skin at all—he liked the song. But she had disturbed Jarrett.

"I'm not your concern. Why did you follow me? Why couldn't you just leave me be?"

"Billy was about to come after you—he said he warned you to stay closer to the grounds of the house."

She shook her head, staring at him. "You're in danger. I'm not. I serve with the Rebel militia. No one is angry at me."

"You don't need people to be personally angry at you to attract violence, I'm afraid. But I told you before— *I'm* angry with you."

"Well, are you a threat?"

"Oh, yes. I've certainly warned you of that, too."

"But you've given me your word that you will not reveal my secret."

"As long as you keep *your* word."

"I said I would."

"But will you? You like to play with fire."

She sighed, then stared at him. "Why is it that a man is brave and a woman foolish when they both want to fight for something in which they believe?"

"I don't consider all women fools."

"Only me? How selective of you!" She shook her head angrily, loosening the coil that had held the length of her hair. It rumbled down her back. He rose, but she saw him coming and jumped off her log, retreating from him. She backed into a tree, and he reached around her, capturing a long tendril of her hair. It curled around his fingers like a silk sheath. "I should slice this off here and now, force you to keep your word."

"My father would kill you."

"For what—assault upon your hair?"

She tugged at the lock. "Let go."

"Maybe. After we have a conversation. Tell me, Miss McKenzie, who do you know better? Weir—or me?"

"What on earth are you talking about, Colonel?" she demanded impatiently. "We've known Colonel Weir forever; he is a friend of the family."

He leaned toward her, laying his free palm flat against the tree at her back. "No, Miss McKenzie, you misunderstand me. Who do you know better? Was there a serious relationship between you two?"

"It's none of your business, is it, sir?"

"Perhaps."

"How can it be?"

"Well, I feel that I've come to know you rather well. And having learned how well versed you are in the art of seduction through intimate experience, I feel obliged to ask. Does he know your lips the way that I do? Or the feel of your bare breast in his hands—"

She was quick. She very nearly caught his cheek with a serious slap—one which might have left it reddened for hours to come.

But, she realized, he had goaded her on purpose, he had expected the slap—and so he had caught her hand in the nick of time.

She lifted her chin, her eyes flashing. "You tell me, sir—how does the feel of my bare breast compare to that of your wife?"

She might as well have managed to strike him, the sudden pain that seared him was so very sharp.

Abby was dead. For what felt like many years now.

Yet her question seemed to rob him of breath, to tear at his heart, his soul.

*She didn't realize that his wife was dead.*

But he had no desire to inform her. He stared at her blankly, fighting the reminder of the pain and impotent rage that had filled him at her death. He had learned to live with it. He'd been with other women since her death. He didn't understand what affected him so, until he thought, *she's like Abby in this, too much like Abby.*

He hadn't seen it at first, because they were so different. Abby was pale in her beauty, golden, with eyes bluer than the morning sky. But she could be so stubborn as well. Set on her own course, refusing to see the danger . . .

He could still hear her, crying out that she could reach the injured men. He could hear himself shouting to her, "Abby, no!"

She had turned to smile, but had kept hurrying forward.

"I can reach them."

But he couldn't reach her.

"Abby, no!"

He had run after her. The day remained loud with the sound of fire. So loud that he didn't hear the individual shot. Her eyes were still on his.

Abby, Abby . . .

Huge, blue eyes, so very wide on his . . .

But she was falling, and when he caught her, confused, unable to believe what had happened, he lowered her to the ground. Pulled his hand away.

And it was red, so very red; God yes, a sea of blood seemed to drip from his hand, blood from the hole that had pierced·through her back, and straight into her heart . . .

His fingers tightened. He didn't realize that he had unintentionally pulled Tia's hair until she cried out.

He eased his hold. Stared at her hard. Yes, in her way, she reminded him of Abby. And then again, she did not. She attracted and intrigued him. She didn't know the power of her own passion. She made him feel a hunger stronger than what he'd felt with even the delicate wife he had loved so much. She infuriated, compelled, repelled him. She was the daughter of a friend; not a woman to be any man's plaything, and yet, she didn't know what she did. Best get the hell away. He had no power over her, no power to stop the tempest that surged around her. He gave himself a mental shake. Let go. Stepped back.

"Everything about Abby brings perfection to mind, Miss McKenzie, her breasts included. Turn around. Get on your horse. Ride back to the property where those who love you can protect you."

"You can't tell me what to do. Go tend to your own perfect Abby!"

She spun around and walked away—just in time, perhaps. He was knotted with the anguish and fury she reawakened within him.

*Let her go, let her walk away. You couldn't change fate for a woman who loved you, who listened to you. Here you are the enemy, loathed and despised . . .*

He didn't make a move to stop her. Staring into the water, he swore that he would ride away, and leave her to her own destiny.

When he awoke on Christmas day, Brent thought that he would turn and find her gone, or discover that the night had been a dream. But it was not. She lay beside him, curled into the covers, appearing as innocent and untouched as she had come to him, and yet forever changed.

He slid carefully from the bed, washed and dressed. Without awakening her, he left the house and walked the distance to the hospital. His aides greeted him with coffee. His patients, even those dying, seemed to awaken with a certain cheer for Christmas. Nurses and orderlies gave him home-cooked treasures, often small but given with love. He attended to his men, and the time passed far more quickly than he had known.

At last, he could return to the house, and again, he feared that she would be gone.

But there were delicious aromas arising from his house. When he entered, he found her in the kitchen. She offered him a beautiful smile. "No turkeys, I'm afraid. Nor could I get my hands on a ham. We've a rather sickly chicken, but there are two of us, so I think he will do."

He followed her with his eyes, and then came to her, taking her into his arms when she turned toward the stove with knit wool potholders in her hands. "The chicken will be the best I have ever tasted, though I admit to my greatest hunger wandering in other directions."

She flushed, telling him, "It will burn . . ."

"Rescue the chicken."

She did. She had sweet potatoes, turnips, and canned tomatoes as well. Canned peaches rounded out their feast. Conversation was polite; she asked about his current patients, and he told her what he could. They didn't talk about the war, or the ravaged South, or the fact that they might well be losing, or that this time, Lee might fail and Grant might take Richmond.

When they were done eating, he helped her to pick up the dishes, but then, in the kitchen, he could wait no longer. He pulled her into his arms, kissed her. She fumbled with the buttons on his jacket. He nearly tied her into her apron for all time. And still, breathless, laughing, they shed their clothing on the way to the bedroom. They made love, and made love again, and sated for the time, Brent stoked the fire, and she had risen with him, so he wrapped her in the blanket and sat with her in the chair before the flames, watching them burn.

"Mary . . . why did you really come here?"

"I told you—because I wanted to be with you."

"But I thought you wanted to be alone."

"I needed to be alone for a while. Because of my father. But I also needed to be with you. Because I can't just be somewhere and pretend the war doesn't exist. And because I can't just be somewhere . . . and forget that you exist."

"You're sure?"

"Of course, I'm sure."

"You have to marry me," he said gravely.

She touched his face. "No, Brent. You don't have to marry me because I came here, because I wanted to be with you. I knew what I was doing. You don't owe me anything. I was afraid that raised as a gentleman, you would think you owed me for my innocence, but you will not marry me for that reason!"

He smiled. "What about the reason that I want to be with you?"

"Brent, there is a war, you were alone—"

"Alone all my life until I met you."

"That is so kind."

"It is also true. Marry me . . . because I love you," he said firmly.

"Oh, Brent . . ."

"Well?"

"Well . . ."

"Say it!"

She smiled. "Yes, I love you!"

"It wouldn't be at all proper for a respected surgeon to live in sin!" he told her.

"Not at all!"

"And I simply won't let you seduce me anymore if you don't intend to do the right thing!" he teased.

She stared at him, and started to laugh.

And she kissed him, and they made love again, and it was the best Christmas he might have ever imagined.

# Chapter 10

Tia returned to the house, riding hard. When she saw Billy, she realized that she had really frightened him.

She dismounted from Blaze, and set her hand on Billy's upper arm. "I'm sorry. Honestly, Billy, I wouldn't want you upset."

He nodded. "Please, Miss Tia, become aware of what is going on around you."

"Billy, I've been gone from home most of the war."

"But the war changes every day."

"I'll be careful, Billy, I promise."

"Your father came here, looking for you."

"Thank you, Billy, I'll find him."

"I told him you were with Colonel Douglas."

Billy said the words as if her being with Taylor had made everything all right. She tried to swallow down her feeling of hostility. She couldn't. It galled her to remember the morning by the river, when she had set out to seduce him so that her green Rebel boys could take him down. She grew infuriated with herself when she thought of the things that had happened between them, the way that she had felt being with him, how quickly she had fallen to the force of his touch, how she had felt his kiss, his hands . . .

And he was married.

She forced a smile for Billy and hurried back toward the house, clenching and unclenching her fists. She reached the house, ran up the porch steps and into the front hallway.

Her father's office was to the right. She walked to it,

tapped on the door. There was no response. She opened the door and stepped in. Her father wasn't about.

With a sigh she went to the large plush leather chair his mother had ordered made for his last birthday. The leather was soft; the chair was deep and encompassing. She sat in it and leaned back, wondering why it should seem her soul was in such a tempest. She opened her eyes. A cut glass decanter of sherry sat on the occasional table across the room. She leapt up, and helped herself to a large glass of sherry.

Her father chose that minute to enter the room.

She was, as her mother had told her, her father's daughter. She knew that her dark eyes were his, that she had inherited his rich ebony hair. But he was very tall, and though gaining more silver in his hair with every year, the expanse of his shoulders remained broad while his torso was as lean and hard as ever. He had been a wonderful parent, stern, a teacher. But she had always felt that she could run to him, and he could solve all problems. In many ways, she had certainly been a spoiled and privileged child. But he had expected manners, intelligence, ethics, and compassion from his children. They had all been taught courtesy, to give way to the elderly and injured, no matter their color or ethnic derivation. His employees worked hard for him, and they were rewarded for their labors. He was, however, a typical father in many ways. His sons had certainly enjoyed a few days of carousing. His daughter he had always protected and pampered—and he expected her to behave with modesty, even if he had encouraged her education and even her free speech in almost every conversation.

He arched a very dark brow at her, eyeing the sherry she'd poured.

"A bit early for you, isn't it?" he said, moving on into the room, his hands folded at his back. He went to the window. His office looked down the river at the far slope of the land. His back remained to her.

"I'm sorry, Father!" she cried.

She wanted to go to him. His back seemed stern and aloof.

He turned around. She saw his eyes and knew that he loved her—but that he was baffled. She set the sherry glass down and ran to him, feeling his arms around her. He kissed the top of her head. "Whatever demon got into you today?" he asked her. He tilted her chin so that he could meet her eyes. "I was always grateful that Julian was a doctor, that he joined the militia as such. And though it tore at every paternal muscle in my body, I knew that you needed to go with him. But I have never lost sight of the fact that we were becoming a strong nation because we were so many states together, and though we went to war over states rights, the argument had always been over slavery—an institution that is obviously morally wrong, and should be legally wrong. And I can't believe that you don't agree with me."

"I do agree with you!" she said. "I just don't agree with . . ."

"With what?" he asked.

At the moment, she couldn't remember.

"Father, it's our state I support. My God! Dozens of men were against secession, but when their states seceded—"

"Yes, yes, I know, even the great Robert E. Lee was against secession!"

"Well, yes, I wasn't going to mention his name, but since you did . . ."

"Men from both sides are guests in this house," he told her. "We were to show no offense to either. Ian has managed to be very circumspect."

"Ian is treading on dangerous territory!"

"Not in my house," her father said firmly. "Then there is the matter of danger to you."

"I'm in no danger here."

"I've held on to this plantation, Tia, because I've held on with an iron fist. Everyone knows that my employees include Seminoles who are familiar with war—they fought the government long enough to become excellent soldiers. My men also include immigrants I supported

from their first step on this soil, ex-gunfighters, High-
landers, fighting Irish, and more. But my scope extends
only so far. The war has grown bitter. Bad things happen, Tia. Rapes, burnings, murders. Bodies are never
found; criminals don't find justice, but blame the war for
every deprivation. God knows, a disgruntled commander
could come after this house one day—he would simply
need a small army to take it. But outside the boundaries
of the house . . . Tia, you *are* in danger."

"Father—you know that I intend to return to Julian's
field hospital."

"Yes, with Julian or his very loyal men accompanying
you at all times."

She didn't protest that statement. Let her father think
that she was always under heavy guard.

"I won't ride into the woods again," she promised.

"Go and get your sherry," her father told her. "I'll
take a brandy, I think."

"Yes, sir."

She walked to the table to pour him a drink.

"Taylor came after you?" her father asked.

"Yes," she said, turning back to Jarrett as she poured
the liquor.

"You apologized to him, I hope."

"Apologized?" She almost spilled the brandy.

"You baited him with that song, Tia."

"Oh . . . I, yes, of course, I apologized."

She suddenly felt as if they were not alone. She turned
to the doorway. Ian and Taylor were just entering the
office. Had they heard her words? She damned herself
for flushing so easily. She tried not to betray her feelings.

"Ian . . . Colonel Douglas. May I pour you a drink?"

"What are you having, Father?" Ian asked, doffing his
plumed hat on his father's desk and taking a seat in the
leather chair. "This is a magnificently comfortable piece
of furniture!" he applauded.

"Yes, it is," Jarrett agreed. "I'm having brandy. Your
sister has acquired a taste for sherry."

"We seldom drink in the surgery, and nothing so refined as this," she told her father.

"I'll have a brandy with you, Father."

"Taylor, what can my daughter get for you?" Jarrett asked.

"I'll join you gentlemen for a brandy, sir. Then I'll be on my way," Taylor said.

Tia poured the brandies, keeping her eyes downcast as she delivered the drinks to her father, brother, and Taylor. Her fingers brushed his as he took the glass. Even that brief contact seemed to cause a rush of blood to her veins. She wanted to throw something at him—or quite simply, tie him up and beat him to a pulp.

"Which way are you going, Taylor? How are you headed out?"

He was silent for a minute, taking the wingback chair opposite Jarrett, too near the occasional table where Tia stood again.

Then she realized that he was looking at her. "I'd rather not say, sir."

"My daughter is not a combatant, Taylor," Jarrett said.

Taylor's eyes were riveted on her father's. "No, sir. But she is friends with many."

"Well, there's an exit line if I've ever heard one!" Tia said with false cheer. "You Yankees just discuss away. I'll remove myself."

"Tia . . ." Jarrett said, frowning.

"It's quite all right, Father!" She returned to him, kissed his cheek, and fled, closing the office door behind her.

She wondered where her mother, sister-in-law, and the children had gotten to. The house itself seemed quiet. Pushing away from the office door, she exited the house by the river side again, thinking they might have gone out on the lawn. She didn't see the children.

She walked down to the docks. Rutger, in charge of the docks and much more in her father's life, waved a hand to her from the bow of one of her father's ships. She waved in turn, and then watched as the men worked along the dock, loading the ship with beef, the Florida beef they raised, that fed so much of the Confederacy.

She sat on the dock, watching for a while. It seemed that life went on here as it always had. Men worked the fields. Horses ran free in the paddocks. Crops grew. It was a good life, a sweet life, and it might have been the same as ever except that she could see armed men at the storehouse windows.

And her father, brother, and Taylor Douglas were discussing Yankee plans in her father's den. Or were they still? She had left sometime ago. Christmas day was fading to dusk.

She rose suddenly, thinking that her mother or Alaina might be around the side of the property. As she walked across the expanse of the lawn, she suddenly found herself drawn to the fence that enclosed the family cemetery. She reached the gate. Strange, it was open. She slipped into the little private plot and thought that, in the dying light, the graves were somehow beautiful.

Before the war, her mother had come here once a week to decorate the graves with flowers. She came more often now, telling Tia that she was grateful every day that none of their family had died in the war, and that the graves were now growing old.

Her father's first wife lay within the cemetery, a grave that was very carefully tended by Tara, who always had a special sympathy for her predecessor. Lisa Marie McKenzie's gravestone was a beautiful sculpture, centermost in the graveyard. There were a number of Seminole graves in the little cemetery as well—most of them relatives of her Uncle James.

Like Taylor Douglas.

She cursed silently to herself. Even coming here, she was reminded of the wretched man.

"Tia."

She turned quickly.

Raymond Weir had followed her. "Raymond," she said.

"I'm glad to find you alone," he told her.

He looked very handsome, in his full dress gray and butternut uniform, his plumed hat in place over his long golden curls.

"Why? What is it, Raymond?"

"I believe they're discussing plans in your father's study."

Her heart skipped a beat. "Raymond, surely not. You are a guest here just the same as Taylor Douglas. If you were to go to the study—"

"No, Tia," he said. Then he looked at her and asked, "I was wondering if you had been in the study."

She inhaled sharply. "I was, and I left. You know, I am passionate myself in the Southern Cause, and I am willing to do a great deal for it, but surely, Ray, you're not suggesting that I spy on my father in his own house?"

"Tia, not only that. I am suggesting that you do something about your father while there is still time."

"Time?"

Raymond shook his head impatiently. "Tia, your father has always been a maverick. When the whites fought desperately to survive during the Seminole Wars, he stayed neutral to foster his half-brother's cause—the Seminole cause."

"Take care where you tread, Ray!" she warned softly. "I love my uncle, and my father prevented untold bloodshed during the Seminole Wars. And, I might add, my uncle's sons have served the Confederacy with sacrifice and honor."

"And I admire your cousins, as you know," he said. "But men such as your father have fostered a line of half-breeds like Douglas—a man who would better himself by joining with the enemy. God knows, most of the Indians have the sense to realize that it was men in Union uniforms who massacred them."

"And those who changed uniforms with secession? Are they different men in different uniforms?" she heard herself asking.

"They have the sense to fight for their state, for a new way of life."

If the South won the war, she didn't think that most white politicians would worry more about the Indians who had helped them.

"Douglas may be half-Seminole or half-savage, Ray, but I believe he went to West Point, and was with the military before the outbreak of war," she said evenly.

"The point is, Tia, that he knows the state. He was bred to the land. He is a dangerous man as an enemy. He knows the swamps, the hammocks, the pine country, the red hill region . . . If you were to know what was happening . . . if we were able to stop Douglas now . . . well, it might be a very good thing."

"I don't think that now would be a good time to attempt to stop Douglas!"

Tia jumped back, dismayed to see that Taylor Douglas was in the cemetery, leaning against a tall oak in the far corner. He must have been there for some time.

He must have heard every word spoken.

*Just what had she said? She'd definitely suggested that he was half-savage.*

He pushed away from the tree, coming forward.

Ray drew his cavalry sword, ready to face Taylor.

"Put your weapon away, sir," Taylor said contemptuously.

"We'll fight—"

"No, Ray!" she cried. "Please, Ray, no, not here."

She started to run toward him. She was stunned when Taylor caught hold her arm before she could reach Ray.

"No, Tia!" he snapped angrily. "This is not your fight."

"It's my father's house!"

"Draw your weapon, man!" Ray demanded.

"No please!" Tia said. Taylor had a hand on her arm. She placed a hand on his, pleadingly. His eyes, glittering gold, touched hers.

"Coward!" Ray accused.

"This is my father's house!" Tia repeated. "Taylor—"

"Be that as it may, you'll not stand between us!" Taylor said. His grip upon her was fierce.

"Let her go!" Ray bellowed. "You let her go. Others in this house may be traitors, but she is not, sir, and you will cease to be so familiar with this *Southern* lady."

"This lady you so cherish—you would suggest she engage in spying?" Taylor demanded.

"Taylor, let go—" she began.

"I will run you through, Douglas!" Ray insisted.

"Yes, well, I will keep you from running her through in your stupid, irresponsible passion!" Taylor returned, but as yet, he held Tia. He had not drawn a weapon.

She dreaded him doing so. The tension in the air was palpable. Ray was determined that blood would be shed there.

In the graveyard.

She was very afraid that if they fought, he would be the one to die!

"Both of you, please . . ." Tia tried. But she didn't need to go further.

Her father had seen them all. He was coming across the lawn to the cemetery. Ian was behind him.

"My God, stop! What is going on here?" Jarrett demanded, swinging the white picket gate open again with such a fury that it nearly snapped on its hinges.

For a moment, no one answered. The squeaking of the gate as it banged shut again was all they heard.

"I repeat, what is going on?" he demanded. "Colonel, why is your sword bared on my property?"

"Because there is war," he said, staring at Taylor Douglas. He looked at Jarrett. "There is a war, sir, and this property is in the state of Florida, and we are at war with the Union! Colonel Douglas should not have been hiding in the cemetery, intent upon spying on your daughter and me—"

"I came to visit a great-great-uncle," Taylor interrupted dryly. "Tia happened upon the cemetery after me, sir—you made the assumption that she was alone."

"You did not make your presence known, Colonel!" Weir snapped. He spun on Jarrett. "This man is a threat to your daughter, sir! See how he holds her? You must order him from your property!"

Jarrett looked at Taylor, a brow arched. Taylor lifted his hands, releasing Tia.

"Colonel Weir!" Jarrett said impatiently, turning from

Taylor to Ray. "I agreed to use my home for your negotiations. I was assured you would both be proper gentlemen—"

Ray was incensed. He interrupted, barking out a command like a drill sergeant. "Order him from your home!"

"I will not!" Jarrett snapped back indignantly.

"Because you are a Yankee, sir!"

"Take care, Raymond!" Ian said, speaking for the first time. He had meant to defer to their father here, Tia knew.

"As your son is a Yankee."

"Colonel Weir, Taylor Douglas is a guest, as you are yourself."

"You refuse to take appropriate measures here?" Weir demanded.

Tia had seldom seen her father so angry. "I repeat, you are a guest in my house, as is Colonel Douglas, and I made a promise to your government, Raymond, that I would host these negotiations and keep the peace. If you wish to do battle, I implore you, return to your battlefield."

"Sir, there is something you continually forget—this is a Southern state. A Confederate state. You are against all that your own land stands for, you—"

"There is no one more dedicated to this state than I am, Colonel Weir. I built what I have out of dreams. I know this land as you never will. I know the people, who grow weary of the conflict, who desire again to build in our paradise, rather than destroy. Don't tell me about my state, sir; I know it as well as any man."

"Then surely you realize you could find yourself under fire—"

"Sir!" Jarrett countered. "Look around you. Look carefully, and well. Down to the river, at points by the pines. My home is defended."

Weir knew the truth of that statement. He sheathed his sword slowly, then stood stiffly, staring long and hard at Jarrett. "Sir, you will deeply regret this day. I will take my leave, and you will have no further threat of trouble here from me this Christmas. Colonel Taylor! I pray for the honor of killing you in battle. Look for me. I always ride at the front of my troops!" He started to walk away, then turned back. Sweeping his hat from his head, he bowed to Tia.

Then he continued on toward the stables.

"I, too, shall take my leave, Jarrett," Taylor said, causing them all to cease watching the departing Weir and turn to face him.

"There is no need," Jarrett protested.

"Oh, but there is, sir!" Taylor told him. "I'd not have it said that I lingered when you argued with a Southern colonel, and that you fraternized with the enemy."

"It is still Christmas day," Jarrett said. "Raymond will say what he will, and there is no way to silence him. But there is no need for you to leave."

"Thank you. However, it is time I moved on."

"Then we'll not hold you," Jarrett said.

Tall, dark, an imposing figure in his navy frockcoat, Taylor Douglas also departed the cemetery, leaving Tia alone with her father and brother.

Her brother, she knew, was puzzled.

Her father was staring at her.

"And what, daughter, caused this near disaster?"

She opened her mouth to explain. Did she tell him that Ray Weir had been suggesting that she spy? Or that she had been surprised by the presence of Taylor Douglas in the cemetery? Did she try to tell him what had happened?

She shook her head, suddenly angry. "Men!" she exclaimed. "Men! They are always harping on women, Father. We're to be careful, we're to be ladies, we're to guard life! Well, men are all fools. They swagger with their swords. They fight like little toddlers in the dirt. Don't look at me so, Father. I did not cause this, I swear it!"

He walked over to her. She bit into her lip, forcing herself to meet his angry dark eyes. "You'll stay out of this war!" he told her harshly. He swung around then, heading back to the house with long strides.

She looked at her brother. "Ian, honestly—"

"You heard him!" her brother interrupted sternly. Blue eyes seemed to bite into her as if she were a child.

"Ian! I didn't do this! Father has a right to his beliefs, and Raymond has been a complete fool, but the state is Confederate! Weir and Douglas have been like a pair of pit bulls since they met. They are, I repeat, like little boys, far too ready to go to war!"

"Raymond is living with some ridiculous ideal of what the South should be," Ian told her, "but Taylor Douglas has seen enough death to last a lifetime. You are baiting a weary man."

He, too, turned and started for the house.

She ran after him. "Ian, wait."

He swung around on her. "Tia! Life is no longer a barbecue or a ball. Don't you understand that?"

"Of course I understand that! How can you say that to me, Ian? You know that I've been with Julian throughout all of this. I've seen the fevers, the saber wounds, the shrapnel, the stumps, the shattered limbs . . . and I've seen my share of death, too!"

He touched her cheek, shaking his head, and she knew that although he understood that she had been as involved as anyone else, he was, after all, the far superior older brother—and a male of the species.

"Then be careful what men you tease, little sister. I would die in your defense, but I would hope not to do so because you played some childish game."

"Ian, I . . . I'm not playing any *games*. I'm grown up, Ian."

"That's what's so scary."

He kissed her forehead, and started for the house again.

She watched him go. Then, feeling a sudden chill settle over her, she left the graveyard, closing the gate behind her. She strode to the house, torn and in a tempest, sincerely hoping that both their Northern and Southern guests were gone.

The breezeway was empty. She went to her father's

study. Alaina was there. Sean was on her lap as she read a book.

"Our guests are gone?" Alaina queried.

"I hope so. I hope that Ray goes and sits in a swamp and that Colonel Douglas—that Colonel Douglas returns to his wife and finds out that she's turned into a real shrew who thinks he's a savage. When he walks into their house in the middle of the night and surprises her, I hope she scalps him for safety's sake alone!"

She felt Alaina staring at her, and she looked at her sister-in-law, puzzled.

"Tia, Abby Douglas is dead."

"What?"

"Taylor's wife is dead. She was shot down by accident at the beginning of the war."

Tia gasped. A strange knot was forming in her stomach.

"Shot?"

Alaina nodded. "It was a terrible situation. Apparently, people in Washington thought that the first major battle was going to be pure entertainment, quickly fought and quickly won. Dozens of politicians and civilians dressed up and came out—and of course, it turned into a deadly conflict, and the Rebels thrashed the Yanks. Abby hadn't thought it would be a picnic, but she came in a carriage with some other cavalry wives. Taylor didn't know she was coming out. When she found Taylor's position and saw all the injured men in the woods . . . she tried to help. She was shot by stray fire. She died in his arms."

"I'm . . . so sorry."

She was more than sorry. She felt ill. Her words to Taylor had been taunting and brutal under the circumstances.

She stared at Alaina, then hurried from her father's study. Racing up the stairs, she found her mother just coming down the landing. "Have you seen Colonel Douglas?" she inquired.

"I believe he's gone to the stables. Tia, what's—"

She tore down the stairs and ran hard across the lawn

again. She slowed as she neared the stables. *Her father might be there, saying goodbye to an invited guest . . .*

Hearing her father's voice from within, she skirted the stables—she didn't want to see Taylor Douglas there. She turned and ran down the slope of the lawn toward the forest, certain he intended to take that trail across the state, where he could surely meet up with many a Yankee unit.

She stood by an old oak and waited in the growing darkness of twilight. A few moments later, she saw Taylor ride out from the stables.

As she had suspected, he came her way. His horse cantered at a brisk pace across the lawn, slowed as it neared the trees.

She stepped from her place by the tree.

"Colonel Douglas!"

He reined in, seeing her. He frowned at the sight of her. "You're at just about the limits of the property, Tia."

"I know; I'm going back."

"Good. Because I did warn you, I will not just give you away if you risk your games anymore. I'll see to it that your father is aware of your actions, and that the authorities—"

"You don't need to threaten me again! I didn't come here to argue. I just—"

She broke off.

"Yes?"

He inched Friar closer to her. Despite his Union frockcoat and plumed cavalry hat, he suddenly seemed . . .

Threatening. The strength of his Seminole blood seemed evident in his features, in the way he watched her. He could move too quickly. Too quietly. Like a savage. Or *half*-savage, as she had called him. And as he had certainly heard. She could see only the stark planes of his face, the dark length of his hair, and the powerful breadth of his shoulders.

She was afraid, she realized. And yet, she was not

afraid of any violence. Force, perhaps, yes, the force of his touch . . .

"I'm sorry."

He inclined his head, his chin tilting, a dark brow lifting, his curious eyes glittering in the half-light. "You're sorry? About . . . ah, calling me savage. A slur on your own relations?" he queried dryly. "I'd no intention of mentioning the matter to our mutual relations, who might have taken offense."

"No! I'm not sorry about calling you savage, and it has nothing to do with my relations! You can be savage and very rude and—"

"Then?" he queried softly.

"I'm really sorry, terribly, terribly sorry about your wife. I didn't know. I thought that, well I thought that . . ."

"Yes, I know what you thought."

"You let me think that . . ."

"Yes, I suppose I did." He was silent for a moment, studying her. "And, I'm sorry for what I let you think. Tell me, then, is it less horrible to be seduced by a widowed enemy than a married one?"

"Oh, what arrogance. I was never seduced by you!"

*"Hm,"* he murmured. "You would have been."

"I beg your pardon!" she said regally, bringing another wry smile to his lips.

"You do know me better than you know Weir, Tia. And you may not believe this, but you want to know me better than you know him."

"You are sadly, sadly arrogant, sir! As are most of your kind!"

"My kind being savage Indians—or Yankees?"

"Unionists! Enemies of a people who seek only their freedom!"

He shook his head. "You don't really believe that."

"I do!"

"Tia, I don't believe that I'm the enemy you want me to be. In fact, I think that I could have had you in the woods. Before you even knew my name."

"Never!" she cried indignantly. "What a wretched, conceited—indecent!—thing to say. Never—"

"What a violent protest!" he interrupted, laughing.

"Look," Tia snapped, trying quite hard to control her temper—and the strange tremors that were suddenly rippling through her limbs. "I came here to say I was sorry, truly sorry about anything rude or cruel I said about your wife—she was very, very beautiful, and apparently kind and compassionate as well." She hesitated. "You must have loved her very much."

"I did," he said simply. His laughter had faded.

The breeze rustled around them. She didn't know what to say then.

She felt him looking down at her, silent for a while. Then, he dismounted, and she backed away—sorry she had come.

But she couldn't back away fast enough. He touched her cheek, lifting her chin, studying her in the red-gold darkness of the dying day. She held very still, oddly paralyzed by this touch.

She couldn't pull away. She felt the gold fire of his eyes. Looking for something within her own.

Finding it, perhaps.

"Thank you," he said after a moment. She felt the bark of the tree at her back. And the heat and form of his powerful stance before her. She didn't think that she had ever been so aware of another human being. His fingertips ran over her cheek. "Take care of yourself, Tia," he said softly.

Then he was gone.

He leapt up on Friar and looked down at her again. "Remember, if I catch you in the woods again, Godiva, you will truly regret the day. I promise you. You will pay for it dearly."

He nudged Friar, and in seconds, he had disappeared into the twilight.

# Chapter 11

Julian arrived at Cimarron toward the end of January, with his wife and newborn son—a very *McKenzie*-looking little fellow with bright blue eyes and a head full of thick dark hair. Rhiannon and the baby, Conar, would spend at least the next several months there, out of the range of danger and fire.

The prisoner exchange took place the day Julian arrived, with different officers, North and South, in charge. Tia was glad that it occurred—the men were a sad-looking group, both Yanks and Rebs. Several were wire thin, suffering from dysentery, and probably too weak to have survived a number of the prison camps. She knew that Andersonville, where most of the Union soldiers would have been taken, had a reputation for being a death camp. Watching the official exchange take place, she slipped an arm through her father's, very proud of him. He played a much bigger role in the war than she had ever realized.

Ian had departed soon after Christmas. Alaina and the children had remained at the house as well for the time being. Tia was glad that her sister-in-laws and nephews and niece were at the house; she knew that made it easier for her parents when the day came for her to ride away with Julian.

Though it was always painful to part from the rest of her family, Tia was glad that Julian needed her. She knew, however, that the battle they were heading for this time would be different from the skirmishes and fights they had faced before—this was a direct assault with the intent to split the state.

It was especially difficult to leave her parents, just as

it had been difficult for her to say goodbye to Ian. She was always afraid that she would be seeing him for the last time. She was glad that he sailed away—she didn't want to think of him fighting in Florida. Too many people grew bitter about the war. It seemed especially dangerous to be a military man many considered to be a traitor.

She hoped that Ian had been ordered to the North. Very far away.

She felt an uneasy certainty, though, that Taylor Douglas was heavily involved in the assault. He had been ordered back to Florida when the Yankee powers had determined that the state must be given far more aggressive attention. As a cavalry officer, he had asked *not* to fight in his native state, and it seemed that his superiors had heeded his request for years yet ignored it now. Ian had often been sent home because of his knowledge of the terrain; she was sure they expected the same expertise from Taylor Douglas. He could move quickly about the state; he probably knew every small Indian trail and cracker pass in the entire peninsula. He could ride circles around troops unsure of the often marshy and swampy landscape, assess the number of the enemy, and give information on positions and strengths as few other men would be able to do.

The closer she and Julian drew to the gathering of troops, the more she began to realize that a good-sized battle would indeed be staged. General Joe Finegan was in charge of the Confederate forces. When the Federal forces arrived in the state, he had only about twelve hundred fighting men, scattered throughout East Florida. He quickly sent out a call for reinforcements, however, and men began moving north from middle Florida and Georgia. Since the battle was taking place near the Georgia border, many of the troops were Georgian. By February thirteenth Finegan had selected a position near Olustee Station, a place that offered the best nature protection in a land that was flat and riddled with pine forests.

On the fifteenth, Julian and Tia had reached the chosen position, and began setting up their field hospital.

By the day of the battle, the Yankees had already done serious damage. They had taken Baldwin, where the railroad met from Fernandina to Cedar Keys, and from Jacksonville to Tallahassee. They had also seized Confederate supplies valued around half a million dollars.

But the Rebel troops had dug in, ready to fight. Their defensive works formed a line from Ocean Pond on the left to a small pond just south of the railroad station.

February twentieth dawned as a beautiful day. Clear, crisp, slightly cool, with rays of sunlight streaming through the pines. The troops raised a cloud of dust, and they became motes in the sunlit air. The battle commenced with the Union sending out a skirmishing party.

General Finegan had ordered forth his own men, convinced that the Union general, Truman Seymour, would be too careful to attack so well defended a Confederate position. As it happened, they came to meet one another on a fairly even playing field. The Federal forces had one cavalry and three infantry brigades, and sixteen big guns. The Confederate had one cavalry and two infantry brigades, and three batteries. The Federals numbered about five thousand five hundred; the Rebs about five thousand two hundred.

Right before twelve, the first cavalry skirmishers met.

After twelve, General Finegan made his decision to send his men out to meet the Yanks on the open field, determining that they couldn't be coaxed to his line.

Soon after, the surgeons were busy.

At her brother's side, Tia quickly felt as if she had been bathed in blood. Word coming in with the orderlies kept them informed about the battle.

The Rebel line had been formed with cavalry on each flank, infantry in the center. Information quickly came that General Seymour had wanted to put his artillery in the center of his line, with infantry on each side.

The deployment of his troops was proving to be his downfall.

A soldier, his left leg riddled with shrapnel, came into the surgery with a smile upon his face despite his pain. "Oh, ma'am, you should see it out there!" he told Tia.

"I'm seeing enough in here, I'm afraid," she told him, busily cutting his trouser leg so that they could see the damage to the limb. A cannon exploded in the pines, far too near. She braced herself, but didn't duck.

"No, ma'am, it's just that . . . well, you know, we're fighting for a victory here! Why, those Yanks are so confused . . . they're hitting their own troops with their fire."

"We're winning the battle?" Tia asked. She flushed, dismayed to realize that she found the thought of a Confederate victory here surprising.

The soldier nodded. "The Georgians and us, ma'am. There's so much bad and sad news coming from Virginia and Tennessee way . . . we're running out of goods and men. But here we are, winning. They aren't going to take our capital ma'am. They will not take Tallahassee!"

"I hope not, soldier!" His pant's leg split, she could see the shrapnel in the leg. One piece was very large, lodged, she feared, against an artery. "This man next!" she called to an orderly, wiping her hands on her apron. She looked beneath the canvas tenting, where Julian was conducting surgery.

They were just removing a young man from the operating table. Her brother was known for his ability to save limbs.

This time, he had not been able to do so. Nor had he been able to many times throughout the day. Sometimes, the screams of those coming under the knife had been deafening. There were several doctors here today. They all worked without pause. There were more women working as well. Officers' wives, some of the privates' wives. There was one woman who Tia had been certain was among the camp followers, but she moved with precision and no thought of hesitation in helping the wounded. Tia had met her eyes once. "I'm good at what I'm doing. I belong here," she had told Tia somewhat defiantly.

"You're very good, and apparently you do belong here," Tia replied.

The woman smiled. She might not have intended to do so, but she had made a friend.

The look on her brother's face was hardened, sad, and grim. He watched his last patient leave the table. With the bottom half of his left leg missing, the young man was singing as the orderlies carried him from the tent to the mule-drawn ambulance conveyance which would bring him south to Confederate-held land and better facilities.

"We've enough morphine?" Tia asked her brother. He had spent part of the last year with the Army of Northern Virginia, and he had grown accustomed to the horrible pace of a real battlefield surgery. She realized she was just beginning to see what he had lived through for months. He had tried once to describe the battle at Gettysburg to her, but words had failed him.

"God knows," he said, waiting for his next patient. There were other surgeons at work. While the soldier with the shrapnel in his leg was set down for the scalpel, another doctor called for help quickly. Tia raced to his side. A lieutenant with a scruffy beard that gave away his youth was spurting blood from a severed artery. She caught the vessel at the doctor's command, using all her strength to exert the needed pressure while the doctor fixed a forceps at the proper point.

"Tia, here."

She hurried back to Julian. Again, her small fingers were needed. "I'm trying to save his limb. I may not be able to. Catch the blood vessel. Hold tight, and be prepared to hold for at least a half a minute." Her brother's eyes touched hers, making sure she understood. She nodded. Once again, she deftly reached through a sudden rain of blood to capture the necessary vessel. The blood was slippery; she nearly lost her hold.

This man was singing as well.

Singing "Dixie."

She didn't know why the sound of the song made her stomach plummet.

"Ease off now . . ." Julian said. "You've got it, fine. Can you stitch up the opening here, Tia?"

"Yes, I've got it."

Their next patient was engulfed in mud; a cannon ball had exploded directly in front of him. Tia busily began cutting off clothes while orderlies soaked cotton cloths in cold water and soothing plant extracts—he was badly burned as well. It was hard to tell what was dirt and what was charred flesh. She talked while she worked on him, cutting cloth while Julian supervised the two orderlies who delivered morphine through a small canvas bag set over the man's mouth and nose. "It's all right, soldier, take it easy, take it easy!" He twitched in his pain, then slowly went still. "Hold on, young man, please hold on . . ." she whispered.

"Miss Tia!"

She looked closer through the dirt.

It was Gilly.

"Gilly, good God . . ."

"I'm dying, Miss Tia."

"No, you're not. I won't allow you to die, do you understand?"

He closed his eyes, tried to smile. "My foot . . ."

She winced, looking at his foot. It had been halfway blown off. She had seen a lot that day, but she nearly vomited at the sight of the bloody stump.

"Julian will take your foot. You'll walk with a crutch. You'll live, do you hear me?"

He stopped twitching. For a moment she froze, biting her lower lip. Had he died?

More cannon fire exploded. She winced. Liam, one of her brother's men, an amazingly capable amputee, came to her side, setting a hand on her shoulder. "He's alive; he's just passed out."

"His foot—"

"Your brother is ready for him."

More cutting. Julian hated being a butcher.

The day was no longer beautiful. It was filled with a miasma of flying dirt, black powder, the screams of dying horses.

The screams of dying men.

A rider came to the hospital, crying out with a bone-chilling Rebel yell.

"We're taking the day, gentlemen! Confederate artillery has riddled the center of the Yankee line! The Rebs are on the move, pushing back the Yanks."

Julian's eyes met his sister's above Gilly's body. She didn't know if either of them felt the general jubilation that quickly spread throughout the surgery. If they were winning, why were they patching up man after man? Losing so many . . .

Finishing with Gilly, Julian told Tia that he thought the boy would make it. "You know as well as I do, though, that it's infection that kills the boys more often than the wounds."

"But you lose fewer men to infection than other surgeons."

"Usually," he told her ruefully. "I always use a clean sponge on each wound. Today . . . we're running out."

That was not all they were running out of. Toward the late afternoon, a man brought in with a broken arm told him that they'd run out of ammunition. His arm had been broken by the strike of a Yankee bayonet—he and the enemy had tried to beat one another to death. The arrival of a friend who had crushed the Yank's skull had saved his own life.

She listened, feeling very sick.

Orderlies were drawn from the hospital to help as officers, and anyone available rode back and forth at utmost speed with supplies from a railcar held far to the rear of the line. Cartridges were carried back in hats, pockets, haversacks, and even the skirts of some of the other women assisting.

New ammunition, and the last of the Southern troops held back at the line, arrived at the front nearly simultaneously.

There was a mighty advance against the Federal line.

Soon after, with night almost upon them, Federal wounded began to be brought in. The Yanks had been forced to leave them behind during their retreat.

"We won! We won!"

Across the field, the shout went up. Among the standing, there was a feeling of victory so great that it seemed like a cry upon the very wind. "We won, Florida won, the Yanks will not be taking Tallahassee, they'll not be taking our state!"

Bugles could be heard.

Shots that signaled victory.

"The battle has been won," Julian said quietly. "Our night has just begun."

The battle could definitely be called a victory, but the fight wasn't over. The Rebs were pressing the Union forces back, back. God knew how far they would follow; what territory they would gain.

The night was horrible. With the fighting over; it was time to search the battlefield. While Julian remained in the surgery, Tia rode out with his orderlies, trying to find the living among the dead.

"Miss Tia?"

Liam, who had learned to ride with his one leg, was with her, ready to summon orderlies with stretchers and litters when they found men who could be saved.

A remnant of the sun remained, as red as the blood that covered the ground.

They dismounted and studied the uniforms on the corpses.

"Mostly Yanks here," Liam said.

"Yes." She turned to him. "I'm so afraid, Liam. Of who I will find."

"Your brother Ian isn't here," he said gently. "He was ordered to Virginia after Christmas."

"You're sure? How do you know?"

"We brought in a cavalryman Julian knew. He told us."

Tia suddenly saw a cavalry officer, lying facedown. He wore a navy frockcoat, and his hair was dark as pitch, straight, long . . .

"Oh, God!" She fell to her knees at his side.

"Tia, I told you, Ian isn't here."

*Yes, but Taylor Douglas is!* she screamed inwardly.

She touched the man, carefully drawing him back toward her. He moaned. He lived. He had a bullet through his shoulder.

He wasn't Taylor.

"We've got one to bring back!" she called to Liam. He nodded, and whistled for the men with the litters and stretchers. Tia moved on.

And on.

During the night, she still thought that she heard the sounds of moans and cries from the battlefield.

She thought that she would hear them forever, for the rest of her life.

During the next six days, the Confederate forces pushed the Union soldiers back to within twelve miles of Jacksonville. The battle had been a disaster for the Union.

Yet the Confederate victory at Olustee Station did little to lighten the mood of the South.

Supplies grew ever scarcer during the spring of 1864. Throughout the South, battles were being waged, and mostly lost. The Union grip was tightening; the Northern generals were considering new ways to tame their Southern counterparts. A "scorched earth" policy became popular—where Yankee armies went, nothing was left for the surviving civilians.

In the weeks that followed the battle of Olustee, Tia could afford little concern for the rest of the Confederacy. Julian was left with the seriously injured to be tended.

During the first few days after the battle, they moved their surgery to an old house at Lake City. Local matrons came to read to the soldiers, to bring whatever food treats they could improvise, and to write letters.

A week after the battle, she and Julian were invited to dinner at the home of General Victor Roper, a septuagenarian who had served during the Mexican War, and a passionate secessionist. A number of officers still in the vicinity had been invited, militia and regular army. The local men brought their wives and daughters. To fill in for those men from other Southern regions, a number of young ladies from the nearby towns were present as well.

It was the closest thing to an old-time Southern party that Tia had attended since the war began. She had been too tired at first to want to come, but Julian had convinced her.

Raymond Weir was there.

At first, she avoided him, but she was glad—after all she had seen on the battlefield—that he was alive. He and his militia troops had been involved at Olustee. His troops had been too far south to be called in for the battle, but he was there because he had ridden quickly northward in anticipation of trouble to follow.

He was persistent, following her until she would listen to him. He apologized for the trouble at Christmas, telling her he was sorry to have ruined her Christmas.

She accepted the apology on the surface.

He did not say that he was sorry for threatening her father, or challenging Taylor Douglas. But to her, he was so earnest and sincere that she couldn't help but forgive him, he seemed so desperate that she understand.

There were musicians from the 2$^{nd}$ Corps of Engineers. Tia danced with her brother, with enlisted men and officers—and with Ray. She was touched again by his affection for her, but equally determined that this was not the right time for her own involvement. To her annoyance, she continued to wonder about Taylor Douglas, and pray that his had not been among the bodies at Olustee that she had not seen.

"Marry me, Tia," Raymond Weir said, looking at her gravely as they danced.

"Raymond, do you think that my father would let me marry you right now?" she asked innocently.

"You're over twenty-one, Tia. You don't share your father's beliefs."

"I share his love," she said softly.

"If he understood what I felt for you, he might readily agree."

"I can't marry until the war is over," she said. "I have to work."

They came to a halt by a table laden with a punch bowl. He poured them both a glass, and looked at her gravely.

"You shouldn't be involved in such work, Tia. It isn't fitting for a proper young woman."

Their hostess, Amelia Roper, a resplendent woman with a huge bosom and assumed dignity to match, stood by the table chatting with a young soldier—until she heard the comment. She tapped her glasses on Tia's arm and joined in, uninvited. "The colonel is quite right, my dear. The work you do is better managed by the order-lies—and by the injured. In Washington, they use the convalescing men to work in the hospitals. The amputees make useful nurses."

"There are never enough nurses. Especially here in Florida," Tia said. "You know that our men are con-stantly drawn from the state to serve elsewhere. Even Julian, who has dedicated himself to his fellow Floridi-ans, was ordered north last year. I believe I can be helpful."

"What are our men fighting for if not our Southern honor—and that of our Southern womanhood, Tia Mc-Kenzie?" Amelia demanded indignantly.

"They are fighting—for us all," Tia said, surprised by the attack on her effort. "And if they fight, then I feel that I must help as I may."

"If you were to marry me, Tia," Ray said, "I would see to it that you were removed from the ugliness and indecency you endure for this passion to work with the wounded."

"Ray, I have said many times: it's work I feel I must do. My father, mother, and brothers know what I do, and they are not appalled. They are proud of my com-mitment to life."

"Even your father and your oldest brother, dear?" Mrs. Roper said tartly. "I imagine they might be happier were you to cease work, and allow for more Confeder-ate dead!"

"No one wants men to die, Mrs. Roper."

"No? Well, it's quite bad enough in the state as it is. Your father and brother aren't the only traitors among us."

"Quite a number of people in the state were against secession, Mrs. Roper," Tia reminded her.

"Oh, I know! And some of our brightest military stars failed to see the error of their ways!" She shook her head, glancing at Raymond, and speaking bitterly. "My husband—a brilliant leader when he was on the field!— has studied the battle at Olustee carefully. Do you know who was one of the first cavalry officers on the field for the Yankees? *Taylor Douglas!* My God, but I remember when that man was a guest in my house. They say he moves like the devil, faster than the wind. He is a traitor to us now—a thorn in our side when he should have been a hero for the state."

Tia didn't want to appear overly interested in Taylor, but she felt as if she were dying within herself, and needed what information she could garner.

"I met Colonel Douglas just before Christmas, Mrs. Roper. He is actually kin to my uncle, my father's brother. I hadn't heard that he was at Olustee."

"Dead center of the battle, dear, leading troops out to the very first of the skirmishing and beyond. It's a wonder he wasn't killed."

*Thank God.*

She almost said the words aloud, but realized that Ray Weir was watching her closely.

"He led troops out—and wasn't injured?"

"Not by our men—or his own!" Mrs. Roper said with a sniff, then smiled. "Though I have heard the Yankees killed nearly as many of their own as they did Rebs! Young lady, don't you go getting it into your head to tend to Yankee men! You will assuredly die with no proper husband!" With another sniff, she shook her head. "This war! It is amazing. The things going on . . . have you heard of the new heroine being hailed by the soldiers? A woman dashing through the woods, leading the Yanks astray. In the buff, completely in the buff.

The little slut! Godiva! They call her—Lady Godiva. Now, there's a girl who will have no husband! There is war, and there is total indecency!"

"Isn't the greatest indecency of war seeing a young human body totally broken and bloodied and maimed? Isn't the greatest horror the destruction of human lives, of dreams, families . . . isn't death the indecent tragedy of it all?" Tia queried, amazed at the tumult suddenly inside her.

"A lack of honor is the greatest indecency! Honor is everything! What is life without honor, without society, without rules of what is proper and what is not? What do men fight for, if not their quality of life—and the honor and chastity and virtue of their womankind?" Amelia Roper demanded, and she waved her reading glasses in the air. "You remember that, young lady!"

"Perhaps we can have honor—and compassion!" Tia said.

Mrs. Roper let out another of her sniffs and turned her back on them.

Ray shrugged to Tia. "Many, many people don't approve of your activities."

For a moment, she froze. *To which activities was he referring? Did he know about Godiva?*

No, Godiva was a story to them here, nothing more. She let go of the breath she had scarcely realized she had held, and answered.

"I thank God, then, that it is only the approval of my own family that matters to me, for as I have said, they are proud of my work with my brother."

"Ah, Tia!" Ray took her hands. "I know that you care for me . . . I feel it when we touch, I see it in your eyes. I wish I could make you see that wrong is just that—wrong. Your work is wrong, and Mrs. Roper is quite accurate in her assessment—many men would refuse to marry you, considering what you have seen and done entirely indecent. And you must realize . . ." His voice tightened suddenly. "You must realize that your father is wrong. Very wrong."

She drew her hands from his. He spoke to her so

earnestly. Her feelings for him were very confused. They had been different before the war. She had liked him . . . she had been tempted. He had liked horses, riding, agriculture, good brandy, and even books. Something had changed with the war; she did care for him, but with a strange reserve. It was still hard to hurt him.

It was made a bit easier, however, by some of the things that he said to her. She was defensive against any criticism of her father.

"If you find my father a fool and me indecent, it's amazing that you would marry me."

"Ah!" he said softly. "But I love you. All men might not. And," he admitted grudgingly, "I know that there are other women working with the wounded. Few of them, though, hold your place in society."

"My father is a man who taught me to respect other men and women for what they do, and how they behave—not how much money or property they possess. Perhaps that's because he was raised by a Seminole woman, my half-breed uncle's mother," she said, the words far too pleasant to convey the reproach and anger she was feeling.

"Your uncle managed to overcome his birth—"

"My uncle is proud of his birth."

"Tia! The Seminole Wars are over, and I don't care to fight them again with you here and now; there are other matters at hand—"

"Just think! Marry me, and you'll be cousin-in-law to *redmen* yourself!"

"Tia, I will tolerate many things for you."

"Tolerate," she mused.

"I believe you have feelings for me as well. There is no need for you to die an old maid. Perhaps what you do is not quite decent, but at least you are not a whore such as that woman the men are all cheering as such a great Rebel—that—that Godiva creature Mrs. Roper was talking about. She has been everywhere, so it is said, leading dozens and dozens of Yankees to their doom."

*A gross exaggeration!* Tia thought.

She longed to slap Ray—then her anger faded. *The*

*things he said were things that he had been taught! And
there was nowhere in him where he might open his heart
and mind to new thoughts, or to understanding . . .*

"If I do not marry, I will not consider my life a dismal
waste. And I would be loathe to marry a man who did
not love me under any circumstances. I appreciate your
kindness, that you would love me enough to marry me
despite my tarnished character. But you have your beliefs, Ray, I have mine—"

"Do they really matter between a man and a woman?
Think about it! Marry me."

"I must refuse you. The war does matter. You can see
that, surely."

"Perhaps. Yet still, I must ask each time I see you!
And if ever you need me, want me . . . you only need
to come to me."

"Thank you. But . . . you must excuse me—I see my
brother waving to me."

She fled from him, hurrying to Julian—who had not
been summoning her. "What's wrong?" he asked.

"I have been hearing about my indecency."

Julian grinned. "The old biddies! What you do is good
work, Tia. You save lives. Don't let anyone ever tell
you differently."

"Thank you, Julian."

"My pleasure. Are you tiring of life here in this bed
of good and decent society?"

"Tonight, yes."

"Good. I'm ready to start back for our old grounds
outside of St. Augustine. I want to take some of the
wounded to convalesce in better circumstances. There
are too many wounded here, and not too many admirable men and women to look after them."

"I'm definitely ready!"

God, yes, she was ready.

# Chapter 12

*She could see the child, a small child, with a quick, mischievous grin, charming, delightful. A handsome little fellow, dark-haired, with a will of his own, and a way of behaving badly in so sweet a manner that he managed to get away with quite a lot. He was playing, as children were wont to do.*

*The dream was murky, as if there were a fog in the bedroom where the child played. There was an open doorway, leading out to the balcony. There were other children, but she couldn't really see them . . . there was the fog, of course, but more. The little boy was the focus of the dream, and so she could see him clearly. He had a dimple . . .*

*There was a balcony. He crawled upon the railing . . .*

*"No! No!"*

*She tossed in her sleep, trying to tell him, trying to stop him. "No, don't do it, oh, God, please, no, no . . ."*

*And then he was falling, falling, falling . . .*

"Rhiannon! Rhiannon! Wake up!" She felt gentle hands on her shoulders, and looked into the concerned, beautiful blue eyes of her mother-in-law.

She jerked up, petrified, terrified. Where was she?

Julian's house, safe in the haven of Cimarron, though Julian was far away. Despatches had already crossed the state; she knew that her husband was safe, that Tia was safe. In his personal letter to her, Julian had sounded very weary, not certain if he cared whether the South won the war anymore. The flow of injured at Olustee Station had seemed endless, almost as bad as when he had been serving with the Army of Northern Virginia, and by sheer numbers of combatants, the battles had been horror-filled from the start. But it was over, Julian was well, her sister-in-law was fine as well, and she was here, recovering as she must, away from Julian, because of their infant son, a Christmas present unlike any she might have imagined. A gift of life in the midst of so much death!

"Conar!" Rhiannon shrieked, leaping from her husband's bed. Heedless of her concerned mother-in-law, she flew to the wicker bassinet where the baby slept. Too panicked to leave him at peace, she swept him into her arms. So brusquely awakened, he started to cry.

"Rhiannon, you're shaking. Let me take him from you," Tara McKenzie said softly.

Rhiannon looked from the baby in her arms to Tara, then handed the baby over and buried her face in her hands.

"It was a dream . . ."

"About the baby?"

"Yes . . ." she said, then hesitated. She sat on the bed, and Tara sat beside her, soothing the baby and still managing to show her concern for Rhiannon.

Rhiannon let out a long breath of relief. "No, not my baby!" she whispered. And yet the pain remained in her heart.

The boy was someone's baby. Someone's beloved baby.

"No, an older baby. A toddler. Not Alaina's Sean! It didn't happen here . . . it was at a different house. A large, beautiful house, on a busy street. People are always coming and going. There's an entry to the house with that wallpaper that is made to look like marble. There's a child's room with a little rocking horse—like the one in the nursery here that was Tia's. There are dolls . . . toys . . ."

"But it definitely isn't this house," Tara said softly.

"No. I'm certain."

"It can't be where Alaina has been living in St. Augustine. She and Risa have just a small place together, without so many rooms, and there is certainly no grand stairway!"

Tara McKenzie had tended many a small child with her own three, nephews and nieces, and grandchildren. Conar's little eyes were already closed again. Rhiannon was tempted to take him, crush him to her, even let him cry again, she was just so grateful to see that her own child lived. Had her dream been of Conar at some later date? No, she would know, surely . . .

"It is someone else's child. If I could only warn her . . ."

"Rhiannon, perhaps the time will come when you can do so," Tara said. She had never doubted her new daughter-in-law's ability to see strange things through dreams. Julian had told her that Rhiannon's predictions had saved many men from sure disaster. Even generals had paid heed to her warnings.

But Tara's heart bled for her daughter-in-law at times.

There was a child, in danger. And she wanted so desperately to help . . .

Tara set the baby back in his bassinet. She took her daughter-in-law in her arms, and rocked with her, smoothing back her long dark hair. "Rhiannon, you mustn't be so upset. It's a blessing to be able to help anyone the way that you have. We'll all be very careful not to let any toddlers we know play unsupervised on a balcony. We will make a difference."

"A difference . . . my God, one day, it's the children who will have to make a difference. The children who will have to lead us from the devastation of this war we have cast upon them!"

"Yes, they will have to make a difference." She drew away and smiled. "In a way, I envy them. They will have to fight and struggle—and forge a new world."

"It will be miserable for years."

"Growth and learning are often difficult. But they are the only ways to forge a new world! Shall I get you a drink, warm some milk, perhaps."

"No, no, thank you, I'm sorry I disturbed you. I know that I'll be able to sleep now."

Tara kissed her on the forehead, and left her.

Rhiannon didn't sleep, but lay awake. In a few minutes she rose, and very gently took her precious child from his bassinet. She didn't wake him, but laid him beside her, and she watched him throughout the night.

Tia and Julian moved southward the day after Mrs. Roper's party. Julian warned her the journey would be long and slow.

It was indeed very tedious; a few of the men were in poor shape. Still, it felt good to be away from the constant reminders of the battle—a field that smelled more and more of decay. Towns where so many men were without limbs. They traveled with the medical supplies they needed, and the days were cool and pleasant, the nights chilly but not too cold.

Toward the end of March, Julian was summoned late at night by a rider sent by General Finegan. One of his most important aides had been wounded by a sharpshooter. "The bullet is lodged in his shoulder," the messenger explained to Julian. "There is no man but you to perform so delicate a surgery."

"I would very much so like to help any man," Julian told him. "Especially an officer the general values. But I have only one whole man among this sorry group!"

Tia, who was at her brother's side, cleared her throat.

"Tia, I don't like leaving you—"

"Sir, will you have some coffee?" Tia asked, addressing their visitor.

"Ma'am, with pleasure."

His name was Arnold Bixby, and he was a Georgian. He sipped his whiskey-laced coffee with real pleasure as Tia tried to sound casual and convince Julian that she would be all right at the same time. Julian hadn't quite seemed to have grasped the concept that he wasn't being *asked* to accompany Bixby, he was being ordered to do so.

"Julian, I can manage very well."

"Tia, I don't like leaving you."

"Julian, we had to split up once before in like circum-

stances, and I was just fine." It was a lie, but he had
never learned that she had met up with any difficulty
before reaching Dixie and his men before Christmas.

"We've just won a major battle! The territory is safe.
Liam is with me."

"Liam has lost a leg."

"Liam remains as fierce as a bulldog," she insisted.

"If you can reach this point by the river here," Bixby
said, drawing a map on the dirt floor of the the tent,
"you'll tie up with Dr. Lee Granger. He's keeping camp
there with more survivors from Olustee. In fact, we can
ride there on our way north and let him know that your
injured will be joining his."

Julian kept staring at his sister. "I don't like leaving
you."

"Julian, I don't *like* being left. There's little choice,
however, and I can manage. I wouldn't perform surgery
without you, but I think that I can manage to keep bandages clean and a party on the road. I've done it before," she reminded him.

"Bixby, I don't like this. If anything happens to my
sister . . ."

"Julian, I'll be fine," Tia insisted. "If we should happen upon the enemy, it might well be men I know. Many
of the officers in this war went to school with Ian or are
friends with Father. Julian, no matter what, I would be
in no danger."

And she would be fine. She would take no chances.
They had sorely beaten their enemy. The Yanks were
like dogs with their tails between their legs now—running away from, not after, the Rebels.

"I'll pack your things," she told her brother.

The next morning was beautiful. Tia awoke feeling
confident, washed at the stream, drank the coffee Gilly
had made, and saw to it that her wounded men at least
sipped some of Liam's hardtack stew before she arranged for them to start out.

Gilly and a man who was fighting an infection were
placed in the back of the wagon. The mules were docile,

and a fellow who had lost his lower leg could manage them easily enough. Tia, Liam, Hank Jones, and Larry Hacker, who had lost his lower arm, would ride.

The day started off very well. They moved very slowly, careful not to jostle Gilly any more than absolutely necessary. By noon, she was proud of the distance they had covered. They could reach Dr. Granger's camp by tomorrow morning if they kept up their pace.

Soon after she congratulated herself on her success, the wagon hit a pothole. The wheel broke; the wagon lumbered, and Gilly screamed.

Frightened, Tia looked at Liam, then hurried to the back of the wagon. Gilly's foot—or rather his ankle—had flown up and crashed down on the planks. It was bleeding profusely.

"Help me get a tourniquet together!" she called to Liam.

Accustomed to working with Julian as well, Liam quickly found her a stick. She ripped up her skirt, and together they wound the tourniquet around the injury. The bleeding stopped. She had Gilly taken down by the water and cleaned the wound. The stump had been cauterized, but the accident had left a tear in it. Gilly fought the pain bravely, but Tia could see the tears in his eyes. "We have whiskey—let's share it." She took a drink first herself; Gilly came next. Liam arched a brow at her then took a long swallow. Returning to the wagon, Tia got out her needle and the surgical thread she was lucky to still have. Sometimes, she sewed wounds with horse hair.

Gilly got enough whiskey in him to pass out, right by the water. Liam set up a camp for the others with Hank Jones. When the camp was done, Liam came back to her. "I'll stay here by the water for a while with him," she said softly. The poor fellow remained passed out. She smiled at Liam. "I think I'm wearing half his blood. I may try to wash out some of this."

"You want me to keep guard, Miss Tia?"

She smiled. "If you will."

Liam watched her for a long moment. "You're a fine leader, Miss Tia."

"No, I'm not, but thank you."

He left her. Gingerly she approached the cold water. She could smell the blood that covered her. She stripped her blouse over her head, shivering. She wore a corset today, but it didn't give her any warmth. Still . . . she slipped out of her skirt. She had to wash her clothing. Liam could bring her the extra set of clothing she carried in her bag. She could leave these to dry on the rocks. She had to bathe. The smell of the blood that covered her made her feel sick to her stomach. She felt as she had the night at Olustee, as if she'd never get the blood out. No matter how cool the night had become, she had stripped down completely and scrubbed until the scent of blood was gone.

She washed her face, then sat back, thinking she could hear something.

She did, and she froze. Looking through the trees, she saw glimpses of blue uniforms. *Yankees*.

She was low against the riverbank. Gilly slept upon it. It was possible that the Yanks on the other side of the trees might pass by without ever noticing them.

But they were close. So close.

"Captain, can we stop here; get some water?" one asked.

"All right, but we can't take long. They say there are Rebs here; we just have to find them."

"What then, Captain? Can we kill them, make it a massacre like Olustee?"

"We're not murdering men, Private Long."

"What if they're half-dead already?" the one named Long asked. "I heard it was nothing but Confederate wounded moving through here."

"Any wounded Rebs we take as prisoners," the captain said sternly.

Tia heard him moving away. Then she heard Long chuckling to a fellow soldier. "Wounded, yeah. So we can't mow them down the way they murdered us. Hell, yes, wounded. Well, they can just happen to die on their way."

There was a slight rustling behind her. She turned

quickly to see Liam coming. She brought her finger quickly to her lips.

Liam didn't see the soldiers, but sensed the danger. She indicated that he should drag Gilly back. He hunkered down by her, catching Gilly's shoulders and frowning.

"Where's Blaze?" she asked him in a hushed whisper.

"Just yonder—"

"Take Gilly. Break camp, and ride through the night. Get to Granger's camp as quickly as you can."

"And what are you going to do?" Liam demanded.

"Lead them astray with Blaze."

Liam shook his head. "No. No. Absolutely no. Your brother—"

"My brother will never know."

"Miss Tia, I'll lead them astray—"

"No!" she said quickly. These particular Yanks were out for blood. "We can't spare you—I can't help Hank lift Gilly and the others; I have to be the one to create a diversion. Besides, I can just be a good local *Unionist* out for a ride. No harm will come to me. All I have to do is mention Ian's name, and I'm perfectly safe with the Yanks."

"No—"

"Liam! You have to listen to me. That is the truth. You all are in danger from the Yankees; I am not. I'll be just fine. If there's a Federal camp near here, I may just sashay in for dinner!"

She spoke lightly, and with assurance. But he frowned, looking at her. "Where's your clothes, Tia McKenzie?"

"On the rock there. Go now, please, please! Get Gilly out of here. Get to Lee Granger's camp, and don't worry about me. I'll deal with any situation as it arises."

Gilly shifted suddenly, moaning.

"Get him out of here, quickly! They'll hear him."

Liam gave her a stern look. She frowned fiercely back. But when Gilly made a deep, moaning sound again, Liam came to life, hobbling on his one leg, but very strong despite that fact. He had barely moved Gilly before Tia saw one of the Yanks come through the trees, heading for the water.

He didn't see her at first. He dipped his head into the cool stream, then made a cup of his hands and drank deeply. She stayed perfectly still, barely daring to breathe.

He drank, and drank. He splashed his face.

Finally, he looked up.

He wasn't old himself, though not as young as most of the Rebs she helped patch up these days. He had a round face, thick beard, and ruby red mouth. He was round himself, as well.

She hadn't seen a heavy soldier in a very long time!

He stared at her; she stared at him.

He opened his mouth as if he would cry out. No sound came at first. She rose slowly. She was in her pantalettes and corset. The latter boasted the tiny pink rose centers of her breasts.

"Ah . . . hello," said the soldier.

"Hello," she returned.

He kept staring at her. She let the seconds go by, hoping she was giving Liam enough time to get moving.

"Ca-Ca-Captain!" he cried at last.

She waited. Waited, counting the seconds. She wanted the captain to see her.

In a minute, the captain appeared. He was more the soldier she expected. Tall, slim, his lean face hardened and saddened by the years of war gone by. She had a feeling he had been in it from the beginning.

He looked across the water at her.

"Are you looking for the enemy?" she called.

"Who do you call the enemy, er-ma'am?" he called back.

"I'll show you!"

She scampered up the embankment, through the trees. She looked to the place where they had been forced to stop.

No sign of the troops.

She whistled; Blaze came trotting to her. The mare wasn't saddled. Tia took a running leap and careened on top of the horse. She headed back through the trees, not wanting to lose the Yankees.

She could hear them, splashing through the trees, shouting. There were at least a half-dozen of them, or maybe more, since she could hear many different voices calling out.

"Where'd she go?"

"Who is she?"

"What's she up to?"

"Where can she lead us?"

"She's naked—"

"Half-naked—"

"Tons of hair—"

"Godiva!"

"My God, yes! Godiva—who has led hundreds of men to their doom."

"That's her, yes!"

Her, yes? Hundreds of men to their doom? Dear Lord, how on earth could truth become so horribly exaggerated?

It didn't matter how she had become such a villain. Her estimate was right—there were six or seven men after her. Seated on Blaze, she tried to count their exact number.

She didn't want to play the wretchedly "dooming" Godiva, adding more fuel to the fire of rumor, but she had to.

She rode hard down to the embankment again.

"This way, fellows!"

She turned Blaze, and started racing first downstream. The Yankees needed to retrieve their mounts. She slowed her gait, making sure they were behind her.

She left the river embankment, heading for the road. She heard them following. She turned, making sure they could see her.

A branch slapped her in the face. Hard. She decided to give more attention to the direction in which she was going.

Ten minutes, twenty. She kept ahead of them by at least fifty lengths, trying to think of a place where she might lose them. Finally, she thought of the pine hammock to the north. The area was riddled with streams and small lakes and ponds. She could plunge into the hammock, follow around the pond, through the pine trails there, cross the stream and the pines on the other side, then head straight out to the copse.

She could hear Blaze breathing as they raced. How long had she run her horse? The Yankees would have to slow when she did, she assured herself.

She reached the hammock, then veered into it. She heard the shouts far behind her when they first followed. They had even lost one another.

She smiled, circling around the pond, at last slowing her gait.

Dismounting from Blaze, she quickly led the horse through the thicket of underbrush, heading again toward the trail of pines along the stream's edge.

She could still hear the Yanks behind her. They remained mounted, without the least idea of where she had gone. They wandered in circles. They couldn't run through this terrain; they didn't seem to realize that neither could she. But she knew where she was going. Once she cleared the pines and passed through the stream, she'd be free. She'd have reached the copse, and so many ways to go it would take a bloodhound to track her. One of the trails led southward. Along that trail there were a multitude of abandoned Indian cabins where she could hide—and perhaps find clothing.

She moved quickly, running through the shallow water, swimming across where it deepened at the river, finding the slender flow of the brook again beyond the main body of the small river. She slipped into the pines, still leading Blaze, but running herself as she realized she neared the copse where she could mount up and ride again.

Yet at the fringe of the trees, she came to a dead stop, startled and dismayed.

There was a camp in front of her.

A Yankee camp.

Tents were pitched; fires burned. It was an organized

camp, with pickets down the length of the pines. A large tent far to her left appeared to be a hospital. Wounded men sat about before it. Elsewhere, soldiers cleaned their weapons, cooked over the fires, smoked pipes and eased back against the trunks of trees. A few had books. Some wrote.

Pickets walked the outer circumference of the camp as well, watching the east and west trails, assuring the men who rested that no large body of men could come crashing through the pines to destroy them.

It was an excellent position; easily defended, well placed for water, food, the best of the sunlight.

She hadn't imagined that the Yanks would know it; it was not an area that had been well mapped in the past.

Ah, but the Yanks were learning the state. And there were, of course, more and more Unionists in the state daily. Those who tired of the war. Those who had voted against secession. Those who might have organized the territory this side of the state into East Florida—with a Unionist government to run it.

She heard the men behind her.

She cursed the camp.

*It would be her death!* she thought.

The soldiers behind her remained lost in the maze of trees, rivers, and ponds.

But they wouldn't stay lost for long.

Dozens of Yanks lay before her.

She hugged a pine, trying not to panic. She searched the camp, shivering. It was growing dark. A large tent, probably an officer's quarters, held a prime position right by a little inlet of water pulsing from the stream. The pines encroached upon the very back of it. The positioning of the tent allowed for privacy within, and escape to the brook—should a man desire his own counsel under the stars.

As she stared at the tent, her heart quickened. A man exited from the canvas flap—tall, dark, imposing. She saw nothing but his back. He wore no jacket, just a bleached muslin shirt and Union-issue cavalry trousers. He had to be an officer; she was certain by the assurance with which he moved. Command was visible in his carriage, in his manner.

He paused by a young, sandy-haired, freckle-faced soldier at a cooking fire some distance from the tent. She didn't hear what he said; he spoke with a deep, low voice and his back remained to her. She did hear the sandy-haired soldier's reply since he was looking in her direction and his voice seemed to carry straight to her.

"Yessir, I understand. You're meeting with Colonel Bryer, and will be with him for some time. If the scouting party returns, I'll tell Captain Ayers that you're with Colonel Bryer, and he may find you there, or wait to speak with you here later, but you wish to see him tonight."

The officer moved on. Tia looked down the length of the pines. She could hear the soldiers coming closer. She ran along the pines, leading Blaze.

Behind the officer's tent, she gave Blaze a firm pat on the rump. "Go on now!"

The horse trotted off as bidden. Tia watched her horse, fingers clenched into her palms. Blaze wouldn't go too far—she hoped. Tia didn't want her horse to give away her position. She hoped, as well, that Blaze would stay deep within the pines, and avoid the copse that was so heavily laden with men and tents.

She didn't want her well-loved mare stolen by the enemy.

"Go on, girl, go on!" she whispered.

Tia watched her go, glad that Blaze soon discovered a nice thicket of grass concealed by the pines.

Sure that the mare had moved on far enough, she plunged quickly through the trees, and then, just as quickly, she drew back, hesitating.

Carefully she viewed the area. She could make it into the tent without being seen, she was certain. She could bide her time, perhaps find more clothing, then slip back through the pines after the soldiers had given up searching for her.

Yes, she could. Easily, if all went well.

But what if the officer who lived within the tent came back before she dared slip back into the pines?

He wouldn't! He had just informed his sergeant that he would be gone for several hours.

She sped the short distance to the tent, fell to her knees on the soft grass, and crawled beneath the canvas wall of the tent.

Within the enclosure she rose, shivering. The night was growing very cool. She was soaking wet. Her hair lay like a cold, damp cloak around her shoulders, trickling little droplets of ice down her spine. Her fear didn't help. Her teeth were chattering. She needed a blanket. Searching for one, she surveyed the strange refuge she had so desperately chosen.

The tent was large, a welcoming place. There was even a throw rug over the earthen floor. A large camp bed lay beside a camp desk. A map of the area was stretched out across the desk. An officer's frockcoat was draped over the folding chair in front of the desk. There was a standing shaving mirror, a chest that housed eating utensils, and a small table that was piled high with books. She found herself looking at the titles. There were military manuals and medical periodicals. Books on engineering and books by Audubon. They were well-read books, and she was tempted to go and look through them. Her father's library at Cimarron was extensive, and he had encouraged his children to read. Her mother loved books; she had told them often enough that books were like luxurious voyages—they could take you wherever you wanted to go from the comfort and warmth of an armchair. Books were teachers as well, opening up the world to those who cared to learn. They were friends with whom to curl up on a rainy day, company when you were lonely, cheer when you were feeling the weight of the world.

She almost walked over to pick up a book. She stopped herself firmly.

She wasn't here to read! she warned herself. She had come to hide—and find clothing. She could not wear a book!

And so, she kept looking around the tent. Another traveling chest was at the side of the first. There was a clean white cotton shirt folded atop it.

Everything in the tent was neat, and yet, the space seemed to have the indelible imprint of a personality upon it. She was intrigued by who might be staying here. The tall, dark-haired officer she had seen leaving. A Yankee, the enemy. Yet the term "enemy" was best when it was a faceless term. Her brother was the "enemy," and yet a cherished face within her life. More than ever, she despised the war.

The second chest, she told herself firmly, probably held clothing. She could use the shirt folded atop it to begin with. There must be trousers within. Too big, certainly, but she could find something with which to tie them on. She hurried to the chest, still shivering. She opened it. Trousers. Nice, warm, navy wool trousers. She lifted them out, then laid them back on the trunk and looked nervously to the flap opening of the tent. She hurried to it, carefully moved the canvas aside, and peeked out. The soldier at the fire seemed to be keeping guard. The other men were busy about the camp. No one knew she was there.

She dropped the canvas, and returned to the trunk where the dry shirt and trousers lay. Seriously cold now, and nervous that she might be interrupted, she quickly stripped off her corset and pantalettes. Her fingers were numb and she could barely untie the strings of her corset and pantalettes. At first, she freed herself from the sodden remnants of her clothing and bent over and reached for the shirt.

As she did so, she froze, a feeling of fear sweeping over her. She was somehow aware that someone had come. No sound, but the air . . . yes : . . she felt a whisper of air from the flap of the tent. Someone had come in with an uncanny silence. Without the sound of a single footfall.

Someone had come, yes. And her back was to him.

She heard the click of a gun as the trigger was set.

"Who are you, and what are you doing?"

The voice was deep, commanding an immediate reply.

She spun around, looked up. She saw the man holding the Colt six-shooter and gasped, horrified.

She was staring at Taylor Douglas. Tall, dark, imposing—as she had noted before. Features betraying no emotion, no surprise, hard-set.

And angry. Merciless.

Yes, he was the officer she had seen leaving the tent. *She should have known, she should have seen, she should have thrown herself in the river before coming here!*

But of course. Taylor was the Yankee officer who knew about this copse, who knew the area, the defensive possibilities of such a position.

And yes . . . the books . . . the sense of clarity here, and of character as well.

Oh, yes, it was his tent.

And he had returned.

# Chapter 13

Instinct.

Foolish perhaps, illogical, but there. Within her soul.

She turned to run.

She didn't get anywhere. His arms were around her waist; he was lifting her from the ground, throwing her down.

The camp bed was hard. It knocked the breath from her as she landed on top of it. She instantly, *instinctively,* attempted to rise again. But he was there beside her, a booted foot on the edge of the bed as he leaned over her.

"Godiva!" he declared.

She gnawed her lower lip, staring at him.

"Well, well. So we meet again."

She couldn't speak. She just stared up into his hazel eyes. She crossed her arms over her breasts, feeling tremors snake along her spine and cause her to begin to shiver anew.

"Cat got your tongue? I never imagined you being silent. But speak up. To what do I owe the pleasure?" he mocked.

She gritted her teeth, swallowed hard, blinked—and then faced him with her own features hard set. "It was a nice night for a ride," she said smoothly.

"Ah, now, that's a poor lie, Godiva, for you. No imagination to it whatsoever."

"This is a social call?" she suggested blithely.

She was amazed that he smiled, yet the amusement didn't reach his eyes. "I warned you, remember, about riding out naked—"

"I didn't come naked!" she said, pointing to her clothes.

He didn't follow the direction of her finger. He arched a dark brow. "Ah, so you came with clothing. You stripped to wait for me? How decadent—and charming, of course."

"Oh, you should truly rot in hell, Taylor Douglas. You're supposed to be having dinner with Colonel Bryer!" she informed him. "You're supposed to be gone for hours."

"Yes, well, forgive my bad manners. I came for some despatches. How rude of me to unexpectedly return while you were stripping—and stealing my clothing, so it appears."

"Borrowing," she murmured.

"You were going to return them?"

"Of course I—" she began, but she broke off, hearing footsteps approach the tent. She paled. If someone entered the tent . . .

"Get under the covers," he told her.

"What?"

"The covers!"

She jumped up, shivering. He pulled up the sheet and blanket, and she crawled beneath them. He tossed both back on her—covering even her head.

"Sir!" a soldier called.

She heard Taylor lift the canvas flap.

"Colonel Bryer was called to the infirmary tent. Colonel McKenzie is on his way here now. He'll take the despatches and join you for dinner in your quarters."

"Thank you, Sergeant Henson."

She heard the footsteps retreating. She didn't move the blanket or sheet that covered her face. A second later, they were ripped away.

"You'll suffocate, you little fool," he told her.

She didn't even look at him. A tempest seared through her heart. Ian. She would be grateful to see her brother. She had learned that she must always be grateful to see him alive.

But . . .

"Ian!" she whispered miserably. "My brother is here—now?"

"Your brother arrived yesterday. Thank God. I'll turn you right over to him. I imagine facing Ian will be worse for you than the prospect of incarceration at unknown Yankee hands. Perhaps he can trim your feathers."

"No, please, Taylor, you can't!"

She didn't look at him. She was dazed. She stared at the canvas roof of the tent. Death, she thought, had to be so much easier than this.

He sat on the edge of the camp bed, caught her chin with his thumb and forefinger, and forced her to look at him. His features were hard and set, eyes damning. "I warned you. You broke your word."

She shook her head, twisting from his touch. "I did not! I swear to you, I never intended to do so. I was covered in blood; I was bathing. I heard the Yanks—"

"You heard men from this camp. You didn't need to lead them on any wild chase. They were looking for injured men."

"If they found Rebel injured, they were going to kill them."

He let out an impatient sound. "Captain Ayers is a good officer and an ethical man. He wouldn't murder injured men, not even enemy soldiers—"

"Maybe Ayers wouldn't—but the men with him would!" she insisted.

"I don't remember allowing you any extenuating circumstances when I asked for your word. You swore you wouldn't do it. You broke your word; you decided to play Godiva."

She shook her head. "I didn't. I had just taken off my shirt and skirt to soak the blood from them. You really can't imagine what it's like, all that blood."

"I believe I could," he murmured darkly.

"The scent of it was . . . never mind. And it all happened so quickly. We were by the river, fixing Gilly's bandages—"

"Gilly?" he said, and she was startled to realize he remembered the young soldier he had met.

"He was horribly burned, and lost a foot at Olustee. Your troops happened upon the exact spot at an importune time."

"And you were convinced they were going to *murder* your injured?"

His disbelief was evident in his tone, in the sharp narrowing of his eyes.

"I'm telling you the truth!"

"With no faith that the men would have a leader who would prevent such butchery?"

"How dare you disbelieve me! You! My mother told me that Federal soldiers—the same army as yours—butchered Seminole women and children during the Seminole Wars. What makes you think that certain men wouldn't consider Rebs as much vermin as they considered the Indians?"

Her angry appeal just seemed to irritate him.

"The same men who were in that army are many of the same men who are in the Confederacy now, and you know it damned well. There were no conditions, Tia. My men just happened upon you. Well, your brother just happens to be here. By God, I warned you that I'd turn you over to him!"

"It was all an accident," she insisted, trying to pull the covers to her breast and rise, and gain some distance from him.

He set his hands on her bare shoulders, pushing her back down, leaning closer. "I take back any insult to your ability to weave a story. You are the most imaginative actress I have met in quite some time, Tia."

"Taylor!" came a call from just outside the tent.

Tia went completely rigid. *Ian!*

Then she felt hysterical laughter rising in her throat. Ian was right outside—no, Ian was coming through the flap. Maybe Taylor would get a chance to tell Ian what had happened. Maybe Ian would kill Taylor.

Maybe Taylor would kill Ian.

"Taylor, I sent word that Bryer was called back to a wounded man—"

Ian was in the tent.

She was in the bed. Naked. Taylor was leaning over her.

*"Tia?"*

Her brother's shock was evident in his voice: the depth of his indignation and absolute fury became evident in his eyes. He looked from her to Taylor. "Douglas, by God, I don't know what's going on here, but I will know and—"

Ian's hand was on his sword hilt.

"Ian!" Tia cried. Taylor stood, facing down Ian. He had instinctively set his own hand on his sword hilt.

Tia grabbed the covers to her chest and leaped from the bed. She didn't know what she was doing, but she rushed to Taylor's side, putting an arm around him, preventing him from drawing his sword.

"Ian, thank God! At Olustee, with all the Union dead and wounded, we were so afraid! I'm so glad to see you. I was told you were out of the state, sent back to Virginia. We were so relieved to hear that . . . there were just so many dead. So many, many men dead." She was babbling, not getting anywhere. She lowered her voice, filling it with feigned emotion. "In fact . . . I had to see Taylor. I was told that he had been part of the battle, and so . . . well, I had to find him. To make sure that he was all right."

Ian's jaw was locked in a way she knew too well. "You had to see Taylor?" he queried, his teeth on edge.

"Of course . . ." Tia said, letting her voice trail off suggestively. "Oh, Ian, of course, I thought you'd realized that we'd met before."

"Tia, when we were last home, I warned you that you couldn't play games! By God, you are my sister and I will defend you at any cost, but—"

"Ian, I swear, I didn't cause the trouble at Christmas. But neither is there trouble here. Oh, God, I have to make you understand. I did know Taylor before Christmas. You see . . . we had become—well, more than acquaintances."

Her brother's scowl at last showed a hint of confusion. "Taylor, what is she talking about?"

"Your sister—"

"He was scouting to the south," Tia interrupted quickly. "We ran into one another. I couldn't say anything at the house during Christmas time. It's all been so very hard for me. You must understand—after all, Alaina was passionately involved with the South when *you* first met. I was angry, confused. I'd come to know Taylor, and . . ." Again, she didn't exactly lie; she just let her voice trail off. "We were so involved, but he was the enemy. Is the enemy. But . . . Ian . . ."

It wasn't enough. Her brother was still as rigid as a steel pike. He was still going to kill her. Or try to kill Taylor. There would be an awful, explosive fight any second. Taylor wouldn't just let Ian kill him because she had decided to take refuge in his tent. She had to say something else, do something . . .

"Ian, we're married," she lied swiftly.

"What?" he said incredulously. "I don't believe you! If so, Tia, someone should take a switch to you, after the way you played with Weir at the house during Christmas. Taylor, good God, explain this!"

Tia held her breath. She stared at Taylor. He stared at her.

Time seemed to go by. An eternity.

Taylor didn't deny her.

Nor was he going to help her. "I'm sure she'll explain," he drawled softly. "Tia is just so—enthusiastic. I'm dying to hear her description of what has occurred myself."

"Tia?" Ian questioned. "Start talking. I really don't understand. Father was upset with your lack of manners to a guest. You were rude and hateful at the house—"

"Oh, Ian! That's what I'm trying to explain. This is so hard for me! I couldn't admit what I was feeling at first. I mean, he is in a Union uniform. Like you. Only you're my brother, and we've managed, except for the awful fear when there's a battle. I didn't want to come here!" It was the first truthful thing she had said. "Though, now, of course, that I see you . . ."

He was waiting. Demanding more of an explanation.

"Ian, I never wanted to care about another enemy! It's bad enough to have my brother . . . fighting against his state. But you've got to understand. There were so many dead, Ian! Yes, I was wretched. And I was afraid. Afraid, terribly afraid, when I'd heard that Taylor was leading cavalry at Olustee. I knew that I couldn't wait, I had to come to him. I had to see him . . . it didn't matter anymore that we were still at war."

Was there even a prayer that he'd believe her?

Taylor slipped behind her, pulling her close to his chest, his arms holding the blanket against her nakedness. "Imagine. Can you believe such a story?" he asked huskily.

She thought it a miracle that Ian didn't hear the sarcasm. But apparently, he didn't.

Because he knew Taylor; trusted him.

He just stared at her, his deep blue eyes troubled, brow knit in a frown.

"Taylor . . . you and my little sister!" Ian said, looking from her to Taylor at last. "Who would have imagined . . ."

"Certainly not me," Taylor added smoothly.

"Oh, right, who would have imagined!" Tia breathed. It was a miracle.

"My God, Taylor! You and my little sister!" Any minute he was going to step forward, pump Taylor's hand, kiss her cheek. But his hand still hovered at his sword hilt.

Ian's hand fell from his sword hilt. He came forward, grinning now from ear to ear.

He shook Taylor's hand. Kissed her cheek. "This calls for a celebration. I've nothing good enough for this occasion, but I did bring a red wine—do our parents know?" he demanded.

"Uh—no. This just happened after Olustee!" she said very softly.

Her brother's palm touched her cheek with real affection. "They'll be glad, Tia, trust me, they'll be glad, I think. Glad of your choice. I think Father was afraid that you were becoming too involved with Ray Weir, and that would have been disaster. Taylor, welcome to the family. Well, you are family to part of the family, but I'm damned happy to have you as a brother-in-law. Good lord, though, I've come at a bad time—"

"No, no! There's no bad time to see you, Ian!" Tia cried out.

"I didn't even imagine that I'd be able to see you at all this trip, Tia. I thought you'd be in the woods with Julian and the wounded."

"No. Here I am," she said lamely.

"Here you are, a married woman, little sister!" he exclaimed. "My congratulations! To you both. I'll go for the wine, and make other arrangements for my sleeping quarters this evening. Tia, get dressed. We will drink a red wine toast. It should be champagne. If only I'd known . . ."

Ian turned and slipped beneath the tent flap, leaving them alone. Tia was suddenly shaking so hard she thought she was going to fall—except that Taylor was holding her with an iron grip. He turned her in his arms. Stared down into her eyes. "Now that was clever. Really clever."

"What should I have told him?" she whispered desperately. The blanket didn't seem like enough of a barrier between them.

"How about the truth?" he queried hotly.

She closed her eyes, opened them, met his gaze again, seeking understanding. "I—I couldn't."

"So you came up with one really damning lie!"

"I'll think of a way out of it."

"Oh, no. I've had it with your fabrications."

He pushed her back against the rear of the tent and walked to the flap, lifting it and exiting. She heard him calling to his sergeant, speaking softly, then, as he reentered the tent, he gave a few last instructions. "Sergeant Henson, tell Father Raphael he must come immediately. And bring Private Allen as well; we'll need another witness. It must all be done very quickly."

"Yes, sir!" Henson called from beyond.

Clutching the covers to her breast like a lifeline, Tia stared at him. "Father . . . Raphael?"

His eyes seemed like knives, cutting into her with irritation and fury. "We're getting married."

"Oh, no, we can't possibly. I can't marry you."

"Oh? You're the one who created this disaster."

"Marriage would be a worse disaster—"

"Well, guess what, my sweet? Your brother is coming back to celebrate. He expects you to be staying with *your husband* through the night. Did you want to become my mistress and continue to pretend to be married?"

"No, of course not—"

"Ian is staying at this camp. You will not be leaving this tent tonight."

"But marriage is a bit drastic—"

"So is death—even in warfare."

"There has to be a way—"

"There is a way, and damn you, I'm offering it to you. This was your lie, not mine. I assure you, I haven't the least desire in the world to marry you."

She couldn't help but take offense. She lifted her chin. "Then why do it?"

He shrugged. She still felt the razor's slash of his eyes. "I have no desire to marry again ever. So . . . since you have begun this charade, we'll carry it through. I don't really give a damn what commitment I make on paper."

She didn't know why she felt so hurt. The situation was a catastrophe she had created herself. She started shaking again, standing at the rear of the tent. Her eyes stung with tears. The truth. She could tell Ian the truth rather than do this. This was serious, awful, forever. If she told Ian the truth about what she had been doing . . . that she was the woman gaining fame as "Godiva," and given credit for far more excursions than she had ever taken . . .

She couldn't do it. She was desperate to find a way out. He seemed to have it for her. Calculated perfectly. But it couldn't work.

"But . . . what about the rest of your camp? They'll

know . . . that I wasn't here before. You're in a scouting and foraging situation—what will your superiors say to the sudden arrival of a Rebel bride?"

"There are no superiors here. Colonel Bryer has equal rank, but I'm the command officer, in full charge of the camp. Colonel Bryer has a daughter here, and there are two young women of excellent reputation working with him in the hospital tent as well, not to mention the laundresses, who also perform other duties for the men. Those with money and inclination. I'm sure you know what I mean. Henson will never breathe a word of when this wedding took place, neither will Father Raphael."

"But . . ."

Outside the tent, a throat was cleared, and there was a call from Henson. "Colonel! I'm out here with Father Raphael."

Taylor threw her the white shirt. "Put it on."

She did so, shaking, managing badly, feeling his hard gaze on her all the while. The shirt was a dress on her. She didn't need trousers.

"This is it. The moment of truth," he said.

"Can it . . ."

"Save you?" he inquired sharply. "Yes."

"I didn't mean that. I mean, can it work, can it be believed . . ."

He was silent for a minute. "Oh, yes. It can work, and be believed. And it will be legal," he added softly, as if in afterthought. "Time, however, is of the essence."

"Call them in," she said.

He stepped beneath the flap of the tent. For a wild moment, she was tempted to crawl beneath the canvas and disappear. But her hands were frozen; she was frozen . . .

He entered again through the flap. Alone. He stared at her. She felt the rage of anger behind the sharp gold glitter of his eyes. "We're just waiting for Private Allen. A few seconds' reprieve! Time to reflect! And I'm really doing you one hell of a service, Miss McKenzie."

Her teeth were chattering. "You don't have to—"

"Yes, you see, that's the point—I do. Yet bear in mind

that you trapped me into this. And I haven't forgotten that you broke your promise. Marry me, and I swear, I'll halfway kill you if you break it again."

She felt flushed. "You don't understand. I didn't mean to—"

"No excuses, or conditions. Marry me, and it isn't a game."

"I don't understand—"

"You're lying; you do."

She shook her head with sudden anger and passion. "I came up with the lie, yes, but you came up with this solution. We don't have to do this."

"We do, unless you want your brother's blood on your hands."

"Ian is damned fine swordsman—"

"You can try to tell him the truth. He still found his sister naked in my tent. His sense of honor and duty will call for him to demand satisfaction from me. He may be a damned fine swordsman, but so am I. You take your chances. It's a pity that any man should die for your recklessness, but there it is."

She felt the gold sting of his eyes a moment longer. Then he turned and moved quickly. He stepped out of the tent and returned with Henson, another soldier, and a man in a white collar. If they were in any way surprised or nonplussed about the strange situation, they gave no sign. "Father Raphael, Tia McKenzie, Ian's sister. Tia, Father Raphael. And these gentlemen are Sergeant Henson and Private Allen. They're two of my best men, discreet in every matter."

"Ma'am!" Henson said, offering her an awkward smile. "We're glad to have you. Mighty glad the Colonel's to have a wife again."

"Thank you, Henson," Taylor said, his voice grating.

Private Allen was a very lean fellow who looked as if he had been called out of an accounting office to serve in the war. He didn't speak, but he smiled at her.

"Father Raphael?" Taylor said.

Father Raphael was a white-haired Frenchman. "You both enter this willingly?"

"Yes, Father," Taylor said.

She would burn in hell, Tia thought. "Yes, Father," she echoed.

"Father, if you please, we need to do this quickly," Taylor reminded him.

The priest cleared his throat. He began to speak. Taylor came to stand beside Tia.

*A white cotton man's shirt. This was to be her wedding gown! She was marrying the enemy in the enemy's own shirt . . .*

There was no elegant ring for her finger; just Taylor's West Point class ring, made to fit her with a piece of string.

The words were all said; she signed the papers the priest carried. He made a hasty exit along with the officers who had stood as witnesses to the event.

When they were gone, she still stood barefoot, shivering, looking down at the ground. "My God, I could die . . ." she breathed. "Just die!"

He didn't intend to let her be at all. He jerked her chin up angrily, staring at her. "Lord no, my love, you're not going to die. You're not going to be allowed to die. There's plenty of torture in store for you before I would begin to let you escape into death! Ian is coming back. You have to play the loving, dutiful wife. You didn't just happen to bring clothing, did you?"

"I told you—"

"Oddly enough, he'll now be expecting you to be dressed. That he interrupted a passionate encounter with us as having been recently married is something he'll accept—he sees his own wife infrequently enough. But now, with you knowing that he is returning, he'll rather naturally be expecting to find you respectably clothed," he told her, then shook his head. "I'll go see if I can find a fairly slim camp follower."

"A camp follower!" she said with dismay.

"Yes, a good, loyal camp follower! One who probably wouldn't dream of doing anything so wanton and dangerous as running around the woods naked."

"You bastard!" she whispered.

"How do I explain to your brother that you haven't any clothing?" he demanded. He didn't expect her to answer. He started from the tent, then ducked back under the flap, tense as wire, voice a whip crack, eyes lethal fire. "Don't leave. Do you understand me? You'll wish you'd thrown yourself on your father's mercy a hundred times over if you take a single step from here and I catch you."

Again, he expected no reply. After he'd left, she sank down on the bed, staring at her ring finger. This couldn't be. She had married hastily in a small canvas tent, wearing only a man's white shirt.

Taylor was back almost immediately with clean clothing.

Chaste clothing. A pale-blue skirt with a blue smocked blouse to match. And a pair of shoes, thank God. He handed her the garments. "You'll have to wear them as is. Godiva's fashion accessories remain quite soaked," he said, indicating her corset and pantalettes, still lying in front of his trunk.

She ignored the comment, rising to dress. Her hands continued to shake; he continued to stare at her. If only he'd leave her alone! But he wasn't going anywhere. His arms were locked over his chest. She didn't attempt to tell him that he was making her so nervous she could barely function; she turned away from him, slipped from the white shirt, and into the new garments. She was struggling with the back hooks when he at last came around to help her. He was fixing the last of the tiny hooks when she heard her brother hailing them again.

"Taylor, Tia!"

"Come on in, Ian," Taylor invited.

Ian carried the wine—and long-stemmed glasses. "They belong to Colonel Bryer," he informed them, setting everything down on the camp desk, then working with a knife to open the bottle. "He is well packed for a surgeon in the field, but a good man, I hear."

"So it appears," Taylor said. He accepted wine from Ian.

"Colonel Bryer had no idea that your wife was here,

or even that you had married my sister," Ian informed Taylor.

"I hadn't told anyone she was here. Well, Sergeant Henson knows, of course, and Father Raphael. He married us. Truthfully, I don't want the matter known. It could cause your father further difficulty with the Confederacy if it's known that his daughter has married the enemy," Taylor to him.

"Perhaps that's true. Well, Tia," Ian said to his sister, providing her with a wineglass. "It might have been far more proper had you asked Father's blessing, or taken the time for an announcement—"

"Oh!" she exclaimed. "You're going to tell me about being proper! If I recall, Ian, you made an appearance at a party with a bride, none of us knowing a thing about it, and rumor circulating that you had seduced your new wife in a spring on our property!"

"Sons are allowed more liberty than daughters, Tia," Ian countered. "But I suppose you do have your point, and I'm delighted for the both of you. Very delighted. I could begin to imagine what situation I might have come upon! To your health! To your long lives, to happiness!"

"Our thanks!" Taylor lifted his glass, took a swallow of the wine. Tia did the same.

"Sirs!" Henson called from just outside the tent. "I've arranged for dinner to be served."

"Please, bring it in," Taylor told him.

Flushed, Sergeant Henson brought in an amazing display of field culinary achievement. He'd managed a snowy tablecloth, China plates, silver flatware. The camp desk became a table complete with a softly glowing candle.

Taylor seated Tia with a mocking, "My love!" whispered at her nape. She sat down to an amazingly complete and intimate meal.

Union foragers had apparently happened upon Florida cattle Tia thought, but she was resigned rather than bitter. They had done an excellent job with it—the cuisine was the finest she had ever tasted in the field. The food consisted of steaks, potatoes, okra, and wild winter berries. Tia thought that she wouldn't be able to eat, but she was famished. And thirsty. Her wine went down quickly. Too quickly. Despite it, conversation was an effort. She had to explain to Ian that Julian had been called to serve one of General Finegan's men, and that no, he wasn't aware that she had left his Rebel troops to find Taylor.

"Tia, that was foolish! You don't know who you might have encountered along the way."

"I came straight to Taylor. Straight to him!" she protested, amazed at how easy it was to smile, then frightened because the smile threatened to turn to laughter, and if she began to laugh, she would cry and she wouldn't be able to stop.

Taylor was staring at her. He looked at Ian. "Oh, yes. She came straight to me."

By the end of the meal, she was giddy and exhausted, worn out with her own efforts at pretense and charade. Her brother had asked about Julian's infant son, and she had happily described him as the spitting image of his own child, Sean. "A little McKenzie pea in a pod," Tia said. "Beautiful blue eyes, thick dark hair—a totally cherubic little face."

"And he and Rhiannon are well?"

"Very well. She was, however, unhappy about staying at Cimarron when Julian left." She shivered suddenly. Many people called her sister-in-law a white witch. She had what they labeled "sight"—sometimes, an ability to see the future. She had seemed to know that Julian would be safe when he had ridden with his sister to join the regulation army for the battle at Olustee.

What a pity she hadn't warned Tia about the dangers of tending to the wounded when Yanks were in the territory! "Though I think she knew," Tia added softly, "that the Rebel forces would turn back the Yankee invasion."

They were both staring at her. She hadn't realized the passion with which she had spoken. She had forgotten that she was in a Union encampment.

"There can be but one finish to the war, I'm certain,"

Ian murmured. "There are things which have now taken place of which you might not be aware."

"What has happened? Our own forces just took the battle here!"

"Surely you've heard that things do not go so well elsewhere."

"Ian, why are you back here so quickly? You were ordered north after Christmas."

"Tia . . ."

He stared at his sister. Tia realized that Taylor was watching him, and she wondered what Taylor knew of the war that she did not. Obviously, Ian wasn't going to share his orders with her, even if she was his sister—and now the wife of a Unionist.

Ian leaned toward her. "Tia, England has officially refused to recognize the government of the Confederacy. No more ships will be outfitted there. The rest of the European powers have refused to recognize her as well—other than the Roman Pontiff. Don't you see—it's over, except for the additional deaths that will follow, on both sides."

"They'll shoot any man—as a deserter?"

"No government has ever had such a harsh law, Tia, and God knows if they can implement it or not. Communications are destroyed in many areas."

She thought he must have seen some deep unhappiness in her eyes then because he suddenly rose. "I pray it ends soon," Ian said briefly, and walking around the table, he pulled her up to her feet, offering her a warm, brotherly hug at last and speaking to her with deep affection, "Enough sorrow for tonight! I wish you every happiness. I'm pleased to see you wed to so fine a man, though you disagree with his beliefs and loyalties. The rest of us have managed under the duress of supporting opposing sides; I imagine you two will do as well. I'll leave you alone now, for I'm very aware of how precious time can be in the midst of war."

"No, no, Ian! You don't need to leave!" Tia said in a panic. She suddenly realized that she was choking on unshed tears. She loved her brother so very much. And with him there, that night, she suddenly thought of the import of his words. She could remember, before the war began, when her brother had scandalously arrived at a party for their father with a new bride himself. And then the violence had broken out, and Alaina had been such a Rebel, and she had believed that her husband would resign from the Union army . . .

But he had not.

"Stay, Ian," she said softly.

He smiled, lifting her chin. "I'll be here in the morning, Tia, though I cannot stay long. We'll be together again."

She desperately wanted to cling to him, and beg him not to leave her.

She couldn't do so.

"I'll walk you out, Ian," Taylor said. He smiled at Tia—like an angry alligator might grin at a crane.

"Good! There are matters we need to discuss."

She couldn't let him go so quickly. She threw herself into her brother's arms, holding him very tightly.

He kissed her cheek, unwound her arms from around his neck. "Good night, little sister!" he said.

He left the tent with Taylor. She paced. She gazed longingly at the canvas at the rear of the tent. The pines were just beyond. Hammocks, rivers, streams—trails that led south and west, back to Cimarron.

"Mrs. Douglas!"

Sergeant Henson was just outside. Calling. Calling her, she realized.

"Yes?"

"I'll just clean out the tent, ma'am," he said, entering. "The dinner things."

"Oh, yes . . . thank you," she said.

He smiled at her and went about his business, quickly and efficiently. "I'm sorry to be a bother," she heard herself telling him.

"No bother, ma'am. Sometimes, other officers have their wives along. Some of the men from St. Augustine are able to have their ladies . . . Colonel Bryer is a New Yorker, but his wife is with him frequently. She defies all Rebel fire! Confidentially, they call her an old battle-ax, but she's a great lady to have in a fray!"

"Well, good for her!" Tia applauded.

He grinned, and slipped out of the tent. Tia turned longingly to stare at the back canvas again. She was startled as she heard another voice in the night. "Colonel! Colonel Douglas!"

A second later, a man was slipping through the tent. It was another man she had seen earlier; the tall, sad-looking captain from the river.

He started, staring at her. "Excuse me, please, I'm so sorry, I didn't know that the colonel had company. I was ordered to report to him this evening."

"He's with Colonel McKenzie," she advised. She bit her lip, wanting to blurt out the fact that his men were monsters.

Yet, he was staring at her equally strangely.

At that moment, Taylor returned to the tent. "Captain Ayers!"

"Yessir," the captain said, saluting. "I have a report for you, sir." He was trying not to stare at Tia.

"Captain Ayers, my wife. Tia, dear, Captain Kenneth Ayers."

"How do you do?" Tia murmured.

"I do apologize for staring. It's just that I'm sure we've met."

"Never, sir," she said, afraid she would choke over the denial.

"I didn't know that your wife was in camp, Colonel Douglas."

"She's just been able to join me," Taylor said smoothly.

"Well, I've come to report—"

"We'll discuss the day's business outside, shall we?" Taylor ordered.

"Certainly, sir."

"Excuse us—my love?" Taylor said, staring at her again.

He and Ayers departed. She paced again, sat on the

bed. She stared at the rear of the tent, then jumped up with horror.

Blaze!

Was she still wandering within the pines? She had to find her horse. She would never let some wretched Yankee killer seize her horse!

She stood, then paused. She'd be right back. She had to come back; surely Taylor would realize that. After all, her brother was in the camp. But she had to find her horse.

She ducked low, plucked at the canvas, and exited the tent by the rear. The moon was half-full, the stars were out, and she had some vision. She slipped quickly into the pines and walked among them. "Blaze! Blaze!" she called. She whistled, dismayed when her horse didn't come. She began running along another path, glad Taylor had provided her with her soft leather slippers along with the clothing.

She came to a halt on the trail, listening. She thought she heard a movement among the trees, and she turned hopefully.

No, Blaze hadn't appeared.

Taylor had.

Arms crossed over his chest, his stance rigid, he watched her with his eyes like the rays of the sun, piercing and hot.

"I told you not to run."

"What? Don't be absurd! I was only—"

She broke off. He was coming toward her. "No! God spare me another of your stories! You have a tale for every occasion; you lie with the same ease with which you breathe."

"I wasn't about to lie to you!" she protested angrily.

"Good," he said. He was almost upon her. Heat seemed to bounce from him like the sun from the earth on a sweltering summer day. She could almost see it on the air. She unwittingly backed away from him. He caught hold of her arm, jerking her to him. "My God, but you have your nerve! You twist me into your wretched games, and then think to escape!"

"No, I didn't—" she tried to protest, struggling against his hold.

"No game, Tia. You forced me to marry you—"

"Forced! Did I hold a gun to your head?"

"No," he drawled sarcastically. "Your brother was about to draw a sword."

"Oh, but you would have killed him with your amazing prowess."

"To my great sorrow, yes, it might have happened."

"Or you might have lain dead."

"Either way, Godiva, you are not worth the bloodshed!"

The words hurt as much as his hold upon her. "You don't understand—" she began.

"No, you don't understand," he assured her. "But you're going to."

It was as if something within him had snapped. He ducked against her midriff even as she struggled, throwing her over his shoulder. A raw sense of panic seized her as she realized the full implications of what she had done. Her chin slammed against his back. She bit her tongue as it did so. Tears stung her eyes. How could things come out so badly when her efforts had all really been so noble?

"Let me down, Taylor, please, now!"

She might as well have not bothered to speak at all.

"Please! I'll cry out, I'll let out a Rebel yell unlike any you have ever heard before. I'll create such a fuss! My brother—"

"Your brother would not interfere between a husband and a wife, Tia. You changed the battlefield today, Godiva. Now I am responsible for you."

Again, he walked with such a fervor that her face slammed against his back. Her nose was crushed. Tears again formed in her eyes. She was unaware when they left the pines. He slipped beneath the back canvas of his tent swiftly and smoothly, as if she were not a burden at all.

He set her down upon the camp bed none too gently, exhaling as he did so with a grunt. She scrambled to a sitting position. They stared at one another. The look in his eyes as they met hers was not at all reassuring. Gold, sharp, incensed, his eyes seemed to cut into her with the sharpness of a bayonet. The veins at his throat and temple pulsed with the depths of his anger. He stood before her, hands on his hips. She could hear his teeth grinding with his efforts to remain still, see the lock of tension that held his body dead stiff from head to toe.

She braced herself for whatever he was about to say—or do. She prepared to fight—a war of words she must win quickly. She was good with words—even he said so. But she couldn't come up with the right ones—despite her innocence at the moment.

She didn't need to speak. He did so.

"All right, Godiva. Here we are."

"Here we are," she repeated. "Look, I tried to tell you—"

"I don't want you telling me anything anymore. Every word out of your lips tends to be sheer fabrication."

"I want my horse—"

"So you said. Well, she is safe, and will be taking you nowhere tonight."

"I didn't mean to run from you—"

"Good. Because you have not managed to do so."

"So . . . ." she murmured carefully, very aware that he still stood less than a foot from her, his temper dangerously explosive.

"So. Well. Get on with it," he said curtly.

Not what she had expected. He suddenly seemed cold and distant, and calculating. Brief in the extreme.

"Get on with what?" she whispered warily.

"My love!" The term was spoken in a voice that was deep, husky, masculine—and so mocking! "You are always so eager to shed your clothing. And I admit," he said wryly, "to have chastised you in the past for your tendency to lose them, but . . . here and now would be the proper time. You *married* me today, Godiva. So here and now, you have your chance. My love, my dearest wife—your constant penchant for carelessly casting your clothing aside is what has brought us here to this—this all-decisive moment in life. So . . . Tia, get on with it. Now."

# Chapter 14

*Just what the hell am I doing?* Taylor wondered. By God, since he'd come back tonight and found her in his tent, he hadn't really known a thing he was doing—until he'd done it.

Actually, his own emotional state didn't matter, he told himself, except that he was angry. He really wanted her to suffer—something like the pain of the damned, which he felt he was enduring now, though he wasn't at all sure why.

"Need help?" he queried, his tone polite. *Talk,* he told himself, *talk. It will keep you from thinking.*

"I'm more than willing to assist you, my love, though one would think you'd have removal of your garments down pat by now, since you so frequently shed them," he told her, and he heard the sarcasm in his voice, knew what he was doing to her, and yet, he couldn't stop himself.

*She* had brought them to this.

He saw the change in her as her temper flared. Burned.

She jumped up, careful that she did so across the camp bed from him, staring at him, hands on her hips, seething. "Say what you will. It's cruel and untrue—"

"Untrue!"

"Yes, untrue. Everything is greatly exaggerated. What you've heard is all lies."

"Tia, I found you tonight," he reminded her. He lifted his hand in a pretense of realization. "We should have consummated the marriage first—done the legal deed later. What a fool I was!"

She shook her head passionately. "I told you what happened tonight. And every word was the truth. You have men who mean to murder injured Rebels if they come upon them. If you weren't such a self-righteous fool, you might at least take the time to wonder if such monsters do exist beneath your nose!"

"I still found you here—"

"Excuse me, sir, but if they had murdered injured Rebels in cold blood and I watched, do you think they would have left me alive?"

"Tia, it is farfetched, and you have lied a dozen times before—"

"It's—"

"Just as you lied to Ian tonight. Well, it was a lie neither of us could live with. A lie which has now become the truth. That being the case, I do intend to reap the benefits."

She didn't intend to respond to that.

She started walking around the camp bed and he realized that she was leaving again—this time, via the tent flap. He caught her arm, swinging her back around to face him. She stiffened, teeth gritting so that they crunched, trying to free herself from him. Flashing dark eyes met his.

"Where do you think you're going now?" he demanded, as angry as she.

"To Ian! I'll tell him we've had a lover's quarrel."

"The hell you will!" he retorted.

He could feel the defiance in every inch of her body, but he had no intention of letting her go. He drew her tightly against himself, one arm pinning her against his length, the other catching her chin.

She meant to protest—wildly. But he didn't allow her to. His mouth crushed down upon hers and he gave her no mercy. She tasted blood where their lips met. His fingers tangled into her hair, holding her, and his tongue pressed past her lips, deep into the crevices of her mouth. He felt her breasts against his chest with her every breath, felt the heat within, the pulsing of her heart, the shivering that had seized her. And he allowed no quarter, could give no quarter, for it was suddenly a battle he meant to win. She tasted sweetly of the evening's wine, of warmth, of slow-building fire, and it seemed, in a matter of seconds, that her lips were molding to his, that they had parted of their accord, that he no longer battled the wall of her teeth for the depths of his kiss.

She was no longer straining against him. Her hands lay upon his chest, but not with struggle or resistance, and when he lifted his mouth from hers at last, her eyes were closed, dark lashes sweeping her cheeks.

"Tia."

She didn't open her eyes. She had decided to play the martyr, he realized, and he couldn't help smiling, because he could see the erratic pulse point beating a mile a minute at her throat. "I have married you, Taylor, and therefore will pay my debts."

His smile deepened. "That you will, Mrs. Douglas!"

He lifted her, swinging her into his arms. With a little gasp, she clasped him around the neck, afraid she would fall. He took the few steps that led to the camp bed and lay down with her, not about to give her another chance to rise. She let out an indignant and garbled protest when he rolled her over to find the buttons at the back of her blouse. "Want to destroy the garment?" he demanded. "I don't know just how many outfits I'll be able to find out here in the midst of nearly nowhere in the middle of the war!" he warned her.

She went still for a moment; he undid the last of the buttons. He could still taste her lips, feel her . . .

He eased the blouse from her. Still at her back, he slipped his arms around her, his hands cupping her breasts. His palms slid over the hard peaks of her nipples, and he feathered the aureoles with the tip of his fingers, stroked them softly, cradled the fullness of her breasts. He pressed his lips to her throat, to the pulse there, and felt the thundering fever of his own arousal begin to pound within him. He stroked the length of her spine slowly with his tongue, and found the buttons to her skirt, opened them, rose enough to drag the garment away. He sat up, drawing his shirt over his head, and cradling her into his arms once again, turning her, so that the stream of her black hair fell away and her breasts teased the flesh of his chest. Her eyes were closed again. He allowed her that, kissing her eyelids, finding her mouth again. Her lips gave way easily to his; he felt her hand upon his shoulder, upon his cheek, touching him, and this time, he felt that her lips melded naturally to his, that she sought as much as she gave, quested, searched.

The length of her shaped itself naturally against him. Their flesh melted together in a sweet inferno. He slid down her body, bathing the tips of her breasts with his tongue, taking the nipples into his mouth, teasing, stroking, sucking, drawing from her lips an exhaled gasp. Her fingers dug into his shoulder. He continued to move against her, nuzzling the satin of her belly, drawing lower, feeling the shaking in the length of her, finding the center of her sex, touching it with his tongue, breathing in the musky scent of sex, tasting the woman, rising to an anguish of desire. His sex throbbed against his trousers. He jerked them open to free himself, shimmying from the length of them, kicking them to the floor. She barely moved, barely breathed, then he touched her, and touched her again, and suddenly she was shaking, and writhing against his wet caress, and murmuring, protesting . . . arching against him. He rose, and hovered over her.

Her eyes were closed.

No mercy . . . and yet, he would allow her that.

He sank slowly into her, and began shaking with the depths of desire she had awakened within him. She went rigid; her nails scraped his chest and she gasped, twisting her head. He saw that she bit into her lower lip to keep from crying out, and for a moment he was shamed, remembering. She had dared the world, risked life and limb—she knew so much about men and war, and yet she was so innocent. He closed his own eyes, feeling the force of his desire trembling like a drumbeat through him. He fought for control, moved slowly, slowly, sheathed in warmth and fever, wanting her . . . every

muscle in his body tortured and rigid. Slowly, slowly,
deeper, withdrawing, deeper . . .

Her fingers tightened upon· him. Breath escaped her
lips. His rhythm increased, and the fierce anguish in his
limbs burned with a greater fever as he sank again, and
again, and felt the subtle change in the woman beneath
him, the hunger awakened in her, the way she began to
move, arching to his stroke, accepting, taking . . .

Wanting.

He cradled her hand against him, and the fever that
swept him seemed to take them like the power of the
wind. Guns might have thundered, swords might have
clashed, the world and war might have exploded around
him, and he would have given them not a care. Compul-
sion ruled him, the searing need, the desperate desire to
reach the pinnacle. He had seen her, yes, he had known
her, tasted her kiss, tasted her flesh. He hadn't imagined
that she could drive him so far, reach so deeply into
him, bring him to a fulfillment of something more than
he had expected or known. Sleek, damp, twisting,
moving . . . she suddenly strained against him, and he
shuddered into her, and into her, and into her again,
flooding her with his seed, with the force of his climax.
He fell to her side, pulling her into his arms again, and
lay there panting, wondering what she had done to him,
what spell she had cast upon him, why there was something so unique about her that . . .

That he could forget.

Not just feel hunger, want sex. But forget . . .

The sound of gunfire. The war all around him.
Abby . . . running.

Abby . . .

The blood on his hands.

He lay in silence. So did she. Soft tangled webs of
ebony hair lay upon his chest. The top of her head was
beneath him. He couldn't see her face. Although he'd
been almost violently certain he hadn't wanted a wife,
he couldn't regret the events of the night. He had
wanted Tia McKenzie. She wasn't a lonely widow, divor-
cee, or prostitute. She was Jarrett McKenzie's daughter,

Ian's sister. There was only one way to have such a woman. Marry her.

She was also Godiva, he reminded himself, and he suddenly felt a greater anger at that fact. She still didn't realize what she had risked, even after tonight.

"Do you think you're going to survive marriage?" he queried.

"Don't!" she whispered.

"Don't what?"

"Don't—talk. Don't, I beg you, add insult to injury!"

Insult to injury? She had taken a heady slug at his masculine dignity and pride, and he wasn't going to ignore it. He turned to her, finding her face hidden in a web of her hair. He delved through it, smoothing it to the side, capturing her hands when she tried to twist away. Being Tia, she put up a fight. He straddled her, leaning low, pinning her wrists down, meeting her eyes. "You were injured?" he demanded.

"This was your idea!" she accused him.

"Marriage was your idea."

"But this—"

"This goes with marriage!"

He saw that her thick dark lashes were spiked with unshed tears. Compassion and anger stirred within him simultaneously. "You were wishing for a gallant Southern gentleman, I take it?"

"You were thinking of your wife!" she accused him in a pained whisper.

Something seemed to thud against the wall of his chest.

"You are my wife now," he told her quietly.

"I have married the enemy."

"So have many women. You will survive it."

"Will I? Will we survive the war?" she asked, and her voice sounded desperate, pained, frightened. He suddenly knew her vulnerability, and the courage it had taken to do the things she'd done. And prickly little enemy that she was, he wanted to protect her.

Enemy . . . wife. *His* wife.

"Yes! We will survive! I will see to it!" he promised

her. Her eyes were beautiful. Shimmering mahogany. And for once, she looked up at him as if she trusted him. He leaned down to kiss her again, and her lips were salty with the taste of tears. But she made no protest to his kiss; indeed, she kissed him in return with a sweet, hungry yearning. Kissed him, and kissed him . . .

It was he who raised his lips. "Insult to injury?" he queried huskily.

"Must you always talk?"

He smiled. "Certain talk has its place . . ." he murmured. "Such as . . . madam, I love the way you move. I love the way you look, the scent of you, and though other wives might be cold and dutiful, making love swathed in voluminous nightgowns, I would not dream of enduring such a situation, since you are quite stunningly beautiful, and you seduce by your very existence."

Her ebony dark eyes were upon him, still glittering with a certain moisture, but his words brought a rueful smile to her lips.

"I don't *dislike* you, Taylor."

"With endearments like that, it is amazing that I can control my ardor at all!"

Her smile deepened. "Taylor?"

"Yes?"

Her cheeks were flushed. She wet her lips. "You . . . are . . . it's not so awful to be with you. You're right . . . you've somewhat seduced me before. I don't think that I could have been with anyone else . . . as I am with you."

"Thank God!" he said.

*She was dreaming again. She saw the big white house with the grand entry. Then the toddler, the boy, the beautiful child, was on the balcony . . .*

*Falling, falling, falling . . .*

She awoke screaming. Once again, her mother-in-law was there, waking her, holding her, arms around her, assurances coming softly from her lips. "It's all right, it's a dream, and we'll take care, we know it's a warning. We'll warn everyone we know with a little boy, Rhiannon. It will be all right, really."

Her mother-in-law wasn't the only one with her. Alaina was there as well, holding little Conar, who screamed in resentment at being awakened again.

"I'm so sorry!" Rhiannon said, "I keep waking you . . . causing so much trouble."

"Waking isn't trouble, Rhiannon," her mother-in-law assured her.

"I just wish that we could help you somehow. Tell us about it," Alaina said. "Perhaps if you talk it out, detail by detail . . ."

And so, Rhiannon talked. Detail by detail. She described all that she had seen in her dream, all that recurred, all that was new.

And when she had finished. Alaina was as pale as the sheets. Her eyes were immense, their deep blue in stark contrast to the ashen shade of her cheeks.

"Alaina, what is it?" her mother-in-law asked with alarm.

"I know the house!" Alaina said. "I know the house she is describing."

When Tia awoke, she was alone, and she lay pensive on the cot for a long time.

The events of the evening seemed overwhelming and unbelievable to her at first. But with the increasing daylight, they became very real.

She didn't dislike Taylor. She was often furious with him, very often wished she could just slap him once really good and force him to listen to her point of view. But he had always intrigued her. And it was true that she had been strangely drawn to him from the beginning, true that she had been fascinated by him, that she had wanted to touch the bronze texture of his flesh. True, she had never imagined that anyone could awaken in her the sensations she had learned in her first night at his side. True, she was even anxious to see him again, feel his gold eyes upon her again, and feel again that sense that she was his, somehow protected, even cherished . . .

Even if he hadn't wanted another wife.

Remembering where she was, she rose quickly then, anxious to wash and dress. A bucket of fresh water and a towel had been left by the camp desk; she assumed they were for her. She also found Taylor's brush in the first compartment of his trunk, and she struggled to brush the mass of tangles out of her hair and wind it into the semblance of a neat chignon.

After making herself presentable, she stepped outside the tent. Sergeant Henson sat on a makeshift chair constructed out of a fallen log, and he whittled a little wooden figure as he tended a fire with a coffeepot. He looked up as she exited the tent, greeting her cheerfully.

"Good morning, Mrs. Douglas." He knew a great deal about her, she mused. What had he thought of her last night, having suddenly arrived in Taylor's tent—and becoming a wife in a large white uniform shirt?

Whatever he thought, he could not have been more cheerful or polite.

"Good morning."

"There's a meeting this morning, occurring in the doctor's tent since your husband wanted to let you sleep."

Because Taylor wanted to let her sleep? She doubted it. *Because no one wanted her around while they discussed Yankee strategy!*

"Thank you, Sergeant."

"Coffee?"

"I would love some."

He poured her a cup, and she sipped it. It was the best coffee she had tasted in a very long time. "Sergeant, is my brother involved in the meeting, too?"

"Why, of course. Your brother arrived with despatches and information, Mrs. Douglas."

"I see." Information they would assuredly not share with her.

Of course, they were both the enemy—her brother, her *husband.* It didn't seem real.

She looked across the camp of army-issue tents, hitching lines for the healthy horses still held by the Union, fires, and men. From a large, extended bleached canvas tent, she suddenly saw a woman hurrying across the grounds. She was young, thin, attractive, and seemed to be coming straight toward them.

"Sergeant," she said softly. "Who is that?"

"Cecilia Bryer, the doc's daughter. A fine young lady, at his side throughout this fight!"

"Mrs. Douglas!" the young woman called, hailing her.

Cecilia Bryer was about Tia's own age, slim, pretty with soft red hair and green eyes. She had a quick smile for Henson, but she looked tired, worn, old for her age, as did most people who involved themselves too deeply in the realities of war.

"Miss Bryer, how do you do," Tia said carefully.

"Well enough, for myself." In a no-nonsense manner, the woman offered Tia her hand. "We heard about your arrival, of course. News travels swiftly in a small camp such as this."

"I arrived unexpectedly."

"Through great difficulty, I understand. Your husband explained the going was quite rough, that you traveled hard to reach him. Those are my clothes you're wearing. I understand that your things were terribly muddied and damp."

"Yes—something like that," Tia said. "And I'm so sorry, I didn't know I had your belongings. Thank you, I apologize . . ."

"There's no need. I'm glad to have the luxury of several changes of clothing. I believe we are far better supplied than our Rebel counterparts."

"We make do," Tia said quietly.

Cecilia arched a delicate, flyaway brow, as if surprised that a woman in a Union camp who was married to a Union colonel would still align herself with the South.

"Well, my father is glad to help any man."

"So is my brother," Tia said quickly. The girl frowned, thinking she was speaking about Ian. "My brother Julian, a Confederate surgeon."

"Oh, yes, we've all heard about Julian—he was spirited into St. Augustine once to help General Magee!"

"Yes."

"Well." The girl smiled suddenly. "Whatever your af-

filiation, Mrs. Douglas, I'm glad that you seem to have
a generosity of the soul. There is a young man in our
infirmary who is dying—and he is an old friend of
yours."

"Who is it?"

"Canby Jacobs. He said his parents have a little cattle
ranch a few miles west of your family home near
Tampa."

"Canby, yes. I went to school with his sister, years
ago."

"Come with me, if you'll see him."

"Of course I'll see him."

"He said that you may not. That you might consider
him a traitor, and not want to have anything to do
with him."

"I will see him gladly."

"Good. Follow me."

Tia followed Cecilia Bryer through a number of single
soldier's tents. She saw in the distance that some of the
men were going through drills. A few were at leisure
about the camp, tending to their laundry, writing at
makeshift desks, reading. One lone soldier played a sad
lament upon a harmonica, but stopped as they passed
him by. "Mornin', Miss Cecilia," he said, nodding to
them both.

"Good morning, Private Benson," Cecilia said. Tia
noted that he had no left foot.

They continued on to the large hospital tent. There
were at least forty, maybe fifty beds in it. Flies buzzed;
men groaned. Orderlies and nurses, male and female,
moved about, changing bandages, talking to the soldiers,
bringing water and what aid they could.

It was not as bad as the battlefield had been. They
were not lying strewn about in pools of blood with
slashed, missing, and mangled limbs.

But the soldier on the bed to which Cecilia led Tia
was in very bad shape. A large, fresh bandage, already
beginning to show the color of blood, covered half his
torso. The left side of his face was covered with a ban-

dage as well. She wouldn't have recognized him as
Canby Jacobs if Cecilia hadn't told her his name.

"His lung is mostly shot away," Cecilia whispered to
Tia. "There's nothing more we can do but keep the
wound moist and clean. Take care if you change the
bandage again."

Staring at Canby, Tia nodded. She walked over to the
bed. His one good eye was closed. His hand was upon
his chest. She clasped it in both her own. His eyes
opened. Deep and blue. The visible half of his lip curled
into a smile. "Miss Tia, can it be!"

"Canby! Yes, it's me. It's good to see you."

"Good to see me, but I don't look so good, eh?"

"You'll get better."

"No, I'm dying," he said flatly. "It's all right. I made
my choice. I knew what I was fighting for, and what I'm
dying for, and I believe that I was right, and that God
will be glad to greet me. I'm awful glad, though, that
you agreed to see me. Thought you might not. My folks
split up over this, you know. My mother is in Savannah
now. Pa died with the Massachusetts Fourth Artillery
last spring."

"Canby, I'm so sorry. I'll write to your mother."

"You needn't write to her, Tia. She said that her son
was dead the day I signed up with the Union."

"She can't have meant it. No mother—"

"Not all folks were like yours, Miss Tia!" he said, then
smiled again. "I always had such a crush on you. Even
now, I can see you when your father had his fine parties
at Cimarron! Why, you danced and you teased—and you
were nice to every fellow there, including ugly poor boys
like me!"

"Canby, you were neither ugly nor poor!"

"So you married Colonel Douglas—now that's mighty
fine. He's a good fellow, Miss Tia. You'll see that more
when the war is over. Reckon, though, I shouldn't be so
surprised that you did come to see me. Your father is
one mighty fine man, one I sure do admire. He loves
both his sons, no matter what path they chose. Guess he
taught you the same."

"I do love both my brothers."

"And Colonel Douglas."

"And my friends, Canby, no matter what side they chose!" she told him. She didn't want him to see the way she was noting how quickly his bandage was filling with blood. "Canby, I need to change this bandage for you."

"No, just leave it be."

But she called to an orderly for a fresh bandage. The limping fellow who glanced her way knew what Canby needed.

As he came over with fresh linen for the wound, Canby said, "Tia, I do need you to write for me—to my wife. I found a right pretty little thing while I was in training camp first of the war, up in D.C. Her name is Darla. Darla Jacobs. And we got us a fine little boy, a real beauty. Can you tell her that I died thinking of her, loving her, and not to grieve too hard or too long, but raise our boy to be a happy child and a good man. Will you tell her . . . tell her that I died with faith and courage."

"Of course, Canby."

The orderly had arrived with fresh linen. Tia carefully started to remove the old bandage. Her heart seemed to stop in her throat. Half his chest had been blown away; the lung was raw and exposed.

She quickly applied the new, dry bandage.

"Sing to me, Tia. 'Amazing Grace.' I remember when you and your ma used to do that at the piano at Cimarron. Your pa would gaze on you both so proud, and you were just like a pair of nightingales, or Rose Red and Rose White, your ma so blond and you so dark! It was so beautiful, I thought the angels could hear!"

"I'll sing, Canby. You save your breath."

"Miss Tia, there ain't nothing to save it for! I got the one lung left, so might as well speak while I can. Father Raphael is on his way over. Most companies have Episcopal ministers, but here we got lots and lots of Irish fellows. So we've got ourselves a Catholic priest!"

"I'm sure he'll be here soon."

"Sing for me. I think the angels will listen to you, Miss Tia, more than a priest."

She smiled, squeezed his hand, and began to sing, very softly. But as she drew in breath for the second verse, another soldier called out, "Louder, please, miss, for all of us!"

And so she did. And when she had finished the last verse and looked down, Canby was already dead. He had died with a slight curve to his lips, as if he had, indeed, seen the angels coming.

She had seen so many men die. They died the same in Union blue as they did Confederate butternut and gray.

She lowered her head, tears sliding down her cheeks as she held his lifeless hand.

In Dr. Bryer's private quarters, Ian had spread a number of maps over the camp desk, describing the main situation of the war as he had seen it in the last meeting he had attended in D.C. "As far as the situation here, little has changed. I have often given my opinion—that nothing less than a major thrust against the peninsula will work. The people here are tenacious, and those who would declare for the Union are often too afraid of repercussions if they state themselves Federals. To win a major battle, you would need a major army. The blockades, however, are tightening. Colonel Bryer, you're to have a few more weeks in the field, then I'm afraid that our captured wounded and missing must be abandoned. You're to return to St. Augustine, the men will be given light duty there, and then returned to heavier duty with the Army of the Potomac."

"These men have been through a lot," Colonel Bryer said. "It was an even battle, and a bloody one, and these men were wounded by swords, cannon fire, bullets, and bayonets, as in any other battle."

"And so the time spent in St. Augustine will be considered a vacation by many of the soldiers," Ian said.

"I fear the war will go on here as it has—with neither side gaining much in victory, but losing many in death,"

Taylor said. He looked at Ian. "I assume you have new orders for me as well?"

Ian nodded, handing him a leather-bound, water-proofed case. Reading the paper within, Taylor looked up at Ian. "This will be like looking for a needle in a haystack!" he said.

"I know. I admit—I'm glad they gave you the duty, and not me."

"And why do you think they have done so?"

Ian stared at him for a minute. "Because you're Indian," he said flatly. "They will always believe that because of your blood, you know the swamp a little better, you are a little craftier—more able to manage such a duty."

"What is the duty?" Bryer asked curiously. "If I am allowed to know. I have served some time now with Colonel Douglas. I have served with no better man."

Taylor glanced at Bryer, somewhat surprised by the crusty old soldier's dedication to him. "Thank you, sir," he said. "But I'm afraid that the mission is to be confidential. I'll be leaving you in a few days' time."

"Colonel Douglas," he began, "I know my rank and I know my work, but I am a medical man, and not prepared to lead this camp as you have done."

"I had thought I was to be leaving this morning," Ian said, "but a messenger arrived from St. Augustine this morning, asking us to delay bringing in so many units of cavalry along with your sorely wounded men. I will be staying here for a time before taking the companies to St. Augustine. Then I, too, will rejoin the Army of the Potomac, just a little later than I had expected." Ian turned back to the maps again. "On the ninth of March, Lincoln put Ulysses Grant in overall command of the armies. These are the goals: Meade remains head of the army under Grant and is to attack Lee's army, as we have attempted throughout the war. General Butler is to take his forces up the south bank of the James River from Fortress Monroe, Siger is to sweep through the Shenandoah Valley, Sherman is to attack Atlanta and Banks is to ride on and assault Mobile." ·

"And it will end the war?" Ayers asked.

Taylor let out a grunt. "If it all succeeds."

"Grant doesn't care how many men he kills," Bryer added.

"Ah, but we complained that too many of our generals were overly cautious! Meade should have chased Lee after Gettysburg. This fratricide might have ended by now," Taylor said.

"But do you think we can win soon?" Bryer asked.

Taylor stared over at Ian, then shrugged and pointed to the map. "Renowned Confederate General P. T. Beauregard is in here somewhere—and he'll do his damned best to detour anyone from Richmond. Jubal Early could catch up with the men in the Shenandoah—"

He broke off suddenly, listening. Someone was singing. A plaintive ballad, in a high, clear voice, both sweet and powerful.

"My sister," Ian murmured.

"I know," Taylor said, rising. He slid his despatch into the inner pocket of his frockcoat and started out of Bryer's living quarters. The small tent was not far from the larger one where the colonel and his nurses tended to the wounded they had managed to gather. Since the day was warm, the canvas walls had been rolled up so that the breeze could cool the injured men.

Tia was seated on a camp chair in the middle of the tent. Someone had supplied her with a guitar; she strummed the chords lightly as she sang her song—one popular with both Northern and Southern soldiers, promoting neither side, but ruing the cruelty of death.

She had a rapt audience.

The soldiers with camp cots lay upon them; amputees with bandaged stumps sat on the ground or leaned against trees just outside the enclosure. Nurses and orderlies had halted in their tasks. And even Cecilia had stopped her busy fretting around "her boys" to enjoy the fact that, for once, they seemed to have forgotten their pain.

When Tia finished her song, they applauded.

"Play 'Dixie'!" someone called to her.

Her eyes shot up with surprise as she looked for the speaker.

"Ma'am, it's me, over here. My name's Corporal Hutchins. I was born right smack on the Suwannee River, though I went to school up in New York. I'm still a Southerner—I just don't cotton to the idea of breaking up the Union. So play 'Dixie' for me, if you will. The boys won't mind."

"You could play any danged thing you want, Mrs. Douglas, and we won't mind a bit!" another man called.

And so she sang "Dixie." Then someone asked her that since she was in a Union camp and they had all enjoyed "Dixie," would she mind terribly doing "The Star-Spangled Banner," and she hesitated, but then she sang the song. And when she was done, she handed the guitar back to one of the men and thanked them.

"Don't you worry none about Canby Jacobs, Mrs. Douglas!" the man who had asked for "Dixie" called out to her. "We fellows will put in money from our pay, get him properly embalmed so that he can be returned to that young wife of his!"

"Maybe he wanted to be buried on Florida soil," she said softly.

"He loved Florida, but he loved his wife more."

"Then that will be very kind, sir, if you can see that his body is returned to his wife. Properly put back together."

She started walking through the tent. Taylor was still some distance from her, and he was sure she hadn't seen him yet.

Captain Ayers, leader of the company he had sent out scouting yesterday, suddenly stepped in front of her.

"Mrs. Douglas, hello, how do you do. Excuse me for waylaying you . . . but I could swear that we've met before."

Taylor saw her hesitate; saw her pallor. *Yes, of course, Ayers had seen her yesterday. As Godiva. Leading him from the Rebs—back to their own camp.*

"My brother is with the camp here, sir. Colonel Ian

McKenzie. Perhaps I bear quite a resemblance to him. He and my other brother, Julian, are so much alike they could be mistaken for one another; even the cousins in my family bear a close resemblance to each other."

Ayers was smiling. "Ma'am, you don't look like any man I've ever met; that is certain."

"Perhaps you've been to my father's home, Cimarron."

"No, ma'am, it's not that . . ."

It had gone too far. Taylor strode through the tent of injured, reaching Tia's side. He set an arm around her shoulders. "Ayers!"

"Sir!" Ayers saluted. He was a fine young cavalry captain, steady, brave, and dependable. "Forgive me. I have this uncanny feeling that I have met your wife before."

"Well, Captain Ayers, I agree that she resembles no man—but if you know her brothers and family as I do, it's true, there are features they share, such as the shape of their eyes, the structure of their faces. I am kin to Colonel McKenzie's cousin myself, and I can tell you, that even the Seminole McKenzies bear a striking resemblance to one another."

"Perhaps that is it. Forgive me," Ayers said again. "It's been a pleasure. It is my understanding that you served with Rebel forces in your brother's field hospital. It was kind of you to bring your talents here today."

"I pity all men maimed by this war, sir," Tia said. With his arm around her, Taylor could feel that she was shaking.

"Amen!" Ayers said.

"Captain, we've yet to fully discuss certain events. Tia, my love, if you'll forgive me, I have business with Captain Ayers. I'll not be long."

"Taylor, you must do your duty!" she said, turning to him. Her dark eyes on his were grateful. Her hand, laid against his chest, felt oddly right.

He stared down at her. Had they reached some strange sort of truce? Brought on by the absurdity of a lie turned real?

He caught her hand, smiled, brushed a kiss on her fingertips.

There was a general call of appreciation from the men—hoots and whistles.

"Aye, there, Colonel, you've found yourself a really wild Rebel to win!"

"That I have!" he agreed.

But smiling still, he stepped around her. And his heart seemed to squeeze. Had he won her? No, he had not really begun to do so.

His future with her, like the war, remained to be seen.

# Chapter 15

With an oath of impatience, Rhiannon ripped up the fifth letter she had tried to write, gnawed at her lip, and started again.

*Dear Mrs. Davis,*
*My name is Rhiannon McKenzie and I am the wife of Colonel Julian McKenzie, surgeon, Florida militia. I believe that the name McKenzie is familiar to you; my brother-in-law, Ian, was well known to President Davis before the division of the states. Ian was a West Point graduate and serving in the army when President Davis was Secretary of War. Jerome McKenzie, a cousin-in-law, is with the Confederate navy and captains one of the most successful blockade runners of the war. Though I admit to grave antisecession sentiment myself, I have worked with my husband in the field saving the lives of Confederate men. I have seen the tragedies of this war, North and South, and have come to put a great value on all life, yet most of all, on the lives of our children. Madam, I have often heard of the love you bear your own. I am sometimes haunted by dreams and visions, and I fear an accident could befall one of your children. Please, I beg you, heed this warning, and do not think me insane from the depravities of war. I see a child falling from a balcony. I have found that though sometimes my dreams are cruel pictures that I can do nothing to stop, sometimes they are but warnings, and so I beg of you, take care with your children on the balcony of your beautiful house. With all prayers and best wishes for you and yours, I can*

*only hope to understand the full burden of all that you
carry with the war.*
  *Sincerely, Rhiannon McKenzie*

She looked pensively at what she had written this
time. The first lady of the Confederacy might very well
think that she was totally insane, and throw the note
away.

It might never reach her.

She still had to try. The dream was far too haunting
to ignore.

Rhiannon laid her head on the table. No, she could
not prevent all the awful deaths of the war! And still,
knowing that a child could needlessly die . . .

Her own sentiments remained staunchly antisecession-
ist—and antislavery. She was comfortable in her father-
in-law's house.

Alaina, though married to a Union officer, remained
a Rebel at heart.

Could either of them make a trip to Richmond?

How could she, with an infant? How could she risk
her own child? And if Julian knew what she was even
thinking . . .

He would say that he would get the letter through.
And surely, he would. But would it be enough?

Alaina could not go. She had her own two small chil-
dren, and since Christmas . . . well, it seemed likely that
Alaina was going to have a third babe. If Alaina could
get to St. Augustine where her new cousin-in-law, Risa
McKenzie stayed, waiting for some word from
Jerome . . .

There was also Sydney, an ardent Rebel—but married
now and in Washington, D.C.

That left . . .

Tia. She was out there somewhere near St. Augustine.
Assisting Julian in her place. If she could just reach her
sister-in-law . . .

Yes. Tia was perfect. The Southern sister of a Southern surgeon who had tirelessly pledged himself to the
lives of so many. Captured for his Cause, in the South,

fighting for life once again. Tia, the daughter of Jarrett McKenzie, respected and consulted by leaders from both sides.

Who could not be faulted for going to Richmond.

She rose suddenly, quickly. She would give her letter to Jarrett, and ask him for an escort across the state. To join Julian. She had lingered behind her husband long enough. The baby was strong, big, healthy—and she had never felt better. She was longing to see her husband; her in-laws would understand.

Yet as she swung around, she saw that Alaina was standing in the doorway.

"Rhiannon, what are you up to?"

"I'm going to find Julian."

Alaina stared at her for a minute.

"I'm going with you. You're not really looking for Julian, are you?"

"Of course I am. I love my husband."

"I didn't say you didn't," Alaina told her stubbornly. "I'm still going with you!"

But she paled suddenly, her palm going to her stomach. "Excuse me!" she said, and turned to flee to her private quarters.

Rhiannon got her traveling bag from the wardrobe and started to pack.

Alaina appeared back in her doorway. "A Christmas present from *your* husband, I think," Rhiannon said, flashing Alaina a smile.

"I was never so sick before."

"You never had twins before."

"Twins!" Alaina grabbed the door frame.

Rhiannon had to laugh. "I'm sorry; I was teasing. I don't know. But you can't come with me—and I have to go."

"You're not going to try to get to Richmond, are you?"

"No, I'm just going to find someone who can. Without causing trouble, of course."

"Of course," Alaina agreed. "I'll help you pack."

\*     \*     \*

Tia was exhausted. She had meant to leave the oppression of the hospital tent, feeling as if she had done her duty. She had held Canby's hand as he died; she had sung more songs when the other injured men had asked her to continue for them.

And in the midst of it all . . .

Captain Ayers had recognized her. Thank God, he didn't know why he had recognized her. Taylor had come to her defense. Perhaps he'd had to do so. He had his sense of honor. He had married her. She had cast him into the situation, and he had seemed very bitter, but then . . .

When Taylor had left with Ayers, Cecilia came to her side. "We can use more help, if you're willing."

And so Tia had turned back to assist the wounded. Most were very brave, grateful for the water she brought them, the quinine with which she dosed them, the bandages and poultices she carefully applied. It was at the end of a very long day when Cecilia slipped an arm through hers and led her from the hospital tent.

"We'll walk down to the stream. It's cool and beautiful there. This is a wonderful place, I think! With pines and ponds and a river and little brooks everywhere! I understand why people come here. I had never thought in a hundred years I would want to come to such a new and *uncivilized* place at this, yet I love it!"

"Where are you from?"

"Massachusetts. And it's very, very cold there!"

The soldiers smiled or nodded as the two women walked through the camp. Tia was so accustomed to running that she had to remind herself that no one was after her.

The pines were shadowed as the sun fell. Cecilia knew exactly where she was heading; along a well-trampled trail that must have been used often by the people in the camp. It led to one of the ponds in the pine forest, fresh spring water that was cool and delightfully fresh. She doused her face with it, drank deeply, and sat back on the embankment, feeling the cool spring air wash over her.

"It's wonderful to have you here," Cecilia said, leaning back beside her. "You're so very good."

"I admit to thinking that you are quite incredibly competent, organized, and efficient yourself!" Tia said.

"I am," Cecilia said, laughing.

"You're also well supplied with bandages, quinine, poultices, morphine, laudanum . . ."

"Yes, we're lucky in that."

"Lucky in many way," she said. "Like my own father, yours is willing to risk himself to help others."

"Oh, my father is wonderful. I remember, at the beginning of the war, when I wanted to help him—as I always had before!—I was given such a miserable time by some of the good society matrons. Nursing was not ladylike, so they said. I shouldn't see the soldiers, touch the soldiers—"

"Really?" Tia asked, startled to realize that someone who seemed as serene, feminine, and dignified as Cecilia Ayers could have possibly faced the same censure she had known. "I thought women were persecuted only in the South."

"No, I think we have all been vilified for wanting to be sensible and help. Even though I am a doctor's daughter, I have had my share of criticism. Oh, it was inevitable that women would be needed to help, and when Dorothea Dix was appointed superintendent of women nurses, *some* women were even welcome." She smiled, her dimples showing. "But not me! She said that I was too young and too pretty to work in a hospital in Washington, and she wouldn't have me. Her nurses had to be thirty and plain—no young ladies with romantic notions were going to work with her! So I turned to Father, and although he really hadn't wanted me on the field at that time, he said that no one could tell him who could or could not help him there, so I have been on the field with him ever since. I *hope* that by now I am good."

"I keep hoping that I'm good, too," Tia said. "When I started with my brother, our skirmishes were small, and we could deal with our injured. Then we had off-shore battles, and bombardments, and bigger skirmishes.

I'll never forget the first time we had a large number of injured. Julian told me to wash a soldier's face. The poor fellow was even worse than my friend Canby today—a ball had torn away part of his nose and both eyes. I thought I'd be sick. I somehow managed to clean his face, but then I needed air. Julian had had to amputate a number of limbs, and I tripped over them trying to leave the tent. I fell right into the pile of arms and legs. But I knew then that if I gave way, I'd probably panic and run and never come back. So I stood up, decided I didn't need the air as much as the injured needed me— and I went back. There is still so much that is so painful, so melancholy, and yet now, when I see men shattered by their injuries, there is not much that I flinch from anymore. So many 'niceties' seem nothing more than silly to me."

Cecilia nodded in understanding. "You can't let petty things concern you—I learned that long ago. To be honest, in a way, I did not blame Dragon Six—that is what many of her nurses call her! Some women cannot take the horrors they see. And some do think that they will find romance—not wounds that exude pus and blood and stumps on which one must change bandages without causing arteries to bleed! Some young ladies thought they would find officers to marry—not enlisted men with wives and children poor and dying and needing real help!"

"On both sides, it's the same," Tia murmured.

Cecilia smiled. "Well, I have been in the war all these years, and I am truly afraid that I may end up an old maid! So I have decided what I will do when the war is over."

"What is that?"

"I'm going to medical school. I'm going to be a doctor myself. Father says it's a fine idea. There's a woman named Elizabeth Blackwell who is the first of our sex, they say, to have earned a medical degree, and she was one of the very first to realize that we would need medical supplies and all manner of things for our troops—

including things as simple as socks! There are other
women doctors now, not many, but I intend to be one."

"You should do it. If you have the desire, yes, you
should!" Tia applauded.

Cecilia stood. "Thank you for your encouragement.
But now I must get back to my father. Don't get up—
you look relaxed there at last by the water. Thank you
also for what you have done for our men, be they
your enemies."

Tia smiled at her. "Thank *you*—for trusting me."

"I think you are a friend, a dear friend," Cecilia told
her, and turning, she walked away, back through the
pines.

Tia sat awhile longer, staring at the cool water, feeling
the soft breeze that wafted through the pines. She closed
her eyes, realizing how tired she was.

Then her eyes flew open. She had to go back now.
She had become so involved with the men, she had forgotten that Ian would be leaving.

She leapt to her feet, spun around—and froze. Taylor
was there, had been there, she realized. Leaning against
a pine, watching her.

"I wasn't trying to escape anything," she murmured
defensively.

"I wasn't accusing you of trying to escape any*thing*.
If you were trying to escape, I assume it would be an
any*one*. Me."

"But I wasn't—"

"I didn't say you were."

He continued to watch her, still leaning casually
against the pine.

"I am really well aware that, as you said, you have
done me a tremendous service."

"Nothing so deep and grave that I cannot endure,"
he said lightly. "I apologize if I caused you a tremendous
amount of guilt."

"Well . . . I . . . you made it quite plain how you feel
about marriage."

She backed away awkwardly as he left the pine and
came toward her.

"Actually," he said, a slight smile on his features, "you have somewhat managed to change my mind."

"I'm glad it's not the torment you expected."

"And what is it to you?" he inquired. He'd reached her. She couldn't go anywhere else or she'd be backing into the water.

She hesitated, meeting his eyes. "Not torment."

"That's right. You don't dislike me."

"And I honestly wasn't running."

"I'm glad. I grow wearing of dragging you about."

Her eyes fell. "I need to see my brother. If he's still here, if I haven't missed him. I can't believe I became so involved I forgot that I might not have much time with him before—"

"He isn't leaving anytime soon."

"No?" she inquired, uneasy. He gazed at her in a strange way, not angry, not mocking.

She was surprised when he looked away for a moment, then his eyes were back on hers. "No, he will be with the camp several days here, I believe, then he'll be going in to St. Augustine."

"Oh!" she said, pleased. If she was going to live with the enemy, at least her brother would be among their number.

"Yes," he said, and his voice had a husky and slightly harsh quality to it. "Yes, you'll be with your brother. For a while, at least. So there is no need to hurry to him now."

She felt the breeze again, touching her cheeks. They felt very warm. This was so strange. The night before had been a tempest of emotions, tangled lies, a swiftness of events. But now, seconds stretched out as he stared at her. Dusk turned darker. Though the sky still remained somewhat blue, the moon began to appear as a half-crown about the treetops.

"You managed quite well today."

"Did you think I would falter?"

"You didn't turn away from your enemy."

"We treated Union injured at Olustee Station."

"Of course . . . as we treated Rebs."

She lowered her head. "An old friend of mine was here."

"An old Yankee friend?"

She nodded. "He died."

"You comforted him?"

She nodded. "His . . . lung was blown away. And half his face." She was feeling very uncertain, afraid she was going to cry.

"He talked about my father . . . Cimarron. Times that are now long gone by . . ."

She suddenly covered her face with her hands. And she was glad to feel him pull her into his arms as tears began sliding down her cheeks.

"It's all right, Tia."

"It wasn't all right. He had a wife and a child to live for, and he was so terribly hurt—you could see what remained of his lung. It was amazing he lived so long."

"Sh . . ." he said softly, easing back down to the pine embankment with her. He held her against him, rocking slowly. "Tia, you have done this so long! It's the bitter truth of the war—men die, and they do not do so prettily."

"But his wife, his poor young wife—"

"There are thousands of poor young wives out there. Thousands of young widows who may live another fifty years or so, and who will live those years full of bitterness and regret."

"Widows and . . ." She broke off suddenly, remembering the picture her mother had given him at Christmas. The picture of Abby.

"Oh!" she murmured suddenly. "I'm so sorry, really, I forgot . . ."

Instantly, she felt him stiffen. His arms did not seem to hold her so closely. *He hadn't wanted to marry. She wasn't his real wife; his real wife lay dead. She was the Rebel liar who had cast a shadow upon his honor, and forced his hand.*

"It's all right," he said.

"How can it be?" she whispered, lifting her damp

cheeks to seek out his eyes. "I heard that she was shot, that she died in your arms—"

"It's all right," he said again. "If you don't mind, it's a painful memory, one I don't care to relive."

"But—"

He suddenly set her from him, rising. "I believe that Ian is in his tent. One has been set up for him not far from mine. He is probably anxious to see you as well."

She was embarrassed to realize that she had been dismissed. Cleanly, clearly dismissed.

"Oh, course," she murmured coolly. "Thank you. I'll find my brother."

He didn't say anything. She rose, but he didn't even seem to notice. He was watching the water.

She walked back through the pines.

The camp was busy with dinner preparations. Sergeant Henson waved at her. She waved back, then seeing the large, newly erected tent near Taylor's, she walked toward it with a purpose. "Ian?" she called.

"Tia!" he replied from within, then appeared at the flap. "Come in!"

She did so. His home away from home already bore marks of Ian. A locket with Alaina's likeness and a tendril of hair, a common piece of jewelry, especially for a soldier, lay on his camp desk. Letters lay strewn next to it, along with the manual he was reading, a text on gunshot wounds. His frockcoat hung on his folding chair, and his shaving paraphernalia had been set up at a standing mirror.

"Sit!"

He indicated the foot of the cot. She sat there, and he took the folding chair himself.

"I was so afraid I'd missed you," Tia told him. "The day was strange, passing by so quickly. I'm glad you're still here."

"I never would have left without saying goodbye," he assured her. "And making certain that you were happy, well cared for. And that you understand what you've done."

"What I've done?" she echoed.

Ian was quiet for moment, then he rose and went to the camp desk and fingered the locket carrying the likeness of his wife. "Tia, you've married a very well known Union cavalry officer, renowned for his abilities to find anyone, anywhere, anytime. And for his ability to shoot the wings off a fly at a hundred feet."

"Well," she breathed. "Thank God I did not marry an inept cavalry officer!"

Her brother turned toward her, apparently seeing the attempted humor in her words. "You have gone from working in a Rebel camp—to working in a Yankee camp."

She lifted a hand in a weak gesture. "The men bleed the same."

"And do you treat them the same?"

"Of course! Why would I be any different from Julian or Brent? I worked well today with your Yankees, Ian. Very well. You may ask Miss Bryer—or the men, for that matter."

He came to the bed, sitting down beside her, searching out her eyes and staring at her very sternly. "Tia, I'm sorry, I can't help but find this very suspicious."

Her throat tightened. "Why?"

"You didn't come here to get into Taylor's papers, did you?"

"No!" she denied heatedly, jumping to her feet.

"You're certain?"

"Ian," she said, frowning at him, "it never occurred to me that Taylor would carry papers that meant anything to me. I was tending to wounded Rebel soldiers throughout the war—*not* attending high-level strategy meetings!"

"The point I'm making is this: You have changed your life. Your own side will mistrust you for the Yank you have married; the Yanks will mistrust you for what you have been in the past."

"I've no interest in the opinions of others."

"You should. Opinions make people dangerous."

"I did not marry Taylor to pry into Yankee secrets,"

she said, agitated. "Oh, Ian, I don't want to argue with you."

"I don't want to argue either, Tia. I just want you to understand that there is no turning back."

"I don't want to run anywhere. I served well here today. I didn't even rifle through the pockets of the dead or dying!" she said bitterly. "Though some of *your* men are butchers who would kill helpless Rebels."

"What?"

She paused, horrified at what she had said. How could she explain to Ian that she had heard the men in the woods and that was why she had wound up running here to Taylor?

"Nothing."

"What did you say, Tia? That wasn't nothing!"

"All right. I think that some of your men would just as soon kill an injured Reb as touch him!" she said.

"And why do you think that?"

"I-I heard them talking today." She wished fervently that she wasn't going to have to fall into another length of lies.

Last time she had lied to him, her world had made a total inversion.

"Whom did you hear talking?"

"Just—just a group of the men. By the hospital tent."

"If you see these men again," he said sharply, "show me who they are, and we'll find out the truth of the matter."

"You'll find out the truth? How can you? You're leaving."

"No, the despatches gave different orders."

"But . . . I'm not sure that Taylor will believe this either, and—"

"I will take care of it."

She frowned. "But if Taylor is in full command—"

"Taylor will be—" Ian broke off. "He didn't tell you?"

"No—he didn't tell me! Tell me what?"

"He's been ordered out on special assignment. I'll take his place until these troops return to St. Augustine."

"He's been ordered—out?"

"I'm very sorry. I wish they had given me the assignment. As it is . . . well, you'll have to stay in St. Augustine. Risa is there. She'll be glad to have you with her."

She was surprised at the way her stomach wretched. *He was leaving; Taylor was leaving.*

And he hadn't even thought to tell her.

She shook her head, feeling her fingers clench into fists at her side. "I'll go back to Julian then. It's insane for me to live among the enemy if Taylor isn't with me. I'll—"

She was interrupted by the sound of a deep voice at the entrance to the tent. "You'll go to St. Augustine, as Ian said!"

She leapt up, startled to see that Taylor had come quietly into the tent. And had issued his command.

"I'm sorry, Taylor," Ian said. "I didn't realize you hadn't told her, that she didn't know."

"It doesn't matter. She knows now," Taylor said. "What does matter, Tia, is that you will not return to *your old ways*!"

"*I* will not return to my old ways!" Tia repeated angrily. And suddenly it all irritated her, not just the war, but the world itself seemed unfair. "And Alaina must watch her step as well, and Cecilia shouldn't work in a hospital becase she isn't homely enough! This is all so absurd and bizarre! Oh, the hell with you both!" With angry force, she slipped beneath the tent flap, exiting in a sudden passion.

"She's really upset," she heard her brother say. "I understand, of course. She didn't realize that you were leaving. I honestly thought you'd had time to tell her."

"It's all right," Taylor replied. "Let her go. There is no way out of it."

*Let her go!* he'd said.

So she went.

With long, angry strides, she walked away from her brother's quarters. She headed straight back for the pines, glad of the welcoming darkness that was beginning to fall around her. She stood before the cool pond beneath the pines.

*My horse!* she thought. *Where is my horse? If only I had her—*

She nearly screamed with surprise when a hand landed on her shoulder. Instinctively, she jerked free, backing away in a circle.

Taylor. Damn him. Damn him for his ability to move like a panther in the pines. Too quick, too swift, too silent. Too . . .

She hadn't thought that he would come.

"What the hell are you doing?"

"I am walking through the pines. What does it look like I'm doing?"

"Trying to find a way out of the pines," he said flatly.

"Oh, really? Who will chase me once you're gone? What difference does it really make? You said—*let her go.* I heard you."

He folded his arms over his chest. "So just where was it you thought you were going?"

She crossed her arms over her chest and stared back at him. "Just where was it that you meant I should go?"

"Back to our tent."

"*Our* tent? How generous you've suddenly become. Our tent. A Yankee tent. Thank you—I don't want part ownership in a Union tent."

"Tia, I don't have much time. I'm not going to spend it arguing with you."

"Good. Save yourself any aggravation. Don't spend the time with me at all."

"Tia, walk back, or I'll take you myself."

She stood tall and stiffly, staring at him. And then she was absolutely amazed at her own language when she told him what he should do with himself, and she didn't even understand herself, didn't know why she felt so angry and so much like crying, all at the same time.

"All right. That's it. I've had it."

"You've had it?" she repeated. "*I've* had it!"

"Run, then. Go on, run."

"What the hell is this game you're playing now? Quit

that, or I swear I shall slug you right back, and I have a very good right hook, I grew up with two brothers. I didn't come here to run, you fool. I never intended to run—"

"Oh, yes, you did. You very much so wanted to run. So go on. Do it. Go. Let me give you a little help . . ."

He shoved her shoulder. Outraged and feeling a strange trickle of real fear down her spine, she backed away slowly.

"Do it!"

His fingers were knotted into fists, and she was suddenly certain he intended her real violence.

She turned and ran. She was right on the edge of the pond and she stepped into the shallows. The water flew at the impetus of her flight, it turned to a shower, and she felt it as it catapulted up around her and fell back in huge splatters.

Stupid! she charged herself. He had goaded her into this. She was encumbered by her skirts, growing heavier in the water.

But she couldn't stop now. He was behind her.

Oh, this was insane. Madness.

And yet she ran. She was swift and fleet, and she knew it, but she had chosen the wrong path, and she was quickly bogged down.

She heard him behind her and sped forward then suddenly spun back on him. He was there, just feet away, but he stopped as well, calculating the distance—planning his pounce.

She wondered if she could outswim him.

Not with a heavy, soaking skirt . . .

But she was wearing her pantalettes.

She slipped out of her shoes then reached behind her, keeping her eyes on him. She found the buttons on the skirt—and shed it. His brow shot up with amazement.

"Ah, my love. When in danger—strip?"

"When cornered, use whatever means are available to elude the *enemy*!"

The skirt gone, she plunged into the water.

And she was very, very good. She'd spent a lifetime

in the water, in the rivers, in the bay, in fresh springs, in salt water.

But so had he.

The far side of the pond stretched before her. She realized, far too late, that he probably let her reach the shoreline first.

When she rose, she saw that he had stripped off his frockcoat, shirt, and boots, and was coming behind her. He didn't even seem hurried. Bronzed shoulders were knotted and tight fingers remained clenched into fists at his side. He didn't run; he walked with steady purpose and menace.

She swore and turned to run again. Then she felt him. A touch of energy and heat in the air at her back, a sound like the wind . . .

And he caught her by the flying length of her hair . . . .

# Chapter 16

She cried out. He released the tangle of her hair caught in her hands, but his iron grip wound around her upper arm.

He swung her around and she briefly felt the barely suppressed force of his anger. She cried out again to no avail; they crashed down into the shallows together. The pond erupted. The water cascaded around them. He lay atop her, half in the water, half out, and she shivered. She was soaked, and suddenly cold, as she hadn't been before, as she hadn't been when moving.

*He's gone mad,* she thought, *totally insane,* and she might die right there and then at his mercy. He seemed a misplaced Othello, his length atop her in the ever-darkening chill of the night. The sun hovered barely upon the horizon; the moon was rising. The glitter of his eyes seemed terrifying in the lengthening shadows.

She closed her eyes, gritting her teeth, rigid, yet shaking, waiting. His voice was as tense as the whipcord length of his sinewed body, deep, harsh.

"You can never run so far or so fast that I will not find you," he warned her. "You should know that now. Wherever you go, I will know. Wherever you might be, I will come for you. You have cast us upon this trail; this is your lie come true. So this is your game, but now, there are new rules in the game, and you'll abide by the rules, my love. Do you understand?"

"Whose rules?"

"My rules!"

"And therein lies all my argument!"

"You must understand—"

"I understand that you will not be here, that you are going on a quest for the enemy—your enemy, not mine—and I am suddenly expected to live among the enemy—my enemy, not yours! The Rebel camp is very close. I can find it. I am almost as good as my brothers in the woods."

"You'll go to St. Augustine!"

She shook her head, feeling tears form in her eyes. "Why can't you understand?" she asked him.

"Why can't *you* understand? You brought this about, but I have married you, Tia."

"A paper commitment which means nothing to you!" she reminded him.

Something passed within his eyes; she didn't know what. "My wife doesn't spy on Union soldiers, strip naked, and lead them astray."

"But it's all right for you to trap or kill Rebel soldiers. To spy on them, scout them out—"

"I'm not off to murder any soldiers!" he interrupted harshly.

"Oh? Are you planning on taking your wife with you?" she inquired.

Again, a shadow over the angry gold of his eyes. And his face was suddenly nearer hers; his thumbs moved over her cheeks. "My love, I dare not!"

"Then understand that I must return to Julian—"

"No."

"I'm not asking your permission! I'm telling you what I must do."

"There are some cells available at Fort Marion," he told her.

"What?"

"The castillo. That beautiful old Spanish fort in St. Augustine, now housing Union men! There are cells in it, I'm sure you know. James McKenzie was imprisoned there once with other savages—or *half*-savages."

He took her face between his hands. And he lowered his head even closer to hers. She felt the water wash up on the shore around her, shivered, and was then warmed. His lips came down upon hers, passionate and hard. Her face lay imprisoned within the walls of her hands. His very passion forced her lips to give way to his; the hot sweetness of his assault seemed to permeate swiftly within her. The depth of his tongue seemed to reach to unexplored places, newly discovered. The deep searing stroke of his kiss elicited fire; she had wanted to touch him—now she yearned, itched, ached to feel more.

Pinned to the embankment, she felt a rush of cold, a rush of hot. The pond against the lightning texture of his body, the air against the inferno of his kiss. She briefly recalled that the blouse she wore was borrowed; then it didn't matter because he was so determined to free her from it, and quickly. The thought touched her mind as well that this did not seem real, possible, to want someone so much, to feel such raging hunger, when she had so recently learned what such a hunger could be like to be appeased. She murmured just one protest. A sound in her throat against the force of his kiss. But he didn't seem to hear. His mouth remained upon hers, lifted, returned, touched, drank, penetrated . . . all while his fingers found buttons, ties, and ribbons. She shivered in the air, against the water, writhed when his fingers covered her breasts, when his mouth opened wetly over her nipple, that dampness so hot, so wickedly hot, where the other had been so cold . . .

His hand slid between her legs, pressing them apart. She felt his fingers there, probing. Felt a burst of sweetness erupt, a fire between her legs. Still he kissed her lips, then her breasts. His thumb moved deeply within her. She writhed, arched, longed to escape, longed for more. Even where the air touched her now, the sensation seemed erotic. He stroked mercilessly within her. Touched, stroked, excited. She had longed so for his touch. Her hands moved wildly over his shoulders. Down along his spine.

He shifted, tore at his trousers. Pressed her deeper and deeper into the embankment, then he was within her, hot, slick, vital, moving like a thunder in the earth, drawing her into the fever of his tempest. They seemed to burn at a million degrees, move more swiftly than the winds of a storm, fly higher than the sky. It was a fever seized and ignited, then burned with an energy of passion born of fury. She lost all thought of past and future, even of the present, for the damp ground did not matter, the pond did not matter, nor the onslaught of night, the concept of intrusion. She simply wanted him, wanted to feel every sensation of him within her, every pulse, every thrust, and each escalating her higher, steering her toward the ecstasy that, once tasted, became ever sweeter. Elusive, so barely known, yet awakened with the scent of his flesh, the feel of his kiss, a brush of her fingertips against the sleek bronze texture of his skin. And culminated with this so very intimate feel of him inside her, the length of him flush against her, lips, hands, sex . . .

She felt the jack-knifing of his body as he climaxed. The warmth filled her, permeating her, erotic and sweet, creating the same sweet lightning within her. Bursting sweet, erasing the world, the war, the embankment, the night . . .

So wonderful, so good. Almost a taste of death, and surely, almost a glimpse of heaven. With her eyes closed, she could see the velvet of the night, the bursting of the stars. There was a plain upon which she drifted, and she stayed there . . . stayed, not wanting to come down. And yet, at first, when she did, she did not mind so much, for she still felt him with her, in her, reposed, not yet withdrawing. She loved the feel of his body still pressed to hers, the intimacy of his arms around her, the scent of him, the way his arms remained around her . . .

Then she felt the water. Cold now. Each little lap of it against her seemed to chill her more. A night wind was coming indeed; the breeze picked up with every passing second. He seemed not to notice the cold until she began to shiver. He withdrew at last, rising, while she drew into herself. He adjusted his trousers and collected the damp clothing he had strewn about, then he came to her, reaching down a hand to her. She didn't accept it at first, but she took her wet pantalettes from him. Shivering violently now, she stepped into them, then he helped her into the corset, his fingers working the ties where hers most certainly could not, and then buttons of her blouse as she donned that wet piece of attire as well. Yet, when she was dressed in her sodden clothing, she found out that she could soon get wetter.

"It's shortest and safest to return the way we came."

"Safest?"

"There may be pickets around the opposite shore, but your skirt and my frockcoat are there. We need to swim back."

She nodded, starting out. She was still shivering. She felt him at her side and she knew that she would never escape him on land—or water.

He didn't know that she really had no desire to escape him, but it was best that he not learn such details.

She reached the shore from where she had begun her reckless plunge, yet as she hovered in the water, too cold now to exit, she wondered if he had not purposely baited her. Perhaps neither of them had known it; they had achieved the outcome they'd desired.

"You're not going to get any warmer remaining in the water," he told her, taking her hand, helping her to her feet. She stumbled, having to cling to him as she rose.

He had her skirt. It was thoroughly soaked, yet she put it back on—the easiest way to return to camp. Which was what she wanted to do quickly now. She was numb with cold, her borrowed clothing as drenched and heavy as the midnight mass of hair spilling down the length of her back.

His frockcoat was dry; he slipped it over her shoulders, then collected her shoes and his boots and shirt. With an arm around her, he started leading her through the trees.

"There is a faster way," she told him.

"Oh?"

"The way I came yesterday."

"Lead on."

"You know where it is—you followed me last night."

"Um, I had forgotten." He turned, leading her along the twisting, slender trail through the pines that was scarcely a trail at all. They emerged from the trees at the rear of his tent, hurried across the few feet from the edge of the pines to the tent, and crawled beneath the canvas. A kerosene lamp had been set on his desk and lit, filling the tent with a shadowy yellow light.

He dropped their footwear and his shirt by the trunk, then turned to her.

She was still shaking. He took his frockcoat from her shoulders and ordered, "Get out of those things now."

She felt too cold to move. She wanted to protest, just for the sake of argument. She didn't. She just stood there, and he returned to her, spinning her around to work at the tiny wet buttons and ties. When her clothing fell to her feet, he cast a blanket around her, collected the wet things, and started out of the tent.

"Taylor!" she murmured, pulling the blanket tightly around her.

"What?"

"What—what will you say?"

"That your clothing is wet."

Her cheeks burned. "But—"

"No one will ask questions," he said, then left the tent.

She hugged the blanket tighter, sitting on the cot, trying to get warm. He returned within minutes, bringing with him a small soldier's-issue pot filled with something that smelled delicious and steamed invitingly. "Henson's famous chicken soup," he said, offering her the pot.

She accepted it, glad of the warmth that thawed her fingers first, then filled her inside as she swallowed down some of the contents. It was freshly made.

"Henson's been stealing Southern chickens again, so it seems!" he said with mock concern.

She ignored the bait of his comment and asked, "What about you?"

"I ate earlier with the men."

She didn't argue. She was starving, and Henson's stew—be it made with stolen chickens or not—was delicious.

He watched her for a moment, then turned away, left

the tent, and returned with two cups of coffee. She had finished the soup; he took the pot from her, exchanged it for the coffee.

She drank the coffee as well. She almost felt warm.

He took the cup from her, but she stood, holding the blanket around her, moving away from the bed. She heard him peel away his damp trousers, then lift the glass and blow out the lamp.

She kept her distance from him, standing in the darkness.

She heard him crawl into the camp bed, and then a moment later, sigh.

"Come to bed, Tia."

"When are you leaving?"

"Soon."

"I'm not tired."

"Then come for the warmth."

"I'm no longer cold."

"Get in here then, to be eased."

"I'm not in any pain."

"You will be—damn it! I don't have much time; I refuse to spend it alone. Come to bed."

She walked slowly toward the camp bed. With his hawklike vision, he saw clearly while she was blinded by the darkness. He was up when she came, drawing her down beside him, keeping the blanket around her, drawing her close to warm her. She felt his hands, his touch, the length of him, something wonderful about being with him. She wanted to sleep beside him, awake beside him.

But he did not intend to be there long.

Yet she was surprised to hear him whisper, "Tia, do you think I *want* to go?"

She turned against him, burrowing her face against his chest, breathing in the memory of him. His hand smoothed her hair; she inched closer. And then, in a few minutes, she heard his breath quicken, and she knew that she had been seducing him, her knuckles running against his chest, then the hardness of his belly, grazing her sex . . . just barely, again and again. A hint, a tease . . .

Soon, she was in his arms again, and he made love very slowly then, so, so slowly, and she didn't even know just how thoroughly she had been seduced in return until she found him kissing her suddenly to silence the cry that was escaping her . . .

Then the reality of night was with her again. The night, the darkness, the camp beyond the intimacy of the Yankee tent. And again he repeated to her, "There is nothing I want less than to go."

"Then don't go."

"I must."

"You are *ordered*."

"Because I believe in what I'm doing."

"And so do I," she whispered passionately. "So do I!"

Then she wished that she had not said the words, for she realized that though he didn't answer her, and though he held her, he lay there awake. Thinking that she did believe in what she was doing. And that made her dangerous.

"Taylor, if I swear to you—"

"You've lied too many times!"

"But—"

"You'll go to St. Augustine. And you'll be there when I come for you."

"Good morning."

One very strange fact of marriage seemed to be that she awoke far more tired than she had been when she went to bed. Yet, this morning, the voice that greeted Tia was a startling one. She had barely opened her eyes, but at the sound of these words, they flew open. Gathering her covers around her, she twisted, and to her amazement she saw Risa, her cousin Jerome's wife, seated comfortably in Taylor's camp chair before his folding desk. She looked wonderful—fresh, beautiful, relaxed, out of place and time in the camp, elegant and composed. Her auburn hair was neatly bound at her nape; her eyes, green as the pine forests, were bright and amused. Risa was the daughter of Union General Magee; once, before the war, she had very nearly married Ian. The war made for strange bedfellows, most certainly, because Ian had married Alaina, an absolute paragon of the virtues of the old South, and Risa, who was very nearly a walking, breathing image of the "Battle Hymn of the Republic," had married Jerome—a blockade runner still doing just that, running circles around the Union navy.

"Risa!"

"Tia McKenzie—excuse me, Douglas. My, my, what will this war come to next!" Risa teased.

Tia longed to hop up and hug her cousin-in-law; but in her state of undress, she did not. Risa looked at the book she had been reading. "I admit, I should have been reading *Shoals and Sandbars off the Florida Coast*! she told Tia. "But your husband does have some wonderful literature here, beautifully bound Shakespeare, Bacon, Defoe . . . I wonder if he ever has the time to read for pleasure, though I've heard that many of the men most responsible for the war do find that reading is what allows them to keep their sanity."

"Risa, I'm so pleased to see you . . . but what . . ." Tia began, and then her voice trailed away. She drew the covers to her chest and sat up. "I was about to ask you what you're doing here, but I think I know. Either my brother or my husband sent for you—to keep me under control."

Risa smiled. "Something like that. An escort party arrived for me yesterday. I felt a wee bit guilty myself, leaving a new doctor in St. Augustine with many wounded coming in. But there are a number of male military nurses there to help him at the moment, what with the situation at Olustee Station being recent and so many men from the army still in the state . . ." She broke off, shrugging. "Were you in some kind of trouble?"

"Who sent for you, Taylor or Ian?" Tia asked, rather than reply to the question.

Risa hesitated, but then apparently decided to tell her the truth. "Taylor sent for me. Ian knew about it, but I don't think he was overly concerned. He still sees you as his little sister, and despite your wrong-headed opinions, he assumes you will listen to him. He can't begin to imagine that you would disobey him or your new husband if what they asked was surely for your own safety."

Tia looked away for a moment. "Then, I'm sorry to say it, but my brother is a fool, and he should have learned better dealing with his own wife!"

"But his wife didn't love him at first, did she?" Risa reminded her. "While now . . . they share everything. And he assumes, of course, that you love him."

"I love both my brothers, and they know it. I've been with Julian through the majority of the war and Ian has known it."

"But that was before you married a Federal officer, wasn't it? And then again, Ian has no idea what else you may be doing."

Tia stared at Risa again. "Are you implying—"

Risa leaned toward her. "Yes. I'll tell you exactly what I'm implying. There's a rumor out about a new Southern spy, the likes of whom rival Belle Boyd and Rose Greenhow."

"Oh, that's preposterous."

"If you know nothing about it, how can you deny the rumors so quickly?"

"What did Taylor tell you?"

"Taylor told me nothing. I simply know the war rather well—and I know you."

"I never spied on anyone," Tia said angrily.

"Rumor does have a tendency to become exaggerated," Risa agreed. "You don't have to answer me, but I'll tell you exactly why I'm here. I think that you are this 'Godiva' they talk about—I admit, I've never met anyone else with the hair to create such a disguise, and I'm amazed more people haven't figured it out."

"Now that's ridiculous! Many, many women have very long hair."

"Very long, sleek, raven-black hair, and the form and figure of a Circe! And it has to be someone very, very familiar with the area. Then, I've actually had Godiva described to me. You see, I've met a few of the men led astray by Godiva.''

"Risa, I never—"

She broke off, alarmed by the sudden sound of gunfire and a barrage of shouts. Her eyes met Risa's. Risa, she saw, was as startled as she by the commotion.

"My God, what—"

Tia leapt up in alarm, dragging the covers with her like a cloak. Both Taylor and her brother were out there. She had to find out what had happened.

"Tia, wait—you don't go running out when you hear gunfire!" Risa, always the general's daughter, called. But Tia was already heading out, her heart in her throat. Men were running everywhere. Risa caught hold of her.

"You can't run out like this! At least get dressed."

Torn, Tia wasted several precious seconds thinking that someone may lie dying while she was taking the time for concessions to society. She was totally encompassed in the covers.

"This might not even involve Taylor or Ian!" Risa insisted.

"But it does. I know it. Help me! I haven't anything—"

"Tia, but you do. I brought you all kinds of clothing."

"Then give me something quickly, please!" Tia said.

"All right. I'll help."

Tia stepped back into the tent. Risa was as good as her word, ready with a cotton print day dress to slip right over Tia's shoulders as she let the covers fall.

Tia muttered a quick "Thank you," eschewed the concept of looking for shoes, and went tearing outside. By then she could see that the men were gathering around a large circle by the hospital tent. She wedged her way into the circle, felt hands upon her shoulders, and knew that Risa was there. She became aware that there was a pileup of men in the center of the circle. All around the circumference, the men were cheering—and throwing out suggestions.

"What's going on?"

"Fight—big fight!" one of the soldiers said cheerfully,

then he looked at her. "Oh! Mrs. Douglas, it's . . . um . . ."

Taylor.

Taylor was in the midst of it all. As she watched, she saw that there were actually three other men in the circle, and that the three of them were coming at him. One of the men she recognized. Private Long. The soldier who had talked about killing Rebel injured.

Taylor was in his navy trousers and cavalry boots; his jacket and shirt—and weapons—were gone.

"There are three of them against him!" she said indignantly. "There were shots . . . and now this! What's going on?"

The soldier looked at her again uncomfortably.

"There was an incident . . . with some Rebs," he said uncomfortably.

"Get him, Colonel, get him!" someone cried, and the soldier turned from her again. "That's it, Colonel, damn, sir, but that's a good right hook."

Tia saw her brother then, on the opposite side of the circle. She tried to break through the men.

"Ma'am, you mustn't interfere now," one soldier said politely, stopping her.

She tried to break in elsewhere. A graying sergeant stopped her. "Why, Mrs. Douglas, we couldn't let no harm come to you, ma'am!"

"Tia, calm down, wait!" Risa called to her.

"They'll kill him! And Ian is just standing there!" Tia said indignantly, escaping Risa's touch upon her arm.

Wrenching furiously from the next man who tried to stop her, she made it around the circle to where Ian stood. At that point, one of the men lay on the ground. Two of them were making a calculated and coordinated running leap for her husband.

"Ian! What's happening? Stop this! My God—"

She tried to rush past her brother, but there was no way to do so. He grabbed her back, not in the least afraid of using force with her, as any other man might have been.

"Stop, Tia. Stop here, let it go."

"Let it go! He'll be pummeled—"

"He chose this."

"He chose this! But he'll be killed!"

"Tia, have faith. He knows his business."

Shouts were going out, calls, cheers, jeers.

"Ian . . ."

The men were down in the dirt on Taylor. She struggled with Ian, staring helplessly as fists and earth flew. Then, she was startled when the two soldiers on Taylor went flying. They literally seemed to soar, up and away from him, and into the dirt.

Then Taylor was standing.

Hands on his hips, he looked at the downed men. His torso was muddied; there was a long scrape down his chest. His cheeks bore evidence of the brawl as well. But the three men who had attacked him lay in the dirt without moving. For a moment, Tia thought they were dead. Astounded and confused, she listened to the roar of the men, congratulating their colonel. She could still feel Ian's hands on her shoulders.

She twisted in her brother's hold, anxious to see his face. "What happened?"

"What you wanted, I think."

"What are you talking about?"

Ian's cobalt eyes fell on hers. "They came across some Rebs, wounded at Olustee or during the skirmishing as we were chased back toward the coast."

"And?" she breathed.

"One of them has nearly died."

"Oh?" Her heart seemed to be in her throat. "You said I should be glad for this. Is the Rebel someone we know?"

"Not an old family friend, but if he is an acquaintance of yours, I don't know." He sighed, shaking his head. "We've been on an opposite side for years now. I don't know who you know, Tia," he reminded her.

"But—there was a fight in a Yankee camp over a Rebel prisoner dying?" She couldn't help sounding skeptical. There had to be enough concern here over their own dying men.

Ian's eyes fell sharply upon her again. "His condition has become much worse since he arrived."

"How?"

"A bandage was ripped from him. His sutures gave; the artery was exposed. He nearly bled to death." ·

"A bandage was ripped from him . . ."

"Tia, you said you heard men talking about killing wounded Rebels. Taylor listened to you, more than you realized. He asked some questions among the men, found out who it might have been. The Rebs had just been found and brought in. He kept an eye on the suspects and caught them in the act of trying to kill the fellow. He took them by surprise—and they shot at him. He was furious; he dragged them out here . . . and a crowd gathered."

"They tried to shoot him! He should have shot back—"

"They claim they thought they were being attacked."

"They tried to murder a man!" she whispered. "They shot at him—"

"If he'd shot back, he wouldn't have missed. And he might have faced a court-martial."

"*They* shot at *him*."

"But they claimed to think themselves under attack by Rebels coming for their wounded. And after the fiasco at Olustee . . . Taylor might have faced an inquiry at the very least. This way, the men will be sent to St. Augustine. And they'll stand trial."

She turned back to look for Taylor. He was gone. And the men who had grouped around him were also gone. The soldiers he had fought and beaten were being dragged away by other men.

"Where is he?" Tia asked anxiously.

"By the water, I would think," Ian said. "He'll want to bathe. It looked like he was wearing half the mud in Florida."

"Ian—"

His hands fell from her shoulders. "I think it will be all right if you go to him now."

Freed from her brother's hold, she ran across the camp,

through the men and to the pines. There was a picket on duty near their tent, but he smiled and waved her on. She ran quickly through the trees, bursting out on the copse before the pond where they had been the night before. As Ian had suggested, he was there, his back to her as he sat on a log. He used a yellow regulation-issue cavalry scarf to squeeze water over his shoulder.

She stood dead still for a moment, wondering if he would want her there. But without turning, he knew that she had come, and he talked to her.

"My love, please don't just stand there and gape. Come over here and be helpful."

She walked around to him, inhaling sharply as she saw the depth of the jagged wound across his chest. She'd spent so much of the war treating injuries; it was instinct and habit to fall down on her knees before him where he sat on the log, take the cloth from him, soak it, and dab carefully at the wound. "Ian told me something of what happened, but I still don't understand . . ."

He caught her hand, and still holding it, he placed his fingers under her chin, causing her face to rise, her eyes to meet his.

"You were right. There were a few men determined that the only good Reb is a dead Reb. Last night, a foraging party came across a small band of wounded Confederates, and brought them back. This morning, I thought I should look in on them—I didn't want to believe that there were such men under my command, but I can tell you, it has been a bitter war. I knew the most fanatic of the men serving beneath Captain Ayers, so I knew who to watch for." He lifted his hands. "To kill a man so vulnerable would have been cold-blooded murder. They panicked and tried to shoot me."

"You would have been within your right to shoot back."

"Thank you, no. The temptation was great, but I have no desire to defend myself on any trumped-up murder charge. I think I broke a few bones, made my point. And the men will be out of here, and under arrest."

"But this slash on your chest! This is fairly serious! It should be stitched."

"Ah, I see! And I think I've gotten your gentle touch at last, when all you want to do is stick a needle into me!"

"Taylor, I'm serious."

"So am I," he murmured wryly, but he was smiling.

"I do excellent stitches. And if you're afraid of me, your camp is well enough supplied with morphine!"

He stroked her cheek. "No morphine, not for such a trivial wound, and certainly not now. I want to be in full control of all my senses for the time I have remaining, thank you."

She flushed slightly, her eyes downcast, but persisted. "Taylor, the wound really does need to be stitched. If you don't trust me—"

"But I do trust you," he said, and her heart seemed to warm. Then he added, "In this, I trust you."

Her eyes flew to his again. "Yes, well, I know how you feel otherwise. Risa is here—to keep an eye on me, of course."

"I was under the impression that Risa was a friend, as well as Jerome's wife."

"Yes—the wife of a really wicked Rebel blockade runner."

"That wicked blockade runner is my relative as well, Godiva."

"Don't call me that!" she whispered, dabbing carefully at the wound again. "Take an injury like this too lightly, Colonel Douglas, and you'll find yourself falling prey to a fever. Even with this, gangrene could set in."

"It will be all right." He caught her hand again. "Get what you need from Dr. Bryer. Meet me back in our tent. I just want to wash the rest of this mud off. Go."

She rose, hurrying to do as he had said; the wound needed stitching. As she moved back into the camp, she was surprised when she was suddenly stopped by Captain Ayers. "Mrs. Douglas! I just wanted you to know . . . well, I'm sorry. Most soldiers would never attempt to kill an injured enemy; they know that they, too, could fall into the hands of those they fight. You must believe me. I didn't know I had men capable of such heinous actions. Don't despise all Northerners for the cruelty of a few men who have fought in one battle too many."

"I do not, sir," she said quickly, uneasy with the way Ayers watched her. She couldn't help wondering if he wouldn't one day figure out that she had been the woman he had surprised by the stream that day.

"Excuse me, please, I must see to my husband . . ." she murmured.

When she had obtained what she needed from the hospital tent, she hurried back to their own. Taylor had returned. His trousers and his hair were damp; he had washed away the dirt and blood and mud of the fight. The wound at his chest, cleaned much more briskly by his hand than hers, was bleeding afresh.

He sat at the camp desk, a bottle of whiskey in his hands. He took a long swig from it as he beckoned her to him. "Ready?"

She nodded, bringing sutures and a needle to the desk. He looked at her gravely, then offered her the whiskey bottle.

*"You're* supposed to drink for the pain, not me," she told him. "You want small, neat stitches, right?"

He smiled. "I was handing you the whiskey to pour on the wound," he told her, and poured the whiskey over his chest himself. He winced with the pain, gritting his teeth. She rescued the bottle from his fingers, knelt down beside him, and began to sew. She did so as quickly and efficiently as she could, and when she had finished, tying a careful knot, she met his eyes again. Watching her, he took another long swig from the bottle.

"You did that very well."

"Did it hurt?"

"Did you want it to?"

"I asked you first. Did it hurt?"

"Not too badly. Disappointed?"

"Not really—except that maybe some real pain might have made you more careful in the future!"

He stroked her cheek. "I was careful. I knew what I was doing. And I thought that you would have been pleased that this matter was settled."

Her eyes fell. "I *am* pleased. I was saddened to learn that a vulnerable man was made worse. I am grateful to you."

"Don't be grateful to me for this, Tia. I didn't do it for you—I did it because it was the right thing to do."

She drew away from him, rising. He caught her by the tangle of her hair, not hurting her but pulling her back. She wound up on her knees before him again, and he caught her chin, meeting her eyes.

"I didn't do it for you—but I'm not unhappy if what I've done has pleased you."

"Why did you need to let them attack you?"

"Because I was angry. And I wanted to hurt them for what they had done. But I can shoot the wings off a fly, and God knows, in this war, there are those who might have been against me if it came to a matter of military law. Frankly, I wanted very much to bash in the one fellow's face—and I did so." He hesitated a long moment, his eyes on hers, his fingers moving gently through her hair at her temple. "Tia, it was Gilly."

"What?" She felt the blood drain from her face. Her men, the men she had wanted so badly to protect, had been taken anyway.

"Your friend, one of the young fellows with you when we met."

She started to rise. "I have to go to him! I have to see what I can do."

His pressed her back down, shaking his head. "Colonel Bryer is a really good man, one of the best surgeons I've ever had the pleasure to work with. He is also compassionate. He has done his best. Cecilia is there with him now. Risa is helping out with all the injured. You are surely wanted, and may see him in time. But you're not needed in the hospital tent now."

"But—"

"I need you here."

She nodded, trembling slightly. Her hands rested on

his thighs; she felt very close to him, as if they were almost carrying on a real conversation between man and wife.

"Taylor—"

"He was one of the men you were trying to protect when you played your Godiva act and came here, isn't he?"

"Taylor, I didn't play any act on purpose."

"So you came here, and now you are married and trapped in a lie, and it was all to no avail. Your injured have been taken by the Yanks."

"You know the truth now of what I heard the soldiers say! I had no choice, Taylor."

"That's debatable. You heard the men. If you had brought what they said to Captain Ayers—"

"How could I know that Ayers was any better?"

"But look what your recklessness—or courage—had brought you to."

His eyes were so intently upon her; the almost tender massage of his fingers had not ceased. She lowered her head; then raised her chin. "Well, there were a number of people worried that a woman as decadent as a *nurse* would never find a husband."

"But you've married a half-savage."

"I know," she replied gravely.

He leaned forward, his knuckles grazing her cheeks. "I know your innocence, and your recklessness, I know that you are rash and determined. I know that you are loyal and headstrong, and that though your heart and passion are often in the right place, you are more likely than Robert E. Lee to take chances! Whatever any old biddies might have had to say, you could have acquired dozens of husbands, before, during, or after this war. But you have done the deed!"

"Yes—a commitment on paper," she reminded him.

"A commitment you will live with!" His thumb padded over her cheek as he continued to stare at her. "I have to leave soon," he said.

"I know. In a few days' time—"

"Today."

She was startled by his words, and startled by the pain that seemed to strike deep inside her. "But you're injured—"

"A scratch."

"I warned you—"

"I know how to keep a wound clean. I will not die of gangrene."

She stared down again. "How long will you be gone?"

"A matter of weeks. I don't know what will come when I return; Olustee Station was a total debacle for us—they may give up on penetrating into Florida again, and sit tight with what the Yankees hold along the coast. I may be ordered back to action in Virginia. But I'll return to St. Augustine from the south, and I want you to be there."

She closed her eyes. It almost sounded as if he were *asking*.

"I'll be there," she said softly. She looked at him, shaking her head. "I was with Julian for years without incident," she told him. "I did nothing but help with injured men. I was never in danger." Her head lowered again with the last. "I don't think you understand. We can be so very *desperate* for help. I did nothing wrong."

"No, there was nothing wrong in what you did. But it isn't a matter of right and wrong. To the Confederates, Godiva is a serious heroine. The problem is that what you were doing was dangerous. Very dangerous. Look at me," he commanded.

She did so.

"Swear that you'll not ride out as Godiva again, and I'll believe you."

"I swear!" she said very softly.

"Come into my arms," he said.

"Taylor! You were wounded and bleeding—"

"And I will lie alone with only memory and desire—a far greater injury—in the days and nights to come. I haven't much time left at all. I want it to be with you."

"But Taylor . . ."

"Yes?" His hazel eyes looked gravely at her.

"It's day."

"Tia, trust me. We will not be disturbed."

She stretched higher upon her knees, and wrapped her arms around him. She lay her cheek against his chest where he was not injured. She eased her fingertips down the muscles of his arms. "I'd not hurt you . . ." she said hesitantly.

"My love, you will not hurt me," he assured her.

He rose with her, cradling her into his arms.

And in minutes, she didn't care that it was day.

That the sun rose, that the wind blew, that the war and the world went on. Time was precious, and she didn't know what she thought, or even exactly what she felt.

She only knew that she wanted to be with him.

# Chapter 17

With Taylor gone, Tia thought she'd be very unhappy.

She had no idea of how she could miss a man, none at all, until she lay awake at night, thinking about him, wanting him. He had touched something within her from the first time they'd met. She should have wanted to escape this place, their marriage, all that had happened since her desperate run to this camp.

But she didn't want to escape. She wanted Taylor to return.

Nor could she despise the Yankees here.

Ian was in charge of the camp, and Risa was with her, and Colonel Bryer and Cecilia were wonderful people. Captain Ayers continued to study her upon occasion, but he remained baffled as to why she might be familiar to him. It was beyond the range of his imagination that Colonel Douglas would have married so notorious a Rebel as Godiva.

There was plenty to keep her busy in the hospital tent. Every morning when she awoke, she was glad to be able to assist the injured men. She was especially happy to be with Gilly.

Each day, he grew a little stronger. He seemed to have complete faith that he would eventually get better, because she was with him.

By the third day after he was nearly killed, Gilly was conscious again, his fever was down, and he seemed on the road to recovery.

She sat with him, carefully tending the rebandaged stump of his lower calf.

He watched her, shaking his head.

He had been startled to see her, but then she whispered what had happened to him. He smiled when she said that she was married to Taylor Douglas. Gilly knew perfectly well who he was, and he didn't seem surprised by the marriage part of it all.

"So you married Colonel Douglas!" he whispered to her one day, eyes bright as he shared the secret. "Did you have to?" he whispered.

"Gilly!"

"No, no, I didn't mean, did you *have* to in that manner. I mean, were you in trouble as Godiva?"

"I married him because I chose to," she said, and it might have avoided the truth, but it wasn't a lie.

"He's a darned good fellow. For a Yank."

"A Floridian. A traitor, some might say."

"Like your brother," Gilly reminded her shrewdly.

"Like my brother," she admitted. "But—"

"There's a strong man who can go against the tide of a raging sea to follow the convictions of his own heart and soul. Far harder to see, and understand, the losses, and be willing to fight the battle despite all that. Taylor Douglas, like your brother, may be the enemy, but he's proven himself one good friend to me. And he's been a good and honest man by you as well, Miss Tia McKenzie. Douglas," he added, then smiled. "And he knows about the Confederate secret weapon, eh?" Gilly seemed amused by it all.

"Secret weapon?"

"You."

"I never intended to be a secret weapon," Tia told him in return. "It just happened that way."

"But quite a legend. It will live on and on—with a happy ending, because you'll never be caught and killed now!"

The last gave her a shiver. "Gilly, it's all good, because you're here, and I'm with you, and you're going to get better."

"And be half a man," he said sadly.

"Never half a man, Gilly. A man is on the inside, not the out."

He squeezed her hand. "You tell that to the girls who'll refuse to marry me for being half a man, Miss Tia."

"Gilly, one day, the right girl will know you as I do, and she'll love you, and you'll never be half a man to her. I can promise you that."

"And how can you promise that?"

She decided a little blunt and rough-edged love would be in order then. "Gilly, half of the men won't even be half a man—they'll be dead and buried and six feet under or rotting in a forgotten and abandoned cornfield somewhere. You're going to live. And a woman who wants a man is going to love you one day, and that's that. And you can still have children—that part of you looks to be in fine working order! You're very young, and you're going to live a full and productive life."

"But what do I do?" he asked her.

"Can you write?"

"Of course!"

"Don't go getting huffy there, young man! I know plenty a planter who can barely sign his name and think that the words 'Francis Bacon' refer to a man's favorite pig! But if you can write, you can help me with letters to the families of the men we've lost—North and South. You can be honest about their bravery in battle; you can help their families through their grief, and make them proud."

"I like to write," he admitted.

"Good. You probably have saved the fellow's life," Colonel Bryer told her later that day. "Half the struggle for any soldier is the desire to live. He was convinced that he would die here—murdered probably, and I can't say that I blame him. But with you here . . . well, he believes in me as well."

The men responsible for the attack on Gilly were gone, and the others were really decent enough fellows. When she wasn't with Gilly, Tia helped Cecilia with other men. She wrote to Canby Jacob's wife, as she had promised the first day, and told the young woman how her husband had died a hero to his country, with fortitude, dignity, a deep belief in God, and a tremendous amount of love for her and their child. She hesitated, then wrote as well that her husband's last words instructed her not to mourn too long, but to live a good, long, and happy life for his sake, and to raise their child to be a compassionate man without thoughts of revenge, but with a desire to structure and repair the country.

She found a certain peace in writing letters, and a certain horror in time with nothing to do. During the day, she worked hard with the men. At night, when most bandages had been changed, meals served, supplies inventoried and doled out, she wrote more letters. For the soldiers who lived. She helped them describe the camp, the state, the battle, the situation. She found out that she could aid them in writing vivid descriptions, letters that were personal and informative, without being morbid. Gily followed her lead. In time, in the hospital tent, he became known more for his help than for being a Rebel. And she knew, in this very strange little outpost, that many of the soldiers had come to realize the fratricide of what they were doing. In writing home, they were forced to see all that they shared—love for family, fear of what would come if they were not there to provide when the war ended, fear of the future, regret for the past.

Risa had moved into the tent with her. Her cousin-in-law's company was good; they talked often and long at night.

No one wanted the war over more than Risa. She worried constantly about her father, a Union general, and even more constantly about her husband, a Rebel blockade runner. And now, she missed her baby, Jamie, on top of all else. He had been left behind in St. Augustine with Chantelle, nanny, maid, and housekeeper, when Risa had ridden into the interior.

"You had to leave the baby to come baby-sit me!" Tia said one night after they had both crawled into bed exhausted at the end of a long day. The black of night, beyond the tent, was broken by a full moon, and they lay in shadow and pale, ivory light. Taylor had been gone about a week.

"That's horrible. Taylor had no right—"

"He knew what he was doing," Risa told her firmly. "The baby is fine, and he needs this time to be without me, to learn to share . . . because we're going to have another."

"Oh, Risa, that's . . . so wonderful!" Tia said, but she knew that there was a catch in her throat. Naturally, men and women wanted children. North and South, men wanted sons to carry on their names, while mothers often longed for daughters to love, to dress up, teach, and raise to be beautiful young ladies, their very best friends in the years ahead. But in Tia's experience, childbirth was also dangerous, complications far too often resulted in the death of the mother. She knew of many women who arranged for their babes to be cared for by others long before their babies were born.

"Everything is going to be fine," Risa said, as if reading her mind.

"Of course."

"Rhiannon told me so."

"I wish she'd told me a few things!" Tia muttered.

"She doesn't have a crystal ball; she can't plan what she sees and what she knows," Risa reminded Tia. "Just sometimes . . ."

"Is it a boy or a girl?" Tia teased.

"Another boy."

"Oh, well, we have baby Mary and my little niece to dress up."

"Well, my dear cousin-in-law, there is nothing wrong with boys!" Risa told her.

Tia laughed. "I wasn't suggesting there was—men, yes, little boys, no." Although, she thought, watching those who had fought sometimes, she realized there was often a thin line between the two. "I was merely thinking about keeping the sexes somewhat even here."

"Then you'll have to have a girl."

Tia was startled by the sudden, uneasy pitching of her

stomach. "I—I wasn't planning on children, not in this war."

"I can't say that I actually *planned* my own," Risa said.

"Yes, come to think of it, when did you manage to . . ."

Risa laughed, rolling on her camp bed to look at Tia. "I knew not to leave St. Augustine at Christmas! Jerome came down the St. Johns, slipping past all the Yankee gunboats . . . he left far too quickly, but we did have Christmas!" she said, and her voice, filled with amusement at first, faded to a husky pain.

"I'm glad you had Christmas," Tia said.

"And I hope you get your girl."

"I have barely married."

"Tia! You are no naive little hothouse flower! You don't need to be married at all to have a child; indeed, you need no more than one night. Or morning—or afternoon."

Tia rolled to her side, away from Risa. She loved children. But not in this war.

"Good night," she whispered.

"Sleep well."

She didn't sleep at all.

The next morning, it was determined that the camp had fulfilled its usefulness; all the soldiers who could be found had been found, and it was time to break down and move into the city of St. Augustine.

By horseback, even alone, the trip south would have taken Taylor nearly eight days, and that would have been hard riding, moving Friar along at fifty miles a day.

However, Taylor was able to find passage on a small, three-gunned ship heading from St. Augustine south to Key West. They were able to take him as far south as an abandoned dock fifty miles north of the Miami River. The trouble with taking too many chances close to the coast was that the sandbars shifted frequently, and it was dangerous territory for a gunboat to run aground, even if the Union blockade was strong and the Federal navy

was far more in charge of the seas than the struggling
Rebels liked to admit. There was dockage to be had
south; in fact, even as far south as Taylor eventually
intended to go, but Union navy ships didn't seek safe
harbor near James McKenzie's property. Not that James
McKenzie had proclaimed himself a sworn enemy; his
sympathies were well known and his ties to the Seminole
society were also well known—the Union was fighting
hard there for little enough gain without adding an Indian conflict into the mixture. But no matter what the
possible dockage, the coast offered dangers because of
the shifting sandbars and shallows that had to be navi-
gated. It was because of a shipwreck that Taylor was
going there now, and he didn't want his mission to become the cause of a greater loss. Besides, there were
places just to the north where he needed to go. Popula-
tion in the south of the peninsula was sparse; white pop-
ulation in the south was even sparser. Taking the time
to garner a little information might prove to be well
worth the effort.

On their first evening out, he was standing on deck
before the helm when he noticed the quickly dimmed
lights of a ship that lay southeastwardly of their position.
Before the lights had gone out, though, he'd a moment
to study the ship.

"Colonel!"

He was startled by the whispered call of the helmsman. "Aye?" he replied as softly.

"Did you see her?"

"The ship that lies ahead?"

"Aye, sir, I thought I might be seeing things."

Taylor was quiet for a moment. "I think we need to
steer clear of her!" he said.

A third man, young Captain Henley, who was in
charge of the small gunner, joined them on deck then.
"Colonel, sir! You may have the rank on me as far as
the army goes sir, but this is my ship and we are at sea.
Sir, I offer no insult, but I suggest that you're advising
we avoid her because the ship is a notorious blockade

runner belonging to your own kin, Captain Jerome Mc-
Kenzie, of the *Lady Varina*."

Taylor replied to the captain, leaning against the teak
of the helm. "Indeed, Captain, I think the ship ahead is
the *Lady Varina.*"

"Then, sir, I'm afraid whether she carries your kin or
not, we should attack her."

"Really? I had not suggested we avoid her because
she is captained by my kin."

"Oh?"

"She outguns us by at least three cannons, sir."

Captain Henley flushed. "Perhaps she is wounded already, drawing into shore. Perhaps—"

"Perhaps she has seen us, and thought what a magnificent prize we might make!" Taylor suggested.

Henley's color deepened. "Helmsman, hard to port,
avoid her if we can."

He called orders to his first mate, who called the men
aboard and ordered them quickly to their stations.

A cannon shot was fired from the darkened Rebel
vessel. The shot fell just short of their ship.

"See? We have outrun her!" the captain declared.

"I don't think so. I believe it was a warning," Taylor
said quietly. "If Jerome had meant to hit us, he'd have
fired more than one gun."

Apparently, Captain Henson saw the wisdom in his
words. "Keep her hard to port!" he ordered, and the
command was shouted down the ranks.

They passed by the phantom Rebel ship with no further fire.

The following night, at dusk, Taylor and Friar disem-
barked at an abandoned dock Taylor knew very well.

He was the one who had ordered the dock abandoned,
long ago.

His father had built the dock and that had been even
longer ago.

They had dredged out the inlet to give the bay there
the depth to accommodate a small gunboat. The land on
the coast was his, and since it was mainly undeveloped
and bordered what most white men considered to be a

mosquito-riddled swamp, he doubted if the state government had made any efforts to confiscate the property. Besides, deeper inland, the terrain was considered dangerous. It was alive with cougars, 'gators, snakes—and Indians.

Despite the growing darkness, there was still enough of a moon in the sky for him to move through the beach and shrub, into thick foliage, and deep, lush pine trails. He rode for an hour, soon becoming aware of the sounds in the forest.

There were eyes in the night.

He was being watched, and he knew it.

He called out loudly in the night, a greeting in the Muskogee language. He drew in on Friar. A moment later, a young man appeared. Tall, muscled, with long black hair and strong, dark features. He wore European-style breeches, a patterned cotton shirt, and a handsome headdress of shell and silver. He grinned, his teeth wide and white in the moonlight. He replied in perfect English.

"What is a White Wolf doing so far to the south, especially when he wears the blue of the slaughters?"

"Charlie Otter, wolves come home," he said, dismounting from Friar. He clasped his clansman's arm in a fierce grip. "We always come home," he repeated.

"Then welcome, cousin," Charlie said, and turning, he let out a birdcall. Three children, two young braves and a little girl, came running out of the bushes. "This can't be the baby?" he asked. "She was just a little pea in the pod when I left!"

"This is the baby. She has grown. Time goes slowly in war, doesn't it?" Charlie asked. "Sometimes," he said, "I think it is all we know . . . except that in this war, the whites kill one another, and do nothing but try to persuade us that we should join them and kill again as well."

"So you've joined neither side?"

"I don't choose to kill white men by sides," Charlie said softly. His eyes were hard, and he grinned again. "No, I do not like killing. But as the war goes on . . .

the refuse of the white armies runs here, and when the deserters come after my wife, our women, cattle, food, children . . . yes, then I make war again on the whites. They don't fight with armies against us now, so when I kill a man and he falls, he is buried in the swamp, and the tale of his evil is buried with him as well. A kindness for a white widow, don't you think?"

"If a man has deserted his army and run to the swamps to steal from the Seminole and rape and murder his wife or children, then yes, you, like any man, have a right to defend yourself."

Charlie grinned. "Come to my chickee, quarter-cousin-wolf. Friends remain forever."

Charlie's wife, Lilly, was a shy, gentle girl. She prepared food for Charlie and Taylor and some of the other men of the small village. She served it, but then moved away to the women's chickee, as was the custom. Sitting on the platform that rose about three feet from the ground, Taylor ate deer and a porridge made from the koonti root, and with the men, he shared the black drink, a strong brew, known to give men visions. He was careful to appear to swallow much more than he actually did. He spoke with the men, honestly, telling them what was going on in the white men's world, how the war went on, how many of their number fought for the Confederates—because of the uniform.

The men around him were grave, listening, judging, nodding.

Then Charlie spoke.

"You didn't come here to teach us about the war, Taylor Douglas. You wear your blue uniform but come to us as White Wolf, our cousin. You don't ask our aid to fight white men in the state. So why are you here?"

"I'm looking for a man, a soldier. One who wears this uniform as well. He was on a ship that went down in a storm. The ship was wounded by an enemy gunner, then she was caught by the wind and waves, and wrecked. Some men survived and were picked up by another ship. Some men were drowned, and their bodies were found floating. But one man was carrying papers important to our government, and he carried information in his head that mustn't fall into Rebel hands. I need to find him, or find out if he drowned and if the papers went to the bottom of the sea. Have you heard of such a man, living here somewhere? The swamp is vast, but still, word travels here. News about a white man from the sea would not be common."

He knew, before they answered him, that they knew of the man. His heart quickened; he hadn't begun to pray that he might find the man he was seeking.

"Charlie?" he said.

"White men are not so unusual as you think. More come all the time. Even with the war. They run into the swamps, as we ran into the swamps, to avoid their governments," Charlie told him. "The man you are looking for could easily be dead."

"Is he dead?"

Emathla spoke quietly. "There is a white man, nearly dead from the sea."

"Where?"

Charlie smiled. "You have come to us . . . when the man you seek is south."

"South where? Will I be able to find him?"

"Such a man is with your grandmother's nephew, James McKenzie. A white man, nearly dead from the sea . . . yes, indeed, there is such a man. Go south to your family there, and you will find what you are looking for."

Taylor frowned. "Is he dying? Is James caring for him?" He felt a strange chill. James was a Rebel, and though he would never murder the survivor of a shipwreck for being a Yankee, would he care for an enemy in his own home?

"Go see James McKenzie, and you will understand," Charlie told him. "Will you stay here with us tonight, and ride south tomorrow?"

"I accept your gracious invitation.

"You never need an invitation. You are among your mother's people."

He inclined his head in acknowledgment of Charlie's

words, making no further protest. He was glad to see that his mother's small band was doing well; they had cattle and pigs, and were growing pumpkins and other fruits and vegetables. There were a number of strong, sturdy chickees built in a circle within the copse, space for the band to grow. They had already fought their wars and had come to this place, and though they seemed interested in his news about the war, they were not affected by the war itself.

The night was balmy. Taylor stripped down to his breeches to sleep, and felt the air wrap pleasantly around him. The mosquitoes weren't bad this season, the breeze was light, and the moon continued to give the sky a golden glow. He had a chickee to himself, and in the night, it was like being alone in the world.

From across the copse, he heard soft shuffling and whispers. Charlie and his wife making love. The stars and the air were good. Being alone was not. He felt the air cool as his body burned. Life certainly took strange twists and turns. Godiva had been enticing; she had intrigued him, and he had wanted her. But the reality of Tia McKenzie as his wife was far more than he'd ever imagined—in his most erotic dreams.

Eyes so dark, face so pale, the cascade of her hair a cloak of silk, encompassing them both, feather soft in his hands. She haunted him in the night; thoughts of her flesh, her lips, the way she moved, the way she looked at him, eyes shimmering ebony, like the deepest pond in a tempest of shadow and light, a tempest that spoke eloquently of the strange bond that had formed between them, of the desire that had burned with incredible brilliance, seizing them like the wind, taking them both unawares . . .

He groaned softly and sat up. Not enough of the black drink. He watched the stars.

Wanting her.

# Chapter 18

Long before he reached James McKenzie's home, Taylor knew again that he was being watched.

A breakwater and lagoon shielded the property from the sea; at a distance, the house and grounds could not be seen. On land, the house was surrounded by thick pine forests, and the trails through the forests were known only by those who were familiar with the area.

The place had burned to the ground a year or so earlier, but it had been rebuilt and stood again as a spectacular enhancement to the natural beauty of the landscape. Built of wood, limestone, and coral rock, the house itself was back from the beach, designed to best embrace the north-south breezes, and painted a soft blue-green that blended with the colors of sea and sky. There were long sweeps of tended lawn right around the house, but then the grass grew sparse and sand began to intermingle with shrubs. Sea grapes shaded the lawn; pines and coconut palms dotted the ocean side of the house. In gardens that fringed around the house, Teela McKenzie grew medicinal herbs and beautiful flowering plants. Far from the back of the house, Taylor knew, the lagoon swept around to an entirely private pool, secluded by underbrush and trees, a paradise within an Eden. Before the war, white friends and neighbors had visited by boat while James McKenzie's native kin and friends had ridden the narrow Indian trails, many of them very old, down to the wild area off the bay. Taylor had journeyed to the property both ways. The McKenzies were as he was himself, both Indian and white, and sometimes, feeling like an outcast from both societies.

As a child, he had felt a strong affection for James, Teela, and their children—there were not many men who straddled the fences of such diverse cultures. Yet now . . .

He knew that many men would fiercely fight for James McKenzie, defend this place as they would defend him, if they felt that he were threatened. Taylor might well have been afraid here, but he was not. Whatever James's belief about the war, he would never allow his own kin to be gunned down on his doorstep.

Even as that thought crossed Taylor's mind, he was startled by a sudden sound that whistled through the air. He turned in time to prepare himself for the attack of the warrior who flew at him with a wild impetus of strength from the branch of a sea grape.

Taylor let the force take them both from Friar and down hard upon the ground. He knew how to twist to take the weight from another person in such a fall—and he knew how to twist to give his opponent the disadvantage as well. He did so, straddling the man, pinning the arm that wielded a long-bladed knife. His attacker was a full-blooded Seminole, a wiry, well-muscled fellow with his flesh bear greased and slippery as all hell. He wore nothing but a breech clout, attire often worn by a people who had learned that clothing fragments could cause infection and bring mortality from wounds that might not have been fatal.

The brave was young and strong, and angry. Taylor slammed his arm hard against the ground, aware that he had to force the weapon from his opponent before it became wedged in his own throat. The fellow grunted; Taylor forced the tactic again. The knife slipped, hitting the ground. Taylor reached for it, hurling it far away from them both into a bed of nearby crotons. The brave slammed a fist against Taylor's chin, a stunning blow. Taylor worked his jaw, hoping he didn't have a broken bone. He could have pulled a Colt, sent a bullet straight into the warrior's heart. In fact, such an action might have become necessary to save his own life because the brave beneath him was wild, twisting, trying to strike again. Taylor got in his own blow, however—a good one. Stunned, the brave lay still.

"Dammit, don't come after me again, you fool," Taylor warned him, standing up. "I'm not here to hurt anyone!"

"So why are you here?"

The question, in English, seemed to come from thin air. Taylor turned. A tall, thin Seminole with a remarkably strong and arresting profile stood before him. Taylor recognized the man, known as Billy Bones. In fact, he was a relative, the son of a cousin of his grandmother.

"Billy. It's Taylor."

"So I see," Billy told him gravely.

Billy was carrying a rifle. It wasn't directed at Taylor, but held loosely in his hand. If he chose to fire, however, it would all happen with the speed of lightning.

"I need to see James. I've come alone, not to do harm."

"This is a Southern state. You're wearing a Union uniform. Why have you come here in that uniform?"

"Because I'm not a spy, Billy. I've come as what I am, and I wouldn't pretend to be anything but what I am."

"What you are is not a friend."

"Billy, we are kin, no matter what clothing I wear. If I discard the uniform, I still believe in the cause I'm fighting for."

Billy watched him gravely. "You are sure you are alone?"

"When I had no father, James McKenzie was that to me and more. I would not come to his house except alone."

Billy Bones nodded after a while. Billy spoke in Muskogee, telling the boy to get up. The warrior who had attacked Taylor got to his feet, watching him carefully.

Billy raised a hand, indicating that Taylor should join him.

Taylor did so. Friar obediently followed along behind them. They followed the trail around to the rear of the house, where the porch let out by the lagoon. To the northeastern side of the house were the docks, and Taylor was sure that there were always more men on guard at that point. He was sure, as well, that Jerome often brought his blockade runner, the *Lady Varina,* into these docks.

James McKenzie stood on his rear porch, arms folded over his chest. Like Billy, he had been aware of his coming company.

"Taylor," he acknowledged gravely. Then he said, "Looks like you're acquiring a bruise on that jaw."

Taylor grinned. "But you should see the other guy."

James smiled, eyes downcast for a minute. "If you'd hurt that other guy, you would have been in some severe trouble."

"Did you think I would?"

"No," James said after a moment. "But I had to be sure. So—what are you doing here?"

"I'm looking for a man. A Union soldier. He was on a ship that went down, but he had despatches from Key West that carried a fair amount of information about naval movements."

"And what do you want with such a man?"

"Well, I want the despatches, of course."

"And the man?"

"And the man."

"Does the Union government suspect him of treason, of having changed sides to give the information to the Confederate government?"

Taylor hesitated only a moment. "Probably."

"And if I knew this man, why would I allow you to take him to be hanged?"

"A man who too easily changes sides may also too easily be a traitor to both."

Behind James, a door suddenly opened. A tall, slender young man with gaunt cheeks shuffled out on crutches. He was wearing a bleached white muslin shirt and dark cotton trousers. His one foot was bandaged; his other foot was bare.

James turned, saying firmly, "Michael, I told you to stay inside."

"Yes, sir, you did. But I won't bring the war to your doorstep. Colonel Douglas,. I'm Lieutenant Michael Long. I'm the man you're looking for. The despatches remain in my coat pocket. They have not been touched. If I'm to face a court-martial, I will do so."

"No!"

Behind Lieutenant Michael Long, the door burst open again. Jennifer McKenzie, beautiful straight black hair flying behind her like a sea of ravens, came flying out of the house, slipping an arm around Long, and staring at Taylor with defiant, troubled eyes. "No, he came here half-dead! He can still barely walk. He nearly died of a fever!"

"Jennifer—" James began firmly.

"Jennifer," Long repeated.

The door opened again. Teela hurried out, coming to stand beside James and stare at Taylor. "Taylor, welcome. I think. Oh, dear, this is quite awkward, isn't it?"

From inside, he could hear a wailing. Mary, a little over a year old, the youngest of the offspring of James and Teela McKenzie, didn't like being separated from her mother.

Surveying the group before him, Taylor felt a sense of defeat. This was not what he had expected.

"Perhaps we could go in and talk," he suggested quietly. He smiled at Teela. "I never got to see the baby."

"Oh, she's beautiful!" Teela said. "James . . ."

"Yes, of course," James said after a moment. "Yes, we should go in and talk."

With that, Teela smiled, walked down the porch steps, and greeted Taylor with a hug and a kiss on the cheek. She smelled sweetly of jasmine, as she always had.

"Are you coming in, Billy?" she asked.

"I think I'll see to my nephew," Billy said. He looked at Taylor, nodded, and passed him by. It was the best he could expect. He was the enemy.

But it hurt. Teela slipped her arm through his. They walked to the porch together. He met James McKenzie's eyes, a startling blue against the bronze of his features.

James hesitated, then reached out and embraced him. Taylor closed his eyes.

God, how he was coming to hate the war.

James released him, and they entered the house. Teela went to retrieve her crying baby from the mixed-blood servant who held her. "Taylor, Mary. Mary, meet your distant cousin Taylor."

He was startled when the little girl stopped crying, reached out to him, then wound up in his arms, placed there by Teela. "Hello, Mary!" he said uncertainly. "You are very beautiful, very definitely a little McKenzie!" The baby was all McKenzie, with huge, blue green eyes and ink-dark hair.

"Let me get drinks," Teela said, turning to start down a hallway.

"Mama!" Mary cried, her little arms now reaching out for her mother.

"We're following her!" Taylor said, hurrying after Teela. He liked children, though he wasn't accustomed to them quite this young. Still, she smelled so sweet, like soap and talc. Her eyes were wide and trusting. Holding her, he remembered that once he'd wanted children, then Abby had died and he'd forgotten everything except the business at hand—the war. But now . . .

Now, he had a wife. A McKenzie wife, closer to this child than he was himself . . .

He could hear Lieutenant Michael Long limping after him, James and Jennifer in his wake. A few minutes later, he was seated in James's study, nicely redone after the fire. Mary had been rescued by Jennifer, who was watching Long with tears continually forming in her eyes. Seated in a leather chair with a large whiskey, Long explained the shipwreck, how he'd been unconscious for weeks and still woke up in the night with chills and fever. "The despatches are safe, Colonel Douglas. Completely safe. I'd not have betrayed my country, but . . . but . . ." he looked at Taylor. "I've prayed that the Union government would think me dead."

"They had to find the despatches," Taylor said. "You must have known that."

"Perhaps. Perhaps I just prayed they wouldn't find me." He glanced at Jennifer, then stared at Taylor again. "I don't wish to be a deserter. But neither do I wish to make war against the South anymore. Nor do I think, in all truth, that I may be able. I still can't walk. My ankle was broken and not set quickly enough."

"Taylor, please . . . isn't there something you can do?" Jennifer pleaded.

"You can see that he really can't go back to war," Teela whispered.

What he could see was that Jennifer had fallen in love. And that Michaél Long seemed to be a very decent man. Tired of the war—and not about to fight the people who had saved his life. *He would let me shoot him before taking him from here,* Taylor thought—except that he wouldn't do that now because the man who had rescued him was kin. He wouldn't cause bloodshed among the family.

James seemed to understand Taylor's situation all too well, and maybe he was damning himself for not remembering that though Taylor was kin, he remained the enemy as well. "Do you think that Taylor can go back to the Union military authorities—and lie?" he asked harshly.

Long lowered his head. "There will be no bloodshed here. I will go back."

Jennifer started to weep.

Taylor rose, walking over to her. He hunkered down before her. "I can't lie, but . . . I can take the despatches to the fort at Key West. And see what I can do."

She looked up at him tearfully. "You won't take Michael?"

"No."

"Oh, Lord, Taylor, you'll be taking a risk."

"Well, I might be taking a risk if I tried to seize him as well, right?"

"How's that?"

"Your father could have me shot down."

"My father wouldn't do that."

"And neither, Jennifer, would I hurt a good man who

is wounded already. Or a cousin who has already felt the tragedy of this war too closely."

"Taylor . . ." She set her arms around him, hugging him. "Taylor, I'm so sorry for doubting you . . . I'd forgotten about Abby in my own pain. The war has cost us Lawrence and Abby and left you a widower."

He drew away from her gently, rising. "Well, I'll leave tomorrow and see what can be done. And I guess I should tell you . . . I'm not a widower anymore."

"You've remarried! How wonderful," Teela said. "Who, Taylor? Ah, a Yankee girl, I imagine, someone from the North! Will you stay there after the war, Taylor, do you think? Will there ever be an 'after' with this wretched war?"

"Teela, my love, you've asked him a half-dozen questions. Let him answer one," James advised.

"You know my wife. You know her well. She's your niece. I married Tia McKenzie."

Jennifer's gasp seemed loud enough to be heard at sea.

"Tia—married you?" she inquired incredulously.

He looked at her, arching a brow. "Yes," he said flatly.

"Oh, Taylor, I did not mean that."

"She means that you're a Yankee," James said.

"Um, well, no one is perfect."

"And *you* married *her*?" Jennifer said.

"She married me, I married her. We are married."

"I think I shall have another drink," Teela said.

"I didn't know that you knew one another," Jennifer said. "Well, of course, you and Ian have been friends— you'd been out here with all the boys since you all were young, but I don't remember Tia being around."

"We met recently."

"At Cimarron?"

"And before," he acknowledged.

"Well, perhaps we all should quit staring at Taylor," Teela said. "You'll be hungry. I'll see about dinner. Michael, dear, you really should be back in bed. Jennifer, give me Mary and help Michael along. James . . . Taylor . . . I'll call you as soon as dinner is ready."

Michael Long came up to Taylor. "Thank you," he said gravely.

"I haven't done anything yet. I make no guarantees."

"Thank you for the effort you have promised."

He nodded. Jennifer and Michael left. He was alone with James. He felt James's brooding, dark blue eyes studying him. "You know, Taylor, I feel, at times, that I helped raise you in a way."

"Yes, sir. I feel that myself at times. It was why I dared come here alone."

"I know you very well. Other than the fact that you've chosen the wrong side in this wretched fight, I'm proud of the man you've become."

"Thank you, sir."

"So what is going on? Why did you marry my hellion of a niece?"

"I . . . well, . . . sir, one need only look at her," he said, taken completely by surprise by the question.

"Hm." James studied him still. "What kind of trouble did she get herself into?"

"I—none. Unless you consider me trouble."

"I'm sure my niece does." James stood, walked over to the whiskey decanter, and poured himself another drink. "Tell me. I've heard rumors about a Rebel spy working the state. I would have feared that Jennifer was trying to take on the war herself again, except that she has been with me—and with this wounded soldier, Michael Long. And I would have feared for Sydney, except that she remains in Washington, married to an unknown Yank, but safe, at the very least. So when I heard the rumor and the description, I began to fear for my brother's daughter—it is a ridiculously dangerous game this young woman plays. Does this marriage have something to do with the capture of a spy? If Godiva happens upon the Yanks . . ."

"Sir—"

"Don't lie or hedge, Taylor. I expect more from you, I'm afraid."

"Sir, it isn't my place—"

"You married her. It is certainly your place."

"I am the Yank she happened upon."

James nodded after a moment. "Keep her safe, whatever it takes," he said. "My brother would, I think, lose his mind if anything happened to her. A man loves his boys, but his daughters are his treasures. God knows, it is terrifying enough to wake up knowing your sons may face a barrage of bullets that day. God help you, North or South, keep her safe."

"Sir, I intend to do my best." He hesitated a moment. "And for Jennifer as well. I'll take the despatches to Key West tomorrow."

James lifted his glass to Taylor. "To your success, Colonel Douglas. In all things."

"Aye, sir."

With all of the injured men, the trip to St. Augustine seemed very long, though they had not been more than thirty miles from the city. It took more than two days to travel the rough roads with their crude ambulances and the amputees who needed care that their stumps were not injured all anew by too much jolting. The men were excited, though, to be coming into the city. Tia found that she was pleased herself.

From the time Tia was a little girl, she had loved St. Augustine. When friends from more northern climes had teased her about Florida being new and raw and savage, she could remind them politely that St. Augustine was the oldest continually habited European settlement in the New World.

A Union flag waved above the city now, and it had done so since 1862. Union soldiers marched in the fields, and took their leisure by the water. Some Rebels had remained, determined to hang on to their property. Others had fled, giving everything up for their great Southern Cause. Since the Yankee invasion, Tia had been in and out of the city a few times to see Alaina, Risa, and the children. When they arrived this time, Risa went home immediately to see her son, little Jamie, but Tia stayed with Cecilia Ayers and the doctor. She didn't visit anyone at first, since she was so busy helping to settle the injured soldiers into their new hospital facilities, scattered throughout the city. When at last that night Tia rode with her brother to the place where her family kept apartments, she was as stunned as he was to find Alaina, who was supposedly back at Cimarron, standing by the house, waiting. Ian let out a surprised cry, leapt down from his horse, and went running to his wife.

Tia dismounted from Blaze, collected the reins for both horses, and followed more slowly. Alaina was in her husband's arms. Tia was so close that she had no choice but to hear their intimate whispers. Her brother spoke first, thrilled to see his wife, but chastising her as well.

"My love, my love, I thought you weren't well, that you were staying at Cimarron, not traveling," Ian protested while holding her.

"I knew you were going to be here. I couldn't stay away. God knows when you will leave the state again, when I'll no longer have such a chance," Alaina replied.

"But you shouldn't have come alone."

"I didn't! Rhiannon is with me. And your father arranged for an escort, of course. I had to come, Ian. I didn't intend to leave when I thought you were out of the state, but when you wrote from the camp saying you'd be here . . ."

"I wouldn't have told you if I thought you'd risk yourself and the children."

"But I'm here. Fine. And well. And the children will get to see you again. So soon after Christmas; they'll even remember you!"

Their voices were so filled with emotion. They were beautiful and romantic there—her very tall, dark brother, so handsome in his uniform, and his petite blond wife, framed there with him in the moonlight. It was a picture of the war: a greeting now, but soon it would be a goodbye as well. Tia felt as if she intruded, and she wished she could slip away.

"Tia!" Her sister-in-law noticed her, raced for her,

hugged her. "It's good to see you again! I'm glad you're with Ian; everyone worries about you so much."

"I'm fine, Alaina," she said quickly, not wanting another barrage of questions regarding her appearance at the Yankee camp and her marriage to Taylor. "The children—"

"Are sleeping, Risa's Jamie as well. And little Conar. Rhiannon is here with me. We came eastward together. She's anxious to see you, of course. Oh, and wait until you meet Chantelle. She is wonderful, the apartments are always neat and clean, and she's a marvel with the children. She came in with the new doctor. His name is Jon Beauvais. I think you'll like him very much. Anyway, Risa's door is there, mine is there, the doctor is across . . . and there, that door is yours, Tia. But, of course, Risa has tea on and is waiting for us all."

Tia smiled suddenly. "Alaina, neither you nor my brother want to have tea at the moment." She kissed her sister-in-law on the cheek. "Go with your husband. We'll be fine."

"Oh, no, but you've just arrived."

"Alaina, my brother is a much nicer human being after he's been with you. Go away; we'll manage! Risa, Rhiannon, and I will do very well on our own, thank you!"

Alaina grinned, raced back to Ian, and caught his hand.

"But the horses—" Ian began.

"I can see the stables—and the stable boy!" Tia called. Her brother stared at her, waved back. He slipped an arm around his wife and disappeared through one of the doors of the big old house that had been turned into apartments.

Tia walked the horses to the stable. She'd been here before, and she knew the layout of the street, the surgery, the hospital. She was far more familiar with it all than perhaps Ian realized—it was much easier for a young woman to cross enemy lines than it was for a man.

A young black stable boy took the horses from Tia. As she thanked him, Risa's door opened and her cousin-in-law came out. "Tia, come in now, come on in. You must be so tired." Risa's arm came around her shoulder and she led Tia into the small parlor area of her apartment. As they entered, she saw that Rhiannon was standing in front of the fireplace, her head lowered. But she heard the two of them enter and she turned, walking quickly across the room to greet Tia with a warm hug. "It's so very good to see you again this soon," she said.

Despite her sister-in-law's affectionate greeting, Tia felt uneasy. Rhiannon appeared tired, and Tia didn't think that it was due to the baby keeping her awake.

"What's wrong?" she asked quickly.

Rhiannon shook her head.

"Oh, my God, you didn't hear anything bad? Julian is all right—"

"Julian is fine," Rhiannon said. "I saw him briefly before coming here. I plan on joining him again shortly. He's working alone now."

"Oh, I know! I'm so sorry—"

"I planned on joining him anyway," Rhiannon reminded her, smiling.

"The tea is hot and we've biscuits and soup," Risa said. "Perhaps we should sit down now and eat. And by the way, Tia, your *husband* is just fine as well."

Startled, Tia stared at Risa. Her red-headed no-nonsense cousin-in-law was staring at her as well.

"Oh? And how do you know? Where is he?"

"I don't know where he is now."

"But he was . . ."

"To the south of us."

"And how do you know?"

"I received a letter from my mother-in-law."

"Aunt Teela? Taylor is with Aunt Teela?"

Risa sighed. "James McKenzie's aunt was Taylor's grandmother, you know."

"Or so I've learned!" Tia murmured.

"It's not so strange that he should have gone there."

"Except that Uncle James hates even the sight of a Union uniform."

"Did he ever hate Ian? No. Does he hate your father? No. Does—"

"None of that counts. Taylor was ordered there. Taylor is after something there."

"You'll have to let them all work that out themselves, won't you?" Risa said softly.

"But—"

"He's alive and well, we know that much," Risa reminded her dryly. "If they'd decided to hang him or shoot him instead of inviting him to dinner, I'm sure she would have mentioned it in the letter."

Tia cast her a frown. "This is hardly a joking matter."

"No, it's a war, isn't it? But my in-laws haven't disowned me for being General Magee's daughter, nor did they blame me when radical Union soldiers decided to burn their house to the ground. To fear that they would do some harm to Taylor does them an injustice."

"But what is Taylor doing there?"

"Negotiating, at the moment."

"Negotiating what?"

"They didn't say. But he will be in the south of the state for some time yet."

"Perhaps time enough for you to visit Brent," Rhiannon said.

Tia stared at her sister-in-law, thinking that the whole world was going insane. Risa and Rhiannon both had their reasons for being Unionists. But why Rhiannon should suggest that she travel through the war-torn South to visit Brent seemed ludicrous.

"Visit—Brent. My cousin Brent," she repeated. "You—Miss 'Battle Hymn of the Republic' herself, are suggesting that I go to Brent. The Confederate surgeon."

"I'm suggesting you visit your cousin who is a doctor—not that you carry military information to Longstreet or Lee!" Rhiannon said indignantly.

"Rhiannon! I'm not so sure that this idea of yours is possible at all. Tia can't go just anywhere anymore," Risa said. "She is married to Taylor."

"I know that—you told me that she married him," Rhiannon said with an exasperated sigh. "I'm not suggesting she do anything at all wrong, dangerous—or even pertaining to the war!" Rhiannon said.

"It does pertain to the war—" Risa argued.

"No, it pertains to a child!"

Tia threw up her hands. "What are you two talking about? I'm going to need whiskey instead of tea if someone doesn't start making some kind of sense soon."

"I had a dream," Rhiannon said.

"Oh, God, no! What about—my cousin Brent?" Tia asked, horrified. "Is he in danger? Can't we write to him? No, we'll have to send him a telegraph."

"It's not Brent," Rhiannon said.

"She keeps dreaming about a little boy in a big white house—falling from a balcony."

"A little boy we know?" Tia asked.

"Alaina says she knows the house I described. And Risa agrees. It is the White House of the Confederacy. And the child belongs to President Davis."

"Oh, but . . . are you sure?" Tia asked.

Rhiannon shook her head, distressed. She walked about the small room. "No, of course I'm not sure, I'm not sure at all. I've already written a letter . . . your father has assured me that he has given it to an officer who will get it through to Varina Davis. But what will she think when she gets a letter from a woman she doesn't even know? She may never read it. If she does, she'll think I'm mad, and ignore it. Then . . ."

"What?" Tia asked.

"It's the strangest set of dreams I've ever had. Once, I thought I'd go mad with the dreams, that they would simply torture me with visions I could not prevent. Then your brother showed me that sometimes I could avert tragedy with my sight. Sometimes . . . but this dream came several times. Then, the last time, while I struggled to wake up, I saw a man's face, such a sad face . . . and it was as if he was speaking directly to me . . ."

"And?" Tia persisted. "Please, Rhiannon!"

She shrugged. "He said that some things were fate, maybe not meant to be prevented."

"Rhiannon, who was the man?"

"I think it was the child's father. President Davis, perhaps."

"So you think you're dreaming about the death of a child—that can't be averted?"

"I don't know! But a child died, and I can't bear the thought!" Rhiannon cried.

"So many people die," Risa said softly. "That's part of life, Rhiannon. Death is a part of life."

"But too many are dying now. Saving what we can seems to be the only way to get through this war. I feel that I still must do what I can!" Rhiannon said.

Tia stared at her. "Someone should go to Varina Davis."

"You know her," Risa said. "President Davis was Secretary of War before this madness started. Your father and brothers were friends with him; you visited their home before the war."

"Yes, I visited them with my family before the war. But you've visited them at the White House of the Confederacy, where they're living now. You were there with Jerome at the beginning of the war. You're the wife of a great Southern hero—"

"And the daughter of a Union general. And . . . and I'm not sure I could make the trip right now," Risa said apologetically.

Tia felt a chill snake along her spine. No, she couldn't ask Risa to go. Not if she was expecting another child. And Rhiannon's little Conar was barely a few months old. "Alaina . . ." she murmured softly.

"Alaina is sick," Rhiannon said.

"Sick?"

Rhiannon shrugged. "Alaina is expecting another child as well."

"Another babe? Are we McKenzies trying to repopulate the South all on our own?" she murmured bitterly.

"Tia!" Risa said.

"Oh, I'm sorry. I'm delighted for you all. I just . . ."

"Are you afraid that Taylor will be angry?" Rhiannon asked.

"She should be," Risa said, staring at her sternly.

Tia suddenly felt defensive—and like a child who had been ordered to behave. "No, of course not. I mean, he is off to war, with no explanations for me, there is no reason I shouldn't travel to see Brent . . . but . . ."

"Ian will probably not let her go," Rhiannon said with a shrug.

"Ian will most probably not be here long," Risa said. "They are pulling officers and all the able-bodied men they can back out of Florida, preparing for a new offensive. General Grant has said that war must be hell, and that he intends to make it so."

"As if we were not in hell already," Tia murmured.

"Ian will be preoccupied. With Alaina. If we have to slip you out before he leaves, we can surely do so."

"Well, tonight," Rhiannon said, appearing very nervous and upset, "you should get some sleep. You can decide in the morning. That will be time enough."

Time enough . . .

As it happened, Tia didn't need the morning to come in order to make up her mind. She had barely crawled into bed when there was a pounding at her door. There had been a buggy accident that night. A man's leg had been crushed, his son had an injured arm, and his seven-year-old daughter had been seriously hurt.

The doctor, Jon Beauvais, was a skilled young surgeon. Tia worked with him throughout the night. The man's leg had to be amputated. The little boy's arm was broken, but they set it, and the doctor believed he would be all right. The fight to save the little girl lasted until morning. Tia tried to soothe her. She was very brave.

"Does it hurt badly?" Tia asked her. "The doctor will make it better. The medicine helps, doesn't it?"

The little girl offered her a tremulous smile. "Doesn't hurt too bad! It's all right, I know. If I die, the angels will come for me. They came for my brother, Daniel. He died at Gettysburg, and so he is in heaven, and if I die, he won't be so alone."

"You're not going to die. You're going to live. Listen, hear that? Your mommy is out there, and she's crying. You have to live so that she won't cry."

But no matter how hard the doctor worked with her, and despite the healing touch of Rhiannon's hands, the little girl died. Tia was at her side when, just before dawn, she struggled to draw in one last breath. She was a beautiful child with strawberry ringlets and cherry-red lips. In death, she seemed to sleep. Tia drew her into her arms and cried, unable to believe that the little girl was gone. She still held her tightly, crying, when the doctor came and said the mother needed to be with her child. Tia sat numbly in the doctor's surgery, listening as a photographer was called. It was common practice, she knew, for photographers to take pictures of dead children so that their parents could remember them. The mother sobbed, holding her baby for the photographer. The child did, indeed, look at peace, as if asleep, and yet it all seemed so horrible to Tia that she could scarcely bear it.

Both of her sisters-in-law went back to cradle their own babies. Risa as well went to her Jamie.

Tia sat outside the surgery, feeling ill. She could still hear the mother's sobs. They would haunt her all her life.

When dawn broke, she told Rhiannon she was ready to go to Richmond.

As it happened, things worked out very well. Ian's traveling papers had awaited his return to St. Augustine.

He'd be leaving by a Yankee ship in the harbor.

Tia would be leaving soon after, slipping out of the city and down river to board a blockade runner.

Taylor arrived late, having not received the documents he needed until late that morning. Then, though the weather was excellent and he had moved along at a fair clip, it was still nearly two hundred miles southwest from James McKenzie's home to the Union naval base at Key West. With the captain of the small vessel eternally nervous that he would meet a heavily gunned blockade runner along the sandbars and shoals that haunted the coastline around the islands, it seemed slow going.

Taylor came into the lagoon by dinghy, and though it

was late, again he was being watched. He rowed in alone, planning on rowing back out to meet the ship that night.

As he stepped from the dinghy onto the wet sand of the beach, he almost expected another ambush, but this time, as he dragged the dinghy high up on the sand, it was Jennifer who came running out to throw her arms around him. "Taylor! Taylor, what happened? Please tell me, quickly! Will it be okay, did they believe you, did—"

"Jennifer, Jennifer, whoa!" James McKenzie was right behind his daughter, slipping an arm around her, ready to draw her from Taylor before she could drag them both down into the sand.

Teela was there as well. "Let him get out of the water and into the house!" she chastised. "The night is cool; let's get inside."

But Taylor could see Jennifer's tortured eyes, and he felt a strange pain in his throat, in his gut. She loved the Yankee she had fished from the sea. He had never expected to see it; her first husband had been killed at Manassas. And she had mourned deeply, and recklessly. But seeing her eyes, hearing her voice, the passion, the care, the concern . . .

"Jennifer, they accepted the despatches, and my statement that he was far too ill to be moved."

"Oh, Taylor!" Escaping her father's hold, she threw her arms around him again. She kissed his cheek, hugged him. "Oh, Taylor!"

"Jen, Jen!" James warned quietly. "He'll eventually have to go back—"

"No, sir," Taylor interrupted quietly. "That's part of what has taken me so long. I have an honorable discharge with me. I took the liberty of suggesting that he'd never be much use to the Yankee Cause again. Of course, I swore in turn that he'd never take arms against the Union, as well."

"Oh, my God, I have to tell Michael!" Jennifer kissed his cheek again. "Taylor! Thank you so very, very much!"

She sped off.

Teela and James remained, staring at Taylor. He could hear the lash of the waves against the shore. The moon was dimming, but it still cast a gentle glow down upon them. Palms rustled gently in the breeze, a whisper against the night sky.

"For my daughter's sake, I thank you sincerely," James told him.

Taylor grinned. "Well, I admit, I'd thought about reporting him dead. I had that suggestion made to me a few times, and it did sound like a good idea. But one day, the war will end. And I don't want any of us to be haunted by this in later years. I was afraid . . . it was a gamble, and Jen might have wound up hating me, but the gamble has paid off."

"Come, let's go on into the house," Teela said, stepping forward and taking his arm. "It's a cool night. You need some hot food, and a good night's rest—"

"Teela, I would deeply appreciate sharing a meal with you and James. Afterward, however, I must return to the ship. I am going to be ordered back to Virginia, and I want what time I may have in St. Augustine with Tia."

Teela seemed to pale suddenly. "Um . . . well, let's have something to eat first, shall we?"

She turned and headed quickly for the house. Taylor looked at James, frowning.

"What's going on?"

"We received another letter from Risa. Tia has headed toward Virginia herself, to spend time with Brent at the hospital outside Richmond."

"She . . . what?"

"Perhaps she thought you'd be gone much longer. There was a ship on the river—"

"A Rebel ship?" Taylor asked tightly.

"Yes," James admitted. "Not Jerome's," he added quickly. "Under the circumstances, he might have refused her passage. I don't really know much; all I have is the information in my daughter-in-law's letter."

Taylor felt as if a band were tightening around his insides. Fear and fury combined to make him feel sick.

Damn her. He'd trusted her.

He pulled the papers he carried—correspondence and
Michael Long's honorable discharge—from the inner
pocket of his frockcoat and handed them to James.

"Sir, I beg your forgiveness, but I must forgo dinner."

"What is your intent?"

"I'm going after my wife."

"She will be in Rebel territory."

"I am accustomed to seizing her from Rebel territory."

"Take care, Taylor. Take the gravest care."

"Aye, sir, that I will."

He pushed the dinghy from the shore, hopped into
the small boat, and picked up the oar, rowing with a
vengeance.

What in God's name was she doing? What reckless
game did she play? Was she torturing different troops
now, leading them into an ambush? No matter how good
she was, no matter how swift, how careful, how cunning,
she would eventually be caught.

He felt a tightness clamp around his throat. He
couldn't lose her . . .

He paused in his furious rowing, staring into the dark
velvet of the night, listening to the water lap against the
small boat. His heart slammed bitterly against his chest.

Prison. A Yankee prison camp. It seemed the only
answer.

# *Chapter 19*

Going north was precarious, at best. War was to be hell, the Yanks had determined, and they were practicing a scorched earth policy throughout the South. Train tracks had been destroyed, and travel by rail was very uncertain. The Yanks had constantly been bombarding the forts protecting Charleston, making travel by ship equally dangerous.

But throughout the journey, Tia cared little. She couldn't shake the vision of the beautiful little girl who had died. She couldn't forget the way that the photographer had posed the dead child to take her picture. Memories. Memories that would haunt her a lifetime, she thought.

She'd had little to do with her own travel arrangements, leaving all the details to Risa and Alaina, who argued over her route and just how and when she should travel. In a way, however, there was little choice—she would have to travel by the whim of the war, with little help otherwise. Her sisters-in-law and Risa were rather like a threesome of maternal hens, leaving St. Augustine with her and braving whatever dangers might face them to accompany her south down the river to the blockade runner. They made certain the captain was a respectable man, and obtained his assurances that he would see to Tia's welfare above all else.

The captain, a man named Larson, was a kindly, gnarled little fellow, a man dedicated to the south. Tia took her meals in his cabin, where he talked fondly about his two little girls, the wife he had lost in childbirth, and how he despised the men who claimed to be

Rebels but ran the blockade purely for the profit they could make. They were bleeding the South worse than the Yankees.

Charleston had been under heavy fire. He would best be able to deliver her to Wilmington. He didn't consider the seas a safe way for a woman to travel—not that there was a safe or sure way to travel through the South anymore.

As it happened, she was able to disembark in North Carolina just off of the Virginia border. Captain Larson received word from his contact at the port that Brent had arranged for an escort to bring her to the hospital where he was working, on the outskirts of Richmond. She was disheartened to meet the two men who would take her to her cousin; they were so thin, their uniforms so very threadbare. They had both been wounded, and weren't ready yet to return to the front line, yet were able to take on the duty of protecting one woman along a path that might be peopled by cowardly deserters or a stray Yankee. Both men were polite, courteous to a fault, and determined that she should have decent accommodations each night. Her first evening she spent at a small, still-functioning plantation that had thus far avoided Yankee depredations. Her hostess was the wife of a lieutenant who had known Ian before the war. The woman thought that Tia must now hate her brother.

She was careful not to mention that she had married a Yankee as well. Her blindly loyal hostess might have thrown her right out. Thankfully, the woman seemed to think that her cousin Jerome was single-handedly keeping the South in the war.

The next morning, they started riding early again. They avoided riders when they heard them coming; Sergeant Brewster, the older of her escort, told her that they never really knew just where they might run into a party of scouting Yanks. In the towns, however, they dared the main roads. They were able to buy meals, and there were places where it even seemed that there was not a war on. Everyone, however, seemed to be wearing a mask. They would win the war, yes, of course, the

South could still win the war, and though Europe had refused to recognize the government thus far, well, they would simply be proven wrong. The South could never lose. The spirit of the people still remained too strong. They were still thrashing the Union army at most engagements.

Whether that was true or not, Tia didn't know. The gaunt, weary soldiers helping her across the countryside didn't seem convinced that they were doing so well. Costs for food had soared—what little could be bought.

The second night she slept in a hotel thirty miles south of the city. She awoke the next morning to a fierce pounding on her door. She bolted out of bed in her nightgown, still exhausted from her long ride, startled by the pounding and blinded by the long tangle of her hair.

"Yes?"

"It's me, Tia, Brent."

"Brent!"

She didn't care the least about decorum but opened the door, delighted to see her cousin. She threw her arms around him, hugged him fiercely, then drew away from him. Brent looked good. He was all McKenzie, tall and dark, Seminole in his features but with a touch of his mother in the shade of his eyes and the hint of red in his hair. He was lean, as seemed to be the tendency with men in the South, but there was something about him that made up for his thinness and the slightly frayed quality of his uniform. He seemed alive with hope, as few people did these days, she thought.

"Tia . . . my God, it's been so long since I've seen you! You are still as beautiful as ever, little cousin, though I hear that the beaus of the South will be forever wailing. You have gone off and married a Yank—my own relation—so I am told."

Tia stepped back, still holding his hands, studying Brent. "Taylor, yes, of course. I keep forgetting that he is your relative as well."

"How is Taylor?"

"Very well, the last time I saw him," she murmured,

trying to keep all sound of bitterness from her tone. "I have heard that he went to see your father."

"You sound indignant!"

She shook her head. "Well, he was off on orders, and naturally, he shares nothing regarding his orders with me."

Brent shrugged. "It's a war, Tia. You're not on his side."

"Neither is your father."

Brent smiled. "Well, Risa's letter, informing me that you were coming, arrived just a few days ago, along with a long, long missive from my mother. It seems there was a Yank sailor tossed up on their shore after a storm. He carried confidential despatches. Taylor was sent to find him, and bring him back."

"Did he do so?"

"No. You see, my older sister had decided she wanted to keep the fellow, and so Taylor went off to return the despatches—and report the soldier unfit for duty so that he could get an honorable discharge."

"How wonderful," she murmured.

"So it seems. Jen has now married the young man."

"Jen remarried—a *Yankee?*"

"Ah, well, he's not a military man at all anymore, so I understand."

She lowered her head, amazed at the information about her cousin Jennifer. No one had been more passionately hateful regarding anyone involved with the Federal government. Jen had been ready to lay down her own life rather than give up the fight. And now . . . she had married for a second time. "Everyone is getting married, so it seems. I didn't know about Jen."

"I believe the wedding just took place." He cleared his throat. "Well, I guess I should tell you now—I have just married as well."

"What? Oh, my lord, Brent! We didn't know, we had no idea."

"Well, you didn't ask me about marrying Taylor. You didn't ask your own father, so I hear, young lady!"

"The war changes the way we do things," she murmured. "But tell me! What is her name, where did you meet?"

"Mary. You'll meet her later. I met her at the special hospital where I was last working."

"Brent! I know where you were last working! Did you marry a . . . a . . ."

He laughed, tapping her chin. "Prostitute—is that the word you're looking for? No, I didn't marry a prostitute. But I wouldn't have cared in the least what she did in her past. She's the most wonderful woman in the world. Her father was my patient. He passed away, I'm afraid, but thanks to him, we're together, and it's horribly ironic—I still spend my days patching men together, but I've never been happier in my life."

"Oh, Brent, I'm so glad!" she said.

"Well, you must know what it's like."

Know what it was like . . . to be loved, as Brent loved his Mary? No, she could not begin to imagine being so cherished.

She kept smiling.

"Marriage is . . . different."

He laughed. "It must be—with Taylor. Especially . . ."

"Yes?"

"Well, with you being so opposed on your views of the war. Frankly, I can't see how it ever came about, but then . . ." He shrugged, grinning at her. "Well, actually, I'm just very lucky that I do have Mary, I suppose. Still, you and Taylor! You are the very soul of independence and Taylor . . . well, Abby was the sweetest little thing in the world, living by his very word."

"You knew Abby?"

"Of course. Taylor is what . . . my second or third cousin or second cousin once removed, or something of the like. His family lived further north, but he came south often enough." He grinned at her. "You've got to remember, you're from the all 'white' branch of the McKenzie family—I'm from the branch with the red blood. Taylor has a similar background. Such a history in the world we live in can create a unique relationship."

"So Abby was—sweet?" she couldn't help but asking.

Her curiosity was morbid, she told herself. Abby was dead, gone. Yet Abby remained a ghost in her life. The perfect wife, while she . . . well, she was a decadent, infamous Rebel spy.

"Charming. But very strong when she chose to be. I can't imagine what he felt, watching her die . . . oh, sorry, Tia. Well, of course. That is the past. He's married to you now. And here you are deep, deep in Rebel territory. Does he know?"

She lifted her hands. "I—don't know. You know more than I do. I came here because of Rhiannon. I felt I had no choice."

"Yes, of course. I understand. Well, surely Taylor will understand as well. Pity he isn't on our side. He would have been quite an asset. I've never met a man with sharper vision, clearer hearing. When we were kids, he could put us all to shame in the Everglades. He could hear the flutter of a butterfly's wings, I think. See in pitch darkness. He's the perfect scout—the Pinkerton Agency wanted him to work with them, but he stayed with the cavalry despite his engineering skills."

"Engineering?"

Brent looked surprised. "Engineering. He studied at Oxford for a while, before entering West Point. He's a regular genius with bridges, roads, pontoons . . . his first love is actually architecture. He used to talk about the building that time would bring to Florida. You didn't know?"

"I . . . well, no." She hesitated. She didn't know much about the man she had married. "We haven't had much time together."

"Well, I must admit, I haven't seen him much myself lately, but then, I've barely seen my own folks since the war began. My mother, bless her, must spend hours writing letters—and then hoping they can reach us. Anyway, the letter I received from Risa said that Rhiannon had written to Varina Davis, but that she felt someone should see her in person as well."

"Do you know about the dream?"

"Something about a balcony, and a child. But I

haven't been able to see either the President or Varina
in the last few days. He has been insanely busy, suffering
from insomnia—and from crushing blows. You've heard
that the Europeans have refused to recognize our
government?"

"Yes."

"He is losing too many men—and too many generals.
But I've sent in a request to see Varina. When we arrive,
we'll see her. Set Rhiannon's mind at rest."

"She was so distraught. The dream keeps recurring.
In it, there is always a little boy, falling from a balcony.
She doesn't know whether she's dreaming about any of
the Davis children, but she's so upset. She's described
what she has seen, and both Risa and Alaina are convinced that the house she's seeing is the White House
of the Confederacy."

"Well, cousin, get dressed. We'll go right away. I'll
meet you downstairs. The executive mansion isn't quite
as open as it was at the beginning of the war, but we'll
go straight there and surely, since I sent my note, we'll
get an audience with Varina quickly enough. Maybe Rhiannon's letter has already reached her."

"Thanks, Brent."

"I'll be downstairs."

She watched him go, closed the door, and dressed
quickly. When she hurried downstairs, he was waiting
for her. He had hired a carriage, and as they jolted along
the streets on the outskirts, Tia was amazed at the
changes that had taken place since the war had begun.
All over, there were defense works set up. "In case
Grant gets in close," Brent told her.

"How close has he come?" she asked.

"Close," he replied. He met her eyes, then squeezed
her fingers. "But Lee meets him every time."

She nodded, and looked outside the carriage again.
There were people everywhere. More and more, the
closer they got to the heart of the city. Wounded men
in worn uniforms were in abundance.

So many men without arms . . . without legs . . . limping on crutches. The expressions on their faces were so lost.

"The city has changed, I guess," Brent said. "Strange, I don't see it as you do, since I have watched as it has happened."

"Why is that building burned to rubble?"

"Ah, that was a munitions factory—burned by our own men when it seemed the Yanks might be getting in. People have fled the city, returned, fled the city, returned. It's the capital of a nation at war. This is the price that is paid."

In time, they came to the huge white house that was serving as the executive mansion for the confederacy. The street was lined with carriages there. Civilians and military men hurried about with grave faces. Fashionably dressed women—appearing just a little frayed about the edges—moved about on their business, most still accompanied by slaves and servants. There seemed to be a constant flow of soldiers on horseback.

"Here! We'll alight here!" Brent called to their driver.

He helped Tia from the carriage and they walked from the street to the elegant house. Tia was amazed to see how neglected and overgrown the grounds were.

"Once . . ." Brent said, pausing on the walk.

"Once what?"

"The house was beautiful, freshly painted, the grounds were beautifully cared for . . . Mrs. Davis's coach was usually ready to take her about the city . . . she had such fine horses. She sold them long ago now. She hasn't been about much lately. It's said that Davis considers himself surrounded by foes. Most people believe that spies have penetrated even the White House. Davis has been ill, sleeping badly. He forgets to eat. I was at a meeting with him not long ago. It was a dinner, but he barely touched his food. He has Varina quite concerned as of late."

"He must carry a great weight on his shoulders."

"He does, indeed. You should hear the furor over Fort Pillow—though I must say, whatever happened was terrible."

"What are you talking about?"

"Well—perhaps some of the fury from the Yanks has to do with our accusations against them. General Dahlgren was to attack Richmond—he didn't make it to the city. He had thought himself something of the conqueror, drinking blackberry wine at the home of our own Secretary of War, Mr. Seddon—with Mrs. Seddon. He was led astray by a guide—hanged the guide—but reached Richmond too late to tie up with Kilpatrick, who had already retreated. To make a long story short, he was killed. He had an artificial leg, acquired at Gettysburg, which was stolen—along with papers claiming that his intent was to fire Richmond and kill the Confederate cabinet. Lee sent photographic plates of the papers to General Meade, still directing the Army of the Potomac under Grant, protesting vigorously. The Yanks were up in arms over us, declaring the entire battle a massacre. Then, just a few weeks later, Bedford Forest's famed Reb Cavalry storms Fort Pillow—five hundred some odd soldiers are holding the place with more than a third of them being black troops. About two hundred and thirty are killed, another hundred are wounded, and two hundred something are captured. That is, I must say, an absurdly high ratio of killed to captured. So the Yanks are stating that we're all a lot of murderers, that it was a massacre—which it might have been, since over two hundred of the troops were black soldiers, and many men in the South are bitter and afraid of the blacks fighting against them—it might well have been a massacre. At any rate, all this goes on day in and day out, and there's no good news, so Davis is suffering the torment of the damned."

They had reached the house. Tia looked at her cousin, reflecting on the actions he had just told her about. It was no wonder there was so much hatred in the war. Both sides could be horribly ugly. She wondered if the bitterness would ever be lived down.

*Not in my lifetime!* she thought.

And suddenly, she just wanted to run away. From it all. She had dreamed of visiting the pyramids in Egypt, seeing London, Madrid, Rome. What a pity she hadn't gone! Before she had seen the dead, dying, and maimed soldiers, before she had come to all but bathe in blood. Before she had seen so many people die, the children as well.

"Here we are. Perhaps my message has been received."

They entered the foyer, and Brent gave his name to a servant, saying that they were friends and that he had written ahead to tell Mrs. Davis they were coming. They needed to see her as soon as possible, on a matter of urgency.

They were asked to wait.

Seconds passed, then minutes. The morning waned. Tia knew that Brent was anxious. He had left his patients to the care of others.

They stood outside, waiting. Brent talked more about Richmond, about the war, telling her that he had seen Sydney shortly before Christmas. Tia was glad to hear it, musing on the fact that Sydney remained in Washington.

"Well, she has married a Yank, you know."

"Of course, but . . ."

"No one made her return. She wanted to be in Washington, just in case he made it home for Christmas. There was some fighting then, of course, but the weather was wretched, halting the armies when God and mercy could not. She hoped that, due to the fact that the armies were most frequently up to their necks in snow, he might be spared—especially considering the fact that he had been injured at Gettysburg."

"I knew that he'd been wounded. Julian told me," Tia said.

"Yes, of course, Julian was there to perform the surgery." He tapped his hat against his leg, growing impatient. "I am a colonel," he told her ruefully. "But apparently, there are generals ahead of me."

"Brent, go back to the hospital," Tia suggested. "You don't need to wait for me."

"I had thought we might be more impressive together. Especially as kin to my brother. Jerome is quite the celebrated hero, you know."

"Of course. But you have patients who may be dying."

"There are many other doctors on duty."

"None so good as you."

He grinned. "That's true, of course, but they will manage without me for an afternoon."

She smiled, glad that he was with her.

Yet even as he spoke, they started to hear shouts coming from inside the house. Then, pandemonium. People were running everywhere; cries could be heard. Brent stared at Tia, then tried to regain entrance. They were stopped by a heavyset man.

"No one will enter now!"

"What has happened, man? I'm a doctor!" Brent declared indignantly.

The man shook his head. "It's too late now. There's been an accident. Young Joseph Emory has fallen."

Brent stared at Tia. She felt as if a river of ice suddenly filled her veins rather than blood.

"Excuse me, I will see the child!" Brent snapped forcefully, and pushed his way past the man. Tia followed.

But the boy and his family were on the ground level. There was too much confusion in the house for anyone to stop them as they saw the scene from above, then rushed back out of the entry and around to the ground level in the rear of the residence. As they came around the house, the sounds of sobbing seemed to be everywhere. Servants and children flocked about. They could hear the comments of the crowd that had formed.

"The President has been working so hard . . ."

"Mrs. Davis brought him lunch every day."

"She had just left the children, just left them to bring him his lunch."

"The boy fell."

"He was his father's favorite, so they say."

"He died right in his father's arms."

"Drew his last breath . . ."

"The poor babe!"

And there, beneath the deadly veranda, was Jefferson Davis, president of the Confederacy, down on his knees.

The grown man with worn, harried features held the lifeless body of his child in his arms. Silent sobs wracked his body. His wife was at his side, tears streaking down her face. She cried horribly. Tia bit down on her lower lip, noting that the first lady of the South was noticeably pregnant.

*And in such a condition, she must endure this agony . . .*

Soldiers stood by awkwardly.

"Sir . . ." A messenger had come with a despatch, Tia saw.

"Not mine, oh Lord, but thine!" Davis cried out. "Not mine, oh Lord, but thine! Not mine, oh Lord, but thine!"

Varina, tall, regal—and broken—stumbled to her feet. She said nothing, but looked at the soldier. The man turned away, his head lowered. The hardest heart would have felt a split. The beautiful child, five-year-old Joe, lay in his father's arms. No human enemy could have done the damage to him that God had wrought that day.

Whatever urgent business challenged the Confederacy would have to wait. Varina went back down to her knees by her husband and her dead son.

Brent gripped Tia's arm. She couldn't move. She could only stare at the little boy, so beautiful, so sweet in death. *How could they bear it? There was so much that was so very awful, she had seen young men cut down in their prime, and yet, this loss of a child seemed so unjust, so cruel, that she wondered if there could be a God at all. If there was, He must have been laughing at all of them, perhaps punishing them for the death they practiced so cruelly upon one another . . .*

Brent pulled Tia back, away from the growing crowd of servants and soldiers, onlookers and friends.

"Brent, is there nothing—" she whispered in anguish.

"He's dead, Tia," Brent said softly. "There is nothing I can do for a dead child."

There was nothing he could do for the child, but he and Tia stayed for a while, waiting in the parlor with Mary Chestnut, Varina's very dear friend, and others close to the Davises. Many people had come to help, yet

few knew what to say or do—there was so little to say
or do when a child was lost. As more and more messen-
gers came and went, sent on to the president's military
advisor, Brent and Tia found themselves waiting in Varina's little office on the ground floor. He was startled to
see a pile of unopened mail lying on the footstool by
her sewing basket. The top letter had a return address
upon it: *Rhiannon McKenzie, Cimarron, Tampa Bay,
Florida.*

His heart seemed to catch in his throat. Her letter had
made it, just as they had made it. Too late. Perhaps
destiny remained in God's hands, and He allowed his
people only to think that they could change it.

Tia seemed drained, unaware of anything. Her beautiful fair skin was almost snow-white against the ebony of
her hair and eyes, she was so pale. She hadn't seen the
letter. When she turned away at last in response to
something Mrs. Chestnut said, Brent unobtrusively
picked up the letter and slid it into his jacket pocket.

It could do nothing now but cause the family further
pain.

Taylor arrived in Washington aboard the ten-gunned
steamer *Majesty,* a ship he'd boarded in St. Augustine.
Coming ashore, he heard a newsboy hawking out the
information that God had smitten the President of the
Confederacy—little Joseph Emory Davis was dead.

Disembarking and leading Friar from his confinement
in the ship, Taylor bought a newspaper, anxiously looking for word of Brent or Tia in the story. There was
none. The anger which had begun a slow burn inside
him when he'd heard of Tia's journey had cooled once
he'd returned to the base at St. Augustine—and he'd
spent an evening with the McKenzies, especially Rhiannon, who had seemed more distraught than ever.

Yet, he still felt a churning turmoil within. A feeling
of *helplessness.* Yes, he damned well meant to get down
to Rebel territory and find her. But what then? What
power did he have over her while the war raged? He
wanted her safe.

Out of the range of fire.

She was in Richmond—and he wanted her back. That simple. He damned well meant to find a way to do it.

Reading the dire news regarding Davis, he discovered that the reporter was not nearly so judgmental as the newsboy hawking the papers. There was sorrow in the article for the loss of a child. The writer didn't believe that Davis had lost his child because he had sinned before God—President and Mrs. Lincoln had lost a child during the war as well. The President's beloved little Tad had died of sickness rather than a fall, but the pain endured by the parents had been the same.

Having reached Washington, Taylor reported to Magee's offices, only to discover that the general was in the field. His presence in Washington, however, had immediately been reported to higher places. He was summoned from Magee's base headquarters straight to the White House, where he found that Lincoln himself had decided to see him.

Though it must have been difficult enough just to keep up with the movements of his generals, Lincoln was aware that Colonel Taylor Douglas had been sent back to duty in Florida. Though other losses were far greater, he knew about Olustee, and he knew, as well, about Naval Lieutenant Long who had been lost with important despatches regarding navy movements. Taylor was able to report that his business in the south of the Florida peninsula with Long had been successfully concluded. "The despatches are returned, and he has been discharged, sir. He is in no state of health to continue pursuing this war."

"We have lost him to the other side?"

Taylor shook his head. "We have lost him to the concept of war; he is weary and broken."

"We are all weary and broken."

Indeed, the President had aged greatly since the war had begun. The battles showed on his face, as if the loss of life lay in his heart at all times.

"No, sir, you do not break," Taylor countered, and grinning ruefully, he meant his every word. "I am surprised that you can be so aware of such small events within the magnitude of this war."

Lincoln shrugged, lifting his large, long-fingered hands. "Little things win a war, in the end. The Europeans helped us more than a dozen victorious battles when they refused to recognize the government of the Confederacy. As to Olustee . . . well, I had hoped for Florida to return to the fold."

"I am afraid she will not be so easy, sir."

"But so many of her citizens are Unionists."

"That is true, but my state is divided. And our best military minds have decided that the vast effort needed to win the state is not worth it—not when they have decided that Richmond must be taken and the deep South slashed in half."

"I'm afraid that our greatest military minds are fighting for our enemy!" Lincoln murmured.

"Are you referring to General Lee, sir?"

"And others. But I think I have a man who will fight now."

"General Grant?"

"You know him?"

"No, sir. He was fighting in the western theater; I was in the eastern campaigns until I was ordered to assess strengths when we undertook the Florida campaign."

"You'll know him soon enough. However, if we had Lee . . . I understand he was your good friend."

"A friend to many of us, sir. He was my teacher at West Point. A fine instructor, and a better man."

"It's been said he could be heard pacing a mile away the night I offered to make him head of the Union armies. He had such a beautiful, gracious home—now we bury our dead in his lawn. It is a bitter, bitter war, sparing no one. Old Jeff Davis apparently paced away the night his boy died. God knows, I can sympathize with the poor man, and he is, indeed, in my prayers. It's far too easy to love our enemies and feel their pain—but much harder to know they must be beaten. I'm sorry to see the destruction and death we reap, but God help us, if we can just end it . . . then we will reach out the hand of friendship, we will take our brothers back into our fold, and we will weep for our dead and our lost together."

"I pray it will be so, sir."

"Many men will feel the need for revenge when this is ended. Tell me, Colonel Douglas, will it be so for you? The war has made many widows—you are one of the few men standing to have lost a wife in this sad conflict."

"I did bear a grudge, sir. A bitter grudge indeed."

"Time has healed the wound?"

"Most wounds scar, sir. But like you, I am eager for the conflict to end." He was quiet for a moment. "I have remarried. A woman with Southern sympathies. You know her brother, Colonel Ian McKenzie."

"Indeed, so I had heard. You have married young Miss Tia McKenzie, the belle of your home state, daughter of Cimarron, renowned for its gracious hospitality, far and near. As your new wife is reputed to be a rare beauty, wild-spirited and entirely charming, I am happy for you, Colonel. It is rare to find moments of peace in this war."

"Very rare," Taylor said wryly. Moments of *peace?* "You are remarkable, sir. You not only know your officers, but are able to keep up on their marital affairs!"

"A house such as Cimarron is known far and wide. As are Jarrett McKenzie's services—not in the name of North or South, but in the name of humanity."

"The family is divided in loyalties, you know. Passionately divided."

Lincoln smiled. "You know, most of my wife's family fought for the South. So many are now dead! She has been accused of Southern sympathies herself. Poor Mary—her brother was killed, but because I am who I am, she didn't mourn him. Rather, she announced publicly that he should not have fought against our Union. When this all ends, the wounds will be terrible. And as you say, even with time, there will be terrible scars. Make peace with your Southern wife, Colonel Douglas. God knows, you have fought the war with faith and vigor, and are deserving of peace." He turned from Tay-

lor, writing on his desk. "There will be fierce action
soon, Colonel Douglas, and your expertise will be
needed. Tomorrow you must head out and find General
Grant himself to give assistance in the coming conflict,
but this order which I am now writing will give you three
weeks' leave. The order is undated, sir, and you may
take the time when you feel that duty will allow it and
circumstance demands it. There will be another attempt
to sway Florida—she is a giant breadbasket, and though
it saddens me, there seems no recourse other than to
starve the South. God go with you, sir. I promise, once
you find General Grant, you will no longer deal with the
frustration of running from the Rebs!"

Taylor accepted the orders the President handed him,
the one directing him to General Grant, and the other
allowing him a leave of absence. "Thank you, sir. I've
no desire, however, to leave a war half-fought."

"You won't leave the war, Colonel. But God alone
knows when a man may need time."

Taylor nodded. Watching Lincoln, he wondered if he
didn't have some of the precognition that plagued Julian's wife, Rhiannon. It was said that the President had
dreamed himself in a coffin; good friends said that he
saw his own death. He wondered uneasily if the man
weren't foretelling an occasion—tragic? deadly? dangerous?—when Taylor would need time away.

"Thank you, sir."

"You've a night of leisure in the city, Colonel. Go
home, rest, enjoy your time."

"Yes, sir," he said, but he didn't intend to head home
at all.

When he had left his audience with the President,
Taylor headed straight to a tavern often habited by cav-
alrymen. He would not go to his own Washington town
home—he had avoided it since the beginning of the war.
Abby's clothes still filled the closet; he'd never had the
time nor the inclination to move them. Her touch was
everywhere. She had even begun to knit clothing for the
baby she was going to have, and they'd had a mahogany
cradle carved.

In the tavern, he found a number of injured friends, politicians, men assigned to the forts that circled Washington, and men who had just received a change of command. In March, Grant had been in the city, conferring with Lincoln. Two known assaults would be occurring with the fine weather—the continual, Grant-determined pursuit of Lee and Richmond, and a slash across the deep South, hopefully breaking the backbone of the region. Louisiana had been drawn back to the fold; a new pro-Union government had been formed. South Carolina needed to be beaten to her knees—there lived the heart of the insurrection, and there it should be smashed and damned.

Taylor was in the middle of his second whiskey when a soldier at his side cleared his throat loudly. "Colonel Douglas, sir!"

He turned, not recognizing the man at first. He was old, with gray whiskers and a round face. He wore a sergeant's uniform.

"Sergeant," he said, acknowledging the man.

The old fellow grinned. "It's been a while, sir. I was cavalry back then, a private, with you at Manassas, back at the start of the war. Got a bullet in my leg, never could ride decent after."

"Ah . . . yes. I remember. Granger. Your name is Granger."

"Yes, sir, it is. Sergeant Hal Granger."

"Well, it's good to see you, Sergeant. Glad to see you alive." He swallowed the rest of his whiskey.

"Thank you, sir. And you as well. I don't mean to bother you none, Colonel. Looks as if you and that whiskey bottle are keeping company enough. But I'm assigned down to Old Capitol now, and I heard tell you were kin to folks named McKenzie."

Taken by surprise, Taylor frowned. "That I am, Sergeant. Is there some news about one of the McKenzies?"

"Nothing ill, sir, nothing bad happening at all, I'm glad to say. I've met a number of folks by that name now. Why, the Rebel sea captain was my guest awhile, but he's been back, a devil on the water, for some time, so I hear. Had the Doc McKenzie—Dr. Julian McKenzie—and Miss Sydney McKenzie."

"Sydney was in yes, I'd heard, but . . . Sydney married Jesse Halston."

"Right. But Colonel Halston, he's been at war for some long time now. And Miss Sydney, well . . ."

Taylor's jaw tightened; his features locked into a frown. "What about Miss Sydney?" he asked.

"Ah, well, sir! Nothing's amiss . . . but she doesn't seem to get out much, sir, that's all. Thought she'd be mighty uplifted by a visit from you, if you're able, before riding out."

Taylor nodded. "Where is she?"

Granger gave him the address. Taylor paid his bill, thanked Granger, and left the tavern, suddenly feeling sober and anxious.

Twenty minutes of riding brought him to the street where Sydney had taken her apartment. He frowned, seeing a uniformed soldier seated on her porch. His hat was pulled low and he was leaning back comfortably in his chair. Sleeping, Taylor thought.

Dismounting from Friar, he tossed his horse's reins over the hitch and approached the soldier.

The man didn't move. Taylor kicked the chair.

The fellow came to life. "Hey, what the—"

Straightening, pulling his hat back, he started to bellow—but then noticed Taylor's uniform and rank. "Colonel, sir—" he began, leaping to his feet, saluting.

"What the hell is going on here, Private?"

"I just dozed off, sir. It's traces of the fever. I had the malaria. That's why I'm on this duty, sir."

"What duty is that?"

The private reddened. "Well, the lady who lives here is a known Rebel spy."

"Who says so?"

"Her, uh, her husband, sir."

"Oh?"

The soldier grimaced uncomfortably. "She's been caught in the act, sir."

"Ah. Well, you can doze right back off again, soldier. I'll be watching her tonight."

"Oh, no, colonel, sir. I mean, I can't—I mean—just who are you, sir?"

Taylor folded his arms over his chest. "The lady's cousin, soldier."

"Oh, jeez—you must be Douglas, sir! I should have known, sir!" Suddenly, he was saluting all over again. "We've heard about you, sir. Every soldier has heard about you. Of course, I should have seen it right away. You're also an In—"

"Indian," Taylor finished for him, but he felt no rancor. The young soldier seemed to be a decent enough fellow. "My cousins are Rebels, but I was under the impression that Colonel Halston had vouched for his wife, and that she had been set free."

"Well, yes, sir, but she kept slipping back down to Richmond, sir."

"Doing what?"

"Well, no one rightly knew, sir. That was the problem."

"She's in there now, I take it?"

"Yes, sir."

"At ease then, soldier. I'll be with her now."

Taylor stepped past him, entering the house, closing the door behind him. It was a small but cozy place. It smelled like fresh-baked bread; a fire burned in the hearth. "Sydney?" he called.

There was no answer. He walked to the bedroom door, looked in. The bedroom was darkened. He could see a form beneath the covers.

"Sydney?" he whispered.

He walked over to the bed. Pulled back the covers. The shape of a body had been formed with pillows. No human being slept therein.

Mary was charming. Pleasant, thoughtful, and lovely with her warm, serious, silver eyes and long dark hair. Tia tried, really tried, to greet her with enthusiasm, to appreciate the woman who had made Brent so happy. When they were introduced, Tia hugged Mary and welcomed her to the family. Brent poured Tia a sherry, and she drank it, then started to cry.

She couldn't eat that evening. Brent told her that little Joseph Emory's death was terrible and painful but she couldn't make herself sick over what had happened. She didn't know how to explain to him about the little girl who had died in Jacksonville, how it was all too unfair to be endured. He was helpless, telling her that if she didn't calm down, he'd be wasting good opiates on her to *make* her calm down. Mary understood her better. She and Tia sat together for a very long time, and they cried together, but in the end, Brent did slip laudanum into Tia's drink, and she fell into an exhausted sleep.

In the middle of the night, she awoke. She sat up, staring at the fire, unable to sleep anymore. Unable to cry.

Brent really didn't understand.

She had failed Rhiannon. Rhiannon had known what was going to happen. Tia hadn't managed to move fast enough, and so another child had died.

Brent found her there, hugged her, tried talking to her. "Tia! This isn't like you. Where is your courage, where is your fire?"

"Gone," Tia told him. "Dead—like the children. Like the young men we kill on a daily basis."

"Tia, you're really going to make yourself sick. You're married now; you could be expecting your own child—"

"No!" she told him, swinging on him violently. "No! I will not have children, I will not let this happen, I will not have any more death!"

"Tia, you can't say that. You don't know that you won't have children. You can't will yourself not to have children—"

"I will *not* have them. I don't care what I have to do or not do, but I will never, ever have children!" she swore.

"I'm not sure that will be agreeable to your husband, Tia. Abby was expecting a child when she was killed. Taylor wanted children."

"Then Taylor will have to find a new wife!" she snapped. "Unless . . . unless . . . he gets himself killed!"

Suddenly, it seemed that flood gates were opened and she started to cry again, and cry, and Brent decided not to argue with her anymore. He fixed her a sherry with more laudanum, and he held her until she fell asleep again.

This time, he had assured himself, she would sleep through the next day.

Taylor sat in the rocking chair before the fire in his cousin's room, rocking, watching the blaze. He waited an hour, then grew worried.

Instinct warned him she wasn't returning anytime soon. The smell of the fresh-baked bread was a front. Just like the pillows tucked into the bed.

Maybe she had meant to make it home. Maybe she was in trouble.

He walked to her bedroom window and studied the sill, then opened the window and looked to the ground below. This was obviously the way she had left. A man didn't need to be any kind of a scout to read so clear a sign.

He left by the front door, saying nothing to the soldier on duty. Mounting Friar, Taylor rode around Sydney's street, picked up the trail, and followed it to a livery, where a man on duty remembered Sydney well. She was a beautiful woman who often rented conveyances from him. She had a brother she visited behind the lines, sick relatives just south of Alexandria.

"She's a sweet one, she is, and a beauty, and hey . . ." He paused, studying Taylor in the lamplight. "Colonel, you her brother?" Taylor was certain the man would think that anyone with Indian blood looked like anyone else with Indian blood, but the livery keeper really seemed to admire Sydney, and wanted to help.

"Cousin. And I'm afraid for her. Running into danger behind the lines."

"Well, I found something in a carriage when she returned it one night. Keep forgetting to give it to her. Perhaps it will help you."

The fellow limped into his office. He saw Taylor watching him as he limped back out. "Bullet in the ankle at Antietam," he explained. "Took me out of the army right fast; they thought I'd lose the foot. Here, it's what I found. Don't know why I kept it. It's just an old wrapping—for material, maybe, or a piece of clothing. But there's an address on it. See there? Bailiwick Farm, Virginia. Do you know the place?"

Taylor did. Northeast of Fredericksburg, in continually disputed terrain. He thanked the fellow, and quickly took his leave.

From the livery, he rode out of the city.

He was well aware of the mounting tensions. Washington itself was surrounded by forts. The father he traveled outward, through Alexandria, Union territory by sheer proximity, the more he heard about the way the armies were forming. They would meet soon.

Heading south, he was challenged several times by the Union pickets. He readily stopped at the lines, handing over his papers.

By dawn, he was far past the lines and into Virginia, into no-man's-land. Troops from both the North and the South vied for every advantage here. He avoided the main roads, taking side trails through the foliage. At one point, he barely avoided a small troop of Southern cavalry—scouts and skirmishers, he thought, watching the men from the cover of a huge oak. He could hear only bits and pieces of their conversation, but enough to know that the whole body of Lee's army was not far away.

By noon, he had reached the farm. Time had taught him caution; he watched the house from the untended apple orchard to its northwest side before deciding how to approach it.

The place had never been ostentatious; the house itself had two stories with trellises but no balconies. Spring flowers tried to climb along the trellises, but they were withered and dying. The paddock fences were broken in places; paint peeled there as it did from the house. The place looked neglected and sad.

A few skinny chickens roamed the dirt in front of the front porch area. One bony mule hung its head sadly in the paddock to the left of the house.

There was a large barn to the right. Its double doors were closed.

Taylor placed his hand on Friar's nose. "Stay here, boy. But come for me right away if I whistle, will you?"

He moved quickly from the orchard to the rear of the barn. Flat against the rear wall, he searched the wooden structure until he found an area of rotted planking. Slamming it with a fist, he winced as the beam itself gave with a creak. He pushed through, rolling into a stall filled with stale, damp straw. He immediately came to his feet, surveying the area.

The stables were empty—except for the wagon in the center of the work area. He walked to it; the horses hitched to the wagon were solid workhorses, in far better shape than the mule in the paddock. He moved to the double doors at the front of the structure. They weren't latched; he could push them open and see toward the house. He watched. And waited.

He didn't now how long he'd stood there, but then he saw a slim black girl come out of the house and start toward the stables. Frowning, he turned around and saw the ladder to the loft. He skimmed up it quickly, and went flat against the rotting hay.

A moment later, an older black man came from the house, then two youngsters, and finally a big, well-muscled black man in his prime. A field hand, Taylor reasoned.

As the older man entered the barn, Taylor saw clearly through the doors. A young, strikingly pretty black woman was racing after him—followed by Sydney. What in God's name was she up to?

Even as Sydney ran, he heard the sound of hoofbeats.

"A Rebel patrol!" the black woman cried.

"Get in, I'll fend them off!"

The black woman entered the barn and hovered at

the entrance, hidden against the doors. Even from his perch in the loft, Taylor could see the pulse beating at her throat.

The hoofbeats came to a halt. "Hello!" Sydney greeted them cheerfully. "Gentlemen, tell me, are the Yankees at bay?"

Barely able to see out the slit in the door, Taylor tried to count their number. "Is there about to be a battle near here? Dear Lord, gentlemen, I haven't much, but we've sweet fresh water—"

"Ma'am, there's word you're harboring an ex-slave known as Sissy McKendrick, and that you are committing treason by giving her aid."

"Sir! How dare you accuse me—"

"Check the barn—and if you find that black demon with any other darkees, hang 'em on the spot. I don't care if Jeff Davis thinks they ought to be returned to their masters—I think they're dangerous!"

"Wait!" Sydney protested. "You can't just kill people."

"Maybe I won't quite hang a white woman, miss. Definitely not right away. Maybe I'll just give you a chance to convince me and the boys that you shouldn't hang. Though they say you're a traitor—a Southern woman taken to thievery and spying for Abe Lincoln!"

"No honest soldier under Master Robert E. Lee would ever talk to a woman that way."

"Maybe I just don't care what Bobby Lee would say, ma'am. Bobby Lee isn't here right now, is he?"

The doors burst open. Taylor was able to get a full count of the men. Seven of them, including the leader, who remained mounted, staring down at Sydney. His six men entered the barn. The blacks had tried to hide in the musty hay once they'd known the soldiers were coming in, but one of the soldiers picked up a pitchfork and started to aim at a too-large pile of straw. Sissy cried out, and the man stopped, turned, and grabbed her. "I think we got the one we're after—damned pretty piece of black baggage, sir!"

"Hang her—hang her now, and fast, and get the rest

of them out here. Let 'em know that they'll die for this, and others won't be quite so willing to run!"

"No!" Sydney cried. "Stop it, stop it now, I'll report you—"

"You won't be reporting anything, miss. You're the worst traitor here. When I finish with you, sweet little belle, there won't be a pretty thing about you, and you surely won't have lips and teeth to do much talking."

He dismounted, grabbing Sydney before she could turn to flee. She fought him, catching him in the eye. The blacks in the barn were beginning to scream. One of the soldiers drew his gun. Taylor had wanted a clearer shot, but he didn't dare wait.

He drew his Colts, aimed first for the man getting ready to shoot, and caught him straight through the heart.

Then taking a split second longer to make sure he didn't hit Sydney, he caught her attacker dead center in the forehead. Screams rose all around him as the slaves in the barn feared for their lives. The five remaining soldiers pulled their guns; five more shots from the Colts brought the Rebels down, all dying while still trying to find the position of the enemy.

Sydney saw him. She hadn't moved; the man who had assaulted her lay dead at her feet. She stared at him. "Taylor?" she whispered incredulously.

He came down the ladder quickly. Sissy stood by the doors again, staring at him as well. "Get your people into the wagon fast," Taylor ordered, "and get them the hell out of here as quickly as you can. Stick to the small trails—most regular troops are going to be too concerned with the major battle coming up to mind much about a wagon going by."

"Yes, sir," Sissy replied. "Come on now, people, you heard the man. Get in the wagon, under the straw in back, fast!"

Her elocution was perfect, her voice soft and melodic. She gazed at him with steady brown eyes, and he realized that she had never been really afraid. If they had chosen to hang her, she would have been willing to die.

Sydney, a little wobbly, walked into the barn. "Taylor, I . . . ." She stopped, staring at the dead men around her.

"Sydney," he said flatly. He came to her, stopping two feet in front of her, suddenly sickened by what the war was doing to all of them. "For the love of God, Sydney, what he hell are you doing? Sweet Jesus, you could have died here!"

"Oh God, Taylor, they're all—dead."

Sydney looked at him, stricken. But Sissy came to life with a vengeance. "Sydney , they were going to kill us, every last one of us!"

"But they were . . . Rebels. I never really meant to betray my people."

"Sydney! They weren't your people. They were the scum of the earth!"

Sydney stared at Taylor again. He thought she was going to crack.

"You killed them all," she said.

"I hate killing people, Sydney. I just didn't see a choice."

"No . . . no . . . it was all my fault!" she cried, and she suddenly threw herself at him, and she was shaking very hard. "Taylor, if you hadn't come . . . oh my God, they were going to hang us! Without a judge, without anything legal, without—"

"They were scum. White trash!" Sissy said. She was staring at Taylor. "Thank you, sir. I don't know you, but I am mighty beholden. It's a miracle that you're here."

"Not a miracle. I went to Sydney's house. I thought . . ." He shrugged. "I thought she was running intelligence behind the lines."

Sissy was very still, her chin high for a long moment. "Not intelligence. People, Colonel. Black people. Yes! She's slipped behind Rebel lines. And she's slipped back through Yankee lines. Saving lives, Colonel, saving lives, saving people!"

Taylor drew away from Sydney, slowly arching a brow. Her face flooded with color. She lifted her hands. "Jesse would still want to throttle me!" she said hoarsely. "And if Jerome knew . . . or Brent, or my father . . . Julian. Tia . . ." Her voice trailed.

"You've been working the underground railroad," he said incredulously.

"No!" Sydney said. "Not really. I didn't mean—"

"Yes!" the beautiful black woman declared defiantly. "She has been incredible."

"By accident!" Sydney said. He shook his head. Accident? He'd heard those words before. What happened that people were drawn into this conflict?

He smiled slowly, gravely. "Sydney McKenzie! I will be damned."

"Taylor, you understand then? You won't tell—"

"Sydney, you turned into a *Yankee?*"

"No! I'm a Rebel in all things . . . but this!" she whispered. "Taylor, you must keep my secret, you must—"

She broke off because he was shaking his head. "Sydney, I can't keep your secret. Jesse thinks you're spying for the Confederacy, so what you are doing has to be better. But he'd be angry because what you're doing is really dangerous. You've been branded a traitor. Go home, and stay under house arrest."

"Taylor, you can't mean to tell Jesse—"

"Sydney, I'm afraid that I do."

He leaned forward, giving her a kiss on her cheek. "I think he'll be very proud of you, too. After he throttles you, that is. But no more outings, Sydney. A good soldier knows when to lay down his arms."

Sydney lowered her head. "I know."

"We've got to get moving. I can follow you for about ten miles—that should bring us to a Union outpost, at the least."

Sissy was staring at him, smiling. "You one mighty fine man—for a white boy, that is. Are you married, Colonel?"

"No, he isn't," Sydney said.

"Yes, I'm afraid I am married," he told Sissy, grinning in return. He looked at Sydney to explain. "I've re-married."

"You have? When? Who? I'm so happy for you, Taylor. I know how deeply you were hurt when Abby died. When did this happen, where—"

"Tia."

"Tia!"

"Yes. Tia."

"Tia *McKenzie?*" she asked incredulously.

"The same. But now, if you'll excuse me, you have people beneath straw in that wagon, and God knows if these fellows had any friends following behind them. Sissy, it's been a pleasure meeting you. You are one of the most courageous—and beautiful—women of my acquaintance. Sydney, again, I'm very proud of you, but I've just left your father, and he would want to flay me alive if I didn't make you swear you'd never take such a chance again. Ever."

"I do swear, but—"

"Then let's get going."

"Let's get going, just like that!" Sydney protested, her emerald eyes as wide as saucers. "Taylor, wait, you can't really have married Tia—"

"I did, but we've no time to talk. Sydney, for the love of God, get in the wagon!"

She stared at him, threw her arms around him, and hugged him fiercely. "Thank you, Taylor, thank you so much for being here to save my life! I do swear that I'll guard it now myself!"

He didn't have to tell her again. She slipped from his embrace and into the wagon. Taylor dragged the dead man who lay outside the barn into the center of it, slapped the Rebel horses on their rumps, and whistled for Friar.

He followed the contraband wagon to the first Union picket he could find.

Then he turned back for the battle lines himself.

Tia lay in what felt like a strange state of twilight. She wasn't sleeping, but she wasn't awake. She didn't want to wake up. Waking meant the most awful sensation of loss. Just now, she was numb, and she liked the feeling.

Suddenly, she was being jarred out of sleep.

"Wake up, Tia!"

Brent was shaking her hard. Almost brutally.

"Stop it, Brent!" she protested angrily. "I want to stay here in bed. I want more laudanum."

"Not on your life. I've given you too much already. You've grieved for the dead; it's time to care about the living again. Get out of bed and get dressed. Fast."

"No."

But her cousin wrenched her covers away, caught her arm, and dragged her to her feet. "Tia, there's a major battle going on. Injured men all over. I'm being sent out to a field hospital. You're coming with me."

"No . . . no. You've got Mary. Nurses, orderlies—"

"Mary is coming. And you're coming with me, too. You're experienced. You've worked with Julian. You know me, and you'll be good with me."

"No, Brent, I don't care anymore. I'm sick of injured soldiers and chopped-up men."

"Oh! You're suddenly sick of them? Well, believe me, Tia, they're sick of being chopped up!"

"I don't care." She closed her eyes.

She was startled when her cousin suddenly seized hold of her, shaking her. "Damn you, Tia, now! I need your help—they need help. They're suffering. Not crying over what they can't change!"

"Brent!" She pulled free from him, taking a deep breath, meeting his eyes. What was the matter with her? "Brent, I'm sorry . . . I'll get dressed. Quickly," she told him.

"Good! I really need you, Tia."

Within a few minutes, she was ready.

With Brent and Mary, she rode down the street to the hospital, where dozens of wagons were being prepared with canvas tents and medical supplies. Men were shouting orders, horses were neighing, bugles were blowing, drums were pounding.

"The engagement has begun!"

"The bloody Yanks are everywhere."

"They say there will be thousands fallen."

"The Yanks don't give a bloody damn how many they kill, not even of their own!"

"Lee will beat them back. He always does."

"They're fighting right near Chancellorsville again."

More troops were amassing—cavalry, infantry. The street was filled with those leaving, and with those looking on.

And those afraid that Grant would ride into Richmond.

Soon their wagons were ready, and they were riding. Out to the Wilderness, an area of no-man's-land near Fredericksburg where the forest and foliage were nearly as thick as the earth.

And none of them knew just what kind of an inferno was about to be set loose.

# Chapter 20

Almost a year earlier, the same ground had been traveled by both armies—to fight the battle of Chancellorsville. Both Union and Confederate troops had died in the forests of the Wilderness.

Riding hard along the trails as they sought the best ground to establish their field hospital, Brent, Tia, and their party passed by sad and ghostly remembrances of the deadly battles gone past: bones, bleached white by the sun, stripped of all flesh by prowling creatures, lay in piles far too numerous all about the roads and among the trees and foliage. Tia tried to tell herself that they were the bones of horses, but a human skull kicked forward by her horse's hoof dispelled whatever illusions she might have cherished.

They found a copse far back in Rebel lines. Brent began to shout orders, and men were quickly setting up the tents, folding tables, chairs, stretchers, and instruments. Before they were set up and prepared, the injured began to come in, some screaming in pain, some silent, some awake, some unconscious. There were five surgeons beneath Brent, ten nurses including Tia and Mary, and six husky orderlies.

Within an hour, the tables were stained with blood.

Tia forgot the strange apathy that had seized her, yet it seemed that she remained numb. She was glad, for she worked with an insane speed, fearful only that her haste would cause her to drop and lose the instruments the doctors called for. She was reminded of the battle at Olustee Station, and yet, within a few hours, she felt that Olustee had barely prepared her for this.

The day seemed endless. Tia felt as if she wore a second skin of blood. *Stay numb,* she urged herself. *Yes, numb. Just keep moving, and moving.*

That night, there was no end. Darkness had brought an end to the fighting, but not to the arrival of the injured. Yanks came into the surgery along with the Rebels.

She kept hearing where the different armies, divisions, and brigades were deployed. Information that meant little. The armies had met and clashed in the Wilderness, and it was highly unlikely that any of the commanders really knew where to find their own men.

Tia slept on a saddlebag by the field hospital, but only for a few hours. In the tangle of growth, injured men were lost and forgotten, found when another group of men stumbled upon the same scene of battle.

Dawn came without much light. The woods and copses were so filled with powder from the cannons and guns that it was hard to discern day from night.

She thought that it was midmorning. Mary had left with a wagon of wounded, desperate to obtain more supplies from a railway deposit that had been expected during the night.

Tia worked across from Brent, clamping an artery as he removed a minie ball.

He looked at her over the man's body, shook his head. "We've lost this one."

She lowered her eyes. There was no time for sorrow. The orderlies were already coming to take the man away and bring another in.

Flies buzzed all around them.

In a corner of the tent, a pile of limbs rose very high. The stench of the blood was almost overwhelming.

"Kneecap is shattered; the leg has to go," Brent said.

There was a sudden, whizzing sound that made even Brent flinch. "Who the bloody hell is shooting off artillery into woods like that?" Brent swore.

Soon they began to hear the sounds of screaming.

Then, the smoke began. Worse than the powder, it began to fill the air.

One of the wounded men brought in was shouting wildly. "God, God, God, someone has to stop it, stop it! They're burning alive out there, oh my God, burning alive, burning to death, sweet Jesus, sweet Jesus . . ."

An orderly rushed over to Brent. "Colonel McKenzie! Colonel McKenzie, it's true! The Wilderness is burning. Men are . . . are burning to death. Caught in the trees. The fire is coming this way. We've got to move the hospital. Quickly!"

Taylor left the women at the first Yankee picket post, then turned and rode back for the main army lines. He rode into hell already taking shape.

Owing to the troop movements in place, Taylor rode around half of both armies before finding Grant's headquarters.

He wasn't assigned to ride with the cavalry, or to lead troops, though he discovered that both Jesse Halston and Ian were out there somewhere, both in the midst of the fighting. His orders from the unassuming Grant sent him circling around the rest of the action, trying to discern the positions and number of the enemy. By reaching the general alone, at his headquarters near the woods, he had garnered a lot of the information about the Rebel units that the command had needed.

General Grant, chomping on a cigar, told him quietly that he was weary of the Confederate numbers being exaggerated—something which had happened frequently from the days when McClellan had been leading the Yankee troops on down. Union officers had been far too cautious. And far too often, even after taking a victory, Union officers ordered a retreat.

"We're not going to retreat, Colonel. We're going to fight."

By nightfall after the first day, Taylor had managed to circle a number of the Rebel divisions, discern the leadership, then meet back with Grant and his officers to point out their current situation and how they had come to it. After leaving the general, Taylor found out where some of the captured Rebels were being kept. A number of the men had been taken that morning, and he hoped that someone might have news about Brent McKenzie.

The Rebs were on a small hill, watched over by a number of Union infantrymen. Captured, they were at their leisure, many of them eating Yankee provisions, and most of them looking as if they needed many more decent meals. Their uniforms were more than frayed, and most of them were hardly regulation anymore. Many wore pants taken from dead Yankee soldiers, and ill-fitting boots taken from the feet of the fallen as well. Some were nearly barefoot. Yet when he first arrived among them, they remained defiant, no one answering when he first asked about the surgeon, Colonel Brent McKenzie.

"Why are you askin', Colonel?" an infantry captain asked him.

He turned to the man. Tall, lean, and grave, he watched Taylor with careful eyes.

"Because he's kin," Taylor said. "And I believe that my wife is traveling with him."

The captain was quiet for a minute, then told him. "McKenzie was working at the hospital just outside Richmond; he had been called out to work in a field hospital right after our first skirmishers ran into one another. Last I heard, he was doing just fine, setting up his surgery down the Plank Road." The captain kept studying him. "You're married to Tia?" he inquired.

Taylor had heard that note of skepticism so often. "Yes, captain, I am married to Tia McKenzie. The war does make for strange bedfellows. You know my wife?"

The captain nodded. "There was no finer place to be asked than Cimarron, sir. I hailed from South Georgia, and attended many a ball and barbecue at Cimarron. No one would ever forget the daughter of the house, sir. She possessed such beauty and grace in those days . . . and yet I had heard that she quickly turned to compassion once the war began, discarding fashion and finery for blood and death. My congratulations, sir."

"Thank you, Captain. You are certain she is with her cousin now?"

"No, I'm not certain. I did not see her myself, but I heard from mutual friends that she was with Brent, and I cannot imagine they would be wrong."

He thanked the captain again, then asked him if there was anything he could do for him. The captain hesitated, then pointed to a man seated by a tree. "Private Simms received a wound some time ago that continues to plague him. I know that we will probably be sent to different prison camps in the North . . . is there any way you can see to it that he goes to Old Capitol? I have heard it is the best, since it is beneath the nose of many Southern sympathizers, and that Old Abe is actually a man of compassion himself."

"I will see to it," Taylor told him. "You have my word. And for yourself—"

The captain offered him a hand. "For myself, I am in good health. I am nothing more than weary. I will survive the war and return home, and until then, I will go to bed nightly praying for it all to end."

"Amen to that!" Taylor told him and, soon after, left the man for what sleep he might acquire during the night.

Tomorrow . . .

Tomorrow would bring more savage fighting. And he would follow orders, and do his duty to his country.

And yet . . .

God help him, he would also try to find his wife.

Musket flashes ignited dry timber. Pine and scrub oak immediately caught fire. The woods were blazing.

Pandemonium broke out in the hospital at first. Tia, trying to calm a soldier with a shattered leg, heard her cousin's voice rise above the shouts in a deep tone of command. Order began to return; those who could walk were up. Ambulances were loaded; soldiers threw wet towels over the heads of the panicking horses. The conveyances began to leave. There were still soldiers to be moved when the trees surrounding the hospital began to smoke, smolder, and catch. Tia was busy tying a temporary bandage when Brent came behind her, picked her up by the waist, and set her on one of the wagons next to a soldier with an arm wound.

"Get going."

"Not until you leave."

"Stay on that wagon!"

"Brent—"

"I'm right behind you. I'll make it out much easier without worrying about you. For the love of God! Corporal O'Malley!" he said, addressing the man at her side. "Keep her there beside you! Get her out of these woods!"

"Yessir!" the slender, graying O'Malley said.

"Brent—"

Brent stepped back, shouting to the driver. The reins snapped, and the wagon started off along the trail.

"Brent . . ." Tia said, ready to hop off the rear of the wagon and race back for her cousin, no matter what his command. But she couldn't do so. The soldier at her side had her in a firm grip with his one good arm. "Miss Tia, I've been told to get you out of these woods. That was an order, ma'am."

The wagon moved down the road. Tia stared back toward the place where their field hospital had been. Her cousin was back there. Brent wouldn't leave until every last man had been moved from the path of the fire.

She heard the snaps and crackling sounds of the blaze as more and more of the brush and trees caught fire. The air began to fill more and more with the blinding smoke.

And even as they moved along the trail, above the din of the creaking wagons and the gunfire that remained, they could hear the screams of the dying.

Men caught in the field of trees. Hurt, fallen, not dead . . . seeing the flames.

"Oh, God!" Tia cried, covering her ears with her hands. But she couldn't block out the sounds, and she was suddenly certain that a cry she was hearing was coming from just ahead.

Taking Corporal O'Malley by surprise, she leapt down

from the wagon. "Wait! Give me just a few seconds!" she shouted to the driver.

"Miss Tia!" O'Malley shouted from behind her.

"A few seconds!"

She ran along the trail, desperately seeking the source of the cries she'd heard. Were the cries real? Or were they just more of the awful sounds of the forest, the rat-tat-tat of guns, the thuds, and bumps and crackling of burning, falling trees?

"Help, Jesus, oh sweet Jesus, oh God, if I only had a bullet . . ."

The words were real. She burst through the shrub on the side of the road. "Where are you?"

"Here, here . . . help! Oh, Mother of God, help me! Sweet Jesus, pray for us poor sinners now . . . oh, God, oh, God, and at the hour of our death . . . Amen . . ."

"Where are you! Talk to me, help me find you!" Tia shouted.

"Here, here, are you real, please, for the love of God, my leg . . . can't move it, caught, the branch is burning. The heat, here, here, please, please . . ."

She burst through the trees into a little copse. She saw that already the tinder-dry fallen leaves on the ground were beginning to catch in clumps. Then, across the copse, she saw him.

A Yankee infantryman, down against the bark of one tree, the gunfire-severed limb of another tree down upon him. She rushed across the copse.

"Oh, sweet Jesus!" he cried, seeing her. He was young. As young as some of the Rebel soldiers newly rushed into the ranks of the Florida militia. His hair was platinum-white, his whiskers nonexistent, his eyes powder-blue, making him appear even younger. His pale face was sooted and streaked with tears. "Please . . ." he said, reaching a hand to her.

She came to her knees at his side, aware of the ever-encroaching fire. "I've got to get the branch first," she told him, and she locked her arms around it, straining. Sweat broke out on her forehead. It had not looked so heavy. She changed position, trying to drag it from his thigh. He let out a horrible scream—and passed out. She saw that his leg was not just broken, but a bullet had probably lodged somewhere in his thigh. "God help me!" she whispered, tugging at the branch again. She wasn't going to make it. She could feel the heat of the flames beginning to lick at her now. "Miss Tia!"

She turned around. Corporal O'Malley had followed her. "Miss Tia, it's going to burn!"

"Help me."

"He's a Yankee."

"He's a boy."

"Big Yank, little Yank—"

"I'm not leaving him."

O'Malley sighed, anxiously coming to her side. He gripped the tree limb with his good arm. Gritted his teeth.

The boy's head began to wobble. His blue eyes opened. He quickly realized his situation and looked up at O'Malley. "Shoot me, sir, please shoot me before the fire . . ."

"Both of us at once," Tia said. "For the love of God, O'Malley! Come, man, please, you're a good Irish Catholic, aren't you? You should have heard him saying his Rosary just now. God could be watching this very minute—"

"Miss Tia, you know where to strike a man as the Yanks do not. On the count of three!" O'Malley told her. They both gripped the tree limb. O'Malley counted. The limb moved. They leapt quickly to their feet. "I can't lift him; my arm's broken," O'Malley said.

"Soldier, you'll have to limp with me."

They got the boy to his feet. Aware of the flames close behind, they hurried toward the road. Suddenly, before them, a tree fell, sending sparks flying everywhere. "Turn!" O'Malley commanded. "Run!"

They did so, the young Yankee screaming at the agony in his leg. They burst upon the road. The wagon had already started moving. "Help him!" Tia called to a number of the men. They did so without question, reaching for the boy. She didn't know if they were so

weary and hurt that they didn't care that they reached
their hands out to the enemy—or if they just simply
couldn't tell what he was anymore. The boy was covered
in dirt and soot and ash, making his uniform appear to
be made of gray, Confederate-issue cloth. Now, the
sounds of men coughing were almost loud enough to
cover up the terrible crackling that continued to fill the
air.

"Get O'Malley!" she cried loudly when the boy was
up. "He can't use his arm!" Despite their own wounds,
the injured soldiers responded. When O'Malley was
boarded, the shattering sounds of trees exploding came
from behind them.

Tia gasped. The crash had come from the site of the
hospital. And Brent was still back there. The mules, pulling the wagon, bolted.

She heard the driver shouting, "Whoa!" The wagon
was taking flight as if suddenly airborne.

"Miss Tia!"

She heard O'Malley's cry. And she ignored it. Her
cousin was back in the flames. She was not leaving without him.

The wagon continued its wild race from the inferno.

Tia started to run back.

The continual twists and turns in the path of the fire
had left many men lost, with no perception of the loca-
tions of the poor trails through the woods. Taylor Douglas had been ordered into the Wilderness, to find the
various officers and commanders caught in scattered
pockets in the woods and escort them out.

Moving into the smoke and fire, Taylor thanked God
for Friar; his warhorse was an experienced animal as
seasoned as any soldier. Instinct must have warned the
horse to steer clear of the flames, but he stalwartly followed the course Taylor commanded.

At first, his mission seemed somewhat feasible. And
he was glad of it. His orders coincided with the direction
in which he had anxiously longed to ride—toward what
had been the Rebel line.

He found able-bodied men caught in copses who were able to carry some of the wounded to the roads, and toward safety. Naturally, he had been ordered to salvage what he could of the Union fighting force. But no one had ordered that he should leave any Rebels in danger of burning, and he was more determined than ever to find Brent McKenzie and his field hospital—and Tia. With the fires raging so furiously, he knew that he was on a course that would take him far beyond his basic orders.

He meant either to find Brent and Tia, or at least locate someone who could tell them that the hospital had been moved, and that his wife and kin were safe.

Yet as time went on, the danger grew ever greater, and although he was aware that there were still men caught and trapped, soon, looking for anyone alive in the wildfire of the Wilderness would be madness. By now, every breath of air was filled with smoke.

And worse.

He could not inhale without breathing in the horrible scent of charred and burning human flesh. What devil had thought up this day's outcome to the battle? He could not believe that any man living would have wished such a fate on his enemy. And despite the horrible losses in the burning woods, neither side had gained a real advantage.

Hearing screams ahead, Taylor left the road, moving into the thicket. The smoke was so thick he could barely see. Friar began fidgeting at last. "Just a bit forward, boy, just a bit."

But a wall of flame suddenly rose before him. Beyond it, he could hear shouts. "To the south, see there, a clearing!"

"Take it, men, take it—"

"Try there east—"

"No, see the flames rising?"

"Friar, which way, boy?" he said to the horse. "And I don't mean hightailing it out of the woods."

Friar inched forward, reared back. Finally, the horse turned southward. Taylor allowed him to keep the lead, finally coming around to where he found a space in the wall of flames. "Hello! This way—if you're trapped, there's a space through here . . ."

He broke off, surveying the area. There were no flames there now because the scrub had burned itself out. He gritted his teeth, seeing that what had appeared to be a log were the remnants of a man, blackened beyond recognition.

And beyond North and South. What color he had worn in life, no one would ever know.

He nudged Friar through the slender trail. Coming around into the copse, he found the pocket of men. They had stopped speaking because they were coughing and choking. One had fallen. "This way, through the trail here!" he called out. Dismounting from Friar, he took his canteen, soaked the scarf of one of the men with water, pressed it to the man's face, then offered the canteen around. "Soak your kerchiefs! Head that way, quickly. It looks like a wall of flame but there's a trail through. Go! I'll get the sergeant!"

While the others obeyed him, soaking cloths and turning desperately toward the trail, one of the men came back to him. "Colonel, sir, I'll help with the old timer there!"

Taylor realized suddenly that this man, remaining in the inferno, ready to help the old sergeant who had fallen, was a Rebel captain. The smoke, ash, and constant soot had blinded him to this strange grouping at first.

"You're a Reb," Taylor said.

"Two of us, sir, are Rebs. Three Yanks." He shrugged. "We were busy killing one another in a crossfire when a tree went down. Fellow screamed so that we all dropped our weapons. Then the whole place was burning."

Caught in the flames together, they had looked for a way to live, rather than die.

Taylor studied the man and nodded slowly, looking back at the sergeant. The old, winded man probably didn't have a chance of surviving much more smoke.

"Let me take him, sir. I'll follow your orders; you can lead on!"

"Fine, Captain!" Taylor said, allowing the captain to take the sergeant. He headed toward Friar, took his horse's reins, and pointed out their route of escape. He looked at the young Rebel. "I won't be leading you anywhere. I'm going on a bit farther, looking for—others. You, sir, will give me your word that you'll be leading yourself toward Union forces," he said quietly.

The captain grinned. "Sir, you can lead me straight into prison camp, if you send me from this inferno. I will go, and gladly. Sergeant Foster, we're going to make it. Hang on, old man, hang on!"

Friar was beginning to react badly to the flames, and still, Taylor thought that the horse might be the sergeant's only salvation. He called out to the captain. "Get the sergeant up on my horse. I'll lead the way out and you go on. And so help me, Captain, come hell or high water, you take care of my horse!"

"Aye, sir!" the captain called.

With the sergeant up on Friar, Taylor led his horse out of the forest trail onto the road. Flames were shooting all around them, all but making an archway over the remaining passable road.

He should have gotten out. Gone with the captain and old Sergeant foster. He could not. He felt a strange restlessness in his spirit, as if he knew he could find Tia. And that she would be in trouble.

He heard more cries of anguish, terror, pain. He hesitated on the road, looking back.

"Sir, you should lead your horse out. I'll go back there for you."

"No, Captain, that won't be necessary. You take the sergeant out, sir. But tell me, do you know what troops were back there, and who was leading them?"

"Infantry troops . . . and there was a Rebel field hospital back in a copse. I know, because I was in at first when my calf was hit."

Looking down, Taylor saw that the man had been wounded. Blood seeped from a bandage around his calf.

Despite his wound, the young captain had apparently come back into the fighting.

"Why the hell did you leave?" he asked harshly.

"They were busy. Colonel, we haven't time to debate. I can't just leave, I have to find what men I can. You can shoot me in the back, or let me go do what I can."

"Sir, you can get up on my horse, and get your bleeding leg and this man to some help—I'll go back for your Rebs."

"They might shoot you on sight."

"I'll take my chances. Look after my horse!"

"Aye, sir."

A field hospital.

There were bound to be scores of physicians on the field today, Taylor thought, but his heart was pounding. This was where the Reb prisoner had said he would find Brent.

"Captain, do you know, by any chance, was a Dr. McKenzie at that site?"

"Dr. McKenzie was in charge of the site, sir. He ordered me not to move," the captain said with a shrug. "But then . . . well, there were so many men who were really badly injured. I think the ball passed right through my leg."

"And you may still bleed to death if you don't get help. Go."

The captain saluted him. "On my honor, sir. "I'll bring the sergeant to the Yanks, and turn myself in—and take damned good care of the horse."

Taylor nodded, turned, and started down the road. He was a fool. All around him now, the woods were burning. The sky itself seemed like a sheet of flame. Even if he could avoid the blaze, he'd soon die of smoke inhalation, no matter how he'd soaked his neckpiece.

His lungs were already burning. Brent had surely had the sense to get out by now.

He kept walking.

Finally, ahead of him, he could see the remains of the field hospital, in a copse. At first, it appeared, the hospital hadn't caught fire because it was enough in a clearing to be away from the dry shrubbery that filled the woods. But now, flame had leaped to canvas, the whole of the place had collapsed, and a huge, ancient tree from the forest flank had fallen. Smoke rose everywhere. A team of mules, caught when the tree had covered their wagon, whinnied and neighed with a vengeance, fighting their restraints. From the stalled wagon, wounded men, near death, groaned, their signs of life pale against the onslaught and fury of the fire.

"McKenzie!" Taylor called out. "Brent McKenzie!"

He headed first toward the wagon, saw the charred oak limb that trapped it, and the men lying in the rear of the conveyance.

Some were dead already. He looked away from their faces, from the eyes left wide open in death, and strained to move the fallen tree. Too heavy. Burned wood crumpled in his hands. He tried for better leverage, saw a downed pole from the canvas tenting, and worked it under the limb. Throwing his weight against the pole, he shifted the limb. It fell to the ground in a hail of ash. The heat around him was growing intense. He returned to the wagon, searching the bodies in it. No sign of Brent McKenzie.

Taylor heard the sounds of movement. One of the men in the rear of the wagon had stirred. Taylor shifted to the man's position. "Soldier, can you hear me?"

The man's eyes opened. His face was nearly black from the ash.

"The doctor, soldier, Dr. McKenzie. What happened to him?"

The wounded man tried to respond. His mouth moved. Taylor reached for his canteen, praying he had water enough let after soaking the scarves of the other men. Yes. He moistened the fellow's lips. The man drank then, slowly, carefully. "The . . . tent . . . collapsed," the man said. His eyes closed again.

"Hang on," Taylor said. "We're going to get out of here. I'm going to find McKenzie. We'll make it out."

He didn't know if he was believed or not; the soldier's eyes closed. But then the man spoke again. "Three of them. The boy the doc went back for . . . and the woman. The nurse . . . she went after him when the pole snapped and the canvas fell."

The woman.

Tia.

Who else would have gone after a McKenzie when threatened with certain death, trapped under canvas in the wake of a roaring inferno?

A shudder ripped through him and he turned, looking at the field of charred canvas. He raced for the fallen field hospital roofing, grabbed it firmly with both hands, and started pulling it, managing to move it no more than a few inches. *Naturally, fool,* he charged himself. *It took a dozen men to set it up!*

The woods were burning hotter, closer. He raged against the impotency of his own strength, then he gritted his teeth, his anger calming with the realization that he would lose this battle for sure if he didn't gain control of his fear and fight with logic.

Again, he saw the fallen pole, picked it up, searched until he found another, then slid both under the canvas. He could feel the heat around him continually intensifying as he worked, but he forced himself to take each step, securing the canvas to the poles with rope, then tying the poles to the wagon like a giant travois, and urging the mules farther and farther forward as the great canopy began to move, foot by foot, rather than inch by inch. The mule power gave him the strength he needed to move the fallen tent.

Then he saw her.

She lay on her back, rolled toward him by the shifting canvas, face white beneath the soot, black hair spread out in a giant fan beneath her. He hurried to her, kneeling at her side, brushing a strand of stray hair from her face and seeking a pulse at her throat. She shifted where she lay, groaned. Her eyes opened, and she stared up at him with disbelief.

"Taylor?" she said incredulously.

"Yes, it's me."

She shook her head. "Taylor, you can't be here, you

can't. It's a Rebel field hospital, the canvas collapsed, it's all burning . . ."

"Tia, I am here, you little fool, and it's no strange quirk of fate. I'm here because I was looking for you. *You're* not supposed to be here; you're supposed to be in St Augustine."

"I had to be here. There was no choice."

"There's always a choice. But we can't argue now. Can you move?"

The words came out harshly, spoken with a mixture of fear and relief. Perhaps it was good that he sounded so blunt and angry—his words brought a spark to her dark eyes. "I can move, yes, and I have to—oh, God! Brent . . . Brent!" She struggled up, using him to grab on to, then pushing him away to rise. "Brent, where in God's name is Brent? I saw him, I was trying to help him with the last man when . . ."

Taylor rose to his feet behind her. He realized that he was shaking; he was so very grateful that Tia was alive. She was racing toward a pile of rubble—cots, surgery tables that had fallen when the tent collapsed. Brent was facedown in the debris.

Taylor reached Brent right behind Tia. She fell down beside him, trying to move him carefully, calling his name.

"Brent, Brent . . ."

Something nearby exploded, perhaps a discarded powder bag, a rifle gripped in a dead hand. Flames seemed to shoot all around them.

Taylor reached down for Brent. "Taylor, we don't know his injury—"

"It's death if we don't move now, Tia!" He collected Brent swiftly in his arms, maneuvering through the rubble to get him to the wagon.

It was heavy laden with the dead.

The soldier who had spoken to him earlier had opened his eyes. He saw Taylor grit his teeth in a fleeting dilemma as he tried to find a place in the wagon for Brent.

"Colonel, roll young Ted Larkin there off the wagon. A funeral pyre here is as good as any. You'll have to leave some of the dead, if we're to get through with the living."

The man was right, and finding the spirit and will to live now that there seemed to be hope, he rose as best he could with his newly amputated leg and shoved the body of the dead man off the wagon, making room for Brent. Not even sure that Brent was still breathing, Taylor turned back for Tia, knowing they were truly running out of time. The air was barely breathable at all; the oxygen was being surely sucked from it.

"Tia!"

She was in the rubble. He ran to her. She was trying to lift the shattered pieces of a camp cot from the body of a soldier. Taylor started to help her, then saw that the man's eyes were open, staring heavenward. He was dead.

"He's gone, Tia."

"No, he just had a wound to his foot."

"His lungs were crushed, Tia."

"No—"

"Tia!"

She started struggling wildly against him. Desperate, he slapped her, hard. Stunned, she reeled back. He stepped forward, caught her arms, and threw her over his shoulder. He ran from the canvas and rubble toward the wagon. A large tree, the trunk ablaze, suddenly fell ahead of him. Tia screamed, and he jerked back just in time to avoid it.

"Colonel, move it, move it, move it, move it, sir!" the soldier from the wagon shouted above the renewed roar of the flame. He had dragged himself to the driver's seat.

Taylor didn't need any more encouragement. He ignored the instinctive fear of fire, made a running leap over the tree, and catapulted toward the wagon. He nearly threw Tia atop it, then crawled aboard himself, even as the soldier cracked the whip high over the mules' heads. They leapt forward—spurred by panic and fear. In a matter of seconds, they were tearing down the trail like a pair of racehorses. Someone within the wagon screamed. Taylor, flat on his back at Tia's side, gasped for air, glad at least that a few of the men were alive. He rose quickly then, but Tia had already staggered to a kneeling position in the wildly jolting wagon. She was seeking a pulse from Brent. She looked Taylor's way. "He's breathing!" she said.

"Good. Damned good."

The woods were still on fire, but the intense heat seemed to be fading with the breeze. They were recklessly racing from the worst of it. Explosions from behind them signified the ignition of the trees as the fire spread, but they were leaving the worst of it.

Then, the wagon wheels hit a pothole. The mules kept shooting forward. The wagon began to break up. The injured screamed as they were flung far and wide from the crushing boards. Taylor halfway rose, throwing his body in a brace over Tia and Brent, burrowing against them as they flew through the smoky air.

They landed hard in the dirt. For a second Taylor couldn't move. He heard the groans and cries around him. They had escaped certain death at the hospital site, but as he looked up, the tall oaks in front of them burst into flame. He swore, staggering to his feet, then he bent down and secured the unconscious Brent in his arms. "Stay with me!" he commanded Tia as she rose up, and he started to run, carrying his human burden around the blazing oaks. Miraculously, they had come upon a little pond in the midst of a copse. The damp earth by the pond kept the fire at bay. There were riders arriving there, shouting. Someone met Taylor as he staggered forward with Brent. "I'll take him, Colonel."

He handed Brent to the man. "There are more in there, just beyond the trees."

He turned. Tia had started back. "Tia! Damn you!" She was past the flame. He chased after her. She was wasting no time, reaching for the arms of a fallen amputee, ready simply to drag him around the flames. With others behind him, he wanted only to stop Tia. "I've got him!" he shouted, lifting the man. "Go!"

She ran. He heard a terrible crackling sound. He looked up. A huge branch was coming down.

He looked at Tia. Her eyes met his.

He heard her shrieking . . .

Then the branch fell. With barely an instant to spare, he leapt back. The fire roared and blazed high before his face. He ducked around it quickly. She started racing toward him. "Tia, no, the other way!"

A weakened tree limb snapped and fell. It struck her on the shoulder. She collapsed to her knees. She rose, fell again . . .

Soldiers were coming, finding the injured, sorting them from the dead.

Someone picked Tia up. Another came to Taylor and relieved him of the man he carried. He raced forward with renewed energy, caught up with the man carrying Tia.

"She's my wife!"

The soldier paused, letting him take Tia. Her eyes opened, caught his. Closed again. He kept moving forward until they came to the water. He went down, ripping her skirt, soaking it, cleaning her face. Her eyes opened again. She stared at him.

"Brent?"

"Safe."

"You can't be here!" she whispered.

"But I am here," he told her.

Behind him, a throat was cleared. "I don't mean to interrupt this reunion but . . . you *shouldn't* be here, sir."

Taylor frowned and turned. Behind him stood an officer. Beyond him, the injured had been taken from the wreckage and the flames. There were many soldiers surrounding them now, efficiently moving men into conveyances to bring them farther back from the flames. The night remained filled with the sounds of the dry trees catching and burning, but the sounds were becoming background noise, and even some of the shouts of the men seemed to be fading into the distance.

He noted what he hadn't taken time to realize before.

Like the officer who had just spoken to him, the soldiers here were all Rebels.

"I'm Colonel Josh Morgan, sir," said the Reb addressing him. The man was too young to be a colonel, Taylor thought. He was too young to be out of a military academy. "Your courage, sir, has been extraordinary. I'm sorry to offer you harm or discomfort in any way, but . . . well, sir, we're still at war. And no matter how it grieves me, I must inform you—you are now a prisoner of the Confederate States of America."

He had a chance, and he knew it. He rose, slowly, carefully, assessing the man. The colonel stood by his mount, a bay mare. It was unlikely that any of the men here were going to shoot him in the back. All he had to do was steal the horse, and ride back into the flames.

He saw the colonel's eyes—and knew that young Josh Morgan was trying to give him just that chance.

"Thank you, sir," he said, and he reached past the man, gripping the horse's reins and meeting the young man's stare. Then he burst into action, leaping on the horse.

And desperately—perhaps ridiculously—racing back toward the inferno. There had to be another way out.

But Tia didn't understand. Or she did. He heard her scream his name. "Taylor!" She was racing after him, coughing, choking, stumbling . . . but coming after him. He spun around on the horse. "Tia, go back!"

"Taylor, damn you!"

The fire lit the night. Smoke was everywhere, blinding him. She nearly reached him, then doubled over, coughing, gagging. She fell.

He reined in, came to her, dismounted. Her eyes remained closed as he lifted her into his arms. He didn't know if she was really unconscious, or if it had been a ploy to bring him back.

Whichever, it didn't matter.

He would not risk her life. He might dare the fires again himself, but he would not risk bringing her through the inferno again.

She lay limply in his arms. Perhaps it was just as well; the trail behind him now blazed with such a fury that it would be pure suicide to risk it. He carried Tia, aware that the good warhorse followed him as closely as a well-trained dog. The Rebels watched him return, the red of the blaze painting the night behind him.

He handed Tia over to one of the Rebel medics who had raced toward him. She was one of theirs; they would see to it that she was taken far behind the lines, and given all possible medical attention. Still, he watched the medic walk away, hearing the grate of his own teeth, feeling tense enough to snap.

He walked wearily to the far-too-young Colonel Morgan.

"Sir, it appears I am your prisoner."

# Chapter 21

W hen Tia opened her eyes again, it was to daylight. She had no idea where she was, though she quickly remembered the terrors of the day gone by. She bolted up, and was startled to realize that she was in a house, in a pleasant room with cheerful blue and white wallpaper, polished paneling, and handsome furniture. Her charred, torn clothing was gone. She could smell a faint reminder of the fires—the scent was in her hair, she realized. But she was dressed in a blue-flowered cotton nightgown. It still hurt a little to breathe.

"At last. You're awake!"

Startled, she turned, and found Mary, Brent's wife, smiling at her from a rocker. She had not kept vigil in an idle manner, but was busy winding bandages from cotton reels.

"Mary!" Tia said, sitting up.

"Well, you were out long enough."

"I was? How long? Taylor . . . Brent . . ."

"Um . . . you've been out about a day and a half. Brent is fine; he's already back working."

"But he was unconscious—"

"Not for long. I reached you all soon after Morgan did. Brent was already coming around then—you were the one we worried about."

"And what about . . . Taylor? Taylor . . . he was there, after the canvas fell, and we made it out of the woods, and then he grabbed a horse and ran back into the fire."

"And you ran after him, you were hurt, and he brought you back."

Tia closed her eyes; she could see the flames again,

feel the awful heat. See his eyes as he sat on the horse. The way he looked at her, across the fire. She shouldn't have followed him. Why had she done so?

*Because he was riding back into the flames. It was as if he had lost his mind, the road was becoming an inferno.*

"Then . . . if he brought me back . . ." She hesitated, and looked at Mary. "What did they do with him?"

"They had little choice. He was taken prisoner. He's with a group of men who will probably be escorted to Andersonville. He's at a farmhouse now. Brent will know more later."

"He's—all right?"

"He's fine, Brent was told. The soldiers who took him were very respectful, He dragged Confederate injured out of those woods, you realize."

Tia nodded. "Yes, of course, I know."

"I'm sure when Brent returns tonight, he'll know more. Of course, you'll want to see Taylor. I'm sure Brent can arrange it."

"Mary, where are we now?" Tia asked, looking around.

Mary smiled suddenly. "My father's house. I haven't been back here in two years. But I have a wonderful, wonderful maid. We grew up together. She's just two years older than I am, and my father saw to it that we were taught up in the classroom in the attic. She writes to me, always assuring me that she's kept the house up. When my father died, I didn't care much. But now . . . well, it's good to be home, except that . . ."

"Except that?"

"Well . . . we're not really far behind the confederate lines, and the lines are shifting all the time now. And, well, some of the neighbors have reported that it doesn't much matter which army robs you blind when the soldiers are hungry."

"How close are the lines?"

"Sometimes," Mary said softly, "you can hear the shelling."

"My God, that close? Then more soldiers are dying— near us! We should probably be with Brent."

"He'll come to the house tonight. He said that you were not to leave here under any circumstances."

"Wonderful! Now *Brent* is telling me what to do!"

"Tia, Brent wants you to stay alive. You must take time to heal yourself."

"*I* must take time? What about Brent? He was out cold for hours, but *he's* back to work!"

Mary shook her head, smiling. "You're forgetting— it's Brent's surgery."

"I suppose you're right," Tia said, unconvinced.

"We'll be back with him soon enough." Mary shuddered. "Last night, I died a thousand deaths in my heart, seeing the fires, not being able to reach you, waiting, wondering, praying . . . it is the waiting that is the hardest job of all in this war."

Mary was right.

Waiting was the hardest job of all.

But Tia waited, and wondered, and she was afraid, dying to see Taylor, not wanting to see Taylor, and not understanding herself at all.

Taylor's imprisonment was not too grim; he was treated decently by the Rebs. He'd even heard that his old teacher and friend, Master Robert E. Lee, knew he'd been captured, and had ordered that he be treated with the utmost respect.

Owing either to Lee's intervention or to the reports that he had risked his own life to save Rebel soldiers, he had been sent southward toward Richmond to be held at an old farmhouse with other officers until he could be transported to a prison camp. The farmhouse had apparently stood empty for some time—or housed the headquarters of one army or the other on some previous date. It had a strange feeling of emptiness. Torn curtains, once white and beautiful, drifted in a gray dance when the breeze blew. Dust covered the finely carved mantle. Windows had broken and fallen.

It was said that the men being taken now were to go to Andersonville—reputed to be something of a death sentence. The overcrowding was beyond imagination;

disease ran rampant. The death ratio was horrendously high.

For the moment, however, his prison was not too grim. Days were spent in the fields—the fields had been mowed down at some earlier battle or skirmish, but there were still a few large oak trees offering shade. The Rebs had little but musty, maggot-ridden hardtack to eat, but what his captors had, they shared. Different men came, and shared the information of the war.

Most of the Confederates had thought that Grant would strike and sidle away—as the Army of Potomac usually did.

Grant sidled, but not away. He moved on to Spotsylvania Court House. The fighting continued, fast and furious. Union losses, they reckoned, were over fifteen thousand. Who could really count? The South . . . well, she wasn't losing so many, but then, she could ill afford any losses.

On May 12, the soldiers guarding them went into mourning; Taylor found out that Jeb Stuart, "Beauty," as they'd called him in class, had died on the eleventh, mortally wounded at a place called Yellow Tavern. He'd been the nemesis of the Union cavalry; he'd also been a friend, a good, bold man, cocky, wild, fun to be with, yet loyal to the core. It was a hard loss. The Rebels, he thought, were fighting a bitter battle, indeed. Stuart was lost now—hit not far from where Stonewall had received his mortal blow. Longstreet had been wounded in the conflict, Hill was ill, and Lee himself had gotten very ill.

Grant wasn't going home. He had decided that the army was staying in Virginia. He refused to accept defeat.

The battle at the Wilderness flowed into the battle at Spotsylvania, and when those battles were over, neither side could claim victory. The Union suffered tremendous casualties. The South lost fewer men, but they could afford far fewer men.

And, Grant refused to give up and go home. He wouldn't even leave the area to lick his wounds, so the soldiers complained. He shifted; Lee shifted. Grant was trying for Richmond. Somehow, Lee kept getting his army between the Union army and the Confederate capital.

At the farm, Taylor watched and bided his time. He was not under heavy guard. He listened while some of the other Union officers considered escape routes—tempting, naturally, since their own army was close. Exactly where, no one was certain. Pockets of fighting continually occurred.

He wasn't quite ready to escape himself. He wanted to know where Tia was, and just what she was doing.

His captors, though congenial enough, were pleased to tell the prisoners about the Rebel victories. On the fifteenth of May, a Union force was defeated at New Market. Major General John C. Breckinridge attacked Federal forces under Sigel, at the last minute unwillingly committing the two hundred and forty-seven cadets from the Virginia Military Academy.

It had truly become a war of children, Taylor thought. Ten of the cadets were killed, and forty-seven were wounded.

Toward the end of May, Brent McKenzie arrived to see him. Taylor had been down by the small pond in what had once been a large horse paddock—the horses had been gone for years now. The large oaks offered shade. By twilight, the area was beautiful. It helped him to go there, helped to still his restless spirit—and his self-recriminations. He shouldn't have been idle in a Confederate camp. He should have been out there, scouting positions, reporting on strengths. Every veteran of the war was needed, every experienced soldier. The war needed to end.

So thinking, he leaned against an oak, watching the late-day sun play upon the water.

"Taylor!"

Hearing himself hailed, he turned quickly. Brent was striding toward him. The fact that he wore gray and was among the captors seemed to mean little to him. He walked up to Taylor, embracing him quickly, drawing away. "You look well enough."

"I am, thank you."

"No—thank *you*. I would be cinders now if it weren't for you. I should have come sooner. I haven't been able to."

"Where is Tia, and what is she doing?"

"And why isn't she here with me?" Brent added softly.

"Yes, that is an interesting question."

"She will come soon. We are staying with a family that lives near here, and she is on her way."

Brent was uncomfortable. He felt as if he should apologize for Tia.

"She is anxious to see you, of course."

"Is she?"

"And to convey her deepest gratitude. She knows that you saved our lives."

Taylor was quiet. "I've killed men in battle, more men than I want to remember. But there are few men who would willingly be witness to others—even enemies— being burned to death. And," he added quietly, "I lost one wife in this tempest, a needless tragedy. God help me, if at all in my power, I would not let Tia pay the price for this bloodshed as well."

"Your wife—yes. But your compassion for your enemies has not gone unnoticed or unappreciated," Brent told him. "There were times when the North meant to refuse exchanges—to your side, all men are expendable; to ours, unfortunately, they are not—but still, there is word that certain men will be traded. You are among them. There has been a tremendous demand from those Yanks you saved from the fire—before plucking so many Rebels from the inferno. If I've heard correctly, though, we're getting back two colonels and a lieutenant for you."

"I'm flattered. Do you know when any of this is to take place?"

"No, I'm afraid not. There are pools of blood now being shed at Cold Harbor. The Union army is eight miles from Richmond, but Lee has entrenched, and you know how good our entrenchments are. Perhaps—"

Brent broke off, seeing that Tia had come at last. She stood a distance away, on the little hill that sloped down to the pond. She was slim, and stood very still. Seeing her, Taylor felt a sharp agony as his muscles constricted, and something inside him seemed to rip and tear as well. She knew that he saw her. She started quickly down the hill.

Brent waved to her. "Well," he said. "She has come, more quickly than I expected. I will leave the two of you alone."

But Tia had nearly reached them. She tried to offer a rueful smile. "Brent, you needn't leave us so quickly."

"Cousin, I am already gone," he assured her. "I will await you at the house."

He walked away. Tia stood some distance from Taylor still. He clamped down hard on his teeth and jaw, suddenly tempted to reach out and shake her. She was his wife. Granted he was a Yankee prisoner, but they were all but alone in the copse; his Rebel guards kept watch at the fences, and were pleasant and discreet enough to be looking elsewhere. When he'd last come upon her, they had faced death. Here . . . there was nothing between them but cooling night air. She should have rushed to him, thrown her arms around him. They were both alive. Seeing one another after so much time apart.

He held his distance for the moment, as she held hers. She looked far graver, saddened—even calmer than the wild spirit he had come to know. Very beautiful; appearing slim and sleek in a simple cotton day dress, the length of her hair wound in a twist at her nape. Her eyes were as dark and hypnotic as the promise of night; her features were pale.

"Taylor!" she said softly, then fell awkwardly silent again before she found speech once more. "I'm so sorry; honestly. You saved our lives, and I caused you to be here. Except, of course, that perhaps I should be glad you are a prisoner—there's such terrible fighting going on. Thousands of men are dead. Thousands . . ." She broke off, waiting for him to speak. "Thousands," she repeated. "Not just men—but boys. Real boys." She looked away for a moment. "Taylor, I'm so grateful to you. I want you to understand that, believe me, please."

Her manner was very strange. The tension in him seemed to be increasing. Of course, with his guards at the fences, with others surrounding—with him a prisoner—it would be difficult at best to follow pure instinct and sweep her into his arms and do to her everything that he longed to do. But he did, at the least, want her in his arms.

"Come here," he said.

"Taylor, it's a camp," she murmured. "There are guards."

"The guards won't care." It wasn't the guards. There was another reason she wouldn't come near him.

"Taylor, I—"

He didn't intend to hear it. She wouldn't come to him; he would come to her. He stepped forward, catching her shoulders, drawing her forcefully into his arms. She was soft, smelling more sweetly than he might have dared imagine, clean, feminine. Her hair teased his nose; his senses came to life. He lifted his chin, touching her lips.

She stiffened at first to his embrace, fought the intimacy of his kiss. Yet time made him strong, persistent, and persuasive, and in a few moments it seemed that she thawed, and melted in his hold. Soon his intimate invasion of her mouth was met with a wicked, searing passion that all but matched his own. He held her tightly, felt the supple fever of her form. And for that moment, he felt that, yes, there was something, she was wild and unique, and she was his, and when the war ended . . .

Yet she retreated again, pressing away from him. She didn't even pause to look at the guards, but stared into his eyes.

"Taylor, I've come to tell you that . . . I mean, of course, I came to say thank you, with my whole heart. I know that you came purposely to save me, that you felt it your duty to come for your wife, that you've paid a terrible price for what you did. I know all that, Taylor. My God, for Brent as well! Brent—"

"Brent is my relation, too, Tia. You owe nothing on

his behalf," he said, studying her eyes and feeling again
as if a spring were winding within him.

"Taylor, what I'm trying to say is that I know that . . .
I know that I do, just for myself, owe you so very
much . . . and because of it, well, partially because of
it . . . Taylor, it's all been my fault, I see that, I know
that, but . . ."

"Tia, what the hell are you trying to say?" he grated
out. He was aware, more than ever, that guards surrounded him. That he was a prisoner.

"I . . . plan to give you a divorce. I've decided that I
very definitely don't want to have children."

"What? What does this sudden revelation have to do
with now, with the war—"

"I want you to know that I don't hold you to anything.
You're a hero, Taylor, to both sides, a rather difficult
role in this wretched, bloody war. I know . . . I know
how you felt about Abby, which was why you did marry
me, feeling that . . . that it didn't matter, because you
still loved her so much. But I suppose every man wants
children, most men want children, and if not children,
well . . ." She paused, her face flooding with color, her
eyes falling from his. "Well, I mean, I don't want . . ."

"You don't want what?"

"I have to go, Taylor."

"No, you don't."

"Yes, I do. There are injured children—"

"That's what this is all about? You came to Richmond
to see Varina, and she lost her little boy anyway."

"Taylor, I just don't want—"

"People lose children, Tia, yes. Every little life is very
vulnerable. But where there is pain and tragedy, there
is joy as well. Yes, you will lose in life! But Tia, you will
not deny it while you live it!"

"I have to go!" she said, pulling away from him.

He might be a prisoner, but he'd be damned if he'd
let her go. Not like that. He forced her closer again,
tilted her chin, forced her lips, her hunger, with his passion. Again, she resisted, yet again, after a moment . . .

She fought so hard to deny it. Yet she was on fire,

the passion that had led her to war lived in her spirit, her heart, her soul. She could try to deny anything about herself, or the two of them. She could be his enemy, but she was also his wife, and he could make her realize that she wanted the role, desired his touch . . .

Her arms curled around, fingers wove into his air. She returned his kiss with hunger and yearning . . . then suddenly, she broke away.

"I have to go."

"Tia—"

"I have to go. I'll find a way to get a divorce."

"Tia, damn you—"

"Stop!" She screamed the word. Guards started to turn. She stared at him, seeing the outrage in his eyes. But she slapped him, with speed and with vigor. And she turned and ran.

Naturally, he started after her. She was swift and fleet, but he would have caught her.

Except that he suddenly had two men down upon him, and when he would have fought like a jungle cat, throwing them off, he felt the muzzle of a gun against his temple.

"Colonel! Colonel, please, oh, for the love of God, please!"

One of the guards who had brought him down was almost in tears, looking at him. "Sir, please, oh, please, don't make me shoot you."

He drew in a deep breath and went dead still.

"Sir, I will not put that burden upon you!" he declared.

The guard rose, stretched a hand down to him. Taylor accepted the hand and rose. Tia was just stepping into a covered wagon at the front of the farmhouse.

Taylor closed his eyes, lowered his head, and damned her a thousand times over.

# Chapter 22

Tia was tired, yet determined that what she was doing was right. If she didn't take the time to think about the tragedy of it all, and just worked as hard as she could, all the awful sights she saw were bearable. Making a difference was what mattered.

From the third to the twelfth of June, battle waged at Cold Harbor, Virginia. Grant had brought his troops to within eight miles of Richmond. But the Southerners had dug in, and Lee's army remained between him and his objective.

Tia wasn't just glad to stay busy herself; she was glad to know that Taylor was being kept from the action. Now, each time she saw a Union uniform come into surgery, she had only to hope and pray that the man was not her brother. She knew that Brent feared finding Ian now more than ever, with the armies so constantly at one another, and she realized that he watched for Jesse Halston as well, the man Sydney had married. But either both Ian and Jesse were surviving the carnage intact—or their destroyed bodies remained on the field, or the Union surgeons were looking after their own with the same speed and efficiency the Rebels attempted. Brent worked at a frenetic pace, since men who could be saved far too often perished if left too long upon the bloody fields where the fighting took place.

It was as Mary had said. Waiting was hard. Working was much better. Much, much better for Tia, because she didn't want time to think about Taylor. She didn't want to remember either the way that he had held her, touched her, kissed her—or the way he had looked at her when she told him that she didn't want children and would give him a divorce.

And then, she had slapped him and run, and the Rebels had jumped on top of him, and she had looked back, seen his golden eyes upon her . . .

Much better to work, than to think.

And the work was continuous. From Cold Harbor, Grant began to shift again. The Rebels were praying that he'd decide he had taken his quota of blood for the time being and turn back. He did not.

Lee began to withdraw from Richmond, believing that Grant was heading straight toward the capital. But Grant was not, they discovered, heading toward Richmond. He was after Petersburg, considering it the back door to the Confederate capital.

With the tremendous fighting and the casualties sustained, Tia spent much of her time on the field with her cousin and his wife, using Mary's beautiful old home as a base.

But on the twentieth of June, a messenger arrived, stating they should abandon the house. It might well be in the way of the circling Union army.

Brent and Mary had packed and just finished with the house by late afternoon when Tia returned. She had remained at the Lutheran church turned makeshift hospital in the town center until the last of their young patients had been removed.

"Tia, hurry, we've got wounded waiting at the new facilities," Brent told her, anxiously throwing the last of his supplies on the larger of the two carriages they were taking from the stables.

"You two go on; I'll follow right behind."

"I'm not leaving you," Brent insisted. "There's no one else here."

"And there could be deserters," Mary added. "Yankee scouting parties."

"I just have a few things to take. I can manage the small carriage alone."

Brent looked around. There wasn't a soul in sight on the pretty, residential street. It had become a ghost town.

Dust swirled in the streets, caught by the breeze. The houses around them had been closed down in the hopes that the enemy would find them locked—and go away. The windows that gazed upon them from the street seemed like soulless eyes.

"Brent, go!" She kissed his cheek, then hugged Mary.

"All right, but when we go, you stay in the house. I'll send a soldier back to escort you to us."

"I promise. I'll stay in the house."

Even as she urged him, a rider suddenly burst onto the street, coming hard. "We have a general down, sir, begging we bring you in and quickly!" he said, saluting Brent.

"There you have it, get moving!" Tia said.

"Soldier, I'll go to the general; you stay with my cousin, bring her along the minute she's finished packing."

"Aye, sir!" He dismounted from his horse.

Tia smiled, waved as Brent and Mary departed, and thanked the soldier for staying.

"It's my duty, ma'am. I'll be at the fence, waiting."

"I won't be long."

She opened the gate to the white picket fence, and closed it behind her. The small buggy remained in the stately drive. Hitched to it was the best of their available horses, a tough little mare. "One minute, Suzie, and we'll be out of here as well!"

She should have come back from the hospital sooner, she thought. She suddenly felt a chill, as if the place really had become a ghost town, peopled with soldiers who had perished, who walked the streets wondering what might have come of their lives.

She was glad that Brent had left her an escort.

In the house she rushed into the room she had been using. It seemed so clean and neat and *normal.* She looked from the dressing screen to the hip tub and the bed with its soft, welcoming mattress. So much for luxury. Though she had spent her fair share of nights on the field, she'd had this place to come to as well. A haven for rest, for real baths with hot water, a place for clean clothes and the scent of rose soap, far from the smell of battle—and death.

She opened a brocade carpetbag on the bed and looked around quickly for the things she needed and wanted most. The soap, most definitely. Candles, matches, clean pantalettes, hose, and her freshly laundered blouses, tended by Mary's servants, all gone now as well. How many had gone with Mary and Brent? she wondered.

And how many had fled to the coming Yanks?

She folded her stockings into the bag, then paused, feeling a strange sensation that she was being watched.

Turning toward the bedroom door, she froze. Taylor was there, blocking the doorway. As she stared at him, her mouth dry and a sense of fear invading her limbs, he tossed off his hat and walked into the room. He helped himself to the nearly empty brandy decanter on the occasional table, and walked over to the mantle.

"Hello, Mrs. Douglas. Were you leaving?"

She didn't answer; she didn't move. "What are you doing here?" she cross-queried him. "You were a prisoner at the farmhouse."

"I felt I'd overstayed my welcome," he said with a grin. "Apparently, my captors agreed and were shipping me out—to Andersonville. The place has acquired a nasty reputation, so I decided not to go. The prisoner exchange that Brent was promised never took place."

"Did you escape from the farmhouse?"

"No. We were already en route. Ian and Jesse Halston—you know, he married Sydney—were coming to rescue me, but I'd already freed myself before they met up with me. Afterward, I had a chance to fill Jesse in on his wife's foolhardy exploits."

"How convenient," Tia said flippantly, not wanting to accept the sudden acceleration of her heartbeat. *Taylor was back.*

*But what had happened to the Rebel soldier waiting for her at the fence? Was he watching the house, waiting to recapture Taylor?*

"I missed you, Tia."

"Well . . ." she murmured, and she realized that what voice she had was husky and faint. "I was just leaving."

"But now you're staying," he said flatly.

She shook her head, moistening her lips. "No, I'm leaving. I didn't mean to be so rude and ungrateful when I saw you at the farmhouse, Taylor. I was trying to make you understand, I'm not what you want."

"Oddly enough, at the moment, you're exactly what I want."

"Taylor, I've told you—"

"And I've told you. You made a commitment. You want out of it? Sorry, already done."

"But I forced you into this. You can get a divorce."

"Come here, Tia." With purpose, he set his empty brandy glass on the mantle.

"Taylor . . ."

She backed away from him uneasily, feeling his eyes. A fluttering began in her stomach. Just the way he looked at her . . . she closed her eyes, gritting her teeth. Was she afraid of Taylor? She knew exactly what he intended. She didn't think he cared at the moment whether she was particularly willing or not. She'd slapped him, ignored him—and had him brought down by an enemy with a gun at his head. And still . . .

It wasn't Taylor she feared. It was the way she felt inside, just when he looked at her like that. It was the hunger he awakened when she gazed at his hands, at the bronze of his long fingers. The yearning that swept through her like a storm when he came closer and closer, when she felt his warmth, breathed his scent . . .

"Taylor, you haven't paid the least bit of attention to me. I don't want children. I'm sick of seeing them die. I won't go through what I've watched parents go through."

He caught her by the shoulders, forcing her to break off her words as he gave her a violent shake. "Shut up, Tia. We all play with what we're dealt. Life is the game, and we play it out. Yes, there is loss, and yes, we endure. Can I tell you that you'll never have a child die? That you won't face more tragedy, even when the war is over?

No, my love, there are no guarantees in life, none at all. But I'll be damned if I'll watch you risk your own fool life over and over again, and then turn into the worst kind of coward there is."

"Taylor, don't—"

"You'll deal with life, Tia, and that's the way it is."

"But I don't want this!" she cried, wrenching free from his hold, backing away again. "I don't want you, I don't want this! It was sheer accident, sheer stupidity, and I have said that I am deeply sorry, and deeply grateful, and I have given you your freedom."

"But I have not given you yours!" he snapped angrily.

She turned, trying to escape him around the bed. His hand snaked out, caught her by the arm with a vengeance. He pulled her back, and she fell on the bed. She lay winded. He crawled over her—staring down at her—and shoved her carpetbag off the bed. "Want to slap me? Call for the Rebs?"

She didn't answer him, but stared up at him hard.

He smiled. "Sorry—your Rebel escort isn't coming for you."

"What did you do to that poor soldier?"

"He's alive, Tia, but he won't be escorting you anywhere. There's no one to call, my love. I believe the tables are turned."

"Taylor, I . . ."

He leaned low against her. "You what?"

"I . . ." she began. "I don't love you!" But as she said the words, she knew they were a lie. She had started falling in love with him when she'd first met him. He was different from anyone else in the world. His voice captivated her, his eyes compelled her, his touch, his whisper, aroused her. He was her enemy, but a man who would die for her. An enemy who fought for what he believed was right, who would give his life for his convictions, never back down, never falter. And she did want him, but she was so afraid of pain now . . .

"Then we're even," he said softly. "Because I don't love you. But damn you, Tia, I married you, and you are my wife, and you are not free. I *will* have you."

That simply, he spoke the words. And that simply, he meant to have his way.

And she . . .

He kissed her.

Again, a kiss filled with force, with hunger, with passion. As relentless as a tempest, his tongue forced entry, drank, demanded, delved, and seduced. She tried to twist against the surge of his force, but could not. Tried to fight the rage of feelings that surged within her breast, her blood, her limbs, but could not. Dusk turned to dark red, red to night, and all that remained were the shadows of the moon. He didn't notice the bloodred coming of darkness. He kissed her, seized her lips again and again. Found the pulse point at her throat, touched her, stroked her cheek, her hair. Found the buttons on her bodice and swiftly unfastened them, chipping one delicate little piece of ivory in his haste to disrobe her.

Then he was everywhere . . .

Her shoes were cast aside, skirt all but torn away, pantalettes nearly shredded, stockings—precious stockings—seized like autumn leaves in the winter wind. And surely she should be pushing him away, struggling against this onslaught, but it seemed that she was tugging off his clothing as well. His shirt was open, slipping from his shoulders. Her hands were on his bare flesh as his lips pressed against her shoulders, her throat, and then her breast. She could feel the fever of his body heat against her naked belly as he captured her breast with his kiss, tongue laving her nipple, teeth capturing the pebbled bud, mouth forming fully upon it, suckling, taunting, arousing, creating sensations that caused her to strain against him, protesting, arching, crying out. She was tearing at his hair, cradling his head as he moved against her. His body on hers, between hers, the force of his movement thrusting her thighs apart, his lips running wild and rampant over the bare expanse of her abdomen, lower, upon her upper thighs, between them, touching, demanding, arousing, allowing no quarter in the quest for pure seduction. And he did seduce. At last she realized that she didn't fight, but clung. She didn't struggle, but reached. And she wanted him. Wanted this. Hunger so sweet and erotic it was anguish. What he could do with his touch. His kiss, the brush of his whisper, the sweep of his tongue. And then . . . the force of his body within her. A feeling of completeness, wholeness, part of him, still climbing—no, *soaring*—reaching to a sun that didn't exist, a panoply of stars in the velvet of the night that had come. His eyes on her in the night, gold eyes, cat's eyes, panther eyes, pinning her with the same surge of power as his touch, demanding, more so than the force of her touch, complete and unconditional surrender. She could not win the war.

She could hardly join in the battle, for it had been lost from the beginning, and it had never been the violence she had feared, but the knowledge that she hadn't the will to fight. He had stripped her of her clothing, and her defenses, and she had not just accepted his greater strength, she had embraced her own weakness, wanting him.

Loving him, no matter what her words . . .

Absence, anger, fear, tempest, perhaps they all added in as well. He moved against her with a strength that left her breathless, which seduced anew with every surge and eddy, which brought her flying ever higher, into the darkness, into the realm of lovers, where the world receded and only hunger and need existed. Then the darkness burst into white, blazing light; she closed her eyes and saw it still, and she shook and shuddered as sheer pleasure seized her in its sweet grip, and climax ripped into her with a searing ecstasy that defied the war, the day, the night, and all sanity and reason. His body heat melded into her own, and she was swept with the fire of his ejaculation, enwrapped in the warmth that encapsulated them both for the long, sweet moments as they flew, and drifted, and wound within one another, then came back to the reality of the earth and bed and their sweat-dampened bodies.

Tia lay silent, her heart pounding, in torment. It was frightening to want him this way, so frightening to realize how much she did care about him, what he meant to

her, and who and what he was. She had straightened
her world out—the best she possibly could in the
melee her country had become—and he had come and
twisted her inside out all over again. It had been so
much easier when she had thought him safely locked
away, when she had been able to turn to long hours with
the injured who needed her so much that she wouldn't
have to think about the tempest of her own emotions.
When she had convinced herself that she couldn't want
him, couldn't have him, because she couldn't bear the
consequences. If only he had stayed away . . .

"What now?" she asked him quietly after a long moment. "You are burdened with a Rebel bride you don't
love, who . . . doesn't love you, who costs you way too
dear a price in everything you do. What now?" she challenged. She was going to cry. It was so ridiculous. She
had to be stronger than this, not give way at every turn!

"Perhaps I should be grateful you don't love me.
Heaven help the man you do love; he would probably
die from the ecstasy of your touch."

"Taylor—" she began angrily, trying to roll away from
him and rise.

But he caught her, firmly placing an arm around her.
"What is the scale of your emotion? If I recall, you don't
*dislike* me. But then, that was what you said when you
had promised to stay in St. Augustine."

She was disturbed to hear her voice faltering. "I came
to Richmond because my sister-in-law begged me to do
so. I was trying to save a child. You can't begin to understand—"

"But I did understand."

"No, you really don't. There was a little girl in St.
Augustine, a carriage accident . . ."

"And because she died, you refuse to have children."

"Exactly," she said harshly. "So . . . what now?"

"What now?" he repeated, his voice soft and deep.
"Well, now, as I said, the tables are turned."

Her eyes widened.

"Are you having me arrested?"

"It's a thought," he said with a shrug. "However, I didn't say that."

"So I'm not to be your prisoner?"

"I didn't say that either."

"Then what—"

"I said I'm not having you arrested. But neither will I let you out of my sight for sometime to come."

"I'm to stay with you?"

"We'll arrange something. Here, I'm definitely not in charge, as I was in Florida. Still, my rank is high enough."

"Meaning?"

"I'll be close at all times. Damned close."

She felt his fingers on her shoulders, knuckles running down her bare flesh.

"So . . . you do not want children. They may die. And you do not love me, but lucky me, you do not dislike me. Who was it you might have loved? Our old friend from the blessed Florida militia, Colonel Weir? Do you believe you would have wanted children with him?"

"Weir . . ." she murmured. *Weir?* She hadn't even thought of the man in months.

"Yes, the good Rebel Raymond Weir. Well, if you think you wanted him, you really are a fool."

"Oh, am I?"

He met her eyes, his fingers curling into the strands of her hair. "Yes, you are. He is the type of man who would have admired Godiva—and he would have wanted to sleep with her. But he never would have married her."

"He is constantly asking me to marry him," she replied defiantly.

"Because he doesn't know you're Godiva. He is a man who would think nothing of having a wife and a mistress, and the mistress should be a wild and decadent woman to serve his sexual fancies, while his wife must behave with complete dignity and modesty. Maybe he'd even allow you to wear volumes of clothing in bed. He would tell you what to do all the time—"

"Ah! And you don't?"

"Do you think that he would marry you and allow you to work with Julian? I think not."

"I don't remember you allowing me to work with Julian."

"You were with Brent."

"And now, you say, I am with you."

"My concern isn't that you work with wounded men—North or South. My concern remains that you are reckless, and take far too many chances."

She felt a sudden shiver race down her back. The fact that she could have burned to death in the Wilderness was still a sobering thought. He must have thought that she was cold; though the days were hot, the night still brought in a cooling wind.

His arm came around her, and he turned her toward him. She saw that his hazel eyes were gleaming, and that he was tense, muscles taut, teeth jarring. "You didn't answer me. What if you had married your Rebel beau? Would you want children with him?"

"I didn't marry Ray, so this conversation can go nowhere."

"Would you want children with him?"

"I told you, I simply don't want children," she said, clenching her teeth, steadily meeting his gaze.

He looked at her as seconds ticked by, then abruptly he pushed away from her, rising. She was amazed at how cold she suddenly felt.

She hugged her knees to her chest, dismayed that she felt tempted to cry again, bereft, and as if she had lost more than the warmth of his body beside her own.

"Taylor . . . I don't expect you to understand, to tolerate—a distant arrangement as a marriage. I mean, the war causes *distances.* I mean—"

"I know exactly what you mean," he told her, dressing.

She felt colder, but she had started this, and she felt compelled to press forward. "So you understand, you agree—"

"Get dressed."

"Of course, quickly."

She jumped out of bed. Before she could swing around, he caught her arm. "I don't agree with anything. Your brother and Jesse will be here soon. That's all."

She wrenched her arm free from his grip, turning away, finding her clothing, and dragging her carpet bag back on the bed to repack the clothing which had fallen when he'd so rudely shoved the valise from the bed.

"It's good to see you're packed," he told her, walking to the window.

She realized, moments later, that he had heard hoof-beats long before she became aware that riders were nearing the house. He left the room, walking out front. She heard him call out greetings and she bit her lip, standing very still. Ian was out there.

She allowed herself to forget the Confederacy, dropping the blouse she had been folding, and she ran through the house and out the front door. "Ian!" she cried, seeing her brother dismounting from his horse. She raced to him, throwing her arms around him.

"Tia!"

He picked her up, enclosing his arms around her. She drew away, looking him over carefully, her eyes roaming up and down his length. "You've been well? You're not hurt?"

"Not a scratch," he told her, stepping back. She saw the second horseman who had ridden in with him. A tall cavalryman with brown hair and warm hazel eyes, dashing and good-looking. "Tia, this is Jesse Halston. Sydney's—"

"Husband. Yes, I know," Tia said, extending a hand. "It's good to meet you, Jesse."

He took her hand. His smile deepened. He had dimples, and he was charming. She knew why Sydney had fallen for this enemy.

"Tia. I've heard so much about you. How do you do?"

"I'm not at all sure. You'll have to ask Taylor," she said flippantly.

"She's not pleased to be joining our ranks, I'm afraid," Taylor said.

"Perhaps you'll feel a little differently, Tia, when I tell you that we don't have to go anywhere."

"What?" Taylor said sharply.

"We reported back to Magee already and found out that we're extending the Union line. This house is as good as any for an officers' barracks," Jesse said.

"This is Mary's house," Tia said protectively.

"The Union is moving into town. With any luck, we won't be outranked. Mary's house will fare much better with us using it than others," Ian told his sister. "Tia, is there any food left at all? Did our erstwhile cousin pack it all? Probably, if I know Brent, he didn't allow for much waste. We just shared most of our rations with some other fellows, and it would definitely be nice to have something hot and home-cooked."

"I don't know what's left in here," Tia said, smiling at Taylor with false sweetness. "I was on my way out when Taylor arrived."

"How fortunate he arrived in time!" Ian exclaimed.

"Well, we'll go see what's in the kitchen," Jesse said cheerfully. He smiled again. A very warm, kind, gentle smile. *Sydney must be very happy and love him very much,* Tia thought. She was glad. She loved her cousin, who was almost exactly her own age. They had been best friends throughout their lives.

"How is Sydney?" she asked Jesse.

"Fine!"

She was surprised that Taylor was the one to give her the curt answer. "Looks like there is a stable out back," he continued, talking to Jesse. "We can unhitch that mare of Tia's as well. By the way, did that Reb captain I fished out of the woods keep his word and watch out for my horse?"

"Magee has been keeping Friar, so your man was honorable. He's treated him like his own child," Jesse told Taylor. "I'll take the horses around back."

Taylor was hesitating. Hands on his hips, he stared at the road. "I should report to Magee tonight."

"He'll expect you in the morning," Ian said. "He knew you were working directly for Grant before the

Wilderness, and he's anxious to see you now, glad to have you back—though he doesn't know how long he'll get to keep you. I imagine that he'll move our companies into the field by tomorrow, and stage our reconnaissance from here."

"Well, good. Tia is unhappy enough in Federal company. I wouldn't want her to have to be uncomfortable as well," Taylor said pleasantly. "Shall we all go make this our new home?" He smiled at Tia.

A smile that gave her shivers all over again.

Hours later, they had finished an extremely palatable meal, under the circumstances. Jesse had found a ham left in the smokehouse, and there had been a few cans of fruit left in the larder. There had been some corn bread left over from the day before, and Tia had found a few dandelion greens to pull from the small vegetable garden. She was a rich man's daughter, but as capable in a kitchen as she was in a hospital, Taylor thought, and he realized that Jarrett McKenzie had raised his children to live in the world, not believe that they ruled it.

Tia might not have been happy in Federal company, but she loved her brother and she had no difficulty liking Jesse Halston. She was interested in Jesse, naturally— he had married her cousin. She didn't hide her curiosity, or her assessment, and Jesse seemed to like her in return. Ian had received letters from home in the last few weeks, which Tia had not, and she was anxious to hear about her family. Seeing the way her eyes lit up when she talked about her family to Ian made Taylor feel like the odd man out.

Leaving them to their conversation, Taylor came out to the porch with a good cigar he had found in Mary's father's desk. It had aged well, he mused, leaning against one of the posts to smoke it. He blew smoke rings, watching them on the air. *So she wanted a divorce!*

*Like hell.*

But what was he to do? This was a war. He couldn't have her arrested, even if he wanted to. He wouldn't give away her secret. But what recourse did that leave him? He couldn't be with her constantly; he couldn't force her to stay. When he'd left her the last time, she had even promised to be there when he returned. Now, she wasn't making any promises; she was telling him that she didn't want children and that she wanted a divorce.

The door opened. He saw that Ian was joining him. "Have you ever seen anything as quiet as this night?" Ian asked.

"It will change tomorrow."

"It will. Every house will be taken over. Troops will be camped all over those grasslands. And it will be for a long time, I think."

Taylor looked at him. "We're in for a siege. Petersburg is under attack, and don't think that Grant is going to leave until the city surrenders—no matter what the cost."

"What else have I missed?" Taylor asked. "I heard about the boys from the Virginia Military Institute going to war at New Market. What else?"

"Sherman is marching hard on Georgia—destroying everything in sight, I might add. We probably had a chance to capture Petersburg without a siege, but old Beauregard pushed Meade back too hard."

"Anything from home?"

"Skirmishes, a few naval bombardments. A couple of babies come the fall. Alaina is expecting, and so is Risa."

"So Jerome managed to make it home last Christmas!" Taylor said, grinning, as he leaned back and savored his cigar. But his smile didn't seem to touch his soul. It was a sore subject. He did want children. He hadn't thought about it much since Abby had died. Not even when he'd found himself marrying again in a strange fury.

"So this will be three for you," he murmured casually.

"Jerome's second. Prophesied by my brother's wife."

"Who sees too much, and not enough," Taylor murmured.

"She sees the end of this, but she says it doesn't matter. The Rebs will never believe her until they're beaten into the ground. My brother pays her no heed."

"Maybe he pays more attention than we know. What can he do—quit the army, walk away? He's a doctor. It doesn't work that way, and we both know it."

"But people do change," Ian said suddenly, looking at him. "Like Sydney."

"She claims she hasn't changed."

"But that isn't the truth, is it?"

Taylor shrugged, stubbing out the cigar. "No. She met a really remarkable black woman who opened her eyes to slavery—although Sydney still won't accept it as the major cause of the war."

"Lincoln has fought to preserve the Union, not to free the slaves," Ian reminded him. "As good a man as he may be, he's a politician. He used his Emancipation Proclamation just as much as any politician might."

"He does believe that slavery is an abomination."

"He does, but . . ."

"But what?"

Taylor stared at Ian. "Your father has always, openly and honestly, been against slavery. I can understand the hatred of this uniform where James is concerned, and how Jerome and Brent might have naturally been ready to fight the Union. God knows, there were times when I was young that even I thought all white men were murdering demons—because of this uniform. Why can't your sister realize that the South's fight is wrong, that it would be all but sacrilege to destroy the Union, and slavery is one of the cruelest and most unjust institutions ever twisted into being by man."

"She sees it. She's just fought too long and hard now to admit she's wrong."

"Well, then it's onward to battle I go, Ian. It's been one hell of a long day. Good night."

"Good night, Taylor. Go easy on the South, eh? We really are winning the war."

The house was quiet. Jesse had evidently picked a bed and gone to it. Tia had cleaned the dining room and kitchen, and she had disappeared as well. Taylor walked up the steps wearily. It was past midnight now. God knew what morning would bring.

He entered Tia's bedroom, feeling as if liquid fire coursed through his veins. What if she wasn't there, what if she'd locked the door, what if . . .

He closed the door behind him. The room was cloaked in shadow, but he could see her form on the bed.

He walked slowly over to her. She was on one side of the bed, curled away from him. A sliver of moonlight fell across her back. She only feigned sleep. The pulse at her throat gave her away.

He silently stripped his boots and clothing, crawled onto the bed, and reached for her.

She turned toward him, dark eyes wide, catching a spark of the moonlight. "Taylor, I—"

"I don't give a damn what you want," he told her, taking her into his arms.

She didn't protest. And in a matter of minutes, she was everything he knew, and everything he wanted. She teased and seduced and sated his senses, and in the end, she lay curled in his arms as sweetly as a kitten, seduced and sated and exhausted as well. He held her, suddenly grateful for the night just to sleep beside her, trying not to tremble in a manner that would give away the extent of his pleasure just to be with her. To feel the way she breathed, slept, moved in the night . . .

Later, he awoke, and he wondered why for a moment. He had always awakened to the slightest noise, but . . .

There was nothing. The night was quiet, the breeze was slight. And then he knew.

She still lay beside him, entangled in his limbs.

But softly, almost silently . . . so that he would not hear her . . .

She was crying.

# Chapter 23

~~~~

Whe Tia awoke the following morning, Taylor was gone.

Rising and dressing, she found that he had left the house altogether, as had Jesse.

What had been a ghost town, however, was suddenly filled with people again. Soldiers, servants, wives, laundresses—the inevitable camp followers. The field across from Mary's house was filled with tents; the sound of troop commanders could be heard, along with bugles, harnesses, hoofbeats, and shouts.

The Union had come in full force.

Ian was still at the house, receiving despatches. He'd be leaving soon as well, but he had wanted Tia to know that there was a Private Shelby on the porch, that the house had been designated as their quarters by the proper authorities, and that General Magee had chosen the large Colonial across the street for his own headquarters. The kitchen was being stocked, Molly was the maid and cook who would be looking after them, and Horace was the handyman who would watch the chickens, stock the smokehouse, and do any general handy work they might need around the place.

They had settled in for a long siege at Petersburg.

"Where is Taylor?" Tia asked her brother after she had come down for breakfast.

"Riding," Ian said briefly.

She was about to ask where, but she knew her brother wouldn't tell her. She remained a Rebel, and God alone knew just what she might be capable of doing.

Taylor did not return that night, or the next day, or

the next. At first, Tia remained in the vicinity of the house. When she left, she found that Private Shelby followed her. She felt like telling her brother, who returned to the house at odd hours, that if she chose to escape from Shelby, she could do so easily. However, she managed not to make such a confession.

On the fifth day of Taylor's absence, she could no longer bear the idleness of sitting in the house. The Lutheran church had again been turned into a hospital, so with Shelby at her heels, she walked down to the hospital to offer her services. There were two women in the main body of the church. Pews had been stripped; beds had been brought in. Tia made her way to the side chapel, where the doctor in command was quickly looking through the papers that had come with some newly arrived men. As she passed, the women—Yankee wives, she was certain—paused from their duties to whisper.

About her.

She ignored them.

She walked to the doctor's desk. "Excuse me, but I'm an experienced nurse and I'd like to work here if I may."

The doctor looked up. He was a tall man of about fifty, sturdy, gray-haired, and with a calm, steady manner that inspired trust. His gaze fixed on her despite the confusion and noise around them as another load of injured men arrived.

"And you are . . . ?"

"My name is Tia McKenzie."

"McKenzie Douglas, isn't it?" he inquired, smiling. He rose, offering her a hand. "Reginald Flowers, and I know who you are. You have dark eyes, and you're much, much lovelier, but you do bear a resemblance to your brothers."

"You know both my brothers?"

"Julian was with me after Gettysburg. I wish he were with me still. And Ian is legendary with the cavalry—as is your husband, Mrs. Douglas."

"Of course," she murmured.

The two women had followed her and were staring at

her from the entrance to the small chapel. She turned, staring back.

"They think you're a Rebel who will probably poison the injured men in the middle of the night!" Dr. Flowers said.

"And what do you think, sir?" Tia asked.

"I think they're a pair of plump old biddies!" he said conspiratorially, and she had to smile. "What took you so long in coming?" he asked her.

"Pardon?"

"Colonel Douglas was by several days ago, said your sympathies were Southern but your inclination was to heal. If you're Julian's sister, I haven't a doubt in the world that you'll be a tremendous asset to me. If you'll begin with the fellows who have just come in . . ." he suggested.

And so she did. She bathed wounds, sewed them, bandaged them, and found herself quickly taken in as Dr. Flower's surgical assistant.

The other wives, she was certain, continued to talk about her through the day. She didn't care. Several of the orderlies with Dr. Flowers knew Ian as well—and Rhiannon. The admiration and warmth with which they regarded both her brother and her sister-in-law quickly made them her friends, and by the end of the day, she didn't think at all about it being an enemy hospital.

She was back at the hospital at first light the next morning. Her routine became a twelve-hour day. Private Shelby remained her constant tail, and thereby found himself working at the hospital as well. He was a bit green at first, but was a pleasant enough young man, uncertain but ready to plunge in. Tia was surprised to find him quite bearable.

He seldom came in the house, though. He'd fashioned a hammock on the porch and slept there.

General Magee had set up his headquarters right across the street. Even though he was the enemy, he was Risa's father, and twice, having seen him ride home late, Tia sent messages, asking him to dinner.

One evening, he came. He was polite, charming, and

steady, and she knew why Risa was as assured and confident a young woman as she always managed to be, why she was full of warmth—and also, shrewdly intelligent. He had commanded her brother, Jesse Halston—and her husband. But he didn't talk to her much about Taylor's work in the cavalry, other than to say once that he was such a dead-on shot that it was chilling. Magee talked about the housing plans he had seen Taylor draw, how his real love was architecture—and his home. "He wants to build houses that catch summer breezes, that stand up to fierce storms, that capture the essence of the grass and trees, sea and sand."

"Maybe one day," she told him. And in turn, she talked about Jamie, his grandson, and how well Risa was doing—and that there would be a new baby.

"Ah, now, there's hope, isn't there? Thank God for the little ones. How would we endure the war if it weren't for the hope of the children?"

She didn't answer him. She would have told him that children all seemed to die too.

By the end of her first week at the hospital, she returned home to find that Ian was there before her, working on despatches at the parlor desk.

She watched him write for several minutes before she spoke.

"Ian, where is Taylor?"

He hesitated, watching her. "He was at the front at Petersburg for a while. He's cavalry, but because of his engineering background, he was working with some coal miners planning . . . planning some works at the line."

"He was?"

"He's also been running despatches between Grant, Sherman, and Sheridan."

"Is he coming back here?"

"Yes."

"Is he in danger?"

Ian hesitated. "Tia, it's a war. Everyone is in danger." He sighed. "Tia, he's an extraordinary horseman and a crack shot."

She sighed. "So I've been told."

"How was the hospital?"

"Filled with bleeding and dying men."

"But you'll be working there."

"Until I can go home."

"And what you want is to go home?" Ian said, then he smiled. "You don't actually mean *home,* do you? You want to go back and work in the woods with Julian."

"It's where I belong," she agreed.

"Has it occurred to you that you *belong* with your husband?"

"But he isn't here, is he?" Tia asked.

"He will be soon. You know, Tia, I only want what's best for you. I am your brother, and I love you."

She smiled. "And I love you, Ian—even if you are a sadly misguided individual."

"Ah. That means a Yank, doesn't it?"

"Like I said, big brother, I love you dearly, but you're not a doctor. And this isn't my state. Excuse me, Ian, Molly said that she'd fix me some bath water before dinner."

Thank God for Molly, and thank God for baths. Tia wanted to work with the soldiers; she needed to work with the soldiers. But when she came home, she couldn't get over the feeling of being drenched not just in sweat and blood, but in the anguish of the men. She could stay on her feet forever, help in the direst situation, deal with sick soldiers, gangrene, gut wounds, and the most horrible amputations—but she did dearly love to lie in a hot bath when the day was over. It was July, the summer heat could be stifling, and she loved to sit in the water until it turned cooler than the night air.

That night, she lay in the tub for a very long time. She was especially tired. Molly was a wonderful cook, but Tia hadn't been hungry. Though Ian was there with her that night, and she was glad of her brother's company, she went to bed early. However, she lay there awake, unable to calm her mind.

Around midnight, she heard the door to her room open. By the moonlight trickling through the thin curtains, she saw a tall figure there, heard the door close quietly. *Taylor.* Her heart began to thunder.

He moved about the room like a wraith, discarding his clothing then walking to the window. He stared out at the night for a very long time. Then he came to bed.

He didn't say a word to her, but lay on his back. She thought that his eyes remained open, that he stared up at the ceiling. She tried to keep her own eyes closed, to pretend that she hadn't heard him, that she lay asleep. But he knew, he always knew, when she really lay awake. And suddenly he turned on her. "What was that you said, Mrs. Douglas? How am I? Yes, alive, certainly. Well? I believe so, physically, I'm in excellent shape— no bullets lodged in me anywhere. I mean, that is the least you'd ask out of a man you don't actually *dislike,* isn't it?"

"Taylor, I—"

"Never mind, Tia. Never mind."

Startled by the tears his deep, sarcastic words brought to her eyes, she started to turn away. He drew her back. "I'm sorry, Tia. I don't want you to turn away."

He made love to her that night as if a demon rode his soul. He was still drinking coffee in the kitchen when she woke the next morning, but the way his gold eyes touched hers over his cup, she thought that he had never disliked her more intensely. Her eyes downcast, she strode past him, thanking Molly as she accepted coffee from her. The coffee churned in her stomach. She sipped it anyway.

"Find any good Rebels to save yet at the hospital?"

"No."

"Well, you may today. Goodbye, my dear," he told her. "Molly, thank you!" he called to their servant, then he started out of the house.

"Taylor!" she shouted, startled to find that she was following him. He stopped out on the lawn, turning to wait for her question. Friar, she noted, was at the gate. Good old Friar. He had his horse back. That had to make him happy—if having her didn't.

Private Shelby was leaning against one of the porch

columns, waiting for her. She felt awkward, smiling a good morning to him but not wanting an audience at this moment.

"Are you leaving again for . . . for a long time? Or will you be back soon?"

She felt the sweep of his distant, gold gaze. A slight smile curved his lips. "Did you want me back?" he inquired politely.

Shelby was behind them. She felt her cheeks burn. "Of . . . of course."

He walked back to her. Kissed her cheek. Whispered "Liar!" in her ear. And without giving her an answer, he strode to Friar, mounted up, and rode away.

At the hospital, she learned what demons tormented him. The soldiers, doctors, patients, wives, nurses—everyone—talked about the horrible events at the crater. Union engineers had dug a tunnel to reach Confederate lines. Black troops had been trained to go in—but at the last minute they'd been pulled out. The generals were afraid that it would look as if they were willing to sacrifice their black soldiers.

As it happened, explosives that had been set didn't fire properly. Then the replacement men, too hastily trained, faltered. The Rebels counterattacked. It had been a disaster. One of the injured men, learning that Tia was Taylor's wife, talked to her about what happened.

"Colonel Douglas kept trying to tell them there could be a fault with men being trapped, but somebody said he was cavalry, and even if he'd had training in engineering and architecture, he wanted to build mansions, not military works.

"Colonel Douglas was angry then, saying they shouldn't ask him for information if they didn't want his opinion. He was angry that they changed the troops at the last minute, and angrier still, I think, when so many men were blown to bits. He didn't want to be right. But he was there, ma'am, right there, racing into the action, trying to get men out when it all blew up in our faces.

He later asked to be sent back to General Magee and left alone as cavalry, since that was what he was.

"They say about twenty thousand men were involved and that we flat out lost a full four thousand of them. It was one of the most horrible things I've seen in the war, and I've been in the Army of the Potomac since the beginning. You'll see . . . when the fellows start coming in today. Some of them are in pretty bad shape."

They were. Men came in from the siege line throughout the day.

Rebel soldiers came as well, many of them dying, bodies maimed, limbs blown to bits in the explosion that had rocked the crater.

Tia stayed at the hospital through the night. The next day, she almost passed out at one point; she was nearly sick at another. She ignored her weariness. At dusk, Dr. Flowers made her go home, telling her that she was suffering from exhaustion.

When she reached the house, Taylor was there. She had been bone tired, but the news that he had preceded her home seemed like a stimulant. She was immediately awake and wary. Molly told her he was in her room—in the bathtub. She entered quietly, saw that he was indeed there, leaning back, a washcloth over his face. She started to walk back out. He didn't move the washcloth, but he had heard her, and he knew it was her. "Don't leave on my account."

Awkwardly, she moved into the room. She hesitated near the wooden hip tub. "I heard how many men were lost at the crater. I'm very sorry."

He pulled the washcloth from his face, studying her. "Well, I don't know how many, but I'm afraid a number of Rebs were blown to bits as well. Unfortunately, that's the idea with war. We kill one another. The last man standing wins."

"I heard that you had argued against it."

"I did, but I wish I'd been wrong."

"You were resting. I didn't mean to disturb you," Tia said.

"You disturb me, my love, on a daily basis."

She turned around, determined to leave the room. But before she could reach the door, he was up and out of the tub, water sluicing from his naked body. And when he caught her and swung her around, she was amazed at the way that just the touch of his sleek, bare flesh aroused her, at how she wanted him. "I have just come from the hospital," she told him, feeling that she was obliged to offer some manner of protest.

"Then you should share my bath." He spun her around, working on buttons and ties and closures. Her shoes flew, stockings followed, cloth lay on the ground in a pool of pastel color. He picked her up, plunked her into the tub with him, and when they tried to sit, their knees knocked. They stood again, facing one another in the water, and to her amazement, she found herself laughing. "We don't fit at all . . ."

"We don't, do we?" he inquired, but he cupped her chin, kissed her, and then she felt the soap in his hands against her flesh, and the sleek feel of it moving against her, over her breasts, between her thighs . . . she was shaking, still feeling his kiss. The soap was suddenly in her hands. She bathed his shoulders, his chest, back . . . buttocks, sex. The soap slipped from her hands, splashed into the water. Droplets cascaded around them. They both ducked for more water to rinse out, crashed together, laughed. Then her eyes met his, and she saw the fire, felt as if it touched her inside. He lifted her from the tub, fell instantly upon the bed, and within seconds he was inside her. Tia wondered how she had ever lived without him.

"You really don't ever listen to me, do you?" she murmured.

"I listen, but I simply refuse to agree. You're my wife, and I will be with you. Whether or not I am a Rebel countryman, as you would have liked."

"I told you, I don't *dislike* you."

"You'll have to quit saying so with such passion. I might start thinking you actually do *like* me."

"I just wish that . . . I were home."

"In Florida, you mean. Away from me."

:"In Florida," she agreed. "And I told you . . . I just don't want . . ."

"Don't want what?"

"Children."

Exhaustion then seemed to be overwhelming her. If he said something more, she didn't hear it. Perhaps he was just as exhausted. He remained beside her. Sometime in the night, she awoke, feeling him at her back. The length of him against the length of her. Then he must have known that she had awakened, because he was touching her. His arms were around her, upon her breasts, and he was inside her, and she was soaring into the sweet warm rain of ecstasy, bursting into a field of light and stars, and drifting down into a night of velvet and blackness. "You'll simply have to forgive me," he whispered against her earlobe.

"I'll try," she murmured.

Yet, the next thing she knew, she was shaking. It was summer, it was hot, but she was freezing. She couldn't get warm enough. At first, she was against him, trying to gain his body heat. It wasn't enough. His arms were around her, she soon realized, then he was cradling her in blankets, but she couldn't seem to open her eyes.

Cold, cold, cold . . .

So cold . . . and she was dreaming. She was at Cimarron, by the pool. The sun was shining, but she was shaking.

Someone was calling her. Urgently. The sound was coming from the house. But she could see Taylor. He was standing on the other side of the pool. He seemed very far away. She wanted to go to him. But she was so cold, and they were calling her from the house, and if she could only reach Cimarron, she would be warm again. She would see the sun shine on the river, the way the lawn swept down to the embankment, the way the grass grew so very green, and even the way the white puffs of clouds moved across the heavens.

"I want to go home . . . I have to go home . . ."

"*Sh* . . . it's all right."

Then he wasn't across the freshwater spring from her

anymore. He was holding her again. She was glad; she was where she wanted to be. Except that she was slipping away. She needed to say something, hold on to him. She couldn't. She was falling . . . into darkness.

She couldn't seem to remember, or to feel, until she realized that she hadn't fallen; his arms were around her again. He was urging her to drink; she tasted bitter quinine. She opened her eyes, and she wondered what had happened. She was in a nightgown, and she wasn't alone with Taylor. He was there, in full uniform, but Ian was there, too, and so was Dr. Flowers. The doctor had his hand on her forehead, and he looked grave. "Can you hear me?"

"Yes." Her voice seemed thick. Her throat hurt; it was hard to talk.

"Drink more of this."

She did so, then closed her eyes. She wasn't quite so cold anymore, but she was very, very tired. "You picked up a fever at the hospital, Tia," Dr. Flowers told her gently. "But I think we're through the worst of it. You need to sleep, to rest. Do you understand?"

She nodded. She thought she heard them talking again—all of them. She tried to reach out. She had seen something strange in Taylor's eyes. "Taylor . . ." She managed to murmur his name. And she knew that he was beside her again, holding her hand. Then she felt blackness slipping over her once more.

When she next awoke Taylor was gone. Ian was in the room with her, sitting in a chair by the bed, his sharp blue eyes watching her. She managed a smile and a weak "Hi."

"Hi, little sister. How are you doing?"

"Better, I think."

He reached over, touched her forehead. He seemed satisfied. Rising, he brought her a glass of water. She took it from him, realizing she was tremendously thirsty.

"Thanks."

"I'm going to tell Molly you're awake. She has some tea for you to start with, then you're to go to soup and toast, I believe."

"Sounds good. I'm famished."

He started out of the room. She called him back. "Ian? Where's Taylor? I'm not asking for the secret movements of the Union army or anything, just . . . where is he?"

"He had to leave. Jesse was ordered back to Washington. Taylor is down in Georgia."

"Georgia! When did he leave? When is he coming back?"

"I don't know. But he's arranged passage home for you."

"What?" she murmured.

"He said you wanted to be in Florida. When you're better, General Magee will arrange an escort to the nearest safe port, and you can return to St. Augustine by ship. I'll try to follow, since Alaina's baby is due in September and I'd like to be there."

"He's not coming back?" Tia said. "And I'm just to go?"

"Isn't that what you want?" Ian asked. "It's what you told me."

"Of course," she murmured. Her brother's eyes were on her. Her own lowered.

"Taylor stayed until he knew you were out of danger, but he said that even in your fever, all you talked about was going home." He hesitated. "He was carrying despatches down to Sherman. Once you were on the mend, he couldn't wait any longer."

She nodded. "I see."

Ian started out of the room again.

"Ian?" she said, again calling him back.

He paused. "I'd . . . wait for him," she whispered.

"Tia, I don't know when he's coming back. Sherman is trying to take Atlanta. Taylor could be gone a very long time. I thought you'd be happy about going home."

"I *am* happy about going home," she told him. And she was. But she was dismayed to realize that she was desolate about leaving Taylor. *But I'm not leaving him; he's already gone!* she thought.

"There's a note for you in the desk."

Tia started to rise but fell back, dizzy. She looked at her brother ruefully, seeing that he was hurrying to her side. "I'm all right, just not quite back to normal. Would you . . . ?"

Ian opened the desk drawer, brought her back a folded piece of note paper, and left her alone to read Taylor's words.

They weren't what she had hoped for.

> *Tia,*
> *You've said you want to be in Florida. Under the circumstances, it seems that you should go. A Union ship will bring you to St. Augustine. I know that you can be with family members and find useful occupation there. Don't even think about a hair-cloaked romp about the state. Take care of yourself, stay well—and stay out of trouble. How's that for fair warning? Is this a threat? Yes, my love, it is.*
> *Taylor*

She wouldn't cry—it would be so stupid! He had always made her stay with him. Now, suddenly, he was gone—indefinitely. And though he had left a threat . . .

Did he really care what she did?

This was what she'd wanted. No matter what she was feeling, he remained the enemy. A staunch enemy. And now, a threatening, unforgiving enemy.

So she was going home. Back to where she'd started. She couldn't stay in St. Augustine. She would go back with her brother. And at home, she would find the strength to begin again.

Tia burst into tears.

And then, only then, did she admit to herself that it all hurt so, so badly because she was in love with Taylor Douglas.

It was the middle of the night.

The door burst open.

Sydney bolted upright in a wild panic. What had happened? Had the Rebs stormed the capital? No! She hadn't heard a cannon or even the firing of a single gun.

She leapt from the bed and rushed out to the parlor. In the firelight burning low at the hearth, she saw him. Jesse. In full uniform, his plumed hat upon his head, frockcoat over his snow-white shirt and doublet. Her hand flew to her throat. It had been so long since she'd seen him.

Did he know that she had slipped her guard, left the city, defied his order? Was he here in anger, or . . .

Had he seen Taylor?

"Jesse?" she murmured.

He strode across the room to her. She felt his eyes, saw the lines about his handsome face. She backed away.

"Sydney, damn you, Sydney . . ."

He reached her. She met his gaze, mouth dry, heart hammering. He was alive. Just that seemed a miracle. She was so glad to see him, wanted so much to touch him . . .

"Sydney."

To her amazement, he went down upon a knee, drawing her to him. His arms encircled her waist; he held her like porcelain. She hesitated, her fingers falling on the brown waves of his hair. He stood, arms around her, holding her. His eyes met hers again. He kissed her, and kissed her . . .

"Sydney . . . you're a Yankee."

"I am not!"

He drew away, his smile gentle, beautiful, the smile with which she had fallen in love, from the very first.

"You were sneaking out to smuggle slaves."

"You saw Taylor."

"Yes."

"Did he . . . did he tell you . . ."

"Particulars? No. Don't look so relieved—*you're* going to tell me what happened. Everything. Then, I'm going to throttle you, of course, you little fool. It's every bit as dangerous as what you were doing, it's more dangerous . . . it's . . ."

"Jesse?"

"What?"

"I love you."

"Oh, God!"

He swept her up. She buried her head against his chest. Slipped her arms around his neck. He carried her back to the bedroom and they lay down together. He smoothed her hair back. "I love you, Sydney, I love you, I love you, I love you . . ."

It was many hours later when he warned her again that he was going to throttle her, and by then she simply didn't care. She knew he didn't mean a word of it.

# Chapter 24

~~~~~~

When Tia arrived in Florida, she returned immediately to Cimarron to spend some precious time with her parents. Her father was pleased that she had married Taylor Douglas, which she told herself was natural because her father was, at heart, a Yankee. But she knew it was more than that. Her father liked Taylor, and respected him, and for that, he was glad for his daughter. Her mother was sorry that they would never plan an elaborate wedding, but she was also pragmatic—they were living in wartime, and what was important was that they survived it. Neither of her parents seemed surprised about the marriage. "You were different with him from the beginning, my dear," Tara said. "There was something there . . . you just had to discover it. I'm so glad you did. I don't think that Ray Weir knows you've married, though. He was here just last week, asking for you. You should never have played him along so, dear."

"I never played him along! Did you tell him that I had married?"

"Actually, no. I never had the chance."

"Well, I assume he'll find out soon enough."

"Yes, I imagine." Her mother seemed unhappy then, as if she was hiding something.

"Mother, what is it?"

"He and your father got into another row."

"What happened? Oh, Mother, I wish Father would be careful with his convictions and his temper. We are a Confederate state."

"Tia, it was not your father's fault."

"Ray came in here demanding to know where you were. Your father said that you were with Ian in Virginia, and Ray exploded, saying he had no right to send you up with the Yankees."

"But he didn't *send* me anywhere. Ray is the most infuriating man. And to think that I did fancy I could be in love with him at one time. I've tried several times to make him understand that I am independent, that I *try* to make my own decisions, go my own way—despite Father and two older brothers and bossy cousins to boot and now Taylor. But—"

"Tia, don't worry about it. He came, and he left. Eventually, someone will tell him that you have married, and he will let it all go."

Later that day, she sat with her father by the river, and eventually she asked him, "Was I really such a horrible flirt?"

He looked at her, arching a brow. "Horrible? You were an excellent flirt, my darling daughter."

He was grinning, but she flushed. "Seriously, Father. I mean, I know that I liked to have a good time, and I did tease, but . . . life used to be so different."

"Tia, I'm afraid that Ray is somewhat obsessed. You did nothing wrong. You are beautiful, polite, friendly, you considered his suit . . . but you fell in love elsewhere."

She leaned back against her father's broad shoulder.

"We think so differently," she murmured.

"You and Ray—or you and Taylor?"

She laughed. "Taylor and I don't think the same at all, except . . ."

"Except that you do. You value life, and your belief in what is right and wrong, and the honor in a family, no matter what someone else's opinion may be."

"Perhaps."

"You did fall in love, right?" he asked gruffly.

"Yes, I did," she admitted. "Father . . ." she asked, but her voice faded away.

Jarrett turned to her, lifting her chin. He always seemed so wise to her. He saw so much, and understood so much, even when he tried to let her think out her own life.

"Do I think he loves you?" he asked.

"He sent me away," Tia admitted.

"He sent you where you wanted to be."

She bit her lip. Not really. She wanted to be with him. "The fighting has been fast and furious, Tia," her father said.

"You've heard from him?"

"From Ian. Taylor has been racing around, from Sherman to Sheridan to Grant. He's been in very hostile territory, seldom sleeping in the same place twice. He knew what his orders were going to be. And if he couldn't be with you, he apparently figured you should be with your family."

She smiled. "Thanks, Father."

"I know a little bit about rocky marital relations."

"You?" she inquired incredulously.

"Your mother. She can keep a secret until a man is nearly insane!"

Tara was coming across the lawn. He drew a finger to his lips, and Tia laughed, and she was suddenly very happy to be where she was, and who she was. She was glad to be with her father; she loved him so very much. And it was wonderful, new and fresh, to see him with her mother. They had been very lucky. The world around them had never been easy, but they had weathered it together.

Being home was almost like old times. Except that, sitting with her parents, she could see the man in the lookout tower at the docks, and she knew that Jarrett's men patrolled the ground constantly.

She didn't stay as long as she wanted—only a few weeks—but returned eastward to find Julian and Rhiannon and keep busy with them in the company of the militia. She wanted to help out when the babies were born, and from Julian's position along the river, she knew she'd hear when the time drew near. She did; Alaina sent them a message via a tobacco and coffee trade between the soldiers.

As it turned out, both babies came early. Katie Kyle McKenzie was born on the nineteenth of September. She had a headful of platinum curls, her mother's legacy, and huge blue eyes. Tia thought she was the most beautiful child she had ever seen. But then, Allen Angus McKenzie was born on the twenty-first of September, and he was as handsome as Katie was beautiful, with a touch of red in the thick thatch of dark hair on his head, and eyes already hinting of his mother's green. Tia was glad to be with her sisters-in-law and cousin-in-law and the whole little brood of McKenzies. She was able to fawn over the infants—and be helpful with the toddlers, who were proving to be quite wild under the circumstances.

Sean had taken it to heart that he was the eldest of this brood, a leader who was supposed to be responsible. Still, he had his moments when he wanted his mother's full attention. Ian was due; he had written that he'd received leave to come, but the war was becoming more and more demanding as the Union determined to end it—and the Confederacy fought on to the bitter end. Atlanta had finally fallen at the end of August. Although Tia still hadn't heard a word from Taylor herself, she learned from Risa that he had spent several weeks riding for General Sherman, maintaining tight communications between himself and other commanders in the field, and keeping a sharp eye on Rebel movements.

It wasn't long after she'd left Virginia that Tia began wondering if she herself was going to have a baby. The possibility was just as frightening as she'd feared it would be. She didn't want to lose a child—if she was definitely carrying one. She definitely didn't want to lose Taylor's child. She wanted a baby, as perfect as Alaina's little Katie, as sturdy and charming as Risa's young master Allen Angus McKenzie.

Tia spent most of October in St. Augustine, enjoying the newborns and her toddling little nephews and nieces. At the end of the month, she gave up waiting to hear from Taylor and returned inland with Rhiannon. Alaina told her that Taylor might have written several times—getting letters through was growing harder and harder.

That might have been true, but Alaina continued to hear from Ian.

There seemed to be a general feeling of despair that hung like a swamp miasma over the troops. Julian's hospital camp held three soldiers with gunshot wounds from skirmishing just south of Jacksonville, two sailors with cutlass wounds from a sea battle, and another three soldiers who had been hit with shrapnel during a Yankee bombardment of a salt mine. Although all were doing well, it seemed that they were listless, and waiting. There was hope in the South that Lincoln would be defeated by McClellan in the presidential election, but soon after the election on November 7, the news came that Lincoln had been reelected. The North would not be offering terms of reconciliation and allowing the South to go. President Davis kept making optimistic speeches, some of which filtered south. He believed that Lee's Army of Northern Virginia was invincible, but Tia could see that the fighting men thought otherwise.

In the middle of November, Julian was summoned northward to take care of several members of Dixie's band of militia. Nearly ten men had come down with the chicken pox. With most of the men doing well and Liam there, almost as familiar now with the treating of wounds as a trained surgeon, Tia thought that she would accompany Julian and Rhiannon, but as it happened, her sister-in-law wasn't going, and she also told Tia in no uncertain way that she wasn't going either.

"Tia, we're not going because it is chicken pox. And although I don't believe that I'm expecting another babe yet, I wouldn't want to discover later that I was wrong and that I'd exposed myself to an illness that would affect it. But if I'm not mistaken . . ." Rhiannon smiled knowingly at her sister-in-law.

"Can you tell?" Tia asked.

"Only because I know you."

Tia was quiet.

"Well?"

"I guess we'll stay here together. With Liam, of course."

Rhiannon was pleased. "Julian will understand; he'll manage alone."

Several days after Julian had left, two men who'd caught Yankee fire from the coast were brought in. It was very late at night when they arrived. Rhiannon was sleeping, and Tia decided not to wake her.

She recognized one of the men; he'd been her escort seemingly ages ago when Dixie's men had accompanied her to Cimarron for Christmas. His name was David Huntington and he was a very thin, charming young man who had just managed to grow his first mustache. He had been a brand new recruit with Dixie when she'd first met him; now he had nearly a year of service under his belt. She smiled at him reassuringly. "Bullet in his calf; shrapnel in his thigh. No bones and no blood vessels involved," she told Liam.

"Can you cut them out? Your brother is a day's ride from here. I can go for him," Liam told her.

"I can manage. Don't worry, I would never chance it if I couldn't. Soldier, I have some really fine whiskey for you to imbibe while I cut away! First—a little for the flesh—and then a little for the soul!"

The bullet came out easily; the shrapnel was harder. She winced each time she had to dig, and wondered if she shouldn't have waited for Julian. But then, she fished out the last piece, put in the stitches that were necessary, and bid her tipsy patient good night. Early the next morning, as she looked over her handiwork, she felt his large, anguished gray eyes upon her.

"Miss Tia . . ."

"Yes?"

"Lord love me, ma'am, I ain't no traitor."

"Of course you're not."

"But . . ."

"But what?"

He moistened his lips. Beckoned her closer. "I heard that you've done more than just patch up us boys, Miss Tia. I know your brother has saved hundreds of men. And I've even heard that your father has done nothing more than let officers from both sides meet on his lands."

"That's true," she said, smiling at the soldier to encourage him to continue.

He started talking in a rush then. "Colonel Weir is going to attack Cimarron. He met up with our camp just a few days ago. I don't think that Captain Dixie believed him, I mean, you know what a fine man Dixie is, ma'am."

"I do," she said gravely. "So how do you know—"

"Weir's got some other militia officer all fired up . . . he—he thinks that your father is a traitor, and that he has to be executed for what he's done to Florida."

"What?" Tia gasped incredulously. "Executed! He can't execute my father; he's done nothing wrong—"

"Sh . . . sh . . . don't want no one calling me a traitor, saying I called the whistle on the colonel. Weir thinks he can prove charges that your father is a traitor, and if he thinks he can do it, he'll find a way. He hasn't got any real permission from the Reb army; he's just taking it all into his own hands."

*Weir is going to attack Cimarron? How dare he? Where does he get the nerve, the authority?*

Then Tia knew. And she shouldn't have been surprised. Weir hated her father. Hated his confidence. Hated the fact that Jarrett was so deeply dedicated to his beliefs. Her father's courage was so strong and unfaltering. He had stood tall against the sea of difference all around him, never agreeing to what he thought was wrong just because others thought it was right.

"You're sure about this?" she asked quietly.

"Yes, ma'am, I am." He moistened his lips again. "He's gathering his troops at the old Ellington place. The Ellingtons have all been gone for some time now, you know."

"Yes, I know. They were friends; the house is close to Cimarron."

"Yes, ma'am. Very close. A good place to meet. He's going to attack . . . let's see . . . four days from now. At dusk. The timing is really important, 'cause he's going to coordinate an attack. Some other fellows will come down from the north while he moves up from the south in a pincer movement. Then he'll seize the property. And . . ."

"And what?"

"He intends to hang your father right there. Make him an example, he says, of what happens to Florida traitors."

"He's planning on hanging my father?" she said, outraged. "And my mother?" she asked sharply.

He didn't answer at first. His eyes were shamed, downcast. "She's . . . fair game for the soldiers. I'm not sure what will happen . . . when they're done . . ."

She stood back, horrified. She had to stop Weir. How? Get to him, buy time. Then what? She had to leave word right away; Liam had to get to Julian. Someone else had to get to St. Augustine right away, find Ian. Was Ian even there? Had he reached the city yet? If not, surely he had friends there, friends enough to raise a force against Weir's men. Friends who could get to Cimarron fast and stop what was happening.

"I have four days?" she whispered. Just enough time to get across the state.

"Well, three and a half, I reckon."

"How many men does Weir have?"

"Five companies, if I heard right. But there's maybe only ten to twenty men left alive in each of those companies. Miss Tia, Dixie would never have just let it go if he believed what Weir was planning. Still . . . he is Florida militia. And they're getting bitter, and hanging spies lots of places."

"Thank you, Private. Thank you so much." Impulsively, Tia kissed his cheek, then left him. She started to run to Rhiannon, but hesitated. No, she couldn't tell Rhiannon that she was going to Cimarron herself, that she had to. She would write Rhiannon a note. And she would write to Julian, and to Ian—oh, please, God, make it be that he had gotten to St. Augustine by now! Cimarron was his inheritance, his birthright. He would come, he would fight for it to his dying breath. Save . . .

Save their father. And their mother. Oh, Lord! She had to get to Cimarron; she couldn't risk anyone trying to stop her. She was going to have to race across the state . . .

She had Blaze with her. She knew the way, knew what she was doing. She could make it. She had to reach Weir. Stall him. What then? She didn't know. She just knew that she had to stop him somehow. And if she couldn't stop him, she had to buy time.

She hurried to her tent, wrote her letters. When she came out, she was ready. She went for Blaze, saddled her, bridled her, and started to mount her. Liam came hurriedly limping over to her on his prosthetic leg.

"Miss Tia—"

"Get these letters out for me, Liam."

"Now wait! What do you think that you're doing?"

"Make sure Rhiannon sees this right away. And get to Julian for me. It's a matter of life and death."

"Oh, God, Miss Tia, please tell me you're not going to run and do something dangerous or decadent—"

She was already on Blaze. "Liam! For the love of God! Do as I say."

She turned her horse and started riding hard from the camp.


No man in the whole of Grant's army had moved harder, or faster, Taylor thought, taking the time at last to dismount from Friar, empty his canteen—and look out across the devastated landscape. Damn yes, he was moving hard—and fast. Running. As if it could keep him from thinking, worrying . . . *being afraid.*

He should have made her stay. Strange, but he couldn't get over the longing. The passion they'd had. They'd almost been friends again. *And he had let her go. Like a fool. Why?*

*Because, fool, idiot!* he charged himself. *Because you're in love with her, and it was happening from the first time you saw her. But you're a coward. You don't want to face pain again . . .*

Well, that was it, of course. He had known how she'd

felt about watching the children die, had understood her fear. And scoffed at it, and told her that she was just going to have to live, and accept the tragedy as well as the happiness in life. But when she'd been so sick, tossing and turning, whispering that she just wanted to go home . . .

He hadn't been able to deny her wish. He'd decided that he'd fight harder and harder—as if he, one man, could make the war be over any more quickly.

So . . .

So now he was doing his damned best to follow the wily Confederate General Hood, who, in Sherman's own words, could twist an army around at will.

The problem was, pretty soon Hood wouldn't have much of anyplace left to twist it.

Sherman was destroying everything as he marched. It was said that a crow would have to pack a lunch to fly over Georgia. It was sickening, of course, what war had done there. God had seldom created such devastation with hurricanes, blizzards, tornadoes, floods, or other natural disasters. When Sherman's troops stripped the land, they stripped it good.

Taylor had just reported to the general and, to his surprise, received a personal letter from the general's headquarters. Chewing on a piece of hardtack, he hunkered down by Friar and perused the letter. It was from Jarrett McKenzie, a friendly missive, like one that any man might receive from his father-in-law. Jarrett congratulated him on his marriage and said that he had seen Tia. She had come straight there from Virginia. She must not have told her parents she had been ill, because Jarrett made no mention of the fact. He did, however, mention that Raymond Weir had been to Cimarron, anxiously asking about Tia. They'd argued. Weir had gone on, but Jarrett expected there would be trouble in the future.

Taylor folded the letter and slid it back into his pocket. Though there was nothing in the letter about Weir meaning anything to Tia, Weir was trouble—a fanatic dedicated to his goal.

He shouldn't have sent Tia home.

Then what should he have done? He could still remember the gripping fear he'd felt when he awakened and discovered she was burning up. She was a fighter, had been a fighter from the start, and Dr. Flowers had never thought once that he was going to lose her. But two men had died from the same fever at the hospital, and that had scared him worse than he'd ever been scared since . . .

Since the blood on his hands when he'd reached for Abby.

Tia had pulled through, but watching her, day after day, the beauty of her pale features, the silky sweeping length of her "Godiva" hair, he realized just how much he wanted and needed and *loved* his wife. He could remember telling her that only a fool would love her. He was that fool. And although he admired her passion and conviction and her fighting spirit, he was afraid for her. Afraid that he wouldn't be there to protect her against fanatics like Weir.

"Colonel Douglas!"

Hearing himself called, he stood and turned, frowning. He didn't know the young infantry lieutenant striding toward his position on the little hill.

"Yes, I'm Douglas."

"Hello, sir. Lieutenant Nathan Riley."

"Lieutenant," he acknowledged. "What can I do for you?"

"Sir, I'm hoping I can do something for you."

"Oh?"

"My unit was a bit south of here the other day, down closer to the border. We took some wounded militia boys from North Florida prison. I was hoping to find a way to reach Colonel McKenzie, but then I heard you were kin to him, sir, that his sister is your wife."

"What's this about?"

"The McKenzie property is down by Tampa Bay. Jarrett McKenzie is a Union sympathizer, so I understand."

"Yes, he is."

"One of the Florida boys died just a few hours ago. I took this off him."

Lieutenant Riley passed him a creased sheet of paper. He looked at Riley curiously, then unfolded the paper and studied it. It was a map, he realized, crudely drawn. He saw Tampa Bay, the river, Cimarron. A plantation just south of Cimarron, and another one just north of it. There was a notation of "Major Hawkins" with an arrow coming from the north, and another notation, "Colonel Weir," with an arrow sweeping up from the south. The arrows met at Cimarron. There, a hangman's noose had been crudely drawn, and next to it, a date in November, just four days away. "Coordinated assault, must be timed to coincide from both fronts," was written in the corner.

He looked up. "Lieutenant, have we a working telegraph? I do need to get this information to Colonel Ian McKenzie, in Petersburg."

"As I said, I thought of Colonel McKenzie right away, sir. But he left Petersburg for St. Augustine several days ago."

"Then I need the information to reach him there. I know that lines are down, but Ian may be the only hope."

"I'll get it through somehow, sir."

"And send a message that when he gets this, he should go straight to Cimarron. I'll try to deal with Weir at the Ellington place before he can muster his men together for the attack."

"Aye, sir!" Riley said, saluting.

"Thank you, Riley."

"You're going to stop it, sir, right?" Riley asked. "My home is Tennessee. Some people didn't agree with Pa's dedication to the Union Jack, so they burned him out. I'd hate like hell to see it again. Thought Southerners were supposed to be gentlemanly folk, the last of the cavaliers."

"Many of them are, Riley. But some of them aren't. Hell, yes, if I can stop this, I will. I'm going to get leave from Sheridan, and ask for a number of troops. You want to come along, Lieutenant?"

Riley grinned. "Hell, yes, sir! I can round you up one of the finest companies of scouts and skirmishers in the whole Union army, assuming you can get Sheridan to agree."

He knew he could get Sheridan to agree. He was still carrying the leave papers that Lincoln himself had signed. Sheridan couldn't hold him, and knowing the fierce little man as he did, he was certain the cause would appeal to him—despite the fact that many men had lost their homes in the devastation of the war. Jarrett was a man who had never failed the Union. And securing Florida always remained an intriguing challenge to the Union commanders.

If he couldn't bring troops, he would go himself. But he believed that his own passion would be enough to convince Sheridan.

"Get those messages out for me by telegraph, Riley—and if the lines are down, get a runner. But make sure we get the information through to Ian. Meet me back at the general's headquarters. We haven't much time to travel a hell of a lot of miles."

Riley saluted. "Yes, sir! I'll be mighty proud to ride with you!"

On Friar, Taylor rode hard back toward headquarters, hoping that no recent development in the fighting would prevent him from an immediate audience with Sheridan.

He had to leave, now. As soon as Riley could muster his company together.

*When the hell had militia been given the right to become judge and jury in the state? Was Weir going mad, seizing far too much power, thinking himself the law?*

His heart pounded in his chest like a drumbeat. *Could he make it in time?* Where was Tia? Did she know about any of this?

She would never let men go against Cimarron without doing something.

*How in hell was he going to endure the time it would take to get there?*

# Chapter 25

## A House United

*Fall, 1864*
*The West Florida Coast, Near Tampa Bay*

The sky was strange that night. Though dark, the lingering effects of a storm at dusk had left crimson streaks across the shadowy gray of the sky. A cloud passed over the moon, which seemed to glow with that strange red light. Reaching Ellington Manor, Taylor lifted a hand to signify a silent halt to the men behind him. They could hear the clamor of other men, disbursing supplies, but they were around the back of the property. One lone soldier, leaning against a once-majestic column, guarded the house in front.

Taylor made a sign to Riley, indicating that he would take the fellow on the porch and that they would then move around the rear at his signal. Riley nodded. Dismounting from Friar, Taylor slunk low and approached the house from the northwest side. The guard never looked up. Taylor leaped over the porch banister, came behind the guard, and set the muzzle of a Colt against his neck. "Quiet, soldier. You may find conditions in a Northern prison better than what you'll have with the militia soon, and certainly better than the alternative you face if you so much as whimper now." The soldier lifted his hands in a gesture of surrender.

"Is Weir in there alone?" Taylor asked the guard softly.

"No, sir."

"Who is with him?"

"Miss McKenzie."

Taylor nearly dropped his weapon. "What?"

"Miss McKenzie, sir, Miss Tia McKenzie. A local girl, an old friend." The guard sounded terrified. Taylor realized that he had pressed the muzzle of his gun deeper into the man's neck.

Miraculously, he managed to ease his grip on the gun and let the man talk. "What's she doing here?"

"I don't—"

Taylor pressed the gun more tightly to his flesh. "What's she doing here?"

"She came to marry the colonel."

"Marry him?"

"Except that he couldn't marry her. We have no minister."

"But she's still in there?"

The man surely thought he was going to die. "Yes!" he gulped.

"Doing what?"

"Well, sir, I think she's trying to seduce him."

Taylor felt as if his flesh burned, as if his soul had exploded into a white light of fury. He forced himself to regain control. He gave the man a firm thump on the head. The Rebel fell without a whimper. Taylor hoped he hadn't hit him too hard. He didn't want to kill the fellow just for being the messenger of such tidings. He bent down, put a finger to the soldier's throat, and felt his pulse. He was alive.

Taylor wanted to rush into the house, but he couldn't, not yet, no matter how he longed to do so. This was his mission. He was responsible for these men, and he'd be damned if he'd be surprised by a few Rebels who slipped their cordon once he was in the house—and accosting Weir.

He rose, waving to indicate that Riley and the troops should come around. Again, as prearranged, they split up, coming around the back of the house. As they fanned out, they could hear conversation.

"I still say this ain't right!" a private, tightening the girth on his saddle, complained. "I mean, there's real Yankees in the state—why are we attacking a home?"

"Because there's no Yankee like a Southern traitor!" another man answered, shoving his rifle into the holster on his saddle. "Colonel Weir says this may be the most important work we do this whole war, bringing down McKenzie. McKenzie has been like a knife sticking right in the back of the state, admitting that he thinks secession is wrong and saying that it's immoral to own slaves. When we hang him, we send out a message to all other would-be traitors, to folks who think and feel like him but who have the sense to shut up—they'll know better than to ever become traitors to the South."

"Is he being a traitor to state his mind?" the first man asked.

"He's a traitor to everything we're fighting for!" the second thundered.

"Right! Like freedom of speech, eh, Louis?"

Taylor had heard enough. He didn't have any more time—Tia was in the house with Weir. The men were in position at the sides of the house. Some had crept around the barn, making sure they knew where their enemy lay. He estimated there were about sixty-five men. More than his own company of thirty—all that Sheridan would allow him. But his troops were seasoned scouts who had been following the likes of Jeb Stuart throughout the war. They'd already surrounded their enemy in silence. Time to take them down, and quickly.

He lifted his arm, then dropped it. His men suddenly appeared in a semicircle around the unwary soldiers, repeating rifles raised. Taylor spoke quickly and quietly. "Stay where you are, gentlemen. Don't make a move. Every man with me is armed with a Spencer repeating rifle, and every man is a crack shot. Now, I know you boys are good, and that you can load and fire those Enfields pretty darned fast—but you know that even at top speed, you'll be dead before you get to fire. Lieutenant Riley here will take your weapons. Form a nice line and deposit those Enfields, swords, knives—whatever else you boys might have." He saw that the man who'd called Jarrett McKenzie a traitor was sliding his hand toward the holster on his saddle. "You!" Taylor said sharply, raising a Colt to eye level. "I wouldn't mind shooting you down in an instant!"

The man dropped his arm. The line began to form. "Riley, I'll need some men in a few minutes. Two, to come for Weir. Then two more—yourself and one other."

"My wife is in there," he said flatly, trying to keep the fury and emotion out of his voice.

Yes, she was in there. *Seducing* Weir.

God help them both!

"Tia can't keep herself out of danger. Time the North does it for her."

"Yes, sir," Riley said unhappily. As Taylor started for the house, the lieutenant called out, "A word, sir!"

Taylor paused impatiently. Time, time, time . . . he had to stop time.

"*She* is the one being attacked, sir. They are after her home, her father."

"I know that, Lieutenant Riley," he said.

Taylor slipped through the back door of the house. He could hear movement upstairs. He followed the back stairs up, careful not to let a single board creak.

He heard them in the hallway.

Heard them enter one of the bedrooms. Thankfully, the only light in the room was moonlight—strange red-glowing moonlight. He saw her standing there, near the window. He clenched down his jaw, trying not to let out a sound. She had shed her bodice. The moonlight played upon the sleek lines of her back. Her hair, that wretched wealth of hair that had created a legend, fell about her in a lustrous sheen, like a raven's wings.

"The bed is clean, the sheets are fresh, tended by my men," Weir was saying.

Taylor ached to stop them right then. To pull a Colt, shoot Weir through the head. What if Weir shifted in the shadows at the last second? What if he heard Taylor, and drew his sword?

Against Tia . . .

*He had to wait, let Weir drop his weapon.*

He stood in the shadow by the door, neither of them noting him.

"So you said," she whispered.

"My love . . ." Weir walked up behind her, drawing her against him. He shifted the fall of her hair, pressed his mouth to her shoulder. His fingers were on her skirt; it fell away. Then her pantalettes, and she was naked.

"Come, my love . . ." he said.

"Look at the moon!" she entreated, walking way from him, toward the window.

*His chance! Taylor's hand itched to draw the Colt. No! he wouldn't shoot a man in the back, even if the bastard had the bloody nerve to be touching his wife . . .*

"Tia, the moon, like the war, will come again."

"It's a beautiful moon, yet shaded in red—"

"There's no time for talk."

His scabbard and sword were, at last, cast aside. Taylor prepared to strike.

Weir's cavalry jacket and shirt were shed.

"I need another drink, Raymond," Tia said. "This is new to me."

New to her? At least she was making some attempt to slow things down.

Weir wasn't having any of it. "Madam," he said curtly, running his fingers through his hair. "I remind you—you invited me to this room. Shall I leave?"

"No! You mustn't leave!" Tia cried out.

He lifted her, bore her down on the bed.

"My love!" Weir said again. He kissed her fingertips.

"My—love," she whispered in return.

"Oh, good God!" Taylor's voice, shaking with rage, suddenly filled the room. He approached the bed, his body on fire, shaking, fighting desperately to control his murderous impulses. "That's it—I've had it with this charade!" he lashed out.

"What in the name of the Almighty?" Raymond grated, twisting around to see who'd had the gall to interrupt him. "Taylor! You!" he spat out.

Taylor drew his sword, pressed it against Weir's throat.

Somehow, Taylor kept himself from slitting the man's jugular vein. "Stop. Stop right now." It still sounded to Taylor as if his very voice shook. He kept the sword point resting just at Weir's vein. He stared at Tia; she stared back, her eyes glistening like ebony orbs.

"Ah, good, I have your attention!" he told her. And at last, he had managed to speak softly, mockingly, controlling the shuddering that had seized him and nearly ruled him. "I'm sorry," he continued, "but this charming little domestic adventure has gone quite far enough. Colonel Weir, if you will please rise carefully."

"Damn you, Taylor Douglas!" Weir swore furiously. "You'll die for this. I swear it! How did you get in?"

"I entered by the door, Captain."

He felt Tia's eyes on him. Still huge, so dark, containing so many secrets, lies, truths. He swung the point of his sword around. Laid it between her breasts. She was so beautiful, so still, staring at him. He couldn't endure her lying there, where she had been—if briefly— with Weir.

"Tia, get up. And for the love of God, get some clothing on. I grow weary of finding you naked everywhere I go—other than in our marital bed, of course."

"Marital bed!" Weir exclaimed, stunned.

"Ah, poor fellow, you are indeed surprised. A fact that might spare your life, though I had thought of you before as something of an honorable man, just a fanatic. But yes, I did say marital bed. You hadn't heard? Though it grieves me deeply to admit it, the lady is a liar and a fraud. She can marry no one for she is already married. She is wily, indeed, a vixen from the day we met. All for the Southern Cause, of course. She will play her games! But what of that great cause now, Tia?"

Her eyes seemed to crackle with a dark fire. She was never a coward. She caught the tip of his blade and cast the sword aside as she leapt from the bed. Her eyes touched his—with an amazing pride and hauteur. She searched about in the shadows for her clothing, then dressed very quickly.

"Tia?" Weir asked suddenly. There was a sad crack

to his voice. Weir had loved her, really loved her, Taylor thought. It didn't ease the tempest inside him. "You are *married* to him," Weir said.

"Yes," she said.

"But you came to me . . . tonight!" he cried, his ego demanding that she had come to him because she had always wanted him, no matter what she had said or done before.

Tia lifted her chin. "You were going to attack Cimarron," she told him, her tone cold and brittle. "And kill my father."

Raymond shook his head, trying to appear very earnest to her. "Your father . . . no, Tia. I meant to seize the property, nothing more."

"That's not true!" she said. How she had learned about this, Taylor had no idea. But Weir wasn't fooling her in the least. "My father was to be killed—executed," she said.

"I would have spared his life—for you!" Weir told her.

Taylor had definitely had enough.

"How touching," he interrupted, his voice a drawl that didn't hide his fury. "Tell me, Tia, was that explanation for him—or me?"

"Taylor, you're being a truly wretched bastard. You don't understand anything!" she lashed out at him.

Raymond suddenly made a dive for the sword where it lay on the floor. Taylor was itching to slash it out of his hands.

He forced himself to refrain from cutting flesh. He hit Weir's sword with a vengeance. The blade flew across the room. He pressed the tip of his own sword to Weir's throat once again.

"Taylor!" Tia cried out. "Don't . . . murder him. Please!"

He stared at her, fighting for control.

"Please, don't . . ." she said simply.

He returned her gaze. Remembered that he had come to prevent murder, not to do the deed himself.

He turned his attention to Weir. "I've no intention of

doing murder, sir. We are all forced to kill in battle, but I'll not be a cold-blooded murderer." A bitterness he couldn't control welled up in his throat. "I've yet to kill any man over a harlot, even if that harlot be my own wife."

"Call me what you will," Tia cried to him, suddenly passionate and vital, "but your life is in danger here, and, you fool, there is much more at stake! There are nearly a hundred men outside preparing to march on my father's house."

"No, Tia, no longer," Taylor said. "The men below have been seized. Taken entirely by surprise. Quite a feat, if I do say so myself. Not a life lost, Colonel," he informed Raymond. Weir stared back at him.

"So you'll not murder me. What then?" Weir asked him.

"I believe my men are coming for you now, if you would like to don your shirt and coat," he informed Weir.

Raymond nodded, as if grateful for the courtesy. He reached for his shirt and frockcoat. The latter was barely slipped over his shoulders before Riley and another of Taylor's men, Virgil Gray, appeared in the doorway.

"To the ship, Colonel?" Riley asked him.

"Aye, Lieutenant Riley. Have Captain Maxwell take the lot of them north. Meet me with the horses below when the prisoners have been secured."

"Sir?" the lieutenant said politely to Weir.

Weir looked at Tia and bowed elegantly to her. She stared at him, and kept staring at him as Virgil slipped restraints around his wrists. Then he turned with Riley and Gray, and departed the room.

Then they were alone. Taylor and his wife. After so much time.

*After this!*

She was so still, not facing him now. But again, asking no pardon, no quarter, giving no excuses, saying nothing at all . . .

He came to her suddenly, because he couldn't help himself anymore. He gripped her shoulders, his fingers

biting into her flesh. She met his eyes. He felt as if he
had been seized by every demon in hell, and he wanted
to strike her to her knees. *No!* He pushed her away.
There was more to the night.

It seemed that he stood there forever, wanting to do
some violence to her, wanting to stop the rage that
warred inside him, wanting just to hold her. And finally,
he managed to walk away. The time had finally come
when he didn't dare trust her, himself, or the future.

*Walk away!* he told himself. *Let your men come and
escort her to prison. Get to Cimarron, while there is still
a Cimarron to get to!*

But now, she had suddenly found movement, and a
voice. She came flying after him, catching him on the
stairs. She pushed past him, turning around to face him.
He saw the grief·in her eyes, heard the pain in her voice.
"Taylor, I—I—they said he meant to kill my father."

"Step aside, Tia," he said.

"Taylor, damn you! I had to come her, I had to do
what I could to stop him. Can't you see that, don't
you understand?"

He lashed out, sarcastic and cruel, striking her with
the anguish that ripped through him.

"I understand, *my love,* that you were ready, willing,
and able to sleep with another man. But then, Weir is a
good Southern soldier, is he not? A proper planter, a
fitting beau for the belle of Cimarron, indeed, someone
you have loved just a little for a very long time. How
convenient."

"No, I—"

"No?" he challenged. How many times had she defended Weir to him?

"Yes, you know that—*once* we were friends. But I . . .
please!" she whispered. His heart constricted, fingers
plucked at it, tightened, squeezed. There was so much
in that simple word. And the way she looked at him.

He reached out, lightly stroking her cheek. "Please?
Please what? Are you sorry, afraid? Or would you seduce me, too? Perhaps I'm not such easy prey for you,
for I am, at least, familiar with the treasure offered, and

I have played the game to a great price already. When I saw you tonight . . . do you know what I first intended to do? Throttle you, you may be thinking! Beat you black and blue. Well that, yes. Where pride and emotions are involved, men do think of violence. But I thought to do more. Clip your feathers, my love. Cut off those ebony locks and leave you shorn and costumeless, as it were—*naked* would not be the right word. What if I were to sheer away these lustrous tresses? Would you still be about seducing men—friend and foe—to save your precious family and state? Not again, for until this war of ours is finished, I will have you hobbled—until your fate can be decided."

"I—have seduced no one else. I . . . ." she said. Tears glistened in the darkness of her eyes. "I'm not a harlot, Taylor!" she managed to whisper. There was a wealth of hurt and sorrow and reproach in her words, and he found himself trembling, shaking, glad to find that she was safe, glad that she wanted him to believe her.

He reached for her, drawing her into his arms. He kissed her too hard, with too much violence in his soul. Felt her hair, her flesh, tasted the sweetness, tempest, and passion in her lips. He was in love with her, did love her so much, had sworn that he would not. He wanted nothing more than to be with her. Hold her, forget. Make love then and there, and let the world crash down around them.

No, good God, he could not be seduced now, couldn't forget his anger, didn't dare. He pulled away from her, speaking hoarsely. "Ah, Tia, what a pity! I'm not at all sure of your motives at the moment, but for once, when you are apparently ready to become a willing wife with no argument to give me, there remains too much at stake for me to take advantage of your remorse. There's a battle still to be waged."

"A battle?" Either she hadn't known about the pincer movement planned against her father, or she had forgotten. "But you've stopped Weir from the war he would wage against my father."

"Tia, you little fool! Weir was only a half of it! There's

a Major Hawkins with militia from the panhandle who will bear down upon Cimarron at any moment now. I don't know if Ian ever received word of this, or if Julian knows somehow. You apparently learned about it. But I may be the only help your father will have."

She stared at him, stunned. And terrified, he thought. "Dear God! I'd forgotten there would be more troops. I've got to get home!" she cried, and she turned, running frantically down the remaining steps.

"No! Tia!"

He wasn't going to allow it. She was willing to risk far too much. He ran after her, caught her first by the length of her raven dark hair. She cried out; he ignored the sound, winding her back into his arms, meeting her eyes. "You're going nowhere," he told her firmly.

"My father—my home—"

Yes, they were everything to her. And once, she had probably thought that Weir would be the one to fight for them. "Your enemy will save them for you," he said.

"No, please, you have to let me ride with you. I beg of you, Taylor, in this, I swear, I—"

"Make me no more promises, Tia, for I am weary of you breaking them."

"But I swear—"

"This fight will be deadly, and I'll not have you seized by either side as a pawn in the battles to be waged."

"Please!" she begged.

No, no . . . no. He could not let her be there. She would die to save her family, or Cimarron. He almost explained that to her, but he heard footsteps at the landing. His men had come for her.

"Gentlemen, take my wife to the ship, please. They'll not be surprised to find another McKenzie prisoner at Old Capitol."

One of the soldiers cleared his throat politely. "Mrs. Douglas, if you will . . ."

She lowered her head, stepping away from Taylor's hold.

Now she really hated him, he thought. And again, the

longing was there to pull her to him, to forget everything else.

*No!*

He released her.

She stared at him again. "No!" she said softly. Then
she cried out, "No!"

He had forgotten who she was, how fast, sleek, supple,
and determined. She spun around with such a swift fury
that she tore past him, and the soldiers who would have
taken her.

She raced down those steps. As she did so, he swore,
thinking that Blaze was probably out there; he hadn't
thought to seize her horse when they'd arrived.

"Colonel, sir, sorry! We'll catch her!" one of the men
swore quickly.

"No, you will not. I barely have a chance myself," he
said without rancor. "Tell Riley to leave all the prisoners
with the captain, and to ride hard for Cimarron behind
me."

He burst outside just as Tia leapt up on Blaze. Her
eyes met his.

"Home, girl, home!" she told Blaze, nudging the
animal.

Taylor whistled for Friar, mounted him in a flying
leap. Tia had already filled the air with her dust.

The pounding of the earth beneath him seemed to fill
him. He rode hard a good ten minutes before nearly
catching her. He shouted; she didn't hear him, or
wouldn't stop. He rode abreast from her and leapt from
Friar to Blaze, catching her in his embrace. She resisted
him, twisting in the saddle and bringing them both flying
down from the horse. He pinned her. She fought him
like a wildcat. "Please, Taylor, please, for the love of
God . . . Please, please!" she whispered. "Bring me
home! Let me be there. Bring me home tonight. I'll stay
by your side, obey your every command! I'll surrender,
I'll cease to ride, I'll turn myself in to Old Capitol, I'll
put a noose around my own neck, I swear it, Taylor,
please, I'll—"

Her eyes were, for once, so honest. She loved her

family. If only she felt half that for him. "Love, honor, and obey?" he asked wryly. And it wasn't even that he had chosen to forgive her; it was that they were closer to Cimarron than they were to going back.

He stood, drawing her along with him. "You'll ride with me!" he told her harshly. "And go where I command, stay away from all fire! Blaze can follow on her own—she knows the way."

"Yes!" she promised.

He whistled again. Friar, good old warhorse that he was, had stopped his flight with Taylor gone from his back. He returned. Taylor set Tia upon his horse, mounted swiftly behind her. He kneed Friar. The horse began a hard flight once again.

The night sky remained bathed in blood. Indeed, when they neared Cimarron, coming from the south below the river that would be one line of defense, the white plantation house itself was steeped in the blood.

Before they reached the property, he could hear shouts. Commands being given, responses, men moving quickly. Defenses had been erected against the river, and men were already busy at the work of battle, taking places behind newly erected earthworks.

Ian had arrived with troops; they were positioned behind the earthworks.

But there were Rebels on Cimarron's side as well. And he saw Julian in the midst of them, calling out, giving orders, receiving responses.

They might not have known, might not have made it. But they had. Now that Taylor was there, they had the superior numbers. And for once in the war, the color of the uniform meant nothing.

He was accosted by a guard at the rear of the property. "Halt, or be shot!"

"It's Colonel Douglas, here to defend with the McKenzies!" Taylor shouted, sliding down from Friar.

There was a gunboat out on the river. Men were loading rifles, manning the single cannon.

Behind him, he suddenly heard Tia leap down from

Friar. "Mother!" she shrieked, and she was gone, racing across the lawn.

"Tia!" He thundered in warning, just as he saw Tara McKenzie hurrying across the lawn to her husband's side, ready to duck beneath the earthworks. But the Rebel soldiers had learned to use their Enfields swiftly in this war. The fire could come too fast.

"Tia!" He shouted her name again. She had reached her mother. Throwing herself against her, Tia meant to bring them both down to the ground.

Taylor heard the volley of fire.

And they were both down.

He raced to her like the wind. The Rebs on the river were getting ready for a second volley of fire.

He drew his guns, sliding to his knees beside his wife and her mother. He started to fire rapidly, buying time to move the women. He felt her eyes. She was looking at him. He bent over her, trying to assess the damage. She reached up, touching his cheek. Her eyes closed. "Tia!"

There was blood on her shoulder. He didn't know where the bullet had ripped through her, only that at least it hadn't struck too close to her heart. Tara groaned, trying to rise.

"Down!" he warned. By then, Jarrett McKenzie, his face a mask of fury and concern, was down beside him. And Julian followed.

Jarrett was lifting Tara. "We've got to get them back to the house," he said gruffly.

Taylor started to lift Tia. Julian reached for his sister; he met Taylor's eyes. "Taylor, let me take her. You might know something about bullet wounds, but not as much as I do. And I'm a damned good shot, but you're better. You can cover us."

He wanted to be with her; more than anything he had ever wanted in his life, he wanted to be with her. But Julian was right. Julian was a doctor. He was not. He was a crack shot.

*If she died, he didn't want to live!*

The thought passed through him. No, he wasn't going

out there to kill himself. He was going out there to end this thing.

So that he could go back to her.

He heard his men arriving behind him. Reinforcements. This could be over quickly; they even had Rebel forces on their side. Sometimes, even in the middle of war, men knew the difference between right and wrong. "Taylor!" Julian gave him a shake. "Keep those bloody bastards out of my house so I can tend to my mother and sister!"

He nodded to Julian, rose, and running along the earthworks, started to fire. The cannon suddenly exploded, shattering the dock. Dirt and dust blew everywhere. Running along the dirt, he found Ian's position. Ian didn't know what had happened to his mother and sister. Taylor decided it wasn't the time to tell them.

"Barrage them!" Taylor exclaimed. "I'm going for the cannon!"

Despite the earth and powder that filled the air around them, Ian saw his intent. If he could get to the gunboat and disable the one cannon, the main threat was over. He nodded. He called out orders to his men. "You'll have to watch out for friendly fire."

Guns fired in a continual fury from the shore line, striking the gunners in the boats and the foot soldiers in the fields beyond. Taylor shed his boots and jacket and slipped down by the ruined dock. He dived into the water, keeping low. He could hear the spitting, soaring sounds as bullets whipped by him in the river. He dived more deeply. When he came up behind the gunboat, he saw that the defenders had done their work well.

The boat held numerous corpses. He walked low and silently across the deck to the single gun. When the Rebel cannoneer went to load the weapon, he drew his fist back and caught the man with a deadly right hook. The man fell. A second gunner was drawing a pistol to shoot him. Taylor caught the man's arm, twisted it, and the gun fired into the fellow's gut. Another man flew across the deck at him, bearing a naval cutlass. Taylor dodged the flight, allowing the man to pin himself into the wooden body of the vessel. Then he threw the man overboard, still using the impetus of the man's flight. He heard something behind him and turned. Sweat beaded on his forehead. He would have been run through by a man with a rapier, but the Rebel merely stared at him, then fell, shot from the shoreline.

Taylor quickly overstuffed the cannon and lit the wick. With only seconds, he dived into the water and swam as hard as he could. He was still beneath the water when he heard the explosion. It rocked him toward the shoreline with a massive catapulting action, then sucked him back. For a minute, he thought that, after all this, he was going to drown. Then he found the surface, broke it, and stumbled on to the embankment.

He lay there in the night, feeling the damp earth beneath him. He gasped for breath. He opened his eyes and looked up. An unknown Rebel soldier stood above him. The man grinned, reaching a hand down to him.

"Colonel, sir, that was one of the most remarkable acts I've ever seen! And they say that we're better soldiers and better strategists!"

Taylor just stared at him for a moment. Then he grinned with relief as well. "Unfortunately, sir, most of the time you are. If you weren't so damned good, this wretched war could have been over long ago."

"Let me help you to the house, sir," the soldier said. Taylor saw that he had one good leg and one wooden leg. "Name's Liam, sir. At your service."

He was up, facing the man. The boat on the river continued to burn, adding to the red haze of the night. Men were racing around, stopping by the injured, assessing the damage and the situation.

"It's over?" Taylor queried.

"It's over."

Taylor nodded, and turned instantly for the house. He ran across the lawn, up the porch steps, and into the entry. Still dripping and muddied, he burst into the parlor.

He saw Tia first. Pale as a ghost, laid out on the Victorian sofa. Sheets covered her; she didn't move. A black woman was at her side.

He walked across the room, his heart in his throat. He looked at the black woman, and sat down by his wife.

"Tia . . ."

Her eyes opened. "Taylor?" she whispered.

"I'm here." He took her hand. "It's over Tia, it's over. Your father is safe. Cimarron is safe."

She squeezed his hand back. *"You're safe!"* she whispered.

Her eyes closed again.

"Tia!"

"She's all right!" he heard from the doorway. Julian was back. "Flesh wound, Taylor. She caught it in the upper arm. If she hadn't deflected the bullet, though, my mother might have died. Tia will probably have a nasty scar, but then, when this is all over, we're all going to have some nasty scars, inside and out."

"But she's unconscious," Taylor said.

"A touch of laudanum. It must have hurt like a bitch when I was sewing her up. And she was making me crazy, insisting she had to see Mother. You know your wife."

Yes, he knew his wife.

And she would make him insane forever with her spirit and courage and determination.

But then, that was partly why he loved her so very much.

# Chapter 26

~~~

Three days later, Taylor walked down to the spring pool that was just through the woods on the McKenzie property. Julian had told him that Tia had gone there. It was the family reflecting pond, he said, glancing toward his older brother. "In fact, Ian looked in the water there once, and found Alaina."

"Very amusing, little brother," Ian said.

"Little! I think I have half an inch on you, Ian!" Julian told him.

Taylor grinned, leaving the two on the porch. The bullet that had grazed Tia's arm had lost its impetus and had stopped short of doing any serious damage to Tara, breaking her skin and lodging in the flesh just below her collarbone. Julian had dug it out quickly and easily. Tara had lost a lot of blood, but today, for the first time, she was feeling strong. She knew she couldn't hold her family at home much longer, so she wanted to be with her sons while she could. Most of the Union soldiers had already returned to their posts, Ian's men traveling back across the peninsula, Taylor's recruits taking the prisoners who had survived the attack at Cimarron on the ship north. Julian's band of orderlies and injured remained, while Ian had added men to his own operations, just in case the war should come home again. Taylor doubted that it would; only a personal vendetta had brought Weir's troops here. The South didn't have enough men left anymore to waste on a private war.

He still had days left himself, days given to him by President Lincoln.

He had wasted a few of those precious days dealing

with military matters, cleaning up the dead at Cimarron, sending men and prisoners on. And though he had sat with Tia, he hadn't gone to her room at night yet, and they hadn't really talked. Once she was up herself, she spent her time with her mother. And he hadn't dared get too close to her until Julian had assured him that her arm was healing very nicely.

Once he had felt that he couldn't afford to take time from the battlefield, even when time had been offered to him; the war effort needed him. Now, he needed the time, and the war effort would go on without him.

As he walked to the pool, he paused for a minute to close his eyes. Home. This was home to him, this warmth. A touch, just a touch, of a winter's chill in the air. The whisper of a palm, bending in the breeze. The cry of a heron.

Yes, it was nearly winter, but still the days were warm and beautiful, the sun brilliant. The pines, oaks, and palms offered a gentle relief from the heat of the sun as he headed toward the pool. When he had reached the copse, he saw Tia there. She sat on a log, dangling her bare feet into the cool spring water. She wore a soft blue-flowered cotton gown, with the full length of her hair untied and sweeping around her. She appeared very young, like a little nymph, a water sprite. But when she turned toward him, her dark eyes were far older, and the tension in her beautiful features betrayed the strain she had been under.

He walked to the log and sat down beside her.

"So this is the McKenzie reflecting pool," he said after a moment, aware that she was watching him.

"It is. It's my favorite place here," she said, and he heard her voice tightening. "I love it. I love the birds, and the water—the fresh water, and the river and the sea beyond. I love the heat, and the breezes, and the days and the nights and . . . Taylor, thank you. I . . ." She turned and looked at him. "Cimarron means a lot to me. But . . . but it wasn't the property that made me do what I did. My father has always taught us that there is no *thing,* no object in the world that is worth a man's life. I went to Weir thinking I could stall him. I didn't have anything planned. I . . ."

She didn't finish. She looked away.

"Taylor, why did you send me away?" she asked him.

His heart shuddered and squeezed. "Because you wanted to go home."

"I wanted to be home," she whispered. "But not away from you."

"Every time I made love to you," he said harshly, "it was as if I forced a burden on you. You told me you didn't want children."

"I was afraid! But I—I was glad that you were impatient with my fears. My God, Taylor! You must have known how I felt!"

"I know that you cried!"

"Because . . . because I needed you so much, and you . . ." Her voice trailed. She stared at him. "Well, when you came to the Ellington place, and then let me ride with you—"

"I was an idiot! See what happened."

She smiled. "I'm all right, and my mother is all right. I had to be here, Taylor. That was fate maybe. But you—you could have stopped me. And I said that I'd do whatever you wished—afterward. And I'll keep my word to you, Taylor. I'll go wherever you want—lock myself into prison, if that's your wish."

He stared at her a long time. Then he grimaced in return. "Tempting!" he said softly.

"You mean . . . you . . ." She hesitated, looking away again. "Taylor, another man might have cut my throat that night. I assume that, at the very least, you must want a divorce now."

"True, another man might have been really tempted to skewer you!" he reflected, picking up and throwing a pebble, then watching it skip across the surface of the water. He turned to her again. "But a wife without a throat does not do a man much good."

She looked at him again. "Wife . . . but Taylor . . ."

"We both made a commitment, Tia. I said I wouldn't let you out of it. And I won't."

"And as for prison?" she whispered softly.

"I think your mother is going to need you here for a while," he said.

He felt her eyes, felt the heat and amazement in the way she looked at him. Then, suddenly, he was pitching off the log, totally unprepared as she threw herself at him. "Taylor, oh, my God, Taylor . . ."

He would have to learn never to underestimate her. She straddled him this time, her hair falling all over him, teasing his nose, making him sneeze. Then her lips were on his, sweet with passion, salty with tears. She kissed him, and kissed him, and then he heard her whisper, "Taylor, thank God, thank God. I didn't want our baby born in a prison."

*Baby.*

He still had the strength. He rose swiftly, pinning her beneath him. "What?"

"Sometime in April, I believe," she said. Then her eyes watered again. "Oh, Taylor, I swear that it's ours . . . yours. I . . . love you. I think I started loving you when I met you, you aggravated me so badly, being so damned certain that you were right, being a . . ."

"Yankee?" he supplied.

"But you just wouldn't act badly, you were always so . . . well, determined, but honorable. Passionate . . . but honorable."

"You didn't want children!" he said hoarsely.

"I was afraid, so afraid!" she whispered. "I'm still afraid. So much bad happens, but then, you should see the new little McKenzies, they're so wonderful . . . so beautiful . . . I do want our baby, Taylor. So very much. And I was afraid again, afraid that taking the bullet the way I did might cost us our child, but then again, I couldn't have watched my mother die . . . and I've been thinking, Taylor, and I was so wrong, but if I had to go back . . . I couldn't have let my father die either."

He smoothed her hair from her face. And he understood, and he should have understood her so long ago. No. He couldn't have done anything other than fight for the Union. And she never could have allowed either of her parents to be harmed.

"We just have to be grateful that it's over; that it ended as it did," he said softly, brushing her lips with a kiss.

Her eyes, so huge and dark against her delicate features, locked with his. "Can you really forgive me?"

"Can you forgive *me?*" he asked.

"I never betrayed you!" she whispered.

"You're right. I was just a horse's ass!"

She smiled slowly. Her arms wrapped around him. She drew his head down to hers. She pressed her lips to his, kissing him, slowly at first, sweetly. Then her lips formed to his, her tongue snaked along his, pressing entry, and her kiss became amazingly provocative. He kissed her back, parting her lips further, penetrating her mouth deeply with his tongue in return. Amazing what a kiss could do. He felt it straight to his groin, felt the hunger, the need, the time between them, the sudden desperation to touch more of her. He found the hem of her gown, slid his hand up the length of her bare legs, heard her soft gasp against his lips as his touch teased along her upper thigh . . .

Then, abruptly, he pulled away from her, aware—too late—that they were not alone.

Weir hadn't quite come up to them. He stood five feet away, a pistol in his hand. He had meant to reach them, Taylor realized, and press the gun straight to his temple. His uniform looked torn, ragged, slept in. Weir's cheeks were dusky with a few days' growth of beard. His eyes were wild. Red-rimmed, nervous, darting.

*He had escaped,* Taylor realized, *by diving into the sea. He had come straight to them.*

He had watched and waited until they were alone and absorbed with one another. He had meant to walk right up to the two of them—then pull the trigger. Then, so that Taylor's blood and bone would shatter over Tia . . .

Taylor leapt to his feet, dragging Tia up with him, pressing her behind him.

Weir had the advantage. Taylor had come here unarmed.

"Hello, there—Colonel!" he said contemptuously. "And Miss McKenzie—oh, excuse me, Mrs. Douglas. That's right, you married him, but came to me. Well, well."

"How did you get here, Weir?" Taylor demanded.

"Oh, Douglas! You do seem to think that you're the only man who knows the woods, the streams, the oceans . . . I grew up here, too, you red bastard. No, I don't have the savage blood in me that makes a swamp rat, but I sure as hell can escape a knot, dive into the ocean, make the shore—and then find my way back here."

"You escaped the ship," Tia said.

"My love!" he exclaimed. "Nothing would keep me from you. Having a taste of all that is offered . . . well, I simply hunger and pine for more."

"Raymond Weir, you meant to kill my father. I loathe and despise you."

"And you, Tia, are nothing but a strumpet and a whore," Weir said. "Don't fear. I don't love you anymore, Tia. When I finish with you, there are armies out there who are welcome to you!"

"Call my wife a whore again, Weir, and I'll kill you," Taylor told him. He sounded confident. Fool. What the hell was he going to do? Weir held the cocked gun.

"Douglas!" Weir said. "By God, but I do despise you. Do you want her to die, too? Get away from her. I won't kill you, Tia. I'll just make you wish you were dead. You think you could make a fool out of me? Take down my men, and I would meekly go to prison and forget? Oh, no, my love. You want to be part of this war? You can pay the price of it as well."

"This war is lost!" Taylor said. "Give it up, Weir. The South that you knew is dead and gone, never to come again."

"Never!" Weir said. "The South is a taste and a feel, and it is honor—"

"Yes! The South can be a taste and feel of what is beauty and honor and graciousness. But you would take all that from her. You call yourself honorable?" Taylor demanded harshly.

"You don't understand. The courage to kill McKenzie when others hadn't the strength or power to pluck a viper from our nest is honor, sir! Now . . . Tia! Ah, Tia! You beautiful, beautiful little *whore*, come to me."

Taylor had only one chance. Maybe a stupid chance. But it was all he had.

He drew Tia from around him—astounded to hear her cry out and throw a thick handful of dirt into Weir's eyes. Weir swore, reaching for his eyes.

Taylor catapulted hard against the man. His flying assault threw them both against the earth.

They struggled for the gun. He had Weir's wrist, fighting for control.

There was a sudden explosion of sound. Raymond Weir went deadly still. Taylor looked into the man's eyes as they glazed over.

The gun had gone off. The bullet had barely missed Taylor. It had lodged deep inside Weir's head, taking Weir just as he had intended to take Taylor.

"Taylor!"

Tia screamed his name. She was at his side, and in his arms. He cradled her to him, and held her, and held her, and held her . . .

It was some time later before they could get up and go back to the house, and have someone else go to the pool for Weir's body. It would be some time, Taylor thought, before he would enjoy the pool again.

But not before he would love his wife.

The war had taught him the lesson that life was precious.

He had never learned it so thoroughly as that day.

That night, she touched him with a tenderness greater than any he had ever known. He made love to her with an equal, heartfelt fervor, passionate, forceful, and humbled.

For all the time that they could be together, he held her. Each night he made love to her.

Every moment, he thanked God for her.

Someday, they would have a real future, but . . .

Time, like life, was precious. It slipped away far too quickly.

They both knew it. They cherished the moments they shared. They touched, they talked earnestly, they were passionate, they were tender . . .

It wasn't over.

Soon, he would have to leave.

There was one more skirmish in Florida, occurring in January of 1865. The Florida troops were victorious. Julian wrote Taylor that there had been little of a victory celebration then. The war was lost. To many, many men, it was far too obvious. Many wished they could walk away. Some deserted. Others could not walk away. They had to see it through to the bitter end.

Lincoln's speech at his second inauguration spoke well of the man. He wanted peace, not punishment. He wanted to welcome the South back to the Union. "With malice toward none, and justice for all," he said in his heartfelt, country manner of eloquence.

Grant was finally the man to win the war. He hammered at Petersburg, never giving up until the desperate city was forced to surrender.

The way to Richmond was open. The Southern capital was abandoned. The government ran.

Taylor was at Appomattox Courthouse the day Lee surrendered. He was able to salute his weary old friend as he gave up the battle, and the death. All around him, North and South, soldiers hailed him as one of the greatest generals ever to rise in America. *America.* They had been North and South. And now, again, they were Americans.

On the day that it ended, Taylor, Jesse, and Ian were able to meet up. In the next few days, they were able to find Brent and Mary. It was another few days before they were able to receive leave together and ride home.

At that moment, home meant Cimarron. To all of them. Sydney had gone there soon after Christmas, knowing that she had done all she could for the Underground Railroad, and that her mother and father would be there.

James and his extended family had traveled north after the events at Cimarron. It had seemed a time to be with family.

It was nearly the middle of April when they heard the news that Lincoln had been assassinated. It was a bitter blow. President Johnson might be a good man who would try, but the Congress would stand up against him. They would enter into a bitter struggle. Taylor was bitter himself, but not surprised; President Lincoln had seen his own death coming. He was legend now, a man greater than he had ever imagined himself to be.

A few days later, their long journey home was almost over. They had tried to find Julian in north Florida, since the last of the Florida troops had yet to surrender.

They learned he was at Cimarron.

When they arrived at the property, Julian was waiting in the parlor, having heard they were coming. "I have something for you," he told Taylor.

And the bundle Julian carried was suddenly in Taylor's arms.

"A daughter. If she's anything like her mother, you're in serious trouble. She was born the day we heard about the surrender. Tia named her Hope."

He held his child, shaking. He found the strength to hold her more tightly, afraid that he would drop her. She had a head of dark, curly hair already, and huge, huge dark but multicolored eyes with just a touch of gold.

Taylor cradled his child to his heart, and took the stairs two at a time.

In his wife's room, he fell to his knees at the bedside, and Tia touched his hair, threading her fingers through it, drawing his head to hers. She kissed him with tears, with love, with tenderness, with passion . . .

And at last, with all the promise of a real future stretching before them . . .

The land was torn. Beaten, scarred.

But peace had been declared.

And the healing could come at last.

"Hope?" Tia questioned softly.

"Hope," he agreed. And kissed his wife again.

# Epilogue

*September, 1876*
*Cimarron*

Jarrett McKenzie stood in the graveyard, one booted foot upon an old, weather-worn border stone. The sudden sound of a screech made him wince, but he smiled and shook his head as he did so. There had been a lot of screeches thus far—and there would be many more to follow. Tara had warned him it would be so when he had determined to invite the entire family for a post-Centennial Fourth of July celebration. That's what happened when you had that many children about. Lord, how many of them were there now? They seemed to be all over the place, a new race of being, totally populating the lawn.

"Father!"

It was Tia coming toward him. Still delicate and tiny, despite the five little Douglases she and Taylor had contributed to the family tree.

All these years gone by . . . and he still felt a special warmth in his heart when he saw his daughter. A daughter was definitely a man's jewel, so he had determined with his son-in-law at the birth of Jessica Lyn—a girl after four boys. He adored his sons, he always would; he respected them now as men. But his daughter. . . .

She was flushed, a bit breathless. He had watched her running with the younger children below on the lawn. She was delighted to be back, and with the children, having just returned from a long-planned trip to Egypt with Taylor. They had come home by way of New York and stopped at the Centennial Exposition in Philadelphia on their way home.

Tia's excitement over the exposition was encouraging. War wounds were beginning to heal. More than a decade after the conflict, there were still huge slashes and scars from the bitter divide to mar the country. But most men wanted to look to the future—and peace.

"Father! Why are you standing up here in the cemetery? Mother wants to have birthday cake for the children."

"Which children?" he teased.

"The September children," she said with a laugh. Her dark eyes flashed with humor. She lifted on her toes, hugged him, and kissed his cheek. He slipped an arm around her. They looked down on the lawn together.

Young Anthony Malloy, the oldest of all the McKenzie third generation, was nineteen, and had just returned from classes in Tallahassee. Like his cousin Taylor Douglas, he wanted to be an architect, and he was seated at one of the picnic tables now with Taylor, who was making a point, building with the picnic ware.

Taylor had come home from the war to build many of the houses he had dreamed of creating. He claimed that his wife still loved her family home, Cimarron, above any mansion he had ever tried to build for her—and his brood.

Anthony seemed oblivious to the nearby teasing of his half-siblings, twins Ana and Ashley Long. Good-naturedly, he ruffled the girls' hair as he listened to Taylor. Young master Sean McKenzie was not being so tolerant—when his sisters Ariana and Kelly sprayed him with water from the gardening hose, he turned on them with what might have been a vengeance, but helped by cousins Conar, Allen, and Tia's oldest boy, Robert, they turned the tables on the girls, and the laughter and shrieking rose again, especially after they showered Risa, who was walking across the lawn with fresh lemonade.

Jerome had gone back into shipbuilding, he and Risa owned a marina—and even allowed Yankee tourists down to stay at one of the houses they kept on the beach. Ian had gone into politics, determined to see the state completely repatriated with all due dignity.

Julian and Brent continued to practice medicine. Sydney and Jesse remained in Washington most of the time. Jesse worked with the Pinkerton Agency, while Sydney pursued equal rights for all—men and women. But even Sydney and her brood had come south for this occasion. She sat with her father now, loathe to let go of James's arm, even to show her baby sister, Mary, the correct way to hold yarn.

"There were times when I never thought that I would see such a day as this," Jarrett said softly to his daughter.

"I know," she said. "But we did survive it all, we survived it so well as a family! Thanks to you, and Uncle James, of course."

"We were at odds throughout the war."

"We were all at odds. But you taught us all something we never forgot."

"Oh? And what is that?" he asked, turning to his daughter.

"Love," she said, smiling, and her dimples showed, and he thought again that she was, indeed, his treasure.

"Love, hm. Well."

She laughed. "Courage . . . perseverance! And we made it and oh, Father! You can't begin to imagine the things we saw at the exposition! Dual telegraphs, telephones! New steam engines, new ideas, air-conditioning, motor-vehicles . . . oh, some of them we won't really see for years, of course, but the prototypes are out there."

"Your children will see it all," he told her.

She smiled. "Maybe I'll see it, and maybe it will all come more quickly than you imagine, maybe we'll all see it."

"Maybe, and if I don't, well . . ."

"Father—"

He shushed her. "I've lived to see peace. I've lived to see my family grow, and my children and nephews and nieces become thoughtful, intelligent, and caring adults. I know that whatever the future brings, you will soar along with it, bringing dignity to men and women of different races and colors and creeds."

"Thank you," she told him, smiling at him. She smoothed back a stray strand of dark hair. "The state is booming, Father. But it isn't all peace, yet. Real peace may take many more decades."

"It may. But we're entering a new era. Of invention, of posterity." Another screech rose from the lawn. "Oh, Lord! An era of McKenzies!" he said with a groan.

"You love it all, and you don't even pretend to be an old grouch well!" she teased. "Shall we have cake?" Tia asked.

Jarrett looked at his daughter, and at the lawn of Cimarron, where his family played.

He glanced at his father's grave.

*If you could only see this wild land of yours now, Father! Peopled with those who will love it, who will see it into the future . . .*

"Father?" Tia said, as he still hesitated.

"I was just thinking that my father would be very proud," he said. Then he drew her arm through his and started down the lawn.

"I hope so," Tia said as they walked. "He really believed in people. I think he might be proudest of Sydney. You know, she's working very hard toward women getting the vote."

"What?" he demanded, stopping.

"Father! You know that women are equally intelligent and—"

She broke off, aware that he was laughing. She flushed.

"Well, it's probably a long way off."

"Well, the future waits for no man," he said. "Come, let's go have cake with the children."

"How many of them are there now?"

"You can't count my grandchildren?"

"Well, there are nephews and nieces down there, too—"

"And another one with us now, I think."

He stopped, arching a brow. "Tia . . ."

"Father, it was a very romantic trip down the Nile."

"But . . . six? I had thought there was a time when you didn't want children."

She smiled. "I didn't want death, war, or pain. We're at peace."

"Death and pain still come."

"I know. But we've met so much together . . . I'm not afraid anymore, maybe that's it." She hesitated, glancing to the lawn, smiling at her father again. "I share all that's good with a very special man; he'll stand behind me whatever pain or sorrow we meet in life as well."

"You have everything," Jarrett told her.

"And six little people to share it all with!" she laughed.

He cradled her chin gently. "Your husband must be very happy."

"He is."

"*My* wife and my children have been everything in life," he told her. "Everything. And it's my greatest happiness that you have known the same. But, you're right. Let's head down for cake before those children eat it all, eh?"

And so they did.

War and peace.

Time . . .

Time always went on.

And so it would.

# *Florida Chronology*

## (And Events Which Influenced Her People)

| | |
|---|---|
| 1492 | Christopher Columbus discovers the "New World." |
| 1513 | Florida discovered by Ponce de Leon. Juan Ponce de Leon sights Florida from his ship on March 27th, steps on shore near present day St. Augustine in early April. |
| 1539 | Hernando de Soto lands on west coast of the peninsula, near present day Tampa. |
| 1564 | The French arrive and establish Fort Caroline on the St. Johns River. Immediately following the establishment of the French fort, Spain dispatches Pedro de Menendez to get rid of the French invaders, "pirates and perturbers of the public peace." Menendez dutifully captures the French stronghold and slays or enslaves the inhabitants. |
| 1565 | Pedro de Menendez founds St. Augustine, the first permanent European settlement in what is now the United States. |
| 1586 | Sir Francis Drake attacks St. Augustine, burning and plundering the settlement. |
| 1698 | Pensacola is founded. |
| 1740 | British General James Oglethorpe invades Florida from Georgia. |
| 1763 | At the end of the Seven Year's War, or the French and Indian War, both the East and West Florida Territories are ceded to Britain. |

| 1762–1783 | British Rule in East and West Florida. |
|---|---|
| 1774 | The "shot heard round the world" is fired in Concord, Massachusetts Colony. |
| 1776 | The War of Independence begins; many of the British Loyalists flee to Florida. |
| 1783 | By the Treaty of Paris, Florida is returned to the Spanish. |
| 1812–1815 | The War of 1812. |
| 1813–1814 | The Creek Wars ("Red-Stick" land is decimated. Numerous Indians seek new lands south with the "Seminoles."). |
| 1814 | General Andrew Jackson captures Pensacola. |
| 1815 | The Battle of New Orleans. |
| 1817–1818 | The First Seminole War—Americans accuse the Spanish of aiding the Indians in their raids across the border. Hungry for more territory, settlers seek to force Spain into ceding the Floridas to the United States by their claims against the Spanish government for its inability to properly handle the situation within the territories. |
| 1819 | Don Luis de Onis, Spanish minister to the United States, and Secretary of State John Quincy Adams sign a treaty by which the Floridas will become part of the United States. |
| 1821 | The Onis–Adams Treaty is ratified. An act of congress makes the two Floridas one territory. Jackson becomes the military governor, but relinquishes the post after a few months. |
| 1822 | The first legislative council meets at Pensacola. Members from St. Augustine travel fifty-nine days by water to attend. |
| 1823 | The second legislative council meets at St. Augustine: the western delegates are shipwrecked and barely escape death. |
| 1824 | The third session meets at Tallahassee, a halfway point selected as a main order of business and approved at the second ses- |

sion. Tallahassee becomes the first territorial capital.

1823   The Treaty of Moultrie Creek is ratified by major Seminole chiefs and the federal government. The ink is barely dry before Indians are complaining that the lands are too small and white settlers are petitioning the government for a policy of Indian removal.

1832   Payne's Landing: Numerous chiefs sign a treaty agreeing to move west to Arkansas as long as seven of their number are able to see and approve the lands. The treaty is ratified at Fort Gibson, Arkansas.
Many chiefs also protest the agreement.

1835   Summer: Wiley Thompson claims that Osceola has repeatedly reviled him in his own office with foul language and orders his arrest. Osceola is handcuffed and incarcerated.

1835   November: Charlie Emathla, after agreeing to removal to the west, is murdered. Most scholars agree Osceola led the party that carried out the execution. Some consider the murder a personal vengeance, others believe it was ordered by numerous chiefs since an Indian who would leave his people to aid the whites should forfeit his own life.

1835   December 28th: Major Francis Dade and his troops are massacred as they travel from Fort Brooke to Fort King.
Also on December 28th—Wiley Thompson and a companion are killed outside the walls of Fort King. The sutler Erastus Rogers and his two clerks are also murdered by members of the same raiding party, led by Osceola.

1835   December 31st: The First Battle of the Withlacoochee—Osceola leads the Seminoles.

1836   January: Major General Winfield Scott is ordered by the secretary of war to take command in Florida.

February 4th: Dade County established in South Florida in memory of Francis Langhorne Dade.

March 16th: The senate confirms Richard Keith Call governor of the Florida Territory.

June 21st: Call, a civilian governor, is given command of the Florida forces after the failure of Scott's strategies and the military disputes between Scott and General Gaines.

Call attempts a "summer campaign," and is as frustrated in his efforts as his predecessor.

December 9th: Major Sidney Jesup takes charge.

1837    June 2nd: Osceola and Sam Jones release or "abduct" nearly 700 Indians awaiting deportation to the west from Tampa.

October 27th: Osceola is taken under a white flag of truce; Jesup is denounced by whites and Indians alike for the action.

November 29th: Coacoochee, Cowaya, sixteen warriors and two women escape Ft. Marion.

Christmas Day: Jesup has the largest fighting force assembled in Florida during the conflict, nearly 9,000 men. Under his command, Colonel Zachary Taylor leads the Battle of Okeechobee. The Seminoles choose to stand their ground and fight, inflicting greater losses to whites despite the fact that they were severely outnumbered.

1838    January 31st: Osceola dies at Ft. Marion, South Carolina—A strange side note to a sad tale: Dr. Wheedon, presiding white physician for Osceola, cut off and preserved Osceola's head. Wheedon's heirs reported that the good doctor would hang the head on the bedstead of one of his three children should they misbehave. The head passed to his son-in-law, Dr. Daniel Whitehurst, who gave it to Dr. Valentine Mott. Dr. Mott had a medical and pathological museum, and it is believed that the head was lost when his museum burned in 1866.

May: Zachary Taylor takes command when Jesup's plea to be relieved is answered at last on April 29th.

The Florida legislature debates statehood.

1839    December: Because of his arguments with federal authorities regarding the Seminole War, Richard Keith Call is removed as governor.

Robert Raymond Reid is appointed in his stead.

1840    April 24th: Zachary Taylor is given permission to leave command of what is considered to be the harshest military position in the country.

Walker Keith Armistead takes command.

December 1840–January 1841: John T. MacLaughlin leads a flotilla of men in dugouts across the Everglades from east to west; his party become the first white men to do so.

September: William Henry Harrison is elected president of the United States; the Florida War is considered to have cost Martin Van Buren reelection.

John Bell replaces Joel Poinsett as secretary of war. Robert Reid is ousted as territorial governor, and Richard Keith Call is reinstated.

1841    April 4th: President William Henry Harrison dies in office: John Tyler becomes president of the U.S.

May 1st: Coacoochee determines to turn himself in. He is escorted by a man who will later become extremely well known— Lieutenant William Tecumseh Sherman. Sherman writes to his future wife that the Florida war is a good one for a soldier; he will get to know the Indian who may become the "chief enemy" in time.

May 31st: Walker Keith Armistead is relieved. Colonel William Jenkins Worth takes command.

1842    May 10th: Winfield Scott is informed that the administration has decided there must be an end to hostilities as soon as possible. August 14th: Aware that he cannot end hostilities and send all the Indians West, Colonel Worth makes offers to the remaining Indians to leave, or accept boundaries. The war, he declares, is over.

It has cost a fledgling nation thirty to forty million dollars and the lives of seventy-four commissioned officers. The Seminoles have been reduced from tens of thousands to hundreds scattered about in pockets. The Seminoles (inclusive here, as they were seen during the war, as all Florida Indians) have, however, kept their place in the peninsula; those remaining are the undefeated. The army, too, has learned new tactics, mostly regarding partisan and guerilla warfare. Men who will soon take part in the greatest conflict to tear apart the nation have practiced the art of battle here: William T. Sherman, Braxton Bragg, George Gordon Meade, Joseph E. Johnston, and more, including soon-to-be President Zachary Taylor.

1845    March 3rd: President John Tyler signs the bill that makes Florida the 27th state of the United States of America.

1855–58    The conflict known as the Third Seminole War takes place with a similar outcome to the earlier confrontations—money spent, lives lost, and the Indians entrenched more deeply into the Everglades.

1859    Robert E. Lee is sent in to arrest John Brown after his attempt to initiate a slave rebellion with an assault on Harpers Ferry, Virginia (later West Virginia). The incident escalates ill will between the North and the South. Brown is executed on December 2nd.

1860    The first Florida cross-state railroad goes into service.

November 6th: Abraham Lincoln is elected to the presidency and many Southern states begin to call for special legislative sessions. Although there are many passionate Unionists in the state, most Florida politicians are ardent in lobbying for secession. Towns, cities, and counties rush to form or enlarge militia companies. Even before the state is able to meet for its special session, civil and military leaders plan to demand the turnover of federal military installations.

1861    January 10th: Florida votes to secede from the Union, the third Southern state to do so.

February: Florida joins the Confederate States of America.

Through late winter and early spring, the Confederacy struggles to form a government and organize the armed forces while the states recruit fighting men. Jefferson Davis is president of the newly formed country. Stephan Mallory, of Florida, becomes C.S.A. secretary of the navy.

April 12th–14th: Confederate forces fire on Ft. Sumter, S.C., and the first blood is shed when an accidental explosion kills Private Hough, who then has the distinction of being the first federal casualty.

Federal forces fear a similar action at Ft. Pickens, Pensacola Bay, Florida. Three forts guarded the bay, McRee and Barrancas on the land side, and Pickens on the tip of forty-mile long Santa Rosa Island. Federal

Lieutenant Adam J. Slemmer spiked the guns at Barrancas, blew up the ammunition at McRee, and moved his meager troops to Pickens, where he was eventually reinforced by 500 men. Though Florida troops took the navy yard, retention of the fort by the Federals nullified the usefulness to the Rebs of what was considered the most important navy yard south of Norfolk.

July 18th: First Manassas, or the First Battle of Bull Run, Virginia—both sides get their first real taste of battle. Southern troops are drawn from throughout the states, including Florida. Already, the state, which had been so eager to secede, sees her sons being shipped northward to fight, and her coast being left to its own defenses by a government with different priorities.

November: Robert E. Lee inspects coastal defenses as far south as Fernandina and decides the major ports of Charleston, Savannah, and Brunswick are to be defended, adding later that the small force posted at St. Augustine was like an invitation to attack.

1862   February: Florida's Governor Milton publicly states his despair for Florida citizens as more of the state's troops are ordered north after Grant captures two major confederate strongholds in Tennessee.

February 28th: A fleet of 26 Federal ships sets sail to occupy Fenrandina, Jacksonville, and St. Augustine. March 8th: St. Augustine surrenders, and though Jacksonville and other points north and south along the coast will change hands several times during the war, St. Augustine will remain in Union hands. The St. Johns River becomes a ribbon of guerilla troop movement for both sides. Many Floridians begin to despair of

"East Florida," fearing that the fickle populace has all turned Unionist.

March 8th: Under the command of Franklin Buchanan, the *C.S.S. Virginia,* formerly the scuttled Union ship *Merrimac,* sailed into Hampton Roads to battle the Union ships blockading the channel. She devastates Federal ships until the arrival of the poorly prepared and leaking Federal entry into the "ironclad" fray, the *U.S.S. Monitor.* The historic battle of the ironclads ensues. Neither ship emerged a clear victor; the long-term advantage went to the Union since the Confederacy was then unable to break the blockade when it had appeared, at first, that the *Virginia* might have sailed all the way to attack Washington, D.C.

April 2nd: Apalachicola is attacked by a Federal landing force. The town remains a no-man's-land throughout the war.

April 6th–8th: Union and Confederate forces engage in the battle of Shiloh. Both claim victories; both suffer horrible loses with over twenty thousand killed, wounded, or missing.

April 25th: New Orleans falls, and the Federal grip on the South becomes more of a vise.

Spring: The Federal blockade begins to tighten and much of the state becomes unlivable. Despite its rugged terrain, the length of the peninsula, and the simple difficulty of logistics, blockade runners know that they can dare Florida waterways simply because the Union can't possibly guard the extensive coastline of the state. Florida's contribution becomes more and more that of a breadbasket as she strips herself and provides salt, beef, smuggled supplies, and manpower to the Confederacy.

May 9th: Pensacola is evacuated by the Rebs and occupied by Federal forces.

May 20th: Union landing party is successfully attacked by Confederates near St. Marks.

May 22nd: Union Flag Officer DuPont writes to his superiors, with quotes, that had the Union not abandoned Jacksonville, the state would have split, and East Florida would have entered the war on the Union side.

Into summer: Fierce action continues in Virginia: battle of Fair Oaks, or Seven Pines, May 31st, the Seven Days Battles, May 25th–7th, the battle of Mechanicsville, June 26th, Gaines Mill, or Cold Harbor, June 27th. More Florida troops leave the state to replace the men killed in action in these battles, and in other engagements in Alabama, Louisiana, and along the Mississippi.

Salt becomes even more necessary: Florida has numerous saltworks along the Gulf side of the state. Union ships try to find them, confiscate what they can, and destroy the works.

August 30th: Second Battle of Manassas, or Bull Run.

September 16th and 17th: The battle of Antietam, or Sharpsburg, takes place in Maryland, where the "single bloodiest day of fighting" occurs.

September 23rd: The preliminary text of the Emancipation Proclamation is published. It will take effect on January 1st, 1863. Lincoln previously drafted the document, but waited for a Union victory to publish it; both sides claimed Antietam, but the Rebels were forced to withdraw back to Virginia.

October 5th: Federals recapture Jacksonville.

December 11th–15th: The Battle of Fredericksburg.

December 31st: The Battle of Murfreesborough or Stones River, Tennessee.

1863    March 20th: A Union landing party at St. Andrew's Bay, Florida, is attacked and most Federals are captured or killed.

March 31st: Jacksonville is evacuated by the Union forces again.

May 1st–4th: The Battle of Chancellorsville. Lee soundly beats Hooker, but on the 2nd, General Stonewall Jackson is accidentally shot and mortally wounded by his own men. He dies on the 10th.

June: Southern commanders determine anew to bring the war to the Northern front. A campaign begins that will march the Army of Northern Virginia through Virginia, Maryland, and on to Pennsylvania. In the west, the campaign along the Mississippi continues with Vicksburg under siege. In Florida, there is little action other than skirmishing and harrying attacks along the coast. More Florida boys are conscripted into the regular army. The state continues to produce cattle and salt for the Confederacy.

July 1st: Confederates move towards Gettysburg along the Chambersburg Pike. Four miles west of town, they meet John Buford's Union cavalry.

July 2nd: At Gettysburg, places like the Peach Orchard and Devil's Den become names that live in history.

July 3rd: Pickett's disastrous charge.

July 4th: Lee determines to retreat to Virginia.

July 4th: Vicksburg surrenders.

July continues: The Union soldiers take a very long time to chase Lee. What might have been an opportunity to end the war is lost.

July 13th: Draft riots in New York.

August 8th: Lee attempts to resign. President Jefferson Davis rejects his resignation.

August continues into fall: Renewed Union interest in Florida begins to develop as assaults against Charleston and forts in South Carolina bring recognition by the North that Florida is a hotbed for blockade runners, salt, and cattle. Union commanders in the South begin to plan a Florida campaign.

September 20th: the South is victorious in the Western field of battle when General Bragg routes General Rosecrans at Chickamauga.

November: The Union army is besieged at Chattanooga. On the 24th, Sherman crosses the river and, the next day, the Confederates are forced to flee the field.

1864    February 7th: Union General Seymour comes ashore in Jacksonville, Florida, preparing for an offensive.

February 20th: The battle of Olustee, Florida, takes place. The Southern forces win the battle when the South is weakly faring elsewhere.

April 9th: Union General Grant tells Meade that "Wherever Lee goes, there you will head also."

April 12th: Bedford Forrest's Confederate cavalry storm Ft. Pillow, Tennessee. Many of the soldiers at the fort are black, causing the North to claim that the battle was a massacre. Later, the Confederates involved will be accused of committing horrible atrocities.

April 30th: Joseph Emory Davis, son of Jefferson Davis, dies in a fall from the balcony of the White House of the Confederacy.

May 5th and 6th: The Battle of the Wilder-

ness takes place. The terrible fires that
break out make battle even more horrible
for the men wounded and left to die in the
tangled brush.

The Union does not retreat.

May 8th: Anderson, commanding Longstreet's forces, gets between the Yanks and
Richmond. The Confederates entrench, and
the Battle of Spotsylvania Courthouse begins.

May 10th: Skirmish at Beaver Dam Station.

May 11th: At Yellow Tavern, the great cavalier Dixie, J.E.B. Stuart is mortally
wounded. The South loses another of its
most able commanders.

May 15th: The Battle of New Market. Desperate, Confederate General Breckinridge
commits the 247 cadets of the Virginia Military Academy to the battle. There are ten
dead and forty-seven wounded cadets.

Through the end of May, the Northern and
Southern troops clash in their race south.

June 1st: Grant begins to batter Cold Harbor. The heavy fighting lasts from June 3rd
through June 12th. The cannon fire can be
heard in Richmond. No matter what
Grant's losses, Lee holds. Grant heads
south to try to get to Richmond through
Petersburg. By the end of June, both armies
are entrenched.

July 12th: President Lincoln is on a parapet
at Ft. Stevens where Early's Confederates
are sending sniper fire. "Get down, you
damned fool, or you'll be killed," he is told.
The messenger is a young officer named Ol-
iver Wendell Holmes, Jr. The president
takes no offense. Ducking down, Lincoln
comments that Holmes knows how to talk
to a civilian.

July 30th: The Crater. A Union decision to
mine a crater beneath the Southern lines at

Petersburg goes horribly awry. Hundreds of Rebels are instantly killed, but the attacking Union soldiers become trapped in the crater and are slaughtered by the defenders. Four thousand Federal troops are killed or wounded within three hours of fighting. Confederate losses are about 1500.

August 31st: Hood desperately telegraphs Lee to come to Atlanta—he must abandon the city.

September 2nd: Federal troops occupy Atlanta.

September 5th: Declared a day of celebration by President Lincoln as Atlanta has fallen and Admiral Farragut has taken Mobile Bay.

October 1st: A Confederate soldier finds the body of a woman on the beach. She is Rose Greenhow, the Confederate spy, drowned while escaping her ship from Europe after it was accosted by the Union blockade. The soldier had taken some of the gold she carried; discovering her identity, he gave it back.

November 8th: Lincoln defeats George B. McClellan to win a second presidential term.

November 11th: Union troops in Atlanta begin the systematic destruction of food supplies and arms, anything that might be left behind, for the South. Sherman's "scorched earth" policy is given full measure. November 16th: he begins marching through the heart of Georgia, heading for the sea.

December 22nd: Sherman sends Lincoln the message, "I beg to present you, as a Christmas gift, the city of Savannah."

1865     January 15th: Fort Fisher, at the port of Wilmington, North Carolina, the Confederates last real point of contact with the outside world, surrenders.

February 17th: Columbia is occupied and destroyed. Ft. Sumter, held by the South from the first action, falls back to the Union. Charleston is abandoned.

March 4th: The Battle of Natural Bridge, Leon County, Florida. The "Baby Corps," troops under General William Miller and troops that included boys from the Seminary West of the Suwannee (now known as Florida State University) repel three strong assaults by Union General Newton and save Tallahassee. It is the only Southern capital not taken by Union troops before Lee's surrender. Also on March 4th, President Lincoln is inaugurated for his second term.

March 24th: Lee makes plans to remove his army from Petersburg, knowing all is lost if he does not. On the 25th, a plan to break through the Federal line has a handful of "deserters" appearing to remove Federal defenses while Gordon makes an assault. There are 4,000 Rebel losses—many of whom surrendered rather than face the slaughtering fury of fire set upon them.

March 28th, The Army of the Potomac prepares for its final assault. 125,000 Union troops are gathered to face fewer than 50,000 remaining Confederates. Lee hopes to join Johnston and make a last stand in North Carolina, the "Tar Heel" state.

April 1st: Florida's Governor, John Miton, foreseeing the fall of the Confederacy, commits suicide.

April 2nd: The Confederates abandon Petersburg. A. P. Hill is killed in the fighting. The Confederate capital is lost; Richmond, too, abandoned.

April 9th: The Army of Northern Virginia fights its last battle. Knowing all is lost, Lee, the great commander, surrenders to Grant. He tells his men to go home and be "as good citizens as you were soldiers." On April 10th, the hungry Rebels receive rations from the Union army. The Confederate government receives word of the surrender, and heads deeper into North Carolina. On the 12th, General Gordon leads the official surrender, accepted by Joshua Chamberlain of Gettysburg fame.

April 14th: Lincoln is shot by John Wilkes Booth at Ford's Theater. He survives through the night, and dies on the 15th.

April 16th: Confederate General Johnston surrenders 31,000 Rebel troops.

June 2nd: General E. Kirby Smith surrenders his troops. The most ardent of Southern generals, he is the last to surrender such troops in the field. His mother has remained in St. Augustine throughout the war. One of his officers, General Shelby, will not surrender, but takes his troops south to fight in Mexico.

July 7th: Four of the Lincoln conspirators are hanged; four are imprisoned at Ft. Jefferson on the Dry Tortugas off the Florida Keys. Dr. Mudd, who treated Booth's leg, is later pardoned for his work in the yellow fever epidemic of 1867.

President Johnson tries hard to follow Lincoln's resolves for peace and forgiveness; he cannot help the bitterness that will divide the country for decades to come. Only one man will die a "war criminal," Henry Wirz, who commanded Andersonville, notorious for being a prison where death was prevalent and sometimes preferable to life. He was hanged—slowly. It took him seven minutes to die. President Johnson will see most of the Southern cabinet paroled; Jefferson Davis will suffer imprisonment for several years after the war.

Lee will go on to teach, and, as he had instructed his men, he will look to peace with the same determination with which he fought in the war.

Florida will face Reconstruction as do the other Southern states, but she will be partially saved by those factors that still make men and women love her and hate her—the sun, the heat, and the humidity! Carpetbaggers will come, but not nearly so many as arrive in other areas of the deep South. In the years ahead, Florida will reach her golden age with the rich purchasing their "winter" homes, inventors coming in droves along with the one true saving grace of the state—air-conditioning!

## The Seminole Connection

James McQueen m. Tallasee Woman

Bob m. Seminole Woman
Fullunny
Peter
Poppinger m. Ann

Willie m. Betsy

Polly m. Powell

Billy Powell/
Osceola
1804–

Risa m. Jerome
1837–

Brent m. Mary
1838–

Sydney m. Jesse Halston
1841–

Mary
1862–

James m.2 Teela
1811–

Jamie        Allen
1863–        1864–

Jennifer m. 1 Lawrence Malloy m. 2 Michael Long
1831–

Sara
1829–1836

Anthony
1858–

## The McKenzies

Geneva — m. 1. — Sean — m. 2. — Mary
1770–1807        1766–1825        1785–

Lisa — m.1 — Jarrett — m.2 — Tara
1806–1833        1802–        1812–

Naomi m.1
1808–1836

Tia m. Taylor Douglas
1840–

Hope
1865–

Julian m. Rhiannon
1837–

Ian m. Alaina
1836–

Sean        Ariana        Katie        Conar
1861–        1862–        1864–        1864–

Be sure to look for Heather Graham's next
novel, a breathtaking story of
romantic suspense . . .

*Long, Lean, and Lethal*

Coming soon from New American Library

To M. S. K.

# ACKNOWLEDGMENTS

In addition to the authors who have participated in this presentation, I should like to thank Evelyn Kirby, Diana Clemmons, and Professor William Dunn, State University College at New Paltz, New York, for the help they have given me on translations.

# CONTENTS

# INTRODUCTION

The origin of the expression "total theatre" appears to be derived from Richard Wagner's concept of a *Gesamtkunstwerk* — a "collected," "united," "whole" or "total artwork." Theatre as the place of intersection of all the arts is, then, the meaning of "total theatre." We most often find this totality indicated by a list of components such as music, movement, voice, scenery, lighting, etc. More important, however, is the understanding that there must be an effective interplay among the various elements or a significant synthesis of them. Totality may, in this sense, be more or less extensive, including a greater or lesser number of aspects, but it must always be intensive, effecting an integration of components. While totality as an ideal is extensive and all-inclusive, it is this relationship between elements, rather than an accumulation of means, which actually distinguishes the form.

Another expression, from a title of Wagner's writings, that has been used as a substitute and synonym for *Gesamtkunstwerk* is "theatre of the future." This phrase indicates two important aspects of total theatre: that it has not yet been realized and that its realization is to be a result of history, of a cultural evolutionary process.

The first aspect, in which the true form of total theatre has yet to come into being, is important from the point of view of reference. We shall be speaking here of many forms of production as total theatre, though some are more representative than others. But attention should be directed through the specific examples, none of which is to be considered definitive, for a sense of the basic underlying principles and an awareness of those techniques that will yet contribute to the creation of the theatre of the future.

The second aspect of the phrase "theatre of the future," in which total theatre is associated with a project of cultural evolution, is the point at which we may best begin a study of the form. The narrative of these conditions starts in the Renaissance when the rediscovered ancient civilizations of Greece and Rome were providing new foundations for learning and for the arts. A dominant view, visualizing the ancient world across a discontinuity in history, was that Greek experience had been that of an integrated totality. It was the recovery of this total reality, not a search for theatre form as such, that motivated the intentions toward a theatre of the future.

The Renaissance English masque and the related French ballet were representative of this interest. In estimating the nature of this interest, it is significant that a revival of classicism was embodied in these new forms rather than in the staging of Greek drama as such. It was known that the ancient drama had been a form of total theatre, with an integration of music, voice, dance-like movement, masks, accentuated costumes, and spectacular stage machinery. The Renaissance masque form used these elements, but chose to rearrange them in a new way. This may be understood as due to two causes. One was that the precise relationships of music, dance, and poetry as employed in Greek tragedy were not sufficiently known, nor are they to this day. The second reason seems to have been that Greek tragedy was dominated by its text, by its literary aspect, and the masque emphasized nonverbal, theatrical techniques in order more directly to symbolize a classic, almost preliterary, ur-reality.

A simplified and schematized sketch of a masque would run as follows. Stage machinery provided an effect, such as the opening of a rock or a descent from the heavens, from which mythical

characters emerged as if from another world. The principal
characters were costumed with symbolic insignia and properties
to be interpreted by the audience—sometimes with the aid of a
narrator or a printed key. The basic situation was established by
a brief verse play, and the masquers danced the "Main" dance in
patterns that were composed both as geometrical figures and as
hieroglyphic signs. Social dancing, mixing audience and performers, then provided a mode of experience that Orgel indicates was, in effect, an "allegorization of the audience." [1] Following this, the masquers regrouped to dance the "Going-out"
and returned, as it were, to the "other" reality.

The masque form was more of a ritual than was Greek tragedy, which had purportedly sprung from ritual: it was a mimetic
prayer for the health and renewal of the State. More significant,
however, in our present context are the patterns of the dances.
The use of geometrical figures was based on a pervading interest
in Pythagorean philosophy, a pre-Aristotelian school that had
held that all things were, or were modeled upon, numbers. This
world view could in particular be perceived in the idea that
musical effects and geometrical figures were both based on
mathematical relationships. The correspondences between these
forms indicated a "total reality" that was of great interest to literature and science, and it was this that was symbolized in the
masque.[2]

The hieroglyphic figures of the dance patterns also referred to
an understanding of an original unity that was thought to have
existed in earlier times before writing, music, acting, and other
forms of expression became separated. The hieroglyph itself
represents such a unity, for it combines many different meanings
in a single, rather unwieldy and suggestive, pre-alphabetic sym-

[1] Stephen Orgel, *The Jonsonian Masque* (Cambridge: Harvard University Press, 1965).
[2] The Pythagorean theory of a "harmony of the spheres" was particularly popular among Elizabethan writers. It was this which Kepler tried to
establish scientifically with his treatise on planetary harmonies (*De Har-
monice Mundi,* 1619) in which movements and distances in the solar system were related to musical intervals. Newton approached the same problem from another angle when he attempted to relate the spectrum of light
and the musical octave in his *Opticks* of 1704. If a given color could be
equated with a musical note, sensory experience as well as art forms would
be placed on an absolute basis of Pythagorean correspondences.

bol or emblem. Claude Menestrier, in a history of the dance (1682), indicated this original totality when he wrote that, "The Egyptians, who were sages disciplined in minute detail, made the first of their dances hieroglyphics in action, as they had among them figures to express their Mysteries." [3] One finds that dance actions have often been defined as "hieroglyphic" rather than as representational, and that this term indicates an intersection of symbolic meaning with music and movement that must be considered a basic goal of total theatre.

This idea in turn relates to the geometrical figures that were used in the masque, for in the Renaissance as in ancient Greece the dance was thought to have arisen in imitation of planetary movements, as if representing and reproducing a Pythagorean harmony of numbers and a "music of the spheres."

In a similar manner, the project of a unified integration of literature and music was a central endeavor of Renaissance musical humanism. Representative of this was Baif's *Academie de Poésie et de Musique,* founded in 1570, which sought to merge poetry and music for the purpose of a singular effectivity. The academy's first principle, that "music and verse are to be firmly united," was a corollary to its second, that this union should "produce a revival of the ethical effects of ancient music." This merger of the arts, renewing an ancient totality, would have, it was thought, the power to "arouse and control passions, inculcate and preserve virtue, even cure disease and ensure the stability of the state." [4]

It was this Renaissance heritage that was summarized by Wagner more than two centuries later. He felt that Greek tragedy, the "great unitarian artwork of Greece," had been fragmented and its component parts had become isolated as rhetoric, sculpture, music, and the other arts. He did not, however, describe this prototaotality in any detail, for he felt that it could not be understood by "our bewildered, wandering, piecemeal minds in all its fullness." He emphasized, however, that it could not be re-created, but rather that it "must be *born anew.*" The origina-

[3] John C. Meagher, *Method and Meaning in Jonson's Masques* (Notre Dame, Indiana: University of Notre Dame Press, 1966), p. 83.

[4] *Ibid.,* pp. 73–4.

tion of rationalism, Wagner felt, had "shattered Grecian tragedy" and produced "the great Revolution of Mankind" that was
Western civilization. Only this revolution would be capable of
creating, in its culmination and by its own means, the new total
artwork.

It is impossible in this context to do more than suggest how the
philosophical basis of Western civilization was involved with a
dualism between reason and the senses, though this is relevant
both to Wagner's work and to considerations of total theatre as
such. In general, sense perceptions, feelings, and emotions were
consistently devalued in comparison with rational and objective
modes. Spinoza, for example, defined sense perceptions as well
as passions as "confused acts of thought," and by the time of
Kant's *Critique of the Power of Judgment* (1790) the philosophical situation presented itself in terms of the questions, "How can
the sensuous and the ideal world be reconciled?" and "How can a
pleasurable feeling partake of the character of reason?" [5] These
were, in a sense, the same questions Wagner inherited. Terminology has varied, but attempting to resolve this subject-object
duality in its many aspects has been the project of philosophy
and of aesthetics, and it can also be understood as the essential
project of total theatre.

Wagner's work in relation to this context was directly inspired
by the philosophy of Schopenhauer. Duality as Schopenhauer
described it was a function of a consciousness that was dependent upon two distinct and opposed types of knowing, a knowledge of oneself (which he associated with the will) and a visual
knowledge of the surrounding world. These two modes of knowing were so held in balance that each excluded the other propor-
tionately as it was used.

One aspect of Wagner's theories based upon this model was
the conception that the voice of the individual represented the
expression of the self while the music of the orchestra represented the "voice" of the world, with the resolution in the two
modes of knowing occurring when coincidences in tonality
blended one with the other. He also used the same schema to indicate how both the poet and the composer were victims of this

[5] Bernard Bosanquet, *A History of Aesthetic* (New York: World Pub-
lishing Company, 1957), pp. 183, 187.

duality, with the art of each constantly alternating between feeling (knowledge of self) and reason (visual knowledge) without being able to attain unified forms. To eliminate the adverse effects of this duality, poetry and music were to be united in a way that would be mutually beneficial to both modes of expression.

Poetry and music, as reason and feeling, were to be united through the interposition of another faculty, that of tone. This was, in a sense, a return to origins, to a "tone speech" that Wagner felt had preceded word speech. In their merger, however, both modes were subsumed under feeling to produce an "emotionalizing of the intellect." This was equated with a prerational expression of reason as it was manifest on the level of "mythos."

Wagner's philosophy of the "total artwork," set in a context of history and of metaphysics and projected toward realization as "the theatre of the future," was an impressive formulation that had considerable influence on others. As has been suggested, however, the lines along which he was working had been present in Western artistic intentions since the Renaissance. These produced a development parallel to Wagner's, and at first independent of his influence, that was inherently involved with the merger of the arts. This was the Symbolist movement which spanned the nineteenth century and continued well into the twentieth, while also being a precursor of Surrealism and of modern art in general.

The designation "symbolist" was first applied in 1886 to Mallarmé and his literary group, but the aesthetic itself may be seen to include Novalis and Baudelaire, Rimbaud, Verlaine, Yeats, Valéry, Claudel, and many others. It encompasses painting as well as poetry, with the work of Gustave Moreau and Odilon Redon, for example. In theatre, Maeterlinck was the outstanding Symbolist playwright, and the theories of Gordon Craig and Adolphe Appia were largely determined by this influence.

The dominant characteristic of the Symbolist aesthetic was that it was based on an acceptance of the correspondences between the arts and between the information of the various senses. Baudelaire's poem "Correspondences," which refers to an interblending of perfumes, sounds, and colors, is usually cited in reference to synesthesia as indicating the direct interplay of sensory

impressions. This concept of synesthesia is so important to our theme that we must here parenthetically consider it in more detail.

"Clinical synesthesia" indicates the involuntary transference of representation from one sense to another, as in seeing the colors of sounds or experiencing the taste of colors. As an actuality it is of doubtful authenticity, but it has been associated, quite inconclusively, with psychotic states and with primitive experience. In regard to the latter, it was proposed that the various individual senses had separated themselves from an original "sensory matrix" of "primitive undifferentiated sensitivity" where there was a complete merger and interchange of modes of perception. This theory is clearly similar to Wagner's view of a separation of the arts arising from the fragmentation of an ancient total artwork. "Intersense analogy," on the other hand, implies synesthesia by using comparisons and resemblances that translate the information of one sense in terms of another, as "hot" sounds or "loud" colors. Such analogies are recurring phenomena in word formation. At the hieroglyphic level of representation, a single symbol will often combine references to *clear,* for example, to *bright* and to a *sharp* in music, thus presenting a brief index to Pythagorean correspondences or of a synesthetic reality.[6]

The degree to which Baudelaire's poetry and the Symbolist aesthetic itself are structured on this general basis is highly significant. Baudelaire, in fact, summarized this Symbolist orientation in an article on Wagner when he wrote that:

What would be truly surprising is that sound *should not* suggest color, that colors *should not* be able to give the idea of a melody, and that sound and color should be unfitting to translate ideas; things always having been expressed through a reciprocal analogy, since the day when God uttered forth the world as a complex and indivisible totality.[7]

[6] Glenn O'Malley, "Literary Synesthesia," *Journal of Aesthetics and Art Criticism,* XV:4 (June, 1957) and Alfred G. Engstrom, "In Defence of Synaesthesia in Literature," *Philological Quarterly,* XXV:1 (January, 1946).

[7] Angelo Philip Bertocci, *From Symbolism to Baudelaire* (Carbondale, Illinois: Southern Illinois University Press, 1964), p. 77.

The importance of this passage, beyond the actual context of synesthesia, is that it centers upon the nonobjective properties of the media themselves as accurate vehicles for ideas. The transmission of ideas, like the correspondences between forms, is objective, as Baudelaire indicated when he denied the prevalent theory of the subjectivity of music by pointing out that it creates "analogous ideas in different minds." [8]

The implications for total theatre of the Symbolist aesthetic and technique are outlined in analogy by Angelo Bertocci in his *From Symbolism to Baudelaire*. In one brilliant paragraph he contrasts Symbolist poetic methods with the traditional Aristotelian "linear" form that is usually associated with the narrative and with the drama in particular. He begins with a concise definition of Symbolism which relates indirectly to two modes of synesthesia: the "vertical," in which sense stimuli produce images and thoughts, and the "horizontal," in which sense stimuli interrelate and correspond. He then proceeds to contrast this form of "in depth" realization with the more usual literary or linear form in a way that applies directly to the methods and concept of total theatre. Bertocci writes:

. . . Symbolisme, in its most general sense . . . in that emphasis by which it has exerted its greatest influence, may be seen as the aspiration common to several families of spirit *toward a thoroughgoing poetic unity conceived in terms of the metaphor of "color"* (which, as we have seen, has also its "music") *in a philosophical context which permits interflow and interglow of meanings, both horizontally and vertically, between areas of experience formerly maintained distinct.* For "organic unity" is as old as Aristotle, but though the image was taken from biology, it was translated in terms of structures easy for logic to distinguish. Hence in the arts the emphasis on "plot" and on "line," and the distinctions between genres. But lay stress upon the individual and the particular, upon change and mobility, upon dynamism, upon interfusion, upon an organicism intuited as "life"—

[8] Artaud made much the same point in regard to a total theatre that would use only "shapes, or noise, or gesture." He said that to raise the question of effective intellectual communication by means of these abstract modes is to question "the intellectual efficacy of art." (Antonin Artaud, *The Theater and Its Double*, trans. Mary Caroline Richards [New York: Grove Press, 1968], p. 69.)

and this was the tendency of thought from the Renaissance on—and that unity can be conceived more "coloristically" and more "musically." From "line" to "color"; from "plot line" as the very sinew of unity, to recurrence in patterned shapes of images, events, sounds, rhythms as the real inner "life" of this unity; from the "fable" or "story" developing in linear fashion and conveying "meaning" easily susceptible of paraphrase, to an "import" suddenly, if fleetingly, "coming together" in consciousness, so that the "whole story" or "what the story has to say" consists of a perception distorted if lifted out of context—it is of this development in Western art that Symbolisme itself is for the historian the "symbol." [9]

It is also this description that may best serve as a definition of the techniques of total theatre. It represents not only the particular way in which total theatre is a place of convergence of the arts as sensory modalities but also how it is a theatre of information through integrated effect rather than of narrative as such.

Given this context, it is not surprising that there was sustained Symbolist interest in creating the total artwork itself. This may here be observed principally in regard to the theatrical theories of two men, Stéphane Mallarmé and Adolphe Appia, though total theatre in fact reached one of its highest realizations in the work of Paul Claudel. (See Claudel's "Modern Drama and Music" and Jean-Louis Barrault on *Christopher Columbus*.)

Appia's influence was exercised largely through his writings; principally *La Mise-en-Scène du Drame Wagnérian* (1895), *La Musique et la Mise-en-Scène* (published in German in 1899), and *L'oeuvre d'Art Vivant* (1921). He has been credited with the replacement of painted scenes by solid settings and with the inauguration of flexible area lighting, but these attributions are misleading. Appia sought to extend Wagner's union of music and drama by integrating all visual aspects of the staged presentation in accord with the orders of musical forms. This was to be attained by (1) a stage space realized in terms of a solid geometry that revealed the mathematical correspondences of form to music, (2) the illumination of actors in a way that emphasized their sculptural qualities and directly related them, by means of this illumination, with the forms of the surrounding "musical space," and (3) the movement of this unity, in which the bodies

[9] Bertocci, p. 59.

of actors and the continuous changes in lighting would provide an integrated, plastic and visual equivalent to music.

Much of Appia's theory centered upon the rhythmic movements of the actors. (See Clark M. Rogers, "Appia's Theory of Acting: Eurhythmics for the Stage.") He suggested that a system of hieroglyphic notation would be necessary to record, and I emphasize, *"the effects of the actor's role on the inanimate setting."* [10] He thus indicated the moments and the nature of a hieroglyphic symboling in which actor and his surroundings were related in a single expressive plastic function.

The symbol as "hieroglyph" also played a central role in Symbolist theory and poetic technique. Aspects of obscurity and ambiguity pertaining to the hieroglyph refer one to that sense in which it represented the "mystery" in Elizabethan masques. But more important, the hieroglyph as used here was not only a symbol representing a vague and allusive reality, it was also the "key," the focal point of a number of different references, the coincidence of which produced the insight into multiple levels of reality, the "almost supernatural" "coming together" of meanings that was the goal of the technique.

This type of a method seems to have been the basis of the "total artwork" as Mallarmé conceived it. The element of dance had an important place in this artwork. It was "emblematic" rather than representational, while the drama was "historical." Mallarmé, however, also conceived of a nonrepresentational form of drama; that is, he thought of it as poetry itself. Haskell Block notes that, "If the poet never deviated from his conviction that poetry is the highest of the arts, he envisioned the drama as a combination of dance, music, and poetry, along with mime, décor, and indeed all of the arts of the theatre." [11]

The theoretical function of Mallarmé's projected total theatre was similar to Wagner's, whose conception of the perfect artwork was that it be integrated with all of society as "the great united utterance of a free and lovely public life." Mallarmé's

[10] Adolphe Appia, *Music and the Arts of the Theatre,* trans. Robert W. Corrigan and Mary Douglas Dirks (Coral Gables, Florida: University of Miami Press, 1962), p. 31.
[11] Haskell M. Block, *Mallarmé and the Symbolist Drama* (Detroit: Wayne State University Press, 1963), p. 93.

"artwork of the future" was visualized as sacred and sacramental, providing participation in a "mystery," but it would also be secular, presenting *"la mise-en-scène de la religion d'état"* as an instrument in civil order and education.[12] In this regard, one is directly reminded of the goals of Baif's Renaissance academy of music and of the efficacy to which it aspired.

Symbolist theatre as it was actually practiced, however, was far from being a theatre of effect and far from making use of all the instruments of the stage. The spoken word in poetic form provided, in general, the entire *mise-en-scène* for plays that were largely without action. Maeterlinck's early dramas were presided over by silence, by the presence of "the overwhelming influence of the thing that had not been spoken." His understanding was that "the profounder vibrations of the soul are more easily communicated by silence than by speech." Others, such as Artaud, would turn to the nonverbal forms of expression available to total theatre for much the same reason. But Symbolist theatre in practice remained essentially the presentation of literature.

This was largely due to the fact that Symbolist poetry had, to a certain extent, achieved within itself a representation of the "merger of the arts," as we have already observed. Marcel Raymond points out that when Symbolist poetry came to be arranged explicitly along the lines of music, with "correspondences" in words to strings and brasses, it left behind the more important correspondences to states of mind. Raymond indicates it was for this reason that "For the last thirty years the dream of the 'merger of the arts' has ceased to haunt the imagination of our poets. And the representatives of the young schools have sought to ally themselves with painters rather than with musicians." [13]

It is in this transference of allegiance to painting, and at this point in history, however, that the project of total theatre passes over, intact, to a new school of thought that claimed Baudelaire and Rimbaud among its progenitors, the Surrealists.

The origin of the word "surrealism" was in fact directly related to concepts of total theatre. It was first applied by Apol-

[12] *Ibid.*, p. 86.
[13] Marcel Raymond, *From Baudelaire to Surrealism* (New York: Wittenborn, Schultz, 1950), p. 47.

linaire in 1917 to indicate the new and particular kind of interaction between Cocteau's script, Satie's music, Massine's choreography, and Picasso's cubist designs for the ballet *Parade*. Cocteau had thought of the form as more real than the usual romantic ballet, and had termed it a "realist ballet." But Apollinaire, in a program note, pointed out that; "From this new alliance—for until now costume and scenery on one hand, choreography on the other, have been linked only artificially— there has resulted in *Parade* a kind of *sur-réalisme* . . ." [14] This *surréalisme* would be "the point of departure for a series of manifestations of [the] New Spirit. . . ." [15] The following month, Apollinaire's own *Les Mamelles de Tiresias* was produced. Subtitled "a surrealist drama," the prologue listed the means of total theatre; sound, gesture, color, action, etc., "Often connecting in unseen ways as in life." [16]

Symbolism and Surrealism were alike in that they both sought the means to achieve a higher reality. The basic distinction between them was that attention shifted from the "dream of the senses" to the "dream of reason" or the "dream of the voyage within." Baudelaire had distinguished the dream that a man constantly carries with him from the dream of the sleeper, and identified the former with the "supernatural" in life and with "hieroglyphic" expression. In a similar manner, Mallarmé's *"rêve"* essentially meant "reverie." Breton and the Surrealists, on the other hand, sought the foundations of consciousness in the images of the dream of the sleeper. In that domain was to be found "the hieroglyphic key to the world which more or less consciously preexists all high poetry." [17] Breton's *Surrealist Manifesto* of 1924 attested to the project of "the future resolution of these two states, in appearance so contradictory, which are dream and reality, in a kind of absolute reality, *surreality*. . . ." [18]

---

[14] Michael Benedikt and George E. Wellwarth, ed. and trans. *Modern French Theatre: The Avant-Garde, Dada, and Surrealism: An Anthology of Plays* (New York: E. P. Dutton, 1964), p. xvii.

[15] William S. Rubin, *Dada, Surrealism and Their Heritage* (New York: Museum of Modern Art, 1968), p. 192.

[16] *Modern French Theatre*, p. 66.

[17] Maurice Nadeau, *The History of Surrealism*, trans. Roger Shattuck (New York: The Macmillan Company, 1965), p. 228.

[18] *Ibid.*, p. 89.

The dream and the reality were established by Surrealism as the new poles of the basic duality. Thus the Surrealists rejected the relativistic subject-object relationship that characterized Western rationalism; that "Logical Europe," as Robert Desnos expressed it, that "crushes the mind endlessly between the hammers of two terms." [19] The Surrealist revolution made the mind itself the subject and object of its own evolution. Superior to political action, it conceived of itself as the mental counterpart of Marxism and of its role in history as that of solving the dialectic not in terms of materiality and the things of the world, but in terms of the mind itself. This project, we may infer, was also the project of its "theatre of the future."

This intention becomes crystallized in the writings of Antonin Artaud, a member of the Surrealist movement, in *The Theater and Its Double,* published in 1938. There Artaud invokes a total theatre that is nonrepresentational and nonliterary and that employs "all the means of expression utilizable on the stage." [20] Dance, sounds, lighting, etc., are to create an informational context and a scenic realization on a hieroglyphic level in accord with Far Eastern forms of expression. It is a level of "speech before words" that Artaud understood as the theatre's own plastic or concrete language, the basis for a "very difficult and complex poetry" of the stage itself. Each mode, each form of expression, was itself a language, and the project of total theatre was "to create stages and perspectives from one language to the other." [21] A salient feature of Artaud's "theatre of the future" was an insistence upon efficacy. Like Baïf's academy or Mallarmé's envisioned project, Artaud's total theatre was to be an instrument in the therapeutic alteration of the consciousness of a culture. It was to this end that his "theatre of cruelty" was to present the spectacle of modes of insanity in which man, constrained by space and by matter itself, was again the focal point of superhuman powers and forces—and it was this that Artaud saw represented in Eastern dramas. Essentially, however, Artaud's

[19] *Ibid.,* p. 106.
[20] Antonin Artaud, *The Theater and Its Double,* trans. Mary Caroline Richards (New York: Grove Press, 1958), p. 39.
[21] *Ibid.,* p. 113.

theatre concepts were projected beyond this toward the resolution of the dialectic and of the duality. The stage was to be an "alchemical theatre" for the archetypes of consciousness. Its efficacy was to be identified with the mystery Artaud suggested had been presented at Eleusis, the vision of a Platonic or Pythagorean reality in which, "by conjunctions unimaginably strange to our waking minds," all conflicts and antagonisms "of matter and mind, idea and form, concrete and abstract" would be resolved. The function and the form of Artaud's total theatre was "to teach us the metaphysical identity of concrete and abstract." [22]

This same function might well be the role of modern art in general. It is significant, for example, that modern art is essentially hieroglyphic expression. Representations of hieroglyphs appear in the work of Kandinsky, Miro, and Klee, and the styles are extensions of this type of symboling activity. However, their canvases may still be scanned or "read" in a literary sense. Even more important in this regard is that more recent transition to totally abstract work in which each canvas is fundamentally a hieroglyph, an "utterance," whose effect and meaning is expressed as a unity by the purely plastic dynamics of the whole work.

As a basic characteristic of modern art, this is in turn related to that development in which the milieu of painting produced a theatre form much like that indicated by Artaud's theories. When modern painting achieved a new birth in a previously insular America in the late 1940's, Surrealism was a stimulus that was rapidly absorbed to produce other distinctive modes. With Abstract Expressionism and the styles that followed, painting quite literally enlarged itself to become an environment, extended itself into the room to become sculpture, and began a process of merger with the other arts in a phenomenon characteristic of our time. One of the aspects of this process, derived from action painting, assemblage, and environments, were the performances created by artists and designated "Happenings." [23] Happenings in effect were a spontaneous approach to the necessity for a nonrepresentational total theatre.

[22] *Ibid.*, pp. 52, 59.
[23] Michael Kirby (ed.), *Happenings* (New York: E. P. Dutton, 1965).

An example we may consider here is the work of Claes Oldenburg, which he thought of as a new type of theatre and only reluctantly termed "Happenings." Oldenburg's use of objects and various materials as a basis for action or for images was representative of this first phase of the genre. In his *Store Days I* (1962), things, actions, projections, and sounds were all used, but in a particular way. Each medium was isolated, compartmentalized, and became in this sense a hieroglyphic unit in a series or structure of concrete symbols.

The same technique was used for the action that took place in three separate rooms. One room, for example, was a collage-type environment composed of various materials, the floor littered with newspapers and trash, the space illuminated by bare bulbs. The audience entered to see a man sitting on a bed holding a pair of socks in his hands, and a girl (called "spirit") who rocked in a hammock suspended overhead. Her face was pancake white. Newspapers in her skirt and in the hammock made crinkling sounds as she rocked. When the audience was present the performance began. The script for a brief portion of the action in this one room reads as follows:

The man drops his socks on the floor. A bell rings. A package is passed him from the opening in the left wall. He sits down and unwraps it. It is a pair of socks and a book and a can of tomato juice. What does he care? He lets it all drop on the floor.
(end of period 1)

Blue bulbs during positioning, always lit. Two minutes of near-darkness. The man removes his coat and hangs it on the wall. He lies down and ties himself to the bed with one-inch rope. He lies looking straight up. The hammock continues its gentle undulation.

A hard roll full of jam is dropped on the man's shirt from above. He frees one of his hands and eats it partly. From above and behind him (left wall) a pipe enters. Water runs out of it. He looks up at it. It goes away.

The floor moves (could be a person dressed as the floor). The leg protrudes down again. Milk is poured down around it. The man coughs

violently. He ties himself tighter. The unfinished roll falls off his stained shirt. The radio goes on with distant sentimental music.[24]

There is a kinship here with one of those states of mind experienced by Ionesco, of a universe "encumbered with matter." Beckett used something of this same method of things and a series of actions in *Mime for Two Players*. Oldenburg's style is related to a mode of dehumanization in art which, as Ortega y Gasset describes it, is a connecting link between "the surrealism of metaphors and what may be called infrarealism," occurring when "the small events in life appear in the foreground with monumental dimensions." [25] It indicates Surrealist technique in the sense that Cocteau described it as a concrete and material poetry, not poetry *in* the theatre but *of* the theatre. And it is perhaps the best representation we have had of that hallucinated reality which Artaud meant to portray rather than violence as such; "the much more terrible and necessary cruelty which things can exercise against us." [26]

Since that original form, Happenings have developed in two general directions; they have become staged performances, usually associated with new perspectives on dance or with the use of multi-media, and they have become participational activities. Allan Kaprow, who named them, now defines Happenings only in terms of participation. In his own work this is a symbolic activity in which small groups undertake such projects as building rectangular enclosures from blocks of ice throughout a city. But Happenings as such then no longer relate to theatre.

On the other hand, participation has become a distinct tendency in theatrical production. The dancing together of performers and audience in Richard Schechner's *Dionysus in 69* is a logical conclusion of this tendency. Like environmental theatre, we must consider participational theatre to be one of the directions in which performances have moved in their search for total-

---

[24] Claes Oldenburg, *Store Days: Documents from the Store* (1961) and *Ray Gun Theater* (1962), selected by Claes Oldenburg and Emmett Williams, photographs by Robert R. McElroy (New York: Something Else Press, 1967), pp. 69–70.

[25] Jose Ortega y Gasset, *The Dehumanization of Art and Notes on the Novel*, trans. Helene Weyl (Princeton: Princeton University Press, 1948), p. 35.

[26] Artaud, p. 79.

ity. But I would like to suggest that these directions are to a certain extent metaphors for the modes of experience that have been indicated as their goal by theories of total theatre. That is, participation and environment as aspects of total theatre would also be metaphors for "hieroglyphic" modes of experience and perception.

This situation is best analyzed in terms of Marshall McLuhan's *Understanding Media,* a metahistory of man's communication systems, in which the author in fact looks at our present culture as if it were, or was intended to be, total theatre. Though he refers to no art more recent than Futurism, it is apparent that developments of the past several years substantiate his vision of a "retribalization" in a culture which emphasizes participation, tactility, and sculptural values.

Of primary interest here is the degree to which participation is more actually participation in media and how this relates to an understanding of the term "hieroglyphic."

McLuhan analyzes the amount and type of participation provided by various media. This is communicated, in each case, by means of a limited portion of the spectrum of the senses. What is lacking is an accurate interchange of information between the senses, and hence a satisfactory level of total sensory experience. His primary target for criticism is the use of print and the phonetic alphabet itself, which he feels have excluded us from more rewarding modes of knowing.

McLuhan's intention is precisely that of the theatre of Wagner, the Symbolists or Artaud, a return to archaic, more primitive modes in which sensory experience and abstract information are integrated on an "iconic" level, the level of the hieroglyph or ideogram, so that we may re-obtain the "worlds of meaning and perception" that have been sacrificed to phonetic modes.

The term "hieroglyphic" here indicates the point of intersection of more than one mode of knowing or of more than one medium of communication. This intersection, which "holds us on the frontiers between forms," is a synthesis, a "hybrid," "a moment of truth and revelation from which new form is born." [27]

[27] Marshall McLuhan, *Understanding Media: The Extensions of Man* (New York: McGraw-Hill Book Company, 1965), p. 55.

For Artaud, hieroglyphic expression was formed by "the gesture of a character to the evocation of a plant's movement across the scream of an instrument." [28]

Artaud was here describing Balinese dancers (see "On the Balinese Theatre"), and as might be expected, other forms of Asian dance and drama are rich in hieroglyphic expression. Section V, "The Oriental Stage: Hieroglyphic Form," will give some indication of this. A particularly striking example, however, is the *mie,* a pose used in climactic moments of the Kabuki drama. Significantly for a mode termed iconic or hieroglyphic, the *mie* pose appears to derive from the fierce and dramatic postures of Japanese religious sculptures. In the drama, the approach of a *mie* is usually signaled by an increase in tempo, by vocal effects or by the aural effects produced by wooden clappers, and there are sometimes calls of challenge or encouragement to the actor from the audience. The *mie* itself, of which there are many variations, is comprised of a highly coordinated series of gestures and movements, accompanied by the intense sounds of the percussive rhythms, which arrive at a climax in a forceful, often difficult or awesome, motionless pose. This integration of aural and visual effects in plastic form makes the *mie* an archetype of hieroglyphic expression.

Sergei Eisenstein, however, centered his attention upon other hieroglyphic aspects of the Kabuki drama and compared them in technique with the creation of a montage in cinematography. In "The Unexpected" (Section V), he observes that the Kabuki stage functions at times like a three dimensional montage, providing certain compartmentalized spatial effects that are essentially plastic hieroglyphs formed into a meaningful sequence. In this technique, the meaning of the drama as it is carried by the music can then be passed over into gesture or into voice or can be created by more than one mode in unison or in counterpoint. "To possess this method," Eisenstein emphasizes, "one must develop in oneself a new *sense: the capacity of reducing visual and aural perceptions to a 'common denominator.'* "

Producing this new sense corresponds to the goal of McLuhan's hybridization. It is also the goal of total theatre. This is

[28] Artaud, p. 55.

the reason for the criticism and rejection of the realistic stage by proponents of total theatre. As Artaud noted, the stage has come to be an inferior art form because "the public is no longer shown anything but the mirror of itself." [29] This view is identical with that image of man which McLuhan associates with the whole phonetic syndrome: Narcissus contemplating himself in the mirror of his conventions. The effect of hieroglyphic expression, of the intersection of media or of modes of knowing, is to "snap us out of this Narcissus-narcosis." It is for this reason, and toward this result, that total theatre can be considered a theatre of effects. Hieroglyphic expression, in a wide range of modes, may be considered its principal instrument.

In organizing this study, I have grouped the selections into six sections dealing with different aspects of the subject of total theatre. After the first, which considers the theories of Wagner and Appia in more detail, the sections have been provided with further introductory material. The second and third sections form an integral grouping based on the concept of the "super-puppet" or "abstract man" as this relates to the abstraction of movement, scenic space, effect, and the other aspects of totality. It is in this abstract domain, rather than in realistic forms, that the intersection of the arts takes place to compose a total theatre. The information in the sections that follow contributes in various ways to broaden this understanding and to establish it in depth.

[29] *Ibid.*, p. 76.

PART I  The Foundations of
Total Theatre

RICHARD WAGNER

## Opera Affirms the Separation of the Arts *

As man by love sinks his whole nature in that of woman, in order to pass over through her into a third being, the child—and yet finds but himself again in all the loving trinity, though in this self a widened, filled, and finished whole: so may each of the individual arts find its own self again in the perfect, thoroughly liberated artwork—nay, look upon itself as broadened to this artwork—so soon as, on the path of genuine love and by sinking of itself within the kindred arts, it returns upon itself and finds the guerdon of its love in the perfect work of art to which it knows itself expanded. Only that art variety, however, which wills the common artwork, reaches therewith the highest fill of its own particular nature; whereas that art which merely wills *itself,* its own exclusive fill of self, stays empty and unfree—for all the luxury that it may heap upon its solitary semblance. But the *will* to form the common artwork arises in each branch of art by instinct and unconsciously, so soon as e'er it touches on its own confines and *gives* itself to the answering art, not merely strives to take from it. It stays *throughout itself* only when it *thoroughly gives itself away:* whereas it must fall to its very opposite, if it at last must feed only upon the other: "Whose bread I eat, his song I'll sing." But when it gives itself *entirely* to the second, and stays *entirely* enwrapped therein, it then may pass from that *entirely* into the third; and thus become once more *entirely itself,* in highest fullness, in the associate artwork.

Of all these arts not one so sorely needed an espousal with another, as that of *Tone;* for her peculiar character is that of a fluid nature element poured out betwixt the more defined and individualized substances of the two other arts. Only through the rhythm of dance, or as bearer of the word, could she brace her

* From *Wagner On Music and Drama: A Compendium of Richard Wagner's Prose Works.* Selected and arranged, and with an introduction, by Albert Goldman and Evert Sprinchorn. Trans. H. Ashton Ellis. (New York: E. P. Dutton & Co., Inc., 1964), pp. 121–124, 188–191.

deliquescent being to definite and characteristic corporeality. But neither of the other arts could bring herself to plunge, in love without reserve, into the element of Tone: each drew from it so many bucketsful as seemed expedient for her own precise and egoistic aims; each took from Tone, but gave not in return; so that poor Tone, who of her life-need stretched out her hands in all directions, was forced at last herself to *take* for very means of maintenance. Thus she engulfed the word at first, to make of it what suited best her pleasure: but while she disposed of this word as her willful feeling listed, in Catholic music, she lost its bony framework —so to say—of which, in her desire to become a human being, she stood in need to bear the liquid volume of her blood, and round which she might have crystallized a sinewy flesh. A new and energetic handling of the word, in order to gain shape therefrom, was shown by Protestant church music; which, in the "Passion music," pressed on toward an ecclesiastical drama, wherein the word was no longer a mere shifting vehicle for the expression of feeling, but girt itself to thoughts depicting action. In this church drama, Music, while still retaining her predominance and building everything else into her own pedestal, almost compelled Poetry to behave in earnest and like a man toward her. But coward Poetry appeared to dread this challenge; she deemed it as well to cast a few neglected morsels to swell the meal of this mightily waxing monster, Music, and thus to pacify it; only, however, to regain the liberty of staying undisturbed within her own peculiar province, the egoistic sphere of literature. It is to this selfish, cowardly bearing of Poetry toward Tone that we stand indebted for that unnatural abortion the oratorio, which finally transplanted itself from the church into the concert hall. The oratorio would give itself the airs of drama; but only precisely in so far as it might still preserve to Music the unquestioned right of being the chief concern, the only leader of the drama's "tone."

Where Poetry fain would reign in solitude, as in the spoken play, she took Music into her menial service, for her own convenience; as, for instance, for the entertainment of the audience between the acts, or even for the enhancement of the effect of certain dumb transactions, such as the irruption of a cautious burglar, and matters of that sort! Dance did the selfsame thing,

when she leaped proudly onto saddle, and graciously conde-
scended to allow Music to hold the stirrup. Exactly so did Tone
behave to Poetry in the oratorio: she merely let her pile the heap
of stones, from which she might erect her building as she fancied.

But Music at last capped all this ever-swelling arrogance by
her shameless insolence in the opera. Here she claimed tribute of
the art of Poetry down to its utmost farthing: it was no longer
merely to make her verses, no longer merely to suggest dramatic
characters and sequences, as in the oratorio, in order to give her
a handle for her own distension—but it was to lay down its
whole being and all its powers at her feet, to offer up complete
dramatic characters and complex situations, in short, the entire
ingredients of drama; in order that she might take this gift of
homage and make of it whatever her fancy listed.

The Opera, as the seeming point of reunion of all the three
related arts, has become the meeting place of these sisters' most
self-seeking efforts. Undoubtedly Tone claims for herself the supreme right of legislation therein; nay, it is solely to her struggle
—though led by egoism—toward the genuine artwork of the
drama that we owe the opera at all. But in degree as Poetry and
Dance were bid to be her simple slaves, there rose amid *their*
egoistic ranks a growing spirit of rebellion against their domi-
neering sister. The arts of Dance and Poetry had taken a personal lease of drama *in their own way:* the spectacular play and
the pantomimic ballet were the two territories between which
Opera now deployed her troops, taking from each whatever she
deemed indispensable for the self-glorification of music. Play
and Ballet, however, were well aware of her aggressive self-
sufficiency: they only lent themselves to their sister against their
will, and in any case with the mental reservation that on the first
favorable opportunity they each would clear themselves an exclusive field. So Poetry leaves behind her feeling and her pathos,
the only fitting wear for Opera, and throws her net of modern
intrigue around her sister Music; who, without being able to get a
proper hold of it, must willy-nilly twist and turn the empty cob-
web, which none but the nimble play-seamstress herself can plait
into a tissue: and there she chirps and twitters, as in the French
confectionary operas, until at last her peevish breath gives out,
and sister Prose steps in to fill the stage. Dance, on the other

hand, has only to espy some breach in the breath-taking of the
tyrannizing songstress, some chilling of the lava stream of musical emotion—and in an instant she flings her legs astride the
boards; trounces sister Music off the scene, down to the solitary
confinement of the orchestra; and spins and whirls and runs
around, until the public can no longer see the wood for wealth of
leaves, that is, the opera for the crowd of legs.

Thus opera becomes the mutual compact of the egoism of the
three related arts.

RICHARD WAGNER

## Essence of Drama Is Knowing Through Feeling

Only in the most perfect artwork therefore, in *the drama,* can the
insight of the experienced one impart itself with full success; and
for the very reason that, through employment of every artistic
expressional faculty of man, the poet's aim is in drama the most
completely carried from the understanding to the feeling—to
wit, is artistically imparted to the feeling's most directly recep-
tive organs, the senses. The drama, as the most perfect artwork,
differs from all other forms of poetry in just this—that in it the
aim is lifted into utmost imperceptibility by its *entire realization.*
In drama, wherever the aim, that is, the intellectual will, stays
still observable, there the impression is also a chilling one; for
where we see the poet still *will*-ing, we feel that as yet he *can* not.
The poet's can-ning, however, is the complete ascension of the
aim into the artwork, the *emotionalizing of the intellect.* His aim
he can reach only by physically presenting to our eyes the things
of life in their fullest spontaneity; and thus, by vindicating life
itself out of the mouth of its own necessity; for the feeling, to
which he addresses himself, can understand this necessity alone.

In presence of the dramatic artwork, nothing should remain

for the combining intellect to search for. Everything in it must come to an issue sufficient to set our feeling at rest thereon; for in the setting at rest of this feeling resides the repose itself, which brings us an instinctive understanding of life. In the drama we must become *knowers* through *the feeling*. The understanding tells us, *"So is it,"* only when the feeling has told us, *"So must it be."* Only through *itself,* however, does this feeling become intelligible to itself: it understands no language other than its own. Things which can be explained to us only by the infinite accommodations of the understanding embarrass and confound the feeling. In drama, therefore, an action can be explained only when it is completely vindicated by the feeling; and it thus is the dramatic poet's task, not to invent actions, but to make an action so intelligible through its emotional necessity that we may altogether dispense with the intellect's assistance in its vindication. The poet therefore has to make his main scope the *choice of the action*—which he must so choose that, alike in its character as in its compass, it makes possible to him its entire vindication from out the feeling; for in this vindication alone, resides the reaching of his aim.

An action which can be explained only on grounds of historic relations, unbased upon the present; an action which can be vindicated only from the standpoint of the state, or understood alone by taking count of religious dogmas stamped upon it from without—not sprung from common views within—such an action, as we have seen, is representable only to the understanding, not to the feeling. At its most successful, this was to be effected through narration and description, through appeal to the intellect's imaginative force; not through direct presentment to the feeling and its definitely seizing organs, the senses: for we saw that those senses were positively unable to take in the full extent of such an action, that in it there lay a mass of relations beyond all possibility of bringing to physical view and bound to be relegated, for their comprehension, to the combining organ of thought. In a politicohistorical drama, therefore, it became the poet's business eventually to give out his aim quite nakedly—as such: the whole drama stayed unintelligible and unimpressive, if this aim, in the form of a human "moral," did not at last quite visibly emerge from amid the desert waste of pragmatic motives

employed for sheer description's sake. In the course of such a piece, one asked oneself instinctively: "What is the poet trying to tell us?"

Now, an action which is to justify itself before and through the feeling, busies itself with no *moral;* its whole moral consists precisely in its justification by the instinctive human feeling. It is a goal to itself, insofar as it has to be vindicated only and precisely by the feeling out of which it springs. Wherefore this action can be such a one only as proceeds from relations the truest, that is, the most seizable by the feeling, the nighest to human emotions, and thus the simplest—from relations such as can spring only from a human society intrinsically at one with itself, uninfluenced by inessential notions and nonpresent grounds of right: a society belonging to itself alone, and not to any past.

However, no action of life stands solitary and apart: it has always some sort of correlation with the actions of other men; through which it is conditioned alike as by the individual feelings of its transactor himself. The weakest correlation is that of mere petty, insignificant actions; which require for their explanation less the strength of a necessary feeling than the waywardness of whim. But the greater and more decisive an action is, and the more it can be explained only from the strength of a necessary *feeling:* in so much the more definite and wider a connection does it also stand with the actions of others. A great action, one which the most demonstratively and exhaustively displays the nature of man along any one particular line, issues only from the shock of manifold and mighty opposites. But for us to be able rightly to judge these opposites themselves, and to fathom their actions by the individual feelings of the transactors, a great action must be represented in a wide circle of relations; for only in such a circle is it to be understood. The poet's chief and especial task will thus consist in this: that at the very outset he shall fix his eye on such a circle, shall completely gauge its compass, shall scrutinize each detail of the relations contained therein, with heed both to its own measure and to its bearing on the main action; this done, that he then shall make the measure of his understanding of these things the measure of their understandableness as a work of art, by drawing in this ample circle toward its central point, and thus condensing it into the periphery which gives an under-

standing of the central hero. This *condensation* is the work proper to the poetizing intellect; and this intellect is the center and the summit of the whole man, who from thence divides himself into the receiver and the imparter.

As an object is seized in the first place by the outward-turned instinctive feeling, and next is brought to the imagination, as the earliest function of the brain: so the understanding, which is nothing else but the imaginative force as regulated by the actual measure of the object, has to advance in turn through the imagination to the instinctive feeling—in order to impart what it now has recognized. In the understanding objects mirror themselves as what they actually are; but this mirrored actuality is, after all, a mere thing of thought: to impart this *thought-out* actuality, the understanding must display it to the feeling in an image akin to what the feeling had originally brought to *it;* and this image is the work of fantasy. Only through the fantasy can the understanding have commerce with the feeling. The understanding can grasp the full actuality of an object only when it breaks the image in which the object is brought it by the fantasy, and parcels it into its singlest parts; when it fain would bring these parts before itself again in combination, it has at once to cast for itself an image, which no longer answers strictly to the actuality of the thing, but merely in the measure wherein man has power to recognize it. Thus even the simplest action confounds and bewilders the understanding, which would fain regard it through the anatomical microscope, by the immensity of its ramifications: would it comprehend that action, it can do so only by discarding the microscope and fetching forth the image which alone its human eye can grasp; and this comprehension is ultimately enabled by the instinctive feeling—as vindicated by the understanding. This image of the phenomena, in which alone the feeling can comprehend them, and which the understanding, to make itself intelligible to the feeling, must model on that image which the latter originally brought it through the fantasy—this image, for the aim of the poet, who must likewise take the phenomena of life and compress them from their viewless many-memberedness into a compact, easily surveyable shape—this image is nothing else but *the wonder.*

GEORGE R. KERNODLE

## Wagner, Appia, and the Idea of Musical Design *

I

When Victor Hugo's *Burgraves* failed in 1843, it seemed the end of Romanticism in the theatre. Hugo turned away from the stage, and Paris gave its soul to Rachel and the classical drama. The "grand opera" of Rossini, Bellini, and Donizetti was all over, and Meyerbeer had done his most important composing. Painters and writers were groping toward realism, and even the melodrama was turning from the long ago and far away to explore the slums and factories of the contemporary city.

Yet Romanticism was far from dead. In fact, it was about to enter a new phase, a second life that would carry it on into the newer developments of the twentieth century. In 1842 Richard Wagner left Paris in disgust and returned to his beloved Germany. At the same time, he turned his back on the historical drama—the stock-in-trade of both the Romantic spoken drama and the Grand Opera—and turned toward myth and legend; toward the deeper, more psychological, more abstract; toward a new Romanticism. He had finished with history in *Rienzi*. He was ready for the myth world of *Lohengrin*. In his search for the myth or the soul of man's human experience, Wagner discovered a new expressive basis for music, and at the same time, in his search for a sensuous, theatrical expression of the abstract musical soul, he discovered a new basis for theatre. He thought he was creating a new synthesis, in which all the arts lost their unhappy individual identity and found a glorious salvation in the new society, the composite work of art, *das Gesamtkunstwerk*.

* Reprinted from the *Educational Theatre Journal*, VI:3 (October, 1954).

We might describe his achievement as the discovery of the more abstract, the more primitive, the more psychological patterns of feeling that underlie equally music and theatre. That concept of a soul, of an inner or deeper being, of a basic idea that underlies and pervades the entire production, is the central concept of all our twentieth-century theory—of the spoken drama as well as of the theatre of music and dance.

The turn from history to myth is a romantic turn from the particular fact in order to give fresh expression to the dream world of the imagination. Lohengrin is a combination in supernatural form of the two most striking figures that dominated the Romantic stage. On the one hand, he performs the function of Karl Moor of Schiller's *The Robbers:* he breaks into the gloomy Gothic castle to rescue the innocent heroine from the tyrant. On the other hand, he is similar to the Stranger of Kotzebue's extremely popular drama known in English by that name: he has renounced his claims on humanity and even his name in order to serve those in need. But Wagner has moved his story far into the world of dreams. The nameless rescuing knight comes to Elsa out of the mysterious supernatural nowhere, whither he returns at the end. He is one of the knights of the Holy Grail come to serve suffering humanity, but so far above actual human beings that Elsa fails him and, when he leaves, dies. From the gradually revealed, shimmering first chords of the overture, the music creates a dream world of spiritual dedication, of the Grail, and expresses the longing and anguish of the inner experience of humankind.

The *Ring* develops in mythical and symbolic form the whole complex of Romantic thought. It is a full and consistent mythology of maladjustment. The dilemma of the unhappy idealist is projected into the realm of the ancient Germanic gods, and beyond them into the primitive realm of giants, dwarfs, Valkyries, and Rhinemaidens, on into the Urwelt of water, light, slime, gold, and the basic emotions of greed, longing, vengeance, dedication, and destruction. It is no wonder G. B. Shaw saw it as an allegory of the evolutionary emergence of the creative will and the order of socialism out of half-conscious depths of nature. But Shaw could accept only the "upward" part of the cycle—the Romantic mythology of maladjustment included an espousal of

betrayal and destruction that seemed to make no sense to later "progressive" thinkers.

Siegfried embodied all the revolutionary hopes of the Romantic age, and Wagner throughout the 1840's and 1850's thought and wrote much about the great revolution to come. But after the Terror of the French Revolution, the Romantics chose to develop a far more complex, even mystic, concept of revolution. They just as violently hated conventional social and artistic forms as the Parisians of 1789. But they no longer hoped for a solid band of citizens joyously marching into a new world. They saw loneliness, anguish, betrayal, and defeat for the heroic individual who must strive for the future of the world. In some mystic way his suffering as well as his heroism would gain the redemption and salvation of Man. Even before the abortive outbreak of 1848 and 1849, Wagner was all too familiar with frustration and hatred so bitter that it could envisage the cruel betrayals of the *Götterdämmerung* and the complete destruction of Valhalla and the return to the formless chaos of the waters of the Rhine. When Wagner read Schopenhauer he found already formed that curiously obsessive combination of the exaltation of the will and the pessimistic yearning for destruction. Siegfried, the fearless Romantic hero, who bore the special gifts of the gods, who despised and destroyed the ugly older generation that nurtured him, who reforged a magnificent new weapon for killing off old evils, who took possession of the gold of this world, who walked unscathed through old barriers, who woke the sleeping princess of beauty and creative fulfillment—that Siegfried could also blindly betray his love and in bitter vengeance be killed. For the counterpart of the Romantic longing for redemption and fulfillment is a longing for destruction and death, for carrying the strife and anguish to its last utter moment and achieving peace in the only possible way, by destruction of both the evil and oneself. Only in death could Siegfried find his love again.

Just as the mythological framework carries the drama's implications far beyond individual heroes into the web of intrigue of gods and giants and dwarfs and into the primitive forces of will and desire and matter, so Wagner's music went far beyond particular song to build up a complex web of sounds, of motifs, of

harmonies and intertwining melodies, in which the individual voices are incidental strands. One Wagnerian singer asked the conductor to "give me a sea of sound into which I can plunge." In musical terms, Wagner, following Weber, shifted the center from the singer to the orchestra. The man who declared that opera had been wrong to make music the end and drama the means greatly subordinated the singer and greatly enlarged the function of the orchestra. And some critics gleefully point out that Wagner has had his greatest life in the twentieth century in orchestral concerts with no voices at all.

But the explanation lies not in the musical terms. The center of gravity was really not in the orchestra but in the soul, the abstract form of the drama that underlies both orchestra and voices.

If neither music nor the word was to dominate but all to be controlled by the basic pattern underlying the whole drama, then of course both the recitative and the separate arias must go. Thus in sheer outline of form, Wagner broke up small patterns, each complete in itself, in order to create the freer, larger patterns of a whole scene or a whole act. This concept of the importance of basic musical patterns in the play seems to me of crucial importance for the modern theatre. Wagner distilled it from the new phase of Romanticism that for him started in the 1840's. The search for deeper feeling and the underlying myth led to the concept of a deeper musical pattern underlying the entire play.

II

A half-century passed. The world of the 1890's, when Appia made his appearance, was a very different world from that of the 1840's. Romanticism had moved into Impressionism. The artistic center of gravity had moved from Germany to France. Where the Romantics found their deepest expression in the broad, violent patterns of music, the Impressionists found theirs in the subtle, controlled interplay of light and color in painting. Now the visual elements were given the same profound transformation that the musical drama had undergone, though the feeling was different. Even in music, the Frenchman, Debussy, gained a wide and complex harmony, and gladly paid for that new musical mood by reducing the thunderous intensity of the Germanic

Wagner. In the theatre the idea of the inner soul of the drama, expressed in music by Wagner, had to be explored in the visual realm by the French-Swiss Adolphe Appia. Like Impressionist painting, the new theatre was more interested in a harmonious relationship between foreground and background and light than in the older problems of structure.

Appia never saw Wagner and never worked at Bayreuth. But he felt that the new tone-drama needed a new method of production. He saw his work as completing the work of Wagner. Wagner had accepted the completely inadequate stage mounting of his day, without realizing it was a sharp contradiction to what he wanted to express. He had transformed the actor, the word, the music into flexible media that moved, surged, and changed intensity and tone as expressions of the inner soul of the drama, but the visual elements—the painted cloths and the flat light— remained static and inexpressive impediments to the action. Wagner had developed the descriptive mood elements in the orchestra, but had not realized how bad the settings and lighting were. If the Germans had shown Latin people undreamed-of depths of feeling, it was time for the Latin people to contribute their sense of form, even if it meant reducing the intensity of the music.

Like Gordon Craig, Appia saw that the complete composite artwork would require one creative mind, one lordly dictator as designer-director to bring all the elements of the stage into harmony. He was almost as harsh as Craig in demanding that the actor be subordinated to the whole play, and that he never be allowed to make an independent display. In the music drama, even more than in the spoken drama, the performing actor should be subordinated. Or better to say he would be freed from some of the surface duty of indicating passing emotions—a function taken over by the music; freed to express the larger patterns of the basic idea.

Appia called for acting completely based on dance, not the dance at the extreme of pantomime with realistic representation of the detail of life, but dance that is impersonal, stripped of the accidental and incidental, dance that expresses the deep and nearly musical patterns of feeling. Just as Wagner abhorred the old-fashioned opera aria, with its temptation to display and its

independent forms and patterns that were not integral to the drama, so Appia would have despised much of our theatrical dancing that, sometimes in modern dance and very frequently in ballet, goes its own gaudy way. Appia felt that music and dance should meet in the word-tone drama, approaching from opposite directions. Music starts free from embodiment, expressing the inner life. But as that inner life yearns for definite expression, then music approaches the drama. Dance, starting from the body, seeks a deep and musical expression, and reaches the same meeting place in the musical drama.

Appia's great contribution is the discovery that the visual elements of the play can be made as expressive of the inner idea of the drama as the music of Wagner. Just as Wagner had discarded the separate recitatives and arias that broke up the opera into tiny segments, and had subordinated actors, voices, and melodies to the larger patterns of the drama, so Appia discarded the painted perspective tableaux, the flats and drops that could not move and change intensity with the music, and developed a plastic setting and a flexible lighting system that would make the moving actor as expressive to the eye as Wagner had made him expressive to the ear. Like the Romantics, Appia discovered his new intensity by stripping away the surface details and getting at the deeper patterns of mood and feeling. Like the Impressionist painters, he discovered that light, ever changing with time of day and with the emotional mood, is the dissolving medium—the one radiant, circumambient spirit that can make the cold dead matter of the nineteenth-century physicists sparkle with life, and flow and change with all the subtle moods of the poetic imagination and the surging tides of the soul.

Like Wagner, Appia realized that behind the surface, behind the particular words, moves the basic pattern—the inner life, the soul of the drama. Everything heard or seen must express that soul, must reinforce and intensify its particular texture and quality, and must change, surge, intensify, and subside with that soul. Wagner called it the drama, and insisted that the singer, the melody, the orchestra must never be independent but must exist only to express that drama. Appia called it the music, and insisted that the floor plan, the platforms, the vertical flats, cloths,

and screens, the costumes, and the actors must never be independent but must exist only to express that music.

The new element for Wagner was the colorful orchestra, which he used with unprecedented skill to blend together his other elements. The new element for Appia was light—flexible, controlled light. He saw both the plastic possibilities of directional light and the temporal possibilities of changing intensity. The enemy of both was the painted wings and drops, which called for flat, unchanging light. With plastic light he wanted three-dimensional structures that would take form by casting shadows and would change form and mood and even color as he caught them up with light from different directions and with light of changing intensity and changing color. At those moments when the drama shifted to the inner life of a character, the light could even isolate the actor and let the background fade out of attention. Platforms and steps would provide additional opportunities for expressive movement of the actor. The background could have a simple form that might sometimes include a minimum of details to signify a particular place, but its form should primarily express the underlying mood of the play. The simpler it was and the less specific detail it had, the more it could be changed by light for the changing mood and intensity of the music or the soul of the drama. At last all of the elements of the theatre could be brought under the control of the musical design of the drama. Of course taste in music had changed. Appia, like the other Impressionists of his day, wanted a musical pattern less violent, less assertive, than Wagner's, to take its place in the new *Gesamtkunstwerk* of Impressionism.

We could go further and point out how Antoine, Stanislavsky, Reinhardt, and the other new craftsmen of the theatre were interested in this Impressionist idea of blending setting and actors and sounds and words.[1] They too saw the theatre as having an inner soul, a musical design that lies behind particular words or particular actors. That musical design may be expressed at par-

---

[1] Walther R. Volbach has noted the tendency in several directors of music drama in his article, "The Inception of Modern Opera Production," *Bulletin of the National Theatre Conference,* XI, No. 2 (August, 1949), and in his book *Problems of Opera Production* (Fort Worth, 1953).

ticular moments by words and by actors; but it is also expressed by the texture of all the properties and details of the setting, and by the rhythm and mood of incidental sounds and movements, and by the changing shape, color, and intensity of the light. All have their place in the complex ensemble.

Wagner and Appia worked out their principles for musical drama, and both supposed that those principles would not apply to the spoken drama. But with a little enlargement and modification they have become the basis of production in both modern drama and modern opera. In general, we have had to modify our order and our wording of Aristotle's list of the six elements of drama. In his hierarchy from plot to spectacle, it will be remembered, Aristotle put music next to the last. In a narrow sense the spoken drama of the early twentieth century had no music at all. But in the wider sense of mood and rhythm it was as indebted to musical design as Wagnerian drama was. In fact, many producers and playgoers put mood at the very top, above plot—and above the language of the dialogue, which they considered only one of the subordinate instruments in support of the musical mood.

And it was Appia who showed the age of Impressionism how to use plastic forms and moving light to create the changing mood and subtle rhythms of a play. In some ways he was ahead of the Impressionists and their contemporaries. His settings anticipated Cubism and abstraction in art, and he was more interested in opera and Greek tragedy and poetic drama than in the local color of the realistic stage or of the landscapes painted by the Impressionists. But he did share with the painters of his day a passionate interest in light, and he gave it the central place in the theatre that it still holds. Ever since Appia it is light that on the visual side expresses the soul—the musical design—of a play.

III

There have been many attacks on the idea of a composite musical drama. Some people in every age have thought it an impossible hybrid form. Wagner once thought that by his achievement he had ended all the individual arts. But as Paul Lang has remarked, "Pure drama and pure music stand unimpaired: Ibsen and Brahms could rise in the very hour of Wagner's triumph."

Nietzsche was the first disciple to turn against Wagner, and Jacques Barzun has written the most brilliant attack both on Wagner's mythology and on his mechanical ideal of music drama (in *Darwin, Marx, Wagner,* 1941). Enid Welsford (in her book on *The Court Masque*) and other writers have pointed out the difficulty of combining the arts unless each art is diluted to a very low intensity.

Two great dramatists of the twentieth century have offered alternatives to the Wagnerian theatre—Paul Claudel and Charlie Chaplin. Claudel objected strongly to the Wagnerian orchestra which engulfed the singer in a vast sonorous mist and never permitted him to stand out separately.[2] He preferred the way of the Japanese Kabuki, where the music does not underscore the words but often precedes and provokes them, following a way parallel or even counter to the words and creating an independent surrounding atmosphere that makes its own comment on the action. Two works of Claudel have recently made a strong impression on Americans—his *Christopher Columbus,* newly set to music by Milhaud for Jean-Louis Barrault, and *Jeanne d'Arc at the Stake,* set by Honneger. Against a small orchestra or a chorus Claudel sets the actor to speak out independently in a musical speech that is sometimes song, sometimes a dramatic recitative. The effect resembles oratorio more than realistic drama, but it is powerfully dramatic.

Background music for the movies has more often followed the Wagnerian concept, organizing the separate realistic shots into long sequences and doing far more than the actors to create atmosphere and build emotional climaxes. But Charlie Chaplin broke completely with the Wagner tradition and returned to the pantomime method of nineteenth-century melodrama and the Chinese classic stage. He again made the actor the center and underscored his every movement with sounds that not only reinforced the rhythm but made delightful melodies that correspond exactly to the actor's pattern.

The most recent attack on the Wagner-Appia heritage is by Eric Bentley in his book *In Search of Theater.* He sees the

[2] Claudel's lecture "Le Drame et la Musique" was delivered at Yale in 1930 and published as a preface to *Le Livre de Christophe Colomb* (Paris, 1935).

strongest contrast between the honest, spare realism of the Ibsen tradition and the lush overdecorated tradition he calls the theatre of magic, which he blames on Wagner and Appia. He sees that theatre of magic as a cult of lurid prettiness, of cute symbolism, of semidarkness, of mysticism, illusion, and fantasy. This is a serious attack, and it cannot be denied that the production of both spoken drama and musical drama has sinned seriously in that direction. But what can be denied is that that is the fault of Wagner and Appia. Appia especially called for an extremely spare stage, and denounced the striving for pictorial illusion. He never wanted his platforms, screens, and lighting to be special and individual interests in themselves. Their sole purpose was to free the actor and make clear the meaning of the action. If his famous synopsis for lighting *Tristan and Isolde* calls for leaving much of the stage in darkness, he constantly wants the actors to be seen. And most of his discussion of lighting assumes that both general and specific lighting will be used.

Whatever the failure of Wagner and the stupid shortcomings of the Wagner worshipers, our theatre in the middle of the twentieth century is again lured by the idea of lyric, dancing theatre. Musical comedies have not quite driven the spoken drama off Broadway, but they carry far more of the serious interest of the audience than anyone would ever have predicted a quarter century ago. Professional opera and ballet companies have mainly exploited the romantic patterns of the nineteenth century and have scarcely touched the feelings and emotions of our day. It is in our schools and colleges that the greatest interest is stirring. Opera has become a major activity, and there the modern operas, at least the shorter ones, get a far better chance than they do in New York. Music and theatre departments are learning much from each other. The new poetic drama *Giant from the South,* which we put on at Arkansas last year, made us realize more than ever before that incidental music, song, and dance are basic ingredients of a new kind of lyric theatre we want to see more of.

While both modern dance and the ballet have approached the theatre and the theatre has made considerable use of dance, the whole problem of integrating dance and drama sends us back to the ideas of Wagner and Appia on unity. Like singing, the dance is a whole art itself, and quite worthy of performance indepen-

dent of drama. But the striking achievement of Agnes de Mille, in creating a ballet within a drama, sends us dreaming again of the *Gesamtkunstwerk* and asking again the questions Wagner raised. One might devise an opera-within-a-play by bringing in a different set of performers to sing a symbolic summary or epitome of the play. Strauss and Hoffmansthal tried something of the kind in the *Ariadne auf Naxos* inserted in the *Bourgeois Gentilhomme*. But no one would consider it a complete solution of the problem. We may go on for years thus inserting poetic passages, songs, and dances in our plays, but all our present-day training implies the hope for a new *Gesamtkunstwerk*. Shakespeare showed us long ago that poetry could be the natural language of the drama; Wagner showed one way to use song; Appia made the setting and lighting responsive to the musical soul of the play. It remains to bring dance within the fold to complete our new idea of musical design. And Appia has indicated the kind of simple, free, intensified movement that would best serve a modern lyric stage.

Of course not every production needs to have an equal amount of every appeal. Appia neglected color and kept his designs to a far narrower range of straight lines and geometrical forms than most of us would like. Recent reports from Bayreuth indicate that the grandsons of Wagner have gone to even greater extremes of austerity for their revival of the *Ring,* with no setting, few levels, and only the most restrained simple movements.

But whatever the choice of media, we still make use —in the theatre, in the movies, or in the opera—of a central Wagner-Appia concept, that the inner being of the play has a continuity, a musical design of its own, and that each actor, each word, each violin player, each incidental sound, each color, each tiny property, is but one instrument in the complex score of the whole.

CLARK M. ROGERS

## Appia's Theory of Acting: Eurhythmics for the Stage *

While much learned ink has been spilled to explain the revolution in scene design and lighting pioneered by Adolphe Appia during the late nineteenth century, comparatively little has been written regarding the actor's place in his new theatre. Actors were naturally concerned and often admittedly puzzled over the trend away from realism. One of them wrote that "since it is upon the shoulders of the actor that the final burden has to be carried, I think it is now due to him to find out just what his position is, or is going to be." [1] Actually, Appia himself proposed specific changes in the actor's art, changes based on his view of the theatre as a synthesis of all the art forms in free association. He shared with Gordon Craig the opinion that, in order to achieve a harmonious whole in theatrical production, there had to be strict controls placed on the actor. While Appia hoped that the actor's body could become a depersonalized instrument, Craig wrote that he would replace the actor with a perfectly pliable *über-marionette,* a logical *reductio ad absurdum* of the new theory. "Do away with the actor," Craig promised, "and you do away with means by which a debased stage realism is produced and flourishes." [2]

When Appia and Craig met for the first time, at the International Theatre Exposition at Zurich in 1914, Craig understood that the theatre united them and that music separated them. Jean

* Reprinted from the *Educational Theatre Journal,* XIX:4 (December, 1967).

[1] Claude King, "The Place of the Actor in the New Movement," *Theatre Arts,* VI (July, 1922), p. 200.

[2] Edward Gordon Craig, *On the Art of the Theatre* (Boston, 1925), pp. 87, 81.

Mercier reported that since Craig spoke no French and Appia did not know English, the two men communicated by drawing pictures and designs on a restaurant table cloth during lunch.

Craig wrote his name on the table cloth and next to it that of Appia. He drew a complete circle around Appia on which he wrote the word "music," Admirable symbol of truth! These two pioneers of contemporary dramatic art rested their reforms on the same base—the actor. But Craig was free in reform; the reform of Appia was dominated by a major force—music.[3]

Profoundly influenced by the Wagnerian opera, Appia used music as the point of departure for his ideas relating to production. "Music," he wrote in the 1898 preface for *Music and the Art of the Theatre,* "has been the inspiration of this book." [4] His main goal was to restate the fundamental aesthetics of the theatre in such a way that the actor, playwright, director, and scene designer would be aided by the unifying power of music. Like Wagner, Appia viewed music as a direct expression of man's inner being, and he saw that it could be used as the major regulating device in the theatre. With regret Appia conceded that the spoken drama was probably permanent; however, he insisted that "the art of staging can be an art only if it derives from music." [5]

While he agreed with Wagner's concept of the supreme art as a synthesis of all the possibilities of art (*Gesamtkunstwerk*), Appia was critical of what he believed to be Wagner's essential weakness. That is, he believed that Wagner was wrong to rely on the popular stage conventions of the day in presenting his music dramas: "He did not conceive of a staging technique different from that of his contemporaries. . . ." [6] In order to avoid Wagner's failure, Appia proposed the development of a "word-tone drama" (*Wort-Tondrama*) in which the separate elements

[3] Jean Mercier, "Adolphe Appia, the Re-birth of Dramatic Art," *Theatre Arts,* XVI (August, 1932), p. 627.

[4] Adolphe Appia, *Music and the Art of the Theatre,* trans. Robert W. Corrigan and Mary Douglas Dirks (Coral Gables, Fla., 1962), p. 9.

[5] Adolphe Appia, "The Future of Production," trans. Ralph Roeder, *Theatre Arts,* XVI (August, 1932), p. 657.

[6] Adolphe Appia, *The Work of Living Art,* trans. H. D. Albright, and *Man is the Measure of all Things,* trans. Barnard Hewitt (Coral Gables, Fla., 1960), p. 85.

(music, language, actor, setting, and lighting) are synthesized through the mutual subordination of these elements. Such a harmonious union would, in Appia's view, be made possible through what he called a "hierarchy of expression." The music in word-tone drama would be used for a double purpose: (1) to illuminate the meaning of the drama (*le drame interieur*), and (2) to define the time of each action. Consequently, the author-composer sets a definite limit on the movements of the actors by composing specific music to be followed. All liberty is taken from the performer; music controls his every action, his every utterance. "If music did not so profoundly alter the natural time durations of life," noted Appia, "it could not force the actor to renounce his ordinary activity in order to become a means of expression." The Swiss aesthetician was convinced that the drama controlled by music could be "the supreme illusion, which rational analysis cannot enter. . . ." The transformation which deprived the actor of his personal, arbitrary expression was essential if he was to become a medium of true art.

What the actor loses in freedom will be gained by the stage designer; and the setting, in giving up all pretense at scenic illusion, becomes an atmosphere in which the actor can be totally expressive.[7]

As early as 1895 Appia had foreseen the need for some kind of "musical gymnastics" to give the actor training in time and proportions. He wrote that the success of the performer in his word-tone drama would require "an abnormal versatility and flexibility that is independent not only of the actor's individual temperament, but also of those proportions which he shares with every other human being." The actor, he believed, should be trained in gymnastics as well as voice and diction because such work would provide great "rhythmic suppleness" and would allow the actor to obey "complex rhythmic patterns" in following the directions of the poetic-musical text.[8] His ideas were partly influenced by the popular developers of aesthetic dance and modern ballet; at that time the Russian Ballet, Isadora Duncan, Ruth St. Denis,

[7] *Music and the Art of the Theatre*, pp. 27, 13–16, 36.
[8] *Ibid.*, pp. 29, 37.

and, later, Rudolf Laban and Mary Wigman were demonstrating the beauty of rhythmic movement. Appia himself explained in 1923 that under the influence of the physical culture movement, the dance gradually freed itself from labored and mechanical technique: "Dancing rose to the rank of a self-expressive art." [9]

The most significant influence on Appia's theory of acting, however, came not from the dance but from eurhythmics, a system of education in the arts based on rhythm, musical theory, and gymnastics. In 1906 Appia attended a demonstration of eurhythmics and was delighted to find that his theories of controlled management of the human body through music found explicit realization in the experimentation of his contemporary Emile Jaques-Dalcroze. As a professor of harmony at the Geneva Conservatory, musician and composer Dalcroze had criticized the conventional method of beginning musical instruction with an instrument and theoretical explanation. What was needed, insisted Dalcroze, was a study of music through physical participation so that the student's mind, ear, and body were simultaneously involved in the music. To that end, he began a series of experiments, eventually devising special gymnastics which, he claimed, enabled his students to transform music into bodily movement. The revolutionary ideas of this young instructor were not readily accepted by the authorities in Geneva. Moreover, the active nature of Dalcroze's class soon led to the students' practice of wearing skimpy costumes, without shoes and stockings. The more conservative members of the faculty objected to the radical nature of the training, while the Geneva Calvinist Society objected to the students' dress. Beryl DeZoete, a follower of Dalcroze, later reported that officials at the conservatory "would not stand for such pernicious nonsense; there was something immoral in the suggestion that bare feet and unhampered bodies could have anything to do with musical education." [10]

Opposition grew so strong that Dalcroze was dismissed from

[9] Adolphe Appia, "Living Art or Still Life?," trans. S. A. Rhodes, *The Theatre Annual,* II (1943), p. 40.
[10] Ethel Driver, *A Pathway to Dalcroze Eurhythmics,* introduction by Beryl DeZoete (London, 1951), p. 1.

the faculty in 1904. However, he lost no time in founding his own school with makeshift facilities elsewhere in Geneva.[11] Within a year he presented a demonstration of his work at the music festival in the Canton of Solothurn, Switzerland. At this convention his demonstration aroused interest not only among musicians but among educators in general. Journalists disagreed over the proper classification of the system: some thought it was more like dancing than musical training,[12] while others viewed it as really a system of gymnastics and not dancing at all.[13] Dalcroze himself maintained that neither of these categories described what his method really was. In a lecture from the stage of the Lyceum Theatre in London, he declared that he taught music, not dancing.[14] On another occasion he explained that eurhythmics differed fundamentally from dancing because it did not *interpret* music but *translated* music into exact space durations, so that the music and the bodily expression became one whole. Since pupils were taught to follow and analyze rhythms by using their bodies as instruments, eurhythmics was less like dancing than it was like playing the piano or any other musical instrument.[15] The basic time of the music was usually beaten by the arms, while the legs and body expressed time values or the duration of notes. Thus, one step, or spatial progression, was allowed for each note in the musical accompaniment, but at the same time the value of the note was analyzed and expressed by a variety of movements, such as knee bends and bodily gestures, without progression.[16]

Appia later recorded his recollection of the first eurhythmics demonstration he attended in Geneva:

The public was full of curiosity, but in no way suspected the range of what they [Dalcroze and his students] presented to it. The master

[11] Urana Clarke, "Dalcroze: Rhythm in a Chain Reaction," *Musical America*, LXX (November 15, 1950), p. 25.

[12] "Synthetic Art of the Super-Dance," *Current Opinion*, LV (July, 1913), p. 52.

[13] "To Make Our Lives Rhythmic," *Literary Digest*, XLVII (November 22, 1913), pp. 1006–1007.

[14] W. J. Turner, "Plastic Music," *The New Statesman*, XIV (January 24, 1920), p. 465.

[15] "Dalcroze Explains his Method," *Literary Digest*, LXXVIII (September 1, 1923), p. 31.

[16] Emile Jaques-Dalcroze, *The Eurhythmics of Jaques-Dalcroze* (London, 1917), pp. 44–53.

often had to leave the piano and come to the front of the podium to beseech the audience not to take that for the theatre . . . and to recall for them that it was a question of a new pedagogic attempt, of an attempted transfusion of musical rhythm into the organism. . . .[17]

The study of eurhythmics was, according to Dalcroze, as important for actors as it was for musicians. He did not conceive of separate forms of rhythm for music, movement, gesture, and speech. There was only one rhythm, and, while it was best developed through music, its "impression" on the body through musical sources would inevitably lead to "expression" in movement and speech.[18] Dalcroze eventually stated eight theoretical conclusions upon which he built his system:

1. Rhythm is movement.
2. Rhythm is essentially physical.
3. Every movement involves time and space.
4. Musical consciousness is the result of physical experience.
5. The perfecting of physical resources results in clarity of perception.
6. The perfecting of movements in time assures consciousness of musical rhythm.
7. The perfecting of movements in space assures consciousness of plastic rhythm.
8. The perfecting of movements in time and space can only be accomplished by exercises in rhythmic movement.[19]

Appia was so impressed with eurhythmics that he wrote a letter to Dalcroze, whom he had not yet met. He explained that Dalcroze's work as a teacher and his own work as a scenic artist were curiously based on the same idea: "the exteriorization of music." Praising the eurhythmist for effectively foreseeing future trends in the composition and performance of music, he confidently stated that the system would result in a true renaissance in all the arts. Its significance for actors was suggested in Appia's comment that ". . . the life of the body tends to anar-

[17] Adolphe Appia, "L'Origine et Les Débuts de la Gymnastique Rythmique," *Les Feuillets,* I (November, 1911), pp. 27–33.
[18] Emile Jaques-Dalcroze, *La Musique et Nous* (Geneva, 1945), p. 255.
[19] Emile Jaques-Dalcroze, *Rhythm, Music and Education* (New York, 1921), pp. 83–84.

chy, then to ugliness; and it is music which must free it by imposing its discipline." Dalcroze was delighted by the interest and understanding expressed by Appia and replied immediately, explaining that they shared a common goal: "To give back to the body its good harmony, to make music vibrate in it—as to make music an integral part of the organism. . . ." Dalcroze wanted "to play on this marvelous keyboard which is the muscular and nervous system in order to make plastic a thought measured in space as in time. . . ." Recalling the resistance that his idea had received over the years, Dalcroze thanked Appia for his encouraging letter and concluded with an invitation for the scene designer to dine with him at his home.[20]

From 1906 until Appia's death in 1928, the two men were in close communication. In fact, Appia was for ten years a member of the staff at Dalcroze's school of eurhythmics at Hellerau, Germany. Although his stuttering and shyness prevented him from lecturing regularly, Appia held informal sessions with students.[21] And in April, 1912, he read at Hellerau his essay entitled "Du Costume pour la Gymnastique rythmique."[22] It was at Dalcroze's school that Appia had his most significant opportunity to work on the practical details of staging music drama. Not only did he design sets for eurhythmic recitals and demonstrations but he also collaborated with Dalcroze in staging a number of pageants for patriotic festivals. "In this partnership," explains Walther Volbach, "Appia supplied the ideas while Dalcroze, the more practical man, executed them."[23] Frank E. Washburn Freund, in the English *Stage Year Book of 1914,* graphically describes and illustrates Dalcroze's theatre, which was actually the great hall of the school at Hellerau. Designed by Heinrich Tessenow, the hall combined the stage and the auditorium into one large unit. The stage itself "consisted merely of a platform divided into three parts and connected by flights of steps, which lent themselves splendidly to effective groupings and processions." Both the performer and the spectator were lighted by the

[20] Edmond Stadler, "Jaques-Dalcroze et Adolphe Appia," *Emile Jaques-Dalcroze* (Neuchatel, 1965), pp. 417–419.

[21] Walther R. Volbach, "A Profile of Adolphe Appia," *Educational Theatre Journal,* XV (March, 1963), p. 11.

[22] Stadler, p. 443.

[23] Volbach, pp. 13–14.

same lambent glow produced by hundreds of light bulbs behind translucent walls and so arranged that they could create various gradations of light.[24] The effect created was called by Alexander von Salzmann, who developed the system for Dalcroze, *"Tageslicht ohne Sonne."* [25]

That Dalcroze shared some of Appia's interest in scene design is evident in his numerous remarks regarding the expressive possibilities of stage lighting. He spoke of light as "the sister of music," explaining that effective combinations of sound and light could "provide actors with undreamt facilities of expression." [26] That he was fiercely loyal to Appia is also apparent. When Stanislavsky and Craig collaborated in the 1911 production of *Hamlet* at the Moscow Art Theatre, Dalcroze was in the audience. Fuming with rage he wrote to his friend about "the Englishman who claims to revolutionize theatrical decorative art. . . ." Craig had managed to create some beautiful settings, but, according to Dalcroze, they were all copied from Appia: "I have the impression that this man must have seen your designs but did not know how to use them." [27]

In 1914 a journalist wrote that Dalcroze and Appia "hope that the outcome of their endeavors will be a new style of acting." [28] Particularly successful productions staged by Dalcroze during his association with Appia were Gluck's *Orpheus and Eurydice* and Claudel's *Annunciation,* both performed as a part of the Hellerau festival of 1913. The settings, lighting, and performance of the actors were closely in line with Appia's ultimate theories. At the Milan International Theatre Exposition of 1923, Appia described the arrangement of his ideal theatre as being "the same as that of the Jaques-Dalcroze Institute." [29] It is no wonder that Edmund Stadler concluded that "the spiritual father of the theatre at Hellerau was Appia, although Tessenow had been signed for the architecture and Salzmann for lighting." [30]

---

[24] Frank E. Washburn Freund, "The Theatrical Year in Germany," *The Stage Year Book* (1914), p. 93.

[25] "Theatre Arts Bookshelf," *Theatre Arts,* VI (April, 1922), p. 175.

[26] *Rhythm, Music and Education,* pp. 227–228.

[27] Stadler, p. 441.

[28] Freud, p. 93.

[29] "Living Art or Still Life?," p. 43.

[30] Stadler, p. 438.

The chief characteristic of Appia's theory of acting was the importance he gave to technique. "Technique can not err," he once wrote, "its laws and their connections exceed our understanding; if we despise those laws, it is we who err." [31] He believed that actors should submit to a principle of order, because its dictates were greater than their own personal intuitions: "The human body, if it voluntarily accepts the modifications that music demands, assumes the rank of a means of expression. . . ." [32] The actor, he maintained, needed the kind of rhythmic training that would transfuse his body with the elements of music: "Everybody knows that Jaques-Dalcroze has discovered a way to do this," Appia once remarked. "His body rhythm proceeds from within to without. . . ." As a result of rhythmic training "our body becomes a marvelous instrument of infinite resources." [33] Through eurhythmics Appia saw clearly a new chance for the theatrical art: ". . . there I found the answer to my passionate desire for synthesis!" [34]

In 1923 Appia explained that the final evolution of his theory was toward an art which took the living and moving human body as its object as well as its instrument. He hoped to create an architectural style which used the living body of the actor as its sole point of departure: eurhythmics seemed to provide a technical means to reach this goal of "living art." "In our time," he wrote, "the Eurhythmics of Jaques-Dalcroze is the only discipline which takes this mysterious road. Its beauty is a result, never an end." The application of the principles of acting suggested by eurhythmics would result in a revolution in theatrical art:

The body, at the behest of music, commands and orders space. Little it cares for age-old conventions, for deep-rooted customs—all must be cut to its measure, all must adopt its pattern. Is not man the measure of all things? [35]

[31] "The Future of Production," p. 658.
[32] *The Work of Living Art*, p. 24.
[33] "Living Art or Still Life?," p. 44.
[34] *Music and the Art of the Theatre*, p. 4.
[35] *Man is the Measure of all Things*, pp. 128–130.

## PART II

**Abstract Man:**
The Essence of Total Theatre

Edward Gordon Craig's vision of a huge puppet, an "Über-marionette," that would replace man on the stage, provided an image that has haunted theatre to the present day. The popular stage, as we know, depends upon personality and upon personalization of situation. Thus the super-puppet was an image that struck directly at the "Narcissus-narcosis" which theatre, by and large, serves. And for this reason, the understanding that the super-puppet was a metaphor has been consciously disregarded and the concept generally rejected.

The image was a metaphor for ritual, iconic, hieratic theatre like the ancient Greek and for a theatre of more-than-human, transcendent precision and a pervasive, controlled aesthetic like that of the Orient. Its basis was the mask, which is a common feature of those theatres. Charles Lyons, writing on "Gordon Craig's Concept of the Actor," traces the development and variations in the metaphor. He shows how it led Craig to introduce a distinction between two types of theatre: the Durable Theatre, which was ego-less and controlled, and the Perishable Theatre,

which was improvisational and personalized. These are interesting and useful distinctions in tracing the development and nature of total theatre. Present theatrical tendencies toward totality, as indicated by the productions of O'Horgan and Schechner, for example, are strongly based on improvisational methods and represent a burgeoning of those values outlined by Craig in regard to the Perishable Theatre. However, it is a delineation of the history and techniques of the Durable Theatre which is of primary concern in these pages.

Craig's second great heresy is also pertinent to total theatre. As Lyons indicates, it was Craig's belief that the director, not the script as such, should determine the nature of the production as a work of art. This is considered here in Section IV, "Creative Staging: A Key to Total Theatre."

The point of intersection between the concept of the Übermarionette and the prerogative of the director to create a new *mise-en-scène* has already been indicated in Appia's work. As Clark M. Rogers has described, this considered not only the settings but also the use of dance-like movement as integrated components of a designed totality. This designed totality, as the apotheosis of the Durable Theatre, was developed further in the theories of Prampolini and Moholy-Nagy and in the related work considered in the following section, "Futurism and the Theatre of the Future." Other methods of introducing movement and effective stagings are presented in such selections as those on Meyerhold and Reinhardt.

The replacement of the lifelike actor by an aesthetic of abstraction seems, however, to have been a concept that Craig adapted from the thought of Maurice Maeterlinck, the leading Symbolist dramatist and Nobel prize winner. Maeterlinck reasoned that if the vision of drama was poetic, then the tangible, all-too-human presence of the actor on the stage immediately destroyed that vision. In his *Menus propos, Le Théâtre* of 1890, he wrote:

The stage is a place where masterpieces die: for the production of a masterpiece by means of accidental and human elements has something antinomic in itself. Every masterpiece is a symbol, and a symbol cannot bear the active presence of a man. There is continual discord

between the forces of a symbol and the forces of a man: the symbol of the poem is a center, the rays of which stretch into infinity; and these rays as long as they come from a masterpiece, have an importance that is limited only by the might of an eye following them. But an actor's eye oversteps the sphere of the symbol. In the passive subject of a poem (the spectator) there appears a phenomenon of polarization; he does not any more see the diverging rays, he sees only the converging ones; an accidental thing spoiled by the symbol, and the masterpiece in its essence was dead during the whole time of that presence. The Greeks felt that antinomy, and their masks, which seem incomprehensible to us, served to smooth down the presence of a man and to facilitate the symbol. . . .

The poem begins to retreat into shadow as the man comes forth. A poem wishes to rescue us from the domination of the senses and to give a preponderance to the past and future; man acts only on our senses and exists only as far as he is able to attenuate that preponderance of past and future by interesting us exclusively in the moment at which he speaks. If man enters on the stage with all his faculties and his whole freedom, if his voice, gestures, attitude are not veiled by a great number of synthetic conditions, if even for a moment the human being appears such as he is, there is not a poem in this world which could stand that event. In that moment, the spectacle of the poem is interrupted and we are present at some scene of outward life.[1]

Even this feeling was not new among literary theatre men. Charles Lamb in 1811, Hazlitt in 1817, and Dr. Maginn, author of *Shakespeare's Papers,* in 1860, had expressed much the same opinion for similar reasons, particularly in regard to the Bard. Productions of an earlier time apparently neither convinced nor overly conditioned the independent imagination, which perhaps looked at them as we do at old photographs.

Appropriately for a poet who sometimes wrote, as did García Lorca, for a puppet stage, Maeterlinck's "campaign against 'the presence of man on the stage' " (de Soissons) seems to have indicated the aesthetic advantages of this "dehumanized" figure. But in accord with the evocative, non-concrete and rarefied qualities of Symbolism it was also expressed in the understanding that the figure of man on the stage might come to be replaced "by a shad-

[1] S. C. de Soissons, "Maeterlinck as a Reformer of the Drama," *The Contemporary Review,* LXXXVI (November, 1904), pp. 699–700.

ow, a reflection, a projection of symbolic forms." We will have reason to recall this later in relation to projection techniques and the hopes for the theatre which Claudel expresses at the conclusion of his "Modern Drama and Music."

The basic form of total production that was inherent in the Symbolist aesthetic was provided with an outstanding example in the Kamerny Theatre of Alexander Tairov in Moscow. Tairov's presentations were entirely orchestrated. The tones of the actors' voices were pitched like those of musical instruments. The movement was dancelike, and colors, lighting and sound effects were all patterned on a musical basis. This was, in fact, Symbolist total theatre.

Gorchakov reports, however, that "The audiences found the productions very musical and quite pleasing to the eye and ear, but the presentations did not affect the heart." [2] In a theatre that stresses aesthetic values as such, this comment suggests one way in which "dehumanization" can be present.

On the other hand, the contrary force is also operative in this abstract mode. The "dehumanization" implied by the Übermarionette is also a means of heightening the potential of a "human" affect and making its reality a more moving one. This is indicated by the experience of Walter Kerr in regard to two modern productions that used masks and masklike costumes, as he describes in "Man—As Monster, or God."

[2] Nikolai A. Gorchakov, *The Theater in Soviet Russia,* trans. by Edgar Lehrman (New York: Columbia University Press, 1957), p. 225.

EDWARD GORDON CRAIG

# The Actor and the
## *Übermarionette* *

Inscribed in all affection to my good friends, the actors De Vos
and Hevesi.

> "To save the Theatre, the Theatre must be destroyed,
>   the actors and actresses must all die of the plague. . . .
>   They make art impossible."
>
> ELEONORA DUSE [1]

It has always been a matter for argument whether or not acting is an art, and therefore whether the actor is an artist, or something quite different. There is little to show us that this question
disturbed the minds of the leaders of thought at any period,
though there is much evidence to prove that had they chosen to
approach this subject as one for their serious consideration, they
would have applied to it the same method of enquiry as used
when considering the arts of Music and Poetry, of Architecture,
Sculpture, and Painting. On the other hand there have been
many warm arguments in certain circles on this topic. Those taking part in it have seldom been actors, very rarely men of the
theatre at all, and all have displayed any amount of illogical heat,
and very little knowledge of the subject. The arguments against
acting being an art, and against the actor being an artist, are generally so unreasonable and so personal in their detestation of the
actor, that I think it is for this reason the actors have taken no
trouble to go into the matter. So now regularly with each season
comes the quarterly attack on the actor and on his jolly calling;
the attack usually ending in the retirement of the enemy. As a
rule it is the literary or private gentlemen who fill the enemy's
rank. On the strength of having gone to see plays all their lives,
or on the strength of never having gone to see a play in their lives,
they attack for some reason best known to themselves. I have fol-

* Reprinted from *The Mask*, I: I (April, 1908), Florence, Italy.
[1] Quoted in *Studies in Seven Arts* by Arthur Symons (Constable: 1906).

lowed these regular attacks season by season, and they seem mostly to spring from irritability, personal enmity or conceit . . . They are illogical from beginning to end. . . . There can be no such attack made on the actor or his calling. My intention here is not to join in any such attempt; I would merely place before you what seem to me to be the logical facts of a curious case, and I believe that these admit of no dispute whatever.

Acting is not an art. It is therefore incorrect to speak of the actor as an artist. For accident is an enemy of the artist. Art is the exact antithesis of pandemonium, and pandemonium is created by the tumbling together of many accidents; Art arrives only by design. Therefore in order to make any work of art it is clear we may only work in those materials with which we can calculate. Man is not one of those materials.

The whole nature of man tends toward freedom; he therefore carries the proof in his own person, that as *material* for the theatre he is useless. In the modern theatre, owing to the use of the bodies of men and women *as their material,* all which is presented there is of an accidental nature. The actions of the actor's body, the expression of his face, the sounds of his voice, all are at the mercy of the winds of his emotions; these winds which must blow forever round the artist, moving without unbalancing him. But with the actor, emotion *possesses* him; it seizes upon his limbs moving them whither it will. He is at its beck and call, he moves as one in a frantic dream or as one distraught, swaying here and there; his head, his arms, his feet, if not utterly beyond control, are so weak to stand against the torrent of his passion that they are ready to play him false at any moment. It is useless for him to attempt to reason with himself. . . . Hamlet's calm directions (the dreamer's not the logician's directions, by the way) are thrown to the winds. His limbs refuse, and refuse again to obey his mind the instant emotion warms, while the mind is all the time creating the heat which shall set these emotions afire. As with his movement, so is it with the expression of his face. The mind struggling and succeeding for a moment, in moving the eyes, or the muscles of the face whither it will; . . . the mind bringing the face for a few moments into thorough subjection, suddenly swept aside by the emotion which has grown hot through the action of the mind. Instantly, like lightning, and be

fore the mind has time to cry out and protest, the hot passion has mastered the actor's expression. It shifts and changes, sways and turns, it is chased by emotion from the actor's forehead between his eyes and down to his mouth; now he is entirely at the mercy of emotion, and crying out to it: "Do with me what you will!" his expression runs a mad riot hither and thither, and lo! "nothing is coming of nothing." It is the same with his voice as it is with his movements. Emotion cracks the voice of the actor. It sways his voice to join in the conspiracy against his mind. Emotion works upon the voice of the actor, and he produces . . . the impression of discordant emotion. It is of no avail to say that emotion is the spirit of the gods and is precisely what the artist aims to produce; first of all this is not true, and even if it were quite true, every stray emotion, every casual feeling, cannot be of value. Therefore the mind of the actor, we see, is less powerful than his emotion, for emotion is able to win over the mind to assist in the destruction of that which the mind would produce; and as the mind becomes the slave of the emotion it follows that accident upon accident must be continually occurring. So then, we have arrived at this point; . . . that emotion is the cause which first of all creates, and secondly destroys. Art as we have said, can admit of no accidents. That then which the actor gives us, is not a work of art; it is a series of accidental confessions. In the beginning the human body was not used as material in the art of the theatre. In the beginning the emotions of men and women were not considered as a fit exhibition for the multitude. An elephant and a tiger in an arena suited the taste better, when the desire was to excite. The passionate tussle between the elephant and the tiger gives us all the excitement that we can get from the modern stage, and can give it to us unalloyed. Such an exhibition is not more brutal, it is more delicate; it is more humane; for there is nothing more outrageous than that men and women should be let loose on a platform, so that they may expose that which artists refuse to show except veiled, in the form which their minds create. How it was that man was ever persuaded to take the place which until that time animals had held is not difficult to surmise.

The man with the greater learning comes across the man with the greater temperament. He addresses him in something like the following terms: "You have a most superb countenance;

what magnificent movements you make! Your voice, it is like the singing of birds; and how your eye flashes! What a noble impression you give! You almost resemble a god! I think all people should have pointed out to them this wonder which is contained in you. I will write a few words which you shall address to the people. You shall stand before them, and you shall speak my lines just as you will. It is sure to be perfectly right."

And the man of temperament replies; "Is that really so? Do I strike you as appearing as a god? It is the very first time I have ever thought of it. And do you think that by appearing in front of the people I could make an impression which might benefit them, and would fill them with enthusiasm?" "No, no, no," says the intelligent man, "by no means only by *appearing;* but if you have something to say you will indeed create a great impression."

The other answers, "I think I shall have some difficulty in speaking your lines. I could easier just appear, and say, something instinctive, such as 'Salutation to all men'; I feel perhaps that I should be able to be more myself if I acted in that way." "That is an excellent idea," replies the tempter, "that idea of yours, 'Salutation to all men.' On that theme I will compose say one hundred or two hundred lines; you'll be the very man to speak those lines. You have yourself suggested it to me. Salutation! Is it agreed then, that you will do this?" "If you wish it," replies the other, with a good-natured lack of reason, and flattered beyond measure.

And so the comedy of author and actor commences. The young man appears before the multitude and speaks the lines, and the speaking of them is a superb advertisement for the art of literature. After the applause the young man is swiftly forgotten; they even forgive the way he has spoken the lines; but as it was an original and new idea at the time, the author found it profitable, and shortly afterwards other authors found it an excellent thing to use handsome and buoyant men *as instruments.* It mattered nothing to them that the instrument was a human creature. Although they knew not the stops of the instrument, they could play rudely upon him and they found him useful. And so today we have the strange picture of a man content to give forth the thoughts of another, which that other has given form to, while at the same time he exhibits his person to the public view. He does

t because he is flattered, and vanity will not reason. But all the time, and however long the world may last, the nature in man will fight for freedom, and will revolt against being made a slave or medium for the expression of another's thoughts. The whole thing is a very grave matter indeed, and it is no good to push it aside and protest that the actor is not the medium for another's thoughts, and that he invests with life the dead words of an author; because even if this were true (true it cannot be) and even if the actor was to present none but the ideas which he himself should compose, his nature would still be in servitude; his body would have to become the slave of his mind; and that as I have shown is what the healthy body utterly refuses to do. Therefore the body of man, for the reason which I have given, is *by nature* utterly useless as a material for an art. I am fully aware of the sweeping character of this statement, and as it concerns men and women who are alive and who as a class are ever to be loved, more must be said lest I give unintentional offense. I know perfectly well that what I have said here is not yet going to create an exodus of all the actors from all the theatres in the world, driving them into sad monasteries where they will laugh out the rest of their lives, with the Art of the Theatre as the main topic for amusing conversation. As I have written elsewhere, the theatre will continue its growth and actors will continue for some years to hinder its development. But I see a loophole by which in time the actors can escape from the bondage they are in. They must create for themselves a new form of acting, consisting for the main part of symbolical gesture. Today they *impersonate* and interpret; tomorrow they must *represent* and interpret; and the third day they must create. By this means style may return. Today the actor impersonates a certain being. He cries to the audience "Watch me; I am now pretending to be so-and-so, and I am now pretending to do so-and-so"; and then he proceeds to *imitate* as exactly as possible, that which he has announced he will *indicate*. For instance, he is Romeo. He tells the audience that he is in love, and he proceeds to show it, by kissing Juliet. This, it is claimed is a work of art: it is claimed for this that it is an intelligent way of suggesting thought. Why . . . why, that is just as if a painter were to draw upon the wall a picture of an animal with long ears, and then write under it "This is a don-

key." The long ears made it plain enough one would think, without the inscription, and any child of ten does as much. The difference between the child of ten and the artist is, that the artist is he who by drawing certain signs and shapes creates the impression of a donkey: and the greater artist is he who creates the impression of the whole genus of donkey, the *spirit* of the thing.

The actor looks upon life as a photomachine looks upon life; and he attempts to make a picture to rival a photograph. He never dreams of his art as being an art such for instance as music. He tries to reproduce nature; he seldom thinks to invent with the aid of nature, and he never dreams of *creating*. As I have said, the best he can do when he wants to catch and convey the poetry of a kiss, the heat of a fight, or the calm of death, is to copy slavishly, photographically . . . he kisses . . . he fights . . . he lies back and mimics death . . . and when you think of it, is not all this dreadfully stupid? Is it not a poor art and a poor cleverness, which cannot convey the spirit and essence of an idea to an audience, but can only show an artless copy, a facsimile of the thing itself. This is to be an Imitator not an Artist. This is to claim kinship with the Ventriloquist.[2]

There is a stage expression of the actor "getting under the skin of the part." A better one would be getting *"out* of the skin of the part altogether." "What then," cries the red-blooded and flashing actor, "is there to be no flesh and blood in this same art of the theatre of yours? . . . No life?" It depends what you call life, signor, when you use the word in relation with the idea of art. The painter means something rather different to actuality when he speaks of life in his art, and the other artists generally mean something essentially spiritual; it is only the actor the ventrilo-

[2] "And therefore when any one of these pantomimic gentlemen, who are so clever that they can imitate anything comes to us, and makes a proposal to exhibit himself and his poetry, we will fall down and worship him as a sweet and holy and wonderful being; but we must also inform him that in our State such as he are not permitted to exist; the law will not allow them. And so, when we have anointed him with myrrh, and set a garland of wool upon his head, we shall lead him away to another city. For we mean to employ for our soul's health the rougher and severer poet or storyteller, who will imitate the style of the virtuous only, and will follow those models which we prescribed at first when we began the education of our soldiers." (The whole passage being too long to print here, we refer the reader to Plato, *The Republic,* Book III, 395.)

quist or the animal stuffer who, when they speak of putting life into their work, mean some actual and lifelike reproduction, something blatant in its appeal, that it is for this reason I say that it would be better if the actor should get out of the skin of the part altogether. If there is any actor who is reading this, is there not some way by which I can make him realize the preposterous absurdity of this delusion of his, this belief that he should aim to make an actual copy, a reproduction? I am going to suppose that such an actor is here with me as I talk; and I invite a musician and a painter to join us. Let them speak. I have had enough of seeming to decry the work of the actor from trivial motives. I have spoken this way because of my love of the theatre, and because of my hopes and belief that before long an extraordinary development is to raise and revive that which is failing in the theatre, and my hope and belief that the actor will bring the force of his courage to assist in this revival. My attitude toward the whole matter is misunderstood by many in the theatre. It is considered to be *my* attitude, mine alone; a stray quarreler I seem to be in their eyes, a pessimist, grumbling; one who is tired of a thing and who attempts to break it. Therefore let the other artists speak with the actor, and let the actor support his own case as best he may, and let him listen to their opinion on matters of art. We sit here conversing, the actor, the musician, the painter, and myself. I who represent an art distinct from all these, shall remain silent.

As we sit here, the talk first turns upon nature. We are surrounded by beautiful curving hills, trees, vast and towering mountains in the distance covered with snow; around us innumerable delicate sounds of nature stirring . . . Life. "How beautiful," says the painter, "how beautiful the sense of all this!" He is dreaming of the almost impossibility of conveying the full earthly and spiritual value of that which is around him onto his canvas, yet he faces the thing as man generally faces that which is most dangerous.

The musician gazes upon the ground. The actor's is an inward and personal gaze at himself. He is unconsciously enjoying the sense of himself, as representing the main and central figure in a really good scene. He strides across the space between us and the view, sweeping in a half circle, and he regards the superb pan-

orama without seeing it, conscious of one thing only, himself and his attitude. Of course an actress would stand there meek in the presence of nature. She is but a little thing, a little picturesque atom; . . . for picturesque we know she is in every movement, in the sigh which, almost unheard by the rest of us, she conveys to her audience and to herself, that she is there *"little me,"* in the presence of the God that made her!! and all the rest of the sentimental nonsense. So we are all collected here, and having taken the attitudes natural to us, we proceed to question each other. And let us imagine that for once we are all really interested in finding out all about the other's interests, and the other's work. (I grant that this is very unusual, and that mind-selfishness, the highest form of stupidity, encloses many a professed artist somewhat tightly in a little square box.) But let us take it for granted that there is a general interest; that the actor and the musician wish to learn something about the art of painting; and that the painter and the musician wish to understand from the actor what his work consists of and whether and why he considers it an art. For here they shall not mince matters, but shall speak that which they believe. As they are looking only for the truth, they have nothing to fear; they are all good fellows, all good friends; not thin-skinned, and can give and take blows. "Tell us," asks the painter, "is it true that before you can act a part properly you must feel the emotions of the character you are representing?" "Oh well, yes and no; it depends what you mean," answers the actor. "We have first to be able to feel and sympathize and also criticize the emotions of a character; we look at it from a distance before we close with it: we gather as much as we can from the text and we call to mind all the emotions suitable for this character to exhibit. After having many times rearranged and selected those emotions which we consider of importance we then practice to reproduce them before the audience; and in order to do so we must feel as little as is necessary; in fact the less we feel, the firmer will our hold be upon our facial and bodily expression." With a gesture of genial impatience, the artist rises to his feet and paces to and fro. He had expected his friend to say that it had nothing whatever to do with emotions, and that he could control his face, features, voice and all, just as if his body were an instrument. The musician sinks down deeper into his chair. "But has

there never been an actor," asks the artist, "who has so trained his body from head to foot that it would answer to the workings of his mind without permitting the emotions even so much as to awaken? Surely there must have been one actor, say one out of ten million, who has done this?" "No," says the actor emphatically, "never, never; there never has been an actor who reached such a state of mechanical perfection that his body was *absolutely* the slave of his mind. Edmund Kean of England, Salvini of Italy, Rachel, Eleonora Duse, I call them all to mind and I repeat there never was an actor or actress such as you describe." The artist here asks, "Then you admit that it would be a state of perfection?" "Why of course! But it is impossible; will always be impossible," cries the actor; and he rises . . . almost with a sense of relief. "That is as much as to say, there never was a perfect actor, there has never been an actor who has not spoiled his performance once, twice, ten times, sometimes a hundred times during the evening? There never has been a piece of acting which could be called even almost perfect and there never will be?" For answer the actor asks quickly, "But has there ever been a painting, or a piece of architecture, or a piece of music which may be called perfect?" "Undoubtedly," they reply, "The laws which control our arts make such a thing possible."

"A picture for instance," continues the artist, "may consist of four lines, or four hundred lines, placed in certain positions; it may be as simple as possible, but it is possible to make it perfect. That is to say, I can first choose that which is to make the lines; I can choose that on which I am to place the lines: I can consider this as long as I like; I can alter it; then in a state which is free from excitement, haste, trouble, nervousness, in fact in any state I choose, (and of course I prepare, wait, and select that also) I can put these lines together . . . so . . . now they are in their place. Having my material nothing except my own will can move or alter these; and as I have said my own will is entirely under my control. The line can be straight or it can wave; it can be round if I choose, and there is no fear that when I wish to make a straight line I shall make a curved one, or that when I wish to make a curved one there will be square parts about it. And when it is ready . . . finished . . . it undergoes no change but that which time, who finally destroys it, wills." "That is rather an ex-

traordinary thing," replied the actor. "I wish it was possible in my work." "Yes," replies the artist, *"it is a very extraordinary thing,* and it is that which I hold makes the difference between an intelligent statement and a casual or haphazard statement. The most intelligent statement, that is a work of art. The haphazard statement, that is a work of chance. When the intelligent statement reaches its highest possible form it becomes a work of fine art. And therefore I have always held, though I may be mistaken, that your work has not the nature of an art. That is to say (and you have said it yourself) each statement that you make in your work is subject to every conceivable change which emotion chooses to bring about. That which you conceive in your mind, your body is not permitted by nature to complete. In fact, your body, gaining the better of your intelligence, has in many instances on the stage driven out the intelligence altogether. Some actors seem to say, 'What value lies in having beautiful ideas. To what end shall my mind conceive a fine idea, a fine thought, for my body which is so entirely beyond my control to spoil? I will throw my mind overboard, let my body pull me and the play through'; and there seems to me to be some wisdom in the standpoint of such an actor. He does not dillydally between the two things which are contending in him, the one against the other. He is not a bit afraid of the result. He goes at it like a man, sometimes a trifle too like a centaur; he flings away all science . . . all caution . . . all reason and the result is good spirits in the audience, . . . and for that they pay willingly. But we are here talking about other things than excellent spirits, and though we applaud the actor who exhibits such a personality as this, I feel that we must not forget that we are applauding his personality . . . *he* it is we applaud, not what he is doing or how he is doing it; nothing to do with art at all, absolutely nothing to do with art, with calculation, or design."

"You're a nice friendly creature," laughs the actor gaily, "telling me my art's no art! But I believe I see what you mean. You mean to say that before I appear on the stage and before my body commences to come into the question, I am an artist." "Well yes, *you* are, you happen to be, because you are a very bad actor; you're abominable on the stage, but you have ideas, you have imagination; you are rather an exception I should say. I have

heard you tell me how you would play *Richard III;* what you would do; what strange atmosphere you would spread over the whole thing; and that which you have told me you have seen in the play, and that which you have invented and added to it, is so remarkable, so consecutive in its thought, so distinct and clear in form, that *if* you could make your body into a machine, or into a dead piece of material such as clay, and *if* it could obey you in every movement for the entire space of time it was before the audience, and *if* you could put aside Shakespeare's poem, you would be able to make a work of art out of that which is in you. For you would not only have dreamt, you would have executed to perfection; and that which you had executed could be repeated time after time without so much difference as between two far-things." "Ah," sighs the actor, "you place a terrible picture before me. You would prove to me that it is impossible for us ever to think of ourselves as artists. You take away our finest dream and you give us nothing in its place." "No, no, that's not for me to give you. That's for you to find. Surely there must be laws at the roots of the Art of the Theatre, just as there are laws at the roots of all true arts, which if found and mastered, would bring you all you desire?" "Yes, the search would bring the actors to a wall." "Leap it, then!" "Too high!" "Scale it, then!" "How do we know where it would lead?" "Why, up and over." "Yes, but that's talking wildly, talking in the air." "Well, that's the direction you fellows have to go; . . . fly in the air, live in the air. Something will follow when some of you begin to. I suppose," continued he, "you will get at the root of the matter in time, and then what a splendid future opens before you! In fact I envy you. I am not sure I do not wish that photography had been discovered before painting, so that we of this generation might have had the intense joy of advancing, showing that photography was pretty good in its way, but there was something better!" "Do you hold that our work is on a level with photography?" "No, indeed, it is not half as exact. It is less of an art even than photography. In fact you and I who have been talking all this time, while the musician has sat silent, sinking deeper and deeper into his chair, our arts by the side of his art, are jokes, games, absurdi-ties." At which the musician must go and spoil the whole thing by getting up and giving vent to some foolish remark. The actor im-

mediately cries out, "But I don't see that that's such a wonderful remark for a representative of the only art in the world to make" at which they all laughed, the musician in a sort of crestfallen, conscious manner. "My dear fellow, that is just because he is a musician. He is nothing except in his music. He is, in fact, somewhat unintelligent, except when he speaks in notes, in tones, and in the rest of it. He hardly knows our language, he hardly knows our world, and the greater the musician, the more is this noticeable; indeed it is rather a bad sign when you meet a composer who is intelligent. And as for the intellectual musician, why that means another . . . ; but we mustn't whisper that name here . . . he is so popular today. What an actor this man would have been, and what a personality he has. I understand that all his life he had yearnings toward being an actor, and I believe he would have been an excellent comedian, whereas he became a musician . . . or was it a playwright? Anyhow, it all turned out a great success . . . a success of personality." "Was it not a success of art?" asks the musician. "Well, which art do you mean?" "Oh, all the arts combined," he replies, blunderingly but placidly. "How can that be? How can all arts combine and make one art? It can only make one joke . . . one theatre. Things which slowly, by a natural law join together, may have some right in the course of many years or many centuries to ask nature to bestow a new name on their product. Only by this means can a new art be born. I do not believe that the old mother approves of the forcing process; and if she ever winks at it, she soon has her revenge; and so is it with the arts. You cannot commingle them and cry out that you have created a new art. *If you can find in nature a new material, one which has never yet been used by man to give form to his thoughts, then you can say that you are on the high road toward creating a new art. For you have found that by which you can create it.* It then only remains for you to begin. The theatre, as I see it, has yet to find that material." And so their conversation ended.

For my part I am with the artist's last statement. My pleasure shall not be to compete with the strenuous photographer and I shall ever aim to get something entirely opposed to life as we see it. This flesh and blood life, lovely as it is to us all is for me not a thing made to search into, or to give out again to the world, even

conventionalized. I think that my aim shall rather be to catch
some far off glimpse of that spirit which we call *death* . . . to
recall beautiful things from the imaginary world; . . . they say
they are cold, these dead things, . . . I do not know . . . they
often seem warmer and more living than that which parades as
life. Shades . . . spirits seem to me to be more beautiful, and
filled with more vitality than men and women; cities of men and
women packed with pettiness, creatures, inhuman, secret . . .
coldest cold . . . hardest humanity. For looking too long upon
life, may one not find all this to be not the beautiful, nor the mysterious nor the tragic, but the dull, the melodramatic, and the
silly: the conspiracy against vitality . . . against both red heat
and white heat; and from such things which lack the sun of life it
is not possible to draw inspiration. But from that mysterious,
joyous, and superbly complete life which is called death . . .
that life of shadow and of unknown shapes, where all cannot be
blackness and fog as is supposed, but vivid color, vivid light,
sharp cut form, and which one finds peopled with strange, fierce,
and solemn figures, pretty figures and calm figures, and those figures impelled to some wondrous harmony of movement, all this
is something more than a mere matter of fact; from this idea of
death which seems a kind of spring, a blossoming—from this
land and from this idea can come so vast an inspiration, that with
unhesitating exultation I leap forward to it and behold, in an instant, I find my arms full of flowers. . . . I advance but a pace
or two and again plenty is around me. . . . I pass at ease on a
sea of beauty I sail whither the winds take me—there, there is
no danger. So much for my own personal wish; . . . but the entire theatre of the world is not represented in me, nor in a hundred artists or actors, but in something far different. Therefore
what my personal aim may be is of very little importance. Yet the
aim of the theatre as a whole is to restore its art and it should
commence by banishing from the theatre this idea of impersonation, this idea of reproducing nature; for while impersonation is
in the theatre, the theatre can never become free. The performers should train under the influence of an earlier teaching (if
the very earliest and finest principles are too stern to commence
with) and they will have to avoid that frantic desire to put *"life"*
into their work; for three thousand times against one time, it

means the bringing of excessive gesture, swift mimicry, speech which bellows and scene which dazzles, on to the stage, in the wild and vain belief that by such means vitality can be conjured there. And in a few instances, to prove the rule, all this partially succeeds. It succeeds partially with the bubbling personalities of the stage. With them it is a case of sheer triumph *in spite* of the rules, in the very teeth of the rules, and we who look on, throw our hats into the air, . . . cheer, and cheer again. *We have to;* we don't want to consider or to question;—we go with the tide through admiration and suggestion. . . . That we are hypnotized, our taste cares not a rap. . . . We are delighted to be so moved, and we literally jump for joy. The great personality has triumphed both over us and the art. But personalities such as these are extremely rare, and if we wish to see a personality assert itself in the theatre and entirely triumph as an actor we must at the same time be quite indifferent about the play, the other actors, and beauty.

Those who do not think with me in this whole matter are the worshipers, or respectful admirers, of the personalities of the stage. It is intolerable to them that I should assert that the stage must be cleared of all its actors and actresses before it will again revive. How could they agree with me? That would include the removal of their favorites . . . the two or three beings who transform the stage for them from a vulgar joke into an ideal land. But what should they fear? No danger threatens their favorites—for were it possible to put an act into force to prohibit all men and women from appearing before the public upon the stage of a theatre, this would not in the least affect these favorites—these men and women of personality whom the playgoers crown. Consider any one of these personalities born at a period when the stage was unknown; would it in any way have lessened their power . . . hindered their expression? Not a whit. Personality invents the means and ways by which it shall express itself; and acting is but one (the very least) of the means at the command of a great personality: and these men and women would have been famous at any time, and in any calling. But if there are many to whom it is intolerable that I should propose to clear the stage of ALL the actors and actresses in order to revive

the Art of the Theatre, there are others to whom it seems agreeable.

"The artist," says Flaubert, "should be in his work like God in creation, invisible and all-powerful; he should be felt everywhere and seen nowhere. Art should be raised above personal affection and nervous susceptibility. It is time to give it the perfection of the physical sciences by means of a pitiless method." He is thinking mainly of the Art of Literature; but if he feel this so strongly of the writer, one who is never actually seen, but merely stands half-revealed behind his work, how totally opposed must he have been to the actual appearance of the actor — personality or no personality.

Charles Lamb says; "To see Lear acted . . . to see an old man tottering about with a stick, turned out of doors by his daughters on a rainy night, has nothing in it but what is painful and disgusting. We want to take him into shelter, that is all the feeling the acting of Lear ever produced in me. The contemptible machinery by which they mimic the storm which he goes out in, is not more inadequate to represent the horror of the real elements than any actor can be to represent Lear. They might more easily propose to personate the Satan of Milton upon a stage, or one of Michaelangelo's terrible figures. . . . Lear is essentially impossible to be represented on the stage."

"Hamlet himself seems hardly capable of being acted," says William Hazlitt.

Dante in *La Vita Nuova* tells us that in dream Love in the figure of a youth appeared to him. Discoursing of Beatrice, Dante is told by Love "to compose certain things in rhyme, in the which thou shalt set forth how strong a mastership I have obtained over thee, through her. . . . And so write these things that they shall seem rather to be spoken by a third person, and not directly by thee to her, which is scarce fitting." And again "There came upon me a great desire to say somewhat in rhyme; but when I began thinking how I should say it, methought that to speak of her were unseemly, unless I spoke to other ladies 'in the second person.' " We see then that to these men it is wrong that the living person

should advance into the frame and display himself upon his own canvas. They hold it as "unseemly" . . . "scarce fitting."

We have here witnesses against the whole business of the modern stage. Collectively they pass the following sentence: That it is bad art, or no art, to make so personal, so emotional an appeal that the beholder forgets the thing itself while swamped by the personality, the emotion, of its maker. And now for the testimony of an actress, Eleonora Duse has said: [3] "To save the theatre, the theatre must be destroyed, the actors and actresses must all die of the plague. They poison the air, they make art impossible."

We may believe her. She means what Flaubert and Dante mean, even if she words it differently. And there are many more witnesses to testify for me, if this is held to be insufficient evidence. There are the people who never go to theatres, the millions of men against the thousands who do go. Then, we have the support of most of the managers of the theatre of today. The modern theatre manager thinks the stage should have its plays gorgeously decorated. He will say that no pains should be spared to bring every assistance toward cheating the audience into a sense of reality; he will never cease telling us how important all these decorations are; he urges all this for several reasons and the following reason is not the least. . . . He scents a grave danger in simple and good work; he sees that there is a body of people who are opposed to these lavish decorations; he knows that there has been a distinct movement, in Europe, against this display, it having been claimed that the great plays gained when represented in front of the plainest background. This movement can be proved to be a powerful one—it has spread from Krakau to Moscow, from Paris to Rome, from London to Berlin and Vienna. The managers see this danger ahead of them; they see that if once people came to realize this fact, if once the audience tasted of the delight which a sceneless play brings, they would then go further and desire the play which was presented without actors; and finally they would go on and on and on until *they,* and not the managers, had positively reformed the Art.

Napoleon is reported to have said: "In life there is much that is unworthy which in art should be omitted; much of doubt and

[3] *Studies in Seven Arts;* . . . Arthur Symons (Constable: 1906).

vacillation; and all should disappear in the representation of the hero. *We should see him as a statue in which the weakness and tremors of the flesh are no longer perceptible."* [4] And not only Napoleon, but Ben Jonson, Lessing, Edmund Scherer, Hans Christian Andersen, Lamb, Goethe, George Sand, Coleridge, Ruskin, Pater, and I suppose all the intelligent men and women of Europe (one does not speak of Asia for even the unintelligent in Asia fail to comprehend photographs while understanding Art as a simple and clear manifestation) have protested against this reproduction of nature, and with it photographic and weak actuality; they have protested against all this, and the theatrical managers have argued against them energetically, and so we look for the truth to emerge in due time. It is a reasonable conclusion. Do away with the real tree, do away with the reality of delivery, do away with the reality of action, and you tend toward the doing away with the actor. This is what must come to pass in time, and I like to see the managers supporting the idea already. Do away with the actor, and you do away with the means by which a debased stage realism is produced and flourishes. No longer would there be a living figure to confuse us into connecting actuality and art; no longer a living figure in which the weakness and tremors of the flesh were perceptible.

The actor must go, and in his place comes the inanimate figure—the Übermarionette we may call him, until he has won for himself a better name. Much has been written about the puppet—or marionette. There are some excellent volumes upon him, and he has also inspired several works of art. Today in his least happy period many people have come to regard him as rather a superior doll—and to think he has developed from the

[4] Of sculpture Pater writes:

"Its white light, purged from the angry, bloodlike stains of action and passion, reveals, not what is accidental in man, but the god in him, as opposed to man's restless movement."

Again, "The base of all artistic genius is the power of conceiving humanity in a new striking rejoicing way, of putting a happy world of its own construction in place of the meaner world of common days, of generating around itself an atmosphere with a novel power of refraction, selecting, transforming, recombining the images it transmits, according to the choice of the imaginative intellect."

And again; "All that is accidental, all that distracts the simple effect upon us of the supreme types of humanity, all traces in them of the commonness of the world, it gradually purges away."

doll. This is incorrect. He is a descendant of the stone images of the old Temples—he is today a rather degenerate form of a God. Always the close friend of children he still knows how to select and attract his devotees.

When anyone designs a puppet on paper, he draws a stiff and comic looking thing. Such a one has not even perceived what is contained in the idea which we now call the Marionette. He mistakes gravity of face and calmness of body for blank stupidity and angular deformity. Yet even modern puppets are extraordinary things. The applause may thunder or dribble, their hearts beat no faster, no slower, their signals do not grow hurried or confused; and, though drenched in a torrent of bouquets and love, the face of the leading lady remains as solemn, as beautiful and as remote as ever. There is something more than a flash of genius in the Marionette, and there is something in him more than the flashiness of displayed personality. The Marionette . . . appears to me to be the last echo of some noble and beautiful art of a past civilization. But as with all art which has passed into fat or vulgar hands, the puppet has become a reproach. All puppets are now but low comedians.

They imitate the comedians of the larger and fuller blooded stage. They enter only to fall on their back. They drink only to reel, and make love only to raise a laugh. They have forgotten the counsel of their mother, the Sphinx. Their bodies have lost their grave grace, they have become stiff. Their eyes have lost that infinite subtlety of seeming to see; now they only stare. They display and jingle their wires and are cocksure in their wooden wisdom. They have failed to remember that their art should carry on it the same stamp of reserve that we see at times on the work of other artists, and that the highest art is that which conceals the craft and forgets the craftsman. Am I mistaken, or is it not the old Greek Traveler of 800 B.C. who, describing a visit to the Temple-Theatre in Thebes, tells us that he was won to their beauty by their "noble artificiality." "Coming into the House of Visions I saw afar off the fair brown Queen seated upon her throne . . . her tomb . . . for both it seemed to me. I sank back upon my couch and watched her symbolic movements. With so much ease did her rhythms alter as with her movements they passed from limb to limb; with such a show of calm did she

unloose for us the thoughts of her breast; so gravely and so beautifully did she linger on the statement of her sorrow, that with us it seemed as if no sorrow could harm her; no distortion of body or feature allowed us to dream that she was conquered; the passion and the pain were continually being caught by her hands, held gently, and viewed calmly. Her arms and hands seemed at one moment like a thin warm fountain of water which rose, then broke and fell with all those sweet pale fingers like spray into her lap. It would have been as a revelation of art to us had I not already seen that the same spirit dwelt in the other examples of the art of these Egyptians. This 'Art of Showing and Veiling' as they call it, is so great a spiritual force in the land that it plays the larger part in their religion. We may learn from it somewhat of the power and the grace of courage, for it is impossible to witness a performance without a sense of physical and spiritual refreshment."

This in 800 B.C. And who knows whether the puppet shall not once again become the faithful medium for the beautiful thoughts of the artist. May we not look forward with hope to that day which shall bring back to us once more the figure, or symbolic creature, made also by the cunning of the artist, so that we can regain once more the *"noble artificiality"* which the old writer speaks of. Then shall we no longer be under the cruel influence of the emotional confessions of weakness which are nightly witnessed by the people and which in their turn create in the beholders the very weaknesses which are exhibited. To that end we must study to remake these images—no longer content with a puppet, we must create an Übermarionette. The Übermarionette will not compete with life—but will rather go beyond it. Its ideal will not be the flesh and blood but rather the body in trance—it will aim to clothe itself with a death-like beauty while exhaling a living spirit. Several times in the course of this essay has a word or two about death found its way on to the paper . . . called there by the incessant clamoring of "Life! Life! Life!" which the Realists keep up. And this might be easily mistaken for an affectation especially by those who have no sympathy or delight in the power and the mysterious joyousness which is in all passionless works of art. If the famous Rubens and the celebrated Raphael made none but passionate and exuberant

statements, there were many artists before them and since to whom moderation in their art was the most precious of all their aims, and these more than all others exhibit the true masculine manner. The other flamboyant or drooping artists whose works and names catch the eye of today do not so much speak like men as bawl like animals, or lisp like women. The wise, the moderate masters, strong because of the laws to which they swore to remain ever faithful . . . their names unknown for the most part . . . a fine family . . . the creators of the great and tiny gods of the East and the West, the guardians of those larger times, . . . these all bent their thoughts forward toward the unknown, searching for sights and sounds in that peaceful and joyous country, that they might raise a figure of stone or sing a verse, investing it with that same peace and joy seen from afar, so as to balance all the grief and turmoil here.

In America we can picture these brothers of that family of masters, living in their superb ancient cities, colossal cities which I ever think of as able to be moved in a single day; cities of spacious tents of silk and canopies of gold under which dwelt their gods; dwellings which contained all the requirements of the most fastidious; those moving cities which, as they traveled from height to plain, over rivers and down valleys, seemed like some vast advancing army of peace. And in each city not one or two men called "artists" whom the rest of the city looked upon as ne'er-do-well idlers, but many men chosen by the community because of their higher powers of perception . . . artists; for that is what the title of artist means, one who perceives more than his fellows, and who records more than he has seen. And not the least among those artists was the artist of the ceremonies, the creator of the visions, the minister whose duty it was to celebrate their guiding spirit . . . the spirit of motion.

In Asia, too, the forgotten masters of the temples and all that those temples contained, have permeated every thought, every mark in their work with this sense of calm motion resembling death . . . glorifying and greeting it. In Africa (which some of us think we are but now to civilize) this spirit dwelt, . . . the essence of the perfect civilization. There too dwelt the great masters, not individuals obsessed with the idea of each asserting his personality as if it was a valuable and mighty thing, but content

because of a kind of holy patience to move their brains and their fingers only in that direction permitted by the law—in the service of the simple truths.

How stern the law was, and how little the artist of that day permitted himself to make an exhibition of his personal feelings can be discovered by looking at any example of Egyptian art. Look at any limb ever carved by the Egyptians, search into all those carved eyes, they will deny you until the crack of doom. Their attitude is so silent that it is deathlike. Yet tenderness is there, and charm is there; prettiness is even there side by side with the force; and love bathes each single work; but gush, emotion, swaggering personality of the artist? . . . not one single breath of it. Fierce doubts or hopes? . . . not one hint of such a thing. Strenuous determination? . . . not a sign of it has escaped the artist; none of these confessions . . . stupidities. Nor pride, nor fear, nor the comic, nor any indication that the artist's mind or hand was for the thousandth part of a moment out of the command of the laws which ruled him. How superb! This it is to be a great artist; and the amount of emotional outpourings of today and of yesterday are no signs of supreme intelligence, . . . that is to say, are no signs of supreme art. To Europe came this spirit, hovered over Greece, could hardly be driven out of Italy, but finally fled, leaving a little stream of tears, . . . pearls . . . before us. And we, having crushed most of them, munching them along with the acorns of our food, have gone further and fared worse and have prostrated ourselves before the so-called "great masters," and have worshiped these dangerous and flamboyant personalities. On an evil day we thought in our ignorance that it was us they were sent to draw, that it was our thoughts they were sent to express; that it was something to do with us that they were putting into their architecture, their music, and so it was we came to demand that we should be able to recognize ourselves in all that they put hand to; that is to say, in their architecture, in their sculpture, in their music, in their painting, and in their poetry we were to figure . . . and we also reminded them to invite us with the familiar words "come as you are."

The artists after many centuries have given in, that which we asked them for they have supplied. And so it came about that

when this ignorance had driven off the fair spirit which once controlled the mind and hand of the artist, a dark spirit took its place; the happy-go-lucky hooligan in the seat of the Law, that is to say, a stupid spirit reigning; and everybody began to shout about Renaissance! while all the time the painters, musicians, sculptors, architects, vied one with the other to supply the demand . . . that all these things should be so made that all people could recognize them as having something to do with themselves.

Up sprang portraits with flushed faces, eyes which bulged, mouths which leered, fingers itching to come out of their frame, wrists which exposed the pulse; all the colors higgledy-piggledy; all the lines in hubbub, like the ravings of lunacy. Form breaks into panic; the calm and cool whisper of life in trance which once had breathed out such an ineffable hope is heated, fired into a blaze and destroyed, and in its place . . . *realism,* the blunt statement of life, something everybody misunderstands while recognizing. And all far from the purpose of art. For its purpose is not to reflect the actual facts of this life, because it is not the custom of the artist to walk behind things, having won it as his privilege to walk in front of them—to lead. Rather should life reflect the likeness of the spirit, for it was the spirit which first chose the artist to chronicle its Beauty.[5] And in that picture, if the form be that of the living, on account of its beauty and tenderness, the color for it must be sought from that unknown land of the imagination, . . . and what is that but the land where dwells that which we call Death. So it is not lightly and flippantly that I speak of Puppets and their power to retain the beautiful and remote expressions in form and face even when subjected to a patter of praise, a torrent of applause. There are persons who have made a jest of these Puppets. "Puppet" is a term of contempt, though there still remain some who find beauty in these little figures, degenerate though they have become.

To speak of a puppet with most men and women is to cause them to giggle. They think at once of the wires; they think of the stiff hands and the jerky movements; they tell me it is "a funny little doll." But let me tell them a few things about these Puppets.

[5] "All forms are perfect in the poet's mind: But these are not abstracted or compounded from nature; they are from Imagination," WILLIAM BLAKE.

Let me again repeat that they are the descendants of a great and noble family of Images, Images which were made in the likeness of God; and that many centuries ago these figures had a rhythmical movement and not a jerky one; had no need for wires to support them, nor did they speak through the nose of the hidden manipulator. (Poor Punch, I mean no slight to you! You stand alone, dignified in your despair, as you look back across the centuries with painted tears still wet upon your ancient cheeks, and you seem to cry out appealingly to your dog, "Sister Anne, sister Anne, is *nobody* coming?" And then with that superb bravado of yours, you turn the force of our laughter [and my tears] upon yourself with the heartrending shriek of "Oh my nose! Oh, my nose! Oh my nose!") Did you think, ladies and gentlemen, that these puppets were always little things of but a foot high?

Indeed, no! The Puppet had once a more generous form than yourselves.

Do you think that he kicked his feet about on a little platform six foot square, made to resemble a little old-fashioned theatre; so that his head almost touched the top of the proscenium; and do you think that he always lived in a little house where the door and windows were as small as a doll's house, with painted window blinds parted in the center, and where the flowers of his little garden had courageous petals as big as his head? Try and dispel this idea altogether from your minds, and let me tell you something of his habitation.

In Asia lay his first kingdom. On the banks of the Ganges they built him his home, . . . a vast palace springing from column to column into the air and pouring from column to column down again into the water. Surrounded by gardens spread warm and rich with flowers and cooled by fountains; gardens into which no sounds entered, in which hardly anything stirred. Only in the cool and private chambers of this palace the swift minds of his attendants stirred incessantly. Something they were making which should become him, something to honor the spirit which had given him birth. And then, one day, the ceremony. In this ceremony he took part; a celebration once more in praise of the Creation; the old thanksgiving, the hurrah for existence, and with it the sterner hurrah for the privilege of the existence to come, which is veiled by the word Death. And during this cere-

mony there appeared before the eyes of the brown worshipers the symbols of all things on earth and in Nirvana. The symbol of the beautiful tree, the symbol of the hills, the symbols of those rich ores which the hills contained; the symbol of the cloud, of the wind, and of all swift moving things; the symbol of the quickest of moving things, of Thought, of Remembrance; the symbol of the Animal, the symbol of Buddha and of Man . . . and here he comes, the figure, the Puppet at whom you all laugh so much. You laugh at him today because none but his weaknesses are left to him. He reflects these from you; but you would not have laughed had you seen him in his prime, in that age when he was called upon to be the symbol of man in the great ceremony, and, stepping forward, was the beautiful figure of our heart's delight. If we should laugh at and insult the memory of the Puppet, we should be laughing at the fall that we have brought about in ourselves . . . laughing at the Beliefs and Images we have broken. A few centuries later, and we find his home a little the worse for wear. From a temple it has become, I will not say a theatre, but something between a temple and a theatre, and he is losing his health in it. Something is in the air; his doctors tell him he must be careful. "And what am I to fear the most?" he asks them. They answer him; "Fear most the vanity of men." He thinks, "But that is what I myself have always taught; that we who celebrated in joy this our existence, should have this one great fear. Is it possible that I, one who has ever revealed this truth, should be one to lose sight of it and should myself be one of the first to fall? Clearly some subtle attack is to be made on me. I will keep my eyes upon the Heavens." And he dismisses his doctors and ponders upon it.

And now let me tell you who it was that came to disturb the calm air which surrounded this curiously perfect thing. It is on record that somewhat later he took up his abode on the far Eastern Coast, and there came two women to look upon him. And at the ceremony to which they came he glowed with such earthly splendor and yet such unearthly simplicity, that though he proved an inspiration to the thousand nine hundred and ninety-eight souls who participated in the festival, an inspiration which cleared the mind even as it intoxicated, yet to these two women it proved an intoxication only. He did not see them, his eyes were

fixed on the heavens: but he charged them full of a desire too great to be quenched; the desire to stand as the direct symbol of the Divinity in Man. No sooner thought than done; and arraying themselves as best they could in garments ("like his," they thought), moving with gestures ("like his," they said), and being able to cause wonderment in the minds of the beholders ("even as he does," they cried), they built themselves a temple ("like his" "like his"), and supplied the demand of the vulgar, . . . the whole thing a poor parody. This is on record. It is the first record in the East of the actor. . . . The actor springs from the foolish vanity of two women who are not strong enough to look upon the symbol of godhead without desiring to tamper with it; and the parody proved profitable. In fifty or a hundred years, places for such parodies were to be found in all parts of the land. Weeds, they say, grow quickly, and that wilderness of weeds, the modern theatre, soon sprang up. The figure of the Divine Puppet attracted fewer and fewer lovers, and the women were quite the latest thing. With the fading of the Puppet and the advance of these women who exhibited themselves on the stage in his place, came that darker spirit which is called Chaos, and in its wake the triumph of the riotous Personality. Do you see then, what has made me love and learn to value that which today we call the puppet and to detest that which we call life in art? I pray earnestly for the return of the image . . . the Übermarionette, to the theatre; and when he comes again and is but seen, he will be loved so well that once more will it be possible for the people to return to their ancient joy in ceremonies . . . once more will Creation be celebrated . . . homage rendered to existence . . . and divine and happy intercession made to death.

CHARLES R. LYONS

## Gordon Craig's
## Concept of the Actor *

In 1908, when Edward Gordon Craig demanded that the human actor must leave the stage to be replaced by a nonhuman "instrument," the Übermarionette, he confirmed an exile from the modern theatre from which he has yet to return. Craig projected that revolutionary theory from the Arena Goldoni in Florence, the ancient theatre which became the home of *The Mask,* that erratic, biased, consistently interesting, and occasionally brilliant periodical which in letter is dedicated to the art of the theatre but which in spirit is dedicated to the image of Gordon Craig as the savior of the modern theatre. It was also at the Arena Goldoni that Craig realized his dream of establishing a school, which, unfortunately, found support for only one year. Craig had come to Florence to continue his study of the art of the theatre. Dissatisfied with the aesthetics of the modern theatre, Craig had withdrawn from his eight-year apprenticeship with Henry Irving in 1898; and, from 1900 as *metteur-en-scène, régisseur,* and aesthetic critic, his energies focused upon the consideration and study of the art of the theatre.[1] However, his theories were so revolutionary that he had difficulty finding an opportunity to express them in performance. Consequently, he became a theorist and a critic and published the concepts which he, with only a few exceptions, was unable to demonstrate in the theatre. Yet the theories and practice of this revolutionary figure have exerted

* Reprinted from the *Educational Theatre Journal,* XVI:3 (October, 1964).

[1] Edward Gordon Craig examines the period of his disenchantment as an actor and his growing interest in the aesthetics of the theatre in *Index to the Story of My Days: Some Memoirs of Edward Gordon Craig, 1872–1907* (New York, 1957), pp. 190–221.

such an influence upon the modern theatre that it is impossible to calculate the degree to which the theatre has responded to his demands. The strength and cyclopean simplicity of Craig's designs for the theatre are still realized in almost direct imitation, and his theories of stage design have become commonplaces in the mouths of contemporary designers. Consider, for example, Craig's following statement: ". . . the stage picture can never make an important artistic statement alone, it must always be an adjunct to the expression of the harmony and orchestration of ideas that the poet clothes in words and that the actor conveys through the instrument of his sensibilities." [2]

Craig's artistic judgments are based upon a principle which is fundamental to his theory: that the objective of the theatre is neither intellectual nor emotional but is the evocation of aesthetic pleasure derived from the presence of imaginative beauty.[3] While Gordon Craig is concerned with an infinite number of subjects within the theatre, his revolutionary concepts focus upon three areas and formulate three demands: that the theatrical production must be unified—movement, scene, costume the product of one artistic imagination; that the scene is to be created to project the atmosphere or idea of the play; and that the essence of the art is symbolic movement with the subsequent demand that the human actor, as he presently exists, must be replaced by a more perfect instrument, one capable of perfect movement.

Craig insists that the theatre's primary need is for artists— that the theatre can reach the level of art only if the total production is the design of a single person. He describes the composite art: "The art of the theatre is neither acting nor the play, it is not scene or dance, but it consists of all the elements of which these things are composed: action, which is the very spirit of acting; words, which are the body of the play; line and color, which are the very heart of the scene; rhythm, which is the very essence of dance." [4] In the absolute of Craig's metaphysical conception of the theatre, the play, or scenario for action, would also be a

---

[2] Craig cited in Peter Brook, "The Influence of Gordon Craig in Theory and Practice," *Drama,* XXXVII (Summer, 1955), p. 34.

[3] Craig, *On the Art of the Theatre* (London, 1911), pp. 295–296.

[4] *Ibid.,* p. 138.

product of the mind of the single artistic director. However, at our present stage of the division between drama and theatre, that situation, he admits, is rarely a possibility. In any case, the production should be directed by a single individual who can coordinate its several elements: "That is the only way the work can be done, if unity, the only thing vital to a work of art, is to be obtained." [5] Although the modern theatre still holds few designer-directors, the present function of the stage-director, or producer, as a source of artistic unity, stands—to a large measure—as the theatre's answer to the demands of Gordon Craig.

Covertly inspired by the writings of Adolphe Appia or simultaneously realizing similar concepts in the aesthetics of the theatre, Edward Gordon Craig was among the first to sense the inherent relationship between the idea of a play and the creation of its scene. His objective in the development of the scene is to produce "an atmosphere, not a locality." He rebelled against the decoration of the romantic theatre and the uncommunicative clutter of the naturalistic stage, declaring that it is not the presentation of realistic detail which is the purpose of the stage setting but rather the creation of a "place which harmonizes with the mind of the poet." He insists that the design proceed from a consideration of the whole play in acting, movement, and voice, and produce an imaginative statement supplementing these elements.[6] As Peter Brook has noted, to realize that Craig's concept of simplification is still a vital force in the contemporary theatre, it is necessary only to consider the stage pictures of Bérard, the coordinated and expressive dance patterns of Martha Graham, the work of Wieland Wagner in Bayreuth, and the designs of Noguchi.[7]

Symbolism is the essence of Craig's aesthetic theory.[8] The projection of a unified symbolic design is the motive of his demand for the single powerful stage-director. His second demand, as noted, is that the scene assist the projection of that design. Integral to the exploitation of visual symbolism implicit in the first two demands is Craig's insistence that the theatre develop a new

[5] *Ibid.*, p. 157.
[6] See Craig's instruction to the young artists of the theatre, *Ibid.*, p. 31.
[7] Brook, p. 36.
[8] See "Symbolism," *On the Art of the Theatre*, pp. 293–294.

language of movement, "a new form of acting, consisting for the main part of symbolical gesture." [9] The research for this "new form of acting" led Craig not only to the Übermarionette but also to evoking a critical response which was unwilling to discount the overstatement of youthful enthusiasm and consider the aesthetic value of his ideas. The Übermarionette remains a source of critical amusement, but it is an important aspect of a total aesthetic concept which has provided one of the strongest influences in the modern theatre. As such, the Übermarionette is worthy of our critical attention. Craig's concept of the Übermarionette as the ideal actor is not a consistent one; rather, it is an evolutionary concept. It is the intention of this essay to examine that concept as it evolved.

Gordon Craig makes his first major statement concerning his theory of acting in his little book, *The Art of the Theatre,* which was published in 1905.[10] The basic concept upon which Craig bases his vision of the actor is expressed here: that the stage-director alone has the potential to be an artist of the theatre. It is the stage-director's creative exploitation of action, words, line, color, and rhythm which produces the art of the theatre. One element of his medium is the physical body and voice of the actor, but—when he interprets by means of the actor, through the actor's creative imagination—he becomes merely a craftsman.[11] In this dialogue, written in the Socratic form in which Lope de Vega discussed his view of the theatre in the seventeenth century, Craig claims that "one element of the art is no more important than the other . . . ," [12] it is obvious that his primary concern is undeniably with those qualities of the art which appeal to the eye: ". . . the eye is more swiftly and powerfully appealed to than any other sense; it is without question the keenest sense of the body of man." [13]

To support his implicit emphasis upon action, he traces the

[9] *Ibid.,* p. 61.

[10] Craig, *The Art of the Theatre* (Edinburgh, 1905) was incorporated into Craig's second book, *On the Art of the Theatre* (London, 1911) as "The First Dialogue," pp. 137–181. All further footnotes will refer to the pagination of the second book.

[11] *On the Art of the Theatre,* p. 148.

[12] *Ibid.,* p. 138.

[13] *Ibid.,* p. 141.

origin of the theatre in dance; and he claims that the first dramatists, as "children of the theatre," were firmly trained in the tradition of the dance and appealed to the eyes, depending primarily
upon movement for communication. Consistent with this emphasis upon movement, Craig claims that the human actor as
material for the stage-director is only more significant than the
materials of wood, canvas, and light because he provides the supreme element of movement.

Craig's concept of the presence of the human actor as a threat
to the artistic creation is also introduced in this dialogue: "For
his thoughts (beautiful as they may chance to be) may not match
the spirit of the pattern which has been so carefully prepared by
the director." [14] At this point in his criticism, Craig had not yet
rejected the actor from the theatre; and, in discussing the need
for the stage-director to control the movement of the actor, he
wrote: ". . . the finer the actor the finer his intelligence and
taste, and therefore the more easily controlled." [15] The image of
the Übermarionette, which is not to present itself until the April,
1908, issue of *The Mask,* is anticipated in the following passage
of the dialogue in *The Art of the Theatre.*

PLAYGOER: But are you not asking these intelligent actors almost
to become puppets?

STAGE-DIRECTOR: A sensitive question! which one would expect
from an actor who felt uncertain about his powers. A puppet is at
present only a doll, delightful enough for a puppet show. But for a
theatre we need more than a doll.[16]

Building upon the premise expressed in this little dialogue, Gordon Craig extended and expanded his theory of the perfect actor
in his essay, "The Artists of the Future." [17] A critical examination of Craig's concept of the actor must include attention to

[14] *Ibid.,* p. 167.

[15] *Ibid.*

[16] *Ibid.*

[17] Craig, "The Artists of the Future," *The Mask,* I (March, 1908). This
essay was incorporated into *On the Art of the Theatre* as "The Artist of the
Theatre of the Future," pp. 1–53. Further footnotes will refer to the pagination of *On the Art of the Theatre.*

what appears to be a major inconsistency in this theory. In consideration of the actor as material subject to the artistic design of the stage-director, Craig denies the creativity of the actor; however, in this essay he states: ". . . the ideal actor will be the man who possesses both a rich nature and a powerful brain. . . . It will contain everything. . . . The perfect actor would be he whose brain could conceive and could show us the perfect symbols of all which his nature contains." [18] The perfect actor would not merely exhibit the conventions of gesture and movement, but from the sphere of the imagination he would "fashion certain symbols which, without exhibiting the bare passions, would none the less tell us clearly about them." [19] Implicit in this statement of the ideal is the demand for a new suggestive language of movement in which "the symbols are to be made mainly from material which lies outside his [the actor's] person." [20] Thus it appears that Craig would exploit the creativity of the actor to develop a new symbolic form of movement, but that movement would be, ideally, implemented by something nonhuman: ". . . the actor as he is today must ultimately disappear and be merged in something else if works of art are to be seen in our kingdom of the Theatre." [21] Again, the concentration is upon movement as the primary source and the primary means of expression of the art: "I like to remember that all things spring from movement, even music; and I like to think that it is to be our supreme honor to be the ministers to the supreme force—movement." [22] Again tracing the development of the theatre, "a degenerate development," from the movement of the human form, Gordon Craig recalls "another and a wiser race, who used other instruments." [23] The criticism of the human form here, as before, is based upon its independence, its native inability to be an instrument of the mind. In an extremely interesting passage, Craig explains the limitations of the body as a result of Man's fall from Grace which destroyed the "square deific." He writes: ". . . we have to ban-

18 *Ibid.*, p. 11.
19 *Ibid.*
20 *Ibid.*
21 *Ibid.*, p. 12.
22 *Ibid.*, p. 47.
23 *Ibid.*, p. 48.

ish from our mind all thought of the use of a human form as the instrument which we are to use to translate what we call movement." [24] Craig's disenchantment with the corporeal actor as a material for expressing the perfect thought is reflected in his letter to Madame Eleonora Duse which is contained in the first issue of *The Mask,* a letter which decries the imperfection of the human form as an expression of thought.[25]

However, there is an obvious tension present in Craig's critical thought between his concept of the theatre as the realization of a unified design in the creative mind of the stage-director and his recognition of the creative force and vitality of the living actor. That this tension exists is demonstrated by his denial of the possibility of achieving art with the human actor, almost simultaneously with the affirmation of the potential which Duse held as an artist of the theatre: ". . . and this wonderful woman, Eleonora Duse, she, too, is content with less than perfection. . . . If she were not so, with the force and the beauty, and, as we believe, the strength which is in her, she could create a state in which the creation of art might become possible." [26] Craig's denial of the potential of man's achieving perfection on the basis of his fall from Grace provides a less than conclusive resolution of that tension: ". . . we must realize that no longer is man to advance and proclaim that his person is the perfect and fitting medium for the expression of the perfect thought." [27]

Consistent with that aspect of his criticism which could not reconcile the actor to his vision of what the theatre should be, Gordon Craig vilified the actor in his strongest statement, "The Actor and the Übermarionette," which appeared in the second

[24] *Ibid.,* p. 50.

[25] Craig, "A Letter to Madame Eleonora Duse," *The Mask,* I (March, 1908). Cf. Craig, *The Theatre Advancing* (London, 1921), pp. 267–274, in which the letter is reproduced.

[26] *Ibid.*

[27] Craig, "The Artist of the Theatre of the Future," p. 50. It is not the purpose of this paper to evaluate Craig's theories in terms of their psychological implication; however, it is interesting to note that Craig's denial of the artistic integrity of the actor is based upon an ascetic attitude towards the human body with its "weakness and tremors of the flesh." He blames the limitations of the body upon the Fall and cites Cardinal Manning in stating that the actor's business necessitates "the prostitution of a body purified by baptism." (*On the Art of the Theatre,* p. 81.)

issue of *The Mask*.[28] The basic concepts in this essay can be found in the earlier statements; however, Craig's revolutionary doctrine finds explicit definition here. Obviously sparing no force, the young critic headed his essay with Duse's famous credo for the salvation of the theatre:

> To save the Theatre, the Theatre must be destroyed, the actors and actresses must all die of the plague . . . [sic] They make art impossible.[29]

Gordon Craig again denies the possibility that the actor can be an artist on the grounds that the human being is not a material which the designer can calculate. Expanding his earlier concept that the human body cannot respond fully and consistently to the mind, Craig describes the actor as subject to the spontaneous action of the emotions: "The actions of the actor's body, the expression of his face, the sounds of his voice, all are at the mercy of the winds of his emotions: . . . emotion possesses him; . . ." [30] The necessary action in art is symbolic movement, not the gesture which attempts to reproduce nature. Craig's rejection of the actor is consistent with an aesthetic which forbids imitation as an artistic process; and with this concept in mind, it is not difficult to understand why he attempted to discover or to create a figure which was itself a symbol, replacing the human actor whose actuality confuses the symbolism: "The actor must go, and in his place comes the inanimate figure—the Übermarionette we may call him, until he has won for himself a better name." [31] Craig briefly traces the history of the puppet from its origin in ritual as the first actor to its modern "prostitution" in

[28] Craig, "The Actor and the Übermarionette," *The Mask*, I (April, 1908). This essay was incorporated into *On the Art of the Theatre* under its original title, pp. 54–94. Further footnotes will refer to the pagination of *On the Art of the Theatre*.

[29] Craig, citing Eleonora Duse, *Studies in Seven Arts* (London, 1900), in "The Actor and the Übermarionette," p. 54.

[30] *Ibid.*, p. 56.

[31] *Ibid.*, p. 81. As a corollary symbol to the Übermarionette, Craig uses the figure of the mask. He writes: ". . . the mask is the only right medium of portraying the expressions of the soul as shown through the expressions of the face." (*On the Art of the Theatre*, p. 13.) For the sake of clarity I have not projected an association of the marionette and the mask throughout this essay; however, that association is implicit in Craig's use of the terms, both literally and symbolically.

the grotesque Punch, and he defines the origin of the human actor to be the gross and vulgar imitation of the puppet.

Craig's attack upon the human actor concentrates upon two aesthetic problems: the obtrusive element of the actor's personality and the paucity of discipline which could control this obtrusive element. Craig's attack was consistently supported, of course, by *The Mask,* which in October, 1912, published an essay by Anatole France which included the following statement, supporting Craig's opinion: "If I must fully express my feeling, the actors spoil the play for me. I mean the good actors. I would put up with the others! But it is the excellent actors, such as one finds at the *Comédie Française* that I positively cannot stand. Their talent is too great; it covers everything. There is nothing but them. Their personality effaces the work which they represent. They are prominent." [32] Craig himself decried the lack of discipline which he felt characterized the theatre he was attacking, a lack of discipline which allowed the personality and temperament of the actor to influence, and frequently, to direct the artistic design of a production.[33] He saw the marionette as the symbol for the perfectly disciplined actor. The marionette, as a figure which holds neither animation nor personality apart from that given to him by the stage-director, would provide a flexible and calculable material for the design without obtruding upon it. "There is only one actor . . . nay one man . . . who has the soul of the Dramatic Poet and who has ever served as true and loyal interpreter of the Poet. This is the marionette." [34] As an inanimate object, subject only to the will of the manipulator, the discipline of the puppet would be the ideal: the silent and obedient actor.

As noted previously in this essay, Craig's concentration upon movement as the primary element of the art was accompanied by a disdain for words in the theatre; consequently, the silence of the marionette required the wordless drama which held his fas-

[32] Anatole France, "The Marionettes of M. Signoret," trans. John Lane, *The Mask,* V (October, 1912), p. 100.

[33] Craig, *The Theatre Advancing,* pp. 277–280.

[34] Craig, "Gentlemen, The Marionette!" *The Mask,* V (October, 1912). This essay was incorporated into *The Theatre Advancing* under the same title, pp. 207–212. Further footnotes will refer to the pagination of *The Theatre Advancing.*

cination.[35] In answer to Nietzsche's criticism of the theatre, three objectives for the modern theatre were formulated in an editorial note in *The Mask* of July, 1913:

1. That the Theatre shall become master of its art.
2. That obedience and silence shall always be in the nature of its art.
3. That words shall become blessed after a century of silence.[36]

The perfect actor would be the means to achieve these objectives. To Gordon Craig, whose imagination was trained to think in terms of abstract symbols, the Übermarionette became the symbol of the perfect actor, that actor whose flexible body would perform the movement of the planned design in performance. In 1912, he published an essay in *The Mask* which seems constructed to redirect back onto his critics the ridicule which his earlier statement had generated. It becomes increasingly obvious in this essay, "Gentlemen, The Marionette!," that Craig is thinking of the Übermarionette as a symbol of the perfect human actor rather than as a nonhuman instrument.

The marionette is a little figure, but it has given birth to great ones who, if they perceive the two essentials, obedience and silence, shall preserve their race . . . these children of his I have called Übermarionettes and have written of them at some length. What the wires of the Übermarionette shall be and what shall guide him, who can say? I do not believe in the mechanical . . . nor in the material. The wires which stretch from Divinity to the soul of the Poet are wires which might command him; has God no more such threads to spare . . . for one more figure? I cannot doubt it. I will never believe anything else.

And did you think when I wrote five years ago of this new figure who should stand as the symbol of man . . . and when I christened

[35] Craig considers that drama and poetry cannot be combined in a single entity known as a dramatic poem. He considers the dramatic poem to be complete without performance. See *On the Art of the Theatre*, pp. 139–145, for the discussion of dramatic poetry in "The First Dialogue."

[36] "Editorial Notes," *The Mask*, VI (October, 1913), p. 89. This note was probably written by John Semar, editor of *The Mask*; however, as important a note as this definition of the objectives for the modern theatre would have been approved, in all probability, by Craig, or have been as consistent with his concept of the art of the theatre as his staff could determine.

him the Übermarionette . . . to see real metal or silken threads? I hope that another five years will be long enough time for you to draw those tangleable wires out of your thoughts.[37]

However, a critical examination of Craig's early essays and notes makes it obvious that he originally did think in terms of the development of an inanimate object rather than merely in terms of a new style of acting. But in a new preface to *On the Art of the Theatre* which was published again in 1924, Gordon Craig denied again his intention to substitute a nonhuman figure for the mortal actor:

. . . I no more want to see the living actors replaced by things of wood than the great Italian actress of our day wants all the actors to die.

Is it not true that when we cry "Oh, go to the Devil!" we never really want that to happen? What we mean is, "get a little of his fire and come back cured."

And that is what I wanted the actors to do—some actors—the bad ones, when I said they must go and the Übermarionette replace them. . . . The Übermarionette is the actor, plus fire, minus egoism.[38]

Regardless of Gordon Craig's reinterpretation in 1924 of his own statements made in 1908, the truth of his early intention to replace the actor with an object is substantiated by his direct statement concerning the instrument with which he hoped to translate *Movement* and the art which would consequently evolve:

I wish to leave all open and make no definite rules as to how and by what means these movements are to be shown. This alone let me tell you. I have thought of and begun to make my instrument, and through this instrument I intend soon to venture in my quest for beauty. . . . When I have constructed my instrument and permitted it to make its first assay, I look to others to make like instruments.

[37] Craig, *The Theatre Advancing*, pp. 110–111.
[38] Craig, Preface (1924) to *On the Art of the Theatre* (London, 1924), pp. vii–viii.

Slowly, and from the principles which rule all these instruments some better instrument will be made.[39]

Certainly Craig's dissatisfaction with the contemporary actor, which began as dissatisfaction with his own "artistry" as an actor, led him to project the theory of the Übermarionette.[40] And his implicit faith in the creativity of the actor—and probably an aesthetic dissatisfaction with the limitations of the marionette— provided the motive for the modification of his original concept of the Übermarionette, as a nonhuman instrument, to the use of the Übermarionette as the symbol of the ideal human actor.

Gordon Craig never lost his fascination in the creative force of the human actor even in his dedication to the Übermarionette; and this aspect of the tension between his concept of the actor as a self-sufficient creative force and his concept of the impropriety of the actor in the theatre is present in the essay which introduces the Übermarionette. While Craig denies the possibility of the human actor to achieve the absolute control necessary for pure symbolic movement, he does request the actor to release himself from that limitation which is imposed upon him by emotional acting. He demands that suggestion by symbol replace impersonation: "They [the actors] must create for themselves a new form of acting, consisting for the main part of symbolic gesture." [41]

Craig's concept of the actor as symbol manifested itself in two assertions: the denial of the psychological method of acting of the Western theatre and the affirmation of the symbolical nature of Eastern drama. Craig's rejection of the psychological method of acting is well demonstrated in Constantin Stanislavsky's detailed admission of the failure of the Moscow Art Theatre to achieve a style of acting which was within Craig's concept of the actor. However, Stanislavsky's account of the Craig production

[39] *Ibid.*, pp. 50–51.
[40] See Craig, *Index to the Story of My Days*, p. 218. "And as I became slowly aware that something was not with us, as it was in truth with those who practice the fine arts, I became gradually unfit to attend to my duties. I was losing my belief (right or wrong) in my old religion—my actor's Art."
[41] Craig, *On the Art of the Theatre*, p. 61.

of *Hamlet* at the Art Theatre is also testimony to the ambiguity present in Gordon Craig's approach to the actor.[42] Stanislavsky notes the tension between Craig's concept of the actorless theatre and Craig's vital interest in the living actor:

> Craig dreamed of a theatre without men and women, without actors. He wanted to supplant them with marionettes who had no bad habits or bad gestures, no painted faces, no exaggerated voices, no smallness of soul, no worthless ambitions. . . . But, as it became clear later on, the denial of actors did not interfere with Craig's enthusiasm for the slightest hint of true theatrical talent in men or women. Feeling it, Craig would turn into a child, leap in joy from his chair, propel himself over the footlights. . . . When he saw the absence of talent he would become angry and dream of his marionettes again.[43]

Before beginning actual work on the production of *Hamlet*, Craig spent a year in Florence preparing his design for the production. "Hamlet in Moscow: Notes for a Short Address to the Actors of the Moscow Art Theatre," was published in *The Mask* four years after the production.[44] The contents of this brief essay give some idea of what Craig demands from the living actor. In his notes, he requests the actor to express a sense of royalty, not the theatrical impression of an actor acting on the stage. Craig's instructions do not include rational processes, because he did not feel that the actor could fulfill his function merely through a process of reason; and here Craig's concept of the actor grows ambiguous: the critic who declared that the actor was not a creative force in the theatre and that the actor's emotion destroyed the stage-director's design insists that the actor project his art only through a state of ecstasy:

> . . . if I went further I should say that we must first get into that spiritual state of ecstasy which we can better imagine than tell about.

---

[42] Constantin Stanislavski, *My Life in Art*, trans. J. J. Robbins (Boston, 1937), pp. 505–524.

[43] *Ibid.*, pp. 509–510.

[44] Craig, "*Hamlet* in Moscow: Notes for a Short Address to the Actors of the Moscow Art Theatre," *The Mask*, VII (May, 1915), pp. 109–110. Cf. "The True Hamlet," *The Theatre Advancing*, in which Craig proposes similar ideas.

. . . How to acquire it? . . . I can help you but I cannot teach you. . . . Remember that the acme of ecstasy is not apparent excitement but apparent calm. It is the white heat of emotion; . . . it is almost a trance. . . . You must awaken your imagination and let it possess you entirely. Ecstasy is nothing else than a kind of madness, remember, not any kind of madness. It is all that is Rapid . . . White . . . Glowing . . . Circular . . . Vast . . . Steady.[45]

The theorist who projected the idea of the actorless theatre continues: "It is impossible to believe that you can interpret so great a work without making use of your own greatness. . . . You can do it only by the power of your imagination." [46] Craig's instructions, however, were prepared for his "ideal actor," and when he met the actual members of the company, he did not deliver the prepared notes; he retreated to make one more design for an Übermarionette.

Stanislavsky's company was unable to develop a style which pleased Craig. Craig, of course, rejected the natural style which was based upon a psychological approach to character; but he was equally offended by a theatrical style. "There were no sonorous voice and beautiful speech, harmonic movement and plastics." [47] Stanislavsky himself experimented with a variety of styles before Craig: the conventional French tragic style, the Italian, "the Russian declamatory," "the Russian realistic"; however, Gordon Craig rejected them all. Stanislavsky describes his reaction in *My Life in Art:* "With all his strength he protested on the one hand against the old conventionality of the theatre, and on the other hand he would not accept the humdrum naturalness and simplicity which robbed my interpretations of all poetry. Craig wanted perfection, the ideal that is simple, strong, deep, uplifting, artistic, and the beautiful creation of living human emotion." [48]

Craig's voice during this period was *The Mask,* and concentration upon symbolic movement as the purest language of the theatre led Gordon Craig and *The Mask* into an investigation of the Oriental theatre. As early as 1908, Craig's theories began to

[45] *Ibid.*
[46] *Ibid.*
[47] Stanislavski, p. 522.
[48] *Ibid.,* p. 523.

relate themselves to the nature of the Oriental theatre. In the April, 1908, issue of *The Mask* Jan Van Holt quotes the Dutch actor, Rayaards, in his remarks on the performance of the Japanese actor, Olojiro Kawakami, in Amsterdam: ". . . it does not matter that you do not understand the language of these artists. . . . In seeing his very powerful and always beautiful gestures . . . I understood the Japanese . . . and came to a fuller understanding of something else; that is to say, the aims of Mr. Gordon Craig to subordinate word to gesture in dramatic art." [49] In 1910, *The Mask* became concerned with the Noh drama, which seems to suggest itself as the type of theatre toward which Gordon Craig was moving.[50] In the intensified but abstract communication which the highly conventionalized form of the Noh allows, there is a "form of acting, consisting for the main part of symbolical gesture." [51] Also, because the Oriental drama depends upon conventions existing for several centuries, the possibility of the human actor's obtruding upon the design is slight. As the supreme example of the disciplined actor, the Noh performer is completely subjected by his form.

In October, 1913, Dr. Ananda Coomaraswamy published an essay in *The Mask* which was to exert a profound influence upon the theory of Gordon Craig.[52] Initially Dr. Coomaraswamy celebrates the ancient puppet, ". . . the symbol of man . . . the beautiful symbol of our heart's delight." [53] However, he then counters Gordon Craig's assumption that the human body is not suitable material for the theatre:

Had Mr. Craig studied the ancient Indian theatre he might not have thought it so necessary to reject the bodies of men and women as the material of dramatic art. For those principles which have with great consistency governed all other Oriental arts until recently, have also governed dramatic techniques. The movements of the Indian actor are not accidentally swayed by his personal emotion; he is too perfectly trained for that. His body . . . is an automaton; while he is

[49] Jan Van Holt, "Notes," *The Mask*, I (April, 1908), p. 21.

[50] M. A. Hinckes, "Review of the Japanese Drama," *The Mask*, II (October, 1910), p. 90.

[51] *Ibid.* See *n*. 41.

[52] Dr. Ananda Coomaraswamy, "Notes on Indian Dramatic Technique," *The Mask*, VI (October, 1913), pp. 109–128.

[53] *Ibid.*, p. 109.

acting there is nothing natural . . . that is to say, accidental or inartistic, . . . in his movements or changes of expression. The movement of a single finger, the elevation of an eyebrow, the direction of a
glance . . . all these are determined in the books of technical instruction, or by a constant tradition handed on in pupilary succession. . . . Many of the gestures . . . called *mudra* . . . have
hieratic significance; equally in a painting, an image, a puppet, or a
living dancer . . . , or in personal worship, they express the intentions of the soul in conventional language. . . .[54]

Gordon Craig, however, objected to the extreme limitation
which the Indian drama imposed upon the actor—an objection
which responded to that part of him which recognized the creative force of the living actor.[55] Craig answered Professor
Coomaraswamy's statement that the ideal actor which was symbolized by the Übermarionette could exist in human form with
his plea for a Durable Theatre.[56] The Durable Theatre as described by Gordon Craig is a theatre of rigid convention, a theatre like the Noh drama of Japan and the Indian drama of Professor Coomaraswamy's definition in which the movement and
gesture are established and traditional. It is the theatre, with a
drama established and beyond criticism, performed as a traditional ritual, with which Craig hopes to answer Leonardo Da
Vinci's imperative: "Shun those studies in which the result dies
with the worker." [57]

His plan for a Durable Theatre was possible because Craig
accepted the possible existence of actors whose bodies through
discipline had become flexible and ego-less. Speaking of the
Indian actor described by Coomaraswamy, Craig withdrew his
absolute rejection of the human actor:

I have been told . . . (since I wrote of the Übermarionette) . . .
of a race of actors that existed (and a few today preserve that tradition) who were fitted to be part and parcel of the most durable theatre

[54] *Ibid.,* p. 127.
[55] *Ibid.*
[56] Craig, "A Plea for Two Theatres," *The Mask,* VIII (June, 1918),
p. 15ff. This essay, together with "The Durable Theatre" and "The Perishable Theatre" are incorporated into *The Theatre Advancing.* Further
footnotes will refer to the pagination of *The Theatre Advancing.*
[57] *The Theatre Advancing,* p. 3.

it is possible to conceive. . . . I am not skeptical. I think I would sooner be proved wrong in all my theories and beliefs, than think man unable to rise to any standard known or to be known. And so I accept this information, new though it be to me, and will present it here as a possibility; . . . If the Western actor can become what I am told the Eastern actor was and is, I withdraw all that I have written in my essay "On the Actor and the Übermarionette." [58]

Craig, however, did not attempt to impose the Eastern form on the Western actor; on the contrary, he still believed, or hoped at least, that a conventional, durable form could be developed for the particular use of the Western actor:

I think it is unnecessary to mention the East when speaking of the possible development of Western art; . . . there is no danger in becoming too early acquainted with a matured foreign development of an art which should be evolved afresh from one's own soil.[59]

However, if this evolution is not possible there is always the Übermarionette, not as symbol, but as instrument.

If he, the Übermarionette, arrives it will be no case of my bringing him here, but because no one can prevent him from coming. . . . In the event of man being unable to return to the ancient standard of the East, there is nothing open for us but to fashion something to represent man in this creative and durable art that we are contemplating.[60]

The continuance of Gordon Craig's implicit faith and interest in the human actor is demonstrated by two facts within his critical writing from 1924 to 1930: his plea for a Durable Theatre was accompanied by a plea for a Perishable Theatre in which the actor would become the creative force; and his attention to the extraordinary talent of Henry Irving. In his plan for a Perishable Theatre, he asked for spontaneous creation: an improvisation of words, movement, and possibly music, with—of course—the emphasis upon movement:

[58] *Ibid.*, p. 19.
[59] *Ibid.*, pp. 25–26.
[60] *Ibid.*, pp. 19–20.

. . . a perishable theatre would have to possess its improvised dramas that were elegant and even exquisite. Perhaps here we would drop speech and pass to the dance . . . but dance based upon the movements of perishable things of nature. . . .[61]

The improvisation as Craig sees it would not be an "invention of the moment," but as in the *commedia dell'arte,* it would exist within a defined style.

Gordon Craig's plea for a Perishable Theatre answers that element of his own imagination which recognizes the creative force of the actor, an element in Craig's own aesthetic nature which was never completely purged by his concept of the Über-marionette. At this point in this essay, it would be interesting to return to a letter published by Gordon Craig in the August, 1908, issue of *The Mask*—four months after he demanded that the Übermarionette replace the human actor. Here Craig anticipates the nature of his concept of the Perishable Theatre:

I believe that the great actors possess the power of creating pieces of work without assistance from any one else; that is to say I believe that you, or one of the few others, could, taking some theme or some two themes—let us say the idea of meeting and the idea of parting —out of these things, by movement, scene, and voice, put before the audience all the different meanings of all the joys and sorrows that are wrapped up in the idea of meeting and the idea of parting.[62]

Gordon Craig's idealization of Henry Irving as the most perfect actor is a fact of great importance which might profitably have been introduced at any point in this essay. As early as 1908, Gordon Craig wrote:

. . . do not forget that the very nearest approach that has ever been made to the ideal actor, with his brain commanding his nature, has been Henry Irving. There are many books which tell you about him, and the best of all books is his face. To begin with, you will find a mask . . . I should say that the face of Irving was the connecting link between that spasmodic and ridiculous expression of the human

[61] *Ibid.*, p. 27.
[62] *Ibid.*, p. 255.

face as used by the theatres of the last few centuries, and the masks which will be used in place of the human face in the near future.[63]

However, Craig's major critical evaluation of Henry Irving was published in 1930. This evaluation was made by Craig after he had developed and affirmed his own concept of the actor, which he symbolized in the Übermarionette; and in this study of Irving, Craig celebrates the potential of the human actor to fulfill the demands of the Übermarionette:

. . . Irving was the nearest thing ever known to what I have called the Übermarionette. Now an Übermarionette is all sorts of things at which I have hinted in books and drawings which I have made since 1907. I only hope that I have not worried anybody with the notion of an actor who should be all that a marionette is and much more—and that I do not worry you now. But there is a point that I never touched on. It is a human point, and it is related to Irving, for from Irving the whole notion receives corroboration.[64]

Craig discusses Irving's transposition of English into a unique speech which enriched the sounds of words. However, his primary concern is with the dance-like movement of Irving, the performance of a preconceived symbolic design: "From the first to the last moment that Irving stood on the stage, each movement was significant . . . every sound, each movement, was intentional—clear-cut, measured dance: nothing real—all massively artificial—yet all flashing with the light and the pulse of nature. A fine style." [65] According to Craig, Irving depended upon technique rather than inspiration. Craig quotes Irving as saying "you can . . . *design* a part, a role, so carefully that inspired or not, you'll be deemed interesting." [66]

From the time of his apprenticeship to the actor-manager, Gordon Craig held the opinion that Henry Irving was the most perfect human actor, but his critical evaluation of him as the human personification of the Übermarionette is made from the perspective and detachment of thirty-three years of aesthetic

consideration. Consequently, since *Henry Irving* was published in 1930, it can be said that the great actor fulfilled the requirements of the Übermarionette in terms of Craig's concept as it evolved from 1907 to 1930.

As this essay notes, Craig sees the theatre as a visual art; and his definition of the perfect actor is made primarily in terms of his function as a visual symbol. Craig demands that the performance be the manifestation of a unified design, a design produced in the imagination of the stage-director. That design, according to Craig's aesthetic, should be a symbolic one. His insistence that the actor submit himself to the preconceived design precludes the individual creativity of the actor. The presence of the ego of the actor is a force which obtrudes upon the symbolic design, and the limitations of the human body provide an inadequate material for the implementation of the design. Acutely sensing these limitations, Gordon Craig turned away from the human actor to the drama of a perfect nonhuman "instrument," the Übermarionette. However, even when he believed that his objective of the ideal actor could be reached only in the creation of an inanimate figure, Craig could not deny his fascination with the creative force of the human actor. Thus it has been the purpose of this essay, in its organic development, to examine that tension as it manifested itself in Craig's critical writings from 1905 to 1930.

That aspect of Craig's imagination which sees the actor's ego effaced in the development of a conventional, symbolic, formalized style recognized the Eastern drama, particularly the Indian, as a promise that a Western drama could exist in which the material would be a disciplined, ego-less human actor. This ideal demanded a Durable Theatre. However, he was unable to reject the spontaneous improvisation of the actor as a vital element in the art of the theatre. Gordon Craig has never attempted to resolve that tension into a single concept and definition; and the dichotomy remains: a plea for two theatres, the Durable and the Perishable.

W A L T E R  K E R R

## Man—As Monster, or God *

Suddenly we are learning something about size in the theatre.

Within a very few months we have come to see the value of images swollen close to the proportions of nightmare. They loom at us, and physically threaten us, in the last short play of *America Hurrah* as giant flesh-tinted robots first rip away their clothes and then rip apart the flimsy match-box world they inhabit. They leer at us in Central Park as a locust-faced chorus darts aside to make way for a mile-wide Titus Andronicus, a masked titan of a man whose shoulders seem literally broad enough to bear the burden of having lost twenty-one sons in battle. Above all, they fill the stage of the Tyrone Guthrie Theater in Minneapolis with massive, mobile bronzes that go by the names of Clytemnestra, Apollo, Athena as *The House of Atreus* walks its path of blood to a last universal judgment.

The oversize in each of these productions is achieved—to begin with—by devices we had long thought outmoded and dismissed as primitive: grotesque masks, boots and stilts to push heads toward the heavens, costumes that seem to have been forged rather than sewn, choruses freshly emerged from clay as though a dozen Lazaruses had not yet wholly rid themselves of the earth they'd been bound to, lighting that seeks out sculptured folds rather than flat paint, music like the thin whistling breath of approaching death or like a pounding heartbeat that has invaded the skull. Man—little, trivial man—blows up in our faces to become a monster or a god.

* Reprinted from *The New York Times*, September 10, 1967. Copyright, ©, 1967 by *The New York Times* Company. Reprinted by permission.

To what purpose? If justification for this new—or revived—insight into the nature of the stage were needed, Tyrone Guthrie's extraordinarily impressive production of Aeschylus' *House of Atreus,* in a version by John Lewin, would take care of the matter hands down. The day is won for sheer scale the moment the great, lava-streaked doors of Agamemnon's palace are thrown open so that Douglas Campbell, as Clytemnestra, can stalk in utter silence across the thrust stage, quieting and dispersing the babbling chorus by the archetypal, instantly electrifying, force of his / her presence.

All of the women's roles in the play are played by men, immediately stilling in our minds our habit of watching all encounters domestically, our habit of thinking in relatively trivial psychological terms. We do not look at Clytemnestra as temptable flesh but as naked human will, as vengeful energy incarnate. Neither does this queen become an abstraction: she is an actuality turned into an ultimate, a human drive elevated to demon. Mr. Campbell does not so much walk as cleave space with the irresistible indifference of a glacier, his spattered purple robes falling away from him like the steep sides of a volcano, his broad cubed cheekbones and bent Picasso eyes piercing and then subduing the yielding universe about him.

Speaking, he does not pitch his voice high. He begins, for a line or two, with a contained softness that is neither male nor female, only casual. Then, not more than four lines in, he opens full to his own masculine register. It is as though our perception of the play had dropped from our heads to our bowels, a plunging below polite surfaces to some vast beginning of things in the sea. The content of the evening is bass; we are going to dig; this is the history of a groan, below speech.

The play, moving through the familiar and open excitements of Clytemnestra's baiting murder of her hardheaded warrior-husband ("We were right and therefore ruthless," Agamemnon says before he dies) and then through Orestes' murder of his mother to avenge his father's death, works as it always has: as simple narrative, as sheer situation, it is very nearly unparalleled. If a little bit of Clytemnestra's catlike deviousness is lost in the masking of faces, the loss is more than made up by the unex-

pected mythic power (I don't like that word "mythic" very much, but there's nothing else for it) of Orestes' first meeting with his sister, Electra. In the confrontation of lost souls, so long awaited, so little hoped-for, two poles of the moral and animal world, two necessary complementary forces, seem to stand face to face, towers of the hemisphere, mutual assurances that man, in his exacerbating experience of life, can hope for shape, for joining, for healing.

This promise, and the promise of theatrical power that so much oversize has been leading to, is unbelievably fulfilled in the final and most intractable play of the trilogy. The last section of Aeschylus' masterpiece, *The Furies,* has always been a stumbling block to translators and producers. In it, Aeschylus moves beyond the human savageries of eye-for-an-eye retribution to a superhuman, or supernatural, solution. Now the god Apollo and the goddess Athena enter the action, forced into it by man's inability to cleanse himself of his accumulated guilt, and a theological debate ensues; the theological content is further complicated by Aeschylus' determination to justify Athenian law by giving it a divine origin. In the recent past these issues have seemed arcane, remote, too rooted in a now-dead Greek civilization for easy conversion into contemporary terms.

Miraculously, the production style here adopted not only salvages the last play but, by a process of continuing expansion, makes it the most impressive of the evening. The guilt-ridden Orestes, now a gray, gaunt ghost, is, for a breathtaking moment, cradled in the arms of a sunburst Apollo, a glistening protector modeled in blazing gold who is nearly twice the height of his frightened charge. Man has been larger than lifesize until now; now he is in the grip of something larger. If man is at last to be pitied, there is a vast power capable of pitying him.

But the proportions have not reached their limits yet. The contest between the defending Apollo and the accusing Furies must be turned over to Athena. Athena appears, a flowing winged victory overwhelming enough in her regal hands and space-devouring robes—this is no longer a costume but a piece of inhabited sculpture—to swallow the stage whole. We have moved on, dizzily, climbed still another step to the Parthenon or to

Olympus; instead of losing breath, our lungs seem to have expanded with the view from the heights. (I found myself so dislo-
cated at this point that I began to wonder, practically, exactly
how big and how manageable each image was. Could Athena's
hands move, for instance, or were we simply hearing a voice
through a mountain? I had to shake my head to clear it when they
*did* move.)

In writing this last scene Mr. Lewin has made very free with
Aeschylus, altering diction at will, paring away, daring some tart
courtroom humor ("You know the rules, having made them"
snaps one god to another), but never, in the simplification, really
falsifying intention. What happens to us at last, as we look across
time and space into the face of Aeschylus and into the ultimate
human conundrum—man is trapped in the role of active servant to gods or impulses that do not agree with one another—is
an experience of multiple vision. The air between ourselves and
the actors is filled with a rush of meanings that have come to the
surface since Aeschylus wrote, echoing his concern in a thousand
new ways.

For instance, as the ancient earth urges, the Furies, howled
their claims against the suprarational powers of Olympus, I
found myself not thinking about, but *seeing,* both Darwin and
Freud in the middle distance. A woman with whom I shared a
taxi away from the theatre, and whom I did not know, said that
she had seen Vietnam. "And Orestes was *forgiven!*" she kept repeating to herself, as though stunned by the thought that the
blood-chain was breakable, the dark and light sides of man rec-
oncilable. However you look at it, and whatever you make of it,
this *House of Atreus* is a remarkable achievement. Its distortions
are something like dreaming—except that the dream is telling
the truth.

Because the methods employed are still so unfamiliar, there
are technical lapses to be noted in passing. The chorus at the
Guthrie does not speak well in unison; director Guthrie makes
surprisingly little visual use of his Furies, with their blasted ape's
faces; music comes in when we don't want it to, when we are too
satisfied with the controlled, rolling speech that is holding our
attention unaided. But Mr. Campbell is superb (it is ingenious to
cast him as both Clytemnestra and Athena, making him both the

origin of pain and the end of pain, the double-mother, at once), all of the other principals are excellent, and the unpredictably imaginative Mr. Guthrie has taken a heady leap forward in exploring the outer reaches of the stage.

The individual performers in Gerald Freedman's production of *Titus Andronicus* in Central Park were in general below Minneapolis standard—Moses Gunn as Aaron the Moor and Clayton Corbin as Marcus Andronicus were easily the best of them—and by adopting a rigidity of vocal tone they arrived at a monotony of vocal tone. In many cases, too, they could not open the sound on stage without scratching their throats badly.

But the use of masks, chorus, and a formalized architecture of movement simply and plainly saved Shakespeare's play for us. Done naturalistically, or with any attempt at the kind of plausibility we are most accustomed to on our stages, the violence must have seemed hopelessly penny-dreadful and the psychology ludicrous. Poor Titus's daughter, Lavinia, is so thoroughly and wantonly abused—raped, hands and tongue cut away, flung endlessly hither and yon—that we should, as reasonable theatregoers, have responded with laughter. As it was, we had to exercise a bit of self-control.

Yet when, in Mr. Freedman's staging, the girl ran headlong to the edge of the open-air stage only to be hoisted high in the arms of two neutral forces, while an ever present chorus rolled away to the ground to huddle in sleep or in shame, the crime itself was elevated from the level of simple shocker to that of cold, universal injustice. The use of thin, flying streamers where blood should be was more effective than any amount of greasepaint: we were looking at a happening, not at a painted picture. When Aaron carried his newborn bastard child about, the child was an armature to which no defining plaster had yet been applied; the effect was to make us believe in the child as we would never have believed in the customary rag bundle.

Best of all, the masks became more real than reality. In the play, two of Titus's sons are held captive; they will be returned to him when he hacks off his own arm and offers it to the Emperor. He fulfills his part of the bargain. The Emperor responds by

sending Titus his sons' severed heads on a platter. In the Central Park production, the platter was brought slowly on stage. It contained the two masks, nothing more. At the performance I saw, the audience gasped aloud. The shock was more intense for not being literal. The masks were now *empty;* it was the emptiness itself that was felt at the pit of the stomach.

With no warning at all, the contemporary stage seems to be catching a glimpse of those presences, specters radiating outward from man and hovering over him in successive dimensions like light rings around the moon, that haunted the stage in its very beginnings but which we thought we had conveniently tamed. They are still there, and they can thrust beneath the ribs.

Futurism and
the Theatre of the Future

Craig's Übermarionette had already actually appeared, in a
sense, in 1896, twelve years before his essay, in a form the Symbolist would never have been able to accept. Yeats saw this in
Lugne-Poe's production at the Théâtre Nouveau in Paris where
the players, as a friend explained, were "supposed to be dolls,
toys, marionettes" and were "all hopping like wooden frogs": Alfred Jarry's *King Ubu* was anything but a return of the Apollonian and hieratic ritual of ancient Greece. "After us," Yeats
realized, "the Savage God." [1]

The puppet-like figures in *King Ubu* represented a return of
those satirical and anarchic impulses that had motivated ancient
and medieval maskers and mummers. In the new century, one
form this would take was use of the grotesque, as called for by
Marinetti in his manifesto and as employed by Meyerhold and
Reinhardt. The toilet-brush scepter carried by Ubu prefigured

[1] *Modern French Theatre: The Avant-Garde, Dada, and Surrealism:
An Anthology of Plays,* ed. and trans. by Michael Benedikt and George E.
Wellwarth (New York: E. P. Dutton, 1964), p. xiii.

the tennis racquet Vakhtangov would introduce for his king in *Turandot*. A primitivization as regression would vie with more sophisticated means of surrealizing reality and rendering visible the new "abyss" of the absurd.

Like the artists' cabarets themselves, Marinetti's manifesto "In Praise of the Variety Theatre" represented the spirit of the times, a culture absorbed in a new immediacy. The manifesto implies Happenings and gives some direct and existential suggestions about creative staging, but the aspect I would like to call attention to is that which relates to Surrealism and to a theatre of effect; the "blossoming forth and disappearance of luminous advertisements" of a "marvelousness."

Joseph Cary's incisive "Futurism and the French Théâtre d'Avant-Garde" traces this influence upon the Surrealists. Apollinaire professed surprise at the suggestion that he had used vaudeville techniques in *Les Mamelles de Tiresias*, a play which, incidentally, seems to have been written in large part in 1903, nine years before Marinetti's manifesto. There, as in Cocteau's *Les Mariés de la Tour Eiffel* (1922), a vaudeville-like spirit is created by a directness of presentation and a rapidity of scenes as images. In both plays, megaphones are used and there are representations of the "puppet" as mechanized man of an oracular modernity. Cocteau often used large masks in his plays, and two specific examples of the effects he devised would be the "fugue of footsteps" he composed for the voices of the two robot-like Managers in *Parade*, and the prologue of his *Roméo et Juliette*, which is spoken by an actor who appears, by optical illusion, to be flying. Surrealism transformed the impetus of the Perishable Theatre of vaudeville toward images of a Durable Theatre of integrated effect.

Prampolini's manifesto is more indicative than is Marinetti's of this tendency and of the nature of Futurist theatre itself, which was largely devoted to mechanical ballets, plays and performances. His statement, a lucid compendium of the requirements of total theatre, previsions the work and interests of Moholy-Nagy and others at the Bauhaus. There, totally abstract kinetic light compositions were performed in relation to music, and the abstract stage of light and shadow effects and machine-like figures was developed.

An outstanding example of the formal intentions involved in the geometricizing of the human figure and its movements was Oskar Schlemmer's *Triadic Ballet,* produced at the Bauhaus in 1923. It was divided into three parts, each of which was dominated by a particular color and type of movement: lemon yellow and gaiety, red and majestic solemnity, black and mystical fantasy.[2] Within this grouping twelve abstract dances were composed for twenty costumes. The dancer within the costume did no more than impart to it the movements inherent in its design. S. Giedion described the ballet for a Swiss periodical as follows:

The curtain rose upon a motionless figure before a chrome yellow plane. It wore a many-colored wooden skirt shaped like a top, surmounted by a breastplate of varnished leather; arms and feet were also lacquered and the head was covered by a transparent helmet crowned by a jaunty wooden knob. When the music started, the figure responded with strong rhythmic movements. While the armor-like clothing restricted the range of possible movements and gestures, it at the same time gave added emphasis to every tiny motion—like the action of a pendulum. Every caper, every shake of the head, every movement of the arms became exaggerated and intensified. . . . Dancers appeared with great balls instead of hands or with heads enclosed within gleaming brazen masks and invisible arms, like an Archipenko sculpture. Their bodies were confined within the rigid spirals of their costumes and only their feet retained freedom of movement. It is conceivable that the effect of this strictly disciplined movement, which is in such striking contrast to our customary lack of control, may be to revive in a new way the human dignity that we have lost so utterly.[3]

This observation about obtaining a new human dignity was not inappropriate, for Schlemmer had defined the history of theatre as "the history of the transfiguration of the human form." The ideal is precisely that expressed in Ernst Juenger's classic modern novel *The Glass Bees* in which transcendently lifelike automata are invented and used in plays and movies, extending the range of all experiences immeasurably and giving man a new

[2] *The Theatre of the Bauhaus,* ed. Walter Gropius (Middletown, Conn.: Wesleyan University Press,, 1961), p. 34.
[3] S. Giedion, *Walter Gropius: Work and Teamwork* (London: The Architectural Press, 1954), p. 33.

vision of himself. The narrator recounts his opinion of this effect in the following manner:

Once upon a time statues and painting influenced not only fashion but man. I am convinced that Botticelli created a new race and that Greek tragedy enhanced the human body. That (the inventor) attempted something similar with his automata revealed that he rose far above technique, using media as an artist to create works of art.[4]

The work of the Bauhaus, in all media, perfectly expressed what Gordon Craig meant when he said that "art arrives only by design." It tended toward that vision of the stage which was totally abstract; Schlemmer's *"absolute* visual stage" composed of "kaleidoscopic play, at once infinitely variable and strictly organized," or the "combinations of colors and shapes" which were part of Artaud's understanding of the Mysteries of Eleusis. Essentially, however, it reserved a place for man on that stage, as the selection by Moholy-Nagy indicates.

A present-day version of Bauhaus intentions may be seen in the dance productions of Alwin Nikolais. Electronic music, shadow effects, and the effects of changing colors of light are among the instruments employed to set off dances based on costume; extensions of the limbs, cylindrical containers with lights inside them on arms and legs, balloon-like shapes from ankle to neck, all indicate particular rhythms and evocative images of movement within a very modern, futuristic context. The world that is indicated may be said to be based on the science of Phenomenology rather than on that of interpersonal relationships; man is a space-object in constant transformation. Nikolais intends to shift attention from world to universe, a universe taking place here.

[4] Ernst Juenger, *The Glass Bees,* trans. Louise Bogan and Elizabeth Mayer (New York: The Noonday Press, 1960), p. 137.

F. T. MARINETTI

# Futurism and the Theatre *

In praise of the variety theatre. We have a profound disgust for the contemporary theatre (verse, prose, and music) because it wavers stupidly between historic reconstruction (a pastiche or a plagiarism) and the photographic reproduction of our daily life.

On the other hand we assiduously frequent the Theatre of Varieties (Music Halls, café-chantants or equestrian circuses), which today offers the only theatrical spectacle worthy of a truly futurist spirit.

Futurism exalts the Variety Theatre because:

1. The Theatre of Variety, born with us, has not, fortunately, any kind of tradition; neither masters nor dogmas, and nourishes itself upon actuality.

2. The Theatre of Variety is absolutely practical because it simply sets out to distract and amuse the public with representations of comicality, of erotic excitation, or of imaginative wonder.

3. The authors, the actors, and the machinists of the Theatre of Variety have one sole motive to exist and to triumph: that of incessantly inventing new elements of wonder. Hence the absolute impossibility of stagnation or repetition; hence a hot rivalry of brains and muscles so as to surpass the various records of agility, velocity, strength, complexity, and grace.

4. The Theatre of Variety, being a lucrative medium for innumerable inventive efforts, naturally generates that which I call Futurist *"marvelousness"* produced by modern mechanism. One finds there at one and the same time: powerful caricatures; depths of absurdity; impalpable and delicious ironies; bewildering and definite symbols; torrents of uncontrollable hilarity; profound analogies between humanity, the animal world, the vegetable world and the mechanical world; conclusions of revealing cynicism, the networks of witty sayings, puns, and rid-

* Reprinted from *The Mask*, VI (1913), Florence, Italy. The first unabridged English translation by D. Nevile Lees. By permission of Marinetti & Papini.

dles which serve agreeably to let in fresh air upon the intelligence, all the gamut of the laugh and smile to stretch the nerves: all the gamut of stupidity, imbecility, blockishness, and absurdity which, insensibly, push to the very border of madness: all the new significations of light, of sound, of noise, and of speech, with their mysterious and inexplicable prolongations in the most unexplored centers of our sensibility.

5. The Theatre of Variety is today the crucible in which are stirring the elements of a new sensibility which is coming into being. Therein is found the ironic decomposition of all the ruined prototypes of the Beautiful, the Great, the Solemn, the Religious, the Ferocious, the Seductive, and the Terrible, and also the abstract elaboration of the new prototypes which shall succeed to these.

The Theatre of Variety is thus the synthesis of all that which humanity has up till now refined in its own nerves so as to divert itself in laughing at material and moral suffering; it is, besides that, the ebullient fusion of all the laughter, of all the smiles, of all the jeers, of all the contortions, of all the raillery of future humanity. Therein may be tasted the gaiety which will move men a hundred years hence, the researches of their painting, of their philosophy, their minds and the upward springing of their architecture.

6. The Theatre of Variety offers the most hygienic of all performances owing to its dynamism of form and color (simultaneous movement of jugglers, dancers, gymnasts, varicolored riding troupes). With its rhythm of swift and languorous dance the Theatre of Variety forcibly draws the slowest souls from their torpor and constrains them to run and leap.

It is, in fact, the only theatre in which the public does not remain inert like a stupid onlooker, but noisily participates in the action, itself singing, accompanying the orchestra, communicating with the actor with unexpected quips and extravagant dialogues.

The action is carried on at the same time on the stage, in the boxes, and in the pit. It then continues at the end of the performance, among the battalions of admirers, sugary youths who crowd at the stage door to dispute the *star,* final double victors; . . . a *chic* supper and bed.

7. The Theatre of Variety is an instructive school of sincerity for the male, because it strips from the woman all veils, all the phrases, all the sighs, all the romantic sobs which deform and mask her. It brings into prominence, instead, all the admirable animal qualities of the woman, her powers of capture, of seduction, of perfidy, and of resistance.

8. The Theatre of Variety is a school of heroism by reason of the different records of difficulty to overcome and efforts to be surpassed which create upon the stage the strong and sane atmosphere of danger. (For example: "Looping the loop" on a bicycle, in a motor car, on horseback.)

9. The Theatre of Variety is a school of cerebral subtlety, complication, and synthesis by reason of its clowns, conjurers, thought readers, lightning calculators, mechanicians, imitators and parodists, its musical jugglers and its eccentric Americans, whose fantastic pregnancies bring forth incredible objects and mechanisms.

10. The Variety Theatre is the only school which one can recommend to adolescents and young men of talent, because it explains in an incisive and rapid manner the most mysterious problems and the most complicated political events.

For example: a year ago, at the Folies Bergère, two dancers were representing the wavering discussions of Cambon with Kinderley-Watcher on the question of Morocco and the Congo, by means of a symbolic and significant dance which was worth at least three years of study of foreign politics. The two dancers, turned toward the public, their arms interlaced, the one close beside the other, went on making reciprocal concessions of territory, leaping forward and backward, to right and to left, without ever detaching themselves the one from the other, each keeping his eye fixed upon the object in view, which was, each to entangle the other in turn. They gave an impression of extreme courtesy, of skillful vacillation, of ferocity, of diffidence, of obstinacy, of meticulousness unsurpassably diplomatic.

Besides, the Theatre of Variety explains and luminously illustrates the dominant laws of life:

a) the interweaving of divers rhythms.
b) the fate of lies and contradictions (example: English double-faced dancers; shepherdess and terrible soldier).

*c*) the synthesis of velocity plus transformations (example: Fregoli).

*d*) the formation and disintegration of minerals and vegetables; (the blossoming forth and disappearance of luminous advertisements are a most effectual illustration of this).

11. The Theatre of Variety systematically depreciates ideal love and its romantic obsession, repeating to satiety, with the monotony and automaticity of a daily business, the nostalgic languors of passion. It extravagantly mechanicalizes sentiment, depreciates and healthily scorns the obsession of carnal possession, abases voluptuousness to the natural function of coition, deprives it of all mystery, of all anguish, and of all anti-hygienic idealism.

The Theatre of Variety gives instead the sense and the taste of easy light and ironic loves. The spectators of the open air café-chantants on the terraces of the Casinos afford a most amusing contest between the spasmodic moonlight, tormented by infinite griefs, and the electric light, which strikes violently upon the false jewels, the rouged flesh, the many-colored little skirts, the velvets, the spangles, and the false red of the lips. Naturally the energetic electric light triumphs, and the soft and decadent moonlight is put to rout.

12. The Theatre of Variety is naturally anti-academic, primitive, and ingenuous, hence the more significant owing to the unexpectedness of its researches and the simplicity of its means. (Example: the systematic turn of the stage which the *chanteuses* make, at the end of every couplet, like wild beasts in a cage.)

13. The Theatre of Variety destroys the Solemn, the Sacred, the Serious, the Sublime of Art with a capital *A*. It collaborates in the futurist destruction of the immortal masterpieces, plagiarizing them, parodying them, presenting them just anyhow, without scenery and without compunction just as an ordinary "turn." Thus we approve unconditionally the execution of "Parsifal" in forty minutes which is in preparation for a large London Music Hall.

The Theatre of Variety destroys all our conceptions of time and of space. (Example: a little doorway and gate thirty centimeters high, isolated in the middle of the stage, and through which certain eccentric Americans pass, opening it, and repass,

shutting it, in all seriousness, as if they could not do otherwise.)

14. The Theatre of Variety offers us all the "records" attained hitherto: The greatest equilibristic, and acrobatic feats of the Japanese, the greatest muscular frenzy of the negroes; the greatest development of the intelligence of animals (trained horses, elephants, seals, dogs, birds); the highest melodic inspiration of the Gulf of Naples and of the Russian steppes, the supreme Parisian spirit, the supreme force, in comparison one with another, of the different races (wrestling and boxing), the greatest anatomical monstrosity, the greatest beauty of women.

15. The Theatre of Variety offers, in short, to all countries which have not one great unique capital (like Italy), a brilliant résumé of Paris considered as the sole and obsessing home of ultrarefined voluptuousness and pleasure.

Futurism wishes to perfect the Theatre of Variety, by transforming it into: *The Theatre of Wonder and of Record*.

1. It is absolutely necessary to destroy all logic in the spectacles in the Theatre of Variety, to exaggerate noticeably its extravagance, to multiply contrasts, and to make the improbable and the absurd reign as sovereigns on the stage. (Example: oblige the singers to paint their bare necks, their arms, and especially their hair in all the colors hitherto neglected as a means of seduction. Green hair, violet arms, azure breast, orange chignon, etc.; interrupt a singer, making her continue with a revolutionary or anarchistic discourse; sprinkle a romanza with insults and bad words.)

2. To prevent any kind of tradition establishing itself in the Theatre of Variety. For that reason to oppose and abolish the Parisian "Revues" which are as stupid and tedious as the Greek tragedy, their "Compère" and "Commère" which exercise the function of the ancient chorus, and their procession of political personages and events, distinguished with witty sayings, by a most fastidious logic and concatenation. The Theatre of Variety ought not to be, in fact, that which unfortunately it is today, . . . almost always a newspaper, more or less humorous.

3. To make the spectators of the pit, the boxes, and the gallery take part in the action. Here are a few suggestions: put strong glue on some of the stalls, so that the spectator, man or

woman, who remains glued down, may arouse general hilarity. (The damaged dress-coat or costume will naturally be paid for on going out.) [1]

Sell the same place to ten different people; hence obstructions, arguments, and altercations. [2]

Offer free seats to ladies and gentlemen notoriously whimsical, irritable, or eccentric, calculate to provoke disturbances by obscene gestures, nudges to the women, and other eccentricities.

Sprinkle the stalls with powders which produce itching, sneezing, etc.

4. Systematically prostitute the whole classic art upon the stage, representing, for example, in a single evening all the Greek, French, and Italian tragedies, condensed and comically mixed up.

Enliven the works of Beethoven, Wagner, Bach, Bellini, Chopin, by introducing into them Neapolitan songs. Put side by side upon the stage Zacconi, Duse and Mayol, Sarah Bernhardt and Fregoli. [3]

Execute a Beethoven symphony backwards, beginning with the last note. [4]

Reduce the whole of Shakespeare to a single act. [5] Do the same with the other most venerated actors. Have *Ernani* performed by actors tied up to the neck in so many sacks. Soap the boards of the stage, to produce amusing tumbles in the most tragic moment. [6]

5. Encourage in every way the *genre* of the American Eccentrics, their effects of exalting grotesque, of terrifying dynamism, their clumsy finds, their enormous brutalities, their waistcoats full of surprises and their pantaloons deep as the holds of ships, from which issue forth, with thousands of other things, the great Futurist hilarity which is to rejuvenate the face of the world.

Because, do not forget, we Futurists are of the "fiery young

[1] Yet somehow I hardly see this being done twice to the same public.
[2] Haven't we already once too often pulled grandma's chair away from her just as she was sitting down?
[3] Who will do the putting? . . . Don't all speak at once!
[4] And then . . . ?
[5] And Marinetti's farces reduced to a single phrase, . . . what?
[6] More than usually considerate!

warriors" [7] as we proclaimed in our manifesto, "let us kill the moonlight."

E. PRAMPOLINI

## Futurist Scenography (Manifesto) *

April-May 1915

*Let's reform the stage.* To admit, to believe that a stage has existed up until today is to affirm that artistically man is absolutely blind. The stage is not equivalent to a photographic enlargement of a rectangle of reality or to a relative synthesis, but to the adoption of a theoretical system and subjective scenographic material completely opposed to the so-called objective scenography of today.

It is not only a question of reforming the conception of the structure of the *mise-en-scène;* one must create an abstract entity which identifies itself with the scenic action of the play.

It is wrong to view the stage separately, as a pictorial fact: (a) because we are no longer dealing with scenography but with simple painting; (b) we are returning to the past (that is to say to the past . . . present) where the stage expresses one subject, the play develops another.

These two forces which have been diverging (playwright and scenographer) must converge to form a multiple synthesis of the play.

The stage must live the theatrical action in its dynamic synthesis; it must express the essence of the character conceived by the author just as an actor at once expresses and lives it within himself. Therefore, in order to reform the stage one must:

---

[7] Uno . . . due . . . tre . . . fire!

\* Reprinted from *Archivi del Futurismo,* Volume I, Rome, De Luca Editore, translated by Diana Clemmons.

1. Deny exact reconstruction of that which the playwright has conceived, thus abandoning resolutely every factual relationship, every comparison between object and subject and vice versa; all these relationships weaken direct emotion with indirect sensations.

2. Substitute for scenic action an emotional order which awakens all sensations necessary to the development of the play; the resulting atmosphere will provide the interior milieu.

3. *Absolute synthesis* in material expression of the stage, which means not the pictorial synthesis of all the elements, but synthesis excluding those elements of scenic architecture which are incapable of producing new sensations.

4. The scenic architecture will have to be a connection for the audience's intuition rather than a picturesque and elaborate collaboration.

5. The colors and the stage will have to arouse in the spectator those emotional values which neither the poet's words nor the actor's gestures can evoke.

There are no theatre reformers today: Dresa and Rouché experimented in France with ingenuous and infantile expressions; Meyerhold and Stanislavsky in Russia with revivals of sickening classicism (we leave out the Assyrian-Persian-Egyptian-Nordic plagiarist Bakst); Adolphe Appia, Fritz Erler, Littman Fuchs and Max Reinhardt (organizer) in Germany have attempted reforms directed more toward tedious elaboration, rich in glacial exteriors, than toward the essential idea of interpretive reform; Granville-Barker and Gordon Craig in England have made some limited innovations, some objective syntheses.

Displays and material simplifications, not rebellion against the past. It is this necessary revolution which we intend to provoke, because no one has had the artistic austerity to renovate the interpretive conception of the element to be expressed.

Our scenography is a monstrous thing. Today's scenographers, sterile whitewashers, still prowl around the dusty and stinking corners of classical architecture.

We must rebel and assert ourselves and say to our poet and musician friends: this action demands this stage rather than that one.

Let us be artists too, and no longer merely executors. Let us

create the theatre, give life to the play with all the evocative power of our art.

It goes without saying that we need plays suited to our sensibility, which implies a more intense and synthetic conception in the scenic development of subjects.

*Let's renovate the stage.* The absolutely new feature that our innovation will give the theatre is *the abolition of the painted stage.* The stage will no longer be a colored backdrop, but an *uncolored electromechanical architecture, powerfully vitalized by chromatic emanations from a luminous source,* produced by electric reflectors, with multicolored panes of glass, arranged, coordinated analogically with the swing-mirror of each scenic action.

With the luminous irradiation of these sheaves, of these planes of colored lights, the dynamic combinations will give marvelous results of mutual permeation, of intersection of lights and shadows. From these will be born blank surrenders, corporalities luminous with exultation. These assemblages, these unreal shocks, this exuberance of sensations combined with dynamic stage architectures which will move, unleashing metallic arms, knocking over plastic frameworks, amidst an essentially new, modern noise, will augment the vital intensity of the scenic action.

On a stage illuminated in such a way the actors will gain unforeseen dynamic effects which are neglected or very seldom employed in today's theatres, mostly because of the ancient prejudice that one must imitate, represent reality.

What's the use?

Is it that the scenographers believe it absolutely necessary to represent this reality? Idiots! Don't you understand that your efforts, your useless realistic preoccupations have no effect other than that of diminishing the intensity and emotional content, which can be attained precisely through the interpretive equivalents of these realities, i. e., abstractions?

*Let's create the theatre.* In the above lines we have upheld the idea of a dynamic theatre as opposed to the static theatre of old; with the fundamental principles which we shall set forth, we in-

tend not only to carry the theatre to its most advanced expression, but also to attribute the essential values which belong to it and which no one has thought of presenting till now.

*Let's exchange the roles.* Instead of the illuminated stage, let's create the *illuminant stage: luminous expression which will irradiate the colors demanded by the theatrical action with all its emotional power.*

The material means of expressing this illuminant stage consist in employing electrochemical colors, fluorescent tubes which have the chemical property of being susceptible to electric current and diffusing luminous colorations of all tonalities according to the combinations of fluorine with other such gases. The desired effects of luminosity will be obtained by stimulating these gases (systematically arranged according to the proper design on this immense sceno-dramatic architecture) with electric neon (ultraviolet) tubes. But the Futurist scenographic and choreographic evolution must not stop there. In the final synthesis human actors will no longer be tolerated, like children's jumping jacks, or today's super-marionettes recommended by recent reformers; neither one nor the other can sufficiently express the multiple aspects conceived by the playwright.

In the totally realizable époque of Futurism we shall see the luminous dynamic architectures of the stage emanate from chromatic incandescences which, mounting tragically or showing themselves voluptuously, will inevitably arouse new sensations and emotional values in the spectator.

Vibrations, luminous forms (produced by electric currents and colored gases) will wriggle and writhe dynamically, and these veritable actor-gases of an unknown theatre will have to replace living actors. By shrill whistles and strange noises these actor-gases will be able to give the unusual significations of theatrical interpretations quite well; they will be able to express these multiform emotive qualities with much more effectiveness than some celebrated actor or other can with his displays. These exhilarant, explosive gases will fill the audience with cheerfulness or terror and it will perhaps become an actor itself, too. But these words are not our last. We still have much to say. Let us first carry out what we have set forth above.

JOSEPH CARY

# Futurism and the French *Théâtre d'Avant-Garde* *

Futurism was, above all, a political phenomenon, dedicated primarily to arousing the Italian public from what was felt to be the paralysis of its past achievements and traditions and freeing it for what Filippo Tommaso Marinetti, the movement's founder and loudest voice, considered *sola igiene del mondo,* namely, war. Within Italy, futurism was essentially a high-powered publicity organ in behalf of the bellicose spirit, and, though eclectic in its origins (an ill-digested stew of French romanticism and symbolism, *verismo,* Nietzsche, Bergson, D'Annunzio, Verhaeren, etc.) and hence literary in its rhetoric, its end was, and was meant to be, militant nationalism.

Paradoxically, however, futurism made its bid for attention —if a scream can be called a bid—outside Italy in terms of its programs for the arts, which happened to coincide broadly with certain programs beginning to find currency among various avant-garde groups (particularly in France). Such a coincidence is easily explained by the *oltremontane* roots of the vast majority of futurist notions on art, so that in one sense it is fair to say that the numerous futurist manifestoes on the arts, published throughout Europe between 1909 and 1919, said nothing of any importance that had not already been said better by *stranieri.* The question then becomes: How can one explain the momentary attraction exercised by futurism on such serious artists as Pound, Severini, Kahn, Papini, Soffici, Mayakovsky, Pasternak, and Apollinaire?

Without having recourse to a concept of *Zeitgeist,* it can be said that it was precisely the propagandist or advertising agency

* Reprinted from *Modern Philology* (November, 1959).

side of futurism that made its fortune in Europe. Its calculated overstatements, its will to outrage, its stage Italian garishness, its high exasperation quotient, were offered in behalf of modernity and the liberty to experiment and directed against the confining *isms* of the past. Everywhere on the Continent were groups (cubists, orphists, vorticists, imagists, paroxyists, dynamists, vitalists, expressionists, et al.) struggling for a public, frustrated by the massive indifference of the public that existed (symbolized in that figure of defensive fun, *l'homme moyen sensuel,* canonized in Jarry's Père Ubu). Then Marinetti ("très riche et très fat," according to Gide [1]) dropped from heaven (Milan), burning to spend his money and time on an internationally scaled war against the past; more than happy to *épater le bourgeois* and even punch him in the nose; delighted to issue manifestoes in English, French, and Italian directed against academies, museums, gondolas, Beethoven, Shakespeare, "spiritual" women, solemnity, syntax, logic, etc. If such a process did not educate the public, it at least provoked it, and provocation has notoriously ever been the first step toward interest. On such grounds as these, as an unreasonable facsimile of the Socratic gadfly, was futurism welcomed throughout Europe.

The movement contained very little artistic talent within its ranks. The non-Italians cited above appreciated it opportunistically for its liberating rhetoric of destruction and even occasionally made use of certain of its tenets (e.g., Apollinaire's and Mayakovsky's *parole in libertà* and abolition of punctuation) but saw the logical impossibility of "breaking" with history and the undesirability of art's being used as propaganda for the violent life. The better artists among the Italians (Soffici, Papini, Palazzeschi, Severini) saw, by 1915, that futurism had degenerated into *marinettismo* and broke with it on the grounds that it had no real relation to the future because it lacked all contact with the past. What remained were Marinetti, his temperament, and some untalented but energetic disciples, all absorbed into fascism by the war's end.

Gide writes in his *Journal:* "Marinetti jouit d'une absence de talent qui lui permet toutes les audaces." [2] The *audace* to be dis-

---

[1] André Gide, *Journal, 1889–1930* (Paris, 1954), p. 152.
[2] *Ibid.,* p. 348.

cussed in the following pages is his futurist theatre, not because the plays themselves are of any intrinsic value, but because certain of the ideas behind them (expressed in the two theatre manifestoes of 1913 and 1915) seem to have been taken up and more profitably employed in French avant-garde theatre from 1916 on, notably in the plays of Guillaume Apollinaire and Jean Cocteau. This is certainly not to say that the authors of *Les Mamelles* or *Les Mariés* were thinking of the manifestoes or of such productions as *Poupées électriques* or *Clair de lune* when they composed their pieces—far from it. But *marinettismo* was particularly hard to avoid in the Paris of this decade, and, subliminally at least, its theatre had some effect. The poor in spirit, after all, may contribute heavenly stepchildren.

It is important to note that for the futurists the theatre was simply a means to an end. In 1915 Marinetti wrote:

La guerra, futurismo intensificato, c'impone di marciare e di non marcire nelle biblioteche e nelle sale di lettura. Noi crediamo dunque che non si possa oggi influenzare guerrescamente l'anima italiana, se non mediante il teatro. Infatti il 90% degl'Italiani va a teatro, mentre soltanto il 10% legge libri e riviste. È necessario però un teatro futurista, cioè assolutamente opposto al teatro passatista, che prolunga i suoi cortei monotoni e deprimenti sulle scene sonnolente d'Italia.[3]

It is clear, then, that this is a theatre *à thèse,* the thesis being to infuse the Italian "soul" with a warlike spirit. Since the theatre attracts, on Marinetti's reckoning, nine times as many people as do books and reviews, from the propagandist's viewpoint the theatre is nine times more valuable than reading matter. Ergo futurist theatre.

Marinetti was no stranger to thesis theatre. *Le Roi bombance, tragédie satirique,* written in French in 1905 and produced in 1909 at Lugné-Poë's Théâtre de l'Œuvre, is described by Francesco Flora as "la caricatura del Passatismo . . . del bolscevismo mondiale, della stupidità putrescente, della imbecillità ventripeta, della noia d'una realtà sempre uguale nelle sue rivoluzione senza meta." [4] Bearing down heavily on oral-anal metaphors

---

[3] In a manifesto quoted in F. T. Marinetti, *Marinetti e il futurismo* (Milan, 1927), p. 7.

[4] *Dal romanticismo al futurismo* (Florence, 1924), pp. 197, 201.

("Roi Bombance, Boyau sacré du monde, Intestin des Intestins, grand Estomac du Royaume de Bourdes" [5]), this long, turgid, unfunny piece, full of D'Annunzian declamations, Maeterlinckian allegories (near the Étang du Passé and the Manoir de l'Impossible, the hero Poet-Idiot "fecundates space" with his vatic breath), created a scandal at l'Œuvre by several intestinal sound effects committed by a priest (representing, of course, the church) in the second act and enjoyed a certain celebrity on that account.[6] Antinaturalist, to be sure, employing masks, music, and several laborious *trucs* requiring a staging worthy of Bayreuth, the play was a pastiche of the heaviest styles extant in nineteenth-century Europe, based on a sadism benevolently disguised as romantic irony; it had no successors, not even in the work of Marinetti himself.

1909 also saw another of his plays, *Poupées électriques,* published and played in Paris. This piece, dedicated to Wilbur Wright ("qui sut élever nos cœurs migrateurs plus haut que la bouche captivante de la femme"), had as its thesis the futurist dogma of "manly" *disprezzo della donna,* a theme already announced in his first manifesto (published in *Le Figaro* that year) and his *roman africain, Mafarka le Futuriste* (1905), wherein, wishing to conserve his male energies for the parthenogenic bearing of a superpuppet, Mafarka has all his lushly upholstered courtesans thrown to the sharks. *Poupées électriques* attempts to show the dangers of romantic attachments: the hero, an American engineer whose hobby is constructing life-size automata of his parents-in-law (and having them clear their throats in the room when he is making love to his wife—presumably in order to gain an extra sexual thrill) has his life ruined by his romantic refusal to see his wife as the beast that she is, for failing to use her as a pleasure machine. Such a summary makes the play sound more amusing than it really is; written in the conventional veristic style of boulevard melodrama, complete with "explanatory" dialogue between servants and the inevitable loaded pistol handed to the wife when her infidelity is discovered so that she

[5] Marinetti, *Le Roi Bombance* (Paris, 1905), p. 52.

[6] For a description of this scandal see E. Aegarter and P. Labracherie, *Au temps de Guillaume Apollinaire* (Paris, 1945), pp. 230–31.

may blow her brains out to a falling final curtain,[7] the play sank quickly into merited oblivion, with not even a scandal to its name.

It is clear that such a theatre was not the type of thing that "ninety per cent" of the Italian public went to see. The self-appointed war propagandist, though not a self-critical man, must have realized this too, for in the following years he ceased to write such stuff and turned to the more congenial task of writing manifestoes for others to follow. His subtle advertiser's mentality saw that people did not flock to the theatre to be harangued with a thesis, that it was necessary to *give the public what it wants*. The public at large wants excitement, "laffs," escape from daily routine, sexual "electricity," spectacle; hence this proto-Goldwyn's manifesto *Teatro di varietà* (1913), published first in the London *Daily Mail,* then in Paris, Rome, and Milan.

In this manifesto Marinetti finds variety theatre, vaudeville, circus, burlesque to be "l'unico teatro semifuturista"[8] of his time. He applauds this type of entertainment's pervading *genialità,* its lack of confining tradition, its use of all the arts (notably music, brilliant costuming, lighting and mechanical effects), its dynamic qualities (continuous movement of colors and forms, simultaneity of action on different parts of the stage), its aptitude for ridicule and parody. He sees in its tightrope walkers and acrobats the rudiments of a school for heroism; in its mimes the most pleasant and efficient way to get an abstruse point across; in its essential extroversion a means of captivating the senses of a large audience and involving it emotionally with violence. Its very lack of subtlety and its inherent hostility to psychological or contemplative analysis, are enormous points in its favor. Moreover, the usual gap between audience and proscenium is obliterated by swirling cigar smoke, clowns planted in the audience, the emotional identification with feats of daring; the spectators collaborate, and distinctions between subject and

---

[7] E.g., "Un petit cadeau qui lui sera (*avec ironie*) le plus utile et le plus fidèle des compagnons durant mon absence," from Marinetti, *Poupées électriques, drame avec une préface sur le futurisme* (Paris, 1909), p. 192.

[8] Marinetti, "Il Teatro di varietà," *I manifesti di futurismo (prima serie) lanciati da Marinetti, Boccioni, Apollinaire,* etc. (Milano, 1914), p. 158.

object are overwhelmingly confused. He claims that "il Teatro di Varietà esalta l'azione, l'eroismo, la vita all'aria aperta, la destrezza, l'autorità dell'instinto e dell'intuizione. Alla psicologia, oppone ciò che oi chiamo *fisicofollia*." [9] *Fisicofollia* signifies an infatuation with things in themselves (what he elsewhere called *l'ossessione lirica della materia* [10]) without regard for their function, history, or meaning. This aversion to all process or sequence, whether in space or in time, material or mental, brings him to praise Variety's abolition of all traditional concepts of perspective, proportion, time, and space. It is futurism's task to take hold of these promising features and exaggerate them into a "teatro dello stupore, del record e fisicofollia." [11] Suggestions follow: destroy all vestigial logic and magnify the *inverosimile* and the absurd (paint hair, arms, faces of *chanteuses* all the colors of the rainbow); destroy all plot and references to daily reality; introduce surprise and compulsive action among the spectators by elaborate practical jokes (glue on the seats, redundant seat numbers, obscene remarks on the personalities of members of the audience, stink bombs, etc.); prostitute systematically all classical art on the stage (mix together Greek, French, Italian tragedies, play Beethoven backward, reduce all Shakespeare to a single act, play *Ernani* with the entire cast up to the neck in burlap sacks, etc.); emulate American grossness. The manifesto epigrammatically concludes with "fuoco + fuoco + luce contro chiaro di luna e vecchi firmamenti guerra ogni sera." [12]

Clearly, the aim of such a theatre is, by a constant bullying of emotions, nerves, and senses, to reduce its audience to a rabble, the individualities of its spectators to the anonymity of suggestible robots. Objective thought is outlawed; the human being is willed to be a conglomeration of mobile matter, inferior to the machine because of his unfortunate faculty of memory. To promote such an end, a battery composed of the various arts is leveled at the audience: music, perpetual motion, sounds of airplanes and hyenas, complicated stage machinery, multicolored

[9] *Ibid.*, p. 161.
[10] Marinetti, "Manifesto tecnico della letteratura turista," in *I Manifesti,* etc., p. 92.
[11] "Il Teatro di varietà," p. 162.
[12] *Ibid.*, p. 166.

lights in movement, masks, makeup, paint disguising the humanity of the artists. The *mise-en-scène* becomes everything; the text, the drama itself, next to nothing.

Although assuredly, as Pellizi says, this program stipulated "una maggior libertà di movimenti" in the theatre,[13] it should be remembered that such a purely physical liberty conspired against liberty of thought and that whatever influence the manifesto had beyond the futurists themselves was owing to its convergence with, and suggestibility to, an antinaturalist movement which, for quite other reasons, was spreading through Europe.

The *teatro dello stupore* remained a theory until 1915. In that year Marinetti and disciples Settimelli and Corra released a second theatre manifesto (*Le Théâtre futuriste synthétique—sans technique - dynamique - simultané - autonome - alogique - irréal* [14]) which gave rise to a rash of futurist plays produced in Milan, Rome, and Paris (1914–19). This synthetic theatre was the direct heir to futurist plans for Variety. The manifesto proposes "d'exalter les spectateurs en tirant de force leur sensibilité de la monotonie de la vie quotidienne pour la lancer dans un labyrinthe de sensations d'une originalité exaspérée. . . . L'action théâtrale doit envahir le parterre." It condemns as prolix, static, and pedantic the varied theatres of Ibsen, Maeterlinck, Andreyev, Claudel, and Shaw. It approves of spontaneous improvisation, although the numerous mechanical devices it calls for give evidence of thorough preliminary planning. "Synthetic," first of all, in its reliance on the various nonverbal arts (painted nudes, masks with searchlight eyes, funnel ears, megaphone mouths; continuously moving sets and perspectives; "dynamic" music composed largely of naturalistic sound effects; colored lights, transforming, "as if by magic," the colors of bodies, costumes, sets), the term "synthetic" more properly applies to a radical compression of time and space: "Nous serrons en quelques minutes, quelques mots, et quelques gestes d'innombrables situ-

---

[13] Camillo Pellizi, *Le Lettere italiane del nostro secolo* (Milano, 1929), p. 225.

[14] In *Futurist Manifestoes: A Collection*, a photostatic reproduction of a publication of the Direzione del Movimento futurista 1909–1920 (Milano, n.d.). This collection, to be found in the New York Public Library, does not have numbered pages; hence the résumé I give of this manifesto cannot include specific page references.

ations, sensibilités, idées, sensations, faits et symboles. . . .
Des milieux différents et des temps divers se compénètrent si-
multanément." The wrench with *vraisemblance* is this time given
a quasi-scientific sanction:

> Il faut porter sur la scène toutes les découvertes . . . les plus
> invraisemblables, les plus bizarres que le génie artistique et la science
> font chaque jour dans les zones mystérieuses du subconscient. . . .
> Dans la vie nous ne parvenons jamais à saisir un événement tout
> entier, avec toutes ses causes et toutes ses conséquences . . . la
> réalité vibre confusément autour de nous et sur nous avec ses rafales
> de fragments de faits combinés, encastrés les uns dans les autres,
> mélangés, entrelacés, chaotisés. . . . C'est idiot de renoncer aux
> merveilleux bonds qu'il faut faire dans le mystère de la création to-
> tale, loin de tous les terrains explorés.

It is clear that the *subconscient* and the elusiveness of a peren-
nially vibrant reality to human perception evoked here have
nothing whatever in common with the similar concepts employed
by Baudelaire, Rimbaud, Mallarmé, Apollinaire, and the surrealists. These latter were moved by such ideas to an exploratory
journey inward, away from an invalid common sense, in search
of an epistemological absolute. Marinetti, on the other hand, although he had picked up the lingo of such men as these (in pre-
futurist days he had lectured on the symbolists in Italy and as
late as 1913 had translated Mallarmé into Italian), was not concerned with knowledge or reality, took chaos at its face value,
and employed such concepts as *carte blanche* for irresponsible
*bonds*. The difference between him and the Dadaists was that the
latter did not have political motives and hence operated in the
despair of a universe without values.

Thus when a man like Anton Bragaglia, director of the Teatro
degli Indipendenti in Rome and occasional producer of futurist
synthetic theatre in the 1920's, attributes to such plays "un sug-
gestivo ambiente ideale . . . scene che, per misura di disegno e
di colore, costituiscono una disciplinata e stilizzata raffigura-
zione della realtà ricordata: non ricopiata. . . . [Una] astrazione ideale di forme tipiche," [15] he is repeating an error found

---

[15] *La Maschera mobile* (Foligno, 1926), p. 300.

in most textbooks on modern drama: i.e., finding a concern for truth where none existed. The key to futurist *sinteticismo* is, as it was in the *teatro dello stupore, l'ossessione lirica della materia,* or *fisicofollia.* That is, the demotion (under the name of promotion) of man to mechanism, on the grounds that a thinking man makes a poor soldier. The "astrazione ideale," under such a scheme of things, is the militant state.

The distinguishing feature of the plays themselves was, of course, their brevity. Few run over two pages. Otherwise they are quite unremarkable: laconic *verismo* with perhaps a symbol thrown in. Marinetti's *Clair de lune,* for example, shows a young couple who have left a dance to stroll in the garden, look at the moon, and talk of love. A repulsive old man, invisible to them, appears, and as they converse, he coughs and clears his throat; the night suddenly seems colder to them, and they return to the dance: finis. Boccioni's *La Garçonnière* gives us a young artist waiting in his studio for a prospective customer. She enters, is beautiful, he attempts to embrace her. When she recoils and upbraids him, he acknowledges his grossness; whereupon she settles on the couch and invites him to take her. Curtain on an unmitigated *tranche de vie*.

In the majority of the synthetic plays, however, the text disappears completely, and the *mise-en-scène* becomes an absolute. Objects (tables, chairs, etc.) begin to mutter, murmur, sing; no human actors appear at all. In one play the curtain simply rises, to music, on a retired colonel's apartment. The occupant is not present, we observe his furniture and souvenirs; in a moment the final curtain falls. Another consists of a choreography for hands alone, their owners concealed behind a curtain. Many employ varying intensities and movements of stage lighting to purvey the illusion of living décor. When humans appear, for the most part they are costumed and masked as puppets and move accordingly.

Such plays were produced not only in Italy but in Paris from 1915 on. It remains to be seen if and how these methods fared in French hands.

Assuredly, neither Apollinaire nor Cocteau had any real affinity with futurist beliefs, although they were well acquainted with Marinetti and his manifestations. Apollinaire, who, for reasons of his own, had briefly joined the movement in 1913 and

had even written a manifesto (*L'Antitradizione futurista*), later wrote altogether more seriously that

généralement vous ne trouverez en France de ces «paroles en liberté» jusqu'où ont été poussées les surenchères futuristes, italienne et russe, filles excessives de l'esprit nouveau, car la France répugne au désordre. On y revient volontiers aux principes, mais on a horreur du chaos.[16]

In his significantly titled *Le Rappel à l'ordre,* Cocteau notes that, while Marinetti is charming (he is agreeing with Apollinaire) "par les balles de toutes les couleurs qu'il lance contre les ruines," he is, finally, hopelessly and sloppily romantic: " [il] parle de . . . dreadnought dans le style de Byron." [17] He finds the Futurists to be "victimes du cinématographe," [18] even as Apollinaire calls them *cinématolâtres.*[19] Finally, talking of two perennial tendencies in art (Nietzsche's Dionysian and Apollonian principles), he locates both cubism and futurism under the reign of Dionysius and, again like Apollinaire, remarks that "il m'apparaît que le signe d'Apollon est plus favorable à la mise en œuvre des qualités françaises." [20]

Both Apollinaire and Cocteau differ radically from Marinetti, then, in their "French" esteem for order. They join with the Italian only in the sense that all three rebel against conventional modes of representation; but, while Marinetti's goal in this was vertigo-cum-politics, the other two desire to return, via *dérèglement,* to the principles of all order, the ultimate decorum. Again, while Marinetti despised reason and logic, Cocteau and Apollinaire appreciate them and extend their usage from the world of perception to the new world of apperception. The break with tradition for them meant not the denial of the past but the denial of its stereotypic effect upon creative mind. In this regard Apollinaire wrote: *"la Merde en musique de mon manifeste-synthèse publié par les Futuristes ne s'appliquait pas à l'œuvre des an-*

---

[16] Guillaume Apollinaire, *L'Esprit nouveau et les poëtes* (Paris, 1948), p. 5; see also his remarks in *Anecdotiques* (Paris, 1926), pp. 215–21.

[17] Jean Cocteau, *Le Rappel à l'ordre* (Paris, 1948), pp. 82–83.

[18] *Ibid.,* p. 181.

[19] *Anecdotiques,* p. 219.

[20] *Le Rappel,* pp. 144–45.

ciens mais à leur nom opposé comme barrière aux nouvelles générations." [21]

Hence there is absolutely nothing *in principle* which links these two with Marinetti. In terms of their theatre, the line of descent for both is by way of Alfred Jarry with, for Cocteau, a strong admixture of the Ballets Russes. *Ubu Roi,* a deliberate source of bewilderment and scandal to the public of its time, was partly *épatement* and partly serious experiment away from Ibsen (whom Jarry called "le grand Tortueux") toward representation of *essences.* If Jarry could appear as prologue to his play and seriously inform his audience that

vous verrez des portes s'ouvrir sur des plaines de neige sous un ciel bleu, des cheminées ornées de pendules se fendre afin de servir de portes, et des palmiers verdir au pied des lits, pour que les broutent de petits éléphants perchés sur des étagères.[22]

this is as much a directive to look beneath the surface as it is a mockery. His bitterness stems from the crowd, which, ignorant of the aims of Baudelaire, Mallarmé, Rimbaud, et al., is

un aliéné par défaut . . . dont les sens sont restés si rudimentaires qu'elle ne perçoit que des impressions immédiates. . . . Le progrès pour elle est-il de se rapprocher de la brute ou de développer peu à peu ses circonvolutions cérébrales embryonnaires? [23]

It is clear what a distance separates the aesthetics of Jarry (and with him Apollinaire and Cocteau) and Marinetti.

Jarry's theatre is essentially one of caricature, that is to say, of simplification followed by magnification. His *mise-en-scène,* masks, costumes, sets, and particularly dialogue all adhere to this principle. Apollinaire's *Les Mamelles de Tirésias* and Cocteau's theatre (from *Parade* through *Orphée* in particular) follow this general line. What is different, however, in the theatre of these two (and where, it seems, futurist influence applies) is that

[21] Letter cited in André Billy, "Apollinaire vivant," *Les Écrits nouveaux* (Paris, 1920), no page numbers.

[22] Alfred Jarry, "Présentation, *Ubu Roi,*" *Œuvres complètes,* IV (Monte Carlo, Lausanne, n.d.), p. 25.

[23] Jarry, "Questions de théâtre," *Œuvres,* IV, p. 159.

the devices (*trucs*) become importunate to a high degree and compete with the *surréalité* which was their end.

The *directeur de la troupe* in *Les Mamelles* presents the author's plans for *un esprit nouveau au théâtre* which contains several elements from futurist syntheticism: first a marriage of

> *Les sons les gestes les couleurs les cris les bruits*
> *La musique la danse l'acrobatie la poésie la peinture*
> *Les choeurs les actions et les décors multiples . . .*
> *Les changements de ton du pathétique au burlesque . . .*
> *Il est juste qu'il* [*théâtre*] *fasse parler les foules les objets*
>     *inanimés . . .*
> *Et qu'il ne tienne pas plus compte du temps*
> *Que de l'espace.*[24]

But, unlike the futurist program, this massed "usage raisonnable des invraisemblances" is designed to serve

> *Non pas dans le seul but*
> *De photographer ce que l'on appelle une tranche de vie*
> *Mais pour faire surgir la vie même dans toute sa vérité,*[25]

i.e., reasoned use of eclectic and disparate materials to catch essential truth.

In point of fact, *Les Mamelles,* like *Ubu Roi* and the early work of Cocteau, was fashioned for delectation rather than for any epistemological end. Yet any one of these plays caught more of the moral essence of its characters than did the pieces on the contemporary boulevards. When "magic" creeps in for the sake of magic, however, or when surprise becomes a goal rather than a means of making an audience conscious, then we are justified in seeing there the mark of Marinettian *stupore*.

Apollinaire has balls and balloons, in guise of bosoms, flung at the audience by liberated Thérèse; the people of Zanzibar are contracted into one silent personage in charge of all sound effects; a megaphone is used to indicate asides to the audience; a kiosk moves and speaks. Yet time and space are respected, the

[24] Apollinaire, *Les Mamelles de Tirésias* (Paris, 1946), p. 31.
[25] *Ibid.,* pp. 31–32.

text is of central importance and makes perfect sense, there is a good-humoredly satiric plot. Thus while the *truc* gains in importance, it does not replace the word. The "futurism" of *Les Mamelles* is mainly confined to the syntheticism of the manifesto prologue. While ex-futurist Gino Severini, writing of this play, could say he found "le surréalisme d'Apollinaire était assez près de ce nouveau-réalisme [des futuristes] . . . lequel, tout en s'éloignant du réel (ou plutôt ses apparences), prenait de lui son élan,"[26] he adds (correctly) the crucial name of Baudelaire and the seminal notion of *correspondances* as the real source of this new realism. But the *trucs,* possibly remotely derivable from Baudelaire, were first promoted by Marinetti, and the *multiples tétons* of Thérèse-Tirésias were manufactured in Milan.

The centrality of the *truc* in Cocteau's early theatre has been well dealt with in Neal Oxenhandler's book on his plays.[27] Cocteau has always loved to pose as the apostle of classic order and has always expressed amazement over his theatrical scandals. He has clucked over Apollinaire's penchants for "hasard, la pacotille nègre et les affiches de New-York," sighed over that "snow colder than death" which he finds in Apollinaire's mocking "destruction" of literature. Yet, and very characteristically, he adds: "Cet étrange suicide m'attirait avec ses yeux bleus."[28] One feels that it was scandal which winked its blue eye at Jean Cocteau.

*Parade,* with sets by Picasso and a couple of Roman futurists, is a light gloss on Rimbaud's piece by that name in *Les Illuminations:* "La démarche cruelle des oripeaux!" and "J'ai seul la clef de cette parade sauvage." Cocteau's *ballet réaliste,* done with (besides Picasso, Satie, the Ballets Russes, and Massine) massive masks, acrobats, magicians, the sounds of typewriters, sirens,[29] vain exhortations by all the cast to the effect that the "real show" is further within, has been best, although unwittingly, criticized by Cocteau himself in his preface to *Les Mariés de la Tour Eiffel:*

[26] "Apollinaire et le futurisme," *XX*ᵉ *siecle* (Paris, 1952), pp. 15–16.
[27] *Scandal & Parade: The Theatre of Jean Cocteau* (New Brunswick, 1957); see esp. chap. iii, "Theatre as Parade."
[28] *Le Rappel,* p. 244.
[29] At least these sound effects were intended. In the actual performance they were found to be impracticable.

Toute œuvre vivante comporte sa propre parade. Cette parade seule est vue par ceux qui n'entrent pas. Or, la surface d'une œuvre nouvelle heurte, intrigue, agace trop le spectateur pour qu'il entre. Il est détourné de l'âme par le visage, par l'expression inédite qui le distrait comme une grimace de clown à la porte. C'est ce phénomène qui trompe les critiques.[30]

*Il est détourné de l'âme par le visage,* and the point is: when such a shifting, colorful, eccentric surface is deliberately spread out before one, isn't it logical to neglect its very hypothetical "soul"? Jarry was correct to expect his audience to look within: his parade was not nearly so formidable as Cocteau's. *Parade* is synthetic theatre with, as in the futurist theatre, all the weight put on *matter;* doubtless it was charming, and one would not complain if Cocteau himself did not complain that his audience did not see into his soul.

These same remarks hold good for his subsequent plays: *Le Bœuf sur le toit, Roméo et Juliette* ("prétexte à *mise-en-scène*"), *Antigone* ("contraction"), and *Les Mariés de la Tour Eiffel.* All employ that "grosse dentelle" which Cocteau stipulates for his "poésie de théâtre," [31] i.e., a *truc* theatre, heavily weighted on the scenic-spectacular side, accompanied by a short, telegraphic text (*Le Bœuf,* like *Parade,* has no text at all). In *Roméo,* for example, the actors move as if in rhythm with an inaudible music, Romeo is a somnambulist, all action proceeds on a dark stage backed by a black velvet curtain against which details of the faces and costumes of the actors are picked up by offstage lighting. In *Antigone* the chorus is reduced to one voice issuing from the mouth of a statue; another statue, masked, walks across stage to symbolize the death of Hémon; the costumes are so designed as to evoke "un carnaval sordide et royal, une famille d'insectes." [32] In *Le Bœuf* the actors "portent des têtes de carton trois fois grandeur nature. Ils agissent selon le style du décor. Ils sont *du décor qui bouge.*" [33] In *Parade, Le Bœuf,* and the adaptations, Cocteau says he set out to "exploiter les ressources

---

[30] Cocteau, *Théâtre* (*Antigone, Les Mariés de la Tour Eiffel, Les Chevaliers de la Table Ronde, Les Parents terribles*) (Paris, 1948), p. 44.

[31] *Ibid.,* p. 45.

[32] *Ibid.,* p. 11.

[33] Cocteau, *Théâtre de poche* (Monaco, 1955), p. 16.

du théâtre en soi, négliger jusqu'à nouvel ordre la littérature dramatique en faveur d'une beauté qui ne peut se mouvoir hors les planches." [34] As for *Roméo*, considered as *un texte prétexte*, he finds it "inséparable des surprises visuelles qu'il motivait." [35]

Here, then, as we found sketched in Apollinaire's prologue and in full swing in futurist syntheticism, is a theatre in which the *mise-en-scène* is king, where the text is reduced to a comment on mobile matter; the fact that with Marinetti this surface is everything and with Cocteau is only a means to an end (i.e., beneath the flux) does not gainsay the resemblance. While the stagecraft of Richard Wagner (whose baneful *musical* influence is deplored in *Le Coq et l'arlequin*) and the Ballets Russes (where Cocteau was an intimate and where earlier he had contributed a scenario) and an early love of variety theatre had assuredly great influence on his theatrical predilections, the mode of Marinetti helped to crystallize such tendencies into a veritable tic which only time and theatrical experience could modify.

Cocteau calls this theatre, up to *Orphée*, "sept ans d'études, sous prétexte de pantomimes et d'adaptation." [36] *Les Mariés*, a thoroughly delightful play in the style of Jarry and Apollinaire (i.e., simplification magnified), is an essay to paint

le plus vrai que le vrai. Le poéte doit sortir objets et sentiments de leurs voiles et de leurs brumes, les montrer soudain, si nus et si vite, que l'homme a peine à les reconnaître. Ils le frappent alors avec leur jeunesse . . . [avec] miracle de la vie quotidienne.[37]

Although the *truc*, the sight gag of sleight of hand stage machinery, is prevalent still, the text has at last come into its own, matter is under the control of *esprit*. *Les Mariés*, *Orphée*, and *La Machine infernale* constitute Cocteau's real contribution to theatre, this in large part because of the centrality assigned to text and the relegation of the other arts to their proper stations as tactful ancillaries to the word.

Marinetti's influence, then, on French theatre was *malgré lui*

34 *Théâtre*, p. 37.
35 *Ibid*.
36 "Le Numéro Barbette," *Œuvres complètes de Jean Cocteau,* IX (Genève, 1950), p. 27.
37 *Théâtre*, etc., p. 42.

an exaggeration to be overcome. The "lyric obsession with matter" in the form of *trucs,* spectacle, and the virtual obliteration of
text was, with the futurists, directed toward an essentially political ideal of *automation;* in France, on the other hand, it eventually served as a liberative influence which, if taken *cum grano,*
helped renew a classical tradition.

L. MOHOLY-NAGY

## Theatre, Circus, Variety *

### I. THE HISTORICAL THEATRE

The historical theatre was essentially a disseminator of information or propaganda, or it was an articulated concentration of
action (*Aktionskonzentration*) derived from events and doctrines in their broadest meaning—that is to say, as "drama-
tized" legend, as religious (cultist) or political (proselytizing)
propaganda, or as compressed action with a more or less transparent purpose behind it.

The theatre differed from the eyewitness report, simple storytelling, didactic moralizing, or advertising copy through its own
particular synthesis of the elements of presentation: sound, color
(light), motion, space, form (objects and persons).

With these elements, in their accentuated but often uncon-
trolled interrelationships, the theatre attempted to transmit an
articulated experience.

In early epic drama (*Erzählungsdrama*) these elements were
generally employed as illustration, subordinated to narration or
propaganda. The next step in this evolution led to the drama of

* Copyright, ©, 1961 by Wesleyan University. Reprinted from *The Theater of the Bauhaus,* edited by Walter Gropius, by permission of Wesleyan
University Press.

action (*Aktionsdrama*), where the elements of dynamic-dramatic movement began to crystallize: the theatre of improvisation, the *commedia dell' arte*. These dramatic forms were progressively liberated from a central theme of logical, intellectual-emotional action which was no longer dominant. Gradually their moralizing and their tendentiousness disappeared in favor of an un-hampered concentration on action: Shakespeare, the opera.

With August Stramm, drama developed away from verbal context, from propaganda, and from character delineation, and toward explosive activism.[1] Creative experiments with motion and sound (speech) were made, based on the impetus of human sources of energy, that is, the "passions." Stramm's theatre did not offer narrative material, but action and tempo, which, un-premeditated, sprang almost *automatically* and in headlong suc-cession from the human impulse for motion. But even in Stramm's case action was not altogether free from literary en-cumbrance.

"Literary encumbrance" is the result of the unjustifiable transfer of intellectualized material from the proper realm of lit-erary effectiveness (novel, short story, etc.) to the stage, where it incorrectly remains a dramatic end in itself. The result is nothing more than literature if a reality or a potential reality, no matter how imaginative, is formulated or visually expressed without the creative forms peculiar only to the stage. It is not until the ten-sions concealed in the utmost economy of means are brought into universal and dynamic interaction that we have creative stage-craft (*Bühnengestaltung*).[2] Even in recent times we have been

[1] August Stramm (1874–1915) was a Westphalian poet and dramatist and the strongest of the members of the circle known as the *Sturmdichter*. His works belong to the early phase of Expressionism and are in a radi-cally elliptical, powerful, and antisyntactical style. His plays, *Sancta Susanna*, *Kräfte* (*Powers*, set to music in 1922 by Hindemith), *Erwachen* (*Awakening*), *Geschehen* (*Happening*), seem today less effective than his volumes of poetry, *Du* (*You*), *Tropfblut* (*Dripblood*).—Tr.

[2] *Gestaltung* was among the most fundamental terms in the language of the Bauhaus and is used many times by Schlemmer and Moholy in their writing, both by itself and in its many compounds, such as *Bühnengestal-tung*, *Farbengestaltung*, *Theatergestaltung*. T. Lux Feininger writes: "If the term 'Bauhaus' was a new adaptation of the medieval concept of the 'Bauhütte,' the headquarters of the cathedral builders, the term 'gestal-tung' is old, meaningful, and so nearly untranslatable that it has found its way into English usage. Beyond the significance of shaping, forming,

deluded about the true value of creative stagecraft when revolutionary, social, ethical, or similar problems were unrolled with a great display of literary pomp and paraphernalia.

## 2. ATTEMPTS AT A THEATRE FORM FOR TODAY

a) Theatre of Surprises: Futurists, Dadaists, *Merz*.[3] In the investigation of any morphology, we proceed today from the all-inclusive functionalism of goal, purpose, and materials.

From this premise the Futurists, Expressionists, and Dadaists (Merz) came to the conclusion that phonetic word relationships were more significant than other creative literary means, and that the logical-intellectual content (*das Logisch-Gedankliche*) of a work of literature was far from its primary aim. It was maintained that, just as in representational painting it was not the content as such, not the objects represented which were essential, but the interaction of colors, so in literature it was not the logical-intellectual content which belonged in the foreground, but the effects which arose from the word-sound relationships. In the case of some writers this idea has been extended (or possibly contracted) to the point where word relationships are transformed into exclusively phonetic sound relationships, thereby totally fragmenting the word into conceptually disjointed vowels and consonants.

This was the origin of the Dadaist and Futurist "Theatre of Surprises," a theatre which aimed at the elimination of logical-intellectual (literary) aspects. Yet in spite of this, man, who until

thinking through, it has the flavor underlining the totality of such fashioning, whether of an artifact or of an idea. It forbids the nebulous and the diffuse. In its fullest philosophical meaning it expresses the Platonic *eidolon*, the *Urbild*, the preexisting form."—Tr.

[3] The phenomenon known as *Merz* is closely connected with the Dadaist movement of the post–World War I period in Germany and Switzerland. The term was coined in 1919 by the artist Kurt Schwitters and came from one of his collages in which was incorporated a scrap of newspaper with only the center part of the word "kom*merz*iell" on it. A whole series of his collages was called *Merzbilder*. From 1923 to 1932, with Arp, Lissitzsky, Mondrian, and many others, Schwitters published the magazine *Merz;* and at about the same period the Merz Poets caused a great furor. The movement was characterized by playfulness, earnest experimentalism, and what seems to have been a great need for self-expression and for shocking the bourgeoisie.—Tr.

then had been the sole representative of logical, causal action and of vital mental activities, still dominated.

b) The Mechanized Eccentric (*Die mechanische Exzentrik*). As a logical consequence of this there arose the need for a *Mechanized Eccentric,* a concentration of stage action in its purest form (*eine Aktionskonzentration der Bühne in Reinkultur*). Man, who no longer should be permitted to represent himself as a phenomenon of spirit and mind through his intellectual and spiritual capacities, no longer has any place in this concentration of action. For, no matter how cultured he may be, his organism permits him at best only a certain range of action, dependent entirely on his natural body mechanism.

The effect of this body mechanism (*Körpermechanik*) (in circus performance and athletic events, for example) arises essentially from the spectator's astonishment or shock at the potentialities of his *own* organism as demonstrated to him by others. This is a subjective effect. Here the human body is the sole medium of configuration (*Gestaltung*). For the purposes of an objective *Gestaltung* of movement this medium is limited, the more so since it has constant reference to sensible and perceptive (i.e., again literary) elements. The inadequacy of "human" *Exzentrik* led to the demand for a precise and fully controlled organization of form and motion, intended to be a synthesis of dynamically contrasting phenomena (space, form, motion, sound, and light). This is the Mechanized Eccentric.

### 3. THE COMING THEATRE: THEATRE OF TOTALITY

Every form process or *Gestaltung* has its general as well as its particular premises, from which it must proceed in making use of its specific media. We might, therefore, clarify theatre production (*Theatergestaltung*) if we investigated the nature of its highly controversial media: the human *word* and the human action, and, at the same time, considered the endless possibilities open to their creator—man.

The origins of music as conscious composition can be traced back to the melodic recitations of the heroic saga. When music was systematized, permitting only the use of harmonies (*Klänge*) and excluding so-called sounds (*Geräusche*), the only place left

for a special sound form (*Geräuschgestaltung*) was in literature, particularly in poetry. This was the underlying idea from which the Expressionists, Futurists, and Dadaists proceeded in composing their sound-poems (*Lautgedichte*). But today, when music has been broadened to admit sounds of all kinds, the sensory-mechanistic effect of sound interrelationships is no longer a monopoly of poetry. It belongs, as much as do harmonies (*Töne*), to the realm of music, much in the same way that the task of painting, seen as color creation, is to organize clearly primary (apperceptive) [4] color effect. Thus the error of the Futurists, the Expressionists, the Dadaists, and all those who built on such foundations becomes clear. As an example: the idea of an *Exzentrik* which is *only* mechanical.

It must be said, however, that those ideas, in contradistinction to a literary-illustrative viewpoint, have unquestionably advanced creative theatre precisely because they were diametrically opposed. They canceled out the predominance of the exclusively logical-intellectual values. But once the predominance has been broken, the associative processes and the language of man, and consequently man himself in his totality as a formative medium for the stage, may not be barred from it. To be sure, he is no longer to be pivotal—as he is in traditional theatre—but is to be employed *on an equal footing with the other formative media.*

Man as the most active phenomenon of life is indisputably one of the most effective elements of a dynamic stage production (*Bühnengestaltung*), and therefore he justifies on functional grounds the utilization of his totality of action, speech, and thought. With his intellect, his dialectic, his adaptability to any situation by virtue of his control over his physical and mental powers, he is—when used in any concentration of action (*Aktionskonzentration*)—destined to be primarily a configuration of these powers.

[4] "Apperceptive" signifies here, in contrast to "associative," an elementary step in observation and conceptualization (psychophysical assimilation). E.g., to assimilate a color = apperceptive process. The human eye reacts without previous experience to red with green, blue with yellow, etc. An object = assimilation of color + matter + form = connection with previous experience = associative process.

And if the stage didn't provide him full play for these potentialities, it would be imperative to create an adequate vehicle.

But this utilization of man must be clearly differentiated from his appearance heretofore in traditional theatre. While there he was only the interpreter of a literarily conceived individual or type, in the new *Theatre of Totality* he will use the spiritual and physical means at his disposal *productively* and from his own *initiative* submit to the overall action process.

While during the Middle Ages (and even today) the center of gravity in theatre production lay in the representation of the various *types* (hero, harlequin, peasant, etc.), it is the task of the future actor to discover and activate that which is *common* to all men.

In the plan of such a theatre the traditionally "meaningful" and causal interconnections can *not* play the major role. In the consideration of stage setting as an *art form,* we must learn from the creative artist that, just as it is impossible to ask what a man (as organism) is or stands for, it is inadmissible to ask the same question of a contemporary nonobjective picture which likewise is a *Gestaltung,* that is, an organism.

The contemporary painting exhibits a multiplicity of color and surface interrelationships, which gain their effect, on the one hand, from their conscious and logical statement of problems, and on the other, from the unanalyzable intangibles of creative intuition.

In the same way, the Theatre of Totality with its multifarious complexities of light, space, plane, form, motion, sound, man — and with all the possibilities for varying and combining these elements—must be an *organism.*

Thus the process of integrating man into creative stage production must be unhampered by moralistic tendentiousness or by problems of science or the *individual*. Man may be active only as the bearer of those functional elements which are organically in acccordance with his specific nature.

It is self-evident, however, that all *other* means of stage production must be given positions of effectiveness equal to man's,

who as a living psychophysical organism, as the producer of incomparable climaxes and infinite variations, demands of the coformative factors a high standard of quality.

### 4. HOW SHALL THE THEATRE OF TOTALITY BE REALIZED?

One of two points of view still important today holds that theatre is the concentrated activation (*Aktionskonzentration*) of sound, light (color), space, form, and motion. Here man as coactor is not necessary, since in our day equipment can be constructed which is far more capable of executing the *purely mechanical* role of man than man himself.

The other, more popular view will not relinquish the magnificent instrument which is man, even though no one has yet solved the problem of how to employ him as a creative medium on the stage.

Is it possible to include his human, logical functions in a present-day concentration of action on the stage, without running the risk of producing a copy from nature and without falling prey to Dadaist or Merz characterization, composed of an eclectic patchwork whose seeming order is purely arbitrary?

The creative arts have discovered pure media for their constructions: the primary relationships of color, mass, material, etc. But how can we integrate a sequence of human movements and thoughts on an equal footing with the controlled, "absolute" elements of sound, light (color), form, and motion? In this regard only summary suggestions can be made to the creator of the new theatre (*Theatergestalter*). For example, the *repetition* of a thought by many actors, with identical words and with identical or varying intonation and cadence, could be employed as a means of creating synthetic (i.e., unifying) creative theatre. (This would be the *chorus*—but not the attendant and passive chorus of antiquity!) Or mirrors and optical equipment could be used to project the gigantically enlarged faces and gestures of the actors, while their voices could be amplified to correspond with the visual magnification. Similar effects can be obtained from the *simultaneous, synoptical,* and *synacoustical* reproduction of thought (with motion pictures, phonographs, loudspeakers), or from the reproduction of thoughts suggested by a construction of

variously meshing gears (*eine zahnradartig ineinandergreifende Gedankengestaltung*).

Independent of work in music and acoustics, the literature of the future will create its own "harmonies," at first primarily adapted to its own media, but with far-reaching implications for others. These will surely exercise an influence on the word and thought constructions of the stage.

This means, among other things, that the phenomena of the subconscious and dreams of fantasy and reality, which up to now were central to the so-called "intimate art theatre" (*Kammerspiele*), may no longer be predominant. And even if the conflicts arising from today's complicated social patterns, from the worldwide organization of technology, from pacifist-utopian and other kinds of revolutionary movements, can have a place in the art of the stage, they will be significant only in a transitional period, since their treatment belongs properly to the realms of literature, politics, and philosophy.

We envision *total stage action* (*Gesamtbühnenaktion*) as a great dynamic-rhythmic process, which can compress the greatest clashing masses or accumulations of media—as qualitative and quantitative tensions—into elemental form. Part of this would be the use of simultaneously interpenetrating sets of contrasting relationships, which are of minor importance in themselves, such as: the tragicomic, the grotesque-serious, the trivial-monumental; hydraulic spectacles; acoustical and other "pranks"; and so on. Today's circus, operetta, vaudeville, the clowns in America and elsewhere (Chaplin, Fratellini) have accomplished great things, both in this respect and in eliminating the subjective—even if the process has been naïve and often more superficial than incisive. Yet it would be just as superficial if we were to dismiss great performances and "shows" in this genre with the word *Kitsch*. It is high time to state once and for all that the much disdained masses, despite their "academic backwardness," often exhibit the soundest instincts and preferences. Our task will always remain the creative understanding of the true, and not the imagined, needs.

5. THE MEANS

Every *Gestaltung* or creative work should be an unexpected and new organism, and it is natural and incumbent on us to draw the material for surprise effects from our daily living. Nothing is more effective than the exciting new possibilities offered by the familiar and yet not properly evaluated elements of modern life —that is, its idiosyncracies: individuation, classification, mechanization. With this in mind, it is possible to arrive at a proper understanding of stagecraft through an investigation of creative media other than man as actor himself.

In the future, sound effects will make use of various acoustical equipment driven electrically or by some other mechanical means. Sound waves issuing from unexpected sources—for example, a speaking or singing arc lamp, loudspeakers under the seats or beneath the floor of the auditorium, the use of new amplifying systems—will raise the audience's acoustic surprise threshold so much that unequal effects in other areas will be disappointing.

Color (light) must undergo even greater transformation in this respect than sound.

Developments in painting during the past decades have created the organization of absolute color values and, as a consequence, the supremacy of pure and luminous chromatic tones. Naturally the monumentality and the lucid balance of their harmonies will not tolerate the actor with indistinct or splotchy makeup and tattered costuming, a product of misunderstood Cubism, Futurism, etc. The use of precision-made metallic masks and costumes and those of various other composition materials will thus become a matter of course. The pallid face, the subjectivity of expression, and the gestures of the actor in a colored stage environment are therefore eliminated without impairing the effective contrast between the human body and any mechanical construction. Films can also be projected onto various surfaces and further experiments in space illumination will be devised. This will constitute the new *action of light,* which by means of modern technology will use the most intensified con-

trasts to guarantee itself a position of importance equal to that of all other theatre media. We have not yet begun to realize the potential of light for sudden or blinding illumination, for flare effects, for phosphorescent effects, for bathing the auditorium in light synchronized with climaxes or with the total extinguishing of lights on the stage. All this, of course, is thought of in a sense totally different from anything in current traditional theatre.

From the time that stage objects became mechanically movable, the generally traditional, horizontally structured organization of movement in space has been enriched by the possibility of vertical motion. Nothing stands in the way of making use of complex *apparatus* such as film, automobile, elevator, airplane, and other machinery, as well as optical instruments, reflecting equipment, and so on. The current demand for dynamic construction will be satisfied in this way, even though it is still only in its first stages.

There would be a further enrichment if the present isolation of the stage could be eliminated. In today's theatre, stage and spectator are too much separated, too obviously divided into active and passive, to be able to produce creative relationships and reciprocal tensions.

It is time to produce a kind of stage activity which will no longer permit the masses to be silent spectators, which will not only excite them inwardly but will let them *take hold and participate*—actually allow them to fuse with the action on the stage at the peak of cathartic ecstasy.

To see that such a process is not chaotic, but that it develops with control and organization, will be one of the tasks of the thousand-eyed *new director,* equipped with all the modern means of understanding and communication.

It is clear that the present peep-show stage is not suitable for such organized motion.

The next form of the advancing theatre—in cooperation with future authors—will probably answer the above demands with *suspended bridges* and *drawbridges* running horizontally, diagonally, and vertically within the space of the theatre; with plat-

form stages built far into the auditorium; and so on. Apart from rotating sections, the stage will have movable space constructions and *disklike areas,* in order to bring certain action moments on the stage into prominence, as in film "close-ups." In place of today's periphery of orchestra loges, a runway joined to the stage could be built to establish—by means of a more or less caliper-like embrace—a closer connection with the audience.

The possibilities for a *variation of levels of movable planes* on the stage of the future would contribute to a genuine organization of space. Space will then no longer consist of the interconnections of planes in the old meaning, which was able to conceive of architectonic delineation of space only as an enclosure formed by opaque surfaces. The new space originates from free-standing surfaces or from linear definition of planes (wire frames, antennas), so that the surfaces stand at times in a very free relationship to one another, without the need of any direct contact.

As soon as an intense and penetrating concentration of action can be functionally realized, there will develop simultaneously the corresponding auditorium architecture. There will also appear costumes designed to emphasize function and costumes which are conceived only for single moments of action and capable of sudden transformations.

There will arise an enhanced *control* over all formative media, unified in a harmonious effect and built into an organism of perfect equilibrium.

P A R T  I V  Creative Staging:
A Key to Total Theatre

The function of the stage director is interpretation, not arrangement.
Stage direction is a re-*creative* activity; it is not the rehashing of exist-
·ing patterns and worn-out clichés. For living theatre there can be
only one style—that of its own period. . . . The art of staging
serves the work's creator only when it is constantly rejuvenated.

WIELAND WAGNER [1]

It is appropriate that Wieland Wagner, Richard Wagner's grandson, continued the practice of creative staging that had been
championed by Appia and Craig. His productions of the operas
at Bayreuth eliminated the ponderous, illustrative settings and
placed the dramas in shaped expanses of dimly lit stage where
they were illuminated by extraordinary lighting effects. Naturalistic groupings and action were replaced by stage movement
reduced to a bare minimum in a style that revealed the drama's
essential quality as "scenic oratorio." This was an approach to
"more" totality through reduction, consolidation, and integra-

[1] Everett Helm, "And This from Wagner's Grandson!", *The New York
Times Magazine* (June 5, 1966), p. 69.

tion, along the lines of Appia's theories, and as called for by Prampolini.

Creative staging, however, remains a subject for controversy. This need not affect us here. In terms of the theatre we are considering, creative staging is the translation of a script to a new form, a distinct medium, that of total theatre. This separates it entirely from those considerations that hold theatre to a function of reproduction.

Questions of technique, and of the manner in which all the arts may contribute to the stage, are of primary importance. Many of the same principles as those involved in transforming a play or a novel into a film are operative here. An implementation of images in terms of the various sensory modalities provides one theoretical basis; the variables of time and space, as the common determinants of the arts, provide another. Appia's theories sought the unity of all theatrical forms in these variables. But Meyerhold's stagings show how time and space can be used both as effect, in passages of different tempos, and to give an overall character to a production. His work of the 1920's is described here by Nikolai Gorchakov in "Meyerhold's Theatre."

In staging his plays, Meyerhold used many new and different styles. Among his early productions was one of Ibsen's *Hedda Gabler* (1906) seen in terms of a complete Symbolist aesthetic. Each actor was given a leitmotif for posing, was dressed in his own color, and his movements and poses were composed in relation to the décor, which was dominated by blue, green, and silver, with white furniture. A colored haze seemed to fill the stage. Within this ambience the actors moved like spots of color in a controlled manner, their voices modulated, precise.

This symbolist emphasis on control, precision and containment became, in metaphor, the Übermarionette, as we have seen. Meyerhold created many new modes in which this essential sur-reality of the performer as puppet was revealed. His work, with all its variations, had a single theme. As Gorchakov observes: "He wanted to create a new theatre of the mask."

Of particular relevance to our present context are Meyerhold's methods of segmenting or compartmentalizing the action in various ways, such as his insertion of passages of pantomime between speeches in the method he called "preacting." This re-

lates to the form of expression that has been described here as "hieroglyphic"; it may also be noted in Meyerhold's tendency to freeze action into static poses. These motionless pictures relate to that aspect of the Übermarionette in which the person takes on the nature of a hieratic statue or idol, but they also relate to a method of using the time and space of the stage to present moments of concrete poetry, of visual impact, as hieroglyphic summations of meaning.

These techniques, rather than an accumulation of means as such, indicate why a production such as Meyerhold's *Bubus the Teacher* pertains directly to the project of total theatre, rather than to forms of musical theatre.

Also of particular relevance in this regard is the influence of Oriental theatre upon Meyerhold's work. An interest in expressive movement, particularly of the hands and arms, derived from the Japanese, and a magic poetry of objects from the Chinese. These influences affected even such a highly rationalized and Western style as his biomechanical phase. Oriental influence, and Oriental techniques in general, will be considered in the following section. As noted, the implications of their concern with hieroglyphic realities can be understood as fundamental to the realization of total theatre.

Yevgeny Vakhtangov was an admirer of Meyerhold's work, but his method differed in that it seemed to center upon elaborating interpretations from within the play itself and upon creating contrasts in attitudes and in levels of reality in relation to the particular text. It thus sought totality, not in specifically sensory means but by a "complexification" of meaning in presentation. William Kuhlke's "Vakhtangov and the American Theatre of the 1960's" gives us a close-up view of Vakhtangov's methods in relation to his famous, and still performed, production of *Turandot*. And it sketches the implications for creative staging in relation to our present modes of theatrical activity.

Max Reinhardt, the great German director, seemed to some critics to be too close to creating Wagner's *Gesamtkunstwerk* in terms of a collective eclecticism, a totality of means as such. But his attention to the techniques of an interplay of the senses can be observed both on the level of spectacle, as in his *Everyman* or in *The Miracle,* and also in regard to detail, as in the Death-drum

sequence in the *Great World Theatre*. These are described in Margret Dietrich's fine account of "Music and Dance in the Productions of Max Reinhardt"; we are there provided with a picture of the "acoustical ecstatic" means which were Reinhardt's particular contribution to creative staging and to total theatre.

A present-day artist working somewhat along these lines is the Belgian, Maurice Béjart, the artistic director and principal choreographer of the Twentieth Century Ballet of the Théâtre Royal de la Monnaie in Brussels. His free adaptation of Aristophanes' *The Birds* was performed in a circus ring with dancers speaking the lines of dialogue, and his *Mass* used many different kinds of music and dancing as elements in a very modern scenic spectacle. His work is an indication of how the dance seems now to be closer to realizing the forms of total theatre than is dramatic production. Béjart speaks of "total theatre" as "the magic word that is now on the lips and in the thoughts of all those who are in any way concerned with dramatic art." [2]

In Russia, Lyubimov's Tanganka Theatre represents a realization of the ideal goal of creative staging as it relates to total theatre. The Tanganka is a complete theatre instrument equipped for producing total theatre (called "synthetic theatre" in Russia) and transforming a script in terms of effects. A horizontal curtain of light can be directed out from the stage just over the heads of the audience, and actors can move into columns of light directed upward from the stage floor. The range of theatricalizing, or totalizing, techniques is extensive, and has included many environmental elements, even the use of odors.

[2] "Maurice Béjart and the Total Theatre," *World Theatre*, XIV:6 (November–December, 1965), p. 556.

# NIKOLAI A. GORCHAKOV

## Meyerhold's Theatre *

Vsevolod Meyerhold's Theatre was the Soviet theatre that
launched the period of *Sturm und Drang*.[1] Its first experimental
work was its production of Crommelynck's *Le Cocu magnifique,*
the première of which was April 15, 1922. Meyerhold's forms
and devices in this production exercised a profound and prolonged influence on both the Soviet and non-Soviet European
theatres. He asserted two completely new ideas in the theatre:
constructivism and biomechanics.

How could Crommelynck's "tragic farce" have attracted
Meyerhold? The plot shows that Bruno, the miller, was jealous
of his wife, Stella. This scarcely harmonizes with the end of the
Civil War and the "October in the Theatre" programs that
Meyerhold headed. There was not even a trace of the "social
conflicts" so dear to the hearts of Marxists. Ivan Aksenov's translation was painful and inaccurate, and it often slid over into
"transsense" language. The only feature of the play drawing
the pre-Revolutionary—but not the post-Revolutionary—
Meyerhold was that jealousy was reduced to an absurdity.[2]

* Reprinted from *The Theatre in Soviet Russia* by Nikolai A. Gorchakov, trans. Edgar Lehrman, copyright, ©, 1957, by Columbia University
Press, New York, and reprinted with their permission.

[1] Vsevolod Meyerhold's Theatre was located on Sadovaya-Trium-
falnaya Street in Moscow (the old Zon Operetta Building). Its name was
changed five times in six years: It opened on October 7, 1920, as the First
Theatre of the R.S.F.S.R.; when it staged *Le Cocu magnifique* in 1922, it
was called The Theatre of the Actor—the Free Workshop of Vsevolod
Meyerhold Attached to the State Supreme Theatre Workshops; toward the
autumn of 1922, the title became the Theatre of the State Institute of
the Theatre Arts—Vsevolod Meyerhold's Workshop (the "Experimental
and Heroic Theatre" of Ferdinandov and Bebutov had autonomous status
within this last mentioned "Workshop"); from 1923 through the winter of
1926, the Theatre was called Vsevolod Meyerhold's Theatre; the title was
changed for the last time at the beginning of December, 1926 when it became the Vsevolod Meyerhold State Theatre, which it remained until its
liquidation by the Soviet government in 1937.

[2] Reducing a passion to an absurdity typifies all Crommelynck's work.
In *Tripes d'or,* for example, he has a miser eat his own gold so that it will
not be stolen from him and will always remain at the bottom of his maw.

Basically, Crommelynck's tragic farce was an abstract orchestral score that merely furnished a pretext for the extremely abstract treatment given it by Meyerhold. In *Le Cocu magnifique* he dealt a most merciless and destructive blow to the old "intimate" theatre with its threadbare devices and its handling of the stage like a box camera. The enormous portal of the Zon theatre stage was laid bare. The curtain, the coulisses, the cornices in front of the soffits, the soffits themselves, and even the fly galleries were stripped completely. There was a gloomy haze on the enormous stage, beyond which rose unplastered brick walls. Radiators for central heating hung in the heights of the fly galleries.

Meyerhold then removed all the machinery for creating scenic illusions. He had the actor stand alone on the stage, with no makeup, no wig, and no colored finery on his costumes. He was starting all over again. It was like the first day of creation. No one tried to hide the spotlights from the public or to pass them off as "sunlight" or "moonlight." Babanova, Ilynsky, and Zaichikov enacted Crommelynck's tragic farce without a drop of the "tragic." They used the gay mockery of mischievous comedians and circuslike devices.

This was Meyerhold's most telling blow against "theatricality" and the most "leftist" point in his work. It marked the birth of constructivism within the Russian theatre. It was the only time in his career that he came close to denying the magic of the theatre completely. The experiment reeked of the laboratory. It resembled an anatomic theatre containing only the skeleton of the living person. He destroyed all the ingredients of the theatre, save only the actor—its final and indestructible nucleus. He wanted to say that almost everything else in the theatre could be removed or replaced, but if the actor remains on the bare stage the greatness of the theatre stays with him.

The constructivism that Meyerhold discovered in this presentation merely continued the stripping of the illusory flesh and sinews from the skeleton of the theatre. The skin of illusion was removed from the décor, and only the ribs—the skeleton of the technical construction—remained. There were two stands on the stage, each as tall as a one-storied house. They were connected by a board which also ran down to the stage floor. There

were two staircases and a ramp to glide down along. Beyond the stands were the skeletons of stage properties, from which the canvas coverings had been removed. One of the stands had turnstiles above and below, while a number of crossbeams on the other stand created windows. The driving wheels of the mill were placed beyond the construction, and the enormous disk was also utilitarian rather than decorative. The sole function of the disk was to start turning furiously when the madness of the jealous Bruno began to fume. CR-MM-L-NCK was written in large, white, Latin letters on the disk so that the public would notice its rotation. The disk itself and the shafts supporting it lacked the letters "O," "E," and "Y" to complete the playwright's name.

Such was the external appearance of the first "machine for acting" in the Russian theatre. This was the abstract construction that the magic of acting virtuosity transformed into the miller's house. One and the same place beneath the stand represented a courtyard where the furiously jealous peasant women want to square accounts with Stella, a dining room in which guests are gathering, and an office in which Bruno dictates his verses to Estrugo. One spotlighted flower in Stella's hands furnished the sole stage property for the entire production; it sufficed, however, to turn the bare platform into a terrace that was filled with flowers and bathed in the morning sun. The production was one of Meyerhold's most powerful, and it revived the pure art of acting on the stage.

Meyerhold had made motion, gesture, and pantomime omnipotent in the theatre. His *Le Cocu magnifique* was the first practical realization on a grand scale of the theories and plans that had matured within him back in the days of "Dr. Dapertutto's" Studio. These ideas dealt with the supremacy of motion over language and illusion. There is a direct connection between *Le Cocu magnifique* and all of Meyerhold's pre-Revolutionary experiments at Interlude House and "Dr. Dapertutto's" Studio.

The "Leftist Front" Futurists considered Meyerhold's work on *Le Cocu magnifique* a mere continuation of their own ideas about "productionalism in art" and "constructivism in painting." [3] They asserted:

[3] Boris Arbatov, a theoretician of "constructivism," characterized the origin of the movement in the depictive arts as follows: "The radical and

In the theatre, constructivism united constructive furnishings—such as the décor, the props, and the costumes—designed to show things themselves, or at least their models, with "constructive" gestures, motions, and pantomimes. This last was the biomechanics of Vsevolod Meyerhold; the actors were organized according to rhythms.[4]

The reference to "biomechanics" in the quotation calls attention to another aspect of the production of *Le Cocu magnifique,* an aspect that was to distinguish Meyerhold's later productions. It was a new system of acting that started with the supremacy of motion, which was calculated in a way resembling circus acrobatics. It was diametrically opposed to the Stanislavsky System. Meyerhold's concept was called "biomechanics" and stood for the power of pantomime.

Meyerhold rejected the Stanislavsky System as having overemphasized the "spirit" and "psychologizing" at the expense of the actor's "body." He felt that the actors at the Moscow Art Theatre, for all their refined souls and experiences, were completely incapable of motion. He was striving to restore the lost equilibrium. He wanted to use his biomechanics for creating actors whose bodies would be supple and obedient and who would be highly proficient in gesture and pantomime. He wanted to break with the acting art that used priestly draperies, the fog of the subconscious, the intuitive, and everything else that smacked of mysticism and spiritual charlatanism. He wanted to confirm the harmony of acting through the algebra of reason. In all the rare statements by Meyerhold and his collaborators on the theory of biomechanics, the emphasis is on rationalism and on a mechanistic understanding of the creative process. They tried to

leading part of the new intelligentsia, the so-called technical intelligentsia (to be precise), has been educated in the industrial centers of the present, and has been permeated with the positivism of the natural sciences, and has become 'Americanized'. . . . At the time when the former intelligentsia was soaring above the clouds in its 'pure ideology,' the new and 'urbanized' intelligentsia was concentrating on the material world, the world of things. These people wanted most to build and to construct. . . . The constructivists have declared that the basis and even the sole aim of art is the creative treatment . . . of materials. . . ." (B. Arbatov, "Iskusstvo i klassy," in a collection of his articles, *Sotsiologicheskaia poetika* [1929], pp. 39–40.)

[4] Chuzhak in *LEF,* No. I (1923), p. 30.

base everything on the simple and elementary laws of the reflexes. Two theoretical works of Meyerhold's appeared in the year he staged *Le Cocu magnifique*. They are especially important because they served as a declaration of his new acting system. These works were called *Amplua aktëra* ("The Actor's Role") and *Aktër budushchego* ("The Actor of the Future"). Their approach to the art of acting is decidedly mechanistic. He wrote:

A necessary and special trait in actors is their ability to respond to stimuli applied to their reflexes. . . . The stimulus is the ability to fulfill an assignment received from the outside through feelings, motion, and language. To coordinate the reactions to stimuli is what constitutes *acting*. The separate parts of this are the *elements of acting*, each of which has three stages: (1) Intention; (2) Accomplishment; (3) Reaction.

Intention is the intellectual perception of the assignment received from the outside (from the author, the dramatist, the director, or on the initiative of the performer himself).

Accomplishment is the series of volitional, mimetic, and vocal reflexes.[5]

Reaction is the lowering of the volitional reflex in accordance with the realization of the mimetic and vocal reflexes. The volitional reflex is prepared to receive a new intention and proceeds to a new element of *acting*.

The actor must be able to respond to stimuli. The reflex stimulus is the process of reducing the perception of a task to the minimum ("the ordinary reaction time").

A person who possesses the necessary ability for reflex stimuli can be or can become an actor; he can fulfill one of the roles in the theatre

[5] Meyerhold appends the following note to clarify the term "volitional": "The term 'feeling' is used in its technical and scientific sense, without any narrow-minded or sentimental connotations. The same is true of the term 'volitional.' This is done to separate the exposition from both acting of the 'internal' school (without systematic narcotics) and from the method of 'experience' (the hypnotic training of the imagination). The first of these methods coerces the will with an artificial incitement of feelings which have been enfeebled beforehand; the second coerces feeling through the hypnotic extraction of the will which has been enfeebled beforehand. Both of them must therefore be rejected as worthless and dangerous to healthy people subject to their influence. The term 'mimetic' indicates all the motions which arise on the periphery of the actor's body, as well as the motion of the actor himself within space."

in accordance with his natural and physical talents. He can be given a position that is determined as appropriate by the stage functions.[6]

One must know Meyerhold, with his burning contempt for the old theatre and the Stanislavsky System, to understand all the charm of his sarcasm. He considered the new theory of acting a stylistic mixture of the "Regulations for the Military Disciple" and a textbook for algebra. He reduced all the subtle complexities of the actor's creative activity to the fulfillment of an "assignment received from the outside" and reduced all the mysterious greatness of acting talent to the presence of those "reflex stimuli" possessed by every person and every animal.

These theoretical works set forth the bases of biomechanics that sought to tailor the actor's motions, to subordinate them to the same methods used to organize labor processes scientifically. Biomechanics aimed at removing superfluous and unproductive motions and rhythms and at correctly locating the center of gravity in the body and finding balance. Meyerhold wrote:

The motions constructed on these bases are distinguished by a *dansant* quality. The labor process used by experienced workers always resembles the dance. Here, work verges on art. The sight of a person who is working correctly produces a certain satisfaction.

This applies completely to the work of the actor in the theatre of the future. We are always dealing in art with the organization of material. Constructivism demands that the artist become an engineer as well. Art must be based on scientific principles; all the work done by the artist must be conscious.[7]

All this "stage algebra" and predominance of mechanics becomes comprehensible only if we realize that Meyerhold also decided to try something else in his production of *Le Cocu magnifique*. This effort was quite important but has been little discussed. He wanted to link the theatre arts with the age of the proletarian dictatorship, and so he struck out sharply and mercilessly against the acting "priesthood." A stage is not a temple, he asserted. Its brick walls and "machines for acting" do not distin-

---

[6] Meyerhold, Bebutov, and Aksenov, *Amplua aktëra*, pp. 3–4.

[7] Meyerhold, "Aktër budushchego," *Ermitazh*, No. 1 (1922), pp. 9–10.

guish it in any way from a factory. An actor on the stage is a member of the actors' guild and wears the same proletarian "street clothes" as any worker. His work contains no bourgeois obscurantism of any sort. It is based on materialist science and is subordinated to methodology principles known to every Soviet worker.

This was what Meyerhold, the Communist and the leader of the "October in the Theatre" movement, contributed to the presentation. At the time, he considered that the theatre of "experiences," of "psychologizing," and of the philistine drama was obsolete. He thought that, in a nation with a proletarian dictatorship, the task of the theatre would be to present the ideal person of the new period on the stage. The new person would be a fine model of a human being, whose motions and labor processes were clean cut and skilled. This would be the human being at work. The theatre would have to infect the audiences with a craving to imitate this dextrous and well-organized hero of the age.[8]

The practice, teaching, and staging of biomechanics in the form it took for *Le Cocu magnifique* was much more interesting, however, than the dry and pseudoscientific statements on the subject by Meyerhold and his associates.

First of all, biomechanics was a rebellion that Meyerhold launched against the conversational theatre of the day. In that theatre people wore frock coats or jackets and sat around on armchairs or couches while talking incessantly.[9] It was an angry revolt against a theatre in which philosophizing had destroyed the motions of acting. The actor had retained only the right to step forth on the stage, to bow, to sit at a place which the director had indicated, and to begin his speeches.

Biomechanics marked the first great breakthrough on the stage of the tremendous experimental work that Meyerhold had

---

[8] In striving to show the "model human being of the new era" on the stage, Meyerhold wanted to expand "biomechanics." He wanted to proceed from the physical training of the actor to a new and purely Soviet conception of the beautiful.

[9] "The bourgeois actor of the nineteenth century was basically a 'talking creature.' Meyerhold compared him to a phonograph which played different records every day. Today he uses a text by Pushkin; tomorrow, by Surguchev. In Meyerhold's words: 'With a change only in his wig and costume, an actor talks, talks, and only talks—now one text and now another.' " (Kryzhitskii, *Rezhissërskie portrety*, p. 32.)

accumulated in his laboratories and studios before the Revolution. He had been seeking to revive pantomime and all the richness of motion possessed by comedians. Biomechanics attempted to contrast the subtle and psychological actor (anemic in his motion) with the tempestuous comedian who loved life. The latter was nourished on all the wealth of the pantomimes in the great theatres of the past. He knew about the Roman mimes, the jugglers, the acrobatic virtuosi of the Italian *commedia dell'arte*. Biomechanics thus used the gold reserves to be found in the traditions of the old comedians' art.

There was another element to biomechanics that has not been discussed in other writings on the subject. Devices were borrowed from the Chinese and Japanese theatres—theatres that were unsurpassed in accuracy or in their graphic quality. Gestures were calculated so precisely that they verged upon dancing techniques and circus acrobatics. It was no accident that Inkinzhinomov, a Mongol connoisseur of the Asian theatre, was one of the founders of biomechanics in Meyerhold's Theatre and one of its best teachers. Biomechanics induced the actor to study the secrets of plasticity from the cat family,[10] which Meyerhold felt possessed the highest degree of inborn feelings for economy, accuracy, calculation, suppleness, and lightness in motion.

This new concept was important, not for its influence on the theories of others, but in its results upon the stage. And the results were the lively, mischievous, and unbridled gaiety of the comedians who enacted *Le Cocu magnifique* with a controlled virtuosity over their bodies. It was as if the band of comedians had just raced out of a sunny square into the gloomy theatre, had joined in tossing all the trashy rags out into the street, had taken the stage in battle, and, in unrestrained happiness at having the space of an open stage under their control, had given themselves up to the most "crazy jokes of the theatre." It furnished clear and convincing proof that the actor himself contained the magic power of transforming the wasteland of the stage and the abstract constructions into something living.

[10] Biological plasticity is a trait of every child and of every animal. There is but one difference: the child loses this natural and innate talent in the process of growing up, an adult becomes more and more stable with each passing year, while animals retain it even into old age.

In 1922 Meyerhold also staged *Smert' Tarelkina* ("The Death of Tarelkin"), a comedy by Alexander Sukhovo-Kobylin (1817–1903), in which the director sharpened and deepened his methods of constructivism. The designer, V. F. Stepanova, aided Meyerhold in creating a number of apparatuses that resembled the devices and contrivances used by circus performers. Again like circus devices, these contraptions were strictly utilitarian — they were all covered with a neutral white and were not ornamental in the slightest. The furniture was altered and used for different tricks during the course of the action, according to the principles used by clowns in the circus. When an actor sat on the constructivist furniture, he would either be tossed into the air by a spring in the seat or a torpedo would go off under him, the chair would somehow turn into a board, a policeman would jump out like a jack-in-the-box.

This was Meyerhold's second production of *The Death of Tarelkin*. In 1917 this tragic farce about a man mistakenly put on an obituary list had served as the basis for a presentation by him at the Alexandrinsky Theatre in Petrograd. Sinister and fantastic colors were used, in the style of E. T. A. Hoffmann. In 1922, however, Meyerhold seemed to be mocking his own earlier mysticism. He now presented the work with the bold and happy devices of circus buffoons, which had nothing in common with Sukhovo-Kobylin's gloomy comedy. In the play Tarelkin is a minor and forgotten functionary—like Akaky Akakievich Bashmachkin in Gogol's "The Overcoat." In his second production, however, Meyerhold transformed Tarelkin into a merry prankster who makes fools out of the police. He flies across the entire width of the stage on a cable, like an acrobat, in order to get away from the police.

As he had done with *Le Cocu magnifique,* therefore, Meyerhold viewed the text of Sukhovo-Kobylin's play as a technical excuse for his unique staging ideas. He believed that the object of presenting the play was to show that a construction could bear the same relationship to actors that it did to stars of the circus — that is, it contained devices useful for the presentation. The actors of Meyerhold's Theatre found *The Death of Tarelkin* to be a kind of "textbook." They learned how to use the "machines for acting" to good effect as virtuosi; they learned to work with

things and to calculate their motions and tricks with the precise-
ness of circus performers.

In 1923 the centennial of Alexander Ostrovsky's birth was
celebrated, and in connection with this event Anatoli Lunacharsky, the People's Commissar of Enlightenment, advanced a new
slogan: "Back to Ostrovsky!" This, he declared, was the policy of
the Soviet government toward the theatre.[11] Meyerhold considered such a slogan reactionary and defeatist. It called for the restoration of truth to life, of naturalism, and of psychologizing.
The director rebelled against these things throughout his life.

He answered Lunacharsky's slogan in January, 1924, with a
production that provoked quite a few tempests in the press and in
theatre circles. The play was Ostrovsky's *The Forest,* a very popular work. The production was clearly polemical, as Meyerhold
used it to assert his own views. He thought that the Soviet theatre
must not go "back" to Ostrovsky but must bring Ostrovsky forward, make him contemporary, and revise him in accordance
with the attainments of the theatre. Ostrovsky must not be transformed into a relic, but the material in his plays must be used for
the tasks of the present. Meyerhold proclaimed a most daring revision of the great pre-Soviet dramatist and then carried it out.

The presentation began something new, first in Soviet Russia
and then in other countries as well. A powerful wave of innovation began that was based, for the most part, on the most daring
revisions, "tailorings," and reworkings of the old classics.
Hence, it will be worth our while to examine this version of *The
Forest.*

Meyerhold was no novice at reevaluating the classics. He had
done that quite often before the Revolution, including his important production of Ostrovsky's *The Storm* on the imperial stage.
With *The Forest,* however, he did something new. He not only
destroyed both the treatment given by the author and the flavor
of the period, but he rose up against the inviolability of the classical text. He made himself the coauthor of the classic.[12] Meyer-

[11] "By the slogan 'Back to Ostrovsky,' I wanted to talk about the need
for returning to the realistic theatre which was socially psychological and
. . . socially interesting. This was a suitable technique of expression."
(A. V. Lunacharskii, *Stat'i o teatre i dramaturgii,* p. 125.)
[12] The posters read: "Author of the presentation: Meyerhold."

hold cut the comedy and changed the order of its scenes, dividing it into thirty-three independent episodes. His revision changed *The Forest* from a comedy, in which the "good" and the "bad" people are depicted rather gently and quite humanly, into a malicious satire on the Russia of the landowners. This was *The Forest* as seen by a Bolshevik, with his enormous hatred for the departed world of the Russian gentry.

The "leftist" theoreticians in the Soviet theatre and the "leftist" critics hailed Meyerhold's aggression against the classics enthusiastically. They considered this presentation to be a deserved blow against the "reactionary elements who have protected the age-old traditions in the theatre." They felt it was directed against those who, "in connection with the anniversary of the man who created the true-to-life dramas of the Russian burghers," allowed themselves to hope "for reaction within the theatre." [13] There were even those who subscribed to the idea that "there can be no doubt that if Ostrovsky were alive today he could object to nothing in Meyerhold's edition of *The Forest*." [14] They felt that Meyerhold had acted correctly in destroying "the principle that a literary text is inviolable, in changing that text in accordance with the feelings influenced by the events of the Revolutionary years, and in casting aside respect for the supposedly 'eternal' values of the poet-priests." [15] They felt that a majority of even Shakespeare's greatest works contain strata, insertions, and corrections that the actors and directors do not know about.

Meyerhold's real genius was as a director, however, not as a collaborator of Ostrovsky's. In *The Forest* he rejected the constructivist asceticism of his early productions. Canvas was used to cover the brick walls of the theatre, and the stage was filled with furnishings and other stage properties. Something labeled "a bridge road" was hanging in the air and offered the actors a great range of possible uses. There was a dovecote with many living pigeons. Finally, street clothes were not used, but makeup was. Once again the stage used the variegated luxury of costumes and a variety of wigs and masks.

[13] A. A. Gvozdev, *Teatr imeni Meierkhol'da*, p. 27.

[14] S. Mokul'skii, "Pereotsenka traditsii," in the anthology *Teatralnyi Oktiabr'*, pp. 21–22.

[15] Gvozdev, *Teatr imeni Meierkhol'da*, p. 14.

Meyerhold filled the presentation with acting virtuosity. He used real props and introduced "effects" everywhere, even in places where they contradicted the text and the sense of the action. A single phrase in Ostrovsky's text recalls that Neschastlivtsev had once performed some tricks, so a good number of them were shown on the stage. Aksiusha recalls, "Day and night, since I was six, I have helped my mother work," and so Meyerhold had her constantly working on the stage. When the merchant declares, "I shall give up everything," a flood of furs, shoes, and hats drops down on the stage from above.

Meyerhold loaded lyrical passages in the play with singing, dancing, and accordion music. And this helped to establish what was perhaps the most important aspect of the presentation—his assertion that his theatre was, in terms of style, basically a theatre of the mask. Every character was strictly bounded by a completely definite rhythm for his speech and motions; his gestures and pantomime were given a rhythm that was his alone. When he first appeared on the stage, he quickly acquainted the audience with his leitmotif, which remained standard in all situations.

*The Forest* began to crystallize the basic style of this most rebellious director. It clarified his pre-Revolutionary work and his innumerable excursions into the traditions of the *commedia dell'arte* in Italy, into the Spanish, Japanese, and Chinese theatres, and into the folk farce and Attic comedy. During all the years when he was becoming famous in arguments and for his agonizing experiments, he had been seeking a single path. He wanted to create a new theatre of the mask. This new and absolute theatre would be freed from the cheap literature and illusion that had been parasitic upon it. It would be organically hostile to the psychologizing theatre that was true to life, and it would be cleansed of the age-old scum that was alien to it.

The human character was shown by means of the leitmotif and the scheme—the rest of the complex and variegated human heart was omitted. Meyerhold went through the years faithful to the idea of symbolism, to which he had been converted at the very start of his career. For him, the world remained an enormous puppet show in which Fate moved the marionettes according to whims of its own, and his theatre always seemed to be a puppet show, with figures from a wax museum come to life in it.

He did not need any actor with life and talent but only ideal marionettes who would be obedient. The chief feature of the actor under biomechanics was the precise fulfillment of the assignment given him by the director.

Meyerhold's work was frequently brilliant in terms of its directorial resourcefulness, and it proved capable of founding dozens of independent schools within the theatre arts. Yet, the same idea goes right through it—there were no authentically living characters. There was rather the coolness of marionettes breathing from behind wonderful masks.

After *The Forest,* Meyerhold produced *The Give-Us-Europe Trust* and *Bubus the Teacher.*[16] These were not among the best presentations of the period, but they are worth examining because they constitute the intervening links in the evolution of Meyerhold and his theatre.

In *The Give-Us-Europe Trust* Meyerhold tried to rework a typical Western "review" into political propaganda. Here, as in many of his other propagandistic presentations, he considered his theatre a model workshop for developing new forms and devices for the entire Soviet theatre, both professional and amateur.

The text of *The Give-Us-Europe Trust* was compiled by M. Podgayetsky from novels by Ehrenburg, Amp, Kellerman, and Sinclair. The play depicted the struggle of an American capitalistic trust with the radio trust of a Soviet republic. The American organization aimed at the complete "destruction" of Europe to eliminate a dangerous competitor. There were seventeen episodes, accompanied by political slogans. They satirized Poland, Germany, and France of the day, which were shown as disintegrating under pressure from "the trust for the destruction of Europe." The production was of interest, but not for its coarse and deliberate propaganda depiction of the "disintegrating" bourgeoisie trembling epileptically from "fox trots." Nor did its interest come from the proletarians and other Soviet people who, in contrast, were healthy, and tanned by the sun that bathes Soviet stadiums. Its interest resulted from the new devices that Meyerhold introduced to the Soviet theatre. He gave stage action

[16] The première of *The Give-Us-Europe Trust* took place on June 15, 1924; that of *Bubus the Teacher* on January 29, 1925.

a quality of almost motion-picturelike impetuosity by his rapid change of scenes, and he created tremendous and dynamic tension.

To attain this, Meyerhold and Ilya Shlepyanov—the set designer—invented something that was as simple as it was effective. They used a system of wooden panels, which moved on rollers. These panels were heaped up in rapid combinations. They permitted the place of action to be shifted rapidly. A lecture hall was quickly transformed into a street with an endless fence. The street then became a chamber of a parliament. And this last was turned into a stadium within a few seconds. Meyerhold was allowed to enrich the theatre with devices that were incredibly dynamic. One of the most wonderful scenes in *The Give-Us-Europe Trust* was a "chase," and during it the spotlights rushed about chaotically and suddenly all the panels began twirling around in different directions, creating an almost unbelievably dynamic picture.

Pantomime came to the fore in this production, even more than in Meyerhold's earlier efforts. There were a number of episodes that lasted altogether about ten or fifteen minutes and contained an insignificant amount of speech but much pantomime.

*Bubus the Teacher* provided Meyerhold with raw material for seeking a new form for a musical show. He was looking for a symphony of the theatre, in which all the elements would be subordinated to rhythm and melody. Everything in the comedy—the motions and speeches of the actors, the props, the lighting, the sound effects, and the music—was a separate instrument in the scenic orchestra performing a synthetic symphony. First of all, the entire production took place to music. High above the decorative furnishings, one of the finest pianists in Moscow sat on a covered platform. During the three acts of the play, this frock-coated musician performed about forty-six pieces by Chopin and Liszt. All the motions of the actors were set against this musical background. At times, they were greatly prolonged, as if they were performing a tragic and solemn dance of the condemned. Meyerhold was aiming to show the doom of the capitalistic world in these careful and prolonged motions that faded into pauses as if the characters were listening to something going on inside them or outside of them.

Many of Meyerhold's earlier presentations had been done with the broadness of the marketplace farce. In *Bubus the Teacher,* however, he created a refined production that was quite subtle. He turned aside from most of his ascetic and constructivist ideas and again used something resembling a pavilion on the stage. This was a semicircle of long, hanging, bamboo poles. The stage was decorated with a large basin and a flowing fountain. The floor was covered with a luxurious carpet. Furniture was brought in and a massive portal was erected at the entrance.

The presentation produced a strange and mysterious impression. There were agonizing leaps and fadings-out set to rhythm. The actors danced their long pantomime scenes slowly. With this production, Meyerhold put into practice his theory of "preacting." Preacting contained long pauses between the speeches. These breaks were filled with pantomime that strove to accomplish two things—to show the transition of the actor from one situation to another and to prepare the audience for a more correct and sharper perception of that which followed the preacting.

Preacting was based on a very important factor peculiar to the inner technique of acting—the laws of human conduct in life. In life a person prefixes his words with a short "overture" of gestures and pantomimes that transmit the sense of what he wants to say. The preacting in *Bubus the Teacher* was hypertrophied and deliberately prolix, as if Meyerhold were dealing with an exercise for actors rather than with a presentation. It was constructed on the same principle that he used for staging the dances in the play—not on a "legato" but rather on short rhythmic bits. After performing these bits, the dancers would pause motionlessly. The characters in the play would also freeze into the numbness of preacting before moving or uttering a word, as if they were trying first to listen for something before moving. The text merely furnished the sense of the pantomime to follow.

There was still another innovation, however, in this extremely subtle presentation. This was the virtuoso technique that Meyerhold used in conjunction with rhythm to reveal the social mask, the nature, and the psychology of his characters. A system of "rhythmic masks" was developed that belonged to Meyerhold's Theatre alone. It revealed the essence of a character through the individual rhythms of his speech, motions, and gestures. Luna-

charsky termed this feature "sociomechanics" in contrast to biomechanics.

Meyerhold staged Nikolai Erdman's *The Warrant* on April 20, 1925. This production revealed what was always one of Meyerhold's strong points—his flair for satire. In his production of *The Warrant* he reveled in his favorite theme—the animated exhibit, the enormous puppet show, the theatre of "funny faces and grimaces," the theatre of the grotesque. Here there was no boring and state-inspired bifurcation of the characters into "positive" and "negative" camps. Everyone was "negative." They were like wax figures from a chamber of horrors who had come to life under the spotlights of the theatre.

Meyerhold gave each character a caricature as his leitmotif. Very frequently the characters betook themselves in their wax-museumlike poses from the blue haze of the stage to the rotating circle, or they froze with their eyes dully directed toward the audience. There were piles of furniture, trunks, coffers, and dresses that Meyerhold used to transmit the idea that the philistine world hoarded trifles and other items greedily.

Meyerhold found a new and somber kind of comedy in *The Warrant*. It was based on the incongruity between idol-like posing of the characters and their sudden transition from motionlessness to gesturing and loud talking. With the power and perception peculiar to him alone, he turned the ridicule of the early acts into a flagrantly grotesque "rebellion of the philistines." They sang the tsarist anthem and, in the catastrophic "Judgment Day" that transformed them into pitiful and unnecessary people, asked "So, how on earth are we going to live?"

Meyerhold used a revolving stage, a system of concentric circles that rotated in opposite directions to aid him in staging this animated exhibit. These circles "drove" persons and things from the rear of the stage to the foreground. Groups in frozen poses would use them to disappear in the fog. The circles often split groups of characters in two: some of them would remain downstage, while the others—no longer needed for the plot—would be carried off into the wings.

The Bolshevik critics considered that Meyerhold's treatment of *The Warrant* depicted the tragedy of "former people" unsparingly. These were individuals who had "slept through the Rev-

olution" and "lost their last pitiful ideological baggage and their final illusions." The Bolsheviks felt that the play seemed to be limited only because it dwelt on the middle class, dreaming of restoring the monarchy and living in the ready expectation that their lands and factories would be returned to them.

Meyerhold's theme in his production of *The Warrant* was, however, broader and more dangerous to the Soviet regime. He, like Vladimir Mayakovsky, felt that the idea behind the Communist Revolution was threatened most seriously from within by pettiness, philistinism, and bureaucracy. Both these great men foresaw that the Revolution would degenerate into a terrible bureaucratic state that threatened to stifle everything living. They foresaw the appearance of a new kind of philistine—the minor Communist functionaries and activists, the teamsters who would remain Stalin's faithful sycophants to their graves.

Guliachkin, with a Soviet "warrant" in his pocket, personified the petty and roguish philistine against whom Meyerhold was in revolt. The director's unsparing struggle through satire against this "Soviet trash" began with *The Warrant* and continued with Erdman's *The Suicide,* a play that the censors forbade.[17]

On December 9, 1926, Meyerhold offered Nikolai Gogol's *The Inspector General* at the Vsevolod Meyerhold State Theatre. This production was his "Song of Songs" as a director. If a description of this masterpiece alone is preserved of all his presentations, it would be quite enough to permit one to understand his creative personality. The production was the key to all the secrets of his work.

This production contained all the greatest features of Meyerhold as a director in classically polished form. Here the bold re-

---

[17] Maxim Gorky wheedled permission out of Stalin to allow Erdman's *The Suicide* to be staged. The Theatre had been working on the comedy for a year and a half when the permission was withdrawn at the insistence of L. M. Kaganovich. The play showed a Soviet philistine who has decided to close out his accounts with life. He assiduously spreads rumors to the effect that his suicide is inevitable. He engenders a whole movement among the "former people" burdened by Bolshevism. "Former people" make pilgrimages to see him and they implore him to use his suicide as an act against the Soviet regime. The main theme running through the work is that a Soviet individual can really feel free from the nightmare of Soviet realities only when he has chosen death. Shortly after *The Suicide* was forbidden, Erdman was arrested and disappeared into Soviet jails.

vision of the classics that accompanied his entire career was at its climax. He decided to reveal all of Gogol's writings in this *Inspector General,* and so rearranged the scenes of the comedy and even incorporated a number of variants from Gogol's notebooks and some sections of Gogol's novel *Dead Souls* into *The Inspector General.*[18]

In revising the play, Meyerhold worked on an enormous scale. He changed the locale from a remote town in serfholding Russia to something that was almost St. Petersburg itself. Hence, all the classical characters in Gogol's comedy took on a new look. The local chief of police was changed from some minor official in the country to a young general who takes bribes on the scale of St. Petersburg or Moscow. His wife, Anna Andreyevna, was transformed from a silly, stupid and overripe lady of "provincial society" into a beautiful and experienced coquette, a hetaera of the St. Petersburg demimonde. Meyerhold introduced some civil servants plus a number of officers, and the result was the brilliant and worldly society of the capital. Khlestakov was changed from a petty, procrastinating landowner's son given to stretching the truth into an unlovable adventurer whose rapacity did not stop at bribetaking, cheating, or flirting in a most underhanded manner. Meyerhold's goal was to show "everything bad in Russia" and to satirize the remote period of Nicholas I most harshly.

He made the presentation pompous throughout. The wood was varnished until it shone; the furniture was luxurious; the candelabra were gilded; the costumes were glittering and magnificent; the rooms and the partitions on the stage were enormous. He populated the comedy with a multitude of characters "introduced by the author of the presentation." They acted without speaking, but the pantomime of such characters as his captain—an officer in transit—were frequently as interesting or as important as that of Gogol's own characters.

[18] After the première, the Bolshevik critics wrote: "Meyerhold's dramatic concept of *The Inspector General* is an interpretation not of Nikolai Gogol's five-act comedy as it was understood by the academic theatre of the nineteenth century, but rather of Gogol's work in general. Gogol's 'truth and malice' is firmly preserved, but his wish 'to collect everything bad in Russia into one heap' was expanded very greatly and was revealed through the rich resources of contemporary directing." (R. Pel'she, in *Novyi zritel',* December 21, 1926.)

Meyerhold gathered, not only all the work of Gogol and "everything bad in Russia" into one presentation, but also what was most important in his own work. *The Inspector General* included the early Meyerhold of the period of "stylization" in the scene where Anna Andreyevna stood before the mirror in her silk dress. Her pose, her coloring, the lighting, and the furnishings transmitted the entire atmosphere of the early nineteenth century as presented in the genre paintings and realistic miniatures of Fedotov. Only Meyerhold could use iconography to such wonderful "effect" in stylization. Let us not forget either the brilliant "crowded setting" for the reading of Khlestakov's letter to Triapichkin. And here, too, we find Meyerhold's predilection for luxurious furniture, vessels, and costumes—which played roles all by themselves throughout the entire work.

For years Meyerhold had been searching for a rhythmical and musical principle to which all the acting could be subordinated, beginning with his work at the Marinsky Theatre and continuing on through his work in *Bubus the Teacher.* His rhythmic principle acquired a symphonic polish in *The Inspector General,* and he had reason to term this production "musical realism." All fifteen episodes of the play were parts of a suite on Gogolian themes. Language and gesture were subordinated to rhythm and a number of scenes were worked out on the lines of a chorus. Khlestakov or the chief of police would "sing" the verses, and the mass of petty functionaries served as a chorus. Meyerhold added to the length of the text by having the chorus repeat the remarks of Khlestakov and of some of the others.[19]

Once again Meyerhold had boldly returned to mysticism in the cruel world of Soviet materialism. This is what he had done

[19] "Thus, in the episode of the Procession, Khlestakov asks: 'What is the name of this fish?' The chorus of petty functionaries answers: 'Salt cod, sir.' This is repeated several times and is worked out by the chorus like a musical phrase. The voice of Zemlianika stands out from the chorus as he finishes the choral phrase with a flattering nasal sound to his 'Salt cod, sir.' And when the famous letter is read at the end of the play, the chorus of guests and petty functionaries grows nervous, making noise, laughs, gloats maliciously, exults, and cackles. Then, they grow quiet. The exertions— the noise, the outcries, and the laughter—start afresh. Such a use of the vocal retorts and gestures to build with can be compared only to the playing of various instruments in a large symphony orchestra." (Gvozdev, *Teatr imeni Meierkhol'da,* p. 53.)

in his first efforts as a director. The entire production contained something invisible, fatal, and "Hoffmannesque." The "officer in transit" whom Meyerhold had introduced was very much like a devil controlling all the threads of what was taking place.[20]

For staging the bribery episode, there were a number of doors which formed a semicircle of redwood framing the proscenium. The ratlike faces of the officials appeared from these doorways and gazed at the drunken Khlestakov as he dozed in an armchair. The enactment of terror and sycophancy, all the wonderfully effective folding doors, and the planning of the approach and disappearance of the bribers constituted one of the greatest feats ever accomplished by a Soviet director. Another such masterpiece was the "silent scene" at the end of the play. This climaxed one of Meyerhold's main themes, the theme of "exhibits," of playing with masks and puppets. The thread of "figures from a wax museum" also attained its most polished form in *The Inspector General,* and this idea was not disguised. Before the start of every episode the characters froze in their poses as they came out to the proscenium on a part of the revolving stage. They paused for a long time under the spotlights and suddenly began to move and to speak. The actors seemed like mechanical figures, while the motors of the revolving platforms hummed. They thus showed themselves to the audience at the start of every scene. In the concluding episode they froze in rigid, distorted poses. The lights went out for a few seconds, and when they came on again the audience saw not actors but mannequins in the same ridiculous poses, mannequins whose costumes had been removed. With this closing chord, Meyerhold for the first time revealed his secret to the audience. For him, the world still possessed the young passions of symbolism. Even in the "proletarian dictatorship" the world struck him as merely an exhibit, a collection of benumbed puppets who were the playthings and victims of Fate.

[20] Here Meyerhold was at last carrying out plans which he had thought of as early as 1908. He wanted "to introduce correctives in the treatment of the characters" according to "the original traits of the characters in *Inspector General* as given by [Dmitri] Merezhkovskii in his penetrating article, 'Gogol' i chёrt' ('Gogol and the Devil')." Meyerhold wanted to create a production of Gogol's comedy based on a realism "which does not flee life but overcomes it because it looks for only the symbol of the thing in its mystical essence." (Meyerhold, *O teatre,* pp. 98–99.)

Perhaps no production of the Soviet theatre called forth such a torrent of polemics in the press as did Meyerhold's *The Inspector General*. The "cursing" critics won out. They accused this artist of "no longer hearing the music of revolution." They called the presentation mystical, reactionary, and symbolical. They said that he had shifted his center of gravity from satiric exposés to a "romantic, Gogolian-Hoffmannesque, and fantastic" treatment. The show was called "nonsocial," "asocial," and blatantly formalistic. The press printed irate protests by academicians and elderly dramatists who demanded that Soviet justice protect Gogol's rights as an author. The press had always howled at every new Meyerhold production, but after *The Inspector General* its noise grew stronger and contained the same surplus of energy that Meyerhold himself had shown.

This was the reception given the greatest masterpiece in the entire history of Russian directing. And even today the Soviet theatre press libels it by calling it "class-alien formalism." The Soviet critics have termed it a dark and shameful page in the history of the Soviet theatre, claiming it was a reactionary phenomenon that "impeded the correct understanding of the classical heritage and the later development of a national and realistic scenic art." [21]

WILLIAM KUHLKE

## Vakhtangov and the American Theatre of the 1960's [*]

When Yevgeny Vakhtangov died at the age of thirty-nine in May, 1922, his recently opened productions of *The Dybbuk* at the Habima and *Princess Turandot* in the Third Studio of the

[21] VI. Filippov, "Otechestvennaia klassika na russkoi stsene," *Teatral'nyi al'manakh*, Book 2 (1946), p. 141.

[*] Reprinted from the *Educational Theatre Journal*, XIX:2 (May, 1967).

Moscow Art Theatre had already earned him recognition as one of the great theatrical innovators of the twentieth century. Yet six months later, fearing that Vakhtangov was already being forgotten, a weekly magazine of the performing arts published a full-page picture and epitaph. The epitaph began as follows:

> When the poet dies—his books remain.
> When the artist dies—his pictures live on.
> But what is left after the director and actor?
> Only memories.[1]

The article went on to point out what we all know, that men are forgetful and art is absentminded; in its frantic pursuit of the shadow of its future, it seldom takes the time to look back along the path of its advance.

Yet we all know, too, that we could, if we only would, profit from past experience, and it is an interesting and ironic fact that many of the theatrical problems which faced Vakhtangov are still with us, and on those rare occasions when they are being solved by contemporary directors, the most striking and successful solutions bear a remarkable resemblance to those worked out by Vakhtangov himself almost half a century ago. The impulse to look back at this particular way station on the "path of our advance," therefore, comes from something more than antiquarian curiosity. Apparently Yevgeny Vakhtangov, now forty-four years in his grave, still has something to teach us.

1. What had Vakhtangov succeeded in doing that by 1922 had already assured him a place among the great theatrical innovators of the twentieth-century? He had demonstrated to the warring factions of the Soviet theatre that there was perfectly tenable ground between the basic positions assumed by Stanislavsky on one hand and Meyerhold on the other. The style of production which he molded from this synthesis of Meyerhold and Stanislavsky he called "fantastic realism."

The assumptions concerning the relation of art to nature upon which fantastic realism is based were not original with Vakhtangov, even in his own time. He had reached his maturity as a

1 *Zrelishche* (November 28, 1922), p. 11.

creative artist during the heyday of futurism and formalism in Russian poetry, and of cubism and surrealism in painting. Although in his published notes and letters Vakhtangov never identified himself as a member of any of these schools, his affinity with some aspects of the formalist point of view concerning the nature and function of art was obvious and has been duly criticized in the official histories of Soviet theatre.[2] Certainly Vakhtangov's correspondence with Vsevolod Meyerhold makes it clear that he admired the work of the futurist director, and his famous deathbed conversations with Boris Zakhava and Xenia Kotlubai indicate that he shared, at least in part, Meyerhold's basic assumptions concerning the relation between art and nature, particularly the concept of creative distortion.[3]

The formalist concept of creative distortion as a mode of artistic expression has been summarized by Victor Erlich as follows: "Not representation of life in concrete images but, on the contrary, creative distortion of nature by means of a set of devices which the artist has at his disposal—this was . . . the real aim of art." [4] Earlier, the futurist poet Mayakovsky had expressed a similar point of view: "Art is not a copy of nature but the determination to distort nature in accordance with its reflections in the individual consciousness." [5] It seems fair to assume that

---

[2] See N. B. Zograf, "Teatr imeni Evg. Vakhtangova," *Ocherki istorii russkogo sovetskogo dramaticheskogo teatra, T. I, 1917–1934* (Moskva: Izdatelstvo Akademii Nauk SSSR, 1954), p. 303: "Vakhtangov, in his creative work, unfortunately did not draw the necessary conclusions from those warnings, contained in party documents, which unmasked the ideologically depraved bases of formalistic art. The influence of formalistic art is unconsciously and detrimentally revealed in a significant measure in the directing works of Vakhtangov and in his evaluations of contemporary theatre art."

[3] Vakhtangov's references to Gogol's *The Inspector General* and the Art Theatre productions of *The Life of Man* and *The Drama of Life* as examples of fantastic realism, and his statement that he was seeking "an incisive form, one which would be theatrical [as contrasted to verisimilar] and because theatrical would be an artistic product," all presuppose a recognition of "creative distortion" as the fundamental method of fantastic realism. See the conversation of April 11, 1922, in *Evgenii Vakhtangov, Zapiski, Pisma, Stati,* ed. N. M. Vakhtangova, et al. (Moskva: Iskusstvo, 1939).

[4] Victor Erlich, *Russian Formalism, History-Doctrine* (The Hague, Netherlands: Mouton and Co., 1955), p. 57.

[5] Vladimir Maiakovskii, *Polnoe sobranie sochinenie* (Moskva, 1939–47), I, p. 268.

these two statements represent the basic premise concerning the relation of art to nature upon which Vakhtangov posited fantastic realism as a style of theatrical production.

If, as an artist, Vakhtangov accepted creative distortion as a basic principle, as a director he recognized certain restrictions to its application in the theatre: (a) The director must not violate the essential nature of the work of the dramatist. (b) At the same time, he must "contemporize" his production, that is, he must make whatever play he is working with answerable to the demands of the immediate present (in Vakhtangov's own case, of course, this meant revolutionary Russia).[6] (c) Finally, his production should be an "organic and natural" expression of his particular theatre, "a manifestation of the artistic personality of the theatrical collective at the given stage of its creative development." [7]

Another basic assumption which regulated Vakhtangov's application of the principle of creative distortion to theatrical production was that no production plan, however striking in its conception, could be successfully executed without the services of actors who had been partners in the creative act and who knew how to "fill form with content and find the necessary justification for [their] conduct on the stage even though this justification had to be found not in the psychological but in the theatrical plan of the spectacle." [8]

It is in this last assumption that Vakhtangov parted company with Meyerhold. In his dialogues with Zakhava and Kotlubai, Vakhtangov charged that Meyerhold "attracted by theatrical truth . . . threw out the truth of feelings." Both Meyerhold and Vakhtangov seem to have been acutely aware of the theatre as a mode of affective communication. Both of them were apparently convinced that such communication could best be accomplished

[6] Vakhtangov shared this concern for contemporaneity with the futurists. However, he was far from willing, as they were, to discard all art previous to his own age. He wanted to use the classics, for instance, but to contemporize them, to make them a part of the present idiom, as he had done in his productions of *Erik XIV* and *The Miracle of St. Anthony*, and as he did most brilliantly with *Princess Turandot*.

[7] N. Bromlei, "Istoria postanovki," in Carlo Gozzi, *Printsessa Turandot: Teatralno-tragicheskaia kitaiskaia skazka v 5 aktakh* (Moskva: Gosudarstvennoe Izdatelstvo, 1923), p. 14.

[8] *Ibid.*, pp. 15–16.

when their "messages" were carried in "sharply expressive," frankly theatrical forms, forms which were the products of the imagination not imitations of phenomenal reality. However, they differed over the place and function of the actor as a part of such forms. Meyerhold tended to see the actor as just another element of the *mise-en-scène;* he did not recognize him as a creative partner.[9] Vakhtangov recognized his actors as creative partners and as the key to successful communication in the theatre. He saw them not as the passive tools of the artist-director but as unique individuals with wills of their own. Vakhtangov was convinced that the form in which his "message" was to be transmitted to an audience had to spring spontaneously, under the director's guidance, from the actors themselves, from their own intellectual and emotional "living through" of the message itself, the given scene and the significance the author and director attached to it. Only then would the final form, however brilliantly conceived by the director, be suitable to them as actors, and only then could they transmit it with the full force of conviction.

The very term "fantastic realism" suggests a paradoxical duality. Such a duality did indeed characterize the style, and Pavel Markov described its manifestation in *Turandot* in 1923.[10] In the first place, wrote Mr. Markov, the manner in which *Turandot* was produced enabled the director to present at the same time both the story and his own attitude as a man and artist to the story, giving full value to both. The story of Calaf and the princess was presented with emotional sincerity to the extent that the audience could, during a given scene, identify with the characters and be deeply moved by their suffering. At the same time, since the King carried a tennis racquet instead of a scepter and the Wise Man wore a hand towel in place of a beard, it was abundantly clear that the attitude of the director and the players

[9] It is dangerous to discuss Meyerhold without indicating to what time in his complicated career one refers. I refer here to 1922, when Meyerhold was involved in the development of bio-mechanics as a theory of acting and a system of actor training. The results of his work on bio-mechanics were first demonstrated in public performance in his production of *Le Cocu Magnifique* in 1922.

[10] Pavel Markov, *"Printsessa Turandot* i sovremenny teatr," in Gozzi, pp. 43–51.

to the story was one of ironic amusement. In *Turandot,* as a matter of fact, Vakhtangov chose to laugh in good natured irony not only at the fairy tale of Gozzi but at theatre in general and "inner realism" in particular. Markov declared that there was not a single problem of contemporary theatrical form which *Turandot* did not touch upon and solve in some fashion or other. But the moment some difficult problem was met and conquered, Vakhtangov and his players immediately laughed at it. For instance, when the actor playing Barach accomplished a small coup of inner realism by weeping real tears as he told Calaf of his mother's death, Tartaglia rushed from the wings with a shaving bowl, collected Barach's tears, and then displayed them to the audience in ironic "proof" of the deep sincerity of Barach's portrayal.

This attitude of irony was the key to Vakhtangov's solution of the problem of "contemporizing" the Gozzi play. It seemed to Vakhtangov that the story as treated by Gozzi, moving though it once was, could not be "played straight" for the Moscow theatre public of 1922. After their horrible experiences of the previous five years, their calloused sensibilities could hardly be touched by a romantic fairy tale as such. Rather than "play it straight," therefore, he presented it in such fashion that the audience could appreciate the tale and all its emotional content and yet laugh at it, at themselves, and at the whole idea of theatrical performance at the same time.

Clearly, fantastic realism made considerable demands on the actor. As *Turandot* demonstrated, it demanded the kind of actor who could deliver a tragic monologue with such depth of inner belief that he shed real tears, then as he finished and the audience applauded, could smile gaily at his admirers, pick up an orange from a vendor in the aisle, sit on the edge of the stage, and peel and eat his orange while the play continued above him. Then, on cue, instantly, he must be able to resume his mask with that same profound inner belief and play another scene, falling in and out of character absolutely at will, completely uninhibited.[11] Finally, as *Turandot* again made clear, the performer had to be so completely sure of his powers as an actor, and so completely confident of his charm as a person, that he was willing

[11] Bromlei, p. 16.

and able to enter into easy, natural, completely uninhibited social and artistic intercourse with the audience. He must be able to play a role and comment on it at the same time.[12]

As one might expect, fantastic realism was realized in scenery by means of something other than the representational box sets of realism. Vakhtangov chose the cubist painter I. Nivinsky to design *Turandot*. Nivinsky had also designed Vakhtangov's production of *Erik XIV* in the First Studio. As both settings indicate, fantastic realism required not representational but boldly expressive and openly functional scenery. The designer was asked not to imitate life but to communicate to the audience his observations on life as it was presented in the play. The sets and costumes for *Turandot* were as frankly theatrical and gaily ironic as was the performance itself.[13]

Apparently, one of the characteristics of the impact fantastic realism was to have on the audience was that no matter how fanciful the settings, the costumes, the stage business might become, the essential, analogical relationship of what was taking place on the stage to what happens in life was never to be lost sight of. In describing her reactions to *The Miracle of St. Anthony*, L. D. Vendrovskaya remarked that in spite of the use of strongly "expressionistic" devices in staging, the audience received the impression of a penetrating and powerful realism.[14] Her opinion was that this impression resulted from the intense inner belief

[12] The similarity to the demands made of actors in the theatre of Bertolt Brecht is obvious. However, Vakhtangov was not after an alienation effect. There is no indication that he saw some need to prevent his audience from becoming emotionally involved in the production. He was simply convinced that there was no need to leave the theatre, transported on the wings of verisimilar illusion, in order to tell a story movingly and believably. The actor could make the audience laugh or cry; he could evoke in them whatever emotion he wished in a few moments, alone, without pretending to be anything but his interpretation of the character, not the character himself.

[13] See Gozzi. This memorial edition of the play and production history of Vakhtangov's work with it is handsomely illustrated with black and white photographs and with color reproductions of the Nivinsky set and costume sketches.

[14] Interview with L. D. Vendrovskaya, August 6, 1964. Madam Vendrovskaya is curator of the archives at the Vakhtangov Theatre and editor of the most recent collection of Vakhtangov materials. Vakhtangov produced Maeterlinck's play twice, in 1918 and 1921. Madam Vendrovskaya saw the second variant.

with which the actors portrayed their roles, even though they wore grotesque makeup and assumed physical mannerisms which went beyond what one might expect to find in real life. This, to her, was the essential effect of fantastic realism.

How did Vakhtangov go about constructing "sharply expressive" forms which his actors could still justify psychologically as well as theatrically? The reports of Ben-Ari and Gorchakov concerning Vakhtangov's work on *The Dybbuk* and *Turandot* reveal that his first goal in working with his actors was to penetrate to the core of the soul of the character—to help the actor to assimilate and, so far as possible, to make his own the thoughts, feelings, and attitudes of the character, filling the empty shell of the physical image with his own sensitive, expressive soul.[15] This was the realistic aspect of the production process of fantastic realism. It was carried out according to the Stanislavsky system. The result was what Stanislavsky called *"perezhivanie,"* that emotional experiencing of the role which results in "inner realism." The next problem was to find a form in which to express these thoughts, feelings, and attitudes so as to make them as clear, as heavily underlined, as unambiguous in their impact on the audience as possible. In accomplishing this task, Vakhtangov found it necessary to shift his attention from the actor to the audience.

Vakhtangov was convinced that his ultimate goal as a theatre artist was not to construct a copy in miniature of some segment of the real world upon the stage; it was rather to stimulate the audience to create in their own imaginations the series of pictures in time which carried the message the theatre company, as a collective interpretative artist, sought to communicate. If the image in the spectator's mind was to be anything at all like the one the company had in theirs when they finally arrived at an interpretation for a given scene, the director must see to it that the stimuli they supplied, above and beyond the words of the playwright, were powerful, unambiguous, and immediately comprehensible.

Knowing his audience thoroughly, and knowing just as thor-

[15] Raiken Ben-Ari, *Habima*, trans. R. H. Gross and I. Soref (New York: Thomas Yoseloff, 1957). N. M. Gorchakov, *Rezhisserskie uroki Vakhtangova* (Moskva: Iskusstvo, 1957).

oughly the capacities of his troupe, having meticulously analyzed the play and characters so that he and his actors knew precisely what it was they wanted to communicate, what messages they wanted to send, Vakhtangov then began searching for the most effective code in which to transmit his messages. The tool with which he conducted this search was the étude. Day after day, under his direction, his actors improvised solutions to the stage tasks of a given scene, selecting through trial and error those solutions which best served their purpose.

In judging the usefulness of the ideas and actions which were developed during this period of experimentation, Vakhtangov did not ask, "Does this prop look real? Is this costume authentic period? Is this a situation or a characterization which we might reasonably expect to meet on the street?" His question was rather, "Will this costume or this pose or this makeup or this situation or gesture not only stimulate the audience to create vividly in their own fantasy the picture of life we are presenting but also make clear to them the conclusions we have drawn about that life?" In other words, "Does it play well?" "Is it successful communication?" L. D. Vendrovskaya described quite vividly the carrying of the hands of the miser in *The Miracle of St. Anthony,* how they were carried palms up, waist high, fingers grasping—a powerful, nonrealistic, expressionistic if you will means of communicating a sense of grasping, avaricious miserliness.[16] Obviously one does not see people carrying their hands in such fashion in real life, but that is not the point. It "played," it communicated. It was a clear, simple, vivid, unambiguous way to make a point about a character, portrayed by a certain actor, as part of a particular company, doing a specific play, in the Soviet Union. And this particular action was specifically designed for an audience who had just carried out a revolution which they believed would rid them of czars and capitalists forever.

Vakhtangov, like Stanislavsky, was holding the mirror up to nature. His goal was to present the life of human beings upon the stage and comment on that life. But Vakhtangov's mirror did more than reflect. It was more like a lens with a filter; it eliminated peripheral detail; it concentrated on essences; it focused on the core of a problem or a character and then communicated

[16] Vendrovskaya interview.

that core in unmistakable terms. Although in this respect Vakhtangov's goals were similar to those of Meyerhold, he differed from the great theatricalist both in the attitude and manner in which his communication was carried out. Instead of pommeling his audience with extravagant physical stimuli as did Meyerhold, Vakhtangov wooed them. He taught his actors to love and respect the audience, to empathize with them, to reach out and draw them into the play, to make of them partners, not victims. The form of his messages may indeed have been just as fanciful as Meyerhold's, but his mode of delivery was a dialogue rather than a harangue.

To Yevgeny Vakhtangov the interpretation and production of a given play was a once in a lifetime affair. It took into account all the given circumstances: place of performance, time, the capacities of the actors, the nature of the audience, the technical potential of the theatre and its staff, the director. All these elements were thrown into the crucible of the combined creative imaginations of the entire theatrical company, melted down, then poured into the mold of the play—a mold, however, which might itself be altered in form as it embraced the molten distillate of the given circumstances. Out of this mold came a unique form, never to be repeated. Indeed, there could never be any reason for trying to repeat it. The river, after all, moves on. The circumstances change. A repetition would only be an anachronism, interesting perhaps as an artifact but not a vital, living work of theatre art.

2. At the beginning of this article I indicated that our interest in Vakhtangov might profitably go somewhat deeper than antiquarian curiosity, that we still might have something to learn from him because we face many of the problems with which he wrestled and, in the opinion of many of his contemporaries, won. As he worked with his contemporaries to make of the theatre a significant cultural force in what was to be a new and free society, his major effort was devoted to freeing himself of the chafing restrictions which realism places on the theatre's means of expression and yet preserving that vital inner realism which he considered to be the underpinning of histrionic communication. Today in the United States, as we work to make of our theatre an

important cultural force in a rapidly changing society, we find ourselves fighting Vakhtangov's battle all over again—struggling to be free of a remarkably obstinate realistic tradition and yet understandably reluctant to turn the theatre over to the seven-foot marionette and the electrical engineer.

To be sure, unlike Vakhtangov, we have no lack of playwrights—mostly foreign admittedly—who recognize the theatre's need for imaginative power rather than verisimilitude, for a release from the necessity to be faithful to "real life" which has bound so much of modern drama to earth and robbed it of the soaring poetry, the vivid evocation of emotion, the great experience through feeling not thinking which art gives and social studies do not. Surely Beckett, Ionesco, Genet, Albee, Kopit, Grass, Frisch, Weiss, Shaffer, and many others have given us a gallery of characters which are conceived in the theatre rather than taken from the street. Their plots treat real human problems, but their method is unashamedly theatrical; their characters are drawn from life but always have an aura of the mask about them. But the playscript is of course only a blueprint, and scripts by such authors require commensurate production techniques. It is here where we have yet to win the battle.

The record of the failure of American productions of the current avant-garde is impressive, and surely I need not document it thoroughly here. Perhaps a single, recent example will suffice. In November of the current season Elizabeth Hardwick reviewed the New York production of Weiss's *The Investigation*. She remarked that it had been directed as though it were written by Arthur Miller and then continued:

What you see in the production of *The Investigation* is our fear of stylization, of "interpretation." Perhaps this clinging, adhesive didactic naturalism, year after year, play after play, had its roots in commercialism. But its development has been peculiar and complex. Stylization, where it is called for, is the work of a free imagination, of a confident spirit, following his singular gleam. The imagination, the person, must be free and yet, by a paradox, stylization is the willingness to be rigid, to control and order, to interpret, even, at times, to wrench and distort in favor of some ruling design or idea. You must of course stand upon it, since it is clearly a decision, an idea. And in that, great risks are involved.

Stylization is too personal as an action, and too refined as a conception, apparently. How much safer to trust the simple flow of "real life," to fall back on sincerity at the expense of truth, to trust earnestness more than inspiration. . . . Perhaps by this time, no power on earth could sever our actors from their "serious," eyes-glinting, next-door realism. The insufficiency, the falseness of this is never more pathetic than when you have a strangely hidden script like *The Investigation*.[17]

Of course we have made our mistakes on the other extreme, too, and have found to our grief that high stylization void of inner belief can be just as disappointing a theatrical experience as that against which Miss Hardwick protests. John Gassner stated the issue quite clearly for us ten years ago in his *Form and Idea in the Modern Theatre:* "A reconciliation of the polarities of realism and theatricalism is indeed inherent in the very nature of dramatic art. . . . The future of our stage depends greatly upon the possibility of turning the present chaotic coexistence of realism and nonrealistic stylization into an active and secure partnership." [18]

It is here, then, that the study of Vakhtangov might be most immediately and practically useful to American theatre artists. Our theatre tradition has been dominated by naturalism. Since the late 1920's it has drawn sustenance and inspiration from Stanislavsky. Our directors have consistently sought to create on the stage that illusion of phenomenal reality which became the hallmark of his early work, and our actors have sought to follow his "system" (albeit in various mutilated forms) in working on themselves and in working up a part. Our directors are still hesitant to "distort creatively," and our actors are too often incapable of doing so without turning into puppets. Vakhtangov's problem was strikingly similar. As a director he had first to free himself from that psychological allegiance to naturalism which he had imbibed at the feet of Sulerzhitsky in the First Studio. But that was just the beginning, for he had inevitably to work with actors of similar training, who, though skilled at penetrating to and emotionally experiencing the soul of a character, were

---

[17] "Auschwitz in New York," *New York Review of Books* VII (November 3, 1966), p. 5.

[18] (New York: Dryden Press, 1956), p. viii.

tongue-tied and hamstrung so far as Vakhtangov was concerned by their ineradicable reverence for "naturalness." His solution, as we have seen, was to take the basic methods of role study from the "system" and supplement them with theatrical means of expression derived from the nonrealistic theatre in order to achieve a synthesis which he called fantastic realism.

3. Vakhtangov and the era which produced him were unique. And perhaps it is true, as he himself insisted, that his productions themselves can now engage our attention only as interesting artifacts, remarkable for their affinity with the work of Barrault perhaps, or D. Esrig's hilarious *Troilus and Cressida,* which won a first prize at the Paris festival last year, or with Peter Brook's *Marat/Sade.* But the methods which produced them do have vital significance for us and may indeed be as applicable to our theatre as they were to Vakhtangov's. Fantastic realism, not so much as a paradoxical name for just another paradoxical style, but as a practical, workable procedure for achieving a synthesis of realistic content with boldly theatrical, "fantastic" forms of expression, might well prove, indeed is proving elsewhere under other names, to be a useful solution to one of the major problems which currently face American directors. In spite of much theorizing and considerable labor, we have yet to produce in this country a theatrical tradition which fully recognizes not only the value of this synthesis but the practical steps necessary to achieve it.

As the American theatre teeters on the brink of becoming at last a significant force in our culture (and the figure is purposely ambiguous), with respect to scenic form we find ourselves, as John Gassner put it, like Matthew Arnold, "wandering between two worlds—one dead, the other powerless to be born." [19] I should think that Yevgeny Vakhtangov might make an excellent midwife.

[19] *Ibid.,* p. 179.

MARGRET DIETRICH

## Music and Dance in the Productions of Max Reinhardt *

When naturalism had taken poetry out of theatre, and it had become the fashion to make productions as bare and cheerless as possible, Max Reinhardt began his stage career. It is significant that right from the start he did productions which were entirely and consciously opposed to the naturalistic spirit and style of the day. With this talent for, and inclination toward the Southern Austrian Baroque Style, he could do little with the Puritan simplicity of the stage. The idea that scenes could be made significant only by tangible or visible means, was contrary to his sense of color and form and music, just as his feeling for art opposed scenes which were inartistic, though historically correct in detail. What the youthful Reinhardt already wanted and was looking for went hand in hand with the antinaturalistic tendencies of his time: life whole, complete, in an artistic form. This comprised all the degrees in between: from that which the naturalistic mind can barely comprehend to that which can only be hinted or imagined. These are the invisible assets, which give reality to existence, in music, in rhythm, in all colors and the dynamic forms which appear artistically on the stage. In order to achieve this, it was necessary to make use of quite other means than those employed by historians and exponents of naturalism in the theatre.

Of course Reinhardt adopted some of the best traditions of the nineteenth century. Above all he took over the idea of the "Gesamtkunstwerk," with music and dance, as it had been developed by the Meiningers and by Richard Wagner. With his Austrian-Baroque temperament, how wonderfully was he able to remodel this idea of the past! Creator of the *Gesamtkunst-*

* Reprinted from *Revue D'Histoire du Théâtre,* MCMLXIII:3 (1963).

*werk,* visionary architect, painter, and director of the stage, how great was his ability to shape the talents of the leading figures among scene designers and composers so as to help him realize his spectacular and musical vision of the play! And how masterly was the art with which he chose his material! He picked only those works which possessed the same musical quality and atmosphere as his own ideas.

Many of his productions were theatrical symphonies in which words and music, lighting and painting effects, and the art of acting were fused in an intoxicating whole which swept all along with it by the strength of its gripping qualities and its atmosphere.

Reinhardt's gift for production, which has often been compared to the genius of Gustav Mahler in the opera, was for a while an inconceivable revolution on the stage; precisely because its origin lay in the spirit of music, of rhythm, and in the sensual qualities of the scene. He himself was a magician of the stage, inexhaustible in finding ways of staging the visions of his dream-world.—Among these ways the preeminent position was held by music and rhythm. This is well illustrated in his production of the *Great World Theatre* by Hugo von Hofmannsthal, and the poet's account of the original performance in the Kollegien-kirche in Salzburg (1922) is unforgettable:

A particular moment in this play was one of the most striking in all the productions of Max Reinhardt. Indeed, its impact was such that a sigh and an half-audible cry of horror went up from the large body of spectators, pressed together in the dim obscurity of the church. For a moment one feared that the impact would be stronger than the nerves of the audience could stand. This was the moment when Death comes to fetch the six persons who represent the "World Theatre," the King and the Beggar, the Rich Man and the Farmer, Beauty and the Nun, one after the other, to lead them off the stage. As each one was taken off, Reinhardt made Death perform a dance with the victim. . . . Before this, the actor playing Death had been standing as motionless as a statue on a high column. At the moment when God orders him to take part in the plot, he leaves his raised pedestal by coming down a concealed ladder, silently as though on spider's legs. At the same time he mimes the beating of a drum, using two long bones as drumsticks, on an invisible, nonexistent drum. The rhythm chills the spectators to

the marrow. It may be unnecessary to add that this terrifying rhythm is in fact being made by the kettledrums in the organ gallery; but anyone in the audience would swear that it came from the small unseen drum fastened at Death's belt. Beating this rhythm unceasingly, with steps that show uncanny grace, he approaches . . . the first of the characters whom he has to summon. It is the King. Stepping backward, with the hollow eye sockets turned toward him, Death forces the King by his drumbeats to descend from the throne and to follow him, step by step.—But the power of this drumming is such that the King is simultaneously attracted and repelled by it. He no longer walks like a living creature being led by an instrument, but as though his soul had gone out of him and is now part of the drumbeats. Like a puppet dangling on wires, whose limbs hang slack, the King follows the drummer and mechanically, as it were, pushes out the verses that he has to say in front of him. In this manner Death leads him toward the audience, then whirls him round and leads him back to his place. Then Death fetches the next figure, the Rich Man or Beauty, and so on, going through the same performance six times, the same ghostly dancing, while the spectators sat as though chained to their seats, and the medieval cry of "Timor mortis me conturbat" (the fear of death confounds me) seemed to rise up and get stuck in their throats.[1]

No less musical and impressive was Hugo von Hofmannsthal's *Everyman* at the Salzburg Festival in 1920, produced by Reinhardt in front of the magnificent Baroque façade of the cathedral. The dignified incidental music was composed by Einar Nilson and Bernhard Paumgartner. Reinhardt's effects with sound were notable: the trumpeters sounding their fanfares on the vast porticoes at the beginning of the play; the cries of *Everyman* echoing unbelievably further and yet further away from the church towers, from the fortress, from the cemetery; the droning of the bells at the end of the play, and last but not least, the orchestrated voices of the actors. This orchestral effect was not only called forth by the dramatic poesy of Hugo von Hofmannsthal, but was also put in by Reinhardt's conscious design. There was the clear, well-marked sound of the voice of the Lord, issuing from the interior of the cathedral; in front, at the richly-laden table a whole orchestra of sound: the soft, musical voice of Everyman, the cooing, enticing voice of the Paramour; the fresh

---

[1] *Aufzeichnungen,* Ges. Werke (S. Fischer, 1959), p. 346ff.

youthful quality of the Good Apprentice's voice; the bugle-like fat voice of Mammon, the faithful but weak voice of Good Works, the unshakable and confident voice of Faith. We can establish from Reinhardt's books on production how much he demanded from musical effects and atmosphere that could be achieved by vocal technique. These books record exactly the changing qualities of the strength of the voices, the pauses of speech and the character of the spoken word, its value both musically and emotionally.[2] Laughter and wailing, ecstatic cries and drunken bawling—all have their own special tone in each scene. Choruses and voices play their parts. Reinhardt played on the broadest register to make use of all the possibilities of the human voice, from dynamic heights to penetrating quietness.

In his production of *The Miracle,* in 1912, written by Vollmoeller, with music by Humperdinck, a significant place is given to such vocal sound effects. With ecstatic rejoicing, the crowd surrounds the cripple who is healed. At the end, the seducer's laughter resounds, sinister and disdainful, through the church. The nun is terrified and attempts to flee; but the terrible laughter surges toward her, now greatly intensified, from all directions as she turns from one to another. As she kneels trembling in front of the picture of the Madonna, the demoniac laughter fades away "and becomes mingled with the deep, majestic voices of deliverance. The choir bringing divine help builds in an extended crescendo to a deepening climax followed by a single voice announcing the grace of God." [3] Here the composer supports the producer's intentions, for he heightens the dramatic sound effect of the laughter by contrasting it with the choir rejoicing before God.

Examples of such effects with voices and musical sound can be found in many other of Reinhardt's colorful productions. One need only consider his equally famous *Oedipus* production in the circus arena in 1910, which attained ecstatic symphonic effects with the chorus. The gestures of the actors, principals and extras,—the way they walked, stood, strode, moved, or fell—the rhythm of a choral movement especially in his big-stage productions (*Grossrauminszenierungen*), all owe much to this same pattern of musical and rhythmic elements, in which pantomimic and

[2] H. v. Hofmannsthal, *op. cit.,* p. 348.
[3] Reinhardt's *Production-Book.*

dancing effects occupy a large place. Again and again Reinhardt felt himself drawn to musical pantomimic spectacle, as he had already shown early in his career with the oriental fairy-tale drama *Sumurun,* adapted by Freksa with music by Hollaender, but which he was not at that time able to carry out very successfully.

He followed up his worldwide success, *The Miracle,* with some less grandiose productions—among which was also a pantomime-ballet, originally created by Rameau, entitled *The Shepherdesses* and performed by Reinhardt in the Kammerspiele (Berlin) in 1916.

In the Josefstädter Theatre of Vienna or the Kammerspiele of Berlin Reinhardt had small, intimate theatres, as acoustically sensitive as the noble body or framework of a violin. This is what he wanted in order to do full justice to the resources he had at hand for sound effects; and here he created and evoked sometimes with the gestures and movement of the actors a visible but inaudible inner music which filled the auditorium with its harmonies and dissonances: Reinhardt's *"Kammerspielstil."*

But there was not only this musical quality which began with the actors. Along with it there came a host of other acoustical effects which played a part in the whole. These sounds ranged from the quiet rushing of the wind, and the sweeping surging sound of organ pipes to thunder and lightning or perhaps sinister hollow knocking on doors, a sound described in *The Miracle* as a low, gentle sigh that glides through the room.

Naturally, the idea of such an ecstatic "total theatre" which Reinhardt created by all these means was not accepted by everyone without murmur. Sometimes criticisms were loudly vocal. An example of this can be seen in the production in a circus arena of *The Prodigal Son* (by Wilhelm Schmidtbonn) in 1914, for which Aladar Radó composed the incidental music. The *Reichspost* says of this production:

Reinhardt's complicated apparatus is well known. We are familiar with the shrieking people, who burst into the room from every entrance, bearing flaming torches. We have already heard this mass of people shout, scream, and yell; and the glaring spotlights sweeping up and down disturbingly are not unfamiliar either, but never before did we dislike them as much as this time. For never before was the gaudi-

ness of the apparatus quite so opposed to the meaning of the play. This delicate little Biblical parable expires under the brutal handling of the great producer. . . . The modest nature of this dramatic parable contrasts sharply with the interpolated confusion of the orgy: the bellydancers of Jerusalem; the seething mass of hands and feet of the shepherds, shambling in a kind of gymnastic display (*Schauturnen*); walkers-on, men and women, uttering cries as in a litany. This bad imitation of the Meininger crowds wounded any feeling of delicacy.

But such judgments cannot detract from the then justified revolutionary and effective character of Reinhardt's productions, called forth by a new feeling for sound and rhythmic effects and for theatrical entirety.

What part does music itself play in Reinhardt's productions? No other than that of sound values in speech, rhythmical movements of the actors and dancers, or the complex patterns of everyday sounds and noises. Music increases the impact of the drama, using counterpoint as a means of building up a climax. It enters into the whole idea of the production, carrying the theme, and is given the task of weaving the separate elements together so as to achieve a final harmony. It is not décor, it is not ornament. It is not an element that creates atmosphere by its intrinsic value alone; but it is absorbed completely into the scene, as were all other means that Reinhardt had at his disposal.

In spite of what has been said above, Reinhardt was far from being an effective producer of opera and operetta, even if he did occasionally produce a work of this kind, as the *Rosenkavalier* in Dresden in 1911, and *Ariadne* at the Deutsches Theater in Berlin in 1917, or even if he attempted to do a successful production of Offenbach's *Orpheus in the Underworld* at the Neues Theater in 1906, or put on a Johann Strauss operetta, *The Fledermaus,* at the Deutsches Theater in 1929. In the opera he may have felt himself too much limited by the music. With his concept of theatre, he was more in his element with spoken plays and pantomimes, in which nevertheless music demanded a large place, which he granted it.

Sometimes he took over existing Old Viennese incidental music, written for such plays as those by Ferdinand Raimund and Johann Nestroy, and hardly to be understood out of the con-

text of Old Viennese traditional popular music. For Goethe's *Fair at Plundersweilen* (*Jahrmarksfest zu Plundersweilen*), at the Deutsches Theater in 1925, he used the original music arranged for the production in Ettersburg. For *Faust II,* also at the Deutsches Theater but in 1911, he asked Eduard Künnecke to arrange music by Schumann. He chose music by Mozart for Goldoni's *Servant of Two Masters,* given in 1924 at the Komödie, with lyrics taken from the text of Kurz Bernardon, the Old Viennese comic actor.

Usually, however, he commissioned composers who were close to him and familiar with his aim, to write special incidental music while he was building up a scene. Among these were Engelbert Humperdinck, Wagner's pupil; Hans Pfitzner, who worked on the production of Kleist's *Käthchen von Heilbronn* in 1905; and Felix Weingartner, who worked on *Faust* in 1909. Einar Nilson and Bernhard Paumgartner, Friedrich von Hollaender, Mischa Spoliansky and Leo Blech contributed— among others—very significantly.

Undoubtedly, Humperdinck and Nilson were for Reinhardt the most important among these composers. With few exceptions (for example, Blech and Paumgartner) Reinhardt worked with them on all his numerous Shakespearean productions. Characteristically we find Humperdinck's name connected with Reinhardt's production of *The Blue Bird* (Maeterlinck), in 1912 in the Grosses Schauspielhaus and, as previously mentioned, with *The Miracle* (Vollmoeller).

Reinhardt's Shakespeare productions best demonstrate his use of incidental music. Beginning in 1908 with Mendelssohn's music for *A Midsummer Night's Dream,* the young producer achieved international fame. With the exception of the overture and the wedding march, Mendelssohn's music was divided by Reinhardt into separate parts, each carrying a theme, and inserted where he felt they belonged, so that they fitted into the light, feathery, vibrant rhythms of the sets and added force to his dramatic scenes. Complete numbers were split up, accentuated, and allowed to be associated, after many repetitions, with particular characters and atmosphere. They lost their own intrinsic value and fitted in perfectly with Reinhardt's conception. Several months later, Humperdinck wrote incidental music for *The*

*Merchant of Venice.* This music also fitted in completely with Reinhardt's ideas, expressing the love of life and the joy of having fun which he intended, and so came to be part of the scene itself; music in the free, playful world of magic and fantasy.[4]

Julius Bab has given us a lively description of Reinhardt's use of a medley of sounds running parallel with Humperdinck's music:

*The Merchant of Venice* begins with a wonderfully blended symphony of noises: this was the awakening of the town: animal sounds, tools rattling, the individual calls of the gondoliers, all the noises of the people of Venice, Queen of the seas, as they greet the new day. . . . This acoustic atmosphere runs through the whole play and, particularly in the street scenes, it sometimes contrives to be in the air—a noise, a cry near or far-off, or actual music.

And Georg Brandes makes a note of his general impression:

When the performance had finished, from this excursion into the Cinquecento one had an experience of a fantastic Venice to such a degree that its melodies hovered in the air and buzzed in one's ears, while colors and shapes flickered before one's eyes.[5]

*A Winter's Tale* in 1906 and *Romeo and Juliet* in 1907 followed *The Merchant of Venice,* both with music by Humperdinck. *A Winter's Tale* with scenery by Emil Orlik, was musically and scenically almost ritual in effect, simpler and with more weight and economy than the great tragedy of the lovers. Again using music and acoustical effects, Reinhardt achieved for *Romeo and Juliet* the hot-blooded atmosphere of the colorful town of Verona. For *Twelfth Night,* at the Deutsches Theater in 1907, Reinhardt achieved great effects with choric production (*Chorregie*), also with music by Humperdinck. This was to lead to his great productions in circus arenas in later years. The sets for this production glide by easily, one by one, with the help of a revolving stage; spoken scenes, pantomime, masquerade, processions, dances by peasants, all flow easily into one another,

[4] Lorentz Stucki, *M. Reinhardts Shakespeare-Inszenierungen* (Dissertation) (Wien, 1948).

[5] Cited by Legband, *Das Deutsche Theater in Berlin,* p. 90.

witnesses of Reinhardt's power to evoke the world of fantasy. *Lear* followed in 1908, intended as a production with sound effects rather than as a play with incidental music. The scene with Cordelia had "the sound of prehistoric music made by muffled drums and muted horns." [6] Also Nilson, who undertook to write the incidental music, invented a music of barbaric tones for Lear's entrance. Although Reinhardt in other productions created scenes of extraordinary lavishness, in this production he concentrated everything on making a setting with a large, monumental, and ghastly effect. In the *Hamlet* of the following year, 1909, this style was again attempted, although a different atmosphere was achieved. Then *The Taming of the Shrew* appeared at the end of 1909 in direct revolt against this dictum. It was a well-planned extravaganza of sound and color, which added Leo Blech's music to the wild commotion of the comic scenes. It is easily seen from Jacobsohn's description of the staging that Reinhardt is here opening new paths:

Throughout the play there are intentionally confused relationships of figures and space, such as result from states of fever or dreams. Human bodies link themselves together or pile up in heaps and then fall apart again with burlesque bumps and crashes. Chests and cases tower in a pyramid on a table, which later begins to sway;

At the end Katharine sits crying high up on this mountain and Petrucchio swings up to her acrobatically. Figures fall down head over heels from painted chairs.

Groups of servants emerge from the earth, become harlequins, eccentrics, snakelike men, make foolish faces, beat one another, disappear into cupboards and through walls . . .[7]

Along with the renewal of the commedia dell'arte tradition, which, as we have seen, had captured Reinhardt's imagination earlier in his career, expressionism plays an important part in this production, and from here on, although Reinhardt never allowed it to master him completely.

After some Shakespeare productions which are of less impor-

6 Stucki, pp. 107f.
7 Stucki, p. 121.

tance for our purpose, the staging of *A Winter's Tale* in 1914 is interesting. Jacobsohn characterizes the production as follows:

> Humperdinck, the fairytale composer, wrote music which resembles Shakespeare as much as it is unlike Wagner! . . . The mature Reinhardt no longer needed to strive for the choral effects of his earlier period. . . . At the end Hermione descends from the pedestal, led by the music, to the level of suffering humanity. Pictures, sounds, words, and theatrical art completely infused with feeling join together in a way that makes the scene a worthy throne for the honorable Melpomene.[8]

Shortly thereafter, in 1916, at the Deutsches Theater, *Macbeth* followed, a production that once again showed Reinhardt as master of sound effects in a scenic production. As his written directions show, Reinhardt handles the text like a musical score:

> As the curtain goes up, drums and fanfares sound in the distance; the drumbeats gradually quicken, becoming thunder from the underworld. Thick fog weaves its way across the stage. The storm begins to rage; then lightning flashes brightly through the fog and the first witch appears; another flash of lightning, and the second witch comes; and finally, in the same manner, the third. The voices of the three witches sound far-off, shrill and terrifying. Then the noises and lights fade away slowly and the stage becomes dark and silent. The powerful overture of Shakespeare combined with Reinhardt's treatment opens the play and at the same time gives it its atmosphere, its perspective, and its style.[9]

In 1920, after the first World War, Reinhardt's acoustic, ecstatic theatre was subjected to harsh criticism on the occasion of a new production of *Hamlet* in the Grosses Schauspielhaus (Berlin), "Hamlet in a Circus."

Jacobsohn called the protest, in which he—who otherwise wrote favorably of Reinhardt—cried out: "Whoever loves art must most hesitate to set fire to this inartistic barn at all four corners!" And he pointed out how the importance of the actor disappeared under the impact of the acoustics, the unsuitable stage, the Wagnerian music, and the eagerness of the public to

[8] Jacobsohn, *M. Reinhardt*, p. 10.
[9] Stucki, p. 167.

see a "show." Jacobsohn made the same criticism of the production of *The Merchant of Venice* in 1921, also in the Grosses Schauspielhaus, calling it "the continuous musical accompaniment, a mixture of opera, ballet, pantomime, and fairytale. . . ."

At this time Reinhardt seems to have become uneasy about these experiments with Shakespeare. He was drawn to Vienna and Salzburg, where he could begin a period of new creative activity, including productions of Shakespeare, but in a more organic theatre space.

When considering the Reinhardt Shakespearean productions as a whole, with their acoustical and musical direction, one may agree with what Jacobsohn said of the 1907 production of *Twelfth Night:*

An optical delight to accompany the acoustical, the latter being the more important. If music be the food of love, Reinhardt presents it in full measure with richness of instrumentation that excludes the danger of monotony.[10]

Reinhardt himself always remained open to new ideas. Again and again he favored the employment of new composers for new productions and explored with them every corner of an imagination which was unusually sensitive to the elements of sound, color, movement, and form.

Finally, let us take a glance at the very peculiar experiment which Reinhardt conducted in collaboration with the composer Mischa Spoliansky in the production of *Victoria* in Berlin and Vienna in 1926. This is a comedy by Maugham about a soldier and prisoner of war returning home, a farce which is charming if not very profound. The evening was therefore not Maugham's but Reinhardt's. We can call this the production of the theatre of lighthearted acting, inspired by Tairoff's experiments with movement, and in the truest sense of the word an adventurous attempt to make use of the motif of the homecoming as a basis for an amusing evening with music and dancing. Only a few years before, Reinhardt's prose performance of *Victoria* in Ber-

10 Stucki, p. 31.

lin had been a complete failure. Now Reinhardt presented this farce, purely through the medium of his production, as a mixture of comedy, operetta, comic pantomime, and cabaret: a kind of speech-dance-operetta without songs and final tableau. A servant girl interrupts the dialogue, *singing,* to announce a visitor. The man at the piano plays a few bars and the dialogue becomes a recitative. The dialogue or the recitative moves easily into a dance. This is an astonishingly sensitive style of production in which Reinhardt intends us to take pleasure in the purely theatrical delights of the stage. Puppet-like movements and pantomime are interspersed in a light and rhythmical way, amiable and satiric as well as fanciful. In the words of Polgar: "The edges of the dialogue are lightly touched with music." The musical arabesques with Spoliansky at the piano lead the actors, at the end of each act, into trios, quintets, septets, and electrifying finales. A dancing master, introduced by Reinhardt, serves as justification for numerous motifs, each character having his own motif. Probability goes by the board and what remains is a playful and extravagant game. Parlandi and choric effects succeed one another with an inexhaustible wealth of inventiveness. The play becomes a featherweight "plaything"—any weighty moments in the plot are pushed into the background. The scene described by Benno Fleischmann is typical:

A group of keyed-up players get more and more excited, stamp out a crescendo with their feet, then beat a crescendo with their hands on their thighs, at the same time, not singing, but giving rhythmic utterances in chorus to their annoyance, impatience, or reluctance,

the music itself being "more than incidental and less than melodramatic."

Whole scenes are composed in dance rhythms, ranging from graceful pas de deux to ensembles, shimmies, and Charlestons. Even in that section of the press whose criticism was unfavorable, the master of stagecraft met with due recognition:

We have reached the point where the director, who ought to serve the author, has become his master. He introduces new scenes, even an additional character, he adds music, he changes rhythm, color, and

character, he reorders, compresses, inflates, he hardly respects more than the poor skeleton of thought.[11]

Test-tube gaiety, stage technique as a substitute for thought . . . Reinhardt replaces the deficient dialogue with a travesty of this deficiency, with a parade of rhythmical tidbits, with tricks of accentuation. A dance of humors and shadows, a puppet-furioso. The actors, exquisitely carved wooden figures, bubbling over; on this occasion the exaggeration seemed valid.[12]

It can be said in conclusion that Reinhardt, the creator of dynamic *Gesamtkunstwerke,* was in his way a master of the stage. Music and dance, sound and rhythm, fitted organically into his scenic fantasies: these things were in every respect stageworthy and were never introduced without scenic or dramaturgic justification, though to us today, with our predilection for more simplicity, they seem to be overloaded with ideas and effects. Yet everything which he created was in the best sense theatrical, which is something that cannot be said of many theatre productions of today.

Thus Reinhardt's strength coincides with the newest tendencies among our authors and directors, though the latter use different means. They see the theatre primarily as theatre, and thus introduce music, dance pantomime, and rhythm as integral parts of the word-drama.

[11] *Neues Wiener Tageblatt,* November 30, 1926.
[12] *Wiener Allgemeine Zeitung,* November 30, 1926.

## PART V

The Oriental Stage:
Hieroglyphic Form

One of the reasons that must have motivated William Butler
Yeats to pattern plays after the Japanese Noh drama was probably its apparent modesty of scale and means: Yeats desired to
create chamber performances for a select audience. The lesson,
however, is a good one in considering total theatre. The designation "total theatre" seems to imply an accumulation of means
and an epic scale that have little to do with the actual concerns of
an artistic interplay of modalities.

A good illustration of this understanding is a short play called
*The Dead Man Rises* which is done by Peter Schumann's Bread
and Puppet Theatre. It is akin to an Oriental play more in feeling
than in form, and its very moving effect depends upon the combination of three not very usual aspects of production; narration,
mime, and huge puppets. A simple drama is enacted by the
"body puppets," figures six to eight feet tall, moved by persons
inside. A woman, traveling with a figure representing the river,
finds a dead man and takes him home with her. Throughout the
pantomime, a hooded figure seated on the floor to one side nar-

rates the woman's thoughts in a whisper through a megaphone, and sometimes rings a small bell. This simplicity, intensifying the visual and aural basis of the stage, indicates the place at which the techniques of total theatre begin. The sensory attention and participation we devote to such a performance is a characteristic of hieroglyphic modes.

Three of the selections in this section describe the forms and influence of Kabuki drama. Kabuki is perhaps the highest development of total theatre. It is a contemplative drama, visually and aesthetically ordered, capable of commanding sustained attention to detail. Yet, as these selections indicate, it is virtually a machine for creating effect and for passing meaning from one sense modality to another.

Sergei Eisenstein likens this technique to passing a ball in soccer and speaks directly in terms that relate this to synesthesia. Leonard C. Pronko compares Kabuki and Elizabethan staging and gives further insights into the particular effects and affective stylizations employed by Kabuki, such as the "pulling-out," a sudden, onstage transformation from one costume to another.

Transformation may, in fact, be said to be a principle of Kabuki staging. It is facilitated by trap doors in the floor equipped with lifts for entrances and exits, by two revolving sections of the stage, one within the other, and by an extensive repertory of scene changing devices, principally those that may quickly raise or lower or reverse whole units of solid scenery. Music is used to dramatize and emphasize these transformations.

It should be noted that Mr. Pronko's essay relates to a portion of his recent and excellent book, *Theater East and West: Perspectives Toward a Total Theater* (Berkeley, Los Angeles: University of California Press, 1967). There he combines a history and analysis of Oriental theatre forms with detailed observations on their effects upon, and correspondences with, Western drama and productions. One vital conclusion reached is that totality must be achieved in terms of meaning as well as of means, so as to relate to all levels of an individual as well as of society. And this, Mr. Pronko feels, is in accord with the achievement of Oriental theatre.

Paul Claudel's classic, "Modern Drama and Music," like that of Eisenstein, centers upon the particularly effective and affec-

tive qualities of Kabuki music and stresses its distinct theatricality. Leonard Pronko's book makes the valuable suggestion that concrete music might now provide a counterpart in using this technique. To be quite certain, however, that Kabuki music has achieved that specific end which is perhaps most closely identified with total theatre intentions, let us consider Earle Ernst's description of the relationship of voice to music as it is there employed. Ernst writes:

There is the greatest freedom of movement between the actor's voice, the narrator's voice, and the music of the samisen. The narrator, like the samisen, can take over the weeping or the laughing of the actor without pause, and the actor similarly begins with no break between his speech and that of the narrator. And since this triad of expression moves within the same range of pitch, and since each has the vocal qualities of the other two, they produce a strong sense of aural continuity. The sound moves, with no break or division, from the stylized line reading of the actor to the more musical style of the narrator to the music of the samisen, which frequently performs, as in the case of "weeping," the function of an abstract human voice. The fluid movement between speech, vocal music, and instrumental music has no parallel in the Western theatre unless perhaps in the aural effect that was produced in Greek tragedy.[1]

Following Claudel's essay, the selection concerning Barrault's production of his *Christopher Columbus* then forms a natural progression. This section then returns to Oriental theatre itself, with Artaud's "On the Balinese Theatre" and Sophia Delza's "The Classic Chinese Stage." I would draw attention here to Artaud's references to hieroglyphic representations, and to the understanding that these also are employed on the Chinese stage, where their form reminds one of Artaud's emphasis upon an "affective athleticism." The "plastic poetry" of the Chinese stage has much in common with Kabuki. Sophia Delza's point of view is visual, rather than explicitly analytic, and we are able to see with the mind's eye many things at once; our own theatre of the future, perhaps, as well as specific Oriental techniques, and a theatre of constant movement and spectacle as well as those methods of playing which relate to the scope of ordinary staging or to chamber performances.

[1] Earle Ernst, *Kabuki Theater* (New York: Grove, 1956), p. 119.

SERGEI  EISENSTEIN

The  Unexpected *

> Hark! the voice of a pheasant
> Has swallowed the wide field
> At a gulp.
>
> YAMEI [1]

Givochini, the famous comedian of the Malii Theatre, was once forced to substitute at the last moment for the popular Moscow basso, Lavrov, in an opera, *The Amorous Bayaderka*. But Givochini had no singing voice. His friends shook their heads sympathetically. "How can you possibly sing the role, Vasili Ignatyevich?" Givochini was not disheartened. Said he, happily, *"Whatever notes I can't take with my voice, I'll show with my hands."* [2]

We have been visited by the Kabuki theatre —a wonderful manifestation of theatrical culture.[3]

Every critical voice gushes praise for its splendid craftsmanship. But there has been no appraisal of what constitutes its wonder. Its "museum" elements, though indispensable in estimating its value, cannot alone afford a satisfactory estimate of this phenomenon, of this wonder. A "wonder" must promote cultural progress, feeding and stimulating the intellectual questions of our day. The Kabuki is dismissed in platitudes: "How musical!" "What handling of objects!" "What plasticity!" And we come to the conclusion that there is nothing to be learned, that (as one of our most respected critics has announced) there's nothing new here: Meyerhold has already plundered everything of use from the Japanese theatre!

---

* Reprinted from Sergei Eisenstein's *The Film Form*, edited and translated by Jay Leyda, copyright, ©, 1949, by Harcourt, Brace & World, Inc. and reprinted with their permission.

[1] Quoted in *Haiku Poems, Ancient and Modern,* translated and annotated by Miyamon Asatarō (Tokyo: Maruzen Company, 1940).

[2] From a collection of anecdotes about Vasili Ignatyevich Givochini.

[3] In its European tour during 1928 a troupe of Kabuki actors, headed by Ichikawa Sadanji, performed in Moscow and Leningrad; in the latter city the magazine *Zhizn Iskusstva* devoted an issue (August 19, 1928), to this visit to which Eisenstein contributed this essay.

Behind the fulsome generalities, there are some real attitudes revealed. Kabuki is conventional! How can such conventions move Europeans! Its craftsmanship is merely the cold perfection of form! And the plays they perform are *feudal!*—What a nightmare!

More than any other obstacle, it is this conventionalism that prevents our thorough use of all that may be borrowed from the Kabuki.

But the conventionalism that we have learned "from books" proves in fact to be a conventionalism of extremely interesting relationships. The conventionalism of Kabuki is by no means the stylized and premeditated mannerism that we know in our own theatre, artificially grafted on outside the technical requirements of the premise. In Kabuki this conventionalism is profoundly logical—as in any Oriental theatre, for example, in the Chinese theatre.

Among the characters of the Chinese theatre is "the spirit of the oyster"! Look at the makeup of the performer of this rôle, with its series of concentric touching circles spreading from the right and left of his nose, graphically reproducing the halves of an oyster shell, and it becomes apparent that this is quite "justified." This is neither more nor less a convention than are the epaulets of a general. From their narrowly utilitarian origin, once warding off blows of the battle-axe from the shoulder, to their being furnished with hierarchic little stars, the epaulets are indistinguishable in principle from the blue frog inscribed on the forehead of the actor who is playing the frog's "spirit."

Another convention is taken directly from life. In the first scene of *Chushingura* (*The Forty-Seven Ronin*), Shocho, playing a married woman, appears without eyebrows and with blackened teeth. This conventionalism is no more unreal than the custom of Jewish women who shear their heads so that the ears remain exposed, nor of that among girls joining the Komsomol who wear red kerchiefs, as some sort of "form." In distinction from European practice, where marriage has been made a guard against the risks of freer attachments, in ancient Japan (of the play's epoch) the married woman, once the need had passed, destroyed her attractiveness! She removed her eyebrows, and blackened (and sometimes extracted) her teeth.

Let us move on to the most important matter, to a conventionalism that is explained by the specific world viewpoint of the Japanese. This appears with particular clarity during the direct *perception* of the performance, to a peculiar degree that no description has been able to convey to us.

And here we find something totally unexpected—a junction of the Kabuki theatre with these extreme probings in the theatre, where theatre is transformed into cinema.[4] And where cinema takes that latest step in its development: the *sound* film.

The sharpest distinction between Kabuki and our theatre is— if such an expression may be permitted—in a *monism of ensemble*.

We are familiar with the emotional ensemble of the Moscow Art Theatre—the ensemble of a unified collective "re-experience"; the parallelism of ensemble employed in opera (by orchestra, chorus, and soloists); when the settings also make their contribution to this parallelism, the theatre is designated by that dirtied word "synthetic"; the "animal" ensemble finally has its revenge—that outmoded form where the whole stage clucks and barks and moos a naturalistic imitation of the life that is led by the "assisting" human beings.

The Japanese have shown us another, extremely interesting form of ensemble—*the monistic ensemble*. Sound—movement—space—voice here *do not accompany* (or even parallel) each other, but function *as elements of equal significance*.

The first association that occurs to one in experiencing Kabuki is *soccer,* the most collective ensemble sport. Voice, clappers, mimic movement, the narrator's shouts, the folding screens—all are so many backs, halfbacks, goal-keepers, forwards, passing to each other the dramatic ball and driving toward the goal of the dazed spectator.

It is impossible to speak of "accompaniments" in Kabuki— just as one would not say that, in walking or running, the right leg "accompanies" the left leg, or that both of them accompany the diaphragm!

[4] It is my conviction that cinema is *today's level* of theatre. That theatre in its older form has died and continues to exist only by inertia. [The author's commentary of eleven years later on this viewpoint can be found in "Achievement," in *Film Form*—JAY LEYDA.]

Here a single monistic sensation of theatrical "provocation" takes place. The Japanese regards each theatrical element, not as an incommensurable unit among the various categories of affect (on the various sense organs), but as a single unit of *theatre*.

. . . the patter of Ostuzhev no more than the pink tights of the prima donna, a roll on the kettledrums as much as Romeo's soliloquy, the cricket on the hearth no less than the cannon fired over the heads of the audience.[5]

Thus I wrote in 1923, placing a sign of equality between the elements of every category, establishing theoretically the basic *unity of theatre,* which I then called "attractions."

The Japanese in his, of course, instinctive practice, makes a fully one hundred per cent appeal with his theatre, just as I then had in mind. Directing himself to the various organs of sensation, he builds his summation to a grand *total* provocation of the human brain, without taking any notice *which* of these several paths he is following.[6]

In place of *accompaniment,* it is the naked method of *transfer* that flashes in the Kabuki theatre. Transferring the basic affective aim from one material to another, from one category of "provocation" to another.

In experiencing Kabuki one involuntarily recalls an American novel about a man in whom are transposed the hearing and seeing nerves, so that he perceives light vibrations as sounds, and tremors of the air—as colors: he *hears light* and *sees sound*. This is also what happens in Kabuki! We actually "hear movement" and "see sound."

An example: Yuranosuke leaves the surrendered castle. And moves from the depth of the stage toward the extreme foreground. Suddenly the background screen with its gate painted in natural dimensions (closeup) is folded away. In its place is seen a second screen, with a tiny gate painted on it (long shot). This

[5] "Montage of Attractions," LEF, 3 (1923); a translated excerpt appears in Appendix 2 of *The Film Sense*.

[6] Not even what is *eaten* in this theatre is accidental! I had no opportunity to discover if it is ritual food eaten. Do they eat whatever happens to be there, or is there a definite menu? If the latter, we must also include in the ensemble the sense of taste!

means that he has moved even further away. Yuranosuke continues on. Across the background is drawn a brown-green-black curtain, indicating: the castle is now hidden from his sight. More steps. Yuranosuke now moves out on to the "flowery way." This further removal is emphasized by . . . the *samisen,*[7] that is — by sound!!

First removal — steps, i.e., a *spatial* removal by the actor.

Second removal — a flat *painting:* the change of backgrounds.

Third removal — an *intellectually*-explained indication: we understand that the curtain "effaces" something visible.

Fourth removal — *sound!*

Here is an example of pure cinematographic method from the last fragment of *Chushingura:*

After a short fight ("for several feet") we have a "break" — an empty stage, a landscape. Then more fighting. Exactly as if, in a film, we had cut in a piece of landscape to create a mood in a scene, here is cut in an empty nocturnal snow landscape (on an empty stage). And here after several feet, two of the "forty-seven faithful" observe a shed where the villain has hidden (of which the spectator is already aware). Just as in cinema, within such a sharpened dramatic moment, some brake has to be applied. In *Potemkin,* after the preparation for the command to "Fire!" on the sailors covered by the tarpaulin, there are several shots of "indifferent" parts of the battleship before the final command is given: the prow, the gun muzzles, a life preserver, etc. A brake is applied to the action, and the tension is screwed tighter.

The moment of the discovery of the hiding place must be ac-

---

[7] ". . . samisen music depends almost completely on rhythm, rather than melody, to interpret emotion. Sound is inexhaustible, and by groupings of sounds in changing rhythms the samisen musicians gain the effects they desire. . . . Ripple-clang-bang; smoothness, roughness, villainy, tranquillity; falling snow, a flight of birds, wind in the treetops; skirmish and fray, the peace of moonlight, the sorrow of parting, the rapture of spring; the infirmity of age, the gladness of lovers — all these and much more the samisen expresses to those who are able to look beyond the curtain that shuts this musical world away from Western ears because of its baffling conventions of sound rather than melody." Zoë Kincaid, *Kabuki, The Popular Stage of Japan* (London: Macmillan and Co., 1925), pp. 199–200.

centuated. To find the *right* solution for this moment, this accent must be shaped from the *same* rhythmic material—a return to the same nocturnal, empty, snowy landscape . . .

But now there are people on the stage! Nevertheless, the Japanese do find the right solution—and it is a *flute* that enters triumphantly! And you *see* the same snowy fields, the same echoing emptiness and night, that you *heard* a short while before, when you *looked* at the empty stage . . .

Occasionally (and usually at the moment when the nerves seem about to burst from tension) the Japanese double their effects. With their mastery of the equivalents of visual and aural images, they suddenly give *both*, "squaring" them, and brilliantly calculating the blow of their sensual billiard cue on the spectator's cerebral target. I know no better way to describe that combination, of the moving hand of Ichikawa Ennosuke as he commits hara-kiri—*with* the sobbing sound offstage, *graphically* corresponding with the movement of the knife.

There it is: "Whatever notes I can't take with my voice, I'll show with my hands!" But here it was taken by the voice *and* shown with the hands! And we stand benumbed before such a perfection of—montage.

We all know those three trick questions: What shape is a winding staircase? How would you describe "compactly"? What is a "surging sea"? One can't formulate intellectually analyzed answers to these. Perhaps Baudouin de Courtenay [8] knows, but we are forced to answer with gestures. We show the difficult concept of "compactly" with a clenched fist, and so on.

And what is more, such a description is *fully satisfactory*. We also are slightly Kabuki! But not sufficiently!

In our "Statement" on the sound film we wrote of a contrapuntal method of combining visual and aural images. To possess this method one must develop in oneself a new *sense: the capacity of reducing visual and aural perceptions to a "common denominator."*

This is possessed by Kabuki to perfection. And we, too—

[8] A professor in comparative philology at the University of St. Petersburg.

crossing in turn the successive Rubicons flowing between theatre and cinema and between cinema and sound cinema—must also possess this. We can learn the mastery of this required new sense from the Japanese. As distinctly as impressionism owes a debt to the Japanese print, and post-impressionism to Negro sculpture, so the sound film will be no less obliged to the Japanese.

And not to the Japanese theatre, alone, for these fundamental features, in my opinion, profoundly penetrate all aspects of the Japanese world view. Certainly in those incomplete fragments of Japanese culture accessible to me, this seems a penetration to their very base.

We need not look beyond Kabuki for examples of identical perceptions of naturalistic three-dimensionality and flat painting. "Alien?" But it is necessary for this pot to boil in its own way before we can witness the completely satisfactory resolution of a waterfall made of vertical lines, against which a silver-paper serpentine fish-dragon, fastened by a thread, swims desperately. Or, folding back the screen walls of a strictly cubist tea house "of the vale of fans," a hanging backdrop is disclosed, a "perspective" gallery racing obliquely down its center. Our theatre design has never known such decorative cubism, nor such primitivism of painted perspective. Nor, moreover, such *simultaneity*— here, apparently, pervading everything.

*Costume.* In the Dance of the Snake Odato Goro enters, bound with a rope that is also expressed, through transfer, in the robe's pattern of a flat rope design, and her sash, as well, is twisted into a three-dimensional rope—a *third* form.

*Writing.* The Japanese masters an apparently limitless quantity of hieroglyphs. Hieroglyphs developed from conventionalized features of objects, put together, express concepts, i.e., the picture of a concept—an ideogram. Alongside these exists a series of Europeanized phonetic alphabets: the Manyō kana, hiragana, and others. But the Japanese writes *all* letters, employing both forms at once! It is not considered remarkable to compose sentences of hieroglyph *pictures* concurrently with the *letters* of several absolutely opposed alphabets.

*Poetry.* The *tanka* is an almost untranslatable form of lyrical

epigram of severe dimension: 5, 7, 5 syllables in the first strophe (*kami-no-ku*) and 7, 7 syllables in the second (*shimo-no-ku*).[9] This must be the most uncommon of all poetry, in both form and content. When written, it can be judged both pictorially and poetically. Its writing is valued no less as calligraphy than as a poem.

And content? One critic justly says of the Japanese lyric: "A Japanese poem should be sooner *seen* [i.e., *represented* visually. —S.E.] than *heard*." [10]

### Approach of Winter

They leave for the East
A flying bridge of magpies
A stream across the sky . . .
The tedious nights
Will be trimmed with hoarfrost.

Across a bridge of magpies in flight, it seems that Yakamochi (who died in 785) departs into the ether.

### Crow in the Spring Mist

The crow perched there
Is half-concealed
By the kimono of fog . . .
As is a silken songster
By the folds of the sash.

The anonymous author (ca. 1800) wishes to express that the crow is as incompletely visible through the morning mist as is the bird in the pattern of the silk robe, when the sash is wound around the robed figure.

Strictly limited in its number of syllables, calligraphically charming in description and in comparison, striking in an incongruity that is also wonderfully near (crow, half-hidden by the

[9] "The measure of the classical stanza is known as the *shichigoto*, or seven-and-five movement, which all Japanese believe to echo the divine pulse beat of the race." J. Ingram Bryan, *The Literature of Japan* (London: Thornton Butterworth Ltd., 1929), pp. 33–34.
[10] Julius Kurth, *Japanische Lyrik*, p. iv.

mist, and the patterned bird, half-hidden by the sash), the Japanese lyric evidences an interesting *"fusion"* of images, which appeals to the most varied senses. This original archaic "pantheism" is undoubtedly based on a *nondifferentiation of perception —a well-known absence of the sensation of "perspective."* It could not be otherwise. Japanese history is too rich in historical experience, and the burden of feudalism, though overcome politically, still runs like a red thread through the *cultural* traditions of Japan. Differentiation, entering society with its transition to capitalism and bringing in its wake, as a consequence of economic differentiation, differentiated perceptions of the world, —is not yet apparent in many cultural areas of Japan. And the Japanese continue to think "feudally," i.e., undifferentiatedly.

This is found in children's art. This also happens to people cured of blindness where all the objects, far and near, of the world, do not exist in space, but crowd in upon them closely.

In addition to Kabuki, the Japanese also showed us a film, *Karakuri-musume.* But in this, nondifferentiation, brought to such brilliant unexpectedness in Kabuki, is realized *negatively.*

*Karakuri-musume* is a melodramatic farce. Beginning in the manner of Monty Banks, it ends in incredible gloom, and for long intervals is criminally torn in both directions.

The attempt to tie these opposing elements together is generally the hardest of tasks.

Even such a master as Chaplin, whose fusion of these opposing elements in *The Kid* is unsurpassed, was unable in *The Gold Rush* to balance these elements. The material slid from plane to plane. But in *Karakuri-musume* there is a complete smashup.

As ever the echo, the unexpected junction, is found only at polar extremes. The archaism of nondifferentiated sense "provocations" of Kabuki on one side, and on the other—the acme of *montage thinking.*

Montage thinking—the height of differentiatedly sensing and resolving the "organic" world—is realized anew in a mathematic faultlessly performing instrument machine.

Recalling the words of Kleist, so close to the Kabuki theatre, which was born from marionettes:

. . . [grace] appears best in that human bodily structure which has no consciousness at all, or has an infinite consciousness—that is, in the mechanical puppet, or in the god.[11]

Extremes meet. . . .
Nothing is gained by whining about the soullessness of Kabuki or, still worse, by finding in Sadanji's acting a "confirmation of the Stanislavsky theory"! Or in looking for what "Meyerhold hasn't yet stolen"!
Let us rather—*hail the junction of Kabuki and the sound film!*

[1928]

LEONARD C. PRONKO

Kabuki and the
Elizabethan Theatre *

There are probably few directors who would want to attempt an archaeological reconstruction in their productions of Elizabethan plays. But we are all interested in finding some style which would give to our performances a spirit as exciting as that the Elizabethans must have found in their theatre. A great deal has been written on the controversial subject of acting styles in the late sixteenth and early seventeenth centuries, but ultimately scholars must admit that there is little that can be proved about that style aside from suggestions that it was indeed stylized or formal (but how?) rather than realistic (in what sense?). Twentieth-century interpretations of these terms, and of others used by

[11] Heinrich von Kleist, "Über das Marionettentheater," trans. Eugene Jolas, *Vertical* (Gotham Book Mart, 1941).
* Reprinted from the *Educational Theatre Journal*, XIX:1 (March, 1967).

writers referring to productions of Shakespeare, Marlowe, Ford, etc., will necessarily be colored by our own understanding of those terms—and by half a century of naturalistic bias. It seems to me that a fruitful approach to the problem might be taken through a living theatrical tradition which arose from historical conditions somewhat similar to those of Tudor England, and—if we can trust reports as they come down to us—which exhibits astonishing similarities to much of what we are told actually took place on the English stage three or four hundred years ago. I am referring, of course, to that form of popular theatre known as Kabuki, a form which, like Elizabethan drama, mingles hair-raising realism with extreme formalism, low farce with high seriousness.

I am not suggesting that we should follow slavishly the styles of Kabuki, dressing our actors in Japanese garb, striking the same kind of poses or using movements which have developed through a way of life utterly different from ours. What I am proposing is that a close study of the Kabuki theatre can wean us away from a style of presentation which is perhaps more fundamentally realistic than we realize. Taking our cue from a theatre which attempts to appeal to the whole man,[1] we might actually achieve a more "authentic" Elizabethan performance. With this in mind, I should like to point out certain parallels in historical background and some striking similarities in techniques which will, I believe, suggest to the imaginative director fresh and exciting perspectives on the production of Elizabethan plays.

### THE HISTORICAL MOMENT

Kabuki arose about 1605 and reached its zenith in the late seventeenth and early eighteenth centuries. About one hundred years later than the Elizabethan drama it reflects a similar historical moment. Tokugawa Japan, like Tudor England, presented a somewhat feudal façade, but there was a sense of change, a bustling activity behind it. It introduces to Japan a long period of unity and peace, and brings with it a growing sense of national

---

[1] And to people of all classes as well. Although it arose as a people's theatre, Kabuki constantly attracted the nobility, who attended in disguise, had love affairs with the actors, and were reprimanded and even restrained by law.

identity. A vigorous commercial life develops, giving the nation a greater economic stability than ever before, but at the same time making the nobility dependent upon the growing merchant class. Indeed, despite clearly defined classes, and a wide breach between noble and commoner, the wealthy middle class begins to play an important role in the life of the community. It was largely in response to the needs of a wealthy leisured middle class that Kabuki developed.

That sense of exuberance which we think of as typically Elizabethan finds its parallel in Japan in the development of popular arts, the importance of the *geisha* and the amusement quarters as a part of life and as a central focus in the literature. Although Japan was mostly closed to foreign trade, the Tokugawa period is marked by a growing interest in things foreign, and by 1720 the ban on Western books was lifted. We must not forget these elements, which formed a kind of balance to the highly formalized life we tend to think of as Japanese. It may well be that a dynamic tension created by a pull between freedom and hierarchy, the new and the old, was largely responsible for the flowering of the arts in that most brilliant of Japanese periods known as the Genroku (1688–1704).

A similar tension was achieved in Elizabethan England. E. M. W. Tillyard reminds us that Raleigh was a theologian as well as a discoverer, that sermons were as much a part of everyday Elizabethan life as was bearbaiting, and ascribes the greatness of Elizabethan England to the fact that "it contained so much of new without bursting the noble form of the old order." [2]

The blending of the old and new, of the refined and the barbaric, is reflected in the life and theatre of the Tokugawa Japanese and the Elizabethan Englishman: unthinkably cruel punishments for what strike us as rather minor offenses, indifference to the suffering of others, enjoyment of the refinements of poetry and ceremony, often in proximity to the pleasures of bearbaiting and prostitution. Before reaching artistic maturity the Kabuki theatre sometimes served as a front to prostitution while in London the theatres were relegated to the south bank of the Thames, near the infamous Stews. The famous actor Edward Alleyn

[2] E. M. W. Tillyard, *The Elizabethan World Picture* (New York, n.d.), p. 8.

seems to symbolize the era in England: creator of Marlowe's major characters, he made much of his fortune by leasing land for bearbaiting, and invested it in the founding of a college.

Prostitution, violence, bloodshed, vengeance, find an echo in many of the major Elizabethan and Kabuki plays. Refinement and barbarism, both occasionally beyond modern taste, shock us by their juxtaposition in Marlowe, Shakespeare, Ford, and Webster, as they do in works of Chikamatsu or Takeda Izumo. Both theatres are characterized by the historical or legendary raised to the level of the heroic, the encounter between natural and supernatural worlds, insoluble problems ending in death jostled by scenes of the utmost gaiety.

## THE ACTORS

The early Elizabethan actor was more versatile than his modern counterpart. Like the Kabuki actor, he was a dancer and an acrobat as well. "In letters dealing with English players on the Continent in the 1580's," Beckerman tells us, "acting is always linked with dancing, vaulting, and tumbling." [3] An Englishman visiting in Germany comments on how the Germans, "not understanding a word [the actors] said, both men and women, flocked wonderfully to see their gestures and action, rather than hear them, speaking English which they understood not." [4] Such an attitude suggests that there was something worth watching more than mere walking and handling of objects. As late as 1592 a man writes from Nuremberg, "The English comedians have wonderful music and are so skilled at tumbling and dancing that I have never heard nor seen the like." [5] I have found no indications that Alleyn or Burbage were tumblers, or dancers. But it is interesting to note that they were part of a theatre which did include dancing and tumbling, and that we may see just such a theatre today, since Kabuki, unlike modern acting, has not divorced itself from its early traditions.

Whether Alleyn and Burbage and the other major actors of their day tumbled and danced or not, they were at any rate mas-

[3] Bernard Beckerman, *Shakespeare at the Globe, 1599–1609* (New York, 1962), pp. 123–24.
[4] Quoted in Alois Maria Nagler, *Shakespeare's Stage*, trans. Ralph Manheim (New Haven, 1958), p. 37.
[5] *Ibid.*, p. 83.

ters of a formal acting style which is lost today. Beckerman characterizes their style as romantic, Harbage as formal, while Joseph feels quite certain that they employed the gestures common in contemporary rhetorical delivery, perhaps exaggerating them for the needs of the theatre. A broad playing style must have been demanded by poorly lighted theatres, as well as by the public in the pit. Thorndike believes that "every means of facial expression and gesture should be employed in the depiction of emotion, making the action somewhat more intense than in the modern theatre." [6] Nagler, quoting a report of a performance of *Othello* by the King's Men at Oxford in 1610, describes how one spectator was impressed by Desdemona's death, "especially when she lay in bed, moving the spectators to pity solely by her face." Such an ability reminds one of the many occasions on which a Kabuki actor, for perhaps minutes on end, will register emotions by contraction of the facial muscles and movement of the eyes, achieving effects of great pathos. It was no doubt this gift which caused French audiences in 1900 to rhapsodize over the "dying" of Sadda Yacco who, they claimed, died even better than Sarah Bernhardt!

The Kabuki actor, using every facet of his body and voice to portray character and emotion, presents himself quite frankly as a theatrical creation on a stage before an audience. Basing all his movements, even the most realistic, on dance, the actor transforms every moment of the drama into a visually artistic experience. The presentational aspect of the Elizabethan actor's performance was underlined by the form of his stage, but in addition to this he might use such techniques as symmetrical blocking, or speaking directly to the audience, delivering his lines facing toward the public rather than toward his interlocutor onstage. Moreover, he tended to play not so much *in* a setting as *against* it. All of this might well be said of the Kabuki actor who still enjoys a stage structure and type of decor which thrust him toward the audience. The bridge stage, or *hanamichi,* which in important scenes, entrances, and exits, brings the actor into close intimacy with the audience, is an acting area of very special strength and emotional appeal, and one which has not yet been used signifi-

[6] Ashley H. Thorndike, *Shakespeare's Theatre* (New York, 1960), p. 403.

cantly in the West, despite the advice of Paul Claudel, who many years ago said of Kabuki:

It is not without analogy with Shakespearian drama, and the revolving stage and particularly the bridge or *hanamichi* which traverses the auditorium and permits unusual effects of distance and surprise, give it advantages which we would do well to imitate.[7]

## SYMBOLIC FORMS AND COLORS

If the Elizabethan actor gave more importance than we do to the meaning of movement and gesture, it was not simply because he enjoyed picturesque movement—although this is a justifiable reason in the theatre—but because he believed that the inner man was manifested in a visible way. The hunchback was not to be pitied but feared, for his disfigured body was a sign of a disfigured soul. "Man carried the mark of his class and his nature, in his walk, talk, features, and costume." [8] Certainly the twentieth-century theatre is aware of this, but perhaps out of fear of exaggeration or overemphasis it often fails to show such marks in any other way than through speech, and occasionally through makeup and a manner of walking. The Kabuki stage, harboring no such fears, gives each man or woman (courtesan, peasant, princess, samurai, merchant, demon) a different way of walking, a distinctive makeup (white-face, brown-face, red lines, black lines, purple lines, high eyebrows, no eyebrows, etc.), varying ways of using the voice (falsetto, broken falsetto, deep bass, musical intonations, guttural sputterings, etc.), and diverse colors and forms of costumes to suggest class, character, and feelings.

In an informative study of costume in Elizabethan drama, Linthicum describes in some detail the many symbolic values of color used on the Tudor stage. Not only costume color was indicative of character. Beards and hair as well might be changed to show changes in emotions:

If evidence of the dramas may be credited, . . . beards were dyed to harmonize with costumes or to reflect the mood of the wearer,

[7] "Une promenade à travers la littérature japonaise," in Paul Claudel, *Oeuvres complètes,* vol. iv (Paris, 1952), pp. 406–07.

[8] Beckerman, *op. cit.,* p. 14.

. . . happiness over the return of a favorite might be expressed by dyeing the beard carnation "speckled with green and russet." Catherine-pear-colored beards indicated a wicked disposition, and cane, straw, French crown, and Abraham-color beards had each a language.[9]

The practice of changing costume or makeup to express changes in character or emotion is a familiar one to the Kabuki spectator. An actor who has been disguised as a commoner but has finally revealed his true noble identity, may turn his back to the audience in order to pencil in the high, thick eyebrows which symbolize noble blood. An even more common practice is that very exciting moment of costume changing known as *hiki-nuki*. The actor's assistant pulls several threads which basted his top kimono together. At a climactic moment the assistant grabs the costume at the shoulders or sleeves while the actor steps forward into a pose, suddenly revealed in a completely different costume.

Lavish costumes immediately impress the foreigner viewing Kabuki. Accustomed to the relatively dull clothing worn on the realistic stage, he is unaware perhaps that the Western theatre was once similarly lavish in its use of costume. "No stage ever cared more for fine clothes than the Elizabethans," claims Thorndike, "or lavished on dress a larger portion of its expenses." [10] He goes on to point out that authenticity was not sought, but rather display. The Elizabethans would indeed be shocked at some of our modern dress performances of Shakespeare, for although they often wore contemporary clothing, it was of a magnitude almost unknown to us: ruffs and farthingales became so wide that they finally had to be regulated by law.

THE WOMEN'S ROLES

Our inability to conceive seriously of boys playing women's roles indicates not lack of imagination but lack of custom. Even as late as the Restoration men were playing the parts of women in England. Thorndike records Pepys' opinion that in Fletcher's *Loyal Subject* the actor Kynaston "made the loveliest lady that ever I

[9] Marie Channing Linthicum, *Costume in the Drama of Shakespeare and his Contemporaries* (Oxford, 1936), p. 14.

[10] Thorndike, p. 394.

saw in my life." [11] And Downes, he tells us, declared that "it has since been disputable among the judicious whether any woman that succeeded him so sensibly touched the audience as he." If a man could be lovely, feminine, and touching in a female role, it indicates not only his own skill, but the conventions of an audience who were willing to accept this particular kind of stylization.

While it would seem absurd to advocate the use of men to play women's parts today in the West, I think it is important for us to bear in mind that a stylized performance, such as this kind of impersonation requires, is not necessarily a cold, "alienated" performance which does not involve the audience. Just as the Kabuki actor can affect his audience, the Elizabethan boy could move his viewers to tears.

The English critic, Kenneth Tynan, goes so far as to suggest that Lady Macbeth is "basically a man's role," and that "it is probably a mistake to cast a woman [in the part] at all." [12]

Whether we would go so far or not, we must agree that the Kabuki actor of female roles can teach us something about what it means to be feminine, for his movements are more gracefully feminine than those of many women in everyday life, even in Japan where women are noted for grace and femininity. He can also remind us of two Renaissance customs which we have failed to use in our modern productions of Elizabethan plays, and which might add to their visual drama: chopines and lead white. Like the high-ranking courtesan or *oiran* in the Kabuki world, the Renaissance courtesan (and sometimes the "nice" women as well) would sometimes strut about in chopines, or thick-soled shoes, which added to her height if not to her grace. Rising from six to fifteen inches, the higher variety of chopines necessitated that the lady (like the *oiran*) be accompanied constantly by someone upon whose shoulder she might lean in order not to lose her balance. Again like the women of Kabuki, the Elizabethan beauty desired nothing so much as a milk-white skin, and often destroyed her complexion to achieve it. The standard cosmetic for this purpose was lead white, which soon marked the skin and

[11] *Ibid.*, p. 372.
[12] Kenneth Tynan, *Tynan on Theatre* (Middlesex, 1964), p. 108.

required even thicker coats of white paint.[13] The white, high-lighted with vermillion lips and rouged cheeks and bosom, might help us today to create some of those theatrical monsters which we have forgotten and which Genet has resuscitated with such effect in his later plays.

PRODUCTION TECHNIQUES

Similar performing conditions bred other resemblances between Kabuki and Elizabethan drama. The fact that short rehearsal periods were the rule, and a fixed group of actors was used in play after play, meant that scenic conventions developed, a kind of repertoire of devices, which probably would be handled in a similar way from play to play. The manner of handling asides, monologues, disguises, observation scenes and the like, was probably readily understood by the experienced actor so that a minimum of time was needed for rehearsing the technical aspects of such a scene. Kabuki exhibits a similar repertoire of devices, including the beautifully choreographed murder scene which is both aesthetically satisfying and spine chilling; the stylized fight scenes, once again a kind of dance in which no physical contact is made and the visual effect is heightened by an attack on our nerves by sharp wooden clappers. Head inspection, suicide, recitation of offstage events accompanied by a pantomimed description of the action, travel-scene dance duets, and pantomime lineup scenes are other devices common to the Kabuki stage.

A convention arising from the daytime performances of both theatres is that of evoking night by means other than actual lighting: by dialogue in the Elizabethan theatre and by the movements of the actors in Kabuki. Today, of course, we have recourse to lighting, and even the Kabuki, in an effort at modernity, will occasionally darken the stage for a night scene.

The two different manners of dealing with this problem are symptomatic of a very basic difference between Kabuki and Elizabethan theatre: the former stresses movement, dance, ges-

[13] See the enlightening chapters in Elizabeth Burton, *The Pageant of Elizabethan England* (New York, 1958), pp. 235–242, and Carroll Camden, *The Elizabethan Woman* (Houston, 1952), pp. 178–186.

ture, color, music, largely discounting literary or poetic values of the text, while the latter gives more importance to the text than it does to visual and musical values of presentation. It is possible, however, that scholars largely concerned with literary values of the texts have tended to give them more importance than the Elizabethans did. Since the contemporaries of Shakespeare and Marlowe were often lax in their preservation and handling of manuscripts (to say nothing of their revisions of them in performance), we are justified in wondering whether they attached to them the importance which we do today. If the acting traditions of Burbage had come down to us in an unbroken line, as the Kabuki techniques have since the middle of the seventeenth century, perhaps we would be better able to determine whether we are putting undue emphasis on the text.

Precisely because of this fundamental difference between the literary (as we have been taught to believe) theatre of the Elizabethans and the nonliterary [14] Kabuki theatre, it seems to me that it is desirable that we attempt to find some way of harmonizing the two perspectives in one "total" theatre. In combining the highly theatrical and sensual techniques of Kabuki with the more literary virtues of poetry, philosophy, and psychology which are offered by the great Elizabethan texts (to say nothing of their own theatrical and sensual values) we might hope to achieve a maximum of appeal to the senses, the emotions, the imagination, and to our atrophied sense of childish wonder, at the same time arriving at a profound, and perhaps painful, perception of human truth.

[14] Actually it is inaccurate to call the Kabuki nonliterary, since the plays of the greatest Japanese dramatists, Chikamatsu, possess no mean literary value. But they are the exception rather than the rule.

PAUL CLAUDEL

# Modern Drama and Music *

Often in the course of my career as dramatist the problem of the union of music and drama, the word and the note, has inevitably presented itself to me as it had done to many of my predecessors in the most different countries and the most remote ages. Everyone will have in mind the voluminous literature devoted to this question by Richard Wagner, and if any man seemed capable of finding a solution, it was certainly that great genius, who was magnificently gifted both as dramatist and musician. And it would be unjust to say that he totally failed in this immense undertaking. *Tannhäuser* is, on the whole, a grand drama, admirably composed, in which the music poignantly amplifies and colors the emotions of the characters. In my opinion it is the work in which Wagner's soul found its most authentic and complete expression. *Lohengrin* would also be a great success if it were possible to stretch it on new canvas, as is done with old pictures, and to strip it of the romantic frippery that renders it nearly unbearable today. As to *Tristan,* I object to its uniform, monochrome tone and also to the dramatic mediocrity of the libretto. When a gentleman and a lady have repeated throughout two whole acts: "I love you"—"You love me," the spectator thinks this enough; if he discovers that in the third act it is all beginning over again, he is driven to despair and seized with a desire to flee that all the solos of the clarionet are incapable of appeasing.

Instead of choosing as my subject the drama and music, I might have chosen love duets, and I should thus have had an opportunity of working off an old grudge, which is probably in the

* Reprinted from *The Yale Review,* XX (1930). It is reprinted by permission of the editors, copyright,© , Yale University Press.

back of your mind as it is in mine. But I might have been carried away by it. I should like, however, to make here a brief comment. The presentation of a love duet on the stage is fraught with difficulties. During the war, everyone witnessed the awkward plight of artists who had to sing a national anthem and—to render their part more heroic—thought it well to carry a flag. But how unwise this was! One can do only two things with a flag: either brandish it at arm's length or passionately crush it to one's breast. When these two gestures—that have nothing very novel about them—have been repeated several times, the audience feels its emotion subsiding. Now, the case is exactly the same with love duets. The actor who takes the lover's part can do only two things with the prima donna: either hold her at arm's length in order to view his good fortune the better—all the while vigorously shaking his head—or passionately clasp her in his arms. And the audience gets about the same pleasure from these two gestures, when they have been made a number of times, as from the business of the flag. It should be added that the two performers, while they are engaged in these minor gymnastics, have a more serious and difficult task to perform—they must attend to a hard, ticklish score. This somewhat detracts from the sincerity and conviction of unreserved plastic expression, especially when the Isolde that Tristan is to handle has, as is generally the case, a certain amplitude of figure.

But to return to my subject, the union of music and drama. —

As the reader has doubtless already become aware, I am not a musician. It is, therefore, not from the point of view of music that I shall approach the question. I go to the opera as rarely as possible, and I have had little experience on this side. So far as I can see, a regular opera is composed of a series of musical numbers, connected by some sort of action: say, solos, choruses, duets, ballets, overtures, trios, septets, and so on, affording an opportunity for the musician to exercise his talent. In short, it is a concert in fancy dress, the intervals and transitions of which are more or less filled up by some vague noise. Only, in a concert, the singers can stand motionless if they choose, while in an opera they feel bound to indulge in conventional, ridiculous gestures of absolutely no use for their essential purpose, such as the long-drawn elaboration of some dizzy F. I shall not speak of the costumes,

the scenery, and staging, which are generally wretched and which will before long become insufferable to the most patient audience. A little while ago I was present at a performance of *Carmen,* and I had the feeling that it is soon going to be difficult to make the public believe that all Spaniards are clad in green boleros and sky-blue tights, even though the latter are adorned with a pretty yellow band.

If you prefer another definition of the opera, I might say that it is a dramatic action offering an occasion for several situations upon which the orchestra and the actors comment lyrically. For whatever a singer may do, his business is not to act but to sing and to express the movements of his soul with his voice rather than with his limbs.

Of course, there is no form of art, however mediocre and absurd, that will not yield to genius or to that mysterious force, often so oddly applied, which we call "conviction." And genius and conviction sometimes manage to do something even with the opera. Of this strange outcome I can give a few examples, such as Gluck's *Orpheus,* Beethoven's *Fidelio,* Berlioz's *Trojans,* Wagner's *Tannhäuser,* Verdi's *Rigoletto.* Recently, however, I had an experience which gave me pause. I was present at a performance of *Don Giovanni,* at the Metropolitan Opera House, and after a few moments devoted to a refreshing nap, I found, to my great amazement, that I was following the piece with some interest. And yet it would have been difficult to imagine a form of art and, I must own it frankly, a kind of music more repugnant to my taste. That mysterious force called "conviction" was operating upon me, and I regretted having to leave before this experience had reached a decisive stage.

Wagner had a clear idea of the hybrid, artificial character of the opera and of the kind of suffering caused an audience by the fact that their minds are divided and that they do not know whether they have been invited to a play or a concert. He tried to increase the importance of the drama, to immerse the actors more deeply in it (forbidding them to turn toward the spectators), and to carry all the action along on an orchestral flood, a continuous torrent of passion and desire sustained by remembrance and a sort of nostalgic remorse. In fact the lyrical commentary, which the old opera simply assigned to a tenor or a

soprano, Wagner reserved entirely for the orchestra. Let us suppose, for instance, that the composer wants to express this idea: "How beautiful the weather is today; I believe it is a good time to take a walk." In an Italian opera, the tenor would come to the footlights, with a hand on his heart, and supported by a few discreet chords would have no difficulty in imparting his feelings. Wagner, on the contrary, would paint for us with the orchestra all surrounding nature in a mist of sonorous dreams, the singer playing a part in them and his voice emerging, as it were, accidentally. In reality a Wagner drama is a vast symphony, in which the true characters are the leitmotifs, and human beings intervene—in general, pretty laboriously—only to explain where we are, what has happened, what is happening, and what will happen. The human mouth therein is far less important than the silver mouth of the flute or the golden one of the trumpet, and it completely disappears in the continual breaking down of the harmonic superpositions in which the great artist delights. There remains only a submerged gesticulating image.

I am far from wishing to suggest that Wagner did not have a dramatic temperament; on the contrary, he had a very profound, if not an unerring, one. But every situation called forth in him sonorous upheavings which swallowed up all the rest, and which subsided somewhat only to swell again into new waves a little farther on.

On the whole, I think that it would not be giving a bad definition of a Wagner drama to say that it is a symphony with a continuous program and less an action than the sonorous memory of an action.

I have said enough of the way in which musicians have made use of the drama in the practice of their art. My real purpose is to examine what use dramatists can make of music.

One use we can discard at the outset: it is the introduction of music in the guise of a prelude or a detached piece as, for instance, when one of the characters sings a little song or when some vocal or instrumental concert must, for some reason or other, take place. Nothing is more dangerous. The musician is never given his share, and he, as a rule, does not care a straw for the play, his only idea being to find a place for a little score. The action is kept standing still, on one leg, so to speak, until the per-

formers make an end of their pleasant noise. Moreover, between the atmosphere of the spoken word and that of music there exists an almost distressing difference, and the passing from one to the other results in a complete destruction of the spell which the poor poet has been at such pains to cast over the spectators.

How is it, then, that not only the Greek theatre but all primitive theatres, up to and including the stage during the period of melodrama from 1840 to 1880, used music?

I got my first explanation of this fact at a performance of *L'Annonce faite à Marie* given in Paris at the Comédie des Champs-Elysées, with the assistance of M. Gémier. There is a scene in this play in which the head of a family, on the point of undertaking a long journey, breaks bread for the last time with his children and his servants gathered around the table. This is an idea which looks natural on paper, but it is difficult for it to escape ridicule when presented on the stage. And indeed at the first performances I never witnessed that touching picture without feeling a shudder run along my spine as if I had heard a false note. Gémier, prompted by his vast dramatic experience, did not hesitate a moment: "We must have some music," he exclaimed. They set going a *glockenspiel* of some sort, and the scene passed off triumphantly, the sound of the bells at once conferring upon it the atmosphere, the ambient, the dignity, and remoteness, which the words alone, in their thinness and bareness, were unable to provide. And the cinema, of course, offers many instances of the same kind. Any pantomime or dumb show is simply impossible without musical support.

I had carried the recollection of this incident to Japan where, for several years, I occupied a diplomatic post, and where I was a constant spectator at the admirable national theatre called Kabuki, now unfortunately on the way to disappearance, like all things of beauty in this world, under the influence of our coarse, materialistic civilization. The long hours which I spent at the Imperial Theatre watching with emotion the unfolding of the heroic epics of the Genroku period were for me a true professional school of drama. Unluckily this was rather late, at a time when I had given up all dramatic ambitions —the more so as the modern stage, taken up by ecstatic debates of amorous psychology, would collapse under the heavy buskin of a hero or a demi-

god. I then understood what dramatic music is, that is to say, music used by a dramatist, not by a musician, not aiming at the realization of a sound picture but giving impulse and pace to our emotions through a medium purely rhythmical and tonal, more direct and more brutal than the spoken word. We are, let us say, at the dénouement of a play. The atmosphere is stormy. Somebody arrives. Something is going to happen. It is one of those situations where in Europe a whole orchestra would be used. In Japan you have only a little yellow man perched on a platform, with a tiny cup of tea by his side and in front a tremendous drum, which it is his rôle to beat. I will call him the director of thunder. Those single hollow thumps, repeated at first at long intervals, then more vigorously and rapidly until the frightful, expected apparition comes at last, racking our nerves, are enough without any orchestra or score to put us in the desired ambient. In the same way, when anger rises and two human cocks are on the point of coming to blows, or when some peremptory intervention occurs, three or four hard, sharp clacks, with a bat on the stage floor are enough to silence speech and to make way for authority. So a teacher raps his desk with his ruler to call his class to attention.

To take another example: in *Tristan and Isolde,* when the lovers, after drinking the fatal potion, cast on each other distracted looks and suddenly feel burning passion take the place of hatred in their souls, the tremolo of the violin, like the vibration of a soul on the verge of breaking, is all the dramatist needs to have, and the rest of the orchestral commentary seems useless. The sound, the rhythm, the tone of cymbals or a bell do not form with the spoken word so sharp a contrast as does music which belongs to another sphere. On the other hand, the directing of a modern orchestra, whose path is implacably traced by little black signs and measure bars on the rigid stave, has not sufficient life and suppleness. On the Japanese stage the musician is himself an actor. He watches the development of the drama, which he freely punctuates, at the right moment, with whatever instrument, guitar, lyre, or hammer, may have been placed in his hand, or simply with his voice —for this is a magnificent element in the Japanese theatre that I have failed to mention. Side by side with articulated voice goes the inarticulate voice —grumbling,

exclamation, doubt, surprise, all the human feelings expressed by simple intonations in charge of those official witnesses of the play sitting squat in their little boxes. When we are in the grip of the play we are grateful to the anonymous fellow who utters cries for us and assumes the task of expressing our feelings by something less conventional than plaudits or hisses.

Music in the classical drama of Japan and of China has also another rôle, which is to express continuity. It is the *current* of the story, as we speak of the *current* of a river. It is the latent revenge of narration upon action, of duration upon incident. Its business is to give the sensation of the flow of time, to create an ambient, an atmosphere, for in life we not only speak or act, we listen, we are surrounded by something vague, diverse, and changing to which we must needs give attention. According to this conception, music does not aim at sustaining and underlining the words; it often precedes and provokes them, it invites expression through feeling, it sketches the sentences leaving to us the task to finish them. It follows a path parallel to our own. It attends to its special business while we, our ears filled with its murmur of memories, forebodings, and counsels, read at sight *our* score. When necessary it weaves behind the drama a tapestry of sounds, the colors of which both divert and relieve the spectators, and suffuse with their pleasing suggestions the dryness of a description or of an explanation. Such music is to the ear what a back-scene is to the eye. In the same way the sound of a waterspout or of cages full of birds agreeably mingles with our conversation and carries along on a stream of reverie the prose of our everyday affairs.

And since the wanderings of my thought have led me to speak of China I should like to say a word about a great actor who recently gave in New York a series of performances and whom I had much pleasure in seeing once more. I mean the famous Mei Lan-fang. Mei Lan-fang takes only women's or girls' parts, but he acts them with such airy grace that, in the manner of a transcendent mirror, he divests them not only of all sexual suggestions but even, if I may say so, of their temporality. He is neither man nor woman: he is a sylph. All the sentiments and emotions, owing to the delightful fluidity of his postures, are not so much expressed as transposed by him—to the domain of music. It is

music, a long melopoeia of the violin emphasized by the drum, which takes possession of that elegant body, from the nervous spring of the legs up to the last articulated detail of his resourceful hands and sharp-nailed fingers, and which regulates the whole outline of the mimic sentence. His feet give the impetus, his arms draw the general line upon which the nimble phalanges inscribe dainty *appoggiaturas.* The very singing of that charming being, like the humming of a flying insect, only serves to associate the man more intimately with the melodious solicitation and the soul with the action of the body. It is an enchanting spectacle.

For a writer theories are only the—often temporary—scaffolding that serves to prop his productions. And so it seems to me that instead of keeping to the domain of dreams and doctrines it might be more interesting if I were to add a few words about a work to which the various ideas just stated served as accompaniment and support. I have in mind a play for which I received an order from a producer who, after showing intemperate enthusiasm, refused to accept it. This fact, by the by, only resulted in advantage to me, for my play, *Christopher Columbus,* thus abandoned by Herr Max Reinhardt, was eventually performed with Darius Milhaud's music at the Staatsoper in Berlin. It is of this play, which has been published by the Yale University Press with Jean Charlot's illustrations, that I should like to speak before bringing this article to a conclusion. The conditions of the contract, laid upon my desk by the invisible powers whose virtual and imperious agent Herr Reinhardt had consented to be, contained interesting possibilities. The work was to be a historical drama, and, up to that time, I had written only works of pure imagination. Music and, it was specified, choruses were to play an important part. So all through the writing of the drama I had to bear with some implied collaborator, a collaborator who, naturally, could be no other than my friend Darius Milhaud, with whom I have been for years on terms of close intimacy in both ideas and feelings. My rôle, then, consisted in looking on Christopher Columbus, in turning over the leaves of his history and legends, in evoking the principal scenes, one after the other, and in waiting for the questions, objections, and comments which the musician, through the collective medium of the orchestra and

chorus, would have to present in the name of the public—that audience surrounding a great man and a great event which is composed of all peoples and of all the generations.

A life, a work, a destiny, the most sublime that can be, that of the inventor of a new world and the welder of God's earth, is unfolded on the stage, and the reactions and emotions provoked in us by that spectacle do not remain unexpressed. By turns murmuring applause and issuing a challenge, the public follows all the incidents of the drama—that anonymous power which we call Opinion, the opinion of which the press today has become the mouthpiece, the opinion of posterity which supports, espouses, opposes, or reinforces the opinion of Columbus's contemporaries.

In such a drama music plays an entirely different part from what it has previously played down in front of the stage. It is no longer a simple resonator; it does not merely accompany a song; it is a true actor, a collective person with diverse voices, whose voices are reunited in a harmony, the function of which is to bring together all the rest and to disengage little by little, under the inspiration of a growing enthusiasm, the elements of the final hymn.

Pascal has very justly said: "Prolonged eloquence is tedious." I am inclined to modify his thought thus: "Prolonged music, prolonged poetry are tedious." The soul is not all the time in the same state of tension, and this applies to the spectators as well as to the actors on the stage. It needs, now and then, to come down to earth, if only to find a new base from which to spring again. For the author, and with him the spectators, it is advantageous to do as the wine tasters do in France, who, at intervals, suck a piece of lemon to wash out their mouths and so be better prepared to appreciate the next sip of nectar. A drama thus understood is not a monotonous flight amidst the uninterrupted purring of the orchestra or the versification. It is a series of outbursts and abatements.

I mentioned Wagner earlier in this article. The glory of that great man was his understanding that all things which partake of sound, from speech to song, are bound together by subtle links reaching across different realms, and that music is inherent in whatever is realized in time, whether it merely imposes rhythm

upon those realizations or gradually colors them with various tones and raises them at last to the full expression of the orchestra and of song. His only mistake was in not establishing degrees between reality and the lyrical state, and by this he impoverished his palette of sounds and narrowed the scope of his flight. With him we do not penetrate little by little a conquered or deserved world; we are placed at the outset, through an enchanted blending of tones and the incantation of the brasses, in a narcotic atmosphere in which everything happens as in a dream.

Milhaud and I, on the other hand, have tried to show how the soul gradually reaches music, how the sentence springs up from rhythm, the flame from fire, melody from speech, poetry from the coarsest reality, and how all the means of sonorous expression, from discourse, dialogue, and debate, sustained by simple beatings of the drum, up to an eruption of all the vocal, lyrical, orchestral riches, are gathered in a single torrent at once varied and uninterrupted. In a word, we wanted to show music not only in the state of full realization, as a cryptic language portioned out among the pages of a score, but in the nascent state, rising and overflowing from some violent feeling.

Christopher Columbus is seen dying in the Valladolid inn, whither he has crawled to ask the King for the means to sail once more. And at that moment, as all his past on the point of reaching its final issue reappears before his eyes, the hero, so to speak, divides into two and becomes for us both spectator and judge of his own epic. Scene follows scene. We see the line of the horizon toward the West! The dove, image of the Holy Ghost, crosses the sea and comes to Genoa, bringing to the hands of a child its fluttering message. The sailor at the Azores receives intercepted revelations from beyond the Ocean and from beyond the Tomb. Genius strives against creditors and courtiers, against the envious and the skeptic. The captain quells rebellion. And then comes the hour of the Passion: the censure and bickering of petty minds; the Discoverer of the Globe lashed by a cook to the mast of his ship and buffeted by the rage of men and the fury of the elements; the prodigious ingratitude of the whole world, one woman excepted. Death approaches, and, finally, the dove, that, as in the days of the Flood, escapes and bears a branch plucked from the newly risen world to the bosom of the Pantocrator!

All this is not performed in the void. Every voice, every word, every act, every event calls for an echo, an answer. They bring about and diffuse a kind of collective, anonymous roaring as of a sea of generations following one another, looking on and listening.

This I have called the Chorus. It is not the Chorus of the ancient drama—that troop of commentators and self-appointed advisers that no protagonist, if he were ever so little eloquent, had any difficulty in enlisting on the Mediterranean quays. It is, rather, the Chorus which the Church, after the triumph of Christianity, invited to enter the sacred edifice to become an intermediary between the priest and the people, the one *officiating,* the other *official.* Between the speechless crowd and the drama developing on the stage—and if I may say so, on the altar—there was needed an officially constituted interpreter.

*Christopher Columbus,* as it was given in Berlin and may be given some day in America, may be interesting also because of another novelty. This novelty originated from a desire to have no walls—for eyes or for ears—to submit to no ready-made stage spectacle, so that instead we might evoke for ourselves our own music and scenery and paint its ever changing surges on the panels of the magic box in which we are confined for an instant. In a musical drama whose characteristic is the transformation, under the action of time, of disconnected events into one melodic line, why should we admit immobile scenery? Why not let the images suggested by poetry and sound be exhaled like smoke and be caught for a moment on the screen, gradually to disappear and give place to other visions? Why, in a word, not make use of the cinema? Everyone has indeed noticed that a fixed piece of scenery, an unchanging backdrop, once the first effect has been produced, tires and displeases the eyes and tends to spoil the poetic illusion by the admixture of an inferior element rather than to keep it up. Then why not treat the scenery like a simple frame, like a conventional foreground behind which a path is open to dreams, to memory, and to imagination? When a stream of music, of action, and poetry is carrying away the soul of the spectator, why meet it with a sham sky as trivial and gaudy as the walls of a coffeehouse? Why not devise, instead of that inert cloth, a surface sensitive to thought? Why not use the screen as a

magic glass in which all sorts of images and of suggestions, more or less dim in outline, may pass, move, join, or part? Why not open the door of that indistinct world where ideas are born from sensations and where the phantom of the future mingles with the ghost of the past? For the expression of the finest *nuances* of feeling, memory, and thought, why not utilize the infinitely subtle harmony of shadows? Movements, values, clusters of forms and appearances continually decomposed and recomposed, this is all the cinema and it is also all music. It seems to me, therefore, that these two arts are naturally destined to contract an alliance, the formula for which America, better than any other country, might help the artist to discover.

JEAN-LOUIS BARRAULT

## On the "Total Theatre" and *Christopher Columbus* *

The theatre is also a show. Around this "man-theatre" who moves, lives, acts, burns, and dies, and who in himself *is the whole theatre,* one is in the habit of calling on the other arts to frame him and pay him homage, just as one is in the habit of framing a picture out of a sentiment of homage and to obtain a more favorable presentation.

And, as a handsome and appropriate frame has never spoilt a fine picture, so a fine production has never marred good dramatic action.

The production itself is composed of the conjuncture of the other arts, of their participation; it is, indeed, what Baudelaire called "the coincidence of the arts." It is up to those concerned with the theatre not to degrade it to the level of "the complicity of the arts" in order to put over bad theatre.

* From *World Theatre,* XIV:6 (1965).

As Copeau said: "Those that get involved in this easy quest (refinements of lighting or décor), on the pretext of "total art," are engaged on a wrong—a particularly deceptive—course. Which means that the "interior decorator" does not participate in the achievement of the "complete theatre."

It happens, however, that the production ceases to be merely a frame and rises to the level of essential theatre: it becomes, in a way, humanized, attains the stature of the characters and participates in the action; then, the production *signifies the work* on a par with the actors.

I also remember certain transformations in the *Soulier de Satin* and in *Antoine et Cléopâtre;* the admirable imbrication, for instance, of Pompey's galley with the characters!

And a given property—armchair, lance, bunch of flowers, etc.—also becomes a presence, at times.

And certain costumes as well.

This applies even more definitely to certain musical interventions of which the themes appear as magical emanations of human nature.

The most important point in the mounting of a play consists, therefore, in finding the means of so raising the level of the production (décor, props, lighting, sound effects, music) that it no longer contents itself with the secondary role of "frame" or mixture of the arts but succeeds, on the contrary, in humanizing itself to such an extent that it virtually becomes part of the action, that it succeeds, in short, in serving the theatre in its totality—at this moment, the total theatre achieves *unity*.

On this score, *Christophe Colomb* is an attempt at total theatre. In this work of Claudel, as we understood and sought to serve it, man's part is preponderant. Our objective is not to discuss the manner in which the performance actually proceeds, which is not our concern, but rather the manner in which we would like it to proceed.

A troop of men and women—although called "actors," all are primarily "human beings"—march onto the stage in procession, singing in unison with joy and pride. For "the fun of it" or for their spiritual nourishment (which comes to the same thing), they decide to reenact the life of Christopher Columbus.

Alternatively spinning wool, playing the guitar, becoming waves, walking, running, undulating on the sea, receiving the wind, dead, living, assuming reality, becoming shade, bellowing as Indian gods, howling like the tempest, murmuring like the breeze, prattling like gossips, indignant as mutineers, singing their joy, shouting their enthusiasm, whispering their advice, becoming motionless as a picture, stamping like maniacs, withdrawing from the action, reentering it, spectators, commentators, actors: these men and women would conjure up a semblance of our dream of complete theatre. We would, in a way, be able to experience "the drama in the state of inception." Another formula!

Ah! the admirable formula! Ah! the two-edged sword! The essential point would be that it all stemmed from a sincere, indispensable, exigent, imperious sensation. And now let us imagine—as we have a perfect right to do as we are dreaming —that our dream came true.

This troop of men operates with the human means at its disposal and then, suddenly, the objects that it utilizes begin to live in unison—the objects humanize themselves: the chains grate with precision, the sail billows like a living creature. Does one need a court dress? Two flaps detach themselves from the dress one is wearing and become a hoop. Does one need peasant garb? The back part of the dress curls up over the head and is transformed by means of petticoating. One rolls up one's trousers and, bare-chested, becomes a sailor.

Let us go on with our dream.

The lighting joins in, the projectors displace themselves, the luminous intensity oscillates, the cast shadows appear, fade away, change shape according to the movements of the object that receives them. As for the music, it behaves like the men of the troop: by turns actor and commentator. It proposes, it intervenes, it traces lines of joy or of distress, it stretches voluptuously, it stamps with impatience or vitality, it is most often the soul of the adventure—human soul.

Men and objects play together: the men playing at being objects and the objects at being men.

But whatever the future attempts we may happen to make, we must never forget that, above all, for the playwright and all those

that serve it, the *theatre is man:* and that "as long as on four raised boards, wherever it may be, a man, with nothing around him, expresses himself with the totality of his means of expression: there will be theatre, and if one wishes, *complete theatre . . .*"

As for innovations in lighting, disposition, setting, and apparatus that pertain to the art of the "interior decorator" and not to that of the creator, these remain useful if restricted to a secondary role, but become dangerous if they are given precedence over the essential. And they can only breed confusion if they are confounded with what, for the needs of the cause, we *provisionally* call "total theatre."

ANTONIN ARTAUD

On the Balinese Theatre *

The spectacle of the Balinese theatre, which draws upon dance, song, pantomime —and a little of the theatre as we understand it in the Occident —restores the theatre, by means of ceremonies of indubitable age and well-tried efficacity, to its original destiny which it presents as a combination of all these elements fused together in a perspective of hallucination and fear.

It is very remarkable that the first of the little plays which compose this spectacle, in which we are shown a father's remonstrances to his tradition-flouting daughter, begins with an entrance of phantoms; the male and female characters who will develop a dramatic but familiar subject appear to us first in their spectral aspect and are seen in that hallucinatory perspective appropriate to every theatrical character, before the situations in this kind of symbolic sketch are allowed to develop. Here indeed

* Reprinted from *The Theater and Its Double* by Antonin Artaud, translated from the French by Mary Caroline Richards, copyright, © , 1958, by Grove Press, Inc. and reprinted with their permission.

situations are only a pretext. The drama does not develop as a conflict of feelings but as a conflict of spiritual states, themselves ossified and transformed into gestures—diagrams. In a word, the Balinese have realized, with the utmost rigor, the idea of pure theatre, where everything, conception and realization alike, has value, has existence only in proportion to its degree of objectification *on the stage*. They victoriously demonstrate the absolute preponderance of the director (*metteur en scène*) whose creative power *eliminates words*. The themes are vague, abstract, extremely general. They are given life only by the fertility and intricacy of all the artifices of the stage which impose upon our minds like the conception of a metaphysics derived from a new use of gesture and voice.

What is in fact curious about all these gestures, these angular and abruptly abandoned attitudes, these syncopated modulations formed at the back of the throat, these musical phrases that break off short, these flights of elytra, these rustlings of branches, these sounds of hollow drums, these robot squeakings, these dances of animated manikins, is this: that through the labyrinth of their gestures, attitudes, and sudden cries, through the gyrations and turns which leave no portion of the stage space unutilized, the sense of a new physical language, based upon signs and no longer upon words, is liberated. These actors with their geometric robes seem to be animated hieroglyphs. It is not just the shape of their robes which, displacing the axis of the human figure, create beside the dress of these warriors in a state of trance and perpetual war a kind of second, symbolic dress and thus inspire an intellectual idea, or which merely connect, by all the intersections of their lines, with all the intersections of perspective in space. No, these spiritual signs have a precise meaning which strikes us only intuitively but with enough violence to make useless any translation into logical discursive language. And for the lovers of realism at all costs, who might find exhausting these perpetual allusions to secret attitudes inaccessible to thought, there remains the eminently realistic play of the double who is terrified by the apparitions from beyond. In this double —trembling, yelping childishly, these heels striking the ground in cadences that follow the very automatism of the liberated unconscious, this momentary concealment behind his own reality

—*there* is a description of fear valid in every latitude, an indication that in the human as well as the superhuman the Orientals are more than a match for us in matters of reality.

The Balinese, who have a vocabulary of gesture and mime for every circumstance of life, reinstate the superior worth of theatrical conventions, demonstrate the forcefulness and greater emotional value of a certain number of perfectly learned and above all masterfully applied conventions. One of the reasons for our delight in this faultless performance lies precisely in the use these actors make of an exact quantity of specific gestures, of well-tried mime at a given point, and above all in the prevailing spiritual tone, the deep and subtle study that has presided at the elaboration of these plays of expression, these powerful signs which give us the impression that their power has not weakened during thousands of years. These mechanically rolling eyes, pouting lips, and muscular spasms, all producing methodically calculated effects which forbid any recourse to spontaneous improvisation, these horizontally moving heads that seem to glide from one shoulder to the other as if on rollers, everything that might correspond to immediate psychological necessities, corresponds as well to a sort of spiritual architecture, created out of gesture and mime but also out of the evocative power of a system, the musical quality of a physical movement, the parallel and admirably fused harmony of a tone. This may perhaps shock our European sense of stage freedom and spontaneous inspiration, but let no one say that this mathematics creates sterility or uniformity. The marvel is that a sensation of richness, of fantasy and prodigality emanates from this spectacle ruled with a maddening scrupulosity and consciousness. And the most commanding interpenetrations join sight to sound, intellect to sensibility, the gesture of a character to the evocation of a plant's movement across the scream of an instrument. The sighs of wind instruments prolong the vibrations of vocal cords with a sense of such oneness that you do not know whether it is the voice itself that is continuing or the identity which has absorbed the voice from the beginning. A rippling of joints, the musical angle made by the arm with the forearm, a foot falling, a knee bending, fingers that seem to be coming loose from the hand, it is all like a perpetual play of mirrors in which human limbs seem resonant with

echoes, harmonies in which the notes of the orchestra, the whispers of wind instruments evoke the idea of a monstrous aviary in which the actors themselves would be the fluttering wings. Our theatre which has never had the idea of this metaphysics of gesture nor known how to make music serve such immediate, such concrete dramatic ends, our purely verbal theatre, unaware of everything that makes theatre, of everything that exists in the air of the stage, which is measured and circumscribed by that air and has a density in space—movements, shapes, colors, vibrations, attitudes, screams—our theatre might, with respect to the unmeasurable, which derives from the mind's capacity for receiving suggestion, be given lessons in spirituality from the Balinese theatre. This purely popular and not sacred theatre gives us an extraordinary idea of the intellectual level of a people who take the struggles of a soul preyed upon by ghosts and phantoms from the beyond as the basis for their civic festivals. For it is indeed a purely interior struggle that is staged in the last part of the spectacle. And we can remark in passing on the degree of theatrical sumptuousness which the Balinese have been able to give this struggle: their sense of the plastic requirements of the stage is equaled only by their knowledge of physical fear and the means of unleashing it. And there is in the truly terrifying look of their devil (probably Tibetan) a striking similarity to the look of a certain puppet in our own remembrance, a puppet with swollen hands of white gelatine and nails of green foliage, which was the most beautiful ornament of one of the first plays performed by Alfred Jarry's theatre.

This spectacle is more than we can assimilate, assailing us with a superabundance of impressions, each richer than the next, but in a language to which it seems we no longer have the key; and this kind of irritation created by the impossibility of finding the thread and tracking the beast down—the impossibility of putting one's ear closer to the instrument in order to hear better—is one charm the more to the credit of this spectacle. And by language I do not mean an idiom indecipherable at first hearing, but precisely that sort of theatrical language foreign to every *spoken tongue,* a language in which an overwhelming stage experience seems to be communicated, in comparison with which

our productions depending exclusively upon dialogue seem like so much stuttering.

What is in fact most striking in this spectacle—so well contrived to disconcert our Occidental conceptions of theatre that many will deny it has any theatrical quality, whereas it is the most beautiful manifestation of pure theatre it has been our privilege to see—what is striking and disconcerting for Europeans like ourselves is the admirable intellectuality that one senses crackling everywhere in the close and subtle web of gestures, in the infinitely varied modulations of voice, in this sonorous rain resounding as if from an immense dripping forest, and in the equally sonorous interlacing of movements. There is no transition from a gesture to a cry or a sound: all the senses interpenetrate, as if through strange channels hollowed out in the mind itself!

Here is a whole collection of ritual gestures to which we do not have the key and which seem to obey extremely precise musical indications, with something more that does not generally belong to music and seems intended to encircle thought, to hound it down and lead it into an inextricable and certain system. In fact everything in this theatre is calculated with an enchanting mathematical meticulousness. Nothing is left to chance or to personal initiative. It is a kind of superior dance, in which the dancers were actors first of all.

Repeatedly they seem to accomplish a kind of recovery with measured steps. Just when they appear to be lost in the middle of an inextricable labyrinth of measures or about to overturn in the confusion, they have their own way of recovering equilibrium, a particular buttressing of the body, of the twisted legs, which gives the impression of a sopping rag being wrung out in tempo; —and on three final steps, which lead them ineluctably to the middle of the stage, the suspended rhythm is completed, the measure made clear.

Everything is thus regulated and impersonal; not a movement of the muscles, not the rolling of an eye but seem to belong to a kind of reflective mathematics which controls everything and by means of which everything happens. And the strange thing is that in this systematic depersonalization, in these purely mus-

cular facial expressions, applied to the features like masks, everything produces a significance, everything affords the maximum effect.

A kind of terror seizes us at the thought of these mechanized beings, whose joys and griefs seem not their own but at the service of age-old rites, as if they were dictated by superior intelligences. In the last analysis it is this impression of a superior and prescribed Life which strikes us most in this spectacle that so much resembles a rite one might profane. It has the solemnity of a sacred rite—the hieratic quality of the costumes gives each actor a double body and a double set of limbs—and the dancer bundled into his costume seems to be nothing more than his own effigy. Over and beyond the music's broad, overpowering rhythm there is another extremely fragile, hesitant, and sustained music in which, it seems, the most precious metals are being pulverized, where springs of water are bubbling up as in the state of nature, and long processions of insects file through the plants, with a sound like that of light itself, in which the noises of deep solitudes seem to be distilled into showers of crystals, etc. . . .

Furthermore all these sounds are linked to movements, as if they were the natural consummation of gestures which have the same musical quality, and this with such a sense of musical analogy that the mind finally finds itself doomed to confusion, attributing to the separate gesticulations of the dancers the sonorous properties of the orchestra—and vice versa.

An impression of inhumanity, of the divine, of miraculous revelation is further provided by the exquisite beauty of the women's headdresses: this series of banked luminous circles, made from combinations of multicolored feathers or from pearls of so beautiful a coloration that their combination has a quality of *revelation,* and the crests of which tremble rhythmically, responding *consciously,* or so it seems, to the tremblings of the body.—There are also the other headdresses of sacerdotal character, in the shape of tiaras and topped with egret crests and stiff flowers in pairs of contrasting, strangely harmonizing colors.

This dazzling ensemble full of explosions, flights, secret streams, detours in every direction of both external and internal perception, composes a sovereign idea of the theatre, as it has

een preserved for us down through the centuries in order to each us what the theatre never should have ceased to be. And his impression is doubled by the fact that this spectacle—popular, it seems, and secular—is like the common bread of artistic ensations among those people.

Setting aside the prodigious mathematics of this spectacle, what seems most surprising and astonishing to us is this aspect of *matter as revelation,* suddenly dispersed in signs to teach us the metaphysical identity of concrete and abstract and to teach us his *in gestures made to last.* For though we are familiar with the realistic aspect of matter, it is here developed to the n power and definitively stylized.

.        .        .

In this theatre all creation comes from the stage, finds its expression and its origins alike in a secret psychic impulse which is Speech before words.

.        .        .

It is a theatre which eliminates the author in favor of what we would call, in our Occidental theatrical jargon, the director; but a director who has become a kind of manager of magic, a master of sacred ceremonies. And the material on which he works, the themes he brings to throbbing life are derived not from him but from the gods. They come, it seems, from elemental interconnections of Nature which a double Spirit has fostered.

What he sets in motion is the *manifested.*

This is a sort of primary Physics, from which Spirit has never disengaged itself.

.        .        .

In a spectacle like that of Balinese theatre there is something that has nothing to do with entertainment, the notion of useless, artificial amusement, of an evening's pastime which is the characteristic of our theatre. The Balinese productions take shape at the very heart of matter, life, reality. There is in them something of the ceremonial quality of a religious rite, in the sense that they extirpate from the mind of the onlooker all idea of pretense, of cheap imitations of reality. This intricately detailed gesticulation

has one goal, an immediate goal which it approaches by effica
cious means, whose efficacity we are even meant to experience
immediately. The thoughts it aims at, the spiritual states it seek
to create, the mystic solutions it proposes are aroused and at
tained without delay or circumlocution. All of which seems to be
an exorcism to make our demons *flow*.

.    .    .

There is a low hum of instinctual matters in this theatre, bu
they are wrought to that point of transparency, intelligence, and
ductility at which they seem to furnish us in physical terms some
of the spirit's most secret insights.

The themes selected derive, one might say, from the stage it
self. They have reached such a point of objective materialization
that one cannot imagine them outside this close perspective, this
confined and limited globe of performing space.

This spectacle offers us a marvelous complex of pure stage
images, for the comprehension of which a whole new language
seems to have been invented: the actors with their costumes con
stitute veritable living, moving hieroglyphs. And these three-
dimensional hieroglyphs are in turn brocaded with a certain
number of gestures—mysterious signs which correspond to
some unknown, fabulous, and obscure reality which we here in
the Occident have completely repressed.

There is something that has this character of a magic opera-
tion in this intense liberation of signs, restrained at first and then
suddenly thrown into the air.

A chaotic boiling, full of recognizable particles and at moments strangely orderly, crackles in this effervescence of painted
rhythms in which the many fermatas unceasingly make their entrance like a well-calculated silence.

Of this idea of pure theatre, which is merely theoretical in the
Occident and to which no one has ever attempted to give the least
reality, the Balinese offer us a stupefying realization, suppress-
ing all possibility of recourse to words for the elucidation of the
most abstract themes—inventing a language of gesture to be
developed in space, a language without meaning except in the
circumstances of the stage.

The stage space is utilized in all its dimensions and, one might say, on all possible planes. For in addition to an acute sense of plastic beauty, these gestures always have as their final goal the elucidation of a spiritual state or problem.

At least that is the way they appear to us.

No point of space and at the same time no possible suggestion has been lost. And there is a philosophical sense, so to speak, of the power which nature has of suddenly hurling everything into chaos.

.    .    .

One senses in the Balinese theatre a state prior to language and which can choose its own: music, gestures, movements, words.

.    .    .

It is certain that this aspect of pure theatre, this physics of absolute gesture which is the idea itself and which transforms the mind's conceptions into events perceptible through the labyrinths and fibrous interlacings of matter, gives us a new idea of what belongs by nature to the domain of forms and manifested matter. Those who succeed in giving a mystic sense to the simple form of a robe and who, not content with placing a man's Double next to him, confer upon each man in his robes a double made of clothes—those who pierce these illusory or secondary clothes with a saber, giving them the look of huge butterflies pinned in the air, such men have an innate sense of the absolute and magical symbolism of nature much superior to ours, and set us an example which it is only too certain our own theatre technicians will be powerless to profit from.

.    .    .

That intellectual space, psychic interplay, and silence solidified by thought which exist between the members of a written phrase is here, in the scenic space, traced between the members, the air, and the perspectives of a certain number of shouts, colors, and movements.

.    .    .

In the performances of the Balinese theatre the mind has the feeling that conception at first stumbled against gesture, gained its footing in the midst of a whole ferment of visual or sonorous images, thoughts as it were in a pure state. To put it briefly and more clearly, something akin to the musical state must have existed for this *mise-en-scène* where everything that is a conception of the mind is only a pretext, a virtuality whose double has produced this intense stage poetry, this many-hued spatial language.

.    .    .

This perpetual play of mirrors passing from color to gesture and from cry to movement leads us unceasingly along roads rough and difficult for the mind, plunges us into that state of uncertainty and ineffable anguish which is the characteristic of poetry.

These strange games of flying hands, like insects in the green air of evening, communicate a sort of horrible obsession, an inexhaustible mental ratiocination, like a mind ceaselessly taking its bearings in the maze of its unconscious.

And what this theatre makes palpable for us and captures in concrete signs are much less matters of feeling than of intelligence.

And it is by intellectual paths that it introduces us into the reconquest of the signs of what exists.

From this point of view the gesture of the central dancer who always touches his head at the same place, as if wishing to indicate the position and existence of some unimaginable central eye, some intellectual egg, is highly significant.

.    .    .

What occurs as a highly colored reference to physical impressions of nature is taken up again on the level of sounds, and the sound itself is only the nostalgic representation of something else, a sort of magic state where sensations have become so subtle that they are a pleasure for the spirit to frequent. And even the imitative harmonies, the sound of the rattlesnake and rustlings of dried insects against each other, suggest the glade of a swarming landscape ready to hurl itself into chaos. —And these

dancers dressed in dazzling clothes, whose bodies beneath seem wrapped in swaddling-bands! There is something umbilical, larval in their movement. And at the same time we must remark on the hieroglyphic aspect of their costumes, the horizontal lines of which project beyond the body in every direction. They are like huge insects full of lines and segments drawn to connect them with an unknown natural perspective of which they seem nothing more than a kind of detached geometry.

These costumes which encircle their abstract rotations when they walk, and the strange crisscrossings of their feet!

Each of their movements traces a line in space, completes some unknown rigorous figure in the ritual of a hermetic formula which an unforeseen gesture of the hand completes.

And the folds of these robes, curving above the buttocks, hold them as if suspended in air, as if pinned to the depths of the theatre, and prolong each of their leaps into a flight.

These howls, these rolling eyes, this continuous abstraction, these noises of branches, noises of the cutting and rolling of wood, all within the immense area of widely diffused sounds disgorged from many sources, combine to overwhelm the mind, to crystallize as a new and, I dare say, concrete conception of the abstract.

And it must be noted that when this abstraction, which springs from a marvelous scenic edifice to return into thought, encounters in its flight certain impressions from the world of nature, it always seizes them at the point at which their molecular combinations are beginning to break up: a gesture narrowly divides us from chaos.

.    .    .

The last part of the spectacle is—in contrast to all the dirt, brutality, and infamy chewed up by our European stages—a delightful anachronism. And I do not know what other theatre would dare to pin down in this way *as if true to nature* the throes of a soul at the mercy of phantasms from the Beyond.

.    .    .

These metaphysicians of natural disorder who in dancing restore to us every atom of sound and every fragmentary percep-

tion as if these were now about to rejoin their own generating principles, are able to wed movement and sound so perfectly that it seems the dancers have hollow bones to make these noises of resonant drums and woodblocks with their hollow wooden limbs.

Here we are suddenly in deep metaphysical anguish, and the rigid aspect of the body in trance, stiffened by the tide of cosmic forces which besiege it, is admirably expressed by that frenetic dance of rigidities and angles, in which one suddenly feels the mind begin to plummet downwards.

As if waves of matter were tumbling over each other, dashing their crests into the deep and flying from all sides of the horizon to be enclosed in one minute portion of tremor and trance—to cover over the void of fear.

.    .    .

There is an absolute in these constructed perspectives, a real physical absolute which only Orientals are capable of envisioning—it is in the loftiness and thoughtful boldness of their goals that these conceptions differ from our European conceptions of theatre, even more than in the strange perfection of their performances.

Advocates of the division and partitioning of genres can pretend to see mere dancers in the magnificent artists of the Balinese theatre, dancers entrusted with the representation of unexplained, lofty Myths whose very elevation renders the level of our modern Occidental theatre unspeakably gross and childish. The truth is that the Balinese theatre suggests, and in its productions *enacts,* themes of pure theatre upon which the stage performance confers an intense equilibrium, a wholly materialized gravity.

.    .    .

Everything in this theatre is immersed in a profound intoxication which restores to us the very elements of ecstasy, and in ecstasy we discover the dry seething, the mineral friction of plants, vestiges and ruins of trees illuminated on their faces.

Bestiality and every trace of animality are reduced to their

spare gesture: mutinous noises of the splitting earth, the sap of trees, animal yawns.

The dancers' feet, in kicking aside their robes, dissolve thoughts and sensations, permitting them to recover their pure state.

And always this confrontation of the head, this Cyclops' eye, the inner eye of the mind which the right hand gropes for.

The sign language of spiritual gestures which measure, prune, fix, separate, and subdivide feelings, states of the soul, metaphysical ideas.

This theatre of quintessences in which things perform a strange about-face before becoming abstractions again.

.    .    .

Their gestures fall so accurately upon this rhythm of the hollow drums, accent it, and seize it in flight with such sureness and at such climactic moments that it seems the very abyss of their hollow limbs which the music is going to scan.

.    .    .

And the women's stratified, lunar eyes:
Eyes of dreams which seem to absorb our own, eyes before which we ourselves appear to be *fantôme*.

.    .    .

Utter satisfaction from these dance gestures, from these turning feet mingling with states of the soul, from these little flying hands, these dry and precise tappings.

.    .    .

We are watching a mental alchemy which makes a gesture of a state of mind—the dry, naked, linear gesture all our acts could have if they sought the absolute.

.    .    .

It happens that this mannerism, this excessively hieratic style, with its rolling alphabet, its shrieks of splitting stones, noises of branches, noises of the cutting and rolling of wood, compose a

sort of animated material murmur in the air, in space, a visual as well as audible whispering. And after an instant the magic identification is made: *We know it is we who were speaking.*

Who, after the formidable battle between Arjuna and the Dragon, will dare to say that the whole of theatre is not on the stage, i.e., beyond situations and words?

The dramatic and psychological situations have passed here into the very sign language of the combat, which is a function of the mystic athletic play of bodies and the so to speak undulatory use of the stage, whose enormous spiral reveals itself in one perspective after another.

The warriors enter the mental forest rocking with fear, overwhelmed by a great shudder, a voluminous magnetic whirling in which we can sense the rush of animal or mineral meteors.

It is more than a physical tempest, it is a spiritual concussion that is signified in the general trembling of their limbs and their rolling eyes. The sonorous pulsation of their bristling heads is at times excruciating—and the music sways behind them and at the same time sustains an unimaginable space into which real pebbles finally roll.

And behind the Warrior, bristling from the formidable cosmic tempest, is the Double who struts about, given up to the childishness of his schoolboy gibes, and who, roused by the repercussion of the turmoil, moves unaware in the midst of spells of which he has understood nothing.

SOPHIA DELZA

The Classic Chinese Theatre *

Wars may come and wars may go, but the Classic Chinese Theatre continues to function in all its ancient glory with impeccable

* Reprinted from *The Journal of Aesthetics and Art Criticism,* XV:2 (December, 1956) with the permission of the editors and of the author.

style, year after year, night after night. For many centuries this art theatre, with unrelenting artistic integrity, has flourished as a dynamic force in Chinese life. The subtle changes gradually incorporated within the limits of a long-established technique imbue this theatre with the power to stand the test of time, for without change there could be no semblance of life within the art.

Old plays and new (those written during the last 100 years), and revised ones, are in continuous repertory in the theatres of China, despite the agitations of former days and the changes in present times. The fact that people sit for hours at a stretch (without intermissions), in freezing or stifling hot theatres, is but one small indication of their interest in and love of this *art form* —and art it is, from the exciting, exacting choreography of the acrobatic "supers," to the significant arrangement of the angle of a sleeve. The people have attended the theatre for many centuries, in open village squares in the early days; later, in roofed tea houses, and now in theatres with tea. Besides being a factor in bringing together the inhabitants of farms and villages and giving them a release from everyday pressure of hard work, the theatre taught the history and the mythology of China. In this way, since the people were deprived of any other means of education from governmental sources, the theatre played a role comparable to the technique of teaching by means of mural paintings in "foreign lands." What child in China doesn't know his heroic Kuan Kung (as we know George Washington) or the villainous T'sao T'sao; or the magnificent battles in the struggle for unity, and the customs and manners of his ancestors? Today, the Western advanced schools are beginning to use the "theatre" technique in education, which is just an old Chinese custom.

On the surface, the audiences in a Chinese theatre may appear less concentrated than do our Western theatregoers, for there is much to interfere with their full attention: girls with steaming kettles nimbly push their ways between narrow rows of seats to furnish the imperative tea; vendors of hot and cold dishes incessantly call their wares; babies stroll up and down the aisles imitating the actors' voices and gestures; latecomers are loudly ushered in; talk buzzes endlessly. But, nevertheless, eyes are always focused upon the stage with concentrated attention. De-

spite conversation much above a whisper, the audience is always on the alert to respond and shout its approval with loud Hao-Hao's (good, fine, bravo) and also its disapproval. The execution of a difficult dance action, a sustained musical note, a finely made gesture—each is critically appreciated, and sometimes with more than a Hao-Hao, for our uninhibited G.I.'s left behind them sharp whistling and applauding. The actors rarely take any bows and the performance ends without ceremony. The actor walks off, and the audience walks out.

The first startled reaction of the Westerner, inexperienced and untutored in the ways of the Chinese stage, is that he has been caught in an Alice-in-Wonderland world, where strangely painted faces and massive costumes belie the ordinary proportions of the human figure; in which the limp and willowy movements of the female players excruciatingly exaggerate women's traditional frailty; where color patterns and designs follow no painter's palette; and where, despite the terrible weight of clothes, fantastic feats are done with the ease of winged creatures. The music, like nothing on our Western earth, adds to the mad illusion of being hurled, not only back to prehistoric eras, but to an undiscovered planet as well; and the voice which violates every familiar conception of human intonation covers the gamut of sound in vibrationless sequences, with the confused nonchalance of an orchestra tuning up on a damp day. But suddenly out of this surrealist pageant a true logic appears.

Even the most prejudiced observer—he who shudders at the intense clash of gongs and cymbals and squirms at the pitch of the stringed instruments (but whose sensitive ear is deaf to the subway screeches and din of radio noises), whose eye (blind to the hideousness of our advertisement-infested streets) becomes confused by the mass of patterns and colors—even he learns eventually to see and appreciate the consummate artistry of the form and structure of Chinese Theatre. Even without comprehending, he becomes aware of the balance of stylized acting conventions and realistic pantomime. He sees the designed arrangement of the form and the emotional significance of the dramatic action; and finally (the most difficult task of all) can even accept the strange voices in speech and song. The costumes and painted faces become inevitable parts of the intrinsic whole.

A newcomer in the Chinese Theatre finds that what goes on around the play is more intriguing than the stage play itself, which he does not understand. But he can understand the inquisitive faces peering through the back curtain, and the quiet children draped on all sides of the stage in as many positions, or those young and old who push their ways in front of the wings and stand in rapt attention, as unaware of the audience as the actors are of them.

The musicians share the stage with the actors as do their guests and offspring. When they light their cigarettes or converse, the newcomer sees it as part of the play. The most impressive characters who divert the attention are the property men, the ubiquitous blue-gowned figures who quietly do their jobs as if they were invisible or transparent. They refresh the singer with a pot of tea. They toss the cushion to an about-to-kneel actor. A discarded sword is caught agilely, a headdress is adjusted, a chair is turned into a prison gate, a canopy properly placed, a curtain swung. Sometimes he is part of the act, tossing flames into the air, or helping a "dead" actor to exit.

The newcomer sees the teapots framing the stage apron as strangely shaped footlights. He sees the clashing colors of tied curtains and the Chinese character writing designing the front walls of the theatre as decorations. He sees everything but the play. But when he does begin to watch the play, when he inquires into the gesture of the actor, learns the importance of the painted face and the ordered significance of the costumes, then the surrounding distractions fade out and he is completely startled when a newer newcomer comments on those extraneous elements which he has begun to take for granted as everyone does the arch of the proscenium.

But never will the activities within the boundaries of the stage become a taken for granted matter, for each evening's attendance extends the scope of one's appreciation. In a single night one can be impressed by the variety of styles and stories that may span the centuries. One might see one play in which the pantomime is so realistic that it transcends any national boundary; the washing of hands, the sewing of a shoe, or the flirtation of a newly met couple is a language familiar to anyone anywhere.

He probably would see a dramatic play: a defeated hero ac-

companying his actions with song and speech, with formal gestures stylized to the degree at which they become a "dance"—trembling fingers at the chest, staggering steps taken on the knees, a complete somersault with a final position on the back for despair. This is true "expressionistic" acting, where the gestures take the place of the words in awakening the emotional responses of the audience.

He would experience a play of "Action" in which the movement is the "body" of the play, the story being only the frame. He might see, this first evening, a white-costumed, pink-and-white-faced young man elegantly expressing his prowess in terms of pure action, the designs and body tensions, rhythms and abstract arrangements being of "dance" nature. The Chinese call it action and so it is because it actively expresses a state of mind. It is also pure dance because the form is so finished in structure as to be completely expressive of the concept which inspires the action. It can therefore be called Dance-Action.

Although the plays are generally divided into Civil and Military, the subdivisions are many, and are not, as ours are, categorized as Comedy or Tragedy. In each classification there may be plays with sad or happy endings, but these emotions are not the central motivation of the plays. The fact that they are historical, legendary, mythical, seasonal or festival, romantic, satirical, ethical, and sociological is the point. All may contain fanciful notions and mythological concepts. Each may use diverse acting styles: realistic, expressionistic, or abstract. But all are constructed so that movement, speech, and song, sound, and music are fused into a balanced unity, resulting in a unique type of theatre—called classic Chinese.

This theatre is not one of suspense, as is our Western theatre. The plot is generally known in advance (if only from a synopsis in the program). The role of each actor is clearly stated by himself in an entrance speech in which he announces his name, character, and intentions. The plot is unfolded, not developed; the conversation is not in itself the play, but only the skeleton for the action, song, and dramatics.

Nor is this a theatre of the "word" as was the Shakespearean to which the Chinese is so superfluously compared. A moment of great triumph is expressed not by verse or poetic prose, but by

gestures or vocalized sounds. Instead of finding a word for it, as the Greeks had done, the Chinese creative mind found an "act" for it. This distinction is of great significance, as our judgment and appreciation must be based on this fact, not on standards dictated by Western customs. The play is not the thing—it is the playing which is.

It is this difference of emphasis between the "word," or literature of the play, and the "act" or the rendition of the playing of the play which has made the Chinese theatre so sophisticated and "modern" in its visual invention. Even in Shakespearean times, the Chinese theatre was a full-fledged art, the form of which continues to the present day. It had, at that early time, a definite history of 800 years and a background of activity for a thousand years before that. The Shakespearean theatre, eminently superior in terms of literature, was primitive in visual effects, using, for instance, word signs on the stage to indicate scenic places and objects. The Chinese had creatively arranged in set style definite objects, musical sounds, symbols, and movements, to serve for the purposes of scenery, place, and time. They thought of the theatre in visual and aural terms, both of which made the functioning of the play intelligible and expressed an aesthetic approach to the arts of action and sound, dance, and music, apart from the storytelling process.

All the activity on the stage is incorporated into the totality of the play's meaning. The tables, piled one on the other simulating a mountain top, the turned over chair as a prison gate, the black flag of the night, the red-clothed decapitated head; the lifted leg movement for stepping over a threshold; the continuous walking around in a circle to indicate distance; the trotting steps to show ascending or descending a stairway: these *are* the play (to mention but a few meager examples from the immense store of symbolic décor and conventionalized and pantomimic forms). No act is extraneous to the design and very few objects purely decorative and without function. The maid who stands motionless, unused, while her mistress sings her personal song for forty minutes is part of the structure of the play. All is—as much as the paper a watercolorist uses is an intrinsic part of the finished painting.

The property man, on the other hand, is not of the play, although he is such an important functionary, without whose con-

stant attendance some of the above-described scenic changes could not take place. He is not necessary to the structure of the play's design, either as décor or actor. He is to the play what one's maid at home is to a party; offering tea and cake at the proper time. She is not essential to the conversation or activities of the guests. The property man functions outside of the artistic requirements of the play. In plays in the West, he, as stagehand, is behind the scenes, unseen. Due to the physical facts of the Chinese theatre, he happens to be needed on the stage, and though ever-present, often he, too, is unseen. Nothing about the property man's clothes and appearance, nothing in his most everyday, natural way of performing his stage duties, nothing about his walk, stance, or posture could in any way be included as part of the stage play or could even remotely be connected with the play's stylized nature. The property man performs his invaluable services as a sturdy, reliable serving-attendant (which, incidentally, is the Chinese name for him).

Throughout the centuries, we know that in Europe the art of performing as dancer, singer, or musician had been considered a low-class, menial occupation by the élite who, though despising the arts socially, attended theatre performances frequently. In this attitude China was no exception. Although theatricals were in constant demand by the courts and by the wealthy, actors were considered so low in "caste" that they and their families were forbidden to enter the "examinations," otherwise open even to the lowliest beggar.

The social status of Chinese theatrical art was the very antithesis of painting. Developing separately, they did not affect each other stylistically or ideologically at any stage of China's history. Painting was an erudite art, a cultured profession, enjoyed by those classes of people elevated by fortune, birth, position, and education. Removed from man's everyday experiences, his passions, trials, triumphs or failures, painting pictured existence as serene, refined, and aloof, in which man was only an insignificant event in nature's creations. Art interpretation of life was confined to the negation of physical activity and emotional change. Contemplation and relaxation were portrayed as being the only desirable states of well-being.

But the theatre grew out of experiences lived by the people. It

was by them, about them, and for those great masses of people for whom "nature" was far from mild and restful; whose rare respite from working with and against nature were those occasions when theatrical troupes performed in their villages. The theatre was their pleasure and means of education. They were the first and last critics, who had to be pleased and who had to understand. That the art of the theatre could have been so discriminatingly developed is a real proof of the people's imagination, appreciation, and encouragement. An art reflects its audience and in turn serves it.

Color, vigor, energy, excitement; violence, bawdiness, humor and satire, heroism, villainy, astuteness, loyalty; wisdom, stupidity, pride, arrogance, honesty, gentleness, robustness; fantasy and reality—all thrust the Chinese people into a powerful world of feeling, experience and action, where man's personality, as soldier, statesman, student, farmer, merchant, artisan, was the dynamic force and center of interest.

The Chinese Opera form is the result of its origin. The early setting for the theatrical troupes was merely an open-air marketplace, and the stage nothing more than a slightly raised wooden platform without curtains. The actors, who already were versatile as singers, acrobats, mimes, dancers, had to add another element to their talents—that of being the scenery. Since the audiences could neither read nor write, the use of the signboard would have been useless. Painted flats would certainly have simplified matters, but the actors were poor. Since they traveled extensively under difficult conditions, carrying sets for hundreds of plays would have been burdensome and expensive.

Because they thought in terms of body movement, design, and rhythm for expressing their fancies, ideas, and feelings, the actors could easily translate even the "immobile" into gesture. With intelligent thinking (and a sense of humor) they created pantomimic imagery as scenic "asides"—such as hiding the face and standing stiffly to be "invisible"; moving in a circle to indicate journeying from one place to another; feeling the air with cautious hand motion to show darkness; contracting the body for cold, and innumerable other acts.

Knowing the limitations both of physical and artistic energy, and having the artist's awareness of the need for variety, they

made use of some concrete objects as well. The actor did not limit his creative vision to the tight confines of a poor purse. With magical twist of fact and fantasy, he turned a few available and easily handled objects into as many places or things as he had need for in his plays. Prosaic pieces of furniture, the table and the chair, procurable in every village, served his practical and economical purposes. And what could have been more sensible than to get someone to manipulate and arrange them into their various and varied forms, since, without curtains, there could be no hidden changes of the scene, and since the actor could not himself move them without sacrificing his acting style. So the property man was born.

He turned chairs upside down, forward and backward, to and fro; piled tables one upon the other, combined chairs and tables in unorthodox manner; pieces of material and flags became as many symbols for representative ideas as were needed, turned a table into a hilltop; a flag into water; a chair into a window; a red envelope into a rich present of gold or ivory; a canopy was a room; a piece of cloth, a wall; a whip symbolized riding on a horse. With the actors' movements, and this series of inter-changeable objects, the stage easily became a prison or a palace, a valley or a mountain, a river or a forest—in heat, snow or rain. With some quick learning on the part of the people, the stage became an intelligible world, lit by their imaginative participation.

But the actor by no means stopped at this point of the stage play. He had the instinct for decoration and knew the psychological need for glamor and brilliance. With artistic taste and economy he transformed those trite and familiar tables and chairs, simply by covering them with gaily embroidered colorful silks. And what is most important of all, he dressed himself in the most sumptuous of costumes, without considering expense. It was more than the superficial desire for spectacular appeal that made the actor so extravagant. The costume and the man, *together,* were the actor. The costume was almost as necessary a part of the action as was the actor in it. Nowhere in the world, and at no time in the history of dance or pageant or theatre, has the costume been used to an artistic degree to compare even remotely with the creativeness of the Chinese Theatre.

With the Chinese actor, the costume is never apart from him —it is always a part of him. Although ribbons, tassels, pompons, jewels, fringes, and dozens of other kinds of trimmings are used for the added excitement of their "natural" movements, the art of costume arrangement in Chinese acting does not depend on the force of gravity and inertia for form and style. The gesture-designs composed by the actor's manipulation of his clothes are as consciously constructed as the floor pattern he traverses or the dance he performs. The sleeve is held, lifted, dropped; the belt is kicked and tossed and whirled; the crown feathers swayed, shaken; the coat panel grasped, flipped—in anger, distress, surprise, scorn, fear, in strength, and in joy. Every motion, growing out of ideas and emotions, is indispensable to the total meaning of the play. Those attitudinized positions become rhythmically and structurally incorporated into the dramatic situation as expressive motifs, fused by the actor's acting-action.

With imaginative inventiveness, the actor had set his stage; with emotional consciousness he had costumed himself; he had thus made "visible" physical space and emotional states of mind. He continued this theatrical imagery by also making his *character* visible, for despite all the elaborate adjuncts of the performance, it was the actor, the human being, who was the central feature of the play. We speak of people showing their true colors! The Chinese took this metaphor at face value, and proceeded to color the face to show his true character color!

He used all colors and combinations of shades and hues, with artistic insight and ingenuity; designs and patterns carried out the basic interpretation of the color idea, to reveal personality. Features, and even the size of the head, were reshaped by the paintbrush to express the necessary and subtle variations of character within the same person. Accentuating, magnifying, distorting, abstracting, elaborating, could make eyes, nose, mouth, cheeks, appear in odd and unnatural places. The natural face was a canvas, and the painting was an abstraction of the whole character of the man, as vital an interpretation as any art picture within a frame. In fine upright and virtuous characters, the real face was accentuated in a more becoming and beautiful way. Lawless, evil, and conniving persons show their thwarted and maladjusted natures in corresponding facial irregularities.

This art of facial makeup was the plastic visualization of the intangible qualities of character.

By means of this very special technique, reality was *emphasized,* not obliterated. There was no mistaking by the audience, the real nature of a character, exposed as it was by dress, movement, and by face: an honest or villainous one, a figure of elegance or vulgarity. The cruel soldier, the trustworthy adviser, the diligent wife, the dissipated emperor, the deceitful man, the honest peasant, the unscrupulous landowner—had their natures written all over their faces, and were recognized as such. Good and evil commanders-in-chief wear the same styled clothes, but their faces have no color in common. Even a future destiny is seen, as in the case of an about-to-die character.

The symbols are very numerous, the color palette extensive, the number of designs seemingly infinite, but the basic groupings are comparatively few (as are the divisions of good and evil) and are easily perceived. The Chinese actor-artist recognized the fact that individuals differ within the boundaries of their special categories, and accordingly noted this in his creative and realistic analysis of makeup, for the faces of no two persons are delineated in exactly the same way. Every one in a group of five generals will each have his personality individualized. Each person in a line of twenty brutal police guards (whom one would suspect of having the same qualities more or less) show those "more or less" differences in their face-line patterns.

There are, however, as is usual in any rule, some exceptions, where the makeup is identical, and irrevocably so: for the young, all of whom are equally innocent, and for the virtuous (young and old), who are equally indestructible.

In the light of today's advanced psychological theories in art and aesthetics, and modern painting inventions by our Western expressionists, cubists, and surrealists, the profound knowledge of how to translate human nature into art, as depicted in Chinese facial painting, is no less than astounding—created as it was more than 500 years ago.

The most outstanding fact in this development of the facial art is that permanent masks did not take the place of paint. How conveniently simple it could have been to fix a form and pick it out of a stage trunk when needed. The use of masks would have

eliminated the element of chance, temperament, or personal whim, and would have saved time and paint materials, too, since makeup is put on fresh at each performance.

But the Chinese actors, stylized, are artists, not mechanics. They could no more leave facial expression to the accident of artificial lighting on a no matter how subtle mask than they would permit costume movement to be determined by the uncertain play of the winds. Their dramatic feeling was basically human —not decorative. The mask is interesting but static, and dehumanizes an actor. With clever appropriateness the Chinese use masks for those roles which have an unhuman nature: animals, ghosts, heavenly gods depicting thunder, etc.

Facial painting is alive and magnifies one's very *human* nature. Man's own features were the truest means for expressiveness. The muscles of his face, as no light could do, gave life to the patterns and lines which could be made to move coordinatedly with every grimace, with every nose twitch, with the vibrations of mouth and eyelids, with every movement of the lips —all means for the actor's ends.

Just as the actor's own face shone through the intricately painted one, so his body projected its action through the immense, complicated costumes —colorful rivals for the audience's admiration. Full trousers, long wide gowns, headdresses, tight belts, flowing ribbands, collars, shoulder capes, heavy hats, tall boots with thick soles, should on the face of it have made it impossible to move, or have obliterated all design, or finally should have substituted for all action —had it not been for the dynamic power, physical and emotional, of the actor himself.

So we have come to the heart of the matter. The heart of Chinese Theatre lies in the dynamic action of the actor who is the superb master of this and of all the form ensuing from it: pattern, gesture, rhythm, and style. Concentration on the technique of body-action is stressed from the first day a child enters an acting school. Whatever the role he is to play eventually, the serious knowledge of this expressive art is the first requirement. This means that the art of body movement is the matrix, the essence of Chinese theatre art. To this action-art is joined the arts of singing and speech and sound, the coordinated harmony of which makes an elaborate orchestration, cemented by the instrumental music.

What is this profound movement, what is the nature of its technique, and of what is it comprised? This action may be defined as an expressive series of gestures so coordinated rhythmically as to give unity of structure to the ideas which inspired it.

The flow of action may be of *acting-realistic* nature, and of *dance-formal* nature, both of which types can be stylized. The placing of an arm and hand across the eyes with head bent and shoulders heaving would be *acting-action* where the rhythm and forms give a style to the natural act of weeping. A *dance-action* way might be, as an example of strength and assurance, a series of turns, a leg lift and a deep charge forward with strong body tensions—no movement of which would be done in *actual* life. The unique quality of the Chinese Theatre is that it moves so artfully and consecutively from one type of action to another— realistic to stylized, from literal to abstract, with the ease with which any of us walks off a curb.

The form of dance-action that is most easily accepted and readily appreciated is the kind which is purely of physical nature. Who hasn't watched with open-eyed astonishment—and gasped breathlessly—the stunning flying leaps, weightless as the grasshopper's; the fantastic falls done with so much skill that they seem easy to do; the spectacular jumps from enormous heights, the curious slow cartwheels without aid of head or hands, defying the pull of gravity; the suave balances on one leg held for countless minutes; the swift turns with deep bends, the leg lifts, the corkscrew-like somersaults executed with the nonchalance with which our Western actors hold a microphone? But if those acts had no more than the physical muscular control aspect to recommend them, the Chinese Theatre would simply be a vaudeville show, with colossal and dazzling acrobatics. But the actor utilizes those actions with the awareness of the expressive and emotional elements inherent in the nature of real art, and uses them to interpret character and situation. Those three aspects, the physical, the emotional, and the intellectual, combine to make the action a complete entity of mind and movement, a *dance-art* and not an acrobatic one.

This method of theatrical portrayal had its roots in the keen observation and study of how the human being behaves in the

actual world of events. The principles that distinguish movements of *art* from those of real life are the extent and rhythm of muscular tensions, the plasticity of the movements as it relates to structure, the gauge of dynamics, the consecutiveness of its design and the elimination of superfluous detail.

With superlative logic and consummate artistry, a Chinese action form has been evolved which does not sacrifice sense for spectacle. The easy fluency with which each actor performs his role, whether he be a dignified old man or a silly young one, a bold, ungracious servant, a retiring modest heroine or a flirtatious maid, is proof that the understanding of character as translated into action is the core of his intensive and rigorous training.

Realistic, stylized, free, naturalistic pantomimic, abstract, expressionistic, symbolic —this entire range of movement styles, to quote the words of the actors themselves, emanates from the eyes (head), the body, the hands (arms), the legs, and the step (space design), all regulated by the body behavior. An obvious example of body behavior is to point out the difference between a serpent's movement and that of a frog's. The body behavior of the actor playing the monkey's role is not the same as when he plays a leopard. The magnificent gait of a mature statesman differs from the magnificent gait of a young hero, even though the latter shows evidence that he will become a mature statesman. The facile ability to reproduce subtle differentiations of character is a severe requirement for the actor in his role of action-player.

Since, as has been stated, theatre comes out of life, it is to be expected that the roles of men and women should differ and the extent to which they do so was caused by the utterly dissimilar positions they held in society, in family life, economically and psychologically. There is no point at which their motions, tensions, body behavior coincides. The male action dance projects itself with assurance and power as master of the situation; his gestures carve the very air away; his muscular tensions are taut as a ship's rope, firm yet pliable.

Female characterization emphasizes grace and modesty. She is exquisite, delicate. The movement is so light and willowy, it looks as if it is the result of an outside force, as a tree gets its

motion from the play of the winds upon it. The gesture and designs are confined to a small area around the body; they are, nevertheless, alert and nimble and smooth as porcelain.

Their every stance differs. The women, with low chests and sloping shoulders curve like an arc—with heads a bit forward. The men square their shoulders and hold heads up; they thrust their arms and legs outward, extended to their fullest capacities. The steps of the women are small as if calling attention to their tiny feet. Their figures undulate with minute rhythms. Their hands and fingers curve sinuously and elaborately. The male actors' hands are strong and emphatic; the designs of the fingers vary with characterizations. Light and charming, the actresses finish their poses with subtle diminuendo, on a soft and gentle note, but the actors project such vitality even into their final positions that they appear to have arrested action, like a moving picture suddenly stopped. The warrior-actress, even when performing action similar to a man's on the battlefield, never loses her natural femininity.

A few specific examples of action might help to visualize the extent of the delineation of character, emotion, and situation. In the play *Death of General Kuan Kung,* we see this hero frantically trying to escape capture. His extraordinary movements have such poignancy that we almost see a real horse which is supposed to have slipped on the ice. We see him ride and fall in broken rhythms and desperate gestures. His companion, unable to help him, acts his frustration in patterns of amazing meaning.

An elderly man, hopping backwards on one leg, vibrating his head incredibly fast, suddenly turns over in a difficult fall onto his back. The futility of the situation is obvious and clear. Anger comes through quick side steps, and staggerings, low on feet and knee.

We see, in *The Crazy Monk,* humorous passages in which the monk, with nonchalance, hypnotizes the enemy in fighting actions designed for laughter.

We recognize the feeling of dizziness as it is expressed by a somersault; desperation by the act of crossed eyes, legs moving in a kind of wavering skip; a beard is blown in exhaustion; a hair braid is whirled by a fast-rotating head in defeat; a wounded soldier does fighting feats never forgetting his handicap. Each of us

knows the feeling of shock when the heart seems to leap out of place; we get that same sensation when a soldier who has discovered his wife has committed suicide does a speedy somersault and fantastic turn and suddenly lies still as if in a faint.

Satirical mimicry, nimble clowning is artfully done with bendings, turnings, acrobatics of all kinds, and with fine special design of hands and head.

In the *Mission to the West,* the famous monkey, through his movement-action, shows his development from an ignorant monkey to a monkey of "man's" estate. The birth of the monkey, his startling emergence from a rock, the weak attempts to move, his gradual accumulation of strength in learning to walk, are rendered through action with magnificent perception of reality and stylization. By a spiraling motion in imitation of the way smoke rises, one can almost see him fly away. The most poignant action in this play comes at the time when his master, the monk, has finally dominated him, having bound him with a head ring, against the monkey's will. The annoyance, despair, rebelliousness, anger, and final resignation as expressed by the monkey's "eyes, legs, hands, body, step" is acting-action of such high order as to be compared with any interpretation of the tragic roles in Shakespeare's plays.

Rich movement with every shade of meaning: a flick of the wrist, a lift of the leg, an angle of the eye, a turn of the fist, the flexed feet, the becking accent of the head, the walk with the speed of a bird and the smoothness of an ice skater—every part of the body speaks communicatively in exuberance, suspicion, flirtatiousness, bawdiness, cruelty, sadness, and suffering.

The elegant heroes are confident, able, and forthright as their clear carved movements and firm steps, their sure arm configurations, their upright carriage clearly show. We see their prowess and their bravery in their deep turns, back bends, flying leg leap turns, and powerful stances.

Puppet figures have their distinctive staccato qualities; we see litheness and intensity in a leopard; a ghost's collapsed looseness and sudden rigidity.

Group action can be as sedate as in a monastery; as turbulent and fierce as on the battlefield; as lively and gay as fish flying excitedly in a net out of water.

Costumes and properties in concerted action; pheasant feathers dramatically thrust between the teeth in anger; braids thrown, tossed, wound around the neck; beards eloquently handled; chains on imprisoned hands, fighting weapons—knives, swords, spears, flags, ribbons, fire, oars, the whip, a mass of material coordinated into form-structure. The interplay of the action of men and materials integrate the theatrical picture.

During all this time, while the eyes have been stimulated by the activity on the stage, by the ravishingly beautiful costumes and by the actors' stunning actions; and the mind has been aroused by the artful facial paintings, by costume characterization and the actors' meaningful actions, the ears have been receiving a succession of instrumental and vocal sounds. For the intervals of silence are very few indeed. There is no play of classic heritage on the Chinese stage which is musicless. Without music a play would be as incomplete as a flower without a stem. To omit the music would be like removing the wall from behind a mural painting—it would fall apart.

Orchestral music, melodic or percussive, pervades the play with feeling insistence and importance. Interwoven into the very warp and woof of the drama's structure, it is at times parallel to the action, at times contrapuntal to it. It outlines the speech, and supports the song; it punctuates an emotion, concludes a statement of action. The orchestra announces the actor at his entrance, and, so to speak, exits with him. Often it anticipates action and prepares the audience for what is to come. The leading musician's attention is glued on the stage, for he must follow with impeccable accuracy the subtleties and nuances of movement, of beat, of sustained holds, which vary with each actor's personality.

Just as the costume's style and color are definitely related to social position and occupation, so the timbre of the instrumentation is pertinent to the style of the play. Music is a vivid and vital part of the personality of the plays, which are always described by their musical content and are typed categorically by the instruments used. The resonance or shrillness of gong or cymbal; the rolling of percussive drums, the sticks and castanets—staccato or sharp; the stringed instruments of varying degrees of acidulousness or sweetness; the soft wind instruments; the

bells of stone or metal are strong foundations in the integrated structure of song, action or dramatic speech. It is not for nothing that the orchestra was called "the face of the play," and occupied a dominating position in the center rear of the stage. Today, however, we see it on left side front stage, a place far more strategic, it seems to me, since from there it is close to the audience as well as to the actors.

Of impressive importance is the singing aspect in Chinese opera in whose long history song styles and forms have undergone little change. From the earliest times, poems were to be sung, not read, indicating that the voice as an instrument of music was of primary consideration. The very nature of art song is a kind of stylization in itself and demands that the singing process be understood and appreciated abstractly as music and voice technique. This aspect of song is certainly exploited in Chinese Theatre, for Mei Lan Fang can render one short sequence in eleven different ways. No matter how emotionally the song may be related to the story (such as a song delivered in praise and grief at the death of a sworn brother), it is the production of the voice in song that arouses the appreciative response.

Folk music from any country can find sympathetic ears anywhere, for it is the direct expression of common-to-all feelings. But the art styles of the different countries are not so easily understood because they are complicated and sophisticated personalized forms and techniques. And there is the rub, for our Western newcomer (who has *not* been forgotten). He can recognize, whether he likes it or not, that clashing cymbals, gongs, and drums are the musical expressions for war. Mimetic music strikes a familiar chord: the neighing of the horse, a baby's wail, a gong sound indicating the time, a nervous noise a wet finger makes running down a thread. But he does not find any touch of sympathy in the art song style—in its pitch, coloration, and rhythm.

And Chinese singing is unique. Its tone-note changes are subtly microscopic. Its ever changing rhythms are very complicated; its phrasing is most irregular and rarely repeated. Its tone and vibrato are of special coloration; its cadences strange. Within these structural limitations, the voice style of singing varies to suit the character types, as do the costumes, as do the

facial designs, as do the character roles themselves. Broad tones and strong are for the energetic, rough character. The young man sings in falsetto to show youthfulness (when the voice is girlish). An older and refined man's voice is almost natural. The young woman's voice has a special high-pitched tang.

Another facet of the aural nature of the theatre lies in vocalization. This, neither speech nor singing, is wordless sound, coming full from the throat, as primitively expressive as the call of our prehistoric ancestors. Varying as to pitch and intensity, these sounds for fear, pride, disgust are startlingly succinct, as emphatic and timeless as basic gestures. Deep-throated, long-drawn A-A-A-Ah's stating, with inimitable clarity, superiority in a conflict; joyous sounding vocalizations at a meeting after long separation; the sound like a trill (done with the tongue) rattles out its triumph; the sustained high-pitched wail expressing tragedy as no action or poem could do (a technique used by Laurence Olivier in *Oedipus Rex*). These aural theatrics heighten the dramatic situation and merge stylistically into the speech and song.

Chinese theatre has its own poetic flavor, blended from the mixture of reality, imagination, symbolism, and expression. If a graph could be made from the lines and masses of sole and group action, and in another dimension, from movement passing from speech to song to sound, we would weave a balanced overall design of architectural proportions somewhat like a modern painting, where objects and people are so interrelated, juxtaposed and superimposed as to deepen our perceptions, broaden our vision and intensify emotional and aesthetic responses.

The entire gamut of the elements that go into the making of a high art is so deeply analyzed and so creatively synthesized and utilized in Chinese Theatre Classic style as to permit us to compare it to the best of art anywhere. Its profound physical science, its sound emotional expressiveness, its keen artistry of designed structure, have as much timeless pertinence in the realm of art history as has Egyptian art, or Gregorian chants, or Gothic architecture, to say nothing of our Western dance arts—including the technique of the classic ballet, and the expressive significance of the twentieth-century modern art dance.

P A R T   V I   Light and Environment:
The Context of Total Theatre

Adolphe Appia's conceptual intention was that light be used in staging as a visual music. He looked forward to the time when the electrical sciences would "put at the disposal of the poet-musician resources which only he can use." This "must be born of necessity," he felt, and indicated that "since such a system is essential to the word-tone drama, the dramatist of the future will have to invent it." [1]

Thomas Wilfred, the man who actually did invent such a system, looked forward to the time when light art would be generally practiced. In "Light and the Artist," written twenty years ago, he precisely predicts the present, prevalent attention to the art of light, and he traces its development in terms of the interest in the correspondences between light and music.

Wilfred's constantly changing Lumia light constructions are shown in the Museum of Modern Art and in other museums.

[1] Adolphe Appia, *Music and the Art of the Theatre*, trans. Robert W. Corrigan and Mary Douglas Dirks (Coral Gables: University of Miami Press, 1962), pp. 30–31.

However, with an instrument called the Clavilux he also applied similar principles to the staging of drama and dance and to the giving of individual concerts, with the flowing patterns of "color music" being "played" from a keyboard. In 1927 he played such a visual accompaniment for Ibsen's *The Vikings at Helgeland* at the Goodman Theatre in Chicago.

The motion abstractions of "light show" artists are the present day equivalent of Appia's light-as-music. Projected over the performers to create a shifting space of light and colors, this technique has been used to striking effect in dances created by Alwin Nikolais and by Robert Joffrey. This is one example of how the dance is now much closer to becoming the total artwork than is the theatre. Says Joffrey: "I look upon ballet as total theatre." [2]

Motion pictures have been used on the stage almost since their inception in the 1890's to produce effects such as storm or fire, to show figures or carriages passing beyond a window and to reproduce scenes which could not be staged. But these, like the projected setting, are adjuncts to the realistic drama and have little to do with total theatre.

The most obvious integration of film with the literary or illusionistic form of drama is the somewhat difficult one of making a direct transition between the filmed scene and the stage action so that characters seem to move from one medium to the other. This was accomplished, for example, at the State Theatre in Posen in 1911 when an actor climbed from a window and a film continued the action, the film having been "so carefully prepared for the work that the actors in the film and on stage could not be distinguished." [3]

Piscator's production of *The Good Soldier,* described here by Mordecai Gorelik, used a projection-stage interplay employing cartoon characters, and it indicates that suggestion, rather than verisimilitude, can be the basis of a technique. This production,

[2] "The Great Leap Forward," *Time* (March 15, 1968), p. 44. With this issue *Time* transferred its reporting of dance from its Music section to its Theater section, feeling that it was better suited to the latter because the present day choreographer has become "the director of a new theatrical form that has a total design for total involvement."

[3] Friedrich Kranich (ed.), *Bühnentechnik der Gegenwart* (Munich, Berlin: R. Oldenbourg, 1963), Vol. II, p. 151.

because of this interplay, is unlike others in the Piscator-Brecht Epic Theatre tradition which made extensive use of projected images in an illustrative way. In Epic Theatre various media are employed as separate systems. The projections expand the immediate and general reference range of the drama, but they do so in terms of literary or dialectical elaboration rather than as a plastic or sensory function. Epic Theatre in general remains a "special case," an adjunct in the search for total theatre form. Much the same is true of the "living newspapers" of Russia and the United States, which made extensive use of projections in an illustrative manner.

The Czechoslovakian State Theatre's *Laterna Magika* productions, designed by Josef Svoboda, have explored a great range of projection techniques. They have used treadmills, as Piscator did in *The Good Soldier,* and have devised a stage composed of motorized, shifting screens which allow projections to be seen at different depths in order to integrate them with the performance space. They have created sequences based on a matching of action between film and stage, and a passing of action between two films and the stage, but these seem to have lacked the test of integration into a dramatic, narrative continuity. From limited descriptions and from photographs it is apparent that other techniques have been used in creating such a unity, as in their production of Offenbach's *The Tales of Hoffmann* in which projections seem to have created moving, dreamlike settings and a flowing "score" of mural sized images. Perhaps there the backdrop became a "surface sensitive to thought" as suggested by Claudel.

One specific use for this technique would in fact be to provide images such as those called for by Claudel in his plays, but which were not able to be staged. For example, in his *Le Soulier de Satin:*

In the original or literary version of the play, the Island of Japan is made to loom up from a globe and to take slowly the form of a warrior in dark armor, which in turn becomes the Guardian Angel. Later the Angel goes back into the planet Earth which grows smaller and smaller until it becomes as large as the head of a pin. This is followed

by the apparition of a glittering image of the Immaculate Conception across the sky. All of this action was omitted in the 1943 production, probably because its realization on the stage was too difficult.[4]

Claudel's suggestion that multiple and shifting images be used in order to create "that indistinct world where ideas are born from sensations" seems to be the technique that will prove the most important for total theatre. Experiments such as those of Ed Emshwiller's *Body Works* and Roberts Blossom's *Filmstage* have merged the films of dancers with the figures of the dancers themselves by overprojecting multiple images so that image and reality become, in effect, indistinguishable and interchangeable. Such effects could provide an "illusionary matrix" that would vastly increase the poetic and visual capabilities of the stage.

Another type of projection effect that is creating interest is the shadow play. We have seen that this was suggested for use on the stage by both Maeterlinck and Claudel. Filmmaker Ken Jacobs now works in this way. Recently, film columnist Jonas Mekas was led to wonder if "the Shadow and Light artists of Persia, of China, of India were the real masters, the real magicians," of the new multi-media art forms. And he saw the work of the new light artists as "the rebirth of this forgotten art of the past, the art of Shadow Play that will become, during these few coming years, the controversial challenger of cinema as we know it today, and a new source of inspiration." [5]

Projections of various kinds, as an instrument of total theatre, can now provide the "movements, values, clusters of forms and appearances continually decomposed and recomposed," which were visualized by Claudel. In this way they can merge the stage with cinema and with music to create an interplay of sensory modalities and a new plastic vocabulary of forms in space, a totality which is now the essential language of the stage itself.

[4] Leo O. Forkey, "A Baroque 'Moment' in the French Contemporary Theater," *Journal of Aesthetics and Art Criticism,* XVIII: 1 (September, 1959), p. 84.

[5] Jonas Mekas, "Movie Journal," *The Village Voice* (New York), December 2, 1965.

Our consideration of total theatre then concludes with "Environmental Theatre." Michael Kirby's thorough and informative study appropriately brings together many of the themes and aspects that have occupied our attention in this direction toward a "theatre of the future."

MORDECAI GORELIK

Piscator's *The Good Soldier* *

Before *Schweik* Piscator had already established his position as a
startling innovator. Perhaps the appearance of the *Schweik* production as the curtain rose on it was at first glance unusually
mild. Three thin portals spanned the depth of the stage —
Baroque fashion —and were closed in with a translucent drop in
the rear. Between the portals, and parallel with the footlights,
were two treadmills (or "conveyors," as Piscator called them),
whose combined widths formed the depth of the stage. That was
all; and as the stage darkened it was filled with the lilt of a Czech
folksong played on a hurdy-gurdy.

But now the backdrop springs into life, turning into a large
motion picture screen as the projector strikes it from the back. A
black dot jumps to the blank screen; it races over the white brilliance with fantastic speed, leaving behind it lines as jagged and
scratchy as barbed wire. Rapidly it traces in the distinctive style
of the artist George Grosz, a mustachioed and puffy Austrian
general. The hilt of a heavy sword appears in the general's right
hand; his other hand clasps that of the neighboring figure, who
emerges as a German field marshal, his aristocratic scowl half
hidden by his *Pickelhaube* helmet. Between this bellicose pair
the figure of a lawyer makes its appearance —severe, long-
nosed, corpselike, holding legal briefs in one hand, a knout in the
other. Finally an ignoble preacher is sketched out, balancing a
cross on his bulbous nose.

The treadmill begins to work. From the left a little corner of a
room trundles on by itself, a flea-bitten room as dog-eared as the
cur in Schweik's lap. Schweik, in shirt-sleeves, puffs away at his
tasseled pipe while his landlady, Frau Müller, sweeps the conveyor belt energetically. Frau Müller recalls some gossip. "It
seems they murdered our Ferdinand!"

She means Ferdinand, Archduke of Austria. The news
arouses Schweik to idle speculation. He wonders if the assassins

* Reprinted from Mordecai Gorelik's *New Theatres for Old,* copyright,
1940, 1962, by Mordecai Gorelik, with the permission of the author.

wore dress suits and high hats for such distinguished quarry. Something like a fox hunt, perhaps. "It's a great loss for Austria," thinks Schweik, as the corner of his room moves off and he rolls into his favorite pub, the Glass of Beer, almost as soon as the bar travels onstage. A new customer, Bredtschneider, is there already, trying to make conversation with Polivec, the owner. "You can't replace Ferdinand with just any damned fool," Schweik explains to Bredtschneider, who happens to be a police spy. Bredtschneider makes a mental note of this somewhat cryptic remark. Schweik will have to accompany Polivec, who has given no satisfactory reason for suddenly taking down the picture of the Emperor that hung over the bar. "The flies specked all over the Emperor!" Not half good enough! Ten years is what Polivec gets, while Schweik comes limping home from the police investigation to find his mobilization papers lying on the table.

They are in a big envelope with a double eagle and official seals; Frau Müller is excited. "Calm yourself, Frau Müller, I'm going to war. . . ." On the screen the invisible pen scratches furiously a hairy hand heaping gold coins upon a figure with the head of a phonograph. The figure types reams of propaganda: *Gott strafe England, Jeder Stoss ein Franzos,* while a fountain pen gives a military salute and screams *Hurra!* In a wheel chair propelled by Frau Müller, Schweik is on his way to medical inspection at the regional Army H.Q. "On to Belgrade!" he shouts, waving his crutches, while the streets of Prague flash by behind him in motion pictures. The Good Soldier is off on his adventures.

In the wings Piscator, small, bright-eyed and sharp-nosed, shakes his head over the rumble of the "conveyor belt." It ought to have been more perfect, he thinks. Didn't the mechanicians swear that it would function as smoothly as a fine automobile? And some of the scenery and properties that speed in on the conveyor tumble down in the opening-night rush. But the audience is not as critical as the director. These episodes seem to have an added charm. The "conveyor belt" is intrinsically a comic idea; added to a story of a wandering soldier it is a device which penetrates to the heart of the action.

The construction of the play into its continuously flowing episodic character had been hardly less difficult than the con-

struction of the treadmills. Before Piscator decided to use it, the
novel had been turned into a play by Max Brod and Hans Rei-
mann, who owned the rights of dramatization. When the director
read their version his worst fears were realized: Haček's satire
had become a musical comedy with a military background. Gas-
barra, Leo Lania and Brecht were added to the council of war
and the script began to change, racing against time. Some of the
episodes, especially the ending, were not decided upon until the
opening night. . . .

But we must return to Schweik. He and his fellow recruits in
grotesque underwear have been lining up for medical inspection,
swapping hints, meanwhile, on how to keep out of the military
draft. Malingering is hard to get away with. A consumptive soldier, no malingerer, is simply falling apart; but the doctors are
callous to every kind of symptom, however alarming. And the
army physician whose face, dueling scar and all, now fills the
whole screen, has a reliable formula for handling all cases.
"Physic and aspirin!" he roars alternating this with "Stomach
pump and quinine!" Schweik nevertheless assures the doctor
that he has a severe case of rheumatism. So now our hero is on
his way again, to start his army hitch in the guard house, where
two soldiers, gigantically padded out, receive him.

Fortunately he does not stay in long. A certain Lieutenant
Lukasch, who needs an orderly, acquires Schweik in a poker
game. For the Lieutenant, war is only an avocation. His real profession is women. In a short time Schweik, following out the
Lieutenant's whims, is involved in so many scandals that official
punishment becomes necessary for appearance's sake. Lukasch
and his orderly are dispatched to the front lines on the Serbian
border. In the painted and cut-out train rushing past moving-
picture scenery, Schweik is arrested for pulling the emergency
cord without good reason. A grilling by the railway police ends
in a stalemate. "Corporal, this halfwit must go on to Budweis to
join his company. Take him to the ticket window and buy his
fare." But neither Schweik nor the Corporal have money. "Then
he can walk!" roars the officer in charge.

Thus Schweik is started on his famous march to Budweis, a
march which is not as straight as the crow flies. For the direction
in which our hero advances is not likely to get him to Budweis

very fast, especially since a paper snow is beginning to fall. He
meets sympathetic peasants, deserters. "Scenery from the right.
A town appears. Policemen are seen through the map on the
screen. Scenery from the left. A town. The map shows Schweik
making a wide detour around the town."

Film: railroad tracks, signal lamps, signal posts, a watchman's
shanty, gates at a crossing, and then the highway. On the left the
lights of Tabor can be seen. The lights travel along for a stretch, keeping pace and shifting toward the middle, slip back into the distance,
then disappear entirely as if behind a hill. In the background the night
sky, against which a hilly, wooded landscape is silhouetted dimly.
Fade into a map showing Budweis. The titles point out Schweik's direction. The following caption appears on the map (white print):
"Xenophon, a general of ancient times, hastened across all of Asia
Minor, without maps, and ended up God knows where. A continuous
march in a straight line is called an anabasis. . . . Far away, somewhere north on the Gallic Sea, Caesar's legions, which had gotten
there also without the aid of maps, decided to return to Rome by a
route different from the one by which they came. Since then it has
been said that all roads lead to Rome. It might just as easily be said
that all roads lead to Budweis—something which Schweik fully believed. And the devil only knows how it happened that instead of
going south to Budweis, Schweik marched in a straight line west.
. . ." (*From the stage directions*)

In custody after many adventures, Schweik is pushed aboard
an "army transport"—meaning an ancient freight car. He is
being shipped to his outfit, under suspicion of attempting to
desert. The freight car, which rumbles along on the treadmill
without every really getting anywhere, is nothing but a platform
masked by a semitransparent setpiece of a railroad car. It is
adorned with chalk scrawls and patriotic witticisms on the order
of *Serbien, diesmal musst Du sterbien!* Schweik and two or three
other hungry soldiers peer out of the open door; the rest of the
*Kanonenfutter* in transit have been drawn by the scene designer. . . .

On a battlefield consisting of a couple of small mounds behind
which Schweik and another soldier, Marek, are hiding, the saga
approaches its end.

SCHWEIK: I think we went the wrong way, the battle is over there.

MAREK: I'll remember this war for weeks.

SCHWEIK: There's plenty of good points to this war, don't forget. After the war there will be good crops around here . . . made out of us. They'll burn us, our ashes will be used for sifting sugar in the sugar factories. A war makes us useful to posterity. Our children will drink coffee with sugar sifted through our remains.

But Marek has taken himself elsewhere. "I'll do my duty for the Emperor to the end," adds Schweik. On the screen a Russian soldier is swimming in a pond. A bush rolls on with the Russian's uniform hanging on it. "A souvenir," thinks Schweik. He puts it on. A shot rings out, and a Hungarian patrol rushes on and seizes him in loud Hungarian tones. "What do you mean, prisoner?" Schweik demands, "I'm on our side. . . ." A shell bursts. Schweik falls. From the upper corner of the screen a procession of crosses starts toward the audience. As the crosses, growing nearer in perspective, reach the lower edge of the screen, a muslin drop, lowered downstage, catches them once more, bringing them still closer to the spectators. A rain of crosses falls upon this wry comedy as the lights begin to go up. . . .

THOMAS WILFRED

Light and the Artist *

Twenty years hence —perhaps much sooner —people will find it hard to believe that, in our atomic generation, many still shook their heads at the thought of an eighth art coming into the world to take its place among the accepted seven; a major fine art at that, in which the artist's sole medium of expression is light.

* Reprinted from *The Journal of Aesthetics and Art Criticism,* V:4 (June, 1947) with the permission of the editors and of the Art Institute of Light.

"Nonsense!" And our children will accord us the same overbearing smile we now bestow on our ancestors who greeted telephone, automobile, radio, and airplane with the same devastating word.

As far back as we care to look, each generation has firmly believed itself at the pinnacle of human achievement—and been as firmly convinced that the young folks were going to the dogs. The reasoning is simple enough. "Why, if such a thing were possible, someone would have thought of it long ago!"

Well, in the case of Lumia, the Art of Light, someone did— twenty-five centuries ago! The recorded history of the art of light began one starry night on the island of Samos when Pythagoras stood contemplating the firmament. The majestic rhythm of heavenly bodies moving in their orbits appeared to him as cosmic harmony, a vast rhythmic sequence of visual beauty—the music of the spheres.

Here we have the first clear conception of a potential aesthetic language of form, color, and motion in their purest manifestation —apart from earthly phenomena and the human body—and precisely the foundation upon which lumia rests.

But, some two hundred years later, Aristotle unwittingly launched the unfortunate changeling "Color Music" with the following passage in *De Sensu:* "Colors may mutually relate like musical concords for their pleasantest arrangement; like those concords mutually proportionate."

This is merely an analogy to illustrate a point, but the advocates of "Color Music" have construed it to mean that Aristotle believed a definite physical relation existed between the vibrations of light and sound; that each note in the musical scale had a definite color. Science has long since disproved this theory, but "Color Music" still pops out at least once a year as a brandnew idea.

Now we must jump a good many centuries to the year 1719 and the garden of His Chinese Majesty, Emperor K'ang Hsi. It is the fifteenth night of the first month, The Feast of Lanterns, and K'ang Hsi is entertaining guests from faraway Europe. In the darkness of the garden one can just make out the gorgeous ceremonial robes; then the Emperor raises his fan and the perfor-

mance of light begins. Here is an eyewitness account by a French missionary.

"It began by half a dozen of large cylinders, which were suspended from long stakes driven into the earth. These cylinders threw up flames in the air, which rose to the height of twelve feet, and afterward fell down in the form of Golden Rain.

"This spectacle was followed by a large box, filled with different works, and suspended from two posts, or pillars, which threw up a shower of fire, with several lanterns, and sentences written in large characters, and afterwards six-branched candlesticks, that formed pillars with different stories of light, ranged in white and silver-colored circles, which made the most beautiful appearance, and in a moment converted the night into day. A great number of lanterns and chandeliers were lighted up in an instant.

"The Chinese are acquainted with our Magick Lantern, which they used in this Festival. Perhaps we have borrowed it from them."

A book-filled room in Paris a few years later. Father Louis Bertrand Castel, Jesuit philosopher and mathematician, is poring over page 136 in Isaac Newton's *Opticks,* greatly intrigued by Query fourteen.

"May not the harmony and discord of Colors arise from the proportions of the vibrations propagated through the fibers of the optic Nerves into the Brain, as the harmony and discord of sounds arises from the proportions of the vibrations of the Air? For some Colors are agreeable, as those of Gold and Indigo, and others disagree."

Practically what Aristotle wrote in *De Sensu,* reflects Père Castel with a glance at his harpsichord. Color with sound, music for the eye while the ear listens—color music!

Père Castel rebuilt his harpsichord. The job took several years, but on St. Thomas' Day, December 21st, 1734, the *Clavecin Oculaire,* the world's first color organ, was played in Castel's study in Paris.

Only meager description of this instrument has survived, but it had a musical keyboard of five octaves. When a key was depressed, a colored strip of paper or silk would appear above a black horizontal screen to the rear. The first octave represented

he pure hues, the next the same hues "one degree lighter," and
he fifth octave the highest values.

Newton had once suggested that c, being the lowest note in the
octave, should be red, the lowest vibration in the spectrum.

Castel decided c should be blue because it sounded blue. For
he same reason he made f yellow-orange, where Newton had
green, and the one choice is fully as justified as the other.

Goethe has stated the case as clearly as anyone. In *Zur
Farbenlehre,* 1810, he writes: "Color and Sound do not admit of
being compared together in any way. They are like two rivers
which spring from the same mountain, but from there on run
their courses under totally different conditions, in two totally
different regions, so that along the entire course of both no two
points can be compared."

Goethe concludes with the statement that color and sound act
"in wholly different provinces, in different modes, on different
elements, for different senses."

Goethe went unheeded. In the century which followed, color
and sound were not only compared together but chained together, and in practically every case the exponent seemed to believe he was the first to conceive of "Color Music."

Among the "rarities" in the P. T. Barnum Museum, at Broadway and Ann Street in New York City, stood a color organ, invented by the American painter, Bainbridge Bishop. It was a
more advanced edition of Castel's *Clavecin Oculaire,* but here
music and color could be played both together and separately.

The evening of June sixth, 1895, in St. James's Hall, London.
A large and select audience has gathered to see the first demonstration of "Color Music," to be performed on the color organ
invented by Alexander Wallace Rimington, Professor of Fine
Arts at Queen's College. There are the Duke of Norfolk, Princess Hohenlohe, Cardinal Vaughan, the painter Alma Tadema,
and many other prominent people.

On the stage a large white curtain of heavy silk has been carefully draped in deep folds, and down in the center aisle towers a
huge cabinet with an attached organ keyboard—the color
organ, with its elaborate mechanism and its fourteen arc lights
within.

The distinguished looking young professor delivers a lecture; then the hall is darkened and the strange performance begins.

Wagner's "Rienzi Overture" is played by a small orchestra and accompanied by the color organ. The draped screen pulsates with changing color; there is no form, only a restless flicker, hue after hue, one for each musical note sounded. As the tempo of the music increases, the accompanying colors succeed one another too rapidly to be caught by the eye, while the ear readily accepts and enjoys the most rapid passage in the music.

The eye seeks an anchorage, a scrap of form to focus on, but none appears. Questions are whispered, heads shaken. Is there really a color for each note? There must be—Rimington is Professor of Art at Queen's. But it hurts my eyes!

The London critics were not kind to Rimington; in other English cities they were even less kind. All commented on the "restless flicker" on the screen, while the music fell smoothly and with clear meaning on the ear. Rimington, who, strangely enough, was a painter, realized too late that form is an indispensable factor in a visual art.

On March 20th, 1915, Alexander Scriabine's symphonic poem, *Prometheus,* was performed in New York City. The composition was scored for full orchestra and *Tastiera per Luce.* Modest Altschuler conducted the Russian Symphony Orchestra and the color organ was supplied by one of the large electric companies. Scriabine had never been specific about the visual part of his work. He had suggested that the entire hall be flooded with changing colored light, but the equipment used in Carnegie Hall on this occasion consisted of a small screen on the stage and a number of colored lamps actuated from a musical keyboard. Scriabine's color scale was the strangest of them all. *E* and *b* were *pearly blue, with shimmer of moonshine,* and *e* flat and *b* flat *steely, with the glint of metal.* The performance was not a success.

Isadora Duncan was in the audience. As the last note sounded and the last flicker died on the screen, she turned to her escort. "Well—do you still believe in color music?" and he answered, "Give it time! This is only the wail of a newborn."

The man was Van Dearing Perrine, painter, teacher, and

member of the National Academy, who had already then made a far more important contribution to the art of light than all the others put together. Perrine had from the beginning rejected all musical analogy theories and experimented with light as an independent aesthetic medium. He built several instruments based on the silent use of form, color, and motion, and was one of the first important pioneers in lumia.

During the period 1900–1920 there must have been many honest attempts to lay a foundation for an independent art of light, but the obstacles were many. The repeated failures of "color music" demonstrations kept obscuring the issue and prejudicing public and press.

Let us reverse the situation for a moment. If each note has a definite color, then each color must have a definite note. We build a "sound organ" by hooking a photoelectric cell to an amplifier with attached loudspeaker and we "tune" the contraption according to the supposed analogy, so that each color scanned by the cell will produce a note of a certain pitch from the loudspeaker. Even if we succeed in getting deep, basso profundo rumblings from a Rembrandt and high, plaintive howls from a Picasso, we shall have proved nothing, except that we might have used our time and energy to better advantage.

My own experiments began in May 1905 in Copenhagen with a cigar box, a small incandescent lamp, and some pieces of colored glass. During my studies in Paris the instrument grew to several wooden boxes, a few lenses and a real screen—one of my bedsheets tacked up on the wall. One day I invited my teacher of painting to a demonstration. He scowled, "This is an utter waste of time. With this on your mind you will never learn to paint." Well—I didn't. Eventually I became a singer of folk songs and player of the lute, but only in order to support my experiments with light; I would sing till I had money, experiment till I was broke, then sing some more. In 1914 I was honored with a Royal Command to sing at the English Court. After this the engagements multiplied, but three months later World War I cut career and experiments short; within a week I was in uniform and on my way to camp. Mustered out in 1916, I continued my concert work and experiments in the United States. But no one

can serve two masters. In 1919 I gave up my career as a singer to devote all my time to the building of an instrument with which I could materialize something of my fourteen-year-old dream: a silent and independent art of light. Late in 1921 my first real instrument stood ready and I named it Clavilux. The visual compositions came readily enough, they had long been before my inner eye, but I had to learn to play them, develop a technique, and the instrument was not nearly flexible enough.

Finally, on January 10th, 1922, I played my first public performance at the Neighborhood Playhouse in New York City; a tense and wonderful evening.

But it was with fear and trembling I went out to buy the morning papers the next day. Years on the concert platform had taught me to take nothing for granted. It was quite possible I would have to spend many more years as a wandering troubadour with a crazy idea.

The reviews were far better than I had dared to hope. In general the critics accepted lumia as a new art and made allowances for its youth and my inexperience at the keyboard. Kenneth MacGowan wrote in *The World:* "This is an art for itself, an art of pure color; it holds its audience in the rarest moments of silence that I have known in a playhouse."

Requests for recitals in other cities came pouring in and I found myself riding the crest of an unexpected wave, with only a most inadequate surfboard to hold me up. Much against my wish, the Clavilux was christened "Color-Organ" by public and press, and it became a novelty, a fad, a thing it was smart to see and discuss that season. It also seemed that everybody wanted it for something. A novelty is worth money and much money was dangled before my eyes at a time when it would have come in very handy—I was newly married and our firstborn had just arrived. Advertising firms offered me tempting contracts for display and signboard use—Stockings, Chewing Gum, Laxatives, Cigarettes. To this day I shudder when I contemplate the harm I might have inflicted on lumia if I had yielded and sold it into slavery.

For a number of years I played lumia recitals during the winters and improved the equipment during the summers. In

1925 I included Europe, and lumia was well received everywhere.

Upon my return to New York I took stock of the situation. This sudden success, all these glowing comments, was enough to turn anybody's head—but the time had come for a stern and sober evaluation.

It was no longer healthy for lumia to be so closely identified with only one person. Many creative minds should be expressing a variety of ideas through it, many inventive minds should supply better instruments.

Thus began the Art Institute of Light, organized in 1930 as a nonprofit center for research in lumia. My patents and research data became the property of the Institute, a supporting membership was built up, and in 1933 a lumia theatre with surrounding studios and laboratories was opened in Grand Central Palace in New York. A program of lectures and recitals was inaugurated and at every opportunity I would invite artists to investigate the new medium and make use of our facilities.

We had quite an influx, but very few artists turned up. To our great disappointment we had to classify most of our applicants into two familiar categories: the Curious, who only wanted to find out how the instruments were constructed, and the Talkers, who only wanted us to listen. Perhaps I should include those who could play the piano and were firmly convinced that, after a few hours of instruction, they would be able to play the Clavilux at least as well as any of us. They lost heart when they found out that lumia is no easier to learn than music. It looked so easy!

But our doors remained open and we kept our eyes peeled for the Real Thing. From time to time our prayers were answered; serious-minded artists came with ideas and preliminary work was done on many compositions.

Meanwhile more and more people became acquainted with lumia through our recitals and lectures. Art classes from Teachers College, Pratt Institute, and many art schools, came regularly, and the seed sown during those ten seasons will some day bear fruit.

Came World War II. The Army took over Grand Central Palace for an Induction Center, our staff was called to the colors and

I was requested to do a special job for the government, a full-time job which was to last for several years. We had no choice; the Art Institute of Light closed its doors "for the duration."

So much for history. Now for a closer analysis.

An eighth fine art is beginning its life in our generation, a silent visual art, in which the artist's sole medium of expression is light. The new art form has been named lumia.

Like its seven older sisters, lumia is an aesthetic concept, expressed through a physical basis of methods, materials, and tools. In a complete definition the two aspects must be stated separately before a composite can yield a clear picture. The aesthetic definition must clarify the artist's conception and intent, the physical one the means he employs in achieving his object.

*a) Aesthetic concept: The use of light as an independent art medium through the silent visual treatment of form, color, and motion in dark space with the object of conveying an aesthetic experience to a spectator.*

*b) Physical basis: The composition, recording, and performance of a silent visual sequence in form, color, and motion, projected on a flat white screen by means of a light-generating instrument controlled from a keyboard.*

The spectator is a necessary factor in the concept: *a materialized vision, beheld by a beholder.* The spectator may be only the artist himself.

We may now fuse imagination and reality. The aesthetic concept is one of form, color, and motion evolving in *dark space,* the physical reality is form, color, and motion projected on a flat *white screen.*

The lumia artist conceives his idea as a three-dimensional drama unfolding in infinite space.

In order to share his vision with others he must materialize it. This he may do by executing it as a two-dimensional sequence, projected on a flat white screen by means of a specially constructed projection instrument controlled from a keyboard. Seated before the keyboard he may, by manipulation of sliding keys, release white light, mold the light into form, add color and imbue the result with motion and change.

But the original vision—the three-dimensional drama in

space—is constantly before him and he strives to add, by optical means, an illusion of the missing third dimension to his flat screen image, and to perform it so convincingly in a spatial way that the screen creates the illusion of a large window opening on infinity, and the spectator imagines he is witnessing a radiant drama in deep space.

Form, color, and motion are the three basic factors in lumia —as in all visual experience—and form and motion are the two most important. A lumia artist may compose and perform in black and white only, never using color. The use of form and color alone—static composition with projected light—constitutes a less important, but still practical field in lumia.

The only two-factor combination that cannot meet the requirements is motion and color, without form. This is because it violates a basic principle in vision. The human eye must have an anchorage, a point to focus on. If a spectator is facing an absolutely formless and unbroken area of color, his two eyes are unable to perform an orientational triangulation and he will quickly seek a visual anchorage elsewhere, an apex for the distance-measuring triangle that has its base between the pupils of his eyes.

The anchorage may be the frame of the projection screen, the head of another spectator, or his own raised hand, but in the process his attention is diverted from the screen simply because it cannot remain there without discomfort.

#### FORM, THE INTEGRATED MANIFESTATION OF LIGHT

In lumia form is a general and basic visual concept. Form is present on a screen if any part of its surface can be distinguished from the remainder. It therefore embraces the line and the point.

Form has four subfactors:

*Location*—Where is it?
*Volume*—How big?
*Shape*—What is it?
*Character*—What is there about it?

#### COLOR, THE FRACTIONAL MANIFESTATION OF LIGHT

In lumia color is an optical phenomenon, nonexistent without light. Color also has four subfactors.

*Hue*—Which color is it—red, green, blue?

*Chroma*—How much gray has been mixed with the pure hue?

*Value*—How much white in that gray?

*Intensity*—How strong is the light it sheds?

In lumia intensity is a necessary fourth factor. In a given combination of hue, chroma, and value these three factors may retain the same relation to each other, while being moved into a higher intensity range by increased illumination.

MOTION, THE KINETIC MANIFESTATION OF LIGHT

In lumia the term motion applies to all phenomena in the time dimension. Motion may therefore occur in a static form, with changes in volume, shape, character, hue, chroma, value, and intensity.

Like form and color, motion has four subfactors:

*Orbit*—Where is it going?

*Tempo*—How fast? Speeding up? Slowing down?

*Rhythm*—Does it repeat anything?

*Field*—Is it constantly visible, or does any part of its orbit carry it beyond the range of vision?

Lumia's theoretical space-stage is divided into *first field:* the visible section of space (screen surface), and *second field:* the remainder of space, not visible to the spectator.

Lumia's twelve subfactors may be arranged in a graphic equation:

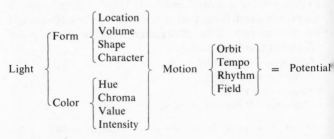

Place this inert potential in a creative artist's hand, supply him with a physical basis—screen, instrument, and keyboard—

and when his finished composition is performed, the last link in the chain has been forged and you have the eighth fine art, lumia, the art of light, which will open up a new aesthetic realm, as rich in promise as the seven older ones.

In composition and execution the potential range of expression reaches from the purely nonobjective to the stark representational; from the diaphanous and amorphous to the solid and sharply outlined; from the very slow to split-second rapidity; from barely perceptible dimness to dazzling brilliance and from the majestic to the grotesque.

In time we shall have lumia virtuosi who can sweep the spectators off their feet with masterly interpretations of a composer's work.

But first the Johann Sebastian Bach of lumia must appear on the scene. Let us hope he is at least a high school student at the moment.

Now for a constructive glance at the future.

What can be done to help and encourage potential pioneer artists and experimenters in this new medium and thus speed its broader development and acceptance?

First of all: those who have acquired a practical knowledge of lumia must be given opportunities to teach what they know to as many interested students as possible. A comprehensive lumia textbook is now being completed. It is here the progressive art museums, art schools, and art organizations may be of real assistance.

Next: an experimental lumia recital hall with adjoining studios and laboratories must be reestablished for practical advanced work. For this purpose the Art Institute of Light organization is available with its equipment, research data, library, and patents—ready to resume its activities interrupted by the war. At the moment we are planning a new building. It is still just a dream, but so many of our dreams have come true that we work as if an endowment had already been granted us.

Included in the plan is the Hall of Light, a miniature theatre seating about fifty spectators. Open day and night, it will present an uninterrupted performance of selected lumia compositions in utter silence. No admission charge, no questions asked, no phi-

losophy propounded. You may walk in at any hour of day and night and remain as long as you like, to rest your ears and bathe your soul in the slowly evolving sequences of radiant form, pure color, and graceful motion.

It is easy to wax poetic on the subject. It is practically impossible to explain lumia convincingly to a person who has never experienced it.

All I can say is that the art of light is here to stay! It has already survived oceans of ridicule and jealousy and it could not have arrived at a time when it was more sorely needed in the world.

Part of the foundation has been laid and seems to rest securely enough. That is about all. The lumia compositions and instruments of today may not even be an indication of what is to come when the first real genius arrives to awaken the Sleeping Beauty.

In *A Primer of Modern Art,* Sheldon Cheney has this to say about lumia: "Here is the beginning, or at least the first serious achievement, of an art as primitive, as complex, as capable of varied emotional beauty as music; and its medium is light—that light which was the earliest god of humankind, which to this day typifies all that is spiritual, joy-bringing and radiant. Perhaps, then, this is the beginning of the greatest, the most spiritual and radiant art of all."

BIBLIOGRAPHY

Aristotle.    *De Sensu.*
Newton.    *Opticks.*
Castel.    *Nouvelles Expériences d'Optique et d'Acoustique.* 1734.
Goethe.    *Zur Farbenlehre.* 1819.
Grosier, J. B.    *De la Chine.* 1818.
Bishop, Bainbridge.    *A Souvenir of the Color Organ.* 1893.
Rimington, A. W.    *Colour Music.* 1911.
Stark Young.    "The Color Organ," *Theatre Arts Magazine,* Jan. 1922.
Vail, George.    "Visible Music," *The Nation,* Aug. 2, 1922.
Cheney, Sheldon.    *A Primer of Modern Art.* 1923. Chapter Ten.
Klein, A. B.    *Colour Music.* London, 1926.
Wilfred, T.    "Prometheus and Melpomene," *Theatre Arts Magazine,* Sept. 1928.
*Encyclopaedia Britannica,* 14th edition.    Vol. 5, p. 784; Vol. 21, p. 289.

MICHAEL KIRBY

# Environmental Theatre *

The medieval theatre-in-the-round made use of raised acting platforms at various spots around the circumference of its circular enclosure as well as employing a central acting space and the radial aisles through the audience. Apparently the arrangement and number of the peripheral towers varied according to the needs of the particular play. In *The Seven Ages of the Theatre,* Richard Southern tells us of an amazing French script, *The Play of the Leafed One,* written by Adam de la Hale in 1276 to be staged in front of the pub in Arras. It not only made use of the real inn, yard, and streets as "setting," but the names of the author and other townspeople were used for "characters" in the play, and actors on stage talked with actors in the audience.

In general, however, we can say that environmental theatre is a recent development. The design of traditional stages is basically functional. It is a practical solution to the problem of presenting a certain type of theatrical material to audiences of various sizes and social characteristics. Even illusionistic developments such as Wagner's "mystic gulf" apply to a type of theatre rather than to individual theatrical works. Environmental theatre, on the other hand, can be viewed as a way in which the spatial characteristics of the stage itself as it is related to the spectator may become a specific aesthetic element of a particular presentation. Environmental theatre, in this sense, makes use of an expressive dimension that is not exploited by traditional performance arrangements.

Two somewhat different meanings of the word "environmental" may be distinguished: one abstract and theoretical, the other

* Reprinted by permission of the author from *The Art of Time: Essays on the Avant-Garde* (New York: E. P. Dutton & Co., Inc., 1969).

concrete and practical. The former is based on pure spatial considerations, while the latter refers to various types of theatre outside of theatres. Taking the more general concept first, we have the definition of "environment" as "the surrounding" and "that which encircles, encompasses." The compass gives us names for every possible point on the horizontal plane that extends away from us in every direction; thus, assuming the traditionally seated spectator, we may say that any theatre is environmental if it presents material from the sides and rear of the viewer as well as from the front.

An annular or ring stage completely surrounding the audience is the simplest model for this concept of environmental theatre. When Guillaume Apollinaire added a prologue to his play *The Breasts of Tiresias* in 1916, he indicated that rather than the "antique stage" that was being used for the performance he would have preferred "A circular theatre with two stages/One in the middle the other like a ring/Around the spectators . . ." This would have allowed "The full unfolding of our modern art."

Several stages that completely surround the audience have been constructed. One example is the Waco Civic Theatre, a project of James Hull Miller who has been very active in proselytizing for more flexible and environmental theatre design. The somewhat egg-shaped seating section, flattened at one end where it faces the primary playing area, is sunk below the level of the main floor so that a continuous peripheral stage actually surrounds it. The 360-degree stage is horizontal, as in our theoretical model.

If the central seating section in this type of arrangement is raked, however, to provide a better view toward the front, sight lines to the side and rear become a problem. One solution is to surround the spectators with motion picture screens that can be hung high enough so that they can be seen easily by everyone. At the New York State pavilion at the recent World's Fair in New York and in an exhibition produced by Walt Disney for Expo 67, contiguous cinemascope screens ringed the circular "auditorium," and synchronized films presented a "single" continuous image within which the spectator was centered. The well-known but unrealized "Total Theatre" that Walter Gropius designed for

Erwin Piscator in 1926 also used projection screens to enclose an audience completely. Thomas Wilfred's "Heptarena" is a similar but more intimate concept using front projection rather than rear projection. Both of these proposed theatres were conceived to extend the scenery ("backdrop") of a play environmentally: In each the physical staging can be varied from proscenium through thrust stage to arena, but the audience is always within the ring of projected setting.

Where live actors are concerned, a solution to the sight-line problem of a raked seating section is to raise the side and rear portions of the surrounding stage. The Nationaltheater in Mannheim, Germany, which uses elevated side aisles as stages, and the Hilberry Classic Theatre at Wayne State University in Detroit, Michigan, in which a stepped metal ramp surrounds the audience, are two examples of this approach.

This elevation of side and rear stages suggests that our simple theoretical model of a horizontal plane extending away from the spectator in all directions is not the most useful one for environmental theatre: the purest archetype is a sphere with the individual spectator at its center. The stimuli that make up the performance may now come from any three-dimensional direction, and, rather than merely the points of the compass referring to the horizontal plane, we now have all the points on a sphere for reference.

Because of the expense and technical difficulties of suspending the individual spectator in space, a "pure" architectural realization of this theoretical model has not yet been built. Frederick Kiesler's "Endless Theatre," designed in 1924, was a huge flattened sphere with a double outer wall of glass or plastic. The architect described his project as "the first continuous shell construction with no foundation to support it." (In many respects it can be compared with Andreas Weininger's proposed "Spherical Theatre," the concept for which was also published in Germany in 1924.) Kiesler's theatre had great flexibility. Permanent seats ringed the shell at its widest point, and lower seats also surrounded a central arena, but that half of the structure above the heads of the audience, the huge smooth dome, could serve as a continuous projection screen. There were three permanent stages in the "Endless Theatre": a round stage in the center of

the arena, and two squarish platform stages that broke the lower ring of seats at either side. Bridges could join the side stages with the central stage. From the very top of the dome, a platform for carrying actors could be raised and lowered; elevators could be positioned anywhere in the space. And great adjustable spiral ramps, inclining at various angles, could be suspended within the shell. (Kiesler pointed out that the "elastic building system of cables and platforms developed from bridge building.") These ramps, rising to a ring stage suspended near the top of the dome, could be used either for the audience—hanging them, in some arrangements, in the very center of the space—or for performance. Or both audience and performance could occupy sections of the same spiral "road." Like so many of his projects, the "Endless Theatre" was never constructed, but Kiesler was allowed to erect a "double spiral stage" in the Vienna Concert House for the Music and Theatre Festival in 1924.

More recently, Jacques Polieri has proposed spherical theatres. In his "Théâtre du mouvement total," small seating sections for spectators are to be inserted into the center of a huge sphere. The performance is to take place on the inner surface of the sphere and within it. In one concept the audience is seated on the "blades" of paddle-like extensions from a central core; in another the platforms are raised on tall metal stalks.

Since the space beneath the spectator is the most difficult to deal with from a practical point of view, we can find examples of "spherical" thought that have been realized only as domes over the audience. In a very small spherical theatre in the French pavilion at Expo 67, a specially photographed film was projected onto a mirror that focused the image onto most of the dome-shaped surface around the spectators and over their heads. The "Space Theatre" that Milton Cohen has built in Ann Arbor, Michigan, roughly approximates a hemisphere by hanging screens for film projection above and around the spectators. *The Night Time Sky* (1965) by Robert Whitman set several small elevated "stages" into the walls of a roughly dome-shaped tent-like enclosure. Elements of the performance also took place on the main floor among the spectators, who were free to move about or recline on mats, and films were projected at various spots in the enclosure, including directly overhead.

Many Happenings have approximated conceptually our spherical environmental model by using for the performance all of the available three-dimensional space, including that occupied by the spectators. In this respect at least, they had a great influence on discothèques. Although I do not consider discothèques as art, they are an example of environmental concern that is widely available and with which many people are familiar. Such an obvious stereotype exists for the light-show discothèque that it is not necessary to name any particular example: projections of various sorts are directed onto the walls, floor, ceiling, and onto the dancers themselves. Other points that make the discothèque worth mentioning are the way in which the volume of the amplified music often seems to "fill" the entire space and the way the individual dancer becomes the center of experience. The kinesthetic and proprioceptive basis of dancing for pleasure rather than to be seen emphasizes the spherical model with a single spectator as its center, in contrast to the consideration of the audience as an undifferentiated mass.

But the spherical archetype is not intended to be taken literally. Being a hypothetical construct, it can "fit" any theatre and any space and serve as a measure of the degree of environmental involvement. Thus it is only when the presentational field and/or performance elements move around, over, or under the spectator that we may call the performance "environmental." From this point of view, thrust and arena staging are not significantly different from proscenium. The spectator sees each from one fixed angle. Of course the visual angle taken up by the stage is inversely related to the viewer's distance from the performance: The visual angle is much greater, for example, for a person in the front row than it is for someone thirty rows back. Nevertheless, all traditional audience-stage relationships are, from the point of view of the individual spectator, *frontal*. Once this basic principle is established, we find that stages actually exist that enclose the spectator to various degrees: "side" or "end" stages move around the auditorium in a variety of ways, "caliper" stages grip the audience between them, and so forth. Since we are involved with a continuum, there is nothing to be gained by specifying the exact angular deviation at which "frontal" theatre becomes "environmental," but the spherical construct indicates a tendency

toward environmental staging as clearly as it represents the extreme examples of the form.

Since any place, theatrical or not, can be examined in terms of our spherical model, the important point is whether or not the sensations coming to the spectator are intrinsic, functioning parts of the performance. These spatial elements may be purely abstract, utilizing the different qualities and characteristics of various viewing angles, for example, or they may relate more literally to the atmosphere or information structure of the presentation.

When *A Sleep of Prisoners* by Christopher Fry is presented, as it often is, in an actual church, the total physical surroundings of the audience are obviously related to the particular piece being presented: The spectator is in the "church turned into a prison camp" for which the script calls. Every element of the real church is justified by the play and becomes a part of it. The spectator is "spherically" involved by the architecture. In this case, the involvement is passive, but the performance, even when the director chooses to place all of the action in a quasi-proscenium arrangement near the altar, therefore can be considered to have an environmental attribute or dimension.

The same kind of passive, physical, environmental involvement exists if a play is presented as being "set" in a theatre. From Pirandello to Peter Weiss we have attempts to use the actual environment of the spectator and integrate it into the intellectual and emotional fabric of the work. The scripts of *Six Characters* and *Marat/Sade* do not call for any active involvement of the audience by the actors, but the spectator is physically "included" in the work, nevertheless.

A slightly more difficult way to achieve this kind of passive architectural involvement is to build a complete enclosure for the audience, extending the setting so that it surrounds the seating section much as the projection screens in Gropius' and Wilfred's proposed theatres would do. When Max Reinhardt staged *The Miracle,* the whole interior of the theatre was turned into an Early Gothic cathedral with tall pillars and arches and huge stained glass windows; when the performance came to this country, Norman Bel Geddes was responsible for the conversion of New York's Century Theatre into a "total setting."

Of course in a play these passive environmental techniques are related to the "suspension of disbelief." We are asked to equate the real church we may perhaps know from our everyday life with the unreal (acted) soldiers, for example. Whether or not this makes the tangible world somehow less real or merely makes the performers seem more artificial depends upon the spectator. And even with the complete integration of the architectural space into the play, it is possible that another physical element will be omitted: the audience. During the performance, the church in *A Sleep of Prisoners* is obviously not empty, as it is represented by the dialogue. The clothes I wear as I watch the Marquis de Sade on the stage of a nineteenth-century mental institution obviously belong to a different time.

In alogical theatre, which does not involve such elaborate use of informational cross-reference, many performances have been presented in complete Environments designed and constructed for the particular piece. Allan Kaprow's *18 Happenings in 6 Parts* took place simultaneously in three adjoining plastic-walled rooms; the spectators changed seats during the two intermissions. A standing audience watched Kaprow's *A Spring Happening* through narrow slits in the side walls of a long "boxcar." In Robert Whitman's *The American Moon,* spectators sat in six tunnels facing a central playing space. Jim Dine's *The Car Crash* enclosed the audience in a completely white Environment: The performers also wore white, and Dine even considered giving the spectators white caps and smocks to wear in order to integrate them with the space.

Of course the environmental aspects of most performances are physically active rather than passive. The aisles, lobbies, and balconies of traditional theatres are used by performers in many different ways. When the spectator is considered to be at the center of a hypothetical sphere, the rest of the audience is part of his "environment," and the device of having actors "planted" as spectators and performing from the house itself rather than from the stage can be seen as an environmental concern. It was used in Andre Antoine's production of *Le Missionaire* in 1894, in the surrealist *The Mysteries of Love* by Roger Vitrac directed by Antonin Artaud in 1927, in *Waiting for Lefty,* and *The Case of Clyde Griffiths* of the 1930's, among many others.

(Although the concept of "audience involvement" is usually employed in discussing the use of the spectators' area for acting purposes, the terminology is tricky. I have been using the word "involvement" in an objective, physical sense, and there is, of course, greater *physical* involvement for the spectator in all environmental theatre: turning to see the actors behind him, for example, is a basically physical act. But physical involvement should not be equated with or misunderstood as *psychological* involvement. It should be obvious that a spectator seated in a top balcony at some spatial remove from the actual performance can be absolutely involved in a psychological sense while, on the other hand, a spectator physically surrounded by a performance or even participating in it may have no psychological involvement at all.)

In environmental theatre the particular three-dimensional spatial relationship between the performance element and the spectator tends to have particular significance in an intellectual or purely plastic sense. Some of the more obvious possibilities of the intellectual use of spatial dynamics, for example, were embodied in the first section of the Canadian National Film Board's "Labyrinth" at Montreal's Expo 67. Spectators stood on four galleries curving along each side of an ovoid space and watched films projected on two huge rectangular screens, one rising vertically at one end of the large room and the other stretching across the floor below. The sensation of looking *down* onto a film was unique and, for many, disconcerting. Feelings of uneasiness were played upon by the authors of the piece with colorful vertiginous action: moving aerial shots; sky divers falling through space; boys climbing an unfinished skyscraper on the vertical screen, while on the horizontal screen the drop to the streets below becomes longer and longer. In Jacques Polieri's *Gamma de 7,* on the other hand, the relationship to dancers seen from beneath the transparent platform on which they are performing is purely a formal one, unrelated to information.

Although a complete documentation of all the possibilities of environmental theatre is not intended here, a description of certain key works and directors can indicate historical progression as well as diversity of approach.

As has already been mentioned, Reinhardt staged *The Miracle,* a wordless play by Karl Vollmoeller, in theatre auditoriums and exhibition halls that had been completely transformed into a cathedral. But there was active as well as passive environmental involvement in *The Miracle.* The *regie book* for the presentation is filled with movement in the aisles, and action takes place in all parts of the space. As The Nun flees into the auditorium in Scene V for example, "Everywhere black shadows step in front of her." Although the performers did not speak, sound was an important element in the performance, and this, too, was treated environmentally, as indicated in the following passages from the production outline.

SCENE 2

31. The Piper then tiptoes to the front and calls as if up into the hills with a mooselike cry.

32. The answer is heard coming from the upper gallery, then the middle one, and soon the lower one.

33. The blowing of horns, the barking of hounds . . .

SCENE 3

43. Whispering comes from all parts of the church. High cackling laughter.

. . .

65. The Nun shrieks, but only makes the formation of her mouth; the sound comes from the gallery.

SCENE 5

265. There is a strong menacing knock at one of the doors of the auditorium.

. . .

268. The knocking is repeated in always shorter intervals with increasing vehemence.

269. Finally it resounds from all the doors round about and ends at last in a mighty, growing, threatening thunder.

In February 1923, Vsevolod Meyerhold staged a play adapted by Sergei Tretyakov from *The Night* by Marcel Martinet, the title of which is variously translated as *The Earth Rises, Earth on Its Hind Legs,* or *The Restive Earth.* "Audience participation"

apparently began before the performance itself, when waiting spectators took part in organized marching in the lobby. During the presentation—which was set during the civil war and employed soldiers whose full battle equipment included small cannon—cars, trucks, motorcycles, and bicycles drove through the auditorium and to and from the stage across a bridge. Finally, according to René Fülöp-Miller, the Red troops arrived, took possession of "the stage, the auditorium, and the foyer," and the spectators stood while everyone sang the *Internationale*.

In the late 1930's Nikolai Okhlopkov presented several productions at the Realistic Theatre in Moscow that made radical and programmatic use of environmental factors. Having at his disposal a small rectangular theatre hall with a flat floor, a balcony at one end, and a low platform stage at the other, Okhlopkov ignored the direct frontal relationship between audience and performance for which the space had been designed. For each production he created a new and particular arrangement of seats and playing areas, surrounding the audience with the action in various ways.

For *The Start* by Vasili Stavsky (also translated as *The Run*) the audience sat in two sections facing each other across a narrow acting platform that divided the room in half along its short axis. From the end of the room opposite the balcony, a wooden walkway supported by metal posts curved up over the central platform and the two audience sections and then sloped down again to where it had started, making a generally circular "road" in space. Actors not only performed on the central stage and the "skyway" but in the rear of the spectator groups and among them. To emphasize scenically this interpenetration of audience and performance, real fruit trees were placed throughout the hall and flowering branches hung from overhead.

A more austere example of Okhlopkov's spatial concerns was his production of *Mother* by Maxim Gorky. A basic arena arrangement was used with a low, round, stepped acting platform rising from a central square surrounded by raked seats. But aisles at each corner of the square connected with peripheral acting space behind the audience, along the walls of the room. (It was somewhat like the stage Apollinaire had despaired of getting two decades earlier.) Okhlopkov designed the space, in the

words of Norris Houghton in *Moscow Rehearsal,* "to bring about the meeting of actor and audience so that it will be impossible to separate the two—to surround the audience with actors just as the actors are surrounded by audience."

Although some credit Okhlopkov with eliminating the stage and blending the stage and auditorium together, it would seem that he actually "fragmented" *the* stage, dividing it into many small stages placed behind, around, and above the audience as well as in front of it. Apparently in only one production did Okhlopkov do away with the platform that indicates "this is acting area" (although he did not do away with the seats that indicate "this is audience area"). For *The Iron Flood* by Serafimovich, an arching "sky" of blue canvas concealed the walls and ceiling of the Realistic Theatre; rocks, trees, and bushes turned the floor into a hillside. It was as if the audience was on stage and a realistic fourth wall had been dropped behind them: The entire hall was filled with the "setting." The scene was the encampment of a unit of the Red army during the civil war, and action took place in all parts of the space. Not only were the spectators "in" the action, but all the senses were forcefully involved: In *Moscow Theatres* Victor Komissarzhevsky explains that "It seemed that the smells of steppe wormwood, of horses' sweat, and the smoke of fires filled the theatre."

If Antonin Artaud was not able to give tangible shape to his vision, he was one of the most passionate and forceful spokesmen for environmental theatre, and his writings have had a great influence on contemporary thought. In "The Theatre of Cruelty (First Manifesto)," published in *The Theatre and Its Double,* Artaud asks for a "diffusion of action over an immense space." This is to be achieved by remodeling a "hangar or barn" to eliminate any barriers between performers and spectators: The stage and auditorium are to be replaced by "a single site." The spectators would be seated in the middle of the space and action would take place around them, in the four corners of the room, and in the center where diffuse, simultaneous, and distributed action could be concentrated. Galleries around the hall would also carry the performance above the audience, filling the space three-dimensionally.

*Hellzapoppin,* which opened in New York on September

22nd, 1938, was really two shows in one: In part it was a revue headed by Olsen and Johnson (who were "responsible" to an unrecorded extent for the whole show) that included the usual singers, dancers, comics, imitators, magicians, and so forth, and in part an aggressive use of the whole auditorium to "involve" the spectator. John Anderson, in his review in *The New York Journal-American,* said the performance did "everything to the audience except drag it up on the stage and spit in its eye." After a prologue, acclaimed by all the critics, in which Hitler, Mussolini, Roosevelt, and John L. Lewis all appeared on film praising Olsen and Johnson and their revue in dubbed voices— Hitler spoke with a Jewish accent and Mussolini in Negro dialect—much of the performance was carried on by "plants" in the house. Barkers walked up and down the aisles selling toy balloons, candy, gum, and souvenirs; one speculator hawked tickets to the then popular *I Married an Angel.* There were several "running gags": A florist repeatedly attempted to deliver a small plant to "Mrs. Jones," and by the end of the performance it had grown into a large tree he could no longer carry; the audience was told that "The Phantom" would escape from a straitjacket in five seconds, but he did not and spent the rest of the evening struggling on and off the stage; a woman loudly searched for "Oscar," and when, late in the performance, she was invited onto the stage and "killed" (blank pistols were numerous and were frequently used), a man began calling for "Lena." An almost nude man appeared in an upper balcony on a horse; an orangutan watched the show from another box; a man in a gorilla costume dragged a screaming girl out of a stage box and carried her off. The lights went out and puffed rice was scattered over the spectators while a voice on the loudspeaker explained that it was "only bushels and bushels of spiders." At other times, eggs, bananas, and clothing were thrown into the audience. Even at intermission, a clown bothered the spectators. One element of Olsen and Johnson's routine carried audience involvement to a point where it would have great pertinence to some spectators while being completely pointless to others: They went to the trouble of finding out the names of notable people in attendance at the performance and incorporated them into their act.

As Okhlopkov did in the 1930's, Jerzy Grotowski works in a

rather small, rectangular, flat-floored theatre, and he establishes a different audience-performance relationship for each play. His presentations at the Theatre Laboratory in Opole, Poland, show that this relationship can be as creatively expressive of the conceptual core as any other element in the production. His fragmentation of *the* stage into a multiplicity of environmental acting areas reached the point in his version of Adam Mickiewicz' *The Ancestors* that individual spectators were spatially isolated, facing in different directions, and the action took place among them: Performance and audience interpermeated, both filling the entire hall.

Richard Schechner has studied with Grotowski, and he uses Grotowski methods, in part, when working with his Performance Group. *Dionysus in 69* was developed and staged by Schechner in a New York garage rather than in a traditional theatre in order to make maximum use of environmental possibilities. Although much of the action occurred in a central playing space, there were no chairs to distinguish performance-area from audience-area. For the most part, the spectators sat or stood on carpet-covered levels, platforms, and towers that were also used, at times, by the actors.

Earlier in this essay, I indicated that the word "environment" had two slightly different meanings, and I related examples of environmental theatre to that definition which is most pure, theoretical, and abstract. But if the word "environment" indicates the space that surrounds a person and anything that occupies that space, it may also be thought of, in a less theoretical and more concrete way, as "the particular world in which we live" or, as Webster says, "the aggregate of all the external conditions and influences affecting the life and development of a human being." Using this sense of the word in the phrase "environmental theatre," we have a theatre that rejects theatre buildings as "artificial" and that uses the real places and "theatrical equipment" of everyday life.

Of course merely because a play is performed on the street or in the countryside rather than in a theatre does not make it environmental. A theatre is as physically "real" as any other arrangement of spatial limitation. But just as it has been suggested

that the physical elements that surround the spectator must somehow become an intrinsic part of the performance before we can consider that performance environmental, so only the performance in "the everyday world" that makes intrinsic use of the materials of that world can be thought of as environmental theatre.

As Allardyce Nicoll points out, *Iphigenia at Aulis* makes particular early reference to Sirius and, somewhat later, to dawn. Original performances of the play actually started at sunrise when Greek audiences could still see the Dog Star; although the script is not environmental, these early performances certainly were, at least in these two "appropriations" of elements from the natural surroundings.

In 1920 Max Reinhardt staged Hugo von Hofmannsthal's version of *Everyman* in the Domplatz, or square, in front of the great cathedral in Salzburg. As people watched from the streets and from the windows of houses along the square, the whole city, including the medieval castle that rises on a wooded mountain in the center of Salzburg, became part of the performance. It was still daylight when the actors entered from the neighboring squares, but after the sun went down torches moved through the landscape. Von Hofmannsthal has described how "cries uttered by invisible spirits to warn Everyman of his approaching death [were heard] from the church [in front of which the stage had been built] and all the church towers of the city as twilight deepened about the 5000 spectators."

Not unlike the restaging in this country of battles from the Revolution or the Civil War using authentic weapons and uniforms, the Russians reenacted their seizure of the Winter Palace on the actual site in Petrograd. Apparently such dramatic recreations took place on the first three anniversaries of the October, 1917, event. There is some confusion because different sources apply different dates to the same photograph. Perhaps this should not be surprising: At least one photograph of a reenactment of *The Storming of the Winter Palace* has been reproduced in histories of the revolution as representing the actual event. Although the photograph of an infantry charge toward the palace looks quite realistic, the performance itself was inaccurate for two reasons: It intentionally included many obviously

theatrical elements performed on two stages joined by a bridge, and historians now seem to be of the opinion that the Reds did not actually "storm" the palace at all but got in through a poorly guarded back door. At any rate, the actual site of the overthrow of Aleksandr Kerensky's Provisional Government was used for at least two or three mass spectacles that involved thousands of performers—1000 citizens and a fully equipped battalion of infantry in the 1918 performance supervised and designed by Nathan Altman; 8000 "actors" and 500 musicians in the 1920 spectacle staged by Evreinov—and mixed symbolic and decorative aspects with an attempt at a historical naturalism. On the first anniversary in 1918, fifty actors all played Kerensky with identical simultaneous movements because a single human figure would have been lost in the large square in front of the palace. The cruiser *Aurora*, lying in the nearby Neva River, added her gunfire to that of the rifles and machine guns firing at the palace just as she had done the year before. Her ammunition, of course, was identical with that which some authorities say was used in 1917: blanks.

In 1924 Sergei Eisenstein staged a play, *Gas Works,* on the various steel walkways and ladders of the Moscow Gas Works. But the use of a "found" environment is not limited to plays. Many alogical performances have made use of the unique characteristics of a particular place: Allan Kaprow presented *Courtyard* in the tall, roofed, central court of an old hotel in New York; Claes Oldenburg did *Autobodys* in a California parking lot; Dick Higgins' *The Tart* took place in a Queens boxing arena; and Oldenburg's *Washes* in a swimming pool.

The mere fact that a stage is outdoors does not mean that performances on it are necessarily environmental. The *Open Air Theatre* in Tampere, Finland, makes particular use, however, of the potentialities of the surrounding landscape in at least one production. This presentation of a war play involves a camouflaged machine gun nest in the nearby forest, trucks moving about, and even an airplane that plays its part "on cue."

(The *Open Air Theatre,* which seats 800 people, is an interesting variation on the annular stage. The central seating section is motorized so that the audience may be turned to face any portion of the peripheral playing area. It seems that in the existing ex-

amples of this type of staging, the audience is quite steeply raked, channeling perception toward the front. The relationship of the audience to the annular stage—ignoring, for the moment, such environmental embellishments as a plane flying overhead —is essentially frontal, and rotation of the audience seems to be only another way of changing scenery. But the spectator moves, and this movement can easily be made an intrinsic part of the performance, suggesting that all movement of the spectator through space can be considered as yet another dimension of environmental theatre. The spectator might be free to move about, as he was in the 360-degree film presentation at the New York State pavilion or at Whitman's *The Night Time Sky,* for example. Or he might become part of a procession, as it were, asked to proceed through one section of the performance to another, as in Oldenburg's Dallas *Injun.* Or his movement might be achieved mechanically as in the various "rides" at the New York World's Fair in which spectators seated in moving conveyances of various kinds looked at displays as they moved past.)

In terms of our broadest definition of "environment," the *Instantaneous Invasion* section of Marta Minujin's *Simultaneity in Simultaneity* could be considered a unique type of environmental theatre. Elements of the presentation were carried simultaneously by two television stations and a radio station in Buenos Aires, Argentina. Each spectator experienced the performance while alone in his own home, switching television channels when directed in order to follow the piece. During the ten minutes that the program lasted, 500 people in a special audience received a telephone call and 100 of them received telegrams. Minujin was using various mass media to create a kind of private environmental theatre.